Darrienia

Darrienia

The Forgotten Legacies Series Book One

K.J. Simmill

Titles by K.J. Simmill

To my wonderful husband, without your support none of this would have been possible.

Thank you.

Contents

Chapter 1

The Past

In her life, Elly had done many things, both mundane and extraordinary, but helping Marise, the sadistic assassin she had trained, to relocate was the most satisfying thing she had done for centuries.

It had been no small task to flee unseen from Blackwood's mansion, especially given the level of security he maintained. His guards were something she had never understood. They were well-trained, loyal, vigilant, and unnecessary. A waste of resources which could have been put to better use elsewhere.

His home was located in a concealed area behind a circle of volcanoes known as Phoenix Landing. A location known only to those who lived and died there and, of course, to the employees of The Courts of Twilight, which Blackwood liked to think he controlled. Nevertheless, despite his superb security, for Elly, such a minor operation had been simple. She had, after all, travelled not only with skilled people whom this world had never known, but those who, in this time, were remembered as heroes.

She eagerly awaited the day of her reunion with Marise. It would mark the beginning of their greatest adventure. She fought with the curiosity that tempted her to see just how she had settled into her new life, to see if the gradual awakening process had been completed. But until the time came it would be too dangerous. Blackwood still kept a close vigil for any signs she had made contact. For now, she had to wait. Even when they did meet, everything would depend on Marise forgiving her for sealing her away in the darkness. Marise had needed to remain hidden in order for things to revert to how they were before she had existed, otherwise, what must come to pass could never be.

The time of their reunion grew ever closer. Soon their journey would begin and then the people of the world would learn their true place. Elly looked at herself objectively as she fastened her long hair back into a twisted bun. Her hair was by far her most striking feature. Even now, as she checked it for any imperfections, her gaze was drawn to its vivid blue colour; a shade that remained a constant reminder of the ancient punishment she had received. She had grown accustomed to it over time, but the same could not be said for any who looked upon her.

Even as she studied herself critically within the surface of the mirror, she knew Blackwood was finally taking action. The idea—which had been prompted by just the right source—had finally bloomed in his feeble mind. It was a solution so obvious he could not understand why he had failed to consider it before. In that moment of inspiration, he had sent a guard to summon her. A guard who would arrive at any second. All of a sudden, he had been filled with optimism. Just when he had been about to abandon all hope of finding her, the idea had finally come to fruition. Although it *had* taken longer than had been anticipated. She had been ready to leave for days. She had expected him to reach the conclusion far sooner, but he could be a little slow sometimes. Subtlety was not something he understood well.

She knew, as she sat waiting for the messenger to reach her chamber, her need for patience was almost over; and how did she know the guard was on his way to her? It was simple, she knew everything.

"Lord Blackwood has requested your presence immediately!" The guard barked the order, flinging open the door without so much as a knock. Seeing her angry stare, he felt himself retreat slightly. None of the guards liked to address Blackwood's daughter. If asked why, they may venture it was her unnatural hair, or her strange purple shaded eyes. More likely, however, was that their ancient instincts recognised she didn't seem quite human. Despite this fear they also respected her. She had always defended them when confrontation occurred. A number of them owed her their lives, even if they didn't realise it. "Please, forgive the intrusion," he added, seeing the unmistakable annoyance. He was new. She would forgive this mistake just once. She always allowed the recruits time to learn their place.

"Very well, inform him I am on my way." A slight smile teased her lips as she smartened her appearance. It was finally time.

There was no time wasted in reaching Blackwood's audience room. It was a simple room which overlooked the rise and fall of the mountains and volcanoes in the distance. In order to give the impression of great knowledge, to any who would stand before him, the room had been lined with bookshelves filled with both common and rare texts, none of which he had so much as cast his gaze over. For those outside his small fiefdom, there was but one reason a person would be invited to this hidden mansion, their time and usefulness had expired. Concealed within this room were numerous nooks and passageways which could be used either as a means of a quick escape or, as was more often the case, to allow his assassin to carefully observe her next target.

Although Elly had been aware of her destination, she had been surprised he had not requested this audience in his 'throne room'. A room which gave him delusions of the powers he thought he was destined to possess. Upon entering, she offered him a quick smile. He sat in his habitual place behind a wooden desk that was currently littered with various papers that, given their contents of advanced sciences, seemed to be far above his level of comprehension.

"You requested me, my lord?" She gave a half-hearted bow as she approached. More than anything else it was an action to satisfy his ego. For now it was vital he continued to believe she was one of his loyal employees. It seemed over time he had forgotten her true reason for being there and, for the moment, she had no desire to remind him.

"Elaineor." He acknowledged her presence before returning to the silence which had filled the air before her arrival. She waited patiently. A nervous anticipation of what was to follow washed over her. Thoughts of her reunion with Marise filled her mind as she willed him to say the words she longed to hear. Finally, he spoke again. "I miss her you know. I've tried almost everything to find her, but each effort has returned in vain." As the silence descended once more she found herself wondering exactly how long this was going to take. "I was thinking, surely someone must know where she is, and then it dawned on me, you."

"Me, my lord?" She felt her heart pound against the walls of her chest. It was so loud she swore he would hear. Part of her feared he had discovered the truth, maybe even how and where she had sealed his assassin. It was possible the notion could have led him to discover what had actually happened. She calmed her mind. This *was* Blackwood. He was by no means a fool, but he had a great talent in overlooking the obvious. Whilst she may have been filled with such turmoil, there was no betrayal of such feelings. She was an expert at acting how people expected. No one could live the life she had without becoming a master of secrecy and deception.

"Yes, after all you were very close. She spoke to you in ways none of us ever knew. I believe, given the chance, you could find her, after all," he paused once more as if to consider his next sentence carefully, "you were more than just master and student, were you not? I worry, Elaineor. What could have happened, was she defeated, was she injured and could not return? That, I doubt. I think it was something else. You noticed the changes in her before she left. I think whatever happened to her is preventing her returning home, from returning to me."

"So what do you have in mind, my lord? You know I, as much as anyone, long to see her again." Elly sighed. She spoke the truth, only Marise truly appreciated her skills. She was one of the only people worthy of travelling beside her. During her absence she had felt so underappreciated, so bored.

"That is why I want you to find her."

"Me, my lord?" It was a performance of surprise which would have had many travelling theatres begging for her skills, just the right level of shock and excitement mingled together as she drew her hands to her chest in surprise.

"Well you had, a special connection. I am unsure why I failed to think of it before."

"Very well, my lord, I shall leave immediately." Her hand almost rested upon the door when his voice stopped her. She did not look back at him as he spoke, in fear he would see her impatience.

"Bring *her* back with you, Elaineor." Although low and almost silent, his words were filled with warning. Unseen to him Elly smiled. There were but a few things that could intimidate her, and *he* was certainly not one of them.

With his warning she departed. Blackwood sat for a short moment as if to ensure the person, who was publicly recognised as his daughter, had truly left. It was but a brief pause, one which reflected his impatience. Had she lingered outside for even a few seconds she would have heard him address the seemingly empty room.

"Eiji, do you understand your task?" A small wooden panel opened into the room to allow a young man to emerge. His blond hair was ruffled, unkempt, as if his tanned hand had anxiously passed through it many times in the same nervous manner in it did now.

He looked fatigued. Sleep for the last few days had escaped him as he was forced to this unknown place, bound and blindfolded. His brown hide trousers were creased from his less than hospitable journey here, and his linen shirt had fared no better, showing clear signs of the manhandling he had suffered during the long journey. Even should he have tried to escape he knew he would never find his way home. There had been too many twists and turns through his journey. Sometimes it seemed almost as if they backtracked just to fool any internal compass he may have possessed.

Given the situation, if they had simply approached him, he would have willingly accompanied them. He would have had no choice. But instead he had been struck from behind, dragged into the back of a cramped wagon, and left to wonder his fate. The only warning issued being, should he try anything people would die.

He looked to the figure who sat before him. He was known as Lord Blackwood and, for the sake of his master, Eiji had no choice but follow the requests of this corrupt lord.

"Yes, Lord Blackwood," he stated somewhat begrudgingly. Unlike Elly he did not bow, his morals would not permit it.

"You will send word to Knightsbridge the instant she finds the girl." Blackwood had been very careful not to reveal in his conversation who Elly would be looking for. In order for his plan to work, the young Elementalist had to believe he was in no danger. However, as soon as contact with Marise had been established, the appropriate measures would be taken to silence him.

"And my master, can I see him?" Eiji questioned nervously. He had no choice but to help this man. At least it seemed a simple task, confirmation his warrior had been located in exchange for his master's life.

"It's early days and your loyalties are uncertain, but I promise you, no harm will come to him from any of my men while you do what is asked of you. Now, be gone." As Blackwood clicked his fingers the guard stationed outside entered, placed a bag over Eiji's head, and escorted him away in a painfully familiar manner. They were to leave him at the outer parts of the volcanic caves. Blackwood knew no matter where Elly's adventure took her, even with the ability to travel through Collateral, she had no choice but to pass through the labyrinth beneath Phoenix Landing. It was there his little spy would pick up the trail.

* * *

She erupted from the forest, running as fast as her weary legs could carry her. She pushed forwards, despite her fatigue, as if her life depended on it. She was right, it did. She looked desperately around for someone, anyone, who could come to her aid. But she knew the chances of finding someone were slim. This island possessed but a single town, and its location eluded her. She dared not cry out. The only people who would benefit from this would be those who pursued her.

Her tangled dark hair was filled with debris from the forest she had fled from just moments ago. Dirt was encrusted down the front of her tight, finely knit, jumper, and her leather trousers were torn from when their ambush had first been sprung.

She had known they were trouble on the boat, but never did she expect for them to take their prejudices this far. They had overheard the purpose of her pilgrimage as she spoke with the harbour master in Albeth, asking his permission to work her fare during the journey. She was almost certain that the only reason they had boarded the vessel had been to follow her. They had ridiculed her throughout the voyage. She had hoped it would end when the boat had docked and, for a time, it had.

She had not seen them hunting her from the shadows, not until the isolated path had made her the perfect target. She had worked the boat's small bar as a waitress to pay for her passage. The purpose of the pilgrimage was to travel in the footsteps of priestess Cassandra. It was a voyage the temple insisted she make, should she wish to join them. It was a rite normally only required as the final journey of the current high priestess' successor, and she was certainly not that. Due to her father's treason, even the temple had refused to train her unless she completed this ancient rite. Now, because she had been so eager to prove them wrong, to prove she could accomplish something more than her family name would allow, she was going to die.

Fighting her way free from their drunken grasps she had fled into the forest, hoping to lose them, but amongst the camouflage they had gained the advantage. She had been left with no choice but to flee to the open ground, and no alternative but to trust her fate to the hands of the Gods. Even if it seemed they had abandoned her.

She glanced behind her, panic filled her eyes as tears streaked her muddy face. The howls of those who pursued her sent waves of fear through her causing weakness in her burning limbs. They were closer now. Her staggered movements, as she dragged one foot in front of the other, allowing them to close the distance between them rapidly. She could do this no longer. She was so tired, so exhausted. Despite her will to live, her desire to keep pushing forward, her legs could no longer able to hold her weight. Her only hope was to find a safe haven, a town, a traveller, or just some cover in which to hide, but it seemed The Fates were against her. Nothing more than the deserted grassland, with the occasional shrub and bush scattered across the open plain, met her panicked gaze.

Her fingers clawed franticly at the ground as she saw the rays of the morning sun glint of a shard of metal concealed beneath a small patch of shrubbery. It seemed to signal her from the base of the decaying shrub as the sunlight danced across it. She prayed it was a weapon, something she could use to defend herself. Her fingernails, already broken and bloody, clawed frantically at the ground as she tried to pull herself towards the hope of salvation. She dug harder, swearing she heard something more, a whisper on the wind calling to her mind, yet despite her rapid glance around. she could not locate its source.

For a moment, things seem to move in slow motion. She heard the taunting calls of her pursuers as they left the forest. Her fingers scraped around the unearthed metallic object as she tugged it free.

"Please, let it be a weapon," she prayed aloud. Yet once more fates had dealt her a poor hand. Within her grasp she held not a dagger but an ancient charm, a talisman from eras past. She cried out in fear and frustration as her last hope of salvation had been torn from her.

She had no time to admire its intricate design, nor did she care to. Within moments those who pursued her would have won. Even powered by the adrenaline of her own fear, she could do no more to escape the tireless monsters who pursued her.

'*Awaken.*' She heard the strange whisper again. It was louder this time. Its soothing tones filled with her with a calm disassociation as she watched the approaching figures focus their gaze upon her.

An explosion of light surrounded her from a force which seemed to radiate from the talisman itself. Something seemed to encase her in a foggy haze, and a new hope began to rise. Perhaps this charm was the tool of her salvation after all. She felt her energy renew, only to find herself looking down upon her body. Whilst death was indeed a mercy, it was not the salvation she had hoped for. The talisman remained clasped tightly within her lifeless hand. For an instant, as she looked upon herself, she thought she saw her body move. Not that it mattered the men were nearly upon it, and Hades had sent an escort for her. She took her mother's hand and walked away through the gates to the underworld.

Acha's eyes shot open as alarm filled every fibre of her being. Her father had sent for her, yet, before she could reach him, she had been attacked. She still lay face down, but the area in which she now found herself was not surrounded by the forest. She glanced around filled with panic, searching for the creatures she feared had attacked her as she walked the Fey's domain. Everything seemed so unfamiliar.

There was a moment of clarity. A brief pause as everything seemed to make sense. It had not been a monster who had dealt the blow that rendered her on the brink of death. It had been her father. He had summoned her, the one he had chosen to be his sacrifice. She vaguely recalled the fading words of his offering to Hades as her world was plunged into darkness. Her father had used her, but to what ends she still didn't know.

She recalled remembered the darkness that had bound her in its silent paralysis. A curse she was powerless to fight as she was forced to sleep. But through her dreams she was given the information she had needed. A means to continue her life in a time so far from her own.

Since she had slept, so much had changed yet somehow, in a strange way, so much had remained the same. Within just a few seconds of being able to move and feel again, the life of the body she had taken flashed before her. Memories which revealed some of the history and developments that had come to pass while she slumbered.

She knew now nearly 1300 years had passed since her father had murdered her. She had been a fool not to take his dabbling in magic more seriously. Looking back, she could clearly see that the tools he used were for a higher ambition than to become the next Shaman.

The town she had once called home was now less than dust. The passing of years had taken a heavy toll. Although much time had passed, the villages now were not too dissimilar from those she had known. The owner of this body had been well-travelled. There were more settlements than in her time, but the world had also lost some of its ancient splendour. The events of the young lady's life flashed through Acha's mind at a disorienting pace. Acha could do nothing but watch and be amazed.

Each town still possessed the old dirt tracks which were created by the steps of those who travelled them. The forests, although smaller now, still shone with magic, but the force which sustained such splendour had greatly weakened. The single storey houses were still built from wood or brick, whichever material was in abundance within the settlement's area, yet the houses appeared more stable now than in her time.

The person's life she had taken had spent much time within a city, where those who had built it had somehow balanced one, or even two, buildings on top of each other. She noticed, through these memories, the emergence of a new substance. It covered some of the old dirt tracks, as if a solid unbroken stone had been placed upon the ground. She also noted it had appeared in a few of the houses as flooring instead of the commonplace wood.

Throughout the paths of the city, tall, wooden objects towered at regular intervals. At night they came aglow as the stone cylinders at their top were filled with oil and set alight to illuminate the streets with the power of hundreds of candles. It seemed this style of lighting had worked its way inside on a lesser scale. The houses had smaller versions that hung from the ceilings. These, however, contained a small lid, which they used to extinguish the flame. They had also made lamps from glass; they worked on a similar principal as cloth soaked up the fluid which was stored in a bulb below, and burnt to make portable light. It was incredible, all this new technology, yet with little of the external change she had expected to find when she had seen broken fragments of this world through her dreams.

Now aware of the events that had transpired while she had slept—and having retained the knowledge of this person's life—she felt ready to face this strange new time. This time was her own now. Her home, her family, even her history, was nothing more than a story. Fate had found her a life-force to replace, but at the same time she feared her fate would still meet that planned for the life she had taken.

She knew it had been predetermined that she would take over the life of this body, but she was still as powerless as the one who died trying to evade her attackers. Her muscles ached, her skin throbbed, and to move was almost impossible. But to lie here, to die as the owner of the body would have, surely that could not be fate's plan. She had to think of something, and fast. This young lady was meant to die, so she knew better than to expect a saviour to arrive.

The pursuers were upon her. Their foul breath reeked of the vast quantities of alcohol they had consumed. The stench of sweat filled the air, stifling her with the same heaviness of the void that had previously imprisoned her. Her eyes swam with darkness as her fatigued body began to die. She never saw the face of her attacker. She only felt his coarse hands upon her skin as he lifted her limp body to her feet. She tried to struggle, to fight, but her entire body seemed so heavy.

An agonising cry filled the air. At first she thought it was her own, but then things became a little clearer. Some of the exhaustion had lifted. The screams were those of a man, the one who gripped her. He howled as if her touch burned. With a small amount of resistance returned she struggled weakly to fend him off. Images flashed through her mind. Unfamiliar scenes, images which she couldn't quite make out. The strange pictures passed through her mind so quickly she couldn't distinguish one from another, until the final one. She witnessed a hand reach out to grab her, and then, it was over.

His hands fell from her and the weight of his falling body pulled them both down. She questioned if this strange force could be yet another side effect from her father's incomplete incantation, or whether The Fates intervened to ensure she could fulfil whatever purpose they had chosen for her.

"What you done to him?" Another man stepped forwards only to be stopped as her third assailant extended his arm, blocking further advance. If she could have seen through the dancing swarms of darkness, she would have noticed the two figures looking at her in paralysed horror. She rose slowly to her feet in an attempt to defend herself, aware that, should they continue their assault, she remained defenceless. But the fact she stood seemed to deter them for the moment. Standing was painful. Her legs shook as they strained to support her, and it took great effort to remain upright. She locked her knees to appear more stable, knowing better than to show them weakness.

"Didn't yer see?" one of the attackers whispered. Panic seemed to flood the air around them as he took a slight step backwards, his extended arm forcing his companion to do the same. "She killed him! The witch didn't even touch him! Let's get outta here!"

She heard their footsteps vanish quickly into the distance, but the blackness, dancing before her eyes, made seeing almost as impossible as standing. She gave a slight whimper as her legs collapsed beneath her. The dark patches within her vision swam and grew until she felt the soft arms of the earth supporting her weight. She would rest, just a little.

* * *

"Zo!" The pure panic in Daniel's voice had startled her. She had been in a world of her own as she tended to the small herb garden which Angela, Daniel's mother, used to grow medicines. "Zo, Zo," he called again. His voice echoed through the trees surrounding her home. The urgency in his tones an emphasis of his distress. When he saw her, she was already rushing towards the sound of his cries, her trowel still clutched within her muddy hands. The look on his face reflected his desperation. "Dad... found... need..." he gasped, unable to force a coherent sentence through his large gulps of air. It was a quite a run from the town where he lived to the little cabin, especially when it seemed time was of the essence.

The town Crowley—located on an island of the same name—was about a thirty minute fast-paced walk from where Zo lived. It was a small island possessing a few ruins, an unmanned port, a shrine, and a temple, most of which were all located far from the almost central town. It was an island where everybody knew each other. A community where everyone joined together to do their part. Although Zo was an outsider, she shared the unity of the town she had come to know as her home. She played an active role, part of which was growing and tending to the medicinal herbs used by Angela, the town's physician.

Daniel tried to catch his breath before he attempted the sentence again. His face flushed and his light brown hair, which was normally kept so neat, was ruffled from the run. His dark eyes filled with urgency as he tried to force the words out again, but failed. He managed to make eye contact with her rich blue eyes, but before he could speak, she interrupted.

"Take a breath. Slow down." She placed her hand on his back as he leaned forwards, breathing deeply. He couldn't help but smile as his gaze fell upon the dirt-stained knees of her lightweight trousers. She spent more time on the ground than any person he knew.

"Dad's found a girl, she's really hurt." As soon as he spoke these words, she knew what was needed from her. She rushed into the cabin and emerged just moments later with her battered cloth satchel slung over her shoulder. She wiped her now clean hands down the fresh linen shirt. She had even changed her trousers, although aside from the dirt stain there was no way to really tell they were any different. She always seemed to favour these lightweight clothes, even in harsh weather. She tightened the leather fasten on her brown hair as he continued. "Mum's exhausted. She's done what she can but—"

"Show me." Daniel grabbed her hand. It was an instinctive reaction to stop her from falling behind as he took off in the direction of the town.

By now he should have known better. Whoever she was before she arrived here, she certainly could run. He had thought at one point she may have been a royal messenger, or Herald, both were known for their speed and endurance. He soon came to realise it was more likely she was a trained alchemist, or apothecary, especially when he considered her skills. Given her age her talents were remarkable, and he could confidently conclude no one else in the world possessed the skills she did. Not a person remained who could use her style of magic.

Recently he had found himself thinking back to how they first met. He often wondered how his life would have turned out had she not appeared on that day. Everything had been so much better since she arrived. His hand slid from hers as she out matched him in pace. He continued to run, and pushed aside his fatigue by thinking back to the day their paths had crossed...

...He had returned to Crowley after having spent his normal three days at the College on the Eastern province of Albeth. Daniel, as quite often was the case, had found himself distracted as he thought over the topics they had covered in his classes, specifically in the mythology class. There was nothing that could distract his mind like ancient lore. He had said he would return straight home from the small port with the herbs his mother had requested. But instead he took the awaiting horse only part of the way before he sent it to complete the delivery without him.

Once again he found himself in the forest. Such hikes were something his mother had grown to expect. Although she encouraged his further education in medicine during his spare time—still hoping one day he would take her position as the physician to those here—she was glad he didn't spend his every moment in some form of study. She understood the importance of him having time alone. In fact, she was grateful for the days he came home late. In her mind it meant he was doing something other than burying his head, and emotions, in study. She worried about her son, and often wondered if he had made friends. It had been a long time since her son had really engaged with other people.

It had been weeks since Daniel had last ventured into the forest. It was his place of inspiration, a place where he could focus and think. Every day, at the end of term, he would find himself here, mulling over the work that had been set. Even now, as he walked the forest, his head was buried deep inside a book.

It was a relatively short walk from the forest to his home, yet despite this, it felt as if there was not a soul around for miles. No one seemed to venture here anymore, not since his mother's herb garden—found in a large clearing near the forest's furthest border—had become barren. The forest was known for its myths, tales of forest trolls and fairies, anguish and woe, but so was every forest. It seemed it wasn't possible to have a forest without some dark lore behind it. There was no better way to keep children from straying than with stories of the monsters and demons who preyed on them.

Daniel came here so often he knew each tree and every turn, without the need to look. He walked autonomously, leaving his mind free to study the examples of ancient writings which had been found in the last decade in some underground ruins. He hoped one day to discover its secret and be able to read them. It was something that had not been achieved since Hectarian magic had been lost forever.

It was said the art of this language had been forgotten when the Hectarian power faded, and so too had the ability of magical readings from the text of the ancients. He was certain, if he studied them for long enough, one day he would be able to understand them. He looked for repeated characters and tried to put letters to symbols as he walked. He could spend hours with the text and not get any further, but nor could the most brilliant minds. It seemed this code was impossible to decipher, and that was precisely why he had to do it.

Daniel's books were wrenched from his grasp as he collided with something with such force it caused him to tumble backwards. He sat in confusion for a moment, knowing there was nothing here which should have blocked his path. He was so busy mentally retracing his steps to see where he may have gone wrong that it was a good minute before he looked to see what, or more precisely who, had brought him to such an abrupt stop.

"Sorry." Daniel apologised suddenly as his vision came to rest upon another figure. He studied the young lady, who also sat following their collision. Seeing her, every fibre of his being filled with panic. He jumped to his feet, his eyes wide with fear as he scurried backwards a few paces while his mind took him back to an event of many years ago. A memory that, now it had fully surfaced, caused him to freeze, unable to retreat further or utter another word. He could do nothing but stare in paralysed horror as he relived the fear he had felt then. The young woman was in her mid-twenties—not much older than himself—but it wasn't her he saw, not until his panic began to subside.

Slowly, as he calmed his breathing, he began to see more of reality than the illusion created by his fear. The figure, who sat amidst scattered firewood, had yet to stand. She was clearly terrified of him, and his reaction to her presence had not helped to defuse the situation. She stared at him, afraid to move, afraid to talk, and as frightened of him as he had been of her. She stared at him, eyes wide in deer-like shock, unsure how to respond to this person's presence in the area she had clearly made her home.

It was a long silence, neither talking as their eyes locked on each other. Daniel's mind reasoned with him. It tried to encourage him to say something, anything. His thoughts raced. There was, at best, a subtle resemblance to the person he had recalled, but that person's hair was redder and her eyes a different shade. The sensible side of him began to see reason as he calmed, and surely *she* was much taller than the brown-haired person who sat before him. Besides, fear was not something the person he recalled would know.

She moved slowly to timidly collect his fallen texts, her small movements guarded. She turned her vision towards the ground, fearing to engage him. Her shoulders tensed as something in one of the books briefly caught her attention. She left it open, placing it on the top of the small pile before standing to return them to him.

"You're reading about Metiseous legends?" she questioned softly, breaking the silence. Her eyes skimmed meaningfully down the page as she passed them back to him. He glanced down to the ancient writing and back to her. It took him a moment to force his arms to reach out to take them, but as her words registered, his excitement drained all the remaining fear.

"You can read this?" he questioned doubtfully, but the excitement in his voice could not be disguised. There was no reason to assume the figure was lying. His instincts told him the words she spoke were true, and if that were the case it made this young lady very interesting indeed.

"Can't you?" She took a slight step back. The look in his eyes unnerved her. First had come his strange reaction at having found her here, and now this complete change in the way he seemed to perceive her. She couldn't place what her mistake had been, but clearly something she had done had upset this person greatly. "With it being in your book, I thought..." Daniel—his fears forgotten—glanced around to get his bearings. He found himself in the small clearing he often visited when he wanted some time to be alone. It was apparent she had been staying here for some time from the makeshift camp, and the scorched stone circle in which she had built her fire. He had not visited this location for a number of weeks, so couldn't be sure of exactly how long she had been here, but it was clear she had not strayed far from this area. She was mostly self-sufficient. There was a small pile of fruits and berries, and she was even growing small plants. He wondered what could have driven her to seek isolation and refuge here.

"You aren't from around here are you?" he questioned calmly, when what he really wanted to ask was, *'who are you, what are you doing here, and how can you claim to read a long forgotten text?'*

"I don't think so," she answered slowly, thinking carefully about her response. All the time she watched him cautiously, matching every step he took towards her in the opposite direction. "I just woke up here." The truth was, she had no idea how she came to be here, or even exactly where here was. She had stayed in this area while she tried to make sense of her situation. She hoped to have had more insight into her past before she needed to explain anything. It was impossible to explain something she herself didn't know.

"Nah, this is a small island. Everyone knows everyone, if you know what I mean." He smiled gently; excitement still lined his voice as he looked down to the ancient text once more. "Woke up here?" he asked approaching her slowly. As she backed away again, she felt herself topple as the fallen tree behind her threw her off balance and forced her to sit upon its rough surface.

"I don't remember much. I think I recall leaving for school. Everything else is a blank, and I think that was over ten years ago," she answered cautiously, unable to elaborate on anything further. With that one sentence she had told this stranger almost everything she knew.

"Ten years?" he repeated in disbelief. "You should come see my mother." He was quick to jump to the conclusion she suffered from amnesia, and found himself instinctively studying her for signs of injuries. What he didn't realise was the ailment afflicting this stranger was far more complex, more danger-ous, than anything he could diagnose. "She's a physician," he added after the curious stares.

Everyone knew his mother. She was a renowned physician, known not only on their homeland but by even the most prestigious areas. It wasn't uncommon for people to travel just for her aid. She was well-known and thus, as her son, he too was often recognised. "She has lots of contacts, you must have a family somewhere." She smiled at him cautiously as he moved to sit at the other side of the fallen tree, leaving a large space between them. She shuffled closer to lift the book from his hands as she started to feel less threatened by him.

"So are you studying Metiseous legends, or magic?" she questioned, quickly changing the subject in order to give herself time to think over his suggestion. Something about him seemed almost familiar.

"Mythology and supernatural studies, amongst other things," he answered dismissively. Daniel studied diligently at the College. He was what some would call a genius. One of his tutors had once said he had the makings of a sage. He retained information like a sponge retained water. Daniel had an unquenchable thirst for knowledge, and had already completed his studies on the basics; mathematics, history, new sciences, and botany, far quicker than anyone had expected, as well as completing his physicians' training to appease his mother. Now he had moved on to his passion, mythology and the supernatural. If possible, he wanted a profession involving something in that field. He had already excelled greatly, one term in, his assessor had told him he needn't study any further. If it was in a book or scroll, he had not only read it, but remembered it. However, Daniel continued to attend the lectures. If for no other reason than his attendance granted him access to the library, which was the second largest in the known world.

Above the forest, the sky began to darken. Hearing the night song of the birds, Daniel suddenly realised how late it had become. His mother was bound to worry if he was not back soon, and he knew enough to know he didn't want to stay in the woods at night; even if the stories *were* only legends. At the same time, he felt compelled to stay and find out more about this stranger. That, in itself, was uncharacteristic. He wasn't a very sociable person. He had acquaintances, but never really pursued friendship. Strangely, after the tension of their initial encounter had dissipated, he found he felt more comfortable talking with this person than he had talking to any of his peers in a very long time.

"So you can really read this?" He moved a little closer to her as she studied his book.

"This?" She smiled giving a slight shrug. "Sure. It tells the story of Metis, of how she and Zeus bore a child. The prophets said if ever she were to conceive another it would be a boy who would then take the place of Zeus, like he had his father before. This troubled him so, to ensure his security, he ate Metis, who at the time was still pregnant with his first child. It goes on to say the child he devoured in Metis was born through Zeus. There's a lot of hearsay, but that's about the idea of it." She passed the book back to him. "Do you always talk about books before formalities?" An easy smile lifted her lips as she rubbed her arms to relieve the chill of the cool of the night air. Realising she should prepare the fire, she stood to position some of the gathered wood, which still lay scattered across the ground.

"Sorry." It was only now he realised he had failed to introduce himself. "I'm Daniel, Daniel Eliot."

"Zoella Althea. Zo," she corrected. Despite everything, her name was one thing she remembered clearly. Once she had finished stacking the remaining wood he offered her a burning stick, which he had been working hard to light as she built the fire. She looked at him questioningly before she gestured for him to approach. As he leaned forward to light it, he stopped before the kindling even had chance to catch the flame.

"Is that camomile?" As he saw the unmistakable flowers all thoughts of the fire extinguished, like the stick held within his hand. He approached the area of greenery, crouching to examine the thriving plant.

"Yes, I grew it myself." She looked towards the small patch of herbs with pride. When she had woken here, she had found herself with many herbs and seeds, some of which she planted. She possessed very little to call her own but, for a reason which escaped her, amongst the contents of her satchel was a strange cork. She couldn't think of any reason to have held onto it although, she had to admit, whatever had been in the bottle it had once sealed was pleasant. She had spent much time inhaling its aromatic fragrance in the hope its smell would stimulate a memory.

"It's nearly impossible to grow in these soils," Daniel stated, pulling her away from her musings. A new thought dawned in his mind as he moved closer to the warmth of the fire. He looked to her in surprise as he realised it was now lit. "My mother has a cabin near the edge of the forest. She once had an incredible herb garden, but the soil went bad and most things died. I'm sure you could stay there a while. It's safer and warmer than sleeping in the woods. In return, perhaps you could tend the garden?" he questioned, wondering how it could be she was not only skilled with botany, but could read a language which, for years, no one had been able to decipher. One way or another he had to ensure he could continue their conversation. He felt compelled to learn everything there was to know about her, which he knew would be difficult, given her condition.

"Okay," Zo answered cautiously. Something about him had almost made her remember something. She stared at him intently, unable to place the forgotten memory, but this strange familiarity told her she could trust him...

...Zo had barely arrived at the door of Daniel's home when Angela had hustled her quickly inside, she glanced behind her, seeing her son just several feet behind. Her voice as she greeted Zo pulled him from his thoughts. It was hard to believe all that had only happened a year and a half ago. He felt like she had always been here, like they had been best friends forever.

"Zoella, thank the Gods." From this alone she knew it was serious, Angela always called her Zo, like everyone else. "I did all I could for now. She's not responding at all. Given the last few days I hoped..." Zo nodded in silent understanding as she made her way to the sink to wash her hands. Angela had been rushed off her feet of late and, although she had helped where she could, Zo often felt more underfoot than of aid. It was clear Angela had been with the patient for some time before sending Daniel for her. Her shoulder length, greying blonde hair spilt out from her ponytail to frame her pale face and darkened eyes which revealed the extent of her labours.

Unable to help any further, Angela took the opportunity to rest. She sat in the chair that faced the stained-glass window. The coloured light from the finely patterned glass spilt into the room and danced across the wooden floor. She knew the patient would be in safe hands. Although Zo was the same age as her son, she had skills with herbs and alchemy that defied her age, and even surpassed her own. She had a natural talent for medicine, something which could never be taught. It was as if the patient and herbs spoke to her, instructing her just what was needed. It was a skill which long ago was called herbal lore. It was a rare talent that Angela herself possessed, but compared to the skill of this young girl she was an intermediate to her mastery. She could rest knowing Zo was with her, and that the young girl appeared to have no life-threatening injuries. After a small rest they could discuss what Zo had found, if anything, and devise a plan from there.

Zo slowly climbed the wooden stairs followed by Daniel. Over the last year and a half, this place had become a second home to her. She found it almost second nature to walk the landing as she made her way to the furthest room. The door lay open allowing light to spill from inside to lighten the darkened hallway.

Daniel's home was the largest in the village. There were but two houses that were built on two layers; theirs—which doubled up as a hospital—and the home of Daniel's old friend, Stephen. In Daniel's home there was a room upstairs for patients who needed to be monitored, his room, his parents' room, and a smaller room for emergencies which couldn't be handled downstairs. There were also a few extra rooms downstairs where surgery could be performed and patients could rest.

Being a small town physician wasn't easy, and being on a remote island meant they needed all the facilities to treat those in serious need of medical attention. His mother had more than the talent required to fulfil all the roles needed of her, and still have time to see those who travelled the sea for a consultation. She was well-known, especially since most physicians were more inclined to practice the more modern science medicine and treatments. Angela, although proficient in both, favoured the old ways.

Inside what they referred to as the recovery room, Daniel's father, Jack, watched the young lady sleeping. His brow wrinkled in a frown. As his vision rested upon Zo, his dark eyes softened a little. He ruffled a hand through his pepper hair as he rose to greet her. After this slight pleasantry he left quickly.

There was something different about Daniel's friend. Something which made him uneasy around her. He had already misjudged her once, and even after such a short time together it was clear Daniel thought the world of her. He had always feared his son would never make friends again after losing Stephen. Since that day he had become withdrawn. He had distanced himself from everyone, but this person had stirred something in him. After he had met her, for the first time in a long time, they had seen Daniel smile.

Jack feared knowing what was so different about her would change his view on her forever. She was just too good to be true. She had turned a dying garden into a flourishing abundance of life in little more than a fortnight, and as for her gifts with herbs, it was beyond belief. His wife had thought about taking her on as her apprentice. Whilst it was clear Zo had no proficiency in the more severe side of medicine, such as sutures and surgery, it seemed her skills in botany were without equal. Whenever a case was in need of researching further, it seemed that, somehow, Zo always knew just what to do.

He couldn't help being surprised such a person could remain missing for so long. She was clearly well-educated. Surely someone, somewhere, had to be searching for her, but there were no reports of missing healers, or of anyone who matched her description.

He looked at Angela, who now sat sleeping in her favourite chair. It was the perfect place for her to rest to ensure she didn't miss Zo before she left. It wasn't surprising she was already asleep. She had arrived home in the early hours of the morning after being called out for the birth of Mrs Hamisley's first child. It had been a painful, complicated, labour which finally resulted in the birth of a healthy baby boy. Prior to that she had been attending to those involved in an accident at the lumber mill. It seemed for days now she had been given no chance to rest and was grateful she had this moment. He covered her with the blanket which was usually draped over the back of the chair, taking a moment or two to watch her sleep.

* * *

Zo knelt beside the patient and moved to rest her hand delicately on her forehead. It was something she often did to read a person's illness, a diagnostic tool known as the sympathetic touch. It was a skill only possible for healers.

Whenever she touched someone she knew if, and how, they suffered. It was both a blessing and a curse.

Daniel grabbed the mortar and pestle from the bedside table as Zo began to rummage through her satchel. She removed three small bags of herbs and instructed him on how much to use, and the order they were to be added. As he mixed the concoction, Zo carefully examined the young lady's injuries.

Some of her wounds were deep, but the blood she had lost was not sufficient to cause the lapse of consciousness she suffered. She looked harder, not with her eyes but deep within her mind, while resting her other hand resting lightly on the young lady's chest. The feelings she received from her were erratic. Even with her skill she couldn't locate the cause of her condition, something which was normally so easy.

"I can't see it," she whispered. Daniel stopped suddenly, resisting the urge to turn to look at her.

"What do you mean?" Concern lined his voice. She always saw *it*, that was what made her so good. She always pinpointed the exact problem within moments of applying her special methods.

"Her wounds are not sufficient to cause this deep a recession in her consciousness." Zo gave a sigh as Daniel handed her the mixed ingredients which had been ground and made into a thick paste. Although Angela had already treated the wounds, this mixture would serve the girl's body slightly better. "Maybe she can tell me something," Zo muttered, her voice trailing off.

"Huh?"

"Never mind." Zo, in theory, knew the routine. She was familiar with it, but it had been so long. At least eleven years had passed since she recalled attempting anything of this magnitude. Then again, this gap in her memories did not mean her talents went unused. When she first arrived here, nothing but darkness had stretched behind her. Recently, she had started to remember small details. She still recalled nothing since the age of twelve, but she knew her mother's face, and the face of her master and friend, Amelia. She knew, against all logic, she used Hectarian artes and, as a child, she had been taught how to. Despite this, she had never recalled the name of her home, or anything which could lead her there.

From that point she remembered nothing, but would think herself a fool if she hadn't used her talents within that time. Her skills came as second nature. She didn't need to remember the words or the rites. They came to her instinctively, and it was an instinct she had learnt to trust.

She steadied her breath as she began to focus. Daniel listened intently as he scribbled down the incantation. The words themselves were spoken in an ancient tongue, but only when the skill she used required the most concentration. The easier spells she spoke in plain language, summoning forth her powers. He sometimes wondered if, in these cases, words were necessary at all.

A sharp pain shot up through her arm. A pain so intense it caused a slight cry to leave her lips as she gritted her teeth against the resistance. Daniel was at her side in an instant. He hovered uncertainly, unsure what he could do if she was in danger. He knew better than to touch her, even a slight interruption could have serious repercussions.

Zo was not aware he stood next to her; in that moment she was somewhere else. She watched as a young lady's life-force, one which looked almost identical to the figure who lay before her, left the body to take the hand of an escort to the other world. She could hear the sounds of people who closed in on her as they emerged from the forest. Suddenly she felt Daniel's hand touch her lightly.

"I don't understand what I am seeing. Is she dead?" Zo spoke with more difficulty than expected. Her breathing was laboured as she once more became aware of her surroundings.

Daniel hesitantly removed his hand. He had been convinced she was ready to collapse. Her breathing had become erratic and shallow as the colour drained from her. He had been unable to do anything but watch, waiting beside her for perhaps thirty minutes, almost convinced her breathing was about to stop. When her lips began displaying the faint blue tinge of cyanosis he had known, regardless of the consequences, he had needed to act.

"I read once about an immortal who had the ability to take the body of another by displacing the essence of the occupant and sending them to Hades. It's rumoured he continued to do so until he had enough power to regain his form. Nothing like this I'm sure." He was unable to hide the relief in his voice as he gave a response, feeling the need to fill the silence with some form of answer. Since she had spoken, most of her colour had returned. It was almost as if her body had needed reminding she was alive which, given his knowledge on magic, shouldn't have been a concern if the person being linked to was alive. Only if the subject of an incantation was dead were there concerns about the caster taking the target's condition, and the lady on the bed before them was clearly breathing.

Zo gasped as the resistance between her and the young lady stopped abruptly. Her legs weakened, refusing to hold her weight any longer as she sank to the floor taking deep, laboured breaths. She quickly wiped her forehead with the back of the arm, removing the beads of sweat.

The patient's eyes opened. Her figure sprang to a sitting position as her alarmed gaze searched the room fearfully.

"It's all right. You don't need to be afraid." Zo's voice was comforting as she reached out to gently squeeze the patient's hand. The fearful brown eyes calmed a little when her vision moved quickly to the hand placed upon her own. "Do you have any family, anyone who needs to know you're here?" The young lady shook her head, all the time watching her surroundings carefully. "Then you will stay with me," Zo announced. "I would enjoy the company and I could do with supervising your injuries for a while." The young lady nodded slowly before speaking.

"I am Acha," she stated shakily. "To whom do I owe my thanks?" It was one of many questions she had, but this was the first she wished answered. She knew much about this time, the when and most of the where, so this seemed to be the most important question of all.

"I'm Zo." She smiled before inclining her head towards Daniel. "And my friend here is Daniel. It was his father who found you." Daniel offered his hand politely. Their skin had barely touched when they felt the charge in the air creating a powerful resistance between them. She pulled away quickly, and in a single movement, also removed her hand from beneath Zo's, her eyes wide with fear as she bit down on her bottom lip.

"I'm sorry I didn't mean to, I didn't. I thought..." She gave a frustrated sigh as she moved her hands to cradle her head.

"It's just as I thought!" He looked to Acha, his excitement failing to still his words. "What I just felt, there was only one other person with a variation of that skill, but that is nothing more than a legend. Her body is protecting itself, absorbing some of the life from those she touches, ultimately killing them. I bet she could possess their form too if she wanted." Daniel's eyes sparkled as he recalled the lore. Zo had seen his expression before, when their paths had first crossed. He was already fascinated by this woman, and the tales she would have to tell.

"By the Gods, I didn't mean to hurt you," she sobbed gently.

"Daniel, stop scaring her." Zo turned her stern gaze towards him, her eyebrows pulled together in disapproval before escorting him from the room. It was not suitable for him to say such things in front of the already terrified girl, but she doubted her ability to silence him.

"Don't you see?" he continued, his tone now hushed. "What you said about her being dead—there's a few things I still don't understand but, from what I can gather, she's like that god I mentioned earlier, but without control. My guess is anyone touching her, and this is the part I don't understand, *anyone* touching her falls prey to her. Her touch steals the very life from them, yet for some reason you seem to be immune. I can only assume one of two things, you're not a suitable host or, more likely, something you did affected her power on a deeper level. What exactly did you do?"

"I gave her what she needed to wake." Daniel pulled his excited gaze from the room where Acha lay to seek further explanation from Zo, an action which reminded him of the toll treating Acha had taken on her. Despite using the wall to support her weight, she seemed barely able to remain standing. Seeing this, he thought it best to ask no more questions, for today at least.

"Shall I ready the horse and cart?" Jack appeared at the bottom of the stairs. His words caused a flutter of nervousness through her stomach. A horse and carriage was not a preferred mode of transport, given the location of Zo's home. It made her question why he had thought to offer one. He had only glanced at her, it caused her to wonder if she looked as terrible as she felt.

"If you would be so kind." She smiled at him gratefully. Jack had always seemed a little cautious around her, yet she could never understand why. He always had some pressing issues to be addressed whenever she was near. She tried to tell herself she was being paranoid, only it truly seemed that way. Even should she stay for dinner conversation was, at best, strained.

"You look tired. I'll have Daniel escort you," he insisted before disappearing from view. Once he had left, she shot a concerned look to Daniel.

"He probably just heard our voices," he reassured, knowing his father's reaction would have been much different if he had the slightest inkling of what had just transpired. Not long after they had first met, Zo had trusted Daniel enough to share the information of her unique talents. They had decided her

24

apparent Hectarian lineage should remain a closely guarded secret between the two of them. After all, people had strange ways of acting towards things they didn't understand. "I will arrange for Acha to come with us, I'll just say she woke up while we were with her. Given her ability, it would be better if she were kept away from people like my mother who fuss over their patients too much." Zo nodded her agreement. A part of her felt as if this young lady was meant to be with her.

* * *

Acha rested inside the cabin, while Daniel helped Zo place the last of the firewood in the furnace located outside under the bathroom. This bath system was revolutionary. It was the first to use wood to heat the water from under the bath itself. It had been developed only ten years ago, and yet each home seemed to possess one.

"Create a fire to soothe her pain, to start with this a ball of flame," she whispered. Even as she spoke the words, she questioned their true meaning. Ultimately, no matter what she said, it would bring about her desire. She felt certain she could call forth her magic without the need for rhymes, but the only memories she had enforced their necessity.

Daniel, as always, watched with awe as a small spark hovered slightly above her hand. Within seconds it had expanded to cover her palm, seeming to swell and ignite within itself until the spherical ball was complete. It took the appearance of a miniature sun, hovering gently as it awaited her command. Manipulating the air around it, she directed the molten ball towards the firewood, releasing the magic only when the wood began to crackle.

Daniel had left in order to allow Acha to make herself comfortable in her new surroundings. When the water was hot enough, Zo helped her into the steaming herbal bath, and left her to relax in peace.

Although Acha stood at least two inches taller, Zo was certain the clothes she had left for her would fit, or at least be acceptable until her own had been cleaned and repaired, a task Zo attended to immediately with her wooden bucket and scrubbing board in the garden.

After the bath, Acha had waited uncomfortably inside the cabin, but as time passed, she finally gathered the courage to step outside. She glanced around, taking in the surroundings, hoping her appearance would be noticed, so she didn't have to disturb Zo. The area around them was thick with forest and the gentle breeze carried the delicate fragrance of the nearby flowers. The cabin itself had been constructed in a large clearing where a large portion of the land had been cultivated to grow herbs, and medicinal vegetation.

She did not have to wait long until Zo saw her and offered a friendly wave and a smile. She blushed, brushing her oak-brown hair behind her ears self-consciously as she made her way towards her.

Zo couldn't help but notice her hair seemed somehow longer than when they first met. There were many subtle differences she put down to the fact the figure was no longer caked with blood, mud and debris from her ordeal. Despite the difference in height, the trousers seemed to fit her perfectly, and the shirt, which Zo felt too self-conscious to wear, seemed almost as if it had been made for her.

"Feeling better?" Zo questioned as she hung Acha's leather trousers over the washing line, which was tied between two large trees. Zo had spent quite some time repairing the rips and tears before she had washed them, and had done so in a manner she hoped would be satisfactory until they could be replaced.

"Thanks." Acha nodded, giving a tired smile. As she spoke, Zo escorted her back inside the bedroom, where she folded back the covers on the soft mat she used for a bed. It wasn't that it was late, there was still at least four hours of light left, but Acha needed to rest, and after the events of the day, she too felt exhausted.

Chapter 2

Familiar Strangers

Just under a month had passed since Acha had returned to the cabin with Zo. The first few days had been difficult. Despite the accomplishments in her past she found herself lacking the confidence she had displayed so easily back then. It had taken time for her to come to terms with the different dialect and customs. But by utilising the experience of the young lady, whose life-force she had replaced, she was able to adapt relatively quickly.

It was different in so many ways to her own time, but now she was more accustomed to it she felt at home in her new surroundings, and her friendship with Zo and Daniel had blossomed. Their socialisation had become a regular routine. She truly felt as if she belonged exactly where she was. It was almost as if this time and these people were always meant to be her home and family.

* * *

Elly was adept in many things, and it was clear her skills were far superior to those of the young man who followed her. He was certainly an amateur. He made far too much noise for someone familiar with this kind of work. She couldn't help but be insulted that Blackwood thought so little of her to send a spy of this calibre to follow her. Clearly, he had let his guard down and forgotten she wasn't really his daughter. It was a façade they had maintained for longer than she cared for, but it still served a purpose.

So far, despite the critical flaws in his tracking and concealment, she had played along. She let him believe she was clueless, that she didn't hear the cracking of twigs beneath his feet, or his laboured breathing when she decided to quicken the pace. In honesty, she was having fun toying with him. It helped to pass the time on what was otherwise a very long journey by foot. After all, she couldn't risk introducing her pursuer to the convenience of Collateral. She wondered how long he could continue at their current pace, after all, *she* didn't need to rest, and only did so when it seemed he could push himself no further.

She made herself comfortable near the fire she had built. This would be the final camp before her reunion with Marise. This resting area was found just off the main path taken by those on pilgrimages to the shrine or temple on this island. Its use saw it had benefited from many modifications left in place by the countless travellers who had passed this way. Large smoothed logs had been placed around the fire pit which had been carefully outlined by pale grey stones. Above it, firmly planted in the ground, stood a timeworn metal stand and spit.

It was a place that provided shelter and convenience to any who passed its way; a place travellers or traders would sometimes meet to conduct business or exchange stories. Many such locations were clearly marked on the maps some, however, you could only find if you knew exactly where to look.

Her uninvited companion had done well to keep moving for fifteen hours. Although his difficulties in doing so meant she was even more aware of his gasping breaths and staggering movements, as he tried desperately not to lose sight of her. Whatever his reason for following her, it was clearly an important one. Most people, even Blackwood's elite, would have long given up regardless of the fee they were being paid. No one would continue to endure this level of punishment without good reason.

She smiled to herself as she rotated a small bird on the metal spit as it cooked above the fire. She could almost feel his hunger as his nostrils flared at the inviting aroma. She had teased him with the delicious scents of her fresh kills for days now. It had been two weeks since they had begun their journey and, while it had been amusing to play the fool, it was time to address the stalker. She could only walk this small island so many times, and she was eager to reach her destination.

"You must be hungry. Your supplies were depleted some time ago. Come and join me, there is more than enough." She smiled as she spoke to add a friendly tone to her voice. There was a long silence as she waited for his reply. She wasn't really surprised when none came, but tonight he *would* reveal himself. She had waited this long, worn him down, led him in circles, all in hope he would tire or lose interest. But the fact he remained close, and pushed himself beyond his limits, meant there was more to this than a simple game.

Tonight was her last chance to discover his motives. If he refused to show himself, she would have to kill him. It would be a last resort, doing so would create a trail, not to mention problems should the corpse be discovered. She could not risk leading him to Marise without having discovered his true intentions.

The call of a night owl was her only reply; there was part of her that suspected this cry had been made by him in an attempt to fill the unforgiving silence. She remained quiet until the bird was cooked. The delicious aroma filled the air, tempting the senses. It was a shame she didn't really enjoy food. To her it almost all tasted the same, but it served a purpose nonetheless.

"I know you have been following me," she continued at last. "I may be his daughter but do not place my intellect on par with *that* imbecile. You may as well reveal yourself, there is little need for further pretence." There was still no response. "I see you require proof, very well. You are a male with fair hair, and you are standing about thirty feet away to my left between a tree and the small bush with the red berries. Yes those," she added knowing he would have looked. "Originally you were carrying a wrap made from leaves containing your supplies, but it has long since been depleted and now you travel empty-handed." She had been granted many opportunities to catch a glimpse of him while he stalked her. The most obvious time had been on the boat across from Albeth. He had tried a little too hard to blend in. A quiet rustle came from the nearby bushes as a shadowy figure emerged slowly, his hands raised slightly as if to show he was unarmed.

"I didn't think y' knew." His blond spiky hair was now less neat than at journey's start. It was filled with the leaves and debris of the forest from all the times he had taken cover in the shrubbery to avoid detection. He moved sheepishly to sit on a log conveniently placed on the opposite side of the fire to that which Elly sat. She passed him part of the bird and watched as he ate hungrily.

"You thought what I wanted you to." He was on his second helping when he stopped in mid-chew. His mouth turned dry. Something was wrong and he had only just realised what.

"Aren't y' eatin'?" His stomach sank as the sick feeling spread from his stomach to encapsulate his whole body. She had not so much as touched the food she had prepared.

"How observant." She gave a short, quick smile. Eiji wasn't sure if it was a trick of the firelight but there seemed something sinister about it. His fears were soon confirmed when she spoke again. "It would be foolish to ingest my own poison, would it not?"

"Wha—" was all he managed to utter before being interrupted.

"Quite a nasty one it is too." She leaned forwards, ensuring he heard her every word. "You see, I need to know why you are following me. I did not think you would volunteer the information so I thought it would be best to skip the pleasantries. You now have two choices. We can wait approximately ten minutes while it seeps into your blood killing you slowly and painfully, by which point delirium will have loosened your tongue." She lingered on her words, her voice strangely soothing despite the serious implications she spoke. Eiji knew for certain he was not mistaking the fire's tricks this time as a sinister smile tickled the edge of her lips as he sat rigid, transfixed by her steely gaze. "Or you can tell me now and I may have an antidote."

This was a lot easier than she had anticipated. He was so young, unwise in the ways of the world. His eyes shone with terror, and power. Yes, there was power there, the likes of which she had seen in but one of his kind before. Although in her many years she had never seen one so young with such potential. It would be a shame to kill him. She had the feeling that, in time, he could accomplish great things.

"I didn't wanna." His voice broke, interrupting the tense silence. It had not taken as long as she had expected. "He made me, said he'd kill my master." He pulled his travelling cape around himself tighter, shivering despite being so close to the fire.

"Who made you?"

"Y' father, Lord Blackwood." Elly had known as much, but she had wanted to ensure she could trust his words. Those loyal to Blackwood always attempted to conceal this simple truth. Having obtained her answer, she now leaned forwards to take a piece of the cooked bird.

"Your master? You are an Elementalist are you not?" He nodded, as she spoke; fear swelled within him as he wondered how she knew so much about him. "I assume your master set you free to learn from the elements?" Again, she was answered with a fervent nod. "Did he never tell you what becomes of a master once he has taught the student all he can?" The same affirmation followed her question. "*And* he released you from your training?" She tried to prompt him to reach the same conclusion she had some time ago, but wondered why she bothered. It seemed impossible that this boy knew the answers but didn't understand the implications. Perhaps she was mistaken about his potential after all.

"Yes." His voice was etched with uncertainty. "But it's not what y' thinkin'. I've still much t'learn."

"If he released you then, obviously, he did not believe so. Elementalists pass on their power to the next generation. As he trained you, and you mastered a skill, you took the ability to perform that action from him. There can only ever be one master of any elemental skill at any time. It is how these forces work. Once you have learnt all his skills and teachings, his body returns to the elements which gave him life." Elly watched the painful realisation spread across his face. He had finally pieced together the truth, although she *had* needed to explain it to him. She saw the pain in his eyes as he understood; his master was already dead.

"He was usin' me!" he snapped in a tone which reminded her once more of how young he was. The rage across his face at being exploited was replaced quickly by panic as his stomach cramped, forcing him to remember the reason behind this conversation. "The antidote." He looked to her desperately. He had given her what she wanted, surely she would spare him. Something about the way she smiled at him made him question the trust he had placed in her words.

"What antidote?"

"But y' said..." he stopped in mid-sentence, his stomach cramps vanishing as he realised that, since speaking the name of the one who had tricked him, she had been helping herself to part of the 'poisoned' bird. She raised an eyebrow as understanding washed over his expression. She had wondered how long it would take before he noticed.

"I lied. You have followed me since I left, where could I have obtained poison?" All at once he felt rather foolish. He *had* followed her and since the first day she had carried nothing but a sword, which she never unsheathed, and the weapon she had used to hunt her food.

"I notice y' carry a sword," he said in an attempt to divert the attention from his stupidity. He was thankful for the firelight, it disguised his reddened face. "It doesn't suit y'."

"Oh, I am a master of swordplay. However, you are correct, this one is not mine. I am returning it to a friend." She turned the sheathed sword over in her hand effortlessly as she examined it. This time last year it had seemed far heavier, as had the burden she carried. "So tell me, who did my father tell you we were looking for?" Elly wondered how much this boy knew. *'Boy'*, she thought to herself. He was probably around the same age as she appeared, but he was still so young in many ways.

"He didn't, he said I'd know when y' found her," he volunteered, despite feeling cheated by her previous ambush.

"I see, well, I may as well tell you since you are part of this now."

"Whaddya mean?" Elly shook her head slightly. He really had no idea of the consequences behind his actions. She realised she would once more have to explain things to him.

"Well, if you return to Blackwood, he will surely slay you for failing. You have no reason to assist him following his deception and you know too much. You are now worth more to him dead, than alive." She heard him gasp as if this thought hadn't occurred to him. "Of course, I will offer you protection, *if* you help me."

"Help y' with what?"

"Well you see, this sword belongs to Mari. A renowned assassin who left his command some time ago." With this one sentence she had sealed his fate. He could not live knowing what he did, not unless he chose to help her.

"Mari, Mari," he mulled over the name. When his eyes widened, she knew he had arrived at the correct conclusion. "Y' don't mean Marise Shi?"

"The one and only," she confirmed, unable to hide the pleasure in her voice. "Now before you get all flustered, you *will* listen." He drew a slow breath and nodded.

"I've little choice. If I go back, I get killed. If I try t'escape, I get killed, and I assume y'd kill me if y' don't like my answer." His voice was filled with the distinct question, 'How do I get myself into these situations?' "Anyway, I heard she was defeated," he continued. He was torn; he had often wondered what she was like, ever since his master's paths had crossed with hers. The notion both terrified and enthralled him. He wiped his damp palms down his trouser legs. "Why'd y' wanna return it t'her? She's lethal."

"That is an understatement." She smiled proudly, an action which obviously alarmed him as she met his gaze. "However, when she left, she was different. She was no longer a killer."

"Now that I don't believe. A leopard can't change its spots. Y' expect me t'believe she woke up one day and thought, 'Hey I've had enough of killin' now I'll go do somethin' else'?"

"I do not expect you to believe anything. To be honest I do not know what to expect myself." Elly wondered if she was perhaps being too nice to him. Normally she would resolve inconveniences such as this and be on her way, but something told her this boy could prove useful. She wasn't sure what it was about him, but she had travelled with enough people throughout the years to know when someone was worth keeping on side, even if only for a short time. It was an instinct she knew to trust. "The truth is, following the rumours regarding Night's movements, my father is attempting to reclaim her before Night seizes the opportunity to take her himself. I, however, wish to protect her."

"By takin' her back?" His voice was outraged as he questioned how she could claim to be protecting someone by returning them to the one who created her, the one who put a child on the path to becoming a bloodthirsty assassin. His master once had the misfortune of crossing paths with her and, although there was little spoken, he had learnt much of her origins. It was knowledge he had passed on to him. Besides, if it really was Marise Shi she spoke of, it was doubtful she needed protection.

"No. I have no alliance with my father. Before you leap to conclusions, meet her. I am certain you will find staying with us is worth your life." She realised how difficult it actually was being nice to people. There was a big difference between this and the familiar mask of indifference she had adopted as Blackwood's daughter. However, for some reason, she wanted to encourage this person to travel with her for a while, and to do that she had to be nice. She gave a silent sigh, trying to keep her body language friendly. Being nice was hard work and she was out of practice.

"Some choice." He rested his head on his hands. With a despairing sigh he leaned closer to the fire and wondered where it had all gone wrong. He was meant to leave, learn more about the elements, and return home. Now he had discovered his master was dead, and whatever he did would ultimately result in his own demise.

"I think I am being more than understanding," Elly scolded. "I did not ask for your help remember? As I have said, I will offer you my protection for as long as you choose to travel beside me."

"Very well," he sighed. "Let's see what our legendary murderer has become. Then I shall make my choice." *'Death... or death,'* he thought to himself sceptically.

* * *

"Say Zo, whatcha reading?" Daniel stood in her doorway. He smiled as she looked up from the book held within her hands, a frown still gripped her gentle features. She had been lost in the pages. She couldn't even imagine how long she had sat staring at the tome before her.

"Just something Elder Robert gave me a while ago. I've been promising myself I'd get around to reading it, but..."

"But?"

"Well, he said I should protect it, but..." Daniel roused with curiosity approached her. As he peered over her shoulder, he too frowned, feeling like he was missing something.

"It's blank?" He looked from the book to Zo, and back again, before taking it in his hands and flicking through the pages. He chuckled slightly, remembering how it had come to be in her possession. It was that same day she had revealed her most guarded secret to him or, more precisely, shown him exactly what she was capable of.

"Not quite." She plucked it from his grasp. "I can make out the odd trace mark. Maybe it's an old notepad or something." She grinned, given its source she was uncertain why she had expected anything else.

"Oh you know Elder Robert, there's always a magnificent history behind everything. Even the firewood he cut yesterday originally belonged to some ancient tree who offered him a piece for fending off the wood-eating Snargles of Shale Steppes." They both chuckled. It was true, everything his hand touched had a mystical story behind it, and one of the many things Zo found so charming about him. It was exactly because of his stories and tales that Zo loved nothing more than to sit in his company once a week and listen to him speak of all manner of things, both believable and those which more than stretched the boundary of the possible.

"Still you never know, one day he may be telling the truth." She closed the book, wrapping it in the ivory cloth she had used to practice embroidery on, before placing it inside the small tear in the lining of her satchel. Daniel shook his head at her.

"Tch, you really should stop putting things down there. One day you'll lose something." Daniel waved his finger in the pretence of scolding her.

"But no one would look there," she protested as she tightened the loose stitches she had slid it through. She examined it carefully and, once satisfied the gap was no longer identifiable, tied the long thread in a bow and tucked it from sight.

"Why would anyone want that old thing?" he asked, knowing that since she went to so much effort to hide it, clearly it held some importance for her. "Anyway, isn't it time you were off?"

"I want it," she protested firmly, clutching the satchel to her chest as he asked his second question. "It is the first gift I've ever received." She paused as she looked outside to the position of the sun. "You're right though." She wasn't sure where the time had gone. It was already far later than she had expected. "I'll be back soon. I'll give your regards to Mr Miller."

Mr Miller was the local greengrocer who, very kindly, picked and packed her order every week for collection. Daniel would have gladly collected it for her since he visited her daily, whenever he was not at college. However, Mr Miller was an elderly gentleman, and one Zo was very fond of. She always looked forward to seeing him on the day of Ares.

When she arrived to collect her provisions, she would always find she had arrived just as the 'pot had boiled', ready for a drink. She would spend a good hour or more with him and his wife as they drank tea and updated her with the events of the town. It was a small town, as such everyone knew everyone's business; not that too much happened. The gossip was normally along the lines of who said what about whom, and plans to rebuild the river barricades. A long time ago someone had drowned there. It was a topic often avoided and she respected their need to leave some things in the past where they belonged.

More recently, the conversation had turned to her and Daniel. It seemed Mr Miller had decided they would make a great coupling, and was even trying to push them together. Tentative plans for their wedding were already under discussion, despite their objections. Mr Miller couldn't seem to understand that they could just be really good friends. They had tried to explain to him, but he merely went off on a tangent about where they could hold the ceremony. They had been tempted to tell them she was already promised to someone, just to stop all the fuss, but neither of them cared to lie. So they allowed him to imagine the exquisite settings and the different flowers. Everything he suggested did sound beautiful. As he described his ideas his wife would sit smiling. She knew by now no such event would happen, but she loved to hear him describe the details which held so close to that of their own wedding so many years ago.

Zo waved to Daniel as she flung her satchel over her shoulder before she left in the direction of town.

"Look after Acha for me," she called back. She hadn't been in the cabin when Zo had left, but she was due back at any minute.

Once Acha had fully recovered from her injuries, Zo had asked her if she would consider staying with her more permanently. It seemed she had no home or family. It only seemed fitting she should offer hers to another person who seemed lost and alien to these lands. She had been quite uncomfortable with the idea at first, but when Zo had explained that, with tending the herb garden and helping Angela about the town, she could use some help to keep things in order, she had happily agreed.

Zo and Daniel usually crossed paths near the town as she went to collect her supplies, or deliver the fresh trimmings of herbs to his mother. This was now part of their routine. Before Acha had joined them she and Daniel would walk back to her home together, and spend the evening chatting about nothing and everything. Now Daniel would arrive earlier than before to spend some time questioning Acha about the past. At first Zo worried that Acha would feel like she was being interrogated, but she soon became accustomed to his passion for knowledge.

"Sure," Daniel called out to no one in particular, since Zo had long vanished from view. He enjoyed the day of Ares. It was the first full day of his time away from Albeth, when he returned home from his three days of study. This was a day he put aside to listen to Acha's tales and for the three of them to share stories and ideas into the early hours of the morning. He had arrived a little earlier than normal today. Acha was still out gathering firewood for the bath and the small wood-burning stove, which Zo would use later to cook for them. He normally started out at the same time, but would encounter Zo on her way into the town and, of course, they would have a brief conversation on the roadside. Today she had been so engrossed in that book, she was running late. He had to wonder exactly how long she would have sat there, staring at the blank pages, if he hadn't arrived when he did.

* * *

As they waited for Zo to return, Acha continued to tell Daniel about her life before the talisman. She told him how—unlike most women at that time—she had been allowed to work the fields and attend to her family's affairs. Whilst other women were sent away to the castle to become ladies in waiting, maids, cooks, and other roles which were deemed more suitable, she remained home labouring in the fields, or taking the long journeys to deliver the produce and taxes. There were times, especially when seeking passage from her home to Albeth, she had needed to disguise herself. Women were thought to bring ill fortune to seafaring vessels, but living on Crowley had meant, in order to pay their monthly tribute to the King, and trade their excess produce for things they needed, passage across the water was required.

When Zo returned, they would normally be at least halfway through their first bottle of wine. They would exchange words of greetings before she listened with interest to whatever the topic of conversation had turned to, whilst preparing a meal for them to share.

Zo asked more questions than anything else, after all, having only vague memories of her past she felt she had little offer. But that's not all they would talk about. They would talk about science, folklore, the stories behind the stars, legends, anything and everything was discussed at that table. Except for things best left buried in the past, such as what occurred with Acha's father, and that Daniel was not the only child they had assumed him to be. There were secrets which none of them would utter. Secrets for one reason or another that would stay buried, despite the strength of their friendship.

Today's particular conversation had started on the topic of shamanism; in particular, the strange amulet which Acha had been found with. Daniel noticed she now wore this charm around her neck on three woven pieces of leather, identical to those used by Zo to tie her hair back. They had been intertwined to form a strong loop to fit over her head like a chain, and wrapped artistically until they split to hold the talisman securely. The twists then continued a little further until it was fastened, leaving a few tassels. There was no doubt in Daniel's mind this particular necklace had been made by Zo.

Acha explained it was the talisman itself that secured her life-force within a given host and, if not for it, she could not imagine what would have become of her. She referred to her sealing as a curse from a practitioner of the arcane. It was true enough, and far easier than explaining the situation. How she explained it, she had simply been at the wrong place at the wrong time. She went on to inform them that if something were to happen and she were to lose it, she would be sealed within it once more until it came in contact with another living creature, or something near her died to create an opening for her life-force to occupy. Even if something nearby did die, she could only keep its body if she retrieved the charm in time to bind her to it.

The open door creaked in the wind as a shadow from outside was cast across the small table. The figure seemed to linger in the doorway for a moment. Seeing the hesitation, Daniel turned to greet Zo, wondering if perhaps she needed a hand with her supplies.

"That was—" But his eyes failed to rest upon Zo as he expected. The opening was filled by an enormous figure, taller and wider than anyone Daniel had seen before. He was so large that only small fractions of light could penetrate past the gigantic frame. Ducking, he invited himself over the threshold as his eyes assessed them both in turn. From head to toe, this giant was covered in body armour, only his scowling face was absent from any form of protection which allowed his matted beard to fall upon his breastplate. He raised his thick arm to point at Acha.

"I've come for her," he boomed. For a moment it seemed as if the walls shook under the force of his voice. It took a few seconds for them to accept he was actually standing there. He was more like a figure from a story than an actual living being.

As the figure's presence and words registered, Acha's eyes widened in pure terror. She stood slowly from her place at the table, her eyes transfixed on the stranger. She backed away, her feet tangling in the chair's legs as her movement forced it aside. Daniel moved to form a barrier between them. The questions of who he was and why he wanted Acha were secondary to his desire to protect her. Daniel's hands wrapped around one of the thick wooden posts Zo had fashioned in order to fence the garden. He held it as if it were a staff which, to Daniel, was not much of a comfort. Despite the fact he held a vast amount of knowledge in regards to the theory behind fighting and techniques, he had never successfully put any to practice, and there had been a *lot* of practice.

"Acha, run!" Daniel glanced towards her through the corner of his eyes. His trembling hands grew moist, but all that mattered was making sure she reached safety. Before she could even move, the giant's arm grabbed him by his throat to fling him through the open door. Acha winced at the sound of his body as it hit the ground. His motionless figure lay sprawled across the damp grass, the wooden post still gripped tightly in one of his hands. She looked desperately for an escape, but her only exit had been blocked.

* * *

"Excuse me." Elly stepped out from the trees to address the person who had just run past them in the direction of the town. The figure stopped as she heard her call. "I see you are in a hurry, but I wondered—" Elly's voice seemed to fail as the young lady turned towards them. Shock registered on her face as she met the girl's familiar blue eyes.

Unable to believe what she saw, Elly found herself speechless. The thought that Marise would have completely reverted back to her original persona hadn't even been a consideration. She had expected at least some traces of the assassin to remain, be it her fiery red hair, or sea-green eyes.

To look at the figure now it was as if all those years had never transpired. It seemed they had been very proficient with the seal, perhaps too proficient. Zo smiled at her politely, showing no sign of recognition as she waited for her to continue.

"Are you all right?" she asked as the colour seemed to drain from Elly's face. She seemed to utter something, but neither Zo nor Eiji, could determine what. They looked to her curiously as they tried to make out the inaudible word and waited for her to speak again. It didn't seem like she could.

"We're lookin' for town. Y'll hafta forgive my friend, she's not been feelin' t'well." Eiji stepped in to avoid the long uncomfortable silence from extending further. He frowned at Elly as he did so. She didn't seem like the kind of person who would falter like that.

"Anything serious? I know a good physician."

"She'll be fine," he stated rather dismissively.

Elly had already begun to regain some of her composure. The impact of seeing her like this had been overwhelming. It had never been the intention to destroy the assassin, for her to be so completely removed there had to have been some mistake. From her understanding, Marise should have already resurfaced. The concoction had been made to specification, yet it appeared something had gone wrong. There was not even a hidden shadow of the woman Elly knew.

"Okay, well I'm heading into town now if you want to—" Zo choked on her words as she gasped painfully. Her hands gripping her stomach as her vision snapped back towards her home. Before Eiji could ask if she was all right, she whispered a name. "Acha." Zo had been aware of the decaying magical trace joining them since she had woken her. It had almost faded completely, but there were times when her friend's powerful emotions were still relayed by the sensation of physical discomfort. Something was wrong. This pain was too powerful of a reaction to be stirred by conversation alone. "Town is that way." She gestured. "Please excuse me," she called back, her legs propelling her in the direction of home.

"What was that all about, do y' think we should follow her? Somethin' seemed wrong," he observed as Elly's vision stayed fixed to the spot where the figure had stood just moments ago.

"Mari," she uttered again this time a little louder than before. She couldn't believe it. She had stood face to face with her and had been unable to speak a single word. She couldn't explain why, but seeing her like that had rendered her incapable of action. So many thoughts had raced through her mind. One of which was questioning if it would be possible to recreate what she had lost.

"Y' mean that was Marise Shi?" Surprise edged his voice. His vision moved towards the tree line, his mouth agape. "I expected her t'be..." He paused, as he thought over his next word very carefully. "Taller, t'say the least." He watched curiously as the slender figure disappeared from sight.

"Not anymore. I made her forget. I cannot believe how much she has—"

"Shouldn't we go after her? Somethin' didn't seem right." Eiji turned his focus to Elly, who stood motionless. "Hey." he prompted, finally gaining a response in the form of a slow nod. Elly blinked, shaking her head slightly as if to dispel her surprise. There was too much to do. The next time they met she knew she would have to tell her everything, and take her away from this island. It was the only way to ensure they could finish what they had started together all those years ago.

* * *

Driven by Acha's fear, Zo reached home in record time. Her vision drawn instantly to Daniel's motionless body sprawled upon the grass a fair distance from the house. The world seemed to descend into an uneasy silence as she approached him. Her senses communicated with her on levels she had never imagined possible; even so, the bombardment of such overwhelming information made it difficult to process anything accurately. She pushed her feelings aside, relying on her eyes to give her all the information needed.

"Daniel?" Her voice faltered as she crouched over him. She checked him quickly for injuries before glancing towards her home, even her touch did not rouse him. The eerie silence was replaced with the sound of a terrified scream, and once more Zo felt the discomfort.

Visible through the open door, Acha stood backed into a corner, her chest heaving in panicked breaths. The table which, until then, Acha had used as a barrier between them, shattered as he flung it effortlessly aside, its wooden legs splintering under the power of his throw. Without a second thought Zo charged into the house, grabbed a bottle from the sideboard, and flung it towards Acha's attacker.

"Get away from her!" Zo yelled, the splintering of glass causing the figure to turn his attention to her. Her hands balled into tight fists as a seething anger began to burn deep within her. "Now," she growled.

"What are you going to do little girl?" his voice boomed mockingly. With his attention distracted, Acha's legs began to respond. She trod carefully, quietly, as Zo tried to keep his attention from her escape. "She couldn't stop me, what hope's a child like you got?" Zo felt her posture slacken slightly as Acha stepped through the opening into the bathroom. She knew from there she could climb through the window to safety.

The giant growled, not oblivious to her attempt to flee, and lunged forward. In what seemed like only a few steps he had covered the length of the room, grabbing Zo before she had a chance to react. He lifted her into the air. His giant hand clasped around her neck as she coughed and struggled to break his grip. She kicked frantically, yet was unable to make contact through the thick armour. He gave a snort, launching her struggling body backwards through the window. Light glinted across the splinters of glass, giving the illusion of rain as it fell.

Zo coughed and groaned, forcing herself to move only to find herself a matter of feet from where Daniel lay. Pain exploded through her. For a moment something else seemed to take control. It scolded her for lying in pain, scolded her for being so weak. As she lay there, the feeling of helplessness changed to anger. An anger which would not permit her to surrender. She began to move, despite the protests of her entire body. The pain now fuelling the raw seething energy she felt rise within her.

Her hand touched Daniel's lightly in order to release the pole still clutched within his helpless grasp. With its support, slowly, she managed to pull herself to stand. Her voice had already found the ancient words of magic as she summoned her fire. She altered it, merging it with another force to forge a spell crafted from fire and wind, a devastating cyclone which caused the air to whip around her in order to take the fiery form she desired before being unleashed.

The impact with the creature, although accurate, seemed to cause it nothing more than a minor annoyance. The adept spell was barely noticed, yet at least it had managed to distract its attention briefly from the place where Acha now hid. The powerful energy, that had helped her to stand, seemed to fade as the creature once more turned to face her. The inner promise of strength was stolen as her courage faltered under the gnarled gaze.

He struck her viciously. The force of his backhand thrust her spinning into the air as his armoured foot connected painfully as she bounced on the ground. Pain radiated through her side under the weight of his kick as she failed to evade his further advance. The ground slipped beneath her feet as she tried desperately to scrabble away. The gentle rain, which hours earlier had seemed so soothing, had now turned even the terrain into an enemy as it hindered her attempts to escape. She had barely fought her way breathlessly to her feet when she felt the figure snatch her back by her hair. He lifted her to face him, unleashing a powerful punch to her stomach, knocking the air from her lungs as she felt herself flying backwards once more.

Joining the painful noise of her body's impact came another sound just to her right. It went almost unheard as the pain coursed through her. The figure still advanced with the intention of finishing what it had started. Her panicked gaze desperately sought an escape as she tried to force her objecting body to move. She caught sight of the long object which had struck the ground. It seemed like a gift from the Gods. Almost as if they had granted her this weapon to defend those she loved. Once more she forced her way unsteadily to her feet, somehow seizing the sword in the process and attaching it with such speed it was almost as if she had executed this motion a thousand times before. Her fingers, as if by memory, had performed the action of arming herself in but a few seconds.

She released the catch with her thumb. The sword was light, far lighter than she had expected. Looking down she saw the reason. She had barely drawn it an inch from the sheath and could clearly see the weapon itself lacked a blade. Securing the hilt once more she noticed the perceived weight had come from the scabbard. It was forged from an unfamiliar black metal, although apparently useless as a blade perhaps in its current form it could prove useful. She was unsure what had come first, the thought about using it sheathed as a weapon, or her instinctively unfastening it from the belt. Glancing around she tried to locate the source of her aid. Perhaps this person would also assist her in facing this being. But as her blurred vision panned around the area, nothing was visible, except for the advancing colossus.

Frustration, anger, and fear rose within her. She could not lose. There was too much at stake. Acha depended on her. Somehow, she had to defeat her opponent. It was the only way to ensure their safety. But she knew nothing of combat, and her magic was ineffective, his seemingly impenetrable armour somehow shielded him from all her magical attacks.

The giant was upon her now, striking out once more with his heavy punch. She turned as quickly as her pained body would allow in an attempt to flee. Her right foot slipped in the mud, dropping her to her left knee just seconds before the creature's strike made contact. A splintering crack resonated above her as its armoured hand struck the tree. Without thinking, Zo thrust the sword upwards, catching the figure by surprise as the scabbard grazed his face. Realising what she had done she rolled to all fours, crawling away quickly, trying desperately to summon the strength to stand.

His foot swung forwards. She rolled to the side, barely dodging his deadly blow, and bringing her sword out as she rolled to strike his knee. The creature let out a frustrated howl. His eyes showing the annoyance caused by facing the pest before him. He lunged, striking her squarely once again. Darkness swarmed her vision as she felt him drag her to her feet by her throat. A sickening, splintering crack filled the air as he thrust forwards slamming her into the same tree he had struck just moments before. The darkness closed in around her as she felt herself sliding towards the ground.

Acha saw Zo's limp body sliding down the tree, leaving a red trail of blood upon its bark. Even from this distance, she had heard the deathly sound the impact had made. Tears streaked her face as she pushed herself backwards frantically. The hulking creature, having finished with Zo, now turned its attention once more to her. The giant's steps seemed to shake the ground as she tried to shuffle backwards to find cover somewhere, anywhere. She glanced across to Zo, hopelessly, as the creature advanced. Her friend sat deathly still against the trunk of the tree. Seeing Zo's lifeless body, she realised escape from such a creature was futile. There was nowhere she could hide. She felt her back press firmly against the side of the cabin, seeing the bath's furnace in her peripheral vision. She was certain it was big enough to hide her, but there was little point. The creature advanced on her at speed, it would follow her every move.

Acha screamed as the giant hand extended towards her, her capture inevitable. His fingers were almost upon her when his movement stopped abruptly. Parts of the armour covering his side exploded into fragments as something thrust through his ribcage. Acha heard the creature's breath alter from its injury. But this being had clearly been a veteran of battle, such a wound would do little to slow its pace. It stood upright as the sword was pulled from its body. Seeing her chance, Acha frantically made her escape towards Daniel who had struggled to his feet.

Daniel could scarcely believe what he had seen. He had just moments ago awoken, only to see Zo striking their attacker. She had moved with impossible ease to land the critical blow through the creature's chest plate. He knew, without a doubt, the sword in her possession was magical. The blade seemed to be formed of light itself. Half shone with a light so white it seemed almost blue, whereas the other half, in a complete contrast, radiated an intense black tinted with a faint blood red aura.

Even from his position, Daniel could see the sticky patch of blood which covered the back of Zo's head. It was a miracle she was standing, let alone finding the coordination to move as she did now. He had never seen anything quite like it.

As the giant looked upon his attacker, his eyes held recognition. He had seen through her appearance to her essence, an essence which now held the fighting spirit of a warrior. His heavy cestus struck out in a fearsome attack, his wound doing little to slow his pace despite his laboured breathing. This time Zo moved as she saw the strike. Her footing slid gracefully to dodge with such minimal movement it allowed her sword to exploit the opening, slicing through his armour until once more she inflicted a damaging strike.

Watching the battle, the fight almost seemed surreal. Every movement she made was so precise, so perfect, it seemed to create clean openings for her to exploit. The creature lunged forwards, a foolish move which allowed her to once more duck his strike. She sidestepped behind him, bringing her sword up to slice his hamstring, forcing him to his knees before her. She stepped again following through in an almost fluid movement, striking his face with her hilt before launching an attack so powerful that, when it struck the mighty creature's collarbone, it forced him to the ground.

She stood over him, the clear victor of the battle. Her sword was held poised at the giant's neck, tempting her to deliver the final blow. Her vision fixed on the throbbing arteries as whispers told her to kill him was the only way to keep her friends safe. It told her she had to do it, that there was no other choice. This instinctive part of her seemed to force her hand down towards his throat, telling her how wonderful it would feel. How it would satisfy and calm the anger which burned within her. She was unsure how long she had stood above the figure. Her head throbbed with pain, a reminder she would soon surrender to the darkness which began to return to her vision. She knew that whatever needed to be done to ensure the safety of her friends needed doing, and soon.

The blade vanished into a fine mist as she somehow managed to force it back into its scabbard taking control of her anger, of her desire to kill the one who had threatened them.

"From this battle teach him shame, and send him back whence he came." As she finally spoke, her tone was little more than a whisper. She leaned upon the scabbard to support herself. Her head throbbed and her mind clouded as things began to lose focus. Everything she knew about medicine, about the injury creating the sticky warm patch running down her neck, told her she should not be conscious. Through the cloud of darkness, she heard the giant let out an agonised howl just seconds before he dissipated.

Her knees gave way. She leaned forwards on her trembling arms as they gave their best effort to stop her falling further. Her numb hands still gripped the sheathed sword, fearing to release it in case further danger approached. Her senses warned her not to surrender to the darkness. There was still something here, a power that didn't belong. Her mind warned her it could be an accomplice of their attacker, and if she collapsed now her friends would still be in danger.

Noises and voices became incoherent as her consciousness began to fade. She was vaguely aware of a commotion happening around her. Things grew darker, her senses dulled. They weren't safe, she reminded herself. She couldn't afford to give in, not yet.

"By the Gods, Zo, where did you learn to fight?" It was Daniel. His voice seemed to echo inside her mind as he rushed forward, but something stopped him from reaching her. She struggled to turn, to look at what had frozen him. But the more she moved, the more darkness threatened to envelop her.

She felt the change in the air and knew Daniel had seen whatever threat remained. She could see nothing beyond his fuzzy image. Zo attempted to speak as she felt his anxiety rise. Her senses had been right, that figure was not alone. The tension in her body, the desire to see them safe, was the only thing which prevented her from losing consciousness. Even if she only gave them enough time to run, she had to ensure they were okay. Part of her questioned if she was up to the task, but another part told her to welcome the challenge.

"Where's... Acha?" Her voice seemed almost alien as she spoke. It was so quiet for a moment she feared her question had gone unheard. Someone approached; she could hear their footsteps. There were two of them, and their footfalls were remarkably lighter than the last one who had engaged them. Her trembling grasp tightened on the sheathed sword as she failed to push herself up.

"She is right here. She is safe, you all are." A foggy blue haze passed before her vision. Even through the confusion, she recognised her. It would be difficult for anyone not to. Their paths had crossed in the forest, yet she felt a deeper familiarity towards this figure.

"Oh, Lee, your sword." Zo looked towards the scabbard held between her hands. She would have offered it back to her had she possessed the strength to lift it.

"It is, and always will be, yours." Elly smiled, hearing Zo speak the name only one person had ever called her. She crouched, quickly assessing Zo's injuries.

"But it looks so—"

"No, Mari, you misunderstand. It *is* yours," she whispered, leaning towards her to ensure the words were shared only between the two of them.

"I think, you've mistaken me, for someone else, my name's Zoella." Speaking hurt, and she was unsure the words had been spoken aloud as intended, or simply thought.

"And yet you know my name." Zo opened her mouth as if to answer, but her speech was cut short by the overwhelming dizziness which encompassed her. The realisation that they were out of danger brought tremendous relief from the nightmare. She knew they were safe, but she wasn't sure how. The remaining energy drained from her body. She could no longer fight, and she no longer needed to. She surrendered to the darkness which beckoned, feeling someone's arms break her fall as they caught her.

* * *

Voices swirled around the darkness of Zo's sleep. They chanted and whispered from every direction as they called to her.

'*Yesss,*' whispered one.

'*She's the one,*' another voice echoed. She turned through the darkness as if to face the voice. It was then she noticed the eyes. The darkness was littered with them, and they all seemed to watch her, never blinking as they stared. Their black pupils glared at her as they followed her every movement through the darkness. She could not distinguish the form of those who watched. There were only two shades of colour visible, the blackness of the area which matched the creatures' pupils, and the almost glowing whites of their eyes that warned her of their presence.

'*We will have fun with this one,*' another voice from her side whispered, then another behind her. Each time she turned to face the noise, turning in circles as they spoke.

'*She shall play.*'

"Who are you?" The whispers stopped suddenly, almost as if they hadn't expected her to hear them. "What do you want?" Her hand fell to her side as if hoping to find a weapon. She knew this was nothing more than a dream, yet something seemed strangely real about the place she now found herself. She couldn't place the feeling, but this was no ordinary slumber.

'*Do you want to know the truth?*' the shadow eyes questioned. There was something almost serpentine in the way they spoke. Their tone never rose above a whisper, yet in the empty silence of the darkness even one voice sounded so loud.

'*We could show you,*' another voice whispered tauntingly behind her.

"What truth?" Frustration rang in her voice, annoyance at her invisible visitors. "What can you show me?"

'*Yourself.*' A voice from the left startled her. They had changed the speaking order now as if deliberately trying to unsettle her.

'*Will you play?*'

'*You do want to know, don't you?*'

'*We can feel it.*'

'*That is why we came.*'

'*We only answered your pleas.*'

'*Don't you want to know?*' The voices chanted.

"Yes, tell me," she pleaded at the swirling voices, still turning in an attempt to see the true form of those who watched her from the shadows.

'*We cannot.*'

'*He would not like it.*'

'*But if you would play.*'

'*If you would play, we could show you.*'

"How, how can you show me?" The voices whispered inaudibly for a moment before they answered.

'*In a game.*'

'*An adventure.*'

'*A quest.*'

'*All truths will be revealed.*'

'*Will you play?*'

"Is it dangerous?" The voices laughed in unison. It wasn't until this point she was really sure it was more than one voice addressing her. The laughter was almost deafening. In this moment she remembered the vaguest of notions. There was a reason she couldn't refuse this invitation. There was more at stake than just her memories. She *had* to play their game, and play to win, otherwise the cost would be far too great.

'You fight well.'

'Wonder why?'

'Will you play?'

"All right, I'll play your game. What must I do?" she asked, weakly. A sickness rose in her stomach as she accepted their challenge. There was so much she wanted to know, answers she had never been offered until now. She had to know the truth. The truth behind the darkness, the secrets hidden in her past. She couldn't bear not knowing any longer, only able to guess why she was never sought or why she woke up screaming in the night. The answer made her question her decision, but she knew there was never really a choice to begin with.

'Survive.'

* * *

As she woke, the words had already started to disperse and the memories of the dream began to fade quickly. Her head pounded, her breath was sharp as a sickening feeling rose within her. Glancing around the room, which she normally shared with Acha, brought some relief. She was home. She was safe.

"So you are The Chosen?" The unfamiliar voice startled her into sitting upright. Pain splintered through her side and stomach as her vision swam with the throbbing in her head. "You are our saviour?" His tone was etched with amusement. Finally, her vision found him standing with his back towards her. He turned to face her and for a moment she could only stare, but he too seemed surprised as he gazed upon her. It was almost as if she was not whom he had expected to see.

He was the most beautiful person she had ever seen. His autumn red hair was tied back into a long ponytail, which finished near the centre of his back. He stood around six foot four, and seemed to have perfectly positioned himself so his slender muscular build would be silhouetted by the light which flooded through the window. He wore an opaque white shirt and tight leather trousers, which only served to enhance his frame. But it was none of this which prevented her words escaping. She was captivated by his intense, brown eyes. They were a shade so rich and deep that they consumed her completely.

When he spoke again, his voice was filled with elemental rhythm. "So you think you can be our saviour?" He had lost the underlying tone of sarcasm. Pain returned her to her sense as his words released her from his thrall.

"Saviour?" Her voice shook slightly, wondering how a stranger had been able to approach her unnoticed, and if she had cause to fear him as she had the giant who came before. She unconsciously touched the back of her head—debating if he was but a delusion—and gasped at the splintering pain caused by her hand as it touched the blood-soaked dressing.

"You agreed to their game did you not?"

"Game?" A vague memory of a slipping dream fought to the surface of her mind, yet in that same second it had vanished.

"So, they are playing with mortals again," he stated to no one in particular.

"With mortals, who are you?"

"You may call me Seiken." He paused almost as if he expected some form of recognition. When he received none, he continued. "They think you shall fail their challenges." He glanced over his shoulder towards the window, his shoulders slumped slightly. "There is little time left. It is a game. There are rules they must follow, although they will twist them to their needs. They do not know I am here, that I have come to warn you." Once more he looked outside as he spoke quickly.

"Warn me?" She examined him intensely. She seemed to recognise this stranger, he seemed so familiar to her yet, like many things from her past, she could not place him.

"We shall help all we can." Again, he glanced through her window.

"What do you mean your saviour?" Everything was gradually starting to become clear. The words he spoke seemed more coherent as she unconsciously began to heal her wounds. Had she looked, she would have seen the small threads from the world outside attached to her, giving her their energy, just as they had to a lesser extent whilst she had been sleeping. The figure looked outside once more, but she didn't dare to follow his gaze in fear he would vanish.

"Their game. It is a quest. You have been selected to attempt to release our kind. With our imprisonment, the barrier between our worlds is thinning. You are our last chance, after you there will be no more time. Consider yourself chosen." This time she followed his gaze through the window. She wasn't sure what she expected to see, a dark ominous cloud which meant evil was afoot, or a barrier which now shimmered in the light where there was none before. It seemed this person could see something she could not. The door swung open, startling her.

"Zo, thank the Gods you're awake. Who were you talking to?" Daniel glanced around the room as she did the same. She looked to the place where the stranger had stood, only to find it empty.

"Nobody?" she asserted, whilst questioning her answer. "I had the strangest—"

"You are awake." The blue-haired lady from before rushed to her side. She moved to examine Zo's condition, her eyes scanned the room briefly before focusing on the injuries. They had healed quite nicely, although she hadn't expected any differently. This persona had always been skilled in healing. "Despite the blood loss, it was not as severe as it seemed, just a superficial wound."

"Do I know you?" Zo looked at the stranger questioningly as she spoke. She had expected to be questioned about the speed of healing, and had readied all manner of reasonings for her quickened recovery, but instead this person had protected her secret.

"A lifetime ago, yes." Zo heard a faint knock at the door and noticed the blond-haired person, who had accompanied her before, standing near the doorway in the now crowded room. "I am Elly, and this is Eiji." He nodded politely at his introduction and shuffled further inside.

"You didn't have anything to do with..." Elly followed Zo's gaze outside to the former battleground.

"Him, no. I think Night is also aware that you are here."

"He was after Acha," Zo protested, not really understanding all that Elly had said.

"No." Elly moved closer to kneel on the mat Zo used as a bed to make room for Acha who, as if on cue, had entered the room. "It was a simple case of mistaken identity. He was sent for the woman who lived here. Acha lives here. He saw her first, but you were his intended target," she explained.

"Elly, I think I remember..." Zo felt the same feeling of familiarity towards her that she had when she first met Daniel. It was as if she'd seen her somewhere before. Unlike with Daniel, she managed to grasp something from the darkness. "Did we used to live in the same area?"

"Something like that." She gave a strange smile, its meaning not quite discernible.

"You said Night?" Zo suddenly realised. There were too many people, all of whom seemed to be talking simultaneously. She could hear so many distant voices, mingled with those present in the room, it made her head swim. The whispers suddenly fell silent. Suppressing a shudder, she spoke again. "Who, and why would he be after us?" Elly stared at her with disbelief before bringing herself to answer.

"Not us, just you. Do you really not recall?" Her voice radiated with the same shock registered on her face. As she looked around it seemed as if she was the only person who was unfamiliar with this name. "You know, Night," she stated as if believing saying the name again would rekindle her memory. It didn't. "No?" She gave a frustrated sigh as she questioned if perhaps she had overdone the potion, just a little. "Well, do you at least remember the Grimoire?" Elly shook her head, she already knew the answer.

As she looked around the room she was met with blank stares. Despite the fact it had happened around two and a half decades ago, no one spoke of the events leading to the creation of the seven Grimoire, almost as if fearing what acknowledgement of such a thing would do.

Elly sighed again. This was meant to have been so easy. The time had come to put phase two of the plan into operation. Was it too much to ask for a little cooperation? "Very well. The Grimoire were used to seal away Night, capturing his spirit and his power within seven tomes." Elly paused as she heard a slight guilt within her voice, a tone she quickly corrected. "This was probably before you were born, and since no one speaks of it..." she shook her head in frustration. To her it seemed hardly any time had passed since this had occurred. "Somebody managed to obtain them and released the power within to return it to Night. His power has been growing since. I was sent to find you before he did. It appears I was too late. You must come with me. It is too dangerous for you to stay here any longer."

"Sent by who?" Daniel's eyes narrowed with suspicion. He gripped Zo's hand tightly as he watched Elly carefully from the opposite side of the bed. He had asked the question in Zo's stead to allow her time to make sense of exactly what was being said. It was bound to take time for her to get her thoughts in some semblance of order, especially this. All this time she had lived without so much as a whisper from her past, and now she faced this. It was only natural she found it all a little overwhelming.

"By her lord, Lord Blackwood. He wanted me to return her before *he* finds her. He does not want to lose her." Zo felt herself blush as she envisioned herself in the service of a lord. Doubt began to creep through her mind. If this were true, it failed to explain why there had been no missing person's notice.

"I don't want to go. I'm staying here," she stated quietly, yet firmly. Her being in service to a lord was ridiculous. She would never consent to servitude, to becoming a trophy of power and being displayed before other nobles at whim. Nor, if this were the case, would she have been permitted to simply vanish for so long. There was something amiss about the entire situation. Something was being kept from her.

"I am not taking you back," Elly admitted earnestly. "But you cannot stay here either. Especially since he knows your whereabouts. It is no longer safe."

"But this is my home," she protested. It had taken her mere weeks to feel like a part of the community. Regardless of her past, Crowley was her home, a place she felt safe, and it was a feeling she was reluctant to surrender for anyone.

"So you're asking her to just up and leave everything, her life, her home, the people she loves?" Daniel's voice was more outraged than Zo's. He could hardly believe a stranger could just walk in here and threaten to take her away.

"She is in danger. If she stays, he will tear the village apart, killing everyone, if that is what it takes to find her."

"All that effort for a witch?" Daniel forgot himself in a moment of disbelief. He covered his mouth as he looked to Zo apologetically. She shrugged, knowing it would have been apparent to everyone here exactly what she was. Besides, she had the strangest feeling these people already knew at least that much about her, and from their expressions it was clear they knew a lot more.

"You're a witch?" Acha's voice trembled as she looked upon her friend with terror. Zo hadn't realised she hadn't known, but for some reason, her heritage had never come up in conversation. Perhaps because she and Daniel had been careful for so long, that it had become second nature. Although she couldn't remember hiding it from her, as she thought back, she realised Acha had never been around on the occasions she and Daniel had discussed it. "A good one, right?" Her voice held underlying tones of panic, she couldn't help it. Witches were known to be evil, which was why those in her own time had feared them. Magic was not something to be crossed lightly. Zo opened her mouth to answer but was interrupted abruptly.

"It's not the witch he's after," Eiji revealed, but further explanations were cut short by the weight of Elly's stare. It was a warning he didn't need twice, it reminded him not to forget himself. He looked down to his feet, sheepishly.

"I don't want to leave," she repeated. The noise of the room swam through her head as it became louder. Everyone seemed to have something to say on the matter, so much so that it all became a jumble until one very clear sentence pierced through the rabble.

"Stay and you are signing the death certificate of this town and everyone within. You are selfishly endangering all the people you claim to love," Elly declared. The room fell silent.

"Why, why go to all that?" She shook her head. Tears spilt down her cheeks, coming of their own accord, regardless of how hard she had tried to stop them.

Everything had happened so quickly. Her day had started out as normal. It was scarcely halfway through and already these strangers had torn her life to shreds with all the delicacy of a hurricane.

"Because you are unstoppable. That is why they both want you. You could tip the balance—" Before Elly had a chance to finish, Daniel interrupted.

"Zo, this town can take anything thrown at it. How do you know you can trust her? It could be a trick." Daniel wrapped his arm around her and pulled her close to him.

"Do not be a fool. Next time it will be more than one weak hunter. He will send an army. Nothing would survive. Can you really live with that? Could you live with the knowledge that everyone you have ever spoken to, or cared for, had to die because *you* were too selfish to leave, too selfish to put their needs first? You have no choice. *He* has decided it is time, therefore, we *must* move you. Unless, that is, you want to be digging the graves of everyone here before you are taken away by force. At least this way you can keep everyone safe. If your actions can protect them surely there *is* no choice."

Despite his previous misgivings, Daniel now had no doubt in his mind that this stranger not only knew Zo, but knew her personally. Only someone with an intimate knowledge of her could have worded their argument in such a way that refusal was not an option. This person knew her well, or at the very least, how to manipulate her.

"I have no choice," she repeated emptily as she thought it over. "You're right." Her voice seemed alien to her ears. She knew she couldn't stay here, not if it meant it would bring danger to those she cared for, those who had welcomed her into their homes.

"Zo you can't leave. The people here need you." Daniel's voice was filled with desperation. He didn't want to lose her. She was his best friend. Without her, he would never have been able to trust again. He already knew he was fighting on the losing side. Elly's last argument had made the case. One way or another she would leave. He doubted there was a single thing he could say to stop her. Worse still, he questioned how much of what Elly had said was the truth. Her timing had been just a little too perfect. Perhaps everything that had occurred was merely a ruse, a way to ensure she left peacefully to fulfil whatever their own agenda was.

"No, they don't need me." Zo forced a smile but Daniel could not manage one in return. "But where do we go from here?" Zo asked. If the situation truly was as desperate as Elly implied, she was glad to have lived in peace for so long, but surely there would be people anywhere she travelled, and her presence would surely be placing their lives at risk too.

"I know of a place you will be safe," Elly counselled, recognising all too well her despair and doubts.

"You're not taking her back to Lord what's-his-name?" Daniel snapped.

"I have no intention of taking her back to Lord Blackwood, ever."

"I'll pack tonight." Zo's voice sounded distant, almost hollow, as she agreed to this stranger's demands. It had happened so quickly. She was leaving, and somehow she knew she would not have a chance to say goodbye.

"We will leave tonight, under the cloak of darkness. *He* may be already watching now he knows for certain you are here," Elly stated, glancing outside as if to enforce her point. Despite this convincing action, she knew for a fact that no more assailants would follow. No one else would come here in pursuit of her; at least not for the moment, not for as long as Zo did exactly what she said.

Chapter 3

Departure

A backpack and a satchel was all Zo needed to carry her life away. She had found it hard to believe a life could be packed away so neatly. Everything she had could be stored in these two bags, and most of the space had been taken up by herbs, food, and a few wooden bowls.

Her vision continually strayed back in the direction of her home, towards a place she had found so much comfort. As she made her way slowly to meet with Elly and Eiji, concerns filled her mind. She wondered if she was really doing the right thing, if her absence would keep those she loved safe. Surely anywhere she lay her head would be in danger of being attacked. If the things she had been told were true, perhaps it would be better to return to Elly's father, to whom she had apparently sworn fealty to. At least he would know the dangers her presence brought.

She wondered—regardless of who she was now— if she would ultimately return to become the stranger she didn't remember, and questioned if would she forget her time on Crowley, like she had forgotten her time before it. She feared her friends and memories would fade into a distant background, and eventually become no more vivid than a forgotten dream. Such concerns preyed on her mind as she walked, and they made each step harder to take.

Pain and guilt knotted her stomach. In just under an hour the sun would be almost ready to set, and Daniel and Acha would return to wish her farewell, but she would not be there to greet them. She had to have left before they came. She was certain that if she faced them, she would lose the strength to do what was needed. Saying goodbye would break her heart. She knew it was better for everyone if she simply slipped away.

As soon as Daniel's father had finished repairing the broken window, she had departed. This was the first time she ever remembered being grateful for their strained relationship. Jack had simply attended to his work, replacing the glass pane without asking a single question as to how it had been damaged.

Earlier that day, after they realised that, regardless of what they said, she *was* going to leave, Acha had begrudgingly left with Daniel. They insisted on getting her a parting gift, something which also gave them the opportunity to accompany Elly and Eiji to the town to gather supplies. Daniel must have asked his father to repair the damage immediately. She suspected his presence was to ensure she couldn't depart before they returned. They hadn't counted on it being such an easy task, after all, it was as simple as inserting another pane of glass. The wooden frame itself had, by some miracle, been left undamaged. She was already packing when Daniel's father arrived. Jack barely spoke to her, and left her to her business as he removed the supporting part of the frame to slide the new sheet of glass into its groove. He didn't even set foot inside the house, he simply shouted his farewell as he left.

Zo had agreed, in private, to meet Elly an hour before dusk. It was the best time. Most predators would expect her to leave when the darkness could provide cover for their departure. They wouldn't even consider the possibility of a daylight escape. She only hoped she would not regret trusting her life, and the lives of those she loved, to the faint recognition she felt.

Zo bit her lip, forcing back the emotions which caused her to hesitate. She had to remind herself she was doing this for them, to keep them safe. She could not afford to stay. It was hard to accept she was never going to see any of them again. Never again would she hear the epic tales of Elder Robert, or help with errands in the village. Never again would she step foot in Crowley, a place which had so quickly become her home.

Her pace slowed further as the clearing, where she and Daniel first met, came into sight. Her eyes lingered upon the stone circle where she had once built her fires. It was in this very place Daniel had given her his friendship. For weeks, months, he had tried desperately to find someone who may have known her. He searched the missing boards and frequently asked for any news relating to missing people, but his search was futile. Zo had been almost relieved when they gave up. She knew that somewhere her mother awaited her return, but each time he came home with no information regarding her past, she was relieved. She had never wanted to leave this place.

Daniel's parents had been accommodating. Without even meeting her, they had given consent for her to use their small cabin as her home, in return for assistance around the town. It was only a few weeks after their brief agreement when Angela had visited. It was at this point she was welcomed into the family. As Angela looked upon the once barren wasteland, which now thrived at the hand of the young lady, it brought tears to her eyes. She had long ago, and with much regret, abandoned this land as lost.

As time passed, they found they had much in common. Zo had seemingly limitless knowledge of alchemy and botany. It was clear she had been well-educated, and it was often commented that her mannerisms were of those found in a well-raised family, making her unpublicised disappearance all the more confusing. They had tried all manner of concoctions and compounds to retrieve her memory, but nothing seemed to fill any of the darkness which clouded her memory. Angela finally decided that something so horrific must have happened that her body was protecting her from the painful recollection, and maybe even explained why there were no reports of her disappearance. Angela's efforts wavered as she came to realise that whatever Zo's past held was better left unknown.

A hand brought Zo back to reality with a start, pulling her from the fond memories of her life on this secluded island. She had been so engrossed in her own thoughts Elly and Eiji's approach had gone unnoticed. It was strange, ending her life here in the very same place it had started. Elly squeezed Zo's shoulder tightly. She understood some of her heartache. It was a despair similar to that she herself had felt when she betrayed Marise in order to bring her to this place.

'*If only things could have been different,*' she thought to herself, seeing Zo's tearful gaze as she stared through the trees longingly towards home. As she looked upon her, she couldn't help but wonder why it was that Marise had not yet awoken, especially when the sealing potion administered was accurate almost to the day. Marise should have been in full control, or at least that was what she had been led to believe. By her calculations, based on the concoction, Marise should have woken six months after her arrival on Crowley. Six months would have been adequate to ensure they had not lost Zoella forever, but Zoella was the one present and, more alarmingly, there wasn't even a trace of Marise visible. Although concerned, she was confident in time things would become as they should be, especially where Marise was concerned. Things would work out exactly as intended.

Zo's mind begged her to reconsider. She had only known this person a day and already she was taking her away from all she knew and loved. Although her unfounded trust for this person strangely reassured her, she couldn't help but question the timing. After over a year and a half she had only now come looking for her, and her arrival had marked the start of trouble. Part of her wanted to ignore the feelings of familiarity, to believe her stories to be nothing but lies, but she knew better than that. For some reason she knew this person spoke the truth and, as much as she wanted to, she couldn't ignore the proven danger.

Elly's hand still rested on her shoulder as she applied an encouraging pressure to turn her to face the direction they walked. Although this action had moved her body, it did little to stray her longing gaze from the direction of her home.

"Are you ready?" Elly's voice ached with concern. She was aware first hand just how powerful the conflicting emotions that she would be feeling, were. "You are doing the right thing you know."

"They will be safe, won't they?" Her eyes filled with worry and concern as she turned to look at Elly who, in response, simply nodded and lifted the backpack from Zo's grasp. "Then, I guess there is no point delaying further." She had already told herself this so many times, but saying it aloud made it seem more definitive. Her friends would be safe, and that was all that was important. With these thoughts she took her first determined step away from all she loved.

Elly was unsure what to say to Zo, and since her thoughts were on other concerns, she remained silent for the next half an hour. She knew any words she could offer would be of little comfort at this moment. Eiji, however, chose not to speak for an entirely different reason. He walked almost shoulder to shoulder with Marise Shi, and although *she* seemed oblivious to this fact, *he* was not.

The thought that he walked side by side with the brutal murderer—whom his master had so often included in horror stories as they sat around the campfire—unnerved him. It was hard to believe this girl and the legendary assassin were one and the same. He was unsure how he would feel when the time came to make his choice. Death or death, he reminded himself.

As they walked, he found he glanced to her repeatedly, worried that she would make a sudden move and end that which he was here to protect, his life. Each time he looked at her, even if the glances were less than twenty seconds apart, he found himself surprised at how young she was. He was easily her elder by three, or maybe four, years. She looked just like any other person. There were no signs of the marks of Hades which were rumoured to scar her body, nor could he see the image of his own death as he looked upon her. He had known the rumours of this person were greatly exaggerated, but still, he had not expected her to seem so normal. She was not at all like the monster he had expected to face.

The atmosphere was beginning to unnerve him. The silence seemed so final, and not even the cries of night animals pierced the air. It was a heavy stifling silence and, against his better judgement, it was he who finally broke it.

"So y' the le—" His words froze as Elly shot him a warning glance, one which cautioned him to rethink his words. Even through the concealing darkness he was stopped in mid-sentence by the weight of the look alone. In the need to break the silence he had forgotten himself and almost said the first thing which came to his mind, something completely inappropriate. Fortunately, she had stopped him in time, before any damage could be done and they were presented with questions that could not yet be answered.

"I'm the what?" she questioned quietly. Elly had hoped she hadn't heard, but such silence was unforgiving to a slip of the tongue.

"Legendary healer around these parts," Elly finished quickly. Another look was directed towards Eiji as silent words were exchanged masked by the darkness. "On our way here, we were told there was a healer whose skill with herbs and potions was beyond all comprehension. I just knew it had to be you, hence why we came here." A quick, but not entirely satisfying rescue by Elly. Even as she looked to Zo, she could tell she was unconvinced by her answer, but her mind was elsewhere. She was too preoccupied to question further, for this she was grateful. Zo did seem to give an answer, something about someone called Angela, but the name was the only thing clearly heard through her lowered tone.

They had not noticed the sound of their boots as they crunched the grass, not until silence was brought upon them by their sudden, sharp, stop. Elly's arm stretched in front of Zo, she seemed a little too preoccupied to have noticed the events around her.

The trees before them danced and swayed, projecting shadows from the firelight in front. They told tales of the company who waited before them, whilst blocking their view of those who could be enemies. It was clear someone had recently set up camp. The wood's air had yet to haze with the dense smoke expected, should the travellers have been there for any length of time.

"The crossroads are just ahead. We get a number of travellers visiting the temple or shrines. Resting here is quite common, given that Crowley has no marked inn. It's nothing to worry about," Zo whispered, trying to convince herself that by firmly stating the figures at the firelight would pose no danger would make it so, but after recent events she was not so sure.

"Then why are you whispering?" Elly raised her eyebrow inquisitively as she handed Zo something, before she had even realised what it was, the sword was fastened around her waist in a smooth, natural movement. Her stomach sank as she realised what she had done. "You had forgotten this," Elly added, slightly relieved as she watched Zoella secure it. At least there were some things the body remembered even if the mind didn't.

'I had not forgotten it,' Zo thought bitterly to herself, remembering her deliberate attempt to leave it behind, despite the fact she nearly left with it in her possession, twice. There was something about this strange item from her past which made her feel uneasy. It left her with a sick feeling deep in the pit of her stomach which surpassed anything she had experienced. As she looked upon the sword she was filled with fear. There was a presence to it she didn't quite like. Something about it seemed almost evil.

As she felt its weight against her hip, she remembered the giant figure from earlier, the one who had started this nightmare. It had been so difficult to prevent the sword from delivering the final blow, almost as if she fought against the weapon's control. She had been left with no choice but to remove her attacker from sight before she gave in to its murderous desire. She never wanted to feel that way again, so angry, so much hatred. The power of those raw emotions had clouded her judgement to the extent she barely remembered the conflict at all. As she had stood with her sword poised above him, she was frightened of herself, of what she may do, and terrified of the voice inside her mind which had urged for her to take his life. She feared their reaction should anyone ever discover how she had felt.

"We should go round, t'avoid any trouble." Eiji's statement seemed more like a question. He looked towards Zo as if seeking an answer. She wondered if there was, perhaps, another thought behind that look, one she couldn't quite place. Even through her distraction she had noticed the strange sideways glances in her direction. Something about the way he looked at her made her feel very uneasy.

"And allow them to get behind us and choose their time to strike?" Elly questioned quietly. "It is better to strike first." Elly's words were delivered in a tone which left no room for debate, and they began to walk towards the firelight.

They *had* attempted a silent approach, which had been instantly sabotaged by Eiji as he seemed to step on almost every root and fallen branch. Each of his footsteps echoed with the snapping of twigs. It was as if the undergrowth itself was attracted to his movement. Even if those they approached had been oblivious to that, or dismissed the noises as rather ungraceful forest creatures, the cry he let out when his foot struck a rock would have certainly revealed them.

"And you wondered how I knew you were following me," Elly whispered as she shook her head in mild amusement. She could not remember travelling with someone so devoid in the skills of walking quietly. It seemed the harder he tried to silence his footfalls, the louder he became. She wondered if advising him to try to make as much noise as possible would have had the opposite effect.

As they approached, they could make out the conversation clearly. One of the voices was a little too loud, almost as if they had wanted to be overheard by those who approached.

"So anyway, I tried to tell her she couldn't sneak away, but still she had to try." Daniel stared at the place Zo now stood. She smiled brightly, her eyes twinkling in the firelight. Even after such a short time apart she felt the lump rise in her throat as she laid eyes on them once more.

Daniel had always been able to read her so well. His presence here served as a reminder of just *how* well. Shock, amusement, and relief all displayed in her face as she looked upon them.

"Hey!" She finally spoke in a playful, yet annoyed, tone. "What if I was waiting back at home for you to come and say goodbye?"

"But you aren't, are you? You didn't think we'd just let you leave with these people, do you?" He gave her a serious look, one which told her he was concerned about where her journey would lead and, that despite any danger, he wasn't just going to let her leave in this manner.

"They *cannot* come with us." Elly had silently watched until this point, and now her voice was firm enough to rule the conversation. "They will be a burden. It will be difficult enough to defend yourself if someone attacks, let alone you having to worry about these two as well." Her tone once more took a 'this conversation is over' tone. It was a tone no one would normally dare to argue with.

"We can take care of ourselves." Acha's voice was timid, yet direct, as it addressed her. They had no intention of allowing this stranger to tell them where they were, and weren't, welcome, especially when it involved their friend.

"As you did earlier?" Elly questioned harshly, reminding them of what had transpired only hours ago. They decided to ignore her comment, in fact, they continued to talk as if she wasn't even there.

"But what about your studies, and the garden?" Zo looked from Daniel to Acha in turn. They each had things they had to do, commitments they needed to attend to, even in her absence.

"My studies concluded yesterday," he advised. She normally recalled his schedule better than he did but, with the events of today alone, he would be surprised if she even remembered the current day. She had more than enough to take in and consider.

"And Angela said she'd happily mind the garden while we followed the lead on your past. We said we were making it into a camping trip," Acha added.

"You really did think of everything. I'm really glad you came but—"

"But this is *not* a game. It is *not* a camping trip either. Her life is in danger, and if you come, so too is yours," Elly snapped, unable to believe their deliberate attempt to ignore her, especially when they knew exactly who she was. They knew her reputation and stature well, as well as the respect her position was owed. It was common knowledge that Elly was the daughter of the one she had named as Zo's lord. It was also true that it was she who attended to the politics and governing of her father's land, whilst he reaped the benefits of her actions.

"We know it'll be dangerous." Daniel once more chose to ignore Elly. "Did you care about it being dangerous when you risked your life for me and Acha? It could easily have turned out another way." He positioned himself to stand between Zo and Elly. A deliberate move to reinforce that both her presence and input were unwanted. This was a choice only Zo herself should make. This stranger had already made enough decisions for her.

"Elly." Something changed in Zo's expression, as she looked from Daniel to her. "You said someone was after me. They've already mistaken Acha for me once and, from my reaction, they'll know we're friends. They could just as easily go after them than come for me directly. If they took my friends... if anything were to happen to them, there is nothing I wouldn't give, nothing I wouldn't sacrifice for them." Zo looked to Daniel and smiled softly. For the first time in this conversation he turned to acknowledge Elly.

"As you say, it's not as if we can look after ourselves, and if you *do* know Zo, you'll know she'd rather die than let anything happen to us, so—"

"Enough," Elly stated. She had decided it would be easier to take them, it was preferential to this long conversation. Besides, perhaps if they were to meet with tragedy it would move things along at a quicker pace. "They can come." She shook her head, her tone filled with annoyance. It seemed they were going to continue until she met their demands anyway, so she thought it was better to spare herself some time. As Zo moved to thank her, she saw Elly smiling in the shadows.

"Besides," Eiji decided to add his opinion already a little too late to aid the debate, "they won't be lookin' for a large group, just the two of y'. It could work t'our advantage." Elly glanced around the group again.

"It might," she stated without any real conviction.

Chapter 4

The Beginning

"So what makes her different from the others?" The voice echoed through a darkened room. It was a large area filled with various life-forces. Even now, despite their imprisonment, they were engaged in heated debate. From the weight of the air alone the severity of the situation was obvious.

"This one will die. The others were fortunate there were more of us free then." Another voice added to the conversation. A low murmur of agreement spread throughout the room. The lack of emotion, and the disinterest placed in their words, would almost have someone believing they spoke of something other than the fate of their entire race.

"Well they had to choose someone I suppose. They have us all now. This would be the last chance," scoffed another. To anyone outside deciphering the conversation would have been nearly impossible. It was difficult to tell exactly who, or what, spoke. Their languages consisted of a combination of sounds relevant to their apparent species, but each life-force understood the others perfectly. Only those in humanoid form spoke in recognisable tones.

"Mew!" The room fell silent as a cat's cry filled the air. Although it had only meowed it had a strange authority to its tone. Pacing back and forth it looked between the countless forms in quick succession.

"Their games will be the end of them. This quest *will* be fulfilled, you'll see. She's different." Seiken argued to deaf ears, pleading for them to listen. He knew faith was one of the most important things they could have. They had to believe in her, or she *would* fail. Despite this, it seemed they had already decided the fate of those chosen. It was frustrating. He was certain if it had been anyone else, they would have been a little more enthusiastic. But it hadn't been someone else. Their last chance of preventing this disaster, their last hope of survival, had been her.

"You think a mortal can succeed where we ourselves failed? When those who came before her also met defeat! I don't think I need to remind you of this, do I?"

"Meow murraouw!" The chatters fell silent again.

"I suppose we have little choice but to hope," the voice replied giving a defeated sigh as he met the annoyed vision of the black and white cat.

"Having us all here like this means only one thing, he controls our world. I've seen it, the boundaries are already thinning." Seiken's voice desperately pleaded for them to listen, but they were too intent on arguing, too insistent on disagreeing to hear him. It was no wonder they hadn't realised what was happening before now. Very few within these confines could work well together. Their role was often a solitary one. Aside from pleasantries, each went about their own business. It was no wonder their dwindling numbers hadn't been noticed before it was too late. When the time had come to cooperate, they had spent too much time in argument and disagreement. By the time their plan was devised they had already lost.

"It will be the end of us all."

"Why would they choose someone who could win?"

"No one ever wins. At best we can hope she'll prove a challenge, but little else. You should know better than to raise our hopes child." Seiken glanced to the figure with venom in his eyes. For the first time since their discussion had begun, they remembered who they were addressing. The figure cringed realising the disrespect to their heir, to the one who would one day be their ruler, assuming there was anything left to rule.

"No! You're not listening. They saw in her the weakness she has, the desire for her forgotten truth, they know the lengths she'll go to find it. They saw her weakness, but in doing so overlooked her strength. *They* do not think she can win but I *know* she can." Seiken assured, but despite their situation they were as stubborn as ever. He didn't know why he was trying, perhaps he was a fool to think that if they believed in those chosen, put their faith in them, it would help them to be victorious. Belief was the very foundation of their world, and if you believed in something enough it became real. Why wouldn't they just offer her the benefit of the doubt? Why did they refuse to put their faith in the ones who it seemed were fated to be The Chosen heroes of this time?

"Seiken," an elder voice, the voice of his father, silenced the room. He, like Seiken, possessed a human form. No one gazing upon him would imagine him to be anything other than a mighty ruler, one who would fight beside his men on the fields of battle. Even his tones were lined with pessimism as he spoke. "You are young," he lied. Seiken wasn't young, he was far older than those in the room thought him to be. Few amongst them knew the truth of his son's origin. "They feel despite your power you are too optimistic, but if you say she is the one then I don't doubt you. It is up to you to assist her. I shall do what I can for the dreamers. We will have to pray our efforts will be enough. You must be careful. Do not stay too long, if our captors discover our astral presence, they will devise a way to inhibit it, and then she will have little, or no chance." In that room, in their entire race for that matter, there were but the two of them who possessed omnipresence. The skill itself was very limited, but it served them well.

"Mew roaw me?"

"Very well, Rowmeow will keep vigil should the task prohibit our real bodies from appearing to function properly." This was a major disadvantage with their astral presence, if a situation encountered by the astral body met with something which required either a lot of concentration, or power, their real body would enter a catatonic state until they resolved the need.

"But I am not experienced in this field," he protested, although with nowhere near enough conviction to convince anyone this was something he did not desire.

"You approached her first did you not?" his father questioned sternly.

"I was simply wondering who they had recruited." He felt now, more than ever, the need to justify how he came to cross the boundaries to stand before one of The Chosen, especially considering all the warnings he had received in the past about her.

"Seiken, you can avail yourself from this prison for periods impossible to myself. Both The Chosen and the dreamers will need all the assistance we can muster. You have created a bond with her already, after all, isn't she the one you have been protecting? If you saw the boundary, as you said, you know this game will be our last."

"It *will* be the last!" The determination in his voice rang through the darkness, yet his enthusiasm did little to convince the sceptical listeners.

* * *

The fire crackled. It was a soothing sound that filled the night air as they sat near to the small dirt track surrounded by trees in every direction. Zo placed a handful of herbs onto the fire, one Elly recognised as a mixture to keep away any wildlife or predators that would think to approach them as they slept. It was commonplace for travellers to carry this mixture. It was these herbs that would generally cause the hazing of the air near a camp, and the almost undetectable odour repelled roaming beasts.

The firelight distorted the undergrowth, shielding anything lurking from sight. More than once they had felt as if something had attempted to approach them. The shadows stretched and twisted to tempt their imagination, reminding them of how unsettled the events of the day had left them.

They had decided to stay by the fire that Daniel and Acha had built and camp for the remainder of the night. They had left the town and that had been the most important part. In fact, Elly reasoned, their delay in departure may even prove to be beneficial. If someone else were to approach Zo's home, they would assume she had already left the island, not that she believed for one moment someone would, but it was worth keeping up the pretence for now. It would provide the extra time needed to ensure they had everything for their journey, just the essentials. By morning she was hopeful Zo would have realised the best option was to leave her friends behind. Perhaps allowing them to spend one last night together would ease any concerns and help them see that their uninvited company would be nothing more than a burden. Yet a lingering feeling that things weren't going to go as planned meant this would be her last chance to persuade Zo. Given the uneasy feel to the air, she realised there may not even be time for that. Things had already progressed quicker than she had expected.

She had considered administering a sleeping potion into their evening meal, and just taking Zo with her. But she had promised Eiji her protection and, knowing him, he would either accidentally expose the plan or, more likely, get caught in the trap himself. So, for the moment at least, she had to accept the possibility of their intrusion.

Elly sat close to the fire, where the contents of Zo's backpack were now spread across the ground. While searching through the supplies, she added various items into the metal pot which sat on the rocks above the fire. The smell of stew began to fill the air as it neared completion. Elly couldn't believe the sheer amount of perishable foods Zo had packed. Had they not been found in the bag so soon, they would have spoilt. It didn't make any sense, Elly knew she had taught her better than this.

"So, anyone know any good ghost stories?" Eiji asked, passing Elly the remaining ingredients for the meal. His question was met with silence. "No one? C'mon y' can't have a campfire without ghost stories." He gestured wildly in what he thought to be an eerie manner. Another silence met his enthusiastic tone. "Oh fine, I'll go first." Now they knew they were no longer in danger of being volunteered to tell a story they gave him their full attention. "It's not a ghost story as such, more like a survival tale, or at least that's what my master called it when he told me." Elly glanced up from the simmering stew. Eiji, satisfied he had caught everyone's attention, continued. "It's a story of legend, although it happened just over seven years ago..." Eiji began. There had been much speculation about what had happened before his master had seen her, but the information he gave was the part of the story which never changed. It was the story of how Marise had obtained the Grimoire of Light and Life-force.

No one knew how the tale came to be known, since all but one within that village were slaughtered on that day. It was a story Elly knew well. She had heard it from its creator, and even she found herself surprised at the tale spun from assumption. His version had forgotten one very important detail. Marise had not been there to seek vengeance on the temple's priest as had been believed. She had journeyed there to retrieve the first of the Grimoire. As Eiji told his version of the tale, Elly found herself recalling the true events of that night...

...The Grimoire of Light and Life-force possessed not only the power to manipulate the mind, but life affecting, and healing magic. Anything relating to physical or emotional magic had been stored within this tome. It was for this reason the Hoi Hepta Sophoi sent this particular tome to Napier village. When Night first found the Grimoire it had been stored in a small bookcase in the town, overlooked by all. It was this very place he discovered he could not, no matter how hard he tried, retrieve it with his own hands.

The villagers, although they did not recognise this stranger, feared him and his interest in this object. Each day he would visit and examine it, and his stature alone was a clear indication of his power. With each passing day he grew more frustrated. He would reach forward, his hand outstretched as if to take the tome, but never did he hold it within his grasp. There was only one way to free themselves of this man before he did something terrible. They had to destroy the object of his fascination. If it was no longer within their possession, he would have no cause to return.

They had taken all necessary precautions before the burning. Having seen how the stranger feared to touch it, they too resisted making contact. With great care they wrapped it in a cloth soaked in holy water and blessed by the priest. They did not want to risk touching anything this stranger had feared to take in his own hands, especially when it was obvious how much he had desired it.

The tome, however, had other plans. It had no desire to be destroyed, and such weak humans could never possess the power to harm it. Had the Grimoire possessed a voice, they were certain it would have mocked them with laughter as the flames burnt away their holy cloth to lick its pages. Hours passed, all manner of fire accelerants were desperately added, yet the book remained unscorched. Anything which could not be destroyed in such a manner had to be evil. There was only one thing left to do.

With no means to destroy it, the people did the only thing they could, they took it to the safe keeping of their temple. When the priest took it, he knew instantly of its power. Any fool could have felt it, but not all of them would be able to resist the whispered commands which echoed in their mind. Whispers that controlled their actions and thoughts. It was this power of persuasion held by the book which had seen it relocated, instead of further attempts being made to destroy it.

The priest protected this book. He wrapped it in a blessed silk cloth and carried it with him through the village. He used it wisely, carefully tapping into its dormant powers to heal those in need. It possessed immense power, and a trait which even the Hoi Hepta Sophoi had not expected; anyone could use that which was sealed within for their own devices. They had sealed the magic of a god within its binding, but a god is a powerful being and they possess a magic so unpredictable that even the Grimoire alone could not contain it. This leakage of energy allowed the person possessing it to utilise a measure of the skills trapped within.

The power of this tome was a secret that the priest did not feel appropriate to share with the one who would ultimately become his successor. He could only hope, before the underworld claimed him, his apprentice would have turned his back on the greed and selfishness he so clearly displayed. If not, he would use its power to control those weaker than him, to force them into doing what he believed was the will of the Gods. He knew these would be his actions. His apprentice reminded him so much of his younger himself and, just as he would have back then, the old priest knew he would abuse its power. He believed, until the day of his death, his apprentice had known nothing of its secrets, but this was not the case.

Since the book had first come into the temple the young priest had been haunted by images of it. It called to him in his dreams and whispered sweet promises of the power and the greatness they could share. The world could be his. With practice he could twist everyone and everything to his whim, but first it had to be surrendered willingly, or pass on to him through inheritance.

As time passed, the young priest realised his master would not share its secrets. In order to inherit the book, he began to poison him. The Grimoire mocked his futile attempts, for each time his master took it within his hands he was cured and the tome would taunt his failure. There was only one option, there was but one time of day in which the tome was not within his possession. During his cleansing, the priest would lock it within his room. The thought of its safety was not even a concern. As the priest bathed in the holy waters purifying his body and soul, he was unaware his apprentice had carefully removed the key from his discarded robes.

He prepared for his master a mighty feast. Seeing the young man's enthusiasm, he had sat to share this meal, unaware seasoning his food was a deadly condiment. By the time he realised what had occurred, the poison had already acted. His pupil watched in silence as he tried to crawl to his chamber through the violent convulsions. Clearing his throat, the young man rotated the chamber key on his finger. This was the last thing he had seen before the gates of the underworld appeared, and Hermes stepped through to collect him.

Hiding his act from the town was not a difficult task. No one would think to question the death of an old man, and if any did, he now possessed the Grimoire, and with it the power to control the thoughts of all who confronted him. It was not long before those in the town obeyed his every whim and fulfilled his every wish. That was, until the fateful day all his obedient pets were slaughtered. His power was absolute. He thought he was unstoppable. He was wrong.

Marise stood on the outskirts of the town. It was a quaint little village, very peaceful. She had arrived in the early evening and the residents were already safely secured in their homes ready for the night ahead. Most of the workers had returned from a hard day in the nearby towns, fields, and mines. There was no need for them to know she was there.

The village itself had been built centuries ago, but the oldest part standing had been constructed little more a few decades ago. It shared its boundaries with desert, mountain, marsh, and plain, constructed on the very place where these four met. The town had visibly suffered many disasters in its time. It was rumoured the damage the town suffered was due to the fact the town possessed a strong link to the Severaine, that and the fact its borders lay on the crossing of such extreme elements. Other people stated the disasters were caused by the immense power which was born there, but the true start of their problems began a long time before. So long ago that everyone, even those who still remembered the pilgrimages of old, had forgotten.

Marise stood on the dirt path for some time. The power of the Grimoire hung heavily in the air. Just one person walked the streets at this late hour, a young priest, who even now hurried towards the temple. He stopped in mid-stride realising the silhouetted figure was watching him intently. He returned her stare for what seemed like an eternity. Neither of them moved, not until finally Marise slowly started to walk towards him.

As the light from the streets illuminated her image her identity became unquestionable. The realisation was reflected in his stiff and panicked posture. Perhaps the Grimoire had whispered her identity to him from its resting place upon the temple's altar. Regardless of how, he knew who she was, and that she had come for him.

It seemed to Marise, more and more people recognised her at first glance. She didn't know whether to thank the wanted posters or her deeds. Sometimes it annoyed her when they ran. It was a waste of her time. That night, she didn't mind in the slightest; she was in exceptionally high spirits.

His hands firmly seized the Grimoire from the altar. With it secure he rushed to the window, ordering the town to take up weapons and do whatever it took to prevent this demon from reaching the temple. The townsfolk scurried from their houses, men, women, and children, all in some way armed, be it with kitchen implements, farming tools, or swords. It seemed not a person remained who had not taken up arms against her. The priest watched from the window fearfully as the demon warrior took the lives of those who stood before her. He watched as she cut a path to the temple, as she hacked her way towards him. Not a single one of his followers, despite their numbers, could connect a single blow. He now understood why people feared this girl, surely, she was a demon taking human form.

Marise smiled. The people of this town were too willing to give their life to someone else, so she took that which they freely offered. Had they been stronger, had they even the slightest desire to think for themselves, such a pitiful manipulation would not have worked. They were ready to die, as long as they weren't to blame. She could have easily spared the town of bloodshed and still reached the temple door unharmed, but such weakness annoyed her. She could have spared them, but she didn't. Not a living soul remained except for the one she had come for. The one who sought sanctuary inside the temple.

As she approached, she felt another life-force enter the village. She knew from the disruption in the elements around her that he was a powerful Elementalist. She could feel the energies which radiated from his aura as it told her of his strength. He was indeed powerful, certainly an advanced manipulator of the forces surrounding him. His essence betrayed the training of the next generation he had started. She could feel the strength of his advanced techniques, but his basic talents had now been passed along to fortify the aura of his student.

Elly had told her that Elementalists would train to master the element they felt the strongest connection with. They would learn to read it, and seek out those who could offer them training in that skill. There were many variations on the elemental skills, but no two manifestations were ever the same. In a past time, Elementalists could draw on light, spirit, and darkness, as well as various other traits, without being confined to those of earth, air, fire, and water, but that was a *very* long time ago indeed, and these skills, as far as she was aware, had been lost through the passage of time.

There were many born who had the potential to become Elementalists but the lack of masters, Elementalists willing to give up their life as they passed their skills on, saw only a few would know of their hidden potential. To fight such a person would prove a challenge. If he stepped further into the village to prevent what was occurring, she would, with only a slight regret, extinguish the remaining talents he possessed from the world.

Marise hesitated outside the temple, wondering if she should go back to face him. He may pursue her in battle, but more likely, on seeing the events which befell the town he would seek to bring aid. They were a few hours away from the nearest town. Even should he leave now, she would be long gone before his return. She decided to finish her business.

Turning her attention back to the temple, she opened the wooden doors by the power of flame. The heavy oak doors disintegrating as her powerful magic connected. The priest stood behind the altar, watching in composed terror as a shadow stepped through the flames like Hades through the gate to the underworld. He turned his eyes to the book which he held clutched within his hands, attempting to appear both calm, *and* innocent, as she approached. It was something he did rather poorly. Even now she could smell his fear. Beads of sweat formed on his forehead as he focused the tome's control onto her. He drew on its powers harder as he concentrated more and more on the force which enabled him to control those of the town. He blanched as the book's power failed to make her hesitate for even a second. Then, she stood before him, only the altar between them.

"Mind games?" She smiled sadistically as she raised her eyebrow. It was a smile which froze his blood. For a moment he was unable to speak, unable to move as he looked upon his own death. She teased her hand through her fiery red hair before she spoke again. "Give me the book," she commanded, leaning forwards onto the altar; as she did so a sudden thought entered his mind. Just as he could not take the book from his predecessor, she could not take it from him. If she were to kill him, it would once more belong to the temple, and thus to the next holy man to cross the threshold and seize it.

Convinced of his safety, he ignored her request and focused all of his will in an attempt to summon a greater strength from the tome. This time she heard the faintest whisper in the back of her mind. It was a voice so faint, so weak, it almost made her laugh aloud. "Very well, two can play at that, I shall wait outside." Her sea-green eyes locked with his for just a moment. There was so much she could do, so much fun she could have. She could simply whisper to his mind and tell him to give her the book, she could have him mutilate himself, kill himself even, but that was not her desire. She wanted to destroy him. "Killing easy, but to destroy someone completely is *far* more rewarding." She smiled coldly, seeing the fear her words brought.

As she reached the door, she heard him cry out as his mind's fears were realised. Creatures like those he had never dared imagine crawled through the floorboards and the ceiling. There were creatures he had always feared, and monsters that sought only his death. He tried to ignore them. He tried to dismiss them as illusions, as fragmented horrific visions, but then, he felt the warm, damp, hungry breath upon his neck which destroyed his logic.

He turned to face them fearfully as they lashed out towards him, sinking their claws deep within his flesh. He was certain now, by the evidence of his own blood, the creatures standing before him were no illusion. Their touch alone had proved them to be as real as the blood he shed. He retreated, clutching his side tightly.

"I shall give you to the count of ten," she smiled once more as she left the temple. She had no intention of staying to watch him fighting with himself. She waited outside, her back towards the door leaning on the temple's stone work and began to count.

Marise was just about to reach ten when, as if on cue, the priest scrambled from the charred remains of the temple door. With a look of pure terror, he fell to her feet. His arms and front were bloody and his clothing torn. Marise sneered, the young priest would not even begin to believe each of his injuries were self-inflicted, not from the illusions which, even now, he thought pursued him with the desire to taste his blood. His hands shook as he pushed the book towards her, she looked down at him questioningly until he found the breath to speak.

"P-p-please, take it." His voice faltered as he glanced nervously behind at the creatures which even now pursued him. "P-p-please, just send away your demons." She took the tome from his grip. The instant he had released it the creatures vanished, leaving his injuries as the only physical evidence of his encounter. She turned slowly to walk away. There was no need to kill him, he was destroyed, a man pushed over the edge into insanity. There would be no life for him anywhere. Although the images which pursued him had vanished, he would be haunted by the events until, born of his own fear, the monsters would return for him.

As she looked down at him she could already see the cracks in his sanity. He hid it well, for the time being, but his sleep, his dreams, would be his downfall. She had, at that point, no intention of killing him. She would have let him live. She liked the idea of the torture and isolation his life would hold, but then he did something which sealed his death. She would have let him live, if not for the thanks he misplaced.

"Thank you. Thank you, Zeus, for sparing me," he cried into the air. He had barely finished his praise when Marise turned sharply with her sword drawn. She swung it in a smooth motion to neatly behead him. The last words he heard as she struck him were so plain, so clear.

"It was not Zeus who would have spared you, it was me." She sheathed her sword and nodded respectfully at Hermes as he collected the priest. She had seen a lot of him lately, today especially.

Just one person, excluding herself, remained with life in their body, and that was the Elementalist. He seemed to be rooted to the spot in fear as he gazed upon her. His already white hair barely a contrast against his pale complexion. She stopped mere feet away from him, and for a moment they simply stared at each other. She saw many things within the depths of his eyes, recognition, fear, and honour. As she studied him, something seemed to shift inside her, something that convinced her to walk away. In that one moment, she lost control.

"Next life, you save me." Marise did not even know she had spoken these words, nor did she remember having left the village. By the time she realised he may have been left alive it was already too late to turn back...

..."He said it was hard t'believe such a sweet voice and heartbroken smile had come from such a malicious person." Eiji began to summarise his far less accurate version of the story as the food had nearly finished cooking. "He was said t'be the only person t'ever survive her gaze."

"Surely, he can't have been the only one, or no one would know who she was. I've never heard such tales." Zo glanced around, aware of the disbelief in everyone's eyes. It was clear she was the only one amongst them who had no idea who Marise Shi was.

"You're kidding right?" Zo's expression told Daniel she was deadly serious. "You've never heard of Marise Shi?" His voice seemed to scream with disbelief. It had only been a few weeks back that he and Acha had discussed the assassin at length even she—or more precisely the person whose body she had taken—had knowledge of Marise and her deeds. As Daniel thought about it, he suddenly realised why she would not know such things. Her amnesia had taken away her memories of the past. She was spared from the curse of knowing, by the curse of not remembering.

"No," she answered as she glanced between them for an answer.

"She was, well, still is, the most feared assassin of all time. She is a legendary warrior who has slaughtered countless numbers and razed cities to the ground. She is feared as a god, but lacking in compassion, she is sometimes deemed to be much worse." There was an uncharacteristic bitterness in his tone as he spoke, one which portrayed his disapproval.

"So what happened to her?" Zo questioned curiously.

"Well, some say when Night returns she will join him. If Elly's tales are true, and he *has* returned, then it stands to reason she would be beside him. Others say she encountered a stronger foe and met her end. Whereas me, I think she's lying low, probably biding her time until she seizes the last Grimoire." Daniel was more familiar with the tale of the Grimoire than he had implied when Elly had questioned Zo about it. However, he had wanted to hear just what this stranger had to say before he gave anything away. By listening to her, he planned to ascertain if the words she spoke were lies or truth. If they were lies, he could have protected Zo, and warned her about the deception. But, so far, it appeared she had spoken only the truth.

Daniel held his friends' attention so well they had been completely oblivious to Elly as she slapped Eiji, very hard, across the back of his head.

"You idiot!" Elly hissed forcefully as Eiji rubbed the back of his head. "What were you thinking?"

"I'm sorry, I wasn't, I forgot. I was just tellin' a story." Eiji bowed his head to her in apology. He hadn't given it much thought. It was always so well received that it was the one he always told around the campfire. He hadn't even paused to consider the people he travelled with.

"Do you *ever* think before opening that mouth of yours?" she scolded. This was not the first time he had received such a warning.

"I said I was sorry," he sulked.

"Be more mindful of your words," she whispered, noticing their low conversation had already moved onto other things. Safe in the knowledge Eiji's indiscretion had not caused any problems, for now, she began to serve the stew. It seemed there were more than enough small bowls, perhaps in some way Zo had anticipated this. Maybe she had known they would follow her, and had planned one last meal together.

* * *

Zo found herself unintentionally withdrawn as they settled around the fire to eat. Her thoughts strayed to Seiken. Something about him seemed so familiar, but even the topic of their conversation had been forgotten, leaving her with only the memory of his image and the fleeting sensation of his importance.

A rustle came from uncomfortably close behind her, snatching her from her thoughts. Oblivious to the sound, her friends continued to talk as they ate. Zo knew, that thanks to the herbs she used on the fire, there should be no wildlife in the area. Even insects would take shelter from the subtle odour created. Something moving in the vicinity was a very bad sign indeed.

Placing her dish slowly to the ground she glanced anxiously, trying to pinpoint the source of the sound. It came from a nearby tree. She already knew it was nothing as harmless as a bird foraging for food, but she didn't want to betray their advantage just yet. As she looked deep into the tree, she saw two large black eyes peering from the shadow. Eyes, for some reason, she thought she should remember, eyes which brought with them danger.

Her hand fell to her sword in a movement she hadn't even noticed until she felt its cool hilt held firmly within her grasp. She pushed the hilt with her thumb slightly, releasing the internal catch with a click.

Everything went deadly quiet. Her friends had stopped in mid-conversation and now watched her with a mixture of expressions as she rose to her feet, holding her weapon ready to draw. She listened intently for signs of further movement. More eyes appeared in the bushes and trees around them. The sound of whispers, which had been nothing but a rustle of wind through the trees, suddenly became noticeable to all.

'*You are chosen.*' Finally, one voice stood out from the rest. It seemed to engulf the air with its words, the quieter voices echoed its statement. Despite the fact that their tone was no higher than a whisper, the voices swelled before crashing over them with all in intensity of a stormy sea shore, battered under the force of the tide.

"There must be hundreds of them," Acha whispered. They were all on their feet now, she turned a full circle as she listened to the same words being spoken over and over.

"It's like they appeared from thin air. What can do that?" Eiji questioned, he too made a similar circular movement to Acha as he tried to determine the exact source of the many whispers.

"Demons?" Daniel gave one of several answers. The first one to enter his mind, an answer which was the closest they would get. They weren't demons, demons could only appear at night when the enchantment, which sealed them to the world, was disrupted by the moonlight. This only happened during the full moon which marked the end of the year, a time known and celebrated as the festival of Hades, or Samhain.

"Chosen for what? Would probably be a better question," Elly stated joining them to form an outward facing circle. Zo, however, still stood at the base of the tree looking at the one whose voice had addressed them so clearly.

'*Are you ready?*' Again, the words crashed over their heads as the question was echoed in, what seemed like, a thousand whispers. '*What fun you'll be.*' With those words, the dream returned to her, as vivid as the creatures themselves. They had promised her the truth. They had promised her answers, if she would accept their quest and play their game, and their 'game' as they called it had something to do with Seiken, and something he needed from her.

She remembered almost everything about the dream, even the subject of conversation between herself and Seiken. Now she remembered she knew the answer to the question they asked. His world was in danger. This quest was their hope, and along the way, as she aided Seiken's people, she was promised the answers about herself she so desperately sought.

"I'm ready," her voice trembled. A chorus of her name and questions filled the air from her friends, their voices so loud they almost drowned out the whispers. It appeared they were shocked she would answer such a question, shocked that she seemed to know what they were referring to, and was ready for whatever it was, without so much as a word to them.

Zo said nothing. This did not involve them. Given the chance there would be time for explanations later, but first there was a need to understand the rules, to understand what was expected of her in order to win. Now she had agreed to their game surely everything would become clear.

'*She's ready.*' The whispers again spoke in unison. '*Ever changing with the sun, your life shall be until you're done.*' A mocking echo of laughter resonated through the air as the world around them erupted in a flash of light, it was a light so bright that no darkness remained, yet with this light came the same blindness which darkness caused.

Zo's hand shot to her shoulder. Although she saw nothing, she felt the skin on the top of her arm begin to burn as if a flame danced across it. It burned with an unnatural pain, as if something was being branded not just upon her flesh but into her essence itself.

She stood paralysed for a moment as the light began to fade. Taking a hesitant breath, she looked to her friends, ready to explain. As her eyes adjusted, an anger burned deep within her. Hers was not the only hand to nurse a wound, her friends, mirrored her posture. The game, or whatever it was, had just started and already they had cheated. They had involved her friends in something that didn't concern them.

"Cheats!" she cried into the now silent air. "You said nothing about them. You asked me, me!" she screamed. Her sword was drawn before she had realised. She hacked at the tree the creature had first appeared in, frustration fuelling her every blow. "Show yourself, I dare you!" she challenged venomously as the blade on her sword flashed wildly, becoming even brighter. Her friends watched her in surprise, shocked by the anger and hatred in her voice as she screamed into the air. The leaves, which were forced from the tree by her violent actions, fluttered through the air in serenity, despite the lack of it at that moment in time.

Daniel placed his hand softly on her shoulder. She spun quickly to face him, her sword raised as if to strike. When her eyes met his, the blade vanished into a fine wisp. Her eyes seemed to change before his stare. He reasoned it was nothing more than a trick of the light, paired with the fast draining anger.

"What was all that about, what just happened?" Daniel asked cautiously as he held contact with her piercing blue eyes. She slowly lowered the hilt, her breathing still erratic from her outburst.

"What does this symbol mean?" Acha asked as she rolled up her sleeve to reveal an upside down Y, but where the top of the down line should finish, it continued down to draw almost level with the bottom of the symbol, it looked a little like an easel.

"It's a rune." Daniel answered when Zo failed to respond to his question. "It's a symbol said to be used long ago by those who were able to travel between worlds. This one is known as Algiz. This one is a means to activate the higher self, but other texts also relate it to boundaries and the setting of limits, since it's reversed, upside down that is, I assume it means just the opposite, the opening of paths otherwise protected." As he spoke, his eyes never for a moment left Zo's. 'You okay?' he mouthed, unable to hide his concern. Never before had he seen her lose her temper, it was uncharacteristic. Zo lowered her head shamefully and sat on the ground as the remainder of the wild energy left her.

"What is going on?" Elly's asked softly, moving to sit beside her. Something about her tone seemed to reveal a deeper understanding. Turning away, Zo jabbed the ground gently with the hilt of the vanished sword.

"We're not playin' games!" Eiji snapped; he covered his mouth, realising who he addressed. When he spoke again his tones were softer. "If somethin's gonna happen, we need all the information we can get." He examined the branding of Algiz on his arm in a ploy to avoid looking at her. He mulled over his choices once more, death, or death. Either way he may as well face it, for the moment he was stuck with them.

"I didn't know. I thought it was just me, I swear." As she looked up to him, tears of frustration ran down her face as she spoke. She was angry at the situation, but angrier at herself for her inability to understand the consequences of her actions. There was no possible way she was going to make things worse by telling them how *they* had tempted her to play. "But I never agreed to this, never. I thought it would just be me."

"You are not making any sense. What exactly is going on?" Elly touched her hand gently, an action to stop her from repeatedly thrusting the sword's hilt into the earth.

"I don't know. The eyes spoke of a game, a quest of some kind, and he... he needed my help. All I know is there is somewhere that needed my help, so I agreed." She tried to explain but failed to put into words a situation she barely understood herself.

"Who needs our help?" she questioned.

"He called himself Seiken. He said I was to be their saviour but you weren't a part of it. They cheated!"

"Saviour?" Eiji almost scoffed at the thought of Marise being a saviour to anyone, but then again, she wasn't Marise anymore. The girl he had spoken to was completely different, apart from her looks. He hadn't even seen the resemblance until just then. He had started to wonder if there had been a mistake, but after having witnessed her outburst, he knew he had to be very careful around her. There was no doubt in his mind, the murderer his master had spoken of lay just below the surface.

"He said something about different worlds, thinning boundaries." Her voice had calmed a little. As she spoke, she tried to make herself remember exactly what had transpired, exactly what he had said, but the harder she thought, the further the answer seemed to retreat. "I don't know," she sighed in frustration.

"Why didn't you say anything to us?" Acha joined the small circle as she sat in front of her.

"I couldn't remember. I thought it was a dream. I saw the eyes, then when I awoke after the attack, Seiken was in my room. But then he simply vanished. I thought it was just delirium. That's all I know. I'm so sorry." She lowered her head again as she examined the ground in an attempt to lessen the force of their looks.

"Well, I'm glad it happened." Zo looked to Daniel in bewilderment as he spoke. "If you're going to explore strange worlds, I want to be with you. You can't have all the fun." He wrapped his arm around her shoulder to hold her tightly.

"I agree." Acha smiled, unaware she and Daniel had become the recipients of Elly's questioning gaze. It seemed she could not understand their reaction, or had expected an alternative response.

"If they're gonna cheat from the start it only makes sense t'have someone watchin' y' back." Zo was even more astounded as Eiji offered his understanding. She was convinced when they had first met, he had taken an instant dislike to her. Yet now, when he had every right to hate her, it seemed he instead offered his assistance. Zo turned to Elly who smiled slightly as Zo's eyes met hers.

"What?" she shrugged. "I expected nothing less. You have never turned down an adventure. You were always getting us into trouble. It will be just like old times." Elly had known this would happen. She had known the naming of The Chosen was about to occur, but she had not expected it to be so early this night. She was aware they had approached Zoella and their doing so had marked the start of an ancient prophecy. Elly's arrival had been timed perfectly to ensure she stood beside her when the time came. The prophecy was destined to begin here, this reason alone was why they had lingered on Crowley. Those with Zoella would be fate's Chosen, and such was the reason the uninvited company had caused concern. But things could still work out as planned, bearing the mark was not a guarantee of longevity.

Gradually as the night passed, they settled down to sleep. Zo watched them for a few moments as she lay awake, she wondered what tomorrow would bring. She could only imagine what dangers lay in wait. At the moment, very little made sense, she could only hope they would understand more of the situation before it was too late, but for now she was grateful to have friends, people who would stand beside her during this journey. With that thought she too settled down to sleep.

Chapter 5

Darrienia

Zo had woken with a start, but she didn't recall having slept. For as long as she remembered she had always taken a few moments upon waking to reflect on her dreams. She would attempt to piece together what they tried to tell her, if she could recall them. Last night, however, there had been none, and that for her was most unusual. For the first time, since her arrival in Crowley, her nightmares had not caused her to stir.

The fire's hot embers shone a dull yet piercing shade of red as they fought the losing battle to live. The world around her seemed darker, colours which should have been bright seemed somehow dull, yet at the same time there was an odd intensity to them. The sun hung fairly high in the sky but despite its position, which indicated it to be early afternoon, the light seemed to suggest it was about to set.

Glancing around the camp it soon became apparent she was alone. Her friends' belongings still littered the ground causing her to wonder where they had ventured. She lay in her blanket a moment longer as she tried to decide if it was warm or cold outside its protection, unusually it seemed neither. With little else to do, she started to collect their things, storing them carefully away in their backpacks. She busied herself, attempting to ignore the denseness to the surrounding air. It confused her senses, made the environment seem unnatural, but she forced herself to dismiss it as a result from last night's strange events.

Given the late hour, she had to wonder why they hadn't woken her, why they had allowed her to sleep so late despite the need for them to leave the island. Glancing around the now cleared camp, she realised how much time had passed since she had first awoken. The longer she remained alone, the more she felt as if something was wrong. The words she had spoken to Elly just yesterday played on her mind.

'*They could just as easily go after them than come for me directly. If they took my friends...*'

What if they had been taken? Something had disturbed the natural spirit of the environment, and the more she thought on it the less convinced she was that it was a result of their branding. Something else had to have happened, why else would she have been left here alone? A disruption like this stifled the senses of people with abilities such as hers. It was a guaranteed means to stop her tracking or pursuing any assailants. She recalled the events of the night, wondering if it were possible something had been added to their food or they had fallen prey to an enchantment. It would certainly explain her prolonged and dreamless sleep.

Her mind filled with panic as she glanced around in the hope of seeing movement, or something that would give some indication of what had happened, but everything was too confused for her to make any sense of it. There was no way they had simply gone to collect supplies, they had more than enough to last until they reached Albeth, which from here was the only place the boat would travel.

The more rational part of her mind tried to suggest that maybe they had wanted to discuss last night's events away from her, where they didn't have to worry about hurting her feelings, and voice their honest opinions about what transpired. Despite this logic she knew they would never leave her like this, let alone disrupt things so badly that she couldn't even tell north from south.

As the fear of what may have happened grew, she decided she had no choice but to venture into the forest, maybe if she walked far enough, the air would clear and she would get some idea of what had transpired.

"Ah, so you have awoken at last." A familiar voice sounded from the shadow of a nearby tree. "I'm glad you came." As Zo looked to Seiken all urgency seemed to drain away as she found herself captivated by his image. Feelings of familiarity washed over her, reinforcing the certainty that their paths had indeed crossed before. Standing with him once more, she knew these feelings were no illusion, they were broken fragments of memories which told tales of their meetings, but the accompanying images were all so distorted, so unreal. The brief glimpses into their past revealed nothing, as was often the case when a memory was formed by magic instead of the mind. Something hidden deep within her remembered him, a part of her which was unwilling to forget him completely.

The memories formed by magic were strange, like prophecies they often appeared jumbled and made little sense. If she were to take the vision literally, he hadn't aged a day since she had first seen him. The harder she tried to grasp the memory, and make sense of the images and words which accompanied it, the more absurd it became. Finally, she surrendered, focusing her attention back on their conversation.

"What do you mean came, came where?" Despite her internal struggle to catch the familiarity, only seconds had passed since he had spoken. She glanced around as if to ensure she still remained within the camp, satisfied she had not moved she returned her gaze to him.

"I have this for you, you would find one sooner or later." He emerged from the tree's shadow, as he did she wondered how many more times she would be rendered breathless by him. He passed her a piece of tattered parchment, without thinking she tucked it deep within the pocket of her trousers. "I just thought I'd try to give you an advantage. The others are already here. I think you should hurry, you are already late." With that, he faded back into the shadows and vanished, as if they themselves had taken him.

'*Of course the others are here,*' she thought to herself shrugging, unaware she had failed to realise the importance of his words. She decided it was time to locate her friends so they could depart. At least Seiken had confirmed they were still in the area, she could only hope no harm had come to them.

She had only travelled a short distance into the trees when an enormous chasm brought her to an abrupt halt, everything that had been in the area it possessed had been sucked into its immeasurable depths. Small vines and moss clung desperately to the side in an attempt to escape the mighty snare. It stretched easily ten feet in diameter, yet, as she watched she was certain that, little by little, it expanded. Some of the vines tumbled down into its stomach doing little to disprove her concerns. Carefully approaching the edge, she peered inside, fearful of what she may find lying broken on the chasm floor, but as she gazed within her vision met with nothing but the dark void which seemed to stretch to the centre of the earth itself. Her panic rose, threatening to consume her as even the devoured foliage seemed to have faded from existence. How could something this large have been created without disturbing their camp, could it be this was the reason her friends had not been there on waking? She called out their names, but silence was her only response.

She walked cautiously around its edge using the nearby trees as support. She had to keep looking, and this could be only the first of a number of carefully concealed traps which surrounded them. Given the structure of this one, it would be foolish to place another one so close, but something more sinister could be just steps away.

Treading carefully, her vision scanned the area for any signs of disturbance which could indicate a further threat. Just before her the trees seemed to thin, her instincts warned of the danger her senses could not perceive. This was the forest they had walked just last night, and she knew for certain there was no clearing ahead. She proceeded with caution.

She rubbed her eyes in disbelief as she stepped from the trees. They had finished abruptly giving way to another unexpected surprise, the inhospitable wasteland of a desert stretched before her puzzled gaze. There was no desert in Crowley. Her head began to ache as she tried to make sense of what lay before her. She had no recollection of having seen a desert before, but it was every bit as derelict as she had imagined. Its pale sands stretched far into the distance, the heat causing the air to shimmer, yet where she stood, it seemed to share the comfortable temperatures of Crowley.

No life could be seen across its desolate waste, with the exception of the occasional cactus. There was something almost strange in the manner they grew, almost as if the area had been created by someone who, like herself, only had an idea of what it should look like. Although she couldn't place why, there was something almost artificial about the landscape and the placing of its scarce landmarks. She felt herself touch the back of her head to check her old injury. The pain along with the wound had vanished so, clearly, this was no hallucination, which left only one option. The reason she found herself near a desert with the slow curve of the trees to her back, was also the reason the air was filled with such heavy magic. Somehow, defying all logic, while she slept, their camp had been moved. Unsure what else to do, she followed the outline of the trees in the hope that along the way she would locate her friends, all the time she called their names at intervals, hoping to hear a response.

She soon discovered the desert wasteland was not the only unexpected terrain to meet her bewildered gaze. The surrounding area was even more bizarre than she had first imagined. As she met with what would be the junction of each major directional change, a major change in climate followed. Between the two completely different climates there was a simple divide. The desert sands ended abruptly almost as if a barrier had been placed between the landscapes which the elements couldn't cross. On the other side of that barrier which, she assumed from the sun's position, was west, luscious green lands stretched far into the distance. Plants thrived and blossomed as heavy rain and thunder echoed through the plains. She blinked a few times, unable to believe a single line could divide the desert from the rain, it was such a dramatic, impossible change. She wondered then, for the first time, if she could be dreaming.

As she continued, she found the same occurrence repeated. To the north the grassy steppes littered with the occasional tree gave way to broken rocky ground, in the distance giant ravines and chasms engulfed the landscape leading to the mountains which towered on the horizon. It was the very depiction of the element of earth, then finally, before she had walked a full circle to return to the desert in the south, came the east. The silhouettes of trees through the heavy fog twisted as their bases sunk in the sodden marshes, their drooping foliage warning of the poison within. Again, when the direction changed, so stopped the fog and mists, never to cross the invisible barrier, it was almost as if some force had taken equal measures of each terrain and merged them to form this new and bizarre landscape.

The layout of the land reminded her of something, but she was too concerned about the disappearance of her friends to think on it further. She only hoped they had not taken it upon themselves to investigate the strange lands. Four friends, four terrains. If that were the case, she feared she would never find them.

With no other option available, unless she wanted to leave the area and risk becoming lost herself, she returned to the camp. She could only hope that if her friends had decided to explore without her, they would soon return.

Arriving at the deserted camp, her mind was now occupied by what she had seen, the desert, the rain, the mountains, and the mist, and suddenly realised why it seemed familiar. It was the depiction of basic magic, each direction was represented by an element, and what she had beheld was simply exaggerated images of the elemental directions.

"Zo!" Acha's voice called from the trees. Acha and Eiji seemed to appear from nowhere to stand just outside the camp. She swore just seconds ago she had been looking in that very place and had seen no movement that would have indicated the presence of anyone, until now she never realised how much she had relied on her senses.

"Something is very wrong here," she stated as they approached. Despite the seriousness of her tones she was unable to hide the relief of seeing at least two of her friends alive and well. She glanced around looking for Daniel and Elly, but they were still nowhere to be seen.

"I know, that pit is..." Acha motioned in its direction as she failed to find the words to complete her sentence.

"Have you seen Daniel?" Elly questioned emerging from the woods behind them. She had been drawn back to the camp by the sound of their conversation, if not for this she too may have continued to walk the forest. "Oh and this, the answer is power." She tossed a small stone tablet, no bigger than the palm of her hand, at Zo, who caught it and read its inscription aloud.

"I am dangerous in the wrong hands, once you taste me you crave more. I can aid or destroy you dependent upon your strength and motivation." Retrieving it back from her, Elly joined them in the centre of the camp.

"It is a riddle. The answer is power," she stated again as if to clarify. "It was by the camp when I awoke, no one was here so I decided I would locate you." For a moment when she had woken, she had been convinced they had tried to leave her behind, her tones were still tainted with the annoyance she had felt.

"That's odd," Eiji stated immediately before Zo could voice the same surprise. "That can't be right, no one was here when I woke either," he muttered. His head began to hurt as he wondered how it could be he had not seen Elly's sleeping figure when he woke at the seemingly empty camp.

"We should get moving. Daniel is still out there somewhere. I have to assume he is the type who *will* venture off alone." Growing pale at Elly's words, Zo gave a nod. She wouldn't be surprised if he had decided to explore one of the outside areas and in his excitement found himself lost. "Their game, their rules. He could be in danger," she added. She wasn't really concerned about their missing group member, there was only one person in the group she was concerned about, and another she was now responsible for. The other two were inconvenient. It would only aid her should they disappear.

"Hey, did I hear my name?" Hearing his voice, they turned to see Daniel descending a nearby tree, until now he had been ignoring the conversation between his friends below, his attention stolen by the vision from the tree-tops. "Something is not right here. I've just been looking around, you won't believe what I saw." His voice was mingled with anxiety and awe as he moved to join them Zo pushed him softly.

"Don't do that, you had me worried," she warned. For a moment the air around her seemed to become a little lighter, almost by instinct she glanced past him only to see the chasm that she had encountered. It was a few moments before she realised it should not have been visible from their camp. "We need to get moving." Zo pointed towards it, concern etched deeply in her tone. It seemed to expand towards them devouring all within its path, but with each movement it made the magic in the air thinner, less stifling.

"It would appear we have outstayed our welcome," Elly observed, something in her tone gave the impression she knew something they didn't but, with the fissure quickly approaching, now did not seem like a good time to question her.

"But which way do we go? How do we know there's not another one right in front of us?" Acha cringed as they broke into a run, charging through the forest in a desperate attempt to escape its ever quickening advance. They paused as they broke free from the cover of the trees, relieved when it too stopped its pursuit. The last of the trees tumbled down into its depths as it appeared to rest, pulsing slightly as if in laboured breath.

Their focus altered as they saw the landscapes that stretched around them. It was only now they realised that Acha's question had four very different answers. The air around them grew lighter as the heaviness dissipated returning things to normal. Although there was still something about the area which Zo's senses found unsettling.

"I don't really care for the desert." Zo was the first to answer. She had thought about this since she had first laid eyes upon the choices they would face. The last thing they needed was to wander this strange land aimlessly and with their limited supply of water, and lack of landmarks, she could only imagine what fate would await them if they were to choose that path. They all wanted to question how they got to be here and where exactly this surreal landscape was, but there were more important things at that moment, such as choosing a path before the chasm decided it was ready for dessert.

"We would do well to avoid the storms and marshland also," added Elly. She too had her own reasoning behind her suggestion. Her last experience with water had not been a pleasant one, and it had delayed her ambitions for months while she had to wait for her body to repair. During that time, she had scared Marise, who had understandably thought she had been claimed by Hades. Although the trauma she suffered hadn't killed her as such, it had been a very painful ordeal and one she was not willing to experience again. Even if there had been precautions taken to prevent such reactions occurring, her mind was unwilling to take the chance.

"That leaves north." Daniel stated firmly. "Perhaps we'll come across a town." He had given the only remaining option, an answer they all agreed on. Their best chance to gain information was to find a traveller, or a town, to help them to understand their situation a little better, this place was like nothing they had seen before.

"I guess it would help if we knew what we were after." Zo sighed as she remembered the only hint they had received, the stone tablet which Elly had deciphered, yet they were still no closer to understanding what exactly power, or the riddle, had to do with them being here.

"Either way, let's not wait round t'see if that thing's still hungry." Eiji nodded in the direction of the pulsing pit. Standing for a moment with their bags, they realised how lucky they had been, if Zo hadn't packed the camp, they would have lost everything. Deep in the recess of their minds, there was a part of them that wondered if perhaps that had been the intention.

* * *

The group trekked across the steppes, with each step the grass, which once fought for life, became healthier. Once they had taken their first intentional step towards their destination, the divide between the landscapes had vanished. Now nothing before or behind them represented the images they had seen. The harsh stony landscape, filled with ravines and chasm had distorted and now before them stretched an open plain. Far on the horizon still lay the mountains, yet the lands leading to them had changed drastically to hold forests and greenery. Along the path they walked stood a few strange looking trees, although if asked, they would have been unable to define how they were strange, except for suggesting they didn't quite look real.

"So where'd you think we are?" Daniel's voice was filled with wonder as he eagerly took in the scenery.

They had been walking for a long time. The sun hung low in the sky indicating they had just a few hours until sunset. Daniel only hoped that by then they had experienced more luck finding shelter than they had so far. He found himself oddly concerned about what terrors may lie in wait when darkness came to this strange land. Being well-read, there was no doubt in his mind that they *should* be afraid of what resides within the dark. Instinctively, as if a primal part of himself reacted to the strange surroundings, he knew nightfall here, unprotected, would be worse than he could even imagine.

"You know," a soft voice called to them, it was one Zo recognised instantly from its elemental rhythm. It was so hypnotic it had stopped her in her tracks. Seiken for the second time made his appearance by a tree. The group, having never seen him before, turned to face him in alarm. The figure moved his hand as if to give a single wave in greeting. He glanced over them as he leaned back casually on the rough bark. The tree, although breath-taking in its magnificent bloom, seemed to pale in comparison to his flawless beauty. "When the sun sets here it rises where you are, it's beautiful." He motioned to the already sinking sun as it hung low in the sky, although he gestured towards it, his eyes never left Zo's gaze. She felt the heat rise to her face as she looked coyly to the ground to avoid his brown eyes. "When your people wake, Darrienia becomes dangerous. When night falls the real danger arrives, during this time you are protected from his hunters, but only if you find somewhere safe before the last ray of light vanishes from the horizon. Stay longer and well, no one ever survives the night."

'*What are these people doing here with her?*' Zo looked up at Seiken in surprise, although he continued talking, she knew it was his voice she had heard just moments ago within her own mind. It was almost as if he spoke to someone else at the same time, someone very far away, and for some reason she could hear him.

"Creatures and monsters born from the imagination of the sleeping are released from the dreamer to this plane as they cross back into your world. These creatures roam the lands as they wait for their next kill."

'*I don't understand, she should have been with those already marked, and yet these four all bear Algiz. Is this part of their trickery?*' He walked closer to Zo, the smell of soft summer rain surrounded his presence, he smiled his captivating smile and all fell silent.

"What do you mean safe?" Acha broke the silence which had seemed to stretch for eternity, yet for Zo it was over in a heartbeat. He took Zo's hand gently. His touch was like fire on ice, burning and freezing where his fingers caressed, while his eyes remained staring deep into hers as if they looked right into her soul. Captured in his gaze she was certain she knew him, and in that moment, along with the recognition, her magic told her what their meeting here meant. From the first time she had laid eyes upon him she had understood how this would end, but despite this knowledge she still couldn't place a single real memory of the figure who stood before her. The almost complete words of a prophecy, only understood by instinct before, echoed clearly through her mind, as if she once again bore witness to its recital.

"I mean, just because *you* can't walk at night doesn't mean everything else isn't on the prowl while you cross over. Once night arrives, his minions, the Epiales, can't capture you, it's against the rules, but there are other dangers to be cautious of."

'*They manipulated the selection. The others were lost to us the very moment she was called upon.*' This voice seemed unfamiliar, like someone gave a reply to his earlier thoughts.

"Between twilight and sunrise you're safe from his minions, but otherwise you're fair game. Being of your upbringings"—he tore his gaze from Zo to glance briefly towards the rest of the small group—"I'm sure you can find somewhere, after all you've read enough books to know the rules."

Daniel, for that brief moment, wondered if they had met somewhere before, he had looked directly to him as if informing him he was the one with the answer. Seiken knew he could have looked at Elly instead, but he had already decided who would be most beneficial by her side. He wanted her to have as little to do with her former friends as possible. He knew all of them, at one point or another their paths had crossed before. That was what made their combined presence here alarming. Other heroes of fate had been selected, and yet it was these five who stood before him. Four of them had somehow lifted the mantle from those once chosen, and each person before him was remarkable in their own way.

'*But was it fate's decision or something forced? It's strange they would select her, but then to involve these people as well, it's almost as if they want us to win.*

There is something more to this, I can't see what it is.' His distant voice seemed concerned at the prospect. Zo couldn't help but feel guilty for eavesdropping on his private conversation, but despite this, she still listened intently, barely catching a word of what he said to the others.

"Evil can't cross running water, but water is out for tonight. There's about an hour remaining until—"

"Can't you help us?" Acha begged. Seiken stared at her heavily as she interrupted, she covered her mouth in embarrassment. She was the only one of the group he had not crossed paths with before. He could make assumptions regarding the rest of them, but he wasn't sure what part she would play in this at all. From their brief encounter in Darrienia previously he knew there was no cause for concern about Eiji, and Seiken himself ensured Daniel's survival, not once but twice, knowing there was a task of great importance before him. He would have felt much better about the situation had Elly not accompanied them. It was her presence that made the situation seem just a little too convenient.

"You need something which both keeps evil in and out, that's all I can say. I can tell you this, although I assume there are a few along the way, not everything here will be an attempt to entrap you."

'They don't even seem to realise Darrienia is the realm of dreamers. The others at least were prepared, they knew the rules.' The stranger's voice answered again as Seiken also wondered how they could not know even the basic premise of the game, after all, there was no way they would understand the rules before nightfall. There were too many questions. This was the first time anyone had appeared without knowing something of their quest. There was a pause as he pondered what this could mean, but he soon spoke again as he realised time was growing short.

"There are those we call non-conscious dreamers, people who are simply sleeping, and I am certain you may come across the occasional lucid dreamer, use them to your advantage. Anything their mind can create could be at your disposal." He produced a small violet flower from the air and passed it to Zo. Her face flushed an even deeper shade of red than when she believed she was somehow eavesdropping on his private conversation.

She looked to the flower holding it tightly to her chest, breathing in its sweet aroma. There was something familiar about its scent, it reminded her of a garden she had visited long ago. Holding it to her nose she breathed deeply, trying to seize the memory, but as always it eluded her. She was so focused on this she failed to notice she had become the centre of everyone's attention. Realising the memory was, as always, just beyond her grasp, she looked up to Seiken, only to discover he had vanished. Aware of the watchful stares, she turned to look at her friends.

"What?"

"She talks! By the Gods she actually talks!" Zo turned to Daniel giving him a playful shove. "Now you've joined us, I wonder if you could make sense of a few things." He knew her expression well, she had almost remembered something, something about that flower had stirred a memory in the back of her mind. It made him wonder if this stranger had somehow known it would. He had, after all, seemed very familiar with her. They started to walk as they continued the conversation.

"What exactly is this place?" Eiji questioned. "That guy gave us the basic idea but..." It seemed they had realised *she* had not been listening to the same conversation as they had.

"Seiken," Zo smiled as she spoke his name, she paused for a second to appreciate the sound of it. "From what I understand, we're in a place called Darrienia, it's the realm of dreamers." She gave an embarrassed smile remembering how she got that snippet of information. "I guess it is kind of like a land of shadows, nightmares, dreams, and imagination. Most things here, I think, were created by belief, collective consciousness, or have come from the minds of other life-forms. Yet at the same time, some of what we see is native to this world, and does not come from within the depths of our world's imagination. I think it's like our world in many respects, but here the sun follows the dreamer, this world is in light as ours is in darkness.

"Also, I think for the last few hours, what we've been seeing has come from our thoughts, or memories, as well as from other people. Darrienia is the world of the mind, wishes, and dreams, all of which is protected by the Oneirois," she explained. She found herself surprised she had knowledge of this place beyond what she had heard, and judging by her friends' expressions it appeared they too shared in this amazement.

"Like that village," whispered Acha gesturing towards a small village just a mile or so away from them. "We can't go there, no matter what, we can't. I-I once lived there, it's bound to be dangerous considering..." she trailed off into an inaudible mumble.

"Considering?" Elly prompted. She was all too aware that during the time they had spent together there was only Zo and Acha who had not spoken at least some details about their past. Zo's silence was understandable, she didn't remember hers, but Acha always seemed to change the subject. It was something she had done so well that until this point no one had really noticed.

"It's not important." She lowered her head slightly to avoid eye contact with anyone. "I have bad memories of that place. I doubt if we went there we would find help or shelter. Speaking of which"—she continued without taking a breath—"don't we need to find somewhere safe before nightfall?" It was not only true, but yet another way to change the topic without being questioned further.

"Well, I've been thinking about that." Daniel ruffled his hair slightly as he spoke. "I vaguely recall reading something along the lines of what Seiken said." Daniel pronounced his name carefully, he looked to Zo relieved to see she nodded at him. "Keeps evil in, keeps evil out, it's called a fairy ring, but I wouldn't know where to look. Although, aside from this poorly located village, this place looks a little like the area in Crowley where my dad found Acha."

"What's a fairy ring exactly?" Eiji asked, seeming rather embarrassed at having to do so.

"It's a circle of mushrooms, on rare occasions flowers. They occur because forest mushrooms grow in circles. The older growths, those in the middle, are the first to die off, as they die a toxin is left behind which inhibits the growth of other plants, therefore it creates a circle in the middle of the mushrooms," Daniel explained.

"In legends, it is said fairies would dance in them, thus creating the circle, which is why they are called Fairy rings," Elly added with no real interest.

"I know what you mean." Acha's voice chimed with excitement. "I used to play in one in the forest by the village when I was little. The local shaman, always used to chase me off and it's near where..." her voice dropped as her mind clouded with thoughts of her father's betrayal. It wasn't that she hated him for what he had done, after all, it was because of him she had come to be in this time, but she still failed to understand how someone could sacrifice their own flesh and blood, to further some unknown desire. "Since the village is here I don't see why it shouldn't be in the forest there." She pointed to the small stretch of woods which ran alongside the village, as she did so, Elly began to wonder if it had actually been there before it had been mentioned.

* * *

The fairy ring, to their astonishment, had been exactly where Acha had described. The furthest growth extended to almost touch the bark of nearby trees, and covered an area large enough to more than comfortably protect them all. The walk had been a tiresome one, and by the time they had entered the forest, and located the mushrooms, the sky had already grown dark in the pre-dusk light.

"Be careful not to step on any of them. I am certain it will not work if the circle is broken," Elly warned, looking towards Eiji. In response he immediately made the extra effort to widen his step over them. He smiled at her once safely inside, still grinning childishly as he stumbled over a backpack which someone had placed behind him. Elly shook her head with an expression of mild amusement.

"So what happens now?" Daniel questioned as the last specks of the light fought for life on the horizon. It grew darker with each passing second as the sun's rays made their final attempt to fend off the encroaching darkness.

"I'm not sure how it works, I guess we have to go to sleep?" Zo volunteered. It seemed a silly thing to say, but it was the only solution she could give. Since they had to sleep to get here it only made sense they had to sleep to return. It was the same thought that had occurred to her earlier at the camp when she thought she may have been dreaming, to her, it made perfect sense.

"That being the case, might I suggest we consume one of these." Elly presented a bag filled with small red berries. She didn't question Zo's knowledge, she simply accepted it as being correct. Reflecting on this, Zo understood a little more of the forgotten relationship she must have shared with this person. It made her more curious about her past, about other relationships she could have forged. She knew she would give almost anything to remember, and wondered how those eyes planned to fulfil their promise. "They induce sleep, rapidly," Elly explained, although none had been needed. The effects were almost instant, and only she and Zo had not yet taken them. "I guess the thought of what they may see after dark is worse than whatever this berry may have done." As she watched them for a moment it seemed as if their bodies slowly faded into the air. She smiled slightly before swallowing her own.

Zo sat mesmerised by the diminishing light beyond the circle. She watched as the last glimmer of the light's rays began to fade from within the safety of her sanctuary. The howls of predators filled the air as the native inhabitants to the land emerged to hunt. Something moved in her field of vision, something so hideous it caused her to close her eyes tightly, like a child trying to imagine away a monster. She turned desperately to Elly who now lay fading. It seemed only she had seen the face of the darkness which had surrounded them.

* * *

Screams echoed through the darkness; tormented, agonised, and distorted cries. A dark red aura consumed Zoella's observing figure, while flames and sparks licked the air around her, casting their light upon the figure of a girl. She held something clutched tightly to her chest as she left the blazing town without so much as a backward glance. Zo didn't want her to look back. She was afraid of this figure, afraid it would realise she was there watching from within the boundaries of that which she had just destroyed. The girl stopped sharply. Zo was no longer in the town but upon the path, just behind the darkened figure. Although she had yet to turn, Zo knew her presence had been noticed. She felt hysteria begin to rise within her as the figure slowly turned. The town's embers illuminated them both through the darkness. Zo tried to scream, but the sound froze in her throat.

"Hey." Zo jumped as Elly's hand touched her shoulder. She sat up quickly, nearly knocking Elly from her feet. "Are you all right?" she asked as Zo gasped for breath. Elly had started to get concerned when, unlike the rest of them, Zo had not awoken straight away after she had reappeared.

"Just a nightmare," she managed to state through her breathless gasps, aware her friends exchanged curious looks. She had wanted to explain but, like always, for the life of her she couldn't think what had scared her so much about the already faded dream. Only vague and disjointed fragments lingered, but the fear still tore at her soul. Suddenly, she found herself looking around in order to avoid the intensity of their stares. The dream was nothing more than a faded memory but a new mystery rose from the darkness. She had absolutely no idea where they were. "Where are we?" Her eyes fell on the vaguely familiar territory, the last remnants of a gentle forest littered the surroundings, grassland fanned out at every angle. Not too far in the distance she could see the rise of the nearby mountains.

"We have backtracked considerably," Elly replied, not even attempting to answer the question, after all, she was meant to be unfamiliar with this island and the landscape they found themselves in. Daniel paced around a broken mushroom circle, muttering to himself, until he finally chose to share his thoughts with the group.

"This is near where..." his voice trailed off as he glanced around once more to confirm his assessment. "This is where my dad found you Acha," he stated, but couldn't imagine how they had come to be here.

"I know." Her voice was little more than a whisper as she spoke. "This is the fairy ring I told you about. My home used to be over there." She pointed to an area of dusty paths and barren sands which seemed void of all life. Despite this, it did not seem to stand out until it had been mentioned. Only Daniel had heard her last sentence, he knew her stating it freely would invite too many questions, after all, how could she explain to them she was actually born in year 150 of Zeus' Era, or as it was more commonly referenced, 150 Z.E?

"That'd mean, somehow, when we slept there we woke somewhere on the boundaries of, here." Eiji deduced, his words expressed the same confusion the others felt. He made a deliberate attempt not to mention what he had overheard Acha say about her home being here. Since Crowley only had one town it was impossible. "So, did we just pack up camp and sleepwalk here or somethin'?"

"Doesn't anyone find it odd? Seiken said our sun rose when theirs set, yet I make it at least two hours after sunrise." As it seemed none of them could respond, Daniel had asked another question. "I wonder if we're safe to—" Before he could finish Eiji interrupted.

"Does that mean we hafta stay here all day!" he exclaimed, his tone once again reminding Elly of how young he was, he had sounded just like a spoilt child.

"I shouldn't think so. Maybe it's just while we pass between worlds that we need to be safe, remember how none of us could see each other when we woke?" Zo paused as she took the time to consider what she had just said. "When I woke Seiken said you'd already arrived, yet none of you saw me at the camp, so if I was the last to wake, or sleep..." Zo paused glad for Elly's interruption as she couldn't quite find the words she needed to explain.

"This circle is broken." Elly pointed to the clear break where the outer section of the mushrooms had died off. "It would offer little protection, even if we were to stay within it, and we need to get moving."

"Is there any point going anywhere if we're just gonna be moved around anyway?" Eiji sighed. He was still not convinced about leaving this circle, broken as it may be, anywhere they would travel would surely be pointless as they would just find themselves in the same place as they had slept in Darrienia.

"Yes, besides..." Elly watched Zo as she stared into the shrubs which grew near the boundaries of the circle. She was surprised she had noticed them so quickly. Little creatures like these weren't of any danger to them, they favoured hunting other animals, besides, eventually as the energy from Darrienia dissipated, so too would their existence on this side fade.

"Who knows what we brought back with us." Zo finished, as she spoke, she became the recipient of their questioning stares. "Keeps evil in, keeps evil out," she reminded them. As they followed her gaze to the bushes, they thought they saw a set of small, nightmarish teeth grin back at them through the shadows.

"Okay, but where we headin'?" Eiji questioned. Surely it made more sense for them to stay right here, that way when night fell, they wouldn't lose any of the distance they had gained.

"From here I know a shortcut, a few hours will see us to our destination." Elly hesitated for a second before taking the first step out of the circle, by her lead they began to follow. The direction of her determined strides seemed to indicate what they sought was near the small cluster of mountains. Daniel was surprised by her actions, it was common knowledge there was just one way to leave Crowley and that was the port. Unlike the larger islands, this one only consisted of a single, unmanned docking area.

"So where are we heading?" Daniel finally questioned as the mountain range grew ever closer. If this was truly their destination, it would have been a far quicker journey than the one they made just yesterday, of course, had they come here instead they never would have had the opportunity to reunite with Zo. If their destination hadn't been the port, it made him question what exactly could be found in two places on this small island. He had taken many trips to the mountains when he was younger. They always had a strange air about them, a mystery, or a forgotten secret seemed to be hidden within them, perhaps he was finally going to discover what it was. Or maybe Elly simply didn't know the area quite as well as she would have liked them to believe.

"You will know when we get there," Elly answered firmly.

Chapter 6

Collateral

"By the Gods!" Daniel exclaimed as he looked down on the small village, a village they all knew shouldn't be there. They had made haste climbing the mountain's slopes and now stood upon its lower peak, gazing down into the valley below where, alien to the known layout of this island, stood a small cluster of wooden houses. It had been a surprise, especially for Daniel. Everybody knew Crowley possessed but a single settlement and now, somehow, they gazed upon a second, a whole new town none of them had seen before.

"How long has this been here?" Daniel stared awestruck into the valley at the modest looking settlement, rubbing his eyes in disbelief. He knew for certain it hadn't been there long, but its aged appearance made him want to doubt his facts. If he and Adam hadn't camped there frequently when he was younger he would have been inclined to believe this impossible situation, but their camp would sit almost exactly upon where this town now stood. "I played around here all the time as a child and I never saw—"

"Forever," Elly interjected bluntly. She began to walk down the steep track that led to the simple town, attempting to avoid further questions. She was already unimpressed at having to lead them here, let alone having to answer their every query.

"Then how come I've never seen it?" Daniel quickened his pace to match hers as she scouted on ahead. It seemed almost as if she anticipated danger. There was something cautious, almost predatory, to her normally relaxed posture. Continuing to match her quickening pace he wondered how she, a stranger to these lands, could know about this place when its existence had eluded him all these years. He also considered what manner of people had remained so expertly hidden within the modest dwellings.

He knew something wasn't quite right. If this town had been their intended destination, they would not have journeyed towards the port initially. They could have saved themselves a lot of time by coming straight here. Had they done that, there would have been no opportunity for them to reunite with Zo and he was positive *they* were not the cause of the detour. He was positive Elaineor knew more about the lay of the land than she implied. He was almost certain she knew exactly where they were when they woke, but for some reason she had pretended otherwise, for a short time at least.

"It's a special village, only certain people can enter." Zo spoke mesmerised as she stared towards it, aware she had answered his question, but unable to place this new-found knowledge.

"You remember it?" Daniel questioned suddenly. It seemed looking upon this place had triggered something, perhaps this meant soon all her memories would return. At least then they would understand her situation fully without having to blindly follow those who had come for her. Since meeting with Elly, she had remembered more, surely it was a good sign, at least there was something positive about her appearance. If this continued, maybe Zo would remember everything and be able to make her own choice about whether or not to continue this journey.

"No, not this one... but at the same time yes." She frowned as she heard the impossible words she had spoken. The longer she looked upon the village, the more familiar it became. Her frown deepened as she fought to remember. Her concentration was broken by Elly, her words making her lose the fragile grip on the fine string attached to the memory.

"What she means is she has been there before, but not from here," she explained. She could understand their confusion since it was likely not one of them had seen such a place before, but having to explain *everything* had quickly become tiresome.

"But how is th—" Acha began, soon to be cut off by Elly's begrudged explanation, she had started to feel more like a guide than a traveller.

"It is simple," she snapped. "What you see before you is not a village, but a gateway. There are hundreds over this world, all of various shapes and images. These doorways exit in a city, an unmapped location, undetectable by beings or creatures of the world. This city was created to be a haven for practitioners of the artes the world over, a place they could be safe. In order for them to be able to get there with minimal delay, portals were erected to allow travel in mere seconds." She gave a sigh leading the group down the path. The unstable terrain had fewer hazards than she had expected. She had hoped at least one of them would have fallen taking an injury which would prevent them from continuing. In fact, she had already decided on the precise order they should leave. Assuming, of course, a freak accident didn't take them all at once. The odds were against it, but she could always hope.

A light mist seemed to radiate around the small village giving it an almost eerie glow, with each step closer it seemed to grow denser. Elly grabbed Zo's hand before she was able to step foot into the representation of the village. She was curious as to whether or not seeing this place would bring back further memories and, if so, whether such things would make the task at hand simpler or harder. It was likely to be the latter. If Zo learnt the true objectives of their mission, it was doubtful she would willingly complete the task at hand. The fact she was needed to fulfil this role was the sole reason she still existed. Things were delicately balanced, which was why there was great care being taken in the information she was given. It was best to ensure nothing could rekindle any undesired memories, memories which lay buried deep within her alternate persona. If their true objective became apparent it was doubtful she could face what lay ahead, not in her current state, she needed to be stronger.

"You may wish to conceal your weapon." Elly took the sword from Zo's belt without waiting for a response, once more she found herself surprised by its weight. Although it appeared its master could carry it with ease, it was clear it did not like to be handled by anyone other than its creator.

During her journey to return it, the sword had seemed to accept her as a temporary measure. This decision was clearly revoked on their reunion. She turned the sword over once in her hand, as if to show it *she* was in control. Reaching forward she grabbed the leather fasten which had, moments ago, held Zo's hair in place. "I will need this too," she stated. As Zo shook her hair free, Elly found herself amazed how little she *really* had changed from times past. She smiled slightly fastening the sword's belt around Zo's midriff to rest firmly against her back, and starting to remove her own long coat in order to conceal the weapon fully.

"Here." Daniel intervened to pass her a soft, handmade cloak that he had just moments before removed from his bag. "I picked up a spare before we set out, I knew you didn't have one." Zo thanked him, wrapping it around herself.

Elly couldn't understand why Zo had left home without protection from the elements, especially when even her friends had the sense to bring their travelling cloaks along. As she reflected on the contents of her bag, and the place Zo had called home, she realised how little she actually owned.

"Thanks, Daniel," she smiled, already feeling the warmth from the cloak as it sheltered her from the cool wind. He passed Acha hers from his bag before swinging his own around him, who knew what conditions they would enter.

"So, what's the deal with this place anyway?" Eiji questioned. "I mean, I've heard rumours but..." Elly gave a sigh as she wondered if this was a sign of things to come, wondering if their entire time together would consist of nothing more than an endless barrage of questions. She looked to Eiji, having Daniel pestering her was bad enough, but if he were to start as well the journey would quickly become unbearable.

"A long time ago, this city housed the most respected Hectarians this world had ever seen, but foolishly, they *all* sacrificed their magic along with the others, to aid the Hoi Hepta Sophoi in the creation of the Grimoire."

"Wait, so how come Zo can use it? If it was all sacrificed surely—" Daniel had taken the question from Zo's lips. It had been something both of them had wanted to ask since Elly had mentioned the sealing of Hectarian magic, after all, it seemed if anyone would know the answer it would be her, but until now the opportunity had never presented itself.

"It is difficult to explain. The Elementalists were unable to assist as their type of magic, stemming from Gaea, was incompatible with the cause. Nyx and Gaea have been allies since creation, and her magic was intertwined with that of Hecate's to create the nine seals erected by the ancients to restrain a mighty power, therefore if both applications of magic from Hecate and Gaea had been compatible there was a high probability the seals may have been destroyed.

"Hectarian magic was most suited to the task, thus was taken in order to bind Night's powers to the Grimoire, however, the Hoi Hepta Sophoi deceived them. Instead of simply taking their powers, they knowingly stripped it straight from the source. The spell they cast had been so powerful that, although Hecate herself was unharmed, it became unlikely any will be born who possess the power again, unless the balance of the magic is restored. This itself is impossible since the Great Spirits will name no Mitéra.

"As for why you still possess the artes, my only thought is you must have been shielded, made invisible to their spell so to speak. Any other Hectarians who remain are also likely to be a result of the same circumstances." She looked to Zo meaningfully, Elly knew no such people existed but had she implied this it would only bring about further questions. Although Marise's powers were, from rumour, believed to be a gift from Hades himself and not Hectarian true to their nature, to give too much information may see them linking the two. It was better to be vague than give an answer no one was ready to hear. She hoped this would be enough to satisfy them, but knew Daniel would push for further information, he was annoying that way. She could only hope the unsure tone in her answer would be enough to dissuade him from continued questioning.

"So in other words you don't know?" Daniel questioned. This had been the first time since meeting her that Elly had seemed unsure of her answer, her tones gave rise to uncertainty. It was disappointing, he had been certain she would have known.

"The exact reason no, but if I were to explain in depth the part I did understand it would far surpass your level of comprehension." Elly snorted her reply, there was something in his tone she had disliked. "Stay close," she warned. A moment later, she passed the first building at the entrance of the town and, as if stepping through a veil, vanished from sight. Her disappearance, as intended, had finished the conversation. They followed quickly in fear of being left behind, each felt the slight pull of resistance as they entered through the portal. The silence of Crowley was broken by the bustling roar of their new surroundings.

They emerged on the outskirts of an enormous city, where towering buildings rose in the distance as far as the eye could see. The portal had brought them out far from the main town, to a place surrounded by a low, broken, stone wall. To their right was a stonemason diligently replacing the fallen bricks along this perimeter. He called out a greeting to the new arrivals before continuing with his labour. In a place like this, a person of his craft was never without work, walls such as these existed throughout the entire city, separating the classes and various areas.

Their current location was considered the poorest of the great city. Merchants littered the broken cobblestones, their blankets outstretched filled with various wares. Seeing the arrival of potential customers their postures stiffened as they readied their most tried and tested sales pitches. Lively banter filled the air, and seemed to follow them wherever they walked.

Some merchants, having no customers at the time, followed them on their walk towards the towering gate, although their cries and pursuit soon stopped as they approached the guarded entrance. Those without the appropriate trade permits could not pass beyond these gates to peddle their wares.

"This area is the merchant district. Here you will find all manner of items. Within this city is every possible item a traveller could want, and even more they do not. Reflecting the nature of the city itself, you will find the trade areas are separated by class." Elly stated, as she began to speak Daniel begrudgingly pulled himself from a nearby merchant to hear what she had to say. "If you have cast your eyes to the north, you have seen the rising residential area. Should you ever be given the grounds to visit the uppermost gardens and residents, you will find the quality of life there beyond anything you could imagine. The area is reserved for people of high stature."

"Like lords and ladies?" Acha questioned joining Daniel by Elly's side. Despite her dislike of explaining things to these people it served its purpose well; whilst she was talking, they were staying close.

"No, that class of people will generally be found on the second tier. The high-class residential areas lack portals, therefore there is no reason for outsiders to intrude. Gaining access to such a place is difficult, there are all manner of political restrictions and permits needed to gain entrance. It is the area with the highest concentration of militia who, you will find, have their centre of operations in the middle eastern sector of the town, near the port."

"This place has a port?" Daniel questioned with disbelief.

"Yes and a beach for that matter. Although I would advise against entering the waters. Just as most roads here lead to somewhere, so too do most bearings on the sea. Alien to the nature of the town-based borders, the sea portals permit the passage of marine life allowing the area to provide a good harvesting ground for the fisherman. You could not imagine some of the unique horrors their nets have snared." As they passed through the stone gateway, she spoke a greeting to the guards. This area, as she had implied, seemed more prosperous than the blanket littered plaza they had exited. The merchants here sheltered beneath brightly coloured tents or sunshades.

"What exactly is this place? It's amazing," Daniel asked; his attention wavering as he stopped to examine the contents of a nearby stall.

"It was a sanctuary, but these days it is more like a bazaar. But as I stated previously, only certain people can enter. Those who enter, if granted leave to do so, may bring guests. Once a person has seen an entrance they can return at any point, assuming they know where to find the portals. Stay close, we are entering the main trade district now," she answered pulling him from a nearby storefront by the back of his cloak, almost choking him in the process.

Through yet another guarded road lay a large trade district. There were stores built on multiple layers with stairs adjoining the walls, allowing access to the higher areas. Merchants sat on their small balconies where they had hung their latest exclusive sale banners.

Until now, she had slowed her pace to permit a small amount of browsing. Or at least, that is how it would have appeared, but her unnoticed movements were predatory as she watched for any threat that may present itself. She was glad this place remained neutral to the conflicts of the outside world. But not everyone who walked here would necessarily abide by the rules, especially if they believed the prize was worth the risk of being permanently evicted. It would take just one person, one unwanted interference, for everything she had carefully prepared to be ruined. They needed to quicken their pace and arrive at their destination, as she had feared, a problem *had* presented itself. From the shadows she had caught sight of a hunter, although she was confident they would not dare approach, if they did it would mean trouble.

"What kind of certain people?" Acha whispered timidly, almost fearful of the answer.

"Invited ones. It is..." Elly stopped, as she had turned to answer Acha, the hunter had made his move and vanished from sight. Despite the regulations created by the council of this metropolis, the law of a hunter was one of their own. There was nothing to say he wouldn't risk being banished for the chance of the bounty; especially *this* bounty. Elly glanced quickly to Zo before once more surveying the area. She knew better than to think he had stopped his pursuit simply because she had lost track of him. It was more likely he would lie in wait and try to ambush them as they left. It was an opportunity which would not be allowed. "What we want is this way." She grabbed Daniel once more from the stores. "Anyone would think you were a child," she scolded. "I am not here to babysit you."

She led them at an increased speed, all narrative now ceased as she focused on getting to their destination as quickly as possible. She backtracked down joining side-streets occasionally, to confuse any who watched from the shadows. Frequently she would hear words of awe and amazement. These tones, much to her annoyance, saw her needing to return to find them at a nearby establishment which had caught their attention. Eventually, when she stopped checking behind her, they stopped browsing, realising there was no choice but to follow, especially should they wish to see the outside world again. As she navigated the maze-like streets, Elly found herself recalling Marise's first visit to these walls. It was the first real confirmation she had received that the precautionary measures taken, to keep troublesome memories at bay, were working. She recalled the memory in Zo's stead...

...."Staying here should prove easier than anticipated." Elly smiled as they left the horses with the Collateral dealer for safe keeping, her words had broken Marise's intense gaze on the stable hand. He was a young boy no older than fourteen, she had been making a mental note of his appearance, from his short scruffy hair, to his cautious brown eyes. Should anything happen to her horse, *he* would be held personally responsible.

"Why is that?" she questioned glancing around. Everyone seemed to be going about their everyday business, merchants peddled their wares and the streets were crowded with people of all persuasions as they hurried to their destinations. Nothing seemed out of the ordinary.

"Well, it seems either they do not know, or do not care, who you are." She smiled, as Marise had noticed, nothing was out of the ordinary. For their safety it would be better it stayed this way. As long as they broke no laws within the confines of this city, they would find very little trouble here. Despite her acts, Marise was not a criminal within this jurisdiction, and she intended to keep it that way. "Come on, let us get to our room." As Elly led the way through the winding paths of the town, Marise soon realised this city, Collateral, was much larger than she had first anticipated.

It was a little past noon and already the streets were filled with people. Entering the main trade district, Elly heard the familiar voice of her favourite waiter call to her in greeting. She was well known to this area, frequenting here often. She had seen this man grow from a young boy to the strapping figure who now worked in his father's establishment. Already he was busily arranging chairs outside ready for the lunchtime patrons. The tempting aromas seeped from the open kitchen door filling the surrounding air with its inviting smells. It was the day of Kronos, as such the traders were only now opening for business.

Elly steered Marise through the bustling streets towards the wall, there, on the outskirts, lay a shop which seemed almost alien, somehow out of place as it stood alone. Outside, a maroon semi-circular tent had been erected. Within it, all forms of goods littered the sturdy looking tables. Most were specialist goods which no thief would dare to steal, possibly due to the words, 'cursed until purchased', being scrawled on a piece of card which hung on the folded back entrance, and given what Elly knew about the owner, she didn't doubt it. The wooden framed and paned casement windows were secured against the outer wall with small latches, showing the stall was open for business.

Through the opening stood the proprietor, a blind man, who offered them a warm smile as Elly removed a coin purse from her trouser pocket. There were numerous things they needed for their upcoming journey, and this was just the place to acquire them. After greeting them he took a seat at his desk just to one side of the window, taking a drink from his battered tin cup as he allowed them to browse his goods. The rear shelves were packed with all forms of oddities, from rope and lamps, to medicines and tinctures. Boxes haphazardly cluttered the right side of the interior. Upon the almost buried shelf was another small note which read, 'Can't see it? Ask'. To the far left stood another door, one Elly knew led into a small business area, otherwise only accessible through the sturdy wooden door concealed to the rear of the tent. It was rare people would be invited within the area that doubled as the merchant's home. He stood unexpectedly as if aware they were ready for his assistance.

"Good day to you, I am Venrent, how may I be of service to you ladies today?" He extended his hand in warm greeting, accepting the gesture Elly found herself impressed he had so accurately assessed who was at his stall, especially when they had yet to speak. Then again, he had been given plenty of time to adapt to his current affliction. "My, your hands are cold, perhaps you need some ginger to aid circulation?"

"No, thank you," she stated politely withdrawing from his touch. "My friend and I are about to embark upon a pilgrimage, I was hoping I may purchase some of your finest rope."

"Indeed you may, what kind of rope are you looking for?" he enquired, not waiting for a response he continued. "I have many kinds, each threaded specifically for terrain. There's mountain rope, dungeon rope, training rope, climbing rope, trap rope—"

"Multi-purpose," Elly interrupted, she didn't wish him to go through all twenty forms of rope she had already noticed on the back shelves. "We are uncertain what we may face." He paused for a moment hearing her words.

"Hmm." She was unsure if his tone was filled with amusement, understanding, or if he was simply being polite. "Adventurer rope it is then." He moved towards the back of the store to select some of the pre-cut ropes.

"What's the difference?" Marise questioned. Hearing her speak he paused briefly, it was only a subtle gesture but he had straightened his posture ever so slightly. Elly quickly realised why, and berated herself for not considering this before they had approached.

"Strength and durability. Depending on how the sections are woven determines whether or not they possess elastic properties, and such. We could do with some more thread. While I conclude business here, go over there and fetch me some." Elly motioned her towards a small, distant storefront, knowing she had to get her away from this place, quickly.

"What kind of thread?"

"For repairs," Elly answered firmly as the gentleman reappeared at the opening holding several lengths of rope. "Go, I will join you shortly."

"If these are not what you require, I will gladly cut you a specific length if you would rather." He motioned towards the rolls at the back of his store.

"No, thank you, this will be fine." Elly stated, taking them from him to size up the ones she wanted before returning the unsuitable ones.

"So where is it you ladies plan on journeying to?" he questioned placing the unwanted ropes on a small shelf next to him.

"We are going on a pilgrimage to follow the steps of the great priestess Cassandra," Elly lied, but there was no way for him to know, nothing in her tone or posture would have given her away even to a great investigator.

"I see, tell me, is your companion's name Zoella?" he questioned hesitantly. He couldn't help himself, her voice was so similar to how he remembered

Kezia's daughter. The mannerisms were harsher than he recalled, but he was certain it had been her. As certain as he could be given the time that had passed.

"No, I am afraid not. Is she also walking the path of the priestess? If we should meet her on our journey, is there anything you wish me to relay?" Elly smiled slightly, he may be blind but his senses were sharp. She would have to be more careful, she still required the aid of this person. Whilst he may have recalled her companion, Elly was now confident he didn't recall their own last encounter. It would make their next meeting much easier.

"Hmm, no never mind, I could have sworn it was her." He gave a sigh rubbing the back of his head as he smiled. "Not to worry. I'm afraid old age has an advantage over me. So that's four adventurer ropes at thirty-two each, that's, let's call it one-twenty shall we, for such a noble pilgrimage." Elly passed him two coins. He weighed them in his hand and smiled, by the weight alone he could tell exactly how much had been presented and, from something as simple as the texture and engravings, he could guess their native land, assuming of course, they carried native currency.

It was a skill he had mastered over the years, one which surprised many travellers when he asked of their homeland. He was well-learned in the outside world, and why wouldn't he be? Before his blindness he had spent a very long time studying it. Each different province used a special picture or mark on the metals they smelted. As time passed and currency mingled this became more difficult, but given the accents of those who visited he could always make an educated guess. Conversation of the outside world was a good way of passing the time. He traced his fingers over them, they were of equal value but of different provinces, and as much as he tried, he could not place the accent she spoke with.

"Thank you," she stated politely as she left to find Marise.

Marise waited patiently outside the small building where she had brought the goods, watching each person as they walked the streets.

"What was that all about?" Marise passed her the bag containing the thread. It had been quite clear she had wanted her to leave in silence, but since they were now free to talk, she felt the need to ask. There had been something about that man Elly had wanted to distance her from, almost as if she had felt anxious about what could be revealed, but the old man certainly didn't seem like he could be much of a threat to them.

"Venrent, the merchant back there, is from Drevera. When you spoke, there was recognition in his posture."

"But *I've* never seen him before," Marise stated, following Elly as she made her way towards the inn.

"True as that may be, I believe he recognised you as your predecessor." All at once things became clear to Marise, and she did not look happy about what had been suggested.

"But he's blind." Her protest only served as a reminder of how young and inexperienced she really was. She had yet to encounter people like Venrent, she didn't know how extraordinary their skills were. They had yet to cover the sensory deprivation training, maybe when she realised herself that when one sense was deadened the others became more sensitive, she would understand.

"But his senses are sharp. There are many things apart from looks which betray a person's identity, you know that," Elly advised as they reached the doors of the inn...

...At the end of the winding paths, they reached a small inn, smaller by far than any of the others they had laid eyes on. It was possibly in one of the worst locations a small business could have been situated yet, despite being difficult to locate, its exterior showed no sign of its poor positioning.

"Elaineor!" The inn keeper welcomed her with open arms as she set foot through the door. "How is my favourite customer? I have reserved the three bedrooms just as you requested." His corpulent arms spread wide as if to embrace her. As he moved forwards, a small amount of light reflected from beneath the hair he had combed over in an attempt to conceal his baldness. His smile faded slightly as he met her cold, unimpressed gaze, his arms lowered quickly. Within seconds, his mercenary smile had once more planted itself on his rounded face. He waddled to the cash register, found just on the other side of the untidy counter. Had it not been for an unusually shaped paperweight holding untidy parchments in an unkempt pile, there would, no doubt, have been none of the rich oaken wood visible through his clutter. He fumbled through the paperwork in search of something before returning to them with a small set of keys in his hand.

It was difficult to look at him for too long, the explosion of clashing colours was painful to the eyes, his attire made him appear more like something you would find at a circus than running an inn. His smile welcomed them each in turn, until his eyes fell upon Zo. He stared at her for some time, darkness wrinkling his brow. "I told you last time Elaineor." His voice, although low, was silenced by a single, dismissive wave of her hand.

"I see you are only a three-bedroom inn and, as you can see, during my travels I seem to have acquired more companions. Perhaps I should take my business elsewhere," she said dismissively, her tone matching her unconcerned posture. It made her companions question why they had covered such distance if the choice of establishments was so unimportant. Having passed so many on the way, they had convinced themselves there was something special about this specific inn.

"No, there's no need, no need at all I tell you. They are double rooms as you well know, of course if there's any—" Another wave silenced him once more; Zo glanced to Daniel, they had both wanted to hear the rest of that sentence.

"Very well, let us try this again. My companions and I wish to rest, we have much to discuss, and in accordance with our prior arrangement, I am awaiting the presentation of the keys and the vacating of any other clients or help. Am I understood?" she questioned sharply.

"Of course, of course. Whatever you wish my dear." He smiled as he rubbed his grimy hands together. "But my silence does not come cheap." Elly nodded placing a tightly wrapped bundle of money on the counter before him. He flicked through it listening to the hum of the notes. He frowned slightly. "You jest, do you not? My silence is not bought so cheaply. I have a reputation to uphold, imagine if people were to find out..." before he could finish his face gleamed as another bundle was placed before him, he took it in his hands tenderly.

"For this, I could purchase my own inn." She sighed tapping the counter with her finger impatiently as he once more listened to the hum of the notes.

"Indeed, but you know very well you cannot guarantee your security in such a place."

"Indeed," she sighed reluctantly. The old magic used to create this structure had long been forgotten. There was little choice but to pay what he asked. Well, there was one other option but it was too messy and would create too many complications, besides, as much as she hated the insufferable innkeeper, this place was, as he said, secure. It was the safest place she knew, and she knew of many. She had spent much time in this inn with Marise, years in fact. "It is said there is no one more honest than a person who is paid highly for

his services. Although I am tempted to seek shelter elsewhere in the future."
She leaned against the wooden counter, unaware that the rest of her group
was watching in awed horror. What she had given him was more than most
people could hope to earn in a lifetime, in fact, it was very rare the vaults
would issue paper notes at all.

Only the rich could afford the luxury of paper money. It was a practical safety measure which prevented the dangers associated with transferring
large sums of gold. Similar to the workings of a Plexus, the paper could be
exchanged in any vault or treasury for the agreed sum. A sum which was
etched onto the paper by enchantments, and bound to the owner by blood
to prevent any forgeries.

"Ah, but should you do that, I have information that may cause more trouble than you wish to confront. Am I right?"

"If any were to care, would the city, or more importantly *you*, survive?
We have been well behaved, until now." Elly turned to smile at Zo before
returning to the conversation. Zo couldn't help but feel there was something
in that look. She frowned, trying to decipher its meaning, trying to grasp
the reason this place seemed familiar to her but was once more distracted by
the innkeeper. She listened carefully, hoping he would reveal further information.

"Very well, my lips are sealed. I shall take my payment and leave you be."
His sticky fingers handed the set of keys to Elly. As she began counting them,
for the second time since their arrival she was recalling more about her first
visit here with Marise. She knew this was a side-effect of her watcher's special
measures. She was glad to have had Annabel take the time to create such
precautions when she had first sealed Marise...

..."Elaineor!" No sooner had the bell above the door sounded than the
greeting from the stout man hailed her. He was, as always, dressed with poor
taste. This time he wore a bright yellow shirt, which seemed to shimmer
green as he rose to his feet from behind the counter. A mercenary smile traced
his robust features. "Could it be you have come to stay once more? It has been
years. How ever did you convince your employer?"

"Blackwood?" she questioned sarcastically. "He is *not* my employer. I ask
if you remember one thing, it is that."

"Well, if you're here does that mean this is..." He looked at the figure who
stood beside her, a frown formed on his face as he took in her every detail. She

must have been no older than fifteen, maybe sixteen, her vivid red hair framed her face giving her something of a wild appearance. She wore a short, soft-leather tasset, almost skirt like in appearance, soft material lay underneath to conceal the areas the leather did not. The front was comprised solely of this black fabric, which was split just below her pelvis by her thighs to allow freedom of movement. His vision traced down her bare legs to her small-heeled, soft-leather, knee-length boots. Despite the obvious manoeuvrability her outfit would allow, she did not look like either a warrior, or an assassin. Her black lace up top had splits in the shoulder leaving them uncovered in a possible attempt to reduce restriction of movement. The top itself was flattering and hugged her feminine curves tightly, yet there was still no escaping she was nothing more than a child, and certainly not a warrior. Elly must be playing with him he reasoned.

"Yes, this is Marise," Elaineor answered coldly. The shock on the innkeeper's face revealed she was clearly not what he had expected. She was not what anyone expected, it was one of the things which made her tasks far easier.

"This, she is Marise?" His tone was filled with light amusement, surely Elaineor was joking. "I expected her to be..." he paused, something about the way the young assassin looked at him almost froze his blood. He swallowed before finding the courage to continue. "Older"—his voice broke—"I-I expected her to be older." How could a child make him feel so weak? He had confronted grown men who did not hold this kind of power over him. Elly had to admire his courage in voicing a criticism, but more than anything, she was grateful for Marise's reserve. She had cut many a man down for less than the words he had spoken.

"I believe longevity should be your concern," Marise whispered quietly, leaning forwards onto the desk. He retreated a few steps.

"Sorry miss," he squeaked, quickly turning his attention back to Elly, who had moved Marise back to stand behind her. "So, what brings you here this time?"

"A mission, that is all you need to know. Now tell me, what do I owe you for the room?" She placed a small box on the desk.

"Normal conditions?" he asked as he rubbed his hands together in anticipation of what was to come.

"No, it seems you already have guests and, as yet, the people of this town have not put the name to a face, nor do we intend to break the edicts of this council. So, for now, just a room will suffice. Besides, it would be difficult for you to explain to your guests why they all must vacate." Elly glanced to the hooks where travellers hung their cloaks. It seemed the inn was almost at maximum capacity, which didn't say too much given it only had three double rooms. There were very few who could afford lodgings here. Like a number of buildings in Collateral it was of special design.

"For you, Elaineor, I could justify anything," he smiled.

"For me, or for my money?" she questioned dryly.

"How long do you plan on staying this time?" He had decided it better not to answer the proposed question, it was an answer she knew too well.

"Indefinitely," she answered, watching as the mercenary smile once more appeared on his face.

"The normal price," he stated.

"The normal price, for just a room?" She shook her head in mild amusement.

"One room or three, it's all the same."

"Please, humour me, explain your logic." She tapped her finger on the box which rested on the counter.

"The way I see it, you're not only paying for a room, you're harbouring a criminal. My silence is a valuable asset."

"I imagine you feel the same way about your tongue," Marise warned. Elly silenced her with a raise of her hand. Marise had become increasingly more aggressive lately, she always seemed to be hunting for blood. It was something Elly would have to address, she may be an assassin but there was a healthy level of desire, and watching everyone for something which would justify a kill was *not* something she taught, or would tolerate from her student.

"For what you are asking I could, of course, buy my own inn."

"True, but as you know, this inn is special," he retorted smugly. "There is no other like it in existence." Elly pushed the box towards him. He grabbed it quickly, his hands fumbling in anticipation of opening the lid to peer inside it. His eyes lit up as he gazed upon its contents before he slid a single key across the desk with his finger.

"Let me know when you require more, and *do not* think I will not be counting," she cautioned.

"Exactly how long is indefinitely?" His eyes flitted from Elly to the box several times. Now he had examined its contents fully, he knew she didn't just plan on staying for a few weeks.

"Now, if I knew that it would not be indefinitely, would it?" she questioned as she walked away.

The room shared the same bad decor found throughout the rest of the inn. The two beds rested by the far wall separated by a chest of drawers, at the base of the bed stood a vanity table filled with strange ornaments. Elly had barely lowered her backpack when Marise questioned her actions.

"Why pay him that much? I could have negotiated a much better offer." She fingered the hilt of her sword, an action Elly had seen too much of recently.

"Enough," she scolded. "I trust him. I have known his family for what seems like forever." She smiled, thinking back over the many centuries to her first stay in this inn. The rates had been a little more reasonable then but, as with everything, it grew more expensive with age. This inn's special feature was difficult to maintain. There were but a handful of people who could even comprehend how to repair such a thing. In fact, the only place with the skill and knowledge for such a feat were her good friends of the Research Plexus, who lived hidden within the city of Knightsbridge. The repairs and maintenance were costly, which meant very few could afford to seek shelter within its walls. Such a thing was of course meaningless to Elly, she had more funds than any would ever realise, and only a fraction of these were stored in the vaults. One with her adventuring expertise knew of far better ways to conceal their riches.

"But he would betray you if the price was right!" she protested. "It would be safer to—"

"Whatever the price it could not compare to what I offer," she stated. "The money is just a technicality." It was true, she only paid the funds as a courtesy. Each of the many previous owners of this establishment knew her worth as a patron, none of them would ever consider betraying her.

"But where do you get such funding?" Marise questioned, she had wondered if perhaps Night paid for their expenses, but something told her she was wrong, and she knew for a fact she certainly didn't get anything from Blackwood.

"For now, let us just say such things are not exactly a concern to someone like me," she responded, fingering each of the ornaments in turn, before searching the rest of the room. By the time she had finished she held several small pieces of ancient technology in her hand. "Come, let us get something to eat." She led Marise to the dining room, which was barely large enough to hold the enormous table which stood within it, motioning for Marise to sit she continued through the door to the reception in order to pay the innkeeper a visit.

"I trust everything is to your liking." He smiled. A fresh bead of sweat formed on his already damp complexion as Elly showed him the technology in her hand. She watched the horror on his face as she dropped it, crushing it beneath her boot.

"It is now," she stated. "How many times must I warn you? My conversations are not for your ears, and if you so much as even think of spying on us in your passageways, so help me, I will allow Marise to deal with you. You are expendable as long as I have your keys, or do you forget I know the secrets of this place possibly even better than you do," she warned as she turned away. "Do not even think about putting it back tomorrow."

"I wouldn't dream of it," he whispered as he looked at the small pieces of broken technology. He should have known better by now. Elly always found his listening devices, but he just couldn't help himself, it was his very nature to be intrusive. "I take it by your warning that you do not expect to be back tomorrow evening?"

"No, I have made other arrangements."

"You know, I will still be charging you for your room. It is all the same to me whether you return or not." Elly nodded, she had not expected anything less. Before approaching Marise, who sat at the table, Elly hung her coat over the enormous portrait of the innkeeper, a portrait which disguised the entrance to one of the many secret passages. She sat with Marise after preparing her a sandwich in the kitchen.

"So we won't be staying here tomorrow?" Despite the quiet tones she had been able to hear every word of their conversation.

"No, we need to follow up on a lead I have."

"You mean a Grim—" Elly raised her hand silencing Marise as two of the other lodgers passed them, and exchanged polite smiles.

Glancing outside, she realised it was getting quite late. The torches, which lit the street corners, had already been burning for some time.

"Tomorrow is going to be a busy day so you need to be rested. We will depart at dawn"...

..."Are you forgetting something?" Elly questioned, sliding the penultimate key slowly over the loop as she pulled herself away from the memory. It was a remarkable thing they had achieved, the detrimental memories would be transferred, by enchantment, to Elly.

The ability to manipulate people's memories, by displacing or altering them, was one of Annabel's greatest skills, and one she had used in her youth for manipulation and crime before finding her true calling. Of course, in most cases the recipient wouldn't understand the flash of images and think it was just their mind deceiving them, but Elly could decipher them perfectly. There was but a single thing which concerned Elly. Annabel had grown old, and all of the safety measures would stop when she was taken to the underworld. She could only hope it didn't happen before it was time for the darkness to be filled. Of course, before that could happen, certain events had to fall into place, and the transfer did not always work on her. It seemed to only work when the memories being recalled were not Zo's. It was a problem they had to be aware of, especially given some of the memories which were free to return.

"I don't think so." The innkeeper paused as he reached the door, turning back to face them. "Blinds drawn, tea is cooking, beds made, you have the keys. No, nothing I can think of." He counted the points on his sausage-like fingers before turning to leave again.

"The passage keys, perhaps?" Elly dropped the final key over the ring, the sound it made as it fell to meet the others seemed to slice through the silence, the accusation in her eyes burning through him.

"Passageways? Your suspicion offends..." he laughed nervously as his gaze fell from hers; he gave a deep sigh before he dug deeply into his pocket to produce three small keys.

"Thank you." She smiled, helping him through the door, locking it as he finally took his leave.

They followed her from the foyer, still in silent horror over the amount of funds she had so carelessly presented. They knew she was of good upbringing, from a rich family, but still, what they had just witnessed surely bordered on insanity, notes were virtually an unseen currency.

"Are y' sure we can trust him?" Eiji was the first to speak, he alone, aside from Elly, understood the threat which had left the innkeeper's lips. He watched her cautiously as they entered the bright red dining room. It was a room which was barely large enough to hold the six place table which had been already prepared with napkins and cutlery.

A large portrait of the owner, wearing the same pink and yellow striped trousers, with and equally grotesque green and blue polka dot shirt, hung on the wall opposite the drawn blinds. Only Elly knew that each day the picture would change to match the attire which the innkeeper wore. In a similar fashion, the interior itself was a reflection of the proprietor's tastes. They were tastes that never improved and seemed to devolve each day.

Elly removed her coat, glancing towards Zo, who warmed herself by the log fire along with Daniel and Acha, who seemed to be sharing a hushed conversation of their own.

"He dare not betray us," she whispered, "he would lose far too much." Her tone returned to normal. "There is nothing as secure as greed. Besides I have used him at least a thousand times, each time we exchange the same playful banter, although, despite the pretence, the price never varies." As she spoke, she hung her coat over the giant portrait, despite its size it concealed the painting completely. "Once he has left the keys in the hands of another, he could not find his way back here, even with sextant readings. This place is like this town but to a lesser degree. Once its keys are secured, no one can enter without reservations, and it cannot be located until the expiry of said reservation, other than by those who reside within of course." She checked under the table. "He is getting lazy." She unhooked and crushed the small piece of ancient technology. "Now I am certain there is no one listening there are a few things you need to know, after hearing them any of you are free to leave, with one obvious exception." She looked at Zo and gave her what she thought to be a comforting smile, a smile which in fact sent shivers down her spine. Eiji knew he wasn't free to leave either, not if he wanted to live.

"What kind of things?" Daniel asked after a prompting nudge from Acha, who now sat to his side at the dining table. Zo took the chair to his other side, leaving Elly and Eiji sitting with a gap between them.

"Well, since you two invited yourselves along," she looked at Daniel and Acha in turn. "And you had no choice but to accompany me," her vision glanced to Eiji. "You should at least know what you are getting yourselves into." She sighed, this wasn't how it was meant to be. It was meant to be just herself and Marise. She hadn't counted on being followed, nor on these other people inviting themselves along. She gave another sigh before continuing. "As you have already gathered, the legends about Night are true, but he *has* been dormant for over two decades, long enough for people to forget the true terror, and motivation, of his work.

"With so long in peace, they now doubt the sincerity of the tales, even his existence, by referring to him as a legend. That, along with the passage of time, dulls the blade of fear. People soon become complacent and adopt the typical apathetic attitude, after all, why should it matter since his powers were sealed away? That is, if they believe the fairy tales at all."

"But you mentioned the Grimoire when we met, so—" Daniel's interruption earned him a scolding look from across the table; he felt himself shrink away slightly as she continued.

"I am getting to it, anyway, his powers *were* sealed away in seven magical tomes called the Grimoire. They were a combined effort of all the Hectarians, who gave their power to the Hoi Hepta Sophoi to aid their creation. The first four sealed away his Elemental magic, the fifth sealed his Destructive or Black artes, the sixth, his Light and Life-force magic, but not even the Hoi Hepta Sophoi knew what was contained within the seventh.

"Night was aware of the plan and set out to face them. He had known ultimately it would come to this, before they could succeed with their plan he would need to confront them, but as the prophecies had foretold, he was overpowered.

"Blood magic, of course, is by far the most potent magic, the Hoi Hepta Sophoi far surpassed it. They gave not only their blood, but life-force and thus created the most powerful seals of all." She looked up to see the blank expressions of those she spoke to, she wondered for a moment if they had been listening at all. "It is easier for me to show you." She removed a small crystal from her pocket, it seemed to grab their attention more than her story had.

"Is that..." Daniel gasped.

"A gossip crystal? Yes," she stated dismissively.

"Where did you get one? I've only heard rumours of such things, only six are said to exist throughout the entirety of the world. When you use it, you see facts as they were, not as history dictates. Each one is empowered with the memories of time itself. It is like watching the past as it happened before it is corrupted by speech." It was a little known fact that all crystals could do such a thing, however, only a gossip crystal could do so, to some extent, in unskilled hands.

"Enough of the lesson, do you want to know why she needs protecting?" Elly scolded; the four companions leaned forwards to stare into the crystal...

..."At last the final spell is complete, Hectarians the world over have surrendered their power for this cause." The middle-aged man now seemed much older than he had when the group had first taken their seats. He leaned breathlessly against the table, using it to assist him as he rose to his feet, his black hair somehow seemed paler than just hours before.

"Surely this method is reckless, if it were to fail." An elderly man, rose to his feet, his shaking hand grasping the cane which stood beside his chair. His cold grey eyes filled with doubt and worry. This man had the hardest task of all, he had to voice everyone's concerns. He had to try to trick the younger man into abandoning the idea.

"It is the only way, what other choice do we have, we are but mortal, he is a god."

"But, to use their powers, to remove it by our method, means Hectarian magic will be dead to the world." The other five sat in silence as they listened to the conversation which volleyed between them. Each stated convincing opinions on why their view was correct, the outcome of this debate would change the world forever one way, or another. They all knew neither change would be ideal, whichever path was chosen, there would be a heavy sacrifice. It was up to them to decide what the sacrifice would be.

"The only chance we have of overcoming him is to take his magic, don't you see? It is our *only* choice, it is our *only* chance to be free." The younger man banged his hand upon the solid oaken table as if to emphasise his point.

"But surely you must consider afterwards, not a single Hectarian will possess the power to even foil a simple attack. The magic powering our homes, our cities, will be lost forever as we are forced to return to the old ways. Even should one who possesses magic emerge by some miracle, they could not develop their power, the lack of users ensures that. To nurse a spark so small, into a flame, would be impossible."

"There will be the Elementalists. True the price is high, but is it really, is it too high a price to pay to ensure tomorrow for our children?"

"If we fail," the old man lowered his head. "If we fail, we have no hope to stand against him. He has done nothing to warrant our action."

"Not yet, but it is only a matter of time, you have seen what he will unleash if left to his own devices. If we do not try to stop him now what hope is there then? You have seen yourself his history, if we leave him bet he will surely repeat his deeds. A pre-emptive strike is our only option." The younger man was still as powerful as ever in his tones as the older man grew weary. He knew almost from the onset that the young man's argument would win, but it was his place to stand against him. After all, to not voice the doubts of the group was to weaken the power. Each member had to be completely committed to the decision, lest the power of their magic be compromised. His job was to put to rest doubt, and if it could not be done, force his opposition to change his mind.

He slowly glanced around the other members, looking at each one in turn, his eye contact pieced the souls of each as he retrieved any remaining questions, concerns, or hesitations. The younger man's eyes stayed focused on his opposition, at least a minute had passed before he spoke again.

"What would happen should he seize the tomes and his power once more be restored?" The younger man broke his gaze for the first time to look down to his battered sandals for but a second. This question had taken him by surprise, he was unsure why, but the possibility felt like a cold icy finger tracing down his spine, he suppressed a shudder.

"There will be none with the magical capabilities who could achieve that, no one with that power will remain, we have seen to that, by the completion of the ritual. The Hectarian power will be no more, the power of a Wizard, Sorceress, or Elementalist would be useless."

"But if there were?"

"You mean should all the forces be penetrated, should he find a Hectarian with enough of the now lost power to diminish the protective barriers, impossible as that may be?" He smiled slightly as he now realised the improbability of this final doubt. The moment of doubt and fear the question had stirred within him now forgotten. The thoughts of such safeguards being defeated, of someone overcoming them all, was impossible. All this question now did was add to his already overconfident tone. "Are you forgetting even should they be obtained, the last book must be taken by his own kin of which he has none. It is impossible, for a being such as he, he could only create a child from love. Something his long dead heart has no capacity for, and besides, why would he interact with a race he finds so disgusting in order to create such a child?"

"He *could* take it himself."

"Only should his heart be pure, then for what purpose would he need it?"

"Still, if that were the case, would he not still possess the other six? The six we were expecting, but not the seventh, we know not the power that will be trapped within this final tome."

"True there is one more than expected," the young man touched the book which had formed before him. Although this would lessen the final seal of the spell, he was confident their plan would work; the magic they possessed now would be enough to seal his powers and banish the Grimoire. "And it is also true that we know not what will be sealed within its binding. But let us not focus on what is impossible, but what is possible, we can stop him now, but time grows short, so I ask you fellow members of the Hoi Hepta Sophoi what be your choice?" The young man returned the respectful nod of his opposition as he took his seat.

"Our concerns were voiced an' argued admirably by the former Elder." The young red-haired girl addressed the room. She was one of the few Méros-Génos who could still wield such power, her magical energy was raw and forceful.

"Indeed, I feel no matter how dangerous it is, it is less hazardous than him remaining unopposed." The gentlemen to her right was the next to voice his opinion, he had pondered this methodically before committing to the act. As the most practical member of the seven he had assessed the long-term implications of both paths, and having reached his well-formulated opinion, nothing could change his mind. He was steadfast, their action was the only logical progression.

"Before you commit on this, there are some other thoughts *I* wish to voice, firstly to thank my elder for a well presented discussion." He bowed his head to the older man whose cane once more rested by his chair as he sat. "Secondly, as with all things, this too carries a cost, you are all aware of the price that must be paid, still, no respect would be lost should any of you wish to leave and not continue, after all, we are the ones to pay the greatest price for this freedom. If any of you have any doubts, I ask that you leave now."

Minutes of silence passed, the young man was relieved to see none left.

"That said, we shall begin the final preparation." He joined them once more to sit at the table, where in front of each of the seven members, there lay a book.

Each tome was a different colour, each possessed a different symbol of unfamiliar origins. Inside the pages were blank, these would be the pages which would secure the seal and hold the words needed to release the bind should it be required. They had wanted to seal the powers completely to ensure they could never be released, but such a thing would have been impossible. In order to ensure the success of their act, there were laws which had to be adhered to, such as the possibility for reversal of their craft.

The timeless room gave pause to their own mortality, before them countless figures had sat in this very place. The endless athenaeum was dedicated to one sole purpose, the obtaining of power. Within the great towers, every tome, parchment, or carving, of magical craft and prophecy could be found. Some mere facsimiles, but nothing, not even a single aged shred of parchment, would further deteriorate within these walls, nothing that was, except for the living.

At this very table, countless warlords had sought the answers to their great battles, wars were waged, victories obtained or lost, depending on how those given the opportunity to enter such a place used the knowledge they acquired. It was a place great strategists, like most mortals, entered only through their dreams, a place they could spend their sleeping hours in the quest for knowledge. This table had seated them all, heroes and villains, the mad and the righteous, all long forgotten like the secrets found within. Its finely crafted hazel wood structure still as pristine as the day it had first been carved, a wood specifically chosen for its knowledge and wisdom giving properties.

Time and light changed within the tower, the focus of those who sat within its spender could not fail to see the movements set in motion by their actions, their very presence here, their undertakings causing such change throughout the cosmos, that even with the tower's physical manifestation of the universe's movements and changes, they still failed to comprehend the consequences of their actions.

The fractured light from the glass tower above, to those who could decipher it, reflected the very nature of existence. Its every change, its every aspect travelled through the countless weave of the spectral glass, down through the seemingly endless tiers of tomes and scriptures to create a complete depiction for any who knew how to look.

Each member seated at the table took the hands of another, the focal light from the tower compressing to illuminate the area between them. The entirety of everything, existence itself central to their invocation as they stripped the very nature of Hectarian power from all it touched. The words of their incantation almost lost in the endless tower as little by little they removed the vital thread from everything, until they reached beyond its very core, an act which would forever silence those using this arte as they stripped the power straight from its source. They did not just take the power of those who bore it now, they took the very gift, the very seed which allowed this power to be born. None from this day forth could call upon this craft. To form a new link to this power now, after all they had done, would surely be impossible.

The light expanded, its image now altered to that reflected just hours before, its illumination now void of a thread so old, so integral, the repercussions were seemingly endless.

The changes had not been unnoticed, there was just one place this feat could have occurred and now, the one they opposed would come for them. The Hoi Hepta Sophoi took one final look at all they were protecting as they prepared for their life-forces to be used as the means of sealing that which they would create. Never would they know the glory of the Elysian fields, not unless the seals were broken and their essence released, something none of them expected to happen.

The leader looked over his allies with pride, they had succeeded, the unimaginable power coursed through each one of them, a power sufficient enough to complete their undertaking. There was but one thing remaining, their victory could only be marked by their death.

Night took form before them, their new-found energy wavered in the mere presence of this god as he granted them the honour of gazing upon his true form. Night had once been an aspect of the goddess Nyx, an ancient deity who had borne many children, inclusive of those known as pain, sleep, dreams, and death, as such these powers were also his to call upon. Just one death was too good for them. He had the means to prolong their suffering for as long as their bodies would endure. The waves of tiredness began to encompass them, stifling their breath. Whilst they would still be aware of the torment endured by their physical bodies, the terrors and agony they would suffer through their dreams would be unimaginable and without reprieve. These seven would live out their remaining days sealed within sleep until death finally took them. It was not the death any of them had anticipated.

He looked upon the figures as the torture of the realm he had created just for them ensnared them, the leader of the Hoi Hepta Sophoi still managing to delay his final moments, but unlike his belief, it was not he who postponed the plagued sleep, but Night who wanted to impart one final terror upon the traitor.

"What were you thinking? I see it all, your thoughts are no secret to me. Do you think you will find peace in knowing your Grimoires shall stop me? The sum of all mortal works and knowledge is here." He watched as the young man smiled. "I knew of your plan."

"Then, why?" he gasped still smiling, he was proud of what they had done and regardless of what would follow, he wanted Night to feel his pride.

"My own tomes rest here wall to wall at your disposal, do they not tell you of the rising of a maiden, or did you learn nothing from me? I shall wait, twelve years is a mere blink of an eye to one such as myself. I shall regain my powers, and claim yours by doing so when she rises." Night knew when he retrieved the Grimoire, and their spells were released, he would not only take back his magic, he would also take the magic of the person who sealed it, and since the seven of them had, before their death, possessed the power of the entire Hectarian culture. It was a power he couldn't resist, even if it meant falling prey to their trap, in fact, it was essential if he were to ensure Gaea was rejuvenated.

"You rely... too much... on hearsay," he smiled weakly.

"That is where you are wrong." Night smiled in amusement as he leaned towards the young man, whispering quietly into his ear. As he heard Night's words the smile faded and his eyes grew wide with terror. It was as he heard that final truth he surrendered to the all-consuming sleep. The bodies of the seven slumped before what they thought to be their final triumph. It would be at least seven days until their life-forces left them to seal the Grimoire, despite this, he knew he could not take the tomes. He would have to wait until the time was right and then, he would reclaim that which he had lost, and so much more. "Patience has always been a strong point of mine"...

...As the image faded Elly placed the crystal back within her pocket and continued the tale where the images left off.

"Despite these words, Night knew that when their lives finally ended, the binding of his powers would be completed. He had been rendered powerless but for his immortality. One day, by sheer chance, he happened upon one of the seven. It was unguarded, hidden within an old bookcase overlooked by all who passed, but he could never touch it. Although none knew his identity, they feared him, and so they handed the book which he had shown such an interest in, into the care of the temple.

"Night's name has been diluted over time, only those who knew his wrath truly feared him, to others, he started to become nothing more than a fairy tale, everything was going according to his plan." She paused as she looked between them. "The first three Grimoire were located in temples which it was thought no human would be able to survive, even if they were gifted with Hectarian magic. One appeared in a town hidden in an ordinary bookcase, another was sent to a place of myth, and another to a place of darkness and rumour. As for the seventh, its whereabouts remains a mystery, but once she seizes the final tome, the last of his power will return."

"By she, y' mean the one who got the other six, right?" Eiji frowned, choosing his words carefully. The last thing he wanted was another blow to the head, he had barely recovered from the last one, although he hadn't made it apparent the pain far exceeded that he had expected. He lowered his arm as he found himself unconsciously rubbing the back of his head.

"Correct, if his final powers were to be released, everything would change." Elly smiled slightly as she contemplated this thought for a moment.

"But Marise Shi disappeared a long time ago." Daniel stated. Elly looked to him in surprise. When they had first met, he had implied he knew nothing of the Grimoire, yet now, he not only showed knowledge of them, but of the one who obtained them. Elly had believed no one knew it was Marise who had collected them. Although Eiji had told the story of Marise Shi's exploits in Napier village, it was never mentioned her target had been the Grimoire. It was always believed, thanks to the Elementalist who told the tale, that she had been seeking vengeance on the temple's priest. She couldn't help but wonder how he had come to possess this knowledge, and if *he* knew, how many others did? His comment showed the need for extra caution. If they were to realise exactly what was happening, things would not run so smoothly. For now she hoped the implications were enough to have them draw their own conclusions. If she had guided them as well as she believed, they would think the reason Zo was in need of protecting was due to her Hectarian linage.

"Indeed," Elly sighed, not only did she dislike the thought of him knowing things he should not, she grew tired of his interruptions. "But that does not mean she, or someone else, still could not retrieve the final Grimoire, I repeat, the first were hidden in impenetrable temples, do I really need to continue? The point is all seven of them were thought unobtainable and all but one has been retrieved. The seventh however, is meant to be the most secure as no one knows its whereabouts."

"Surely someone does. I mean it had to get there in the first place, couldn't Marise just get the information from the person who took it?" Daniel questioned, he knew it was unlikely something could simply vanish, someone, somewhere had to know of it.

"Impossible." Elly sighed as she wondered if they had understood any of what she had just spoken, or even the images they just watched, did he really think the Grimoire had been sent for people to hide? That would have made things *far* easier.

"But the leader of the Hoi Hepta Sophoi said—" Daniel began.

"So you are led to believe, yet I am certain there is a way for Marise to obtain the final tome." Elly this time chose to interrupt Daniel. Unseen, Acha shrunk a little in her chair, the shrouded figure they had seen in the crystal, despite the great expanse of time since her birth was, without a doubt, her mortal father. Although his image was hidden, she somehow instinctively knew it to be him. "You would be surprised what a little ambition and a lot of knowledge can do."

"You talk as if you know her." Acha spoke once she was certain Elly had finished. The thought she knew Marise unnerved her, especially if they discovered her relationship to the shrouded figure, all kinds of problems could arise.

"Yes, I do." Elly's answer, as always, was simple and to the point, it was also a catalyst for a million other questions, she smiled to herself as she ventured into the kitchen.

"What!" Daniel exclaimed. "You've actually met her?" Elly left her answer until she had returned carrying the nicely browned chicken.

"Indeed," she replied, returning to the kitchen to carry in the bread and butter which had been carefully prepared for their arrival. Well surely if she hadn't said something now, Eiji would have betrayed the secret, unintentionally perhaps, but maybe this would give the unwanted company just the reason they needed to part ways. "I asked Mr Francis to prepare a meal for us."

"So you've actually met her, face to face, and lived?" Daniel avoided her attempt to change the topic with ease.

"Yes. Please help yourself, who knows when we will get a chance to eat like this again."

"But I thought none who met her survived." This time it was Acha who pressed the topic further, Elly knew this was one set of questioning she would not avoid easily.

"We were friends." Elly waited for the reaction which was bound to follow her statement as she began to carve the bird.

"Friends!" spat Daniel, almost choking on the bread he had swallowed. "With a bloodthirsty murderer?"

"Yes." Elly passed Zo a plate, she was now the only person who wasn't eating, wherever she was, it wasn't in the room with the others, she seemed so far away, lost in her thoughts. Elly tried to read her concerns as she held the plate a moment longer before placing it before Zo, an action which startled her. "Come see me after you have freshened up later, there is something I wish to give you." They exchanged glances, all curious what this something could be. Zo simply nodded as she stared at the food before her, for some reason, she felt quite peculiar.

* * *

"There's only three rooms, some of us will hafta share." Eiji stated as he emerged from the bathroom to find everyone gathered in the hallway. He rubbed his hair vigorously with a towel, his clean clothes were still warm from the furnace. It was a remarkable invention, more often than not, the washed clothes were dry even before the wearer had finished pumping the water ready to shower.

"I shall stay with Elly then." Zo muttered, her hair still dripping from her own shower, her shortest layer clung to her face for a moment before she brushed it away. Concern flickered through Daniel's eyes, of all people why had she chosen Elly? She could have chosen him, or Acha who she had shared a room with previously. Eiji realised this meant he and Daniel would most likely share the other, he reminded himself to be careful about what he said, he had already realised Daniel was nothing if not persistent in his search for information. Satisfied with this arrangement, they went to ready their rooms, leaving Daniel and Zo alone in the hallway.

"Are you okay?" he asked. Seeing her expression, he touched her shoulder gently, she turned to him with an obviously forced smile, her eyes filled with an array of emotions.

"Yes." Her answer came out more like a question than the positive statement she had intended.

"What did Elaineor want?" He pulled his face as he spoke her name.

"Oh... she, erm, gave me some old clothes of mine," she sighed, "for all I know they could be from the local store." She let out another sigh as she stared blankly towards the floor.

"Say, do you care for a walk before turning in?" he asked, he already knew the answer. Whenever things became a little too overwhelming for her, a walk had always seemed to calm her down, give her a chance to organise her thoughts and clear her mind. There had been many occasions, as parts of her memories returned, when she grew frustrated or tired. She had tried so hard to retain the memories, to keep them coming, but the harder she tried the quicker they left, leaving her frustrated. She wore the same look now as she had all those times.

"Would you mind?" She looked at him gratefully, tying her wet hair into a ponytail. Getting out of here, away from this inn was something she desperately needed. For just a moment she wanted to leave Elly and everyone else behind. "And we could always take a look around the trade district while we're here." She smiled, seeing his face light up at the thought of exploring. Outside Albeth, this was the only place he had encountered which sold trinkets, oddities and vendibles of magical potential. "I saw a few things you just have to get." Daniel couldn't help but feel this new-found enthusiasm was a display for his benefit, he was right, to a certain degree.

"That sounds wonderful." He linked her arm gently as they began towards the door.

"And just where do you think you are going?" Just as they reached the door, Elly's voice echoed from the staircase to stop them in their tracks. For a moment, everything fell silent except for the sound of her footsteps as she approached.

"For a walk, I need some air." As Elly stood before them, her hardened expression seemed to soften a little, for a second it seemed a strange sympathy crossed her features.

"Fine. Hurry back and *do not* draw any attention to yourselves, be back by sunset. Here is a list of supplies we need, you know, rope and food. There is an excellent rope store not far from the tavern." She gave Daniel the list, a hand drawn map to the store, and a small pouch containing some coins, as she did so, she leaned in close to him and whispered something, he nodded, and without wasting any more time, they left.

"What did she say?" Zo asked as she linked him once more as they entered the bustling town.

"She told me not to let you out of my sight." He watched her frown at his words.

"There's something she's not telling me."

"Everything?" He attempted to say it with as little sarcasm as possible, but failed, she knew so much more than she would ever reveal, he had to wonder why, was it because she planned to keep them safe? They still knew nothing more about the situation surrounding Zo and the implied dangers which lay in wait.

"Well, yeah." Zo sighed as she leaned against the side of the tavern, she could feel the music as it vibrated through the walls along with eruptions of laughter. "It's just so frustrating. I mean she knows everything about me, about what's happening. Earlier I thought she was going to tell us something about what was going on, yet instead she told us a story, unrelated to me, maybe even to this situation. It's like she does it on purpose, she knows everything yet..." She gave a frustrated sigh, wrapping her arms around herself.

"Treats you like a child and answers one question with another?"

"Exactly, I mean I don't even know why I'm here, why was I in danger in the first place? It's not as if I have some great power." Zo paused as she suddenly realised why she was being told the story of the Grimoire, perhaps even why she found herself in this situation, it was because of her magic. Daniel saw the realisation in her eyes, he knew she had reached the same conclusion he had, but he couldn't help but feel he had overlooked something.

"She seemed to think differently," he stated after a few moments of silence. He had realised during the tale the relevance of her magic, but all this couldn't simply be due to that, after all, if that were the case, then there would have been people looking for her long before Elly had arrived on their threshold. There was something else, something deeper, but neither of them had any clue as to what it could be.

"Come on Daniel," she sighed as they started on their way again. "This..." A small ball of flame erupted from the air above her hand. "This is the best I can do," she lied. There were other things she knew she could do, things so dark they chilled her to the bone, the conversation of passers-by fell silent as people stopped to look. She quickly willed it to vanish before they continued walking, it was a few moments before the conversation around them resumed at a hushed level. By the time they reached the small store, everything had returned to normal, her actions forgotten. "Even if they want me to get the final book, I do not possess the strength or skill."

"I've seen a lot of things. I've seen your magic, and I've seen you turn a barren wasteland into a thriving herb garden. You use your magic to heal the sick by learning which herbs they need to cure them, instead of treating the symptoms like Kwakzalvers. I've seen the effort and determination you put into every little thing you do, the love and hope you give to others, that's your real power Zo, your heart, not your magic." Daniel stated, glancing over the sheer volume of ropes stored behind this particular counter. He had to wonder if Elly had sent them there just to confuse him with choice.

He was almost certain he had chosen the wrong type, but the elderly man behind the counter had assured him this was the best type for any purpose. Being so close, he couldn't help but overhear their conversation as he measured the rope for them.

"Did you say Zo?" he questioned on his return, before either of them could answer he continued with a wide grin on his face. "Yes, yes, the resemblance is clear." The cashier extended the bag over the counter to Daniel before he reached out to place his coarse hands upon her face.

"Excuse me?" Zo stepped back, away from the unwelcome touch. "Who are you?"

"Forgive me our Zo, you must have forgotten, it's true, time has not been kind to me. I am Mr Venrent, from what I can gather you're just like your mother. Tell me have you finished school then?"

"My mother?" she questioned in alarm, could it be this stranger knew her mother? His face did not seem familiar, yet at the same time there was something about the name, it was a name she had heard before.

"Yes, come through, join me for a cup of tea and we shall talk, come, come." The old man vanished to reappear at the entrance to his home in the shaded rear of the adjoining canopy. He guided them through a small inner room which separated his home from the area he used to conduct more serious business away from prying ears. He motioned them through the faintly lit room, the walls were lined with bookcases and shelves. The glass encased candlelight projecting a limited glow upon his many trinkets and treasures. There, within the confines of this room were relics, ancient technology, and all manner of collectables, it was hard to decide if his living area was simply an extension of his shop, or if these items were a treasure of his own.

He guided them towards the warm glow of the log fire where a number of finely crafted wooden chairs were carefully placed around a table. To the very far side of the room was an equally beautiful wooden dining table, its surface possessing yet more of his rare collectables. As he guided them, his voice seemed filled with a nervous excitement.

"Best not to be seen, hey? Don't want to draw any attention to yourself in these parts, please sit, let me look at you."

She sat where he motioned, as she did so he reached forwards to run his fingers over her face once more. She was about to protest when she realised the reason behind his actions, he was blind. "My, my, you have grown, I heard you talking out there, a good thing too or I may never have known. Anyway, I thought to myself, is that our Kezia? Of course, I realised it couldn't be, I mean, your mother always smelt like rose petals. You, you seemed to favour plum blossom." Zo blushed as she found his comment embarrassing. "Why you haven't been here for at least a decade if not longer, your poor mother, she was heartbroken when you left.

"That reminds me, I have something for you, she gave it me the day you left, never could figure out what the darned thing was. No matter, now you're back it's only fitting you have it." He shuffled to a small recess, his hands excitedly passing over the numerous objects contained within the darkness.

"Does this guy breathe through his ears?" Daniel whispered, as he looked to Zo he smiled, whoever this man was, he was grateful to him, he had returned a smile to her face. It warmed his heart to see her happy.

"So anyhow, she gives me this thing, well maybe I'm missing something here, but it seems to me it's a metal sphere with carvings and a few indents. I'm sure it used to do something mind..." No sooner had the cool metal touched Zo's fingers than it began to play the slow, soothing, gentle chimes of an old melody. "Well, I'll be, what did you do? I've been playing with that thing for years, I just couldn't understand it."

"I just..." Zo shrugged, she hadn't the slightest idea. "So how is my mum?" Venrent seemed to struggle for a few seconds to find the words to continue.

"You know, when you left I told her you'd return, it's been a long time hasn't it?"

"I..." Zo smiled gently as she turned the musical ball over in her hands. She thought about her mother, she was thrilled to finally meet someone who knew her and ecstatic about the thought of being able to return home to see her at last. She had imagined the moment for so long, she had played it out in her mind hundreds of times. Her mother would be waiting for her outside their small cottage, she would take her in her arms they would go inside and talk for hours discussing everything and anything.

"Why did you never come home, why did you wait so long?"

"I don't know where it is," she answered simply. Still after all this time she had been unable to recall the name of the place she called home.

"You're kidding me child, you lost your way?"

"More like my memory, excluding this last year and a half, I have about a ten-year gap, I have no memory at all of the last ten years, and really what I do recall from before is still very fractured. I don't know what happened, if I was ill, or in an accident, I just, can't remember.

"I woke in an unfamiliar place, I knew somewhere I had to have a family, a home. Daniel helped me search Crowley for information before we searched Albeth, but no one knew me, or had heard of any missing people. I began to doubt whether my memories were even real, I mean I remembered so little, even about my childhood, I think I remember leaving for school one day, that's the only clear memory I really have, aside from small fragments of my mum and Amelia."

"Crowley!" Mr Venrent exclaimed. "You did venture far from home, as far as you could be for that matter, you're from Drevera, you can get there from here easy enough, just take the second exit on Boa Street, and there you are. How did you end up so far out?"

"I don't remember," she answered shaking her head. He smiled slightly as he realised he had asked a silly question.

"I tell you, our Zo, that memory of yours, it's worse than mine. Tell you what I'll do, a few weeks back I did a favour for an alchemist, well you know the kind I mean, those who had the seed of magic, he does wonders with potions. Anyway, I happened to mention I was getting a little forgetful and as a joke he made me something for recollection, well he wanted to put something in the phial he gave me, so he thought what better than something we can both laugh at. I don't think I have been to him once without forgetting to take something with me.

"Well, since I don't need it, you're welcome to it. Wait there just one moment I shall fetch it." He left again quickly with what almost seemed to be a nervous spring to his step, returning within seconds with the most breathtaking little phial, it was carefully crafted by a skilled hand. The blown glass was traced with the finest metallic threads she had ever seen, to create a weave of interchanging patterns which even Venrent's hands could appreciate. Within it, a clear syrup glistened. "Here drink this, but could I ask you to do it now, I couldn't bear to give this gift away. It has a lot of sentimental meaning you know, it's kind of my lucky charm, since I had it, good things have happened, best of all running into you and being able to help you as you once did me. Of course, it doesn't work straight away, like everything it needs a little time."

Zo smiled as she carefully removed the top from the phial. She drank its contents without so much as a second thought. She didn't have the heart to tell him about the sheer volume of potions and mixtures she had tried over the last year, it seemed none ever worked.

"It's like ice." She gasped as she felt its freezing liquid slide down her throat, for a second it felt like the icy fingers of death clung to her airway in an attempt to choke her. Daniel, stared at her in paralysed horror.

"Anyway, an old man like me needs his rest, and I'm sure you have much to do am I right?" He felt her hand to locate the phial as she returned it.

"We do have the odd thing, but nothing that can't wait, please tell me of my mother." She touched his hand gently as he slid it from her touch.

"Alas our Zo, youth is on your side, an old man like me, failed vision and aching joints, needs his rest. Please, forgive me I really should rest, this has been far too much excitement for one day."

"If you have a moment, I can make you a remedy for your pains." She started to feel inside her bag for her herbs, she already knew exactly what to make.

"I already have one, after tomorrow I doubt I will need one ever again if this one works as well as I was told. You're such a sweet child," he smiled almost sadly. "Now hurry along, maybe you can visit tomorrow?" He escorted them to the door. "I shall feel much better tomorrow." His wrinkled face stretched into a tired smile as he waited for them to leave. Once they had left, he closed the shop door behind them. His face grew solemn, his hand still rested on the door as he stared into the infinite darkness with a heavy heart.

"You did well, your loyalty will be rewarded." A female's voice echoed from the darkest shadow, he knew it did not share the room with him, not like before, now it simply used the shadow as a means to communicate. He wasn't sure if it would cross through again, he didn't want to find out. The sooner it left, the better.

"You will keep your promise, you won't hurt her. Whatever does he want with such a sweet child?" He knew things could have gone better, he loved that child and all he had done was rambled like an old fool nervous about what he had to do, concerned about the trade and what darker purposes would be hidden behind it.

"He just wants her to remember, anything else is not your concern. A visitor shall call at the stroke of midnight to complete the contract." With that he felt the presence recede, he was alone once more. He sat by the door and sobbed quietly.

* * *

"Are you sure you should have done that? I—" Daniel began to question, worry still framed his brow from her earlier actions. How could she just take something like that without knowing what it was?

"You worry too much, he knew my mum, besides Mr Venrent would never hurt me." She spoke almost as if she remembered him, a clever deception for his benefit, she didn't want him to worry unnecessarily.

"The world is more often than not, very little like your ideals. It could have been poison, or worse."

"Then it's too late to worry now," she smiled. "Besides, he had this." She pulled out the sphere, at her touch it once more began to play. "It was my mum's she used it to lull me to sleep as a child. It's been passed through the females of our family for generations, my mum said that even my father..." she stopped suddenly as she frowned, she had no idea what she was about to say. For a second she had nearly remembered something, something important, it danced on the edge of her mind as if to tease her before it vanished. She was no longer able to finish the sentence. "Mum said she would leave it in the hands of someone she trusted, so when I returned I could find my way home from a place which led to everywhere, I only recalled, when he gave it to me."

"So are you going, home that is?" Daniel had to admit, now he knew how to find her home he was curious to see the place she was raised, the place she had learnt to use magic. He knew she must have the same feelings of excitement at the prospect of finally, after who knew how long, returning home.

"I would like to, but I haven't seen my mum for the longest time. I wonder if she would still know me, I wonder if I'd know her?" The tune from the sphere switched, becoming anxious, nervous, and excitable as it played. It seemed as if the small ball read her moods turning them to music.

"Of course she'd know you, you're her daughter."

"Maybe, but if I visit wouldn't I put her in danger? I'll think about it, as much as I want to go, for now, I don't think I can." She smiled sadly; there was another reason she didn't want to go, a reason she couldn't place, but something in the back of her mind told her returning was not a good idea at all. She had not had the easiest of childhoods, being different had caused her all kinds of problems growing up. The people of her home were less than tolerant towards her, but their reaction to her was not the reason she felt a dark hole in the pit of her stomach at the thought of returning. She hadn't realised until this very moment, but she didn't want to return.

Elly was waiting at the stairway as they stepped into the hall, she leaned against the wall, her arms crossed before her. It was unclear exactly how long she had been waiting for them, but from her expression alone it was clearly longer than she had wanted to. She studied them for a moment before she spoke.

"You were longer than I expected." Although her tone was short the undertone of concern was evident. She had almost been ready to go in search of them, but doing so would have been hard to explain, besides, Annabel had kept an eye on them as best she could. She would have let her know if they had come across any problems. Even so she was not infallible, and the magic of this area meant getting a clear view was almost impossible. Elly would have felt much more comfortable shadowing them herself, she knew exactly what to look for.

"I met someone I know." Zo smiled as she walked past Elly towards the stairs, unaware of the ghastly fear portrayed in Elly's eyes brought on by the words she had spoken. Since Marise had not returned as had been expected, there was no reason Zo would recall a single person from her past outside of Drevera.

"Who, how do you know them?" her voice sounded urgent. "You didn't tell them where we were staying did you?" She grabbed Zo's arm a little too hard, preventing her from taking another step, she forced her to turn to look at her.

"No." Zo gave a frustrated sigh, she moved to break her arm free from Elly's grasp but failed to do so. "He knows my mother."

"And y' know this how? He could'a been lyin', y' a wanted person y' know." Eiji joined the conversation as he emerged from the dining area with the remains of a sandwich in his hand. It had been a difficult mission, but finally he had managed to consume all the remaining chicken scraps from the bones Elly had left, after storing what she felt was worth taking.

"He gave me this." She thrust her free hand into her pocket to remove the metallic sphere, which as if on cue, played an annoyed sounding tune. "It belonged to my mother." Elly glanced over the sphere, her posture relaxed slightly. For a moment she had been worried and not only because Eiji had made yet another thoughtless comment.

"He could have obtained it by any means, surely you realise that? She did not have to *give* it to him!" She released her grip slightly.

"She did! I know she did!" The tune grew angrier as her temper rose. "This is all about you isn't it? You don't like that I remember him and not you!" She turned, snatching her arm free as she ran up the stairs. Daniel moved as if to follow but Elly stopped him.

"You, you are going to tell me everything," she stated, Eiji had disappeared after Zo up the stairs to leave just the two of them alone in the foyer.

"Everything?" he swallowed, somehow he managed to keep his voice from breaking. He knew she wouldn't like what he had to tell her. He didn't want to tell her, but he had a feeling he wasn't going to get the option to refuse.

"Everything," she confirmed as she stared deep into his eyes. He waited for the first question, a prompt or something, but it never came, she just held his gaze for a while before she moved to look up the stairs and finally let go of his arm. "Very well, go and attend to the provisions," she finally spoke, pointing him in the direction of the dining room.

"But—" he paused, why was he going to pursue this? He didn't want to tell her anything, yet was he about to protest when she released him?

"Go, I have more pressing matters to address." She waited until he had left the room before speaking quietly to herself. "Eryx Venrent," she smiled. She had been worried for a moment, there had been so many variables, especially since Annabel hadn't been able to keep a close vigil on her, but it seemed their meeting had gone exactly as she had expected and Zo, as far as she could tell, had not remembered a thing.

* * *

After a single knock, Eiji peered around the bedroom door, Zo sat on the bed she had claimed for her own, her knees hugged tightly to her chest. In the time he had spent hesitating outside her door it seemed she had changed clothes. He had heard her frustrated sighs, sighs which eventually turned into quiet sobs before he mustered the courage to knock. The room had two beds, between them against the wall was a strange vanity table with an assortment of ornaments placed upon it. The room, like every other in the house, was brightly coloured with bad décor. She looked up at him briefly before she turned away wiping her eyes.

"Erm, may I come in?" he asked in what seemed to be a coy manner, of all the places he could have gone, why had he found himself here, why had he ventured to the room of the person behind the situation he found himself in, into the room of a murderer?

"You've come to lecture me too?" she sighed as she tried her best to hide the emotions which lined her voice. She looked at him once again, a look which warned him to stay away. He swallowed with difficulty thanks to the huge lump of fear which rose from that single glance, but still, he found himself sitting next to her.

"No, I came t'apologise, I am sorry, I shouldn'ta said anythin' before. It wasn't my place." He maintained eye contact with his feet as he spoke to her, he never once removed them from their fixed position. "I was just worried, like Elly, I didn't mean t'upset y'."

"It's not that." Zo admitted. "It's just everything has happened so quickly. One day I was leading a normal life, the next I'm here, I don't even know why I'm in danger and I have to trust these strangers. What's worse they know the bits of my past I don't and refuse to tell me, but then hint my past is why I am in danger now. If only I could understand, then maybe..." her voice trailed off.

"T'some extent, I know how it feels, one day y' just mindin' y' own business, the next everything changes."

"I'm sorry." She looked to Eiji. "It must have been hard leaving your master." Eiji looked up and nodded, wondering if he had at some point mentioned this, or if she knew the path of an Elementalist herself.

"It was, but that's not what I meant," he smiled slightly, "I didn't always live with my master. I know what it's like t'be forced t'leave everything behind, with little explanation. It's not easy, but y' have somethin' I didn't, friends. I often wonder the big 'what if', what if things turned out different? What if I had done this, or said that? But ultimately it comes down t'one thing, y' are who y' meant t'be, fight it as y' may, fate has a predestined path chosen for each of us, no matter how y' fight it y' can only be y'self, understand?" Even Eiji was impressed with how wise his words had sounded. Zo nodded as Eiji took her hand in his and smiled, she really wasn't that bad. Now more than ever he found it hard to believe the girl who sat beside him was the legendary murderer.

"Sorry," a small voice came from the door, "I didn't mean to intrude." The door opened a crack more, enough for them to make out Acha's silhouette against the hall light. Eiji rose to his feet and made his way quickly to the door, as he did so he adjusted the valve on the wall mounted gas lamp, filling the room with its warming, gentle light. He stepped aside for Acha to enter.

"It's all right," he smiled. "I was just leavin'."

"I only came to see how you were feeling." Acha walked across the softly illuminated room to sit beside Zo. "Hey are those new?" Acha looked at Zo, the clothes were bold, alien to her normal attire. The black laced top hugged her tightly, accentuating her hourglass figure. The long skirt was split both sides almost to the pelvis and held a leather protection that extended around her hips and back. The knee-length boots, were not only elegant yet simple in design, but seemed far more comfortable and supple than her previous footwear. The clothes were stunning, like those worn by a dancer, but she couldn't imagine what had possessed her to make such a drastic change.

"Yeah." Zo stood up glancing down at herself critically. She felt exposed, self-conscious, and couldn't imagine ever wearing such a thing, it was far too tight. "Apparently they used to be my favourite."

"Oh..." Acha didn't really know what to say and so reverted back to her reason for being there. "Elly said we should start to think about leaving." There was a long silence, finally broken by Zo as she quickly removed her clothes and thrust them carelessly into the bottom of her satchel to revert back into her normal attire. It was strange how something as simple as a piece of cloth could change the way she felt. These were warm, comforting, familiar, yet the ones she had just removed with haste felt cold and unfamiliar. There was something she didn't like about them, she wasn't sure what had made her feel inclined to try them in the first place, had she hoped by doing so she would look at herself in the mirror and everything she had forgotten would come flooding back? But still, the boots were so comfortable she decided to at least leave them on, it was clear from the comfort of fit alone she had walked many a mile in them.

"I'll just put these in here for now." She dressed quickly before carefully replacing the herbs to cover the unfamiliar clothing.

Chapter 7

The Will of a Dreamer

Darkness filled their vision as they awoke in Darrienia, it was a void familiar to all dreamers in that phase between being awake and asleep. A nothingness accompanied by the sleepy paralysis induced by the rousing of the mind and body. After a few moments it cleared, they found themselves looking out over the broken terrain of an unfamiliar land. Before them stretched a mighty courtyard, its once even stone floor sunken and crushed over time to leave large shards of rock protruding from the desecrated ground. The twisted weapons of fallen foes littered the area where it seemed a mighty battle had once raged. Through the crumbled pieces, of what would once have been a protective sandstone wall, lay a littered expanse of discarded metal, large broken metallic plates, twisted ballista, and trebuchet lay mangled in the rusted graveyard. The extent of this debris clearly visible through what once would have been an enormous gateway. The decrepit sandstone wall rose to a mighty arch, fragments of splintered wood still hung near its giant wrought iron hinges. The earth around them seemed to tremble slightly, as if under the sheer weight of the waste it supported.

Just like waking from a deep sleep, not everything became clear at once. It took moments before they felt the cold force of the rock which pressed against their backs, and the coarse metal of the shackles which secured them firmly in place. The chains, which held the shackles, were threaded through the solid rock to secure them in a fixed standing position, allowing them very little freedom of movement.

The question of how they came to be there wasn't even a consideration as they focused on their escape. The chains were so expertly crafted that no join was visible. The shackles, in a similar fashion, remained securely sealed by perfectly sized pegs fitting smoothly against either side of the metal, making dislodging them impossible.

Daniel stretched for Zo's hand desperately, in an attempt to reach her restraints, but no matter how hard he tried he could move no further than an inch. Even that small distance made the metal shackles dig painfully into his flesh. They were actually made to be a rather loose fit, but not so much that they could hope to escape without aid. Whoever had made these restraints was clearly an expert, just enough leeway to offer their prisoners a moment of hope, before their attempt to slide their hand through, would thrust their captives into further despair.

Elly also tugged at the chains finding them unyielding, she glanced over to Zo who seemed deep in thought, clearly thinking over the options. The air around them grew silent, it was only then they realised the sounds of their attempted escape had not been the only noise within their proximity. Something, now silent, had been repeated in the background, but the words of this almost inaudible chant had been lost through their attempts to free themselves.

"Anyone got any ideas how t'—" Another rumble shook the ground, vibrating the loose rocks around them, threatening their balance. The intensity so great it almost felt as if the ground was about to split and swallow them whole. The penetrating screech of metal fragments scraping across each other filled the air. Through the arch they could see the avalanche of metal the most recent tremor had caused. The metal pile swelled as if something beneath it stirred, then rose. It parted to reveal a giant twisted metal paw which sought to find its footing. Eiji cringed as he decided not to finish his question, in favour of re-concentrating his efforts on their escape. No matter how hard he struggled, he did little more than redden his wrists which already throbbed and protested against the pressure from the hard metal. The ear-piercing sound continued as the area just outside the confines of the sandstone wall began to swell further as something enormous stirred from within its depths.

"Zo," Daniel whispered. "Magic?" his voice held hopeful reason. He hoped she would confirm her skills could be used to free them, but he knew even before she replied if it had been an option they would not still be in this predicament, as he looked to her, he could see she was deep in thought.

"I can't," she stated finally. "It would kill us." She yanked at the chains as if to prove her point. If she could summon a fire with the intensity needed to weaken the restraints, she was certain they would be dead before they fell. Her restricted movement would not allow her the control she needed. She pulled against the chains desperately. If they would give even just a few inches there was a chance she would be able to summon a small enough flame to damage her own restraints whilst inflicting serious, but non-fatal, injuries to herself. Once free she could then release her companions. Even with the hope of this possibility, no matter how much she fought against the restraints they wouldn't yield.

Twisted metal rained from the swell as the gargantuan creature within gave one final push to free itself from hibernation. The very sight of it paralysed them. It was not a dragon, or at least, not like any *they* had ever imagined existing. Its large scaly body bore a clear resemblance to one, yet the shape was where all similarities ended. Its enormous paws bore ridiculously long, painful looking, steel nails in place of its claws. Rust spread down the jagged shards starting at the place it first pierced the creature's flesh to extend all the way to the very tip of the steel talon. Its skin was torn and twisted as it hung loosely on the enormous creature. Some of the baggy flesh was gathered into folds and held in place by the enormous twisted nails, which penetrated various parts of its body, driven through its flesh into what they could only assume would be the creature's bone. It was as if these deformed nails were all that stopped the creature's scaly skin from shedding. Its over-large tail seemed to be completely untouched by the rusted spikes, a tail which the creature dragged slowly behind it as it moved, weighted down by the huge mace shaped finish that marked its tail's tip. It was, without question, the most terrifying thing they had ever seen.

It was horrific, but its mouth was by far the most hideous feature. It seemed to sneer at them, forced into a wicked grin by its terrifying teeth, teeth which shone brightly as the millions of, what looked to be, over-sized lances that filled its mouth reflected the sunlight. Within these fine points that it knew as teeth, were the embedded armour shards of its previous meals. The thin teeth overstretched the creature's enormous bite overfilling its mouth with the deadly spikes which spread so far back, that if its meal were to miss the initial row it would be caught in one of the other hundred, to guarantee it the taste of blood, a taste which brought its only release from the eternal torture. It seemed almost as if it were the unfinished project of a long insane alchemist. Laying eyes upon them it gave a deafening roar, harboured within its thunderous tones shrieked the sound of grating metal. With each step it advanced, the ground shook and groaned as it ploughed its way through its rusted nest. Its giant paw reached up planting itself firmly across the stone archway, its sheer weight reducing it to dust. The force of its step further crumbing the shattered wall as the stones broke under the force of its movement.

Exhaling, its putrid breath whipped around them like a strong wind enveloping all within its decayed stench. Standing before them, its nostrils twitched as it took in the scent of fresh food. Zo closed her eyes tightly as it lowered its head to sniff the courtyard, so close to the rock they were imprisoned on.

Just then, as all seemed lost, a cry echoed through the air.

"Unhand those maidens you wretched fiend." Emerging unseen from somewhere to their left, a knight rode into view on his mighty white steed, his silver armour shone brightly as the sun's rays reflected on its highly polished surface. He looked almost alien to the horrific reality of the scene before them, almost fictitious as he rode to their rescue. His voice was filled with heroism which reminded them of the poorly cast heroes in the theatrics performed by the travelling caravans. The knight turned to look towards them offering them a flirtatious wink. "Do not fear, for I, Sir Earnest will protect you. Defender of righteousness, saviour of maidens, hero, knight... lover." He smiled once again at the captives, a silver metal filling in his tooth caught the sun's light as he did so.

"I think, I preferred the dragon." Zo whispered to Daniel, still trying to work free the restraints. Despite the nature of their situation, or perhaps it was simply his nerves, he couldn't help but give a short laugh. Sir Earnest leapt gallantly from his horse using the momentum to target a blow on the dragon's leg. He rolled to the side before springing to his feet evading the path of the monster's mighty paw as it continued its advance. He sprinted forwards, ducking and weaving beneath the belly of the creature as he made its way towards its front.

"Excuse me." Daniel interrupted Sir Earnest's fancy footwork as he danced around the dragon's feet; luckily, as yet, it had failed to notice his arrival.

"How about you cut me down so I can free the others while you do heroic battle with the beast, to save time," he reasoned.

"Do you jest?" he scoffed with mocking laughter. "A real knight would never let a commoner take the glory of the rescue." With those words he turned to face the dragon, who now looked more angry at having being momentarily dazzled by the knight's armour, than the fact only moments before he had lunged forwards thrusting his sword through a small fissure in its ankle. A grinding, earth-shattering roar filled the air once more with the putrid stench of the dragon's rotting breath and their battle began.

"We're all gonna die," Eiji stated loud enough for all to hear. In the meantime, it appeared Elly was still trying to find a means of escape. If required, she was certain she could break these bonds, but she wanted to place her faith elsewhere, she had to know, if she waited long enough, whether Zo's instinct would take over.

"He is getting pummelled," she stated, a strange smile crossed her lips as she watched the dragon swing the hero around with its tail. It was an action Sir Earnest had initiated as he had grabbed it in a futile attempt to stop its movement, or perhaps he had intended to swing it around by this appendage, but he had clearly either underestimated its size, or overestimated his own power. It thrashed its tail from side to side, which he held onto with an amazing display of obstinacy, before it flung him to the ground. "We need to do something before that idiot loses its attention." She looked in Zo's direction as she spoke. They all knew they had to do something, it was just that none of them knew exactly what could be done, as they had already discovered, there was no way to get enough leverage, and magic in such a tight area was too dangerous.

As disturbing as the thought was, it seemed their lives rested in the hands of the knight, Sir Earnest. He gave a cry of victory as the creature brought its enormous paw to the ground, knocking him effortlessly to one side as he tried to lift it in a futile attempt to tip it over, although they had to give him some credit, no matter how much he was being beaten, he always got up for more.

"I wonder if it'll eat us whole?" Acha's voice trailed off as the dragon's jaw began to descend upon their staggering hero. She shuddered as she saw the true extent of the teeth that stretched far back into its throat. A sickening pop filled the air moments before the knight seemed to vanish, mere seconds away from his demise. The dragon sniffed the air around him as it searched for the appetiser which had somehow escaped its jaws. The air seemed heavy, for a moment it was as if the dragon had forgotten their presence as it searched for its lost prey.

"Hey," Eiji shouted, despite their attempts to silence him, was he really so stupid? To call attention to themselves while the dragon was still distracted would only serve to remind it of their presence. They could all see the slowly approaching figure in the distance, they knew calling to him would serve no purpose. Despite their hushing him he shouted again. "Can y' help us?" Eiji had seen Seiken, he stood a short distance away from the dragon, although for some reason it failed to notice him despite the fact he stood clearly in its line of sight, Eiji continued to call, desperate to grab his attention.

The chains which held Daniel suddenly released, without need for instruction he moved quickly and quietly behind the rock, where the remnants of the melted chains still hung loosely. Zo flashed him a quick smile, which he returned.

Seiken slowly began to approach, to Eiji's dismay there was nothing rushed about his actions. Suddenly, his restraints slipped as he tugged against them. With his ability to move returned, he unhooked the pegs to free the shackles from his wrists as Zo hurried to remove the final chains.

"How'd y' get out?" Eiji gave a final tug, freeing himself of the bonds, for some reason, his seemed to fall nowhere near as silently as those of the others, who were freed before him. The creature turned slowly giving an almighty roar in realisation that its dinner attempted to escape. Elly glanced to Zo, she had known, given enough time she would have thought of something, although she had not been willing to wait much longer. At least being freed by these means would not invite unwanted questions. Zo clenched her teeth as she carefully manipulated her thumb to guide it back into place. It made another popping sound, almost identical to the one that marked their hero's departure. She was unsure exactly why she had done it, one minute she was trying to pry the shackles from her wrists, the next she had dislocated her thumb and by doing so had been able to slip her hand through.

"Well, now that you have succeeded in gathering your friend's attention, might I suggest running?" Seiken looked at the dragon as it fixed its vision firmly upon them, his tone was calm despite the size of the creature. It studied them carefully for a moment trying to decide if they too would vanish.

"What in Tartarus just happened?" Elly demanded as they broke into a run. The creature slowly turned to pursue, confident this time he would not be left so unsatisfied with his meal.

"I'm sure I mentioned..." Seiken stayed beside them as they ran, yet unlike everyone else, he appeared to make no effort whatsoever to maintain his pace. "Not only can you interact with the dreamers through your own choice, they too can interact with you, instead of you choosing to involve yourself in their dreams, you become part of them."

"Y' mean we were all just playin' a role in that guy's fantasy?" Eiji gasped, the flat-out running had begun to take its toll. He was painfully aware his pace had slowed. He glanced behind to gain his second wind. The creature was still in pursuit and worse still, it was gaining. Rewording Seiken's explanation did little more than earn him a scornful look, but he was far too concerned with the horrific creature to feel the least bit intimidated.

"What if—" Daniel panted, since he knew where this line of questioning was heading, Seiken had already begun to answer. There was no time to waste. If he were to succeed in his next actions, the timing had to be perfect.

"If he hadn't woken, you would all be dead." He looked at Zo and smiled softly. "Or maybe not."

"If the ruins and area were just part of his dream, then explain why the creature still lingered along with the chains that bound us, once he woke?" Elly questioned, her sentence, unlike those spoken by her comrades, was unbroken by her need to breathe.

"The chains are substance left over from a dream, that feeling you experience in the moment between sleeping and waking. Here we call it dream residue, that is why you found removing the shackles simple once the chains were free, the matter that had created them was already diminishing."

"And the creature?" Zo questioned again as she glanced behind them. Its stride, being far larger than theirs, meant it was gaining on them at a ridiculous speed. She found herself thankful it was too heavy to move more swiftly.

"The creature and its nest, I'm afraid, are native of this world," he stated, never once looking where they ran, only at the one thing he found most intriguing, Zo. Silent words passed between them, giving her the strangest feeling that he was waiting for something.

"I don't know if I understand." Acha panted; she found her motivation to increase her pace from the same source Eiji had previously, the creature was gaining. Even now they could smell its hunger as it approached rapidly. Despite her fear, she found herself faltering, unsure how much longer she could continue at this pace.

"It's simple." Seiken stopped as he glanced around. They hadn't covered as much distance as he would have liked, but here would have to suffice. The dream boundary wasn't that far away, and timing was critical. The ones he knew as The Chosen had also, for some reason, felt compelled to stop. It seemed they were actually just too tired to press on, even had they wanted to. What none of them, except for Seiken, had noticed, was the subtle change in Zo. *He* may have stopped first, but only because he could read her so well. Another few seconds and it would have been she who had brought the group to a halt.

Seiken looked towards them and sighed. Zo had already turned to face the monster, placing herself between it and them. She had known, long before Seiken had stopped, that Acha had reached her limit. He had seen her preparing herself for the battle ahead, planning her tactics to buy them time. Her desire to protect others was one of the many things he admired about her, but at times like this it was not the greatest trait. She would give her life for them in a heartbeat, and he knew one day that bill would come due. Her hand already rested on her sword's hilt as her mind drew on her magic.

She was just about to draw her sword when Seiken placed his hand on her shoulder. The tension she had built, ready to fight, drained from her body as her hand slowly slipped from the sword by its own will. From deep within she felt the magic stir, expanding outward from her core, a silver field stretched until all were concealed within. The creature stopped suddenly and snorted before it began to pace around the area its prey had stood just moments ago. Zo looked to his hand, the feelings of his touch were so familiar, once again a memory deeply rooted in her magic tried to surface, but all it could tell her was she knew him, and they were safe.

"We are in its blind spot, by the time it has moved enough to see us again, this barrier will have completely masked our location. Now, as I was saying, you can utilise things from people's dreams to aid you in your quest, but the reverse is also true. Although you slept in a safe area on your departure the nature of our world is ever changing, so unless you possess the Gods' charms, or stay in one of the seven fixed locations, it is unlikely you will return to the same position. This, of course, invites all manner of dangers, one of which you've just experienced. It is in your best interest to sleep in your own world in the same manner you would here, that way you should be offered at least some protection as you cross into Darrienia." The monster circled the area again, its roar shaking the ground violently. "Creatures such as this dwell deep within the human mind, once something like this is born, it generally resides here. Most creatures that stalk the nightmares of your world, existed here long before they terrorised your dreams."

"Aren't you afraid of them?" Acha asked timidly; it had been obvious as he first approached them that he was unconcerned by the creature's presence.

"No, there's only one creature I have to be cautious of, and it is certainly not a dragon."

"So, what if that guy hadn't woken up. I mean—" Daniel began, only to find himself cut off once more by Seiken.

"I told you, you'd be dead," he stated impatiently.

"No, I mean, why did he wake?" Daniel rephrased his question after he had caught his breath. Had Seiken let him finish, what he was actually asking would have been clear; there was something about this figure he disliked. He wondered if perhaps he was jealous of his friendship with Zo, jealous of what he meant to his friend. He wasn't sure Seiken could be trusted, and the last thing she needed was another person trying to control her. Since Elly's appearance, she had become distant. He felt as if he was losing her, as if there was something important that she wasn't telling him. He couldn't help feeling a little overprotective, given the circumstances.

"That's our role. I am sure at one point you have all experienced a dream in which you were about to die, yet before you see your death you find yourselves awake, safe within your home. That is one of our many functions, to protect you from the reaper who stalks the dreamers. Our race is known as the Oneirois. We are the guardians of Darrienia, and all which is sealed within." It was a well-known rumour of their world, and a truth in Darrienia, that if a dreamer saw themselves die, this dream state would become a reality. "Although we are of different realms, our two worlds are joined more than anyone really cares to realise. One cannot survive without the other. The situation we find ourselves in now is dangerous, since all of our kind have been imprisoned, there are but two of us who possess the ability to protect this world. Even now I must be careful. If he were to discover we possessed this talent he would, no doubt, devise a way to inhibit it, but even so I must continue to protect the boundaries."

"Not everyone dreams of death. Whaddya do the rest of the time?" Eiji cringed as he realised how his question must have sounded. He knew he really had to work on his tact, even without seeing the expression on Elly's face as he engaged his mouth before his brain.

"We do have lives and responsibilities of our own," he stated bluntly. "Watching your people is not our only role, our true purpose is to guard the barrier between our two worlds and ensure the nightmares don't filter over and become real again, and to hunt down those that do and return them to our world.

"If the barrier is weakened further, it's not only death our dreamers will have to fear, every injury or ailment they obtain here will pass over with them, as the barrier falls there will be nothing to distinguish this world from your own. Even the creatures which reside here will cross into your physical world." They had been so focused on his words, they had not noticed the creature had retreated. Seiken glanced around before removing his hand from Zo's shoulder, as he did so, the silver sphere which circled them vanished. She looked at the place his hand had been, somehow, she knew he had touched her like that before. Still touching the place his hand had rested, she realised what he had done. He had reached into her and touched her magic, using it to activate his own, she couldn't help but wonder why he had used this method. It was something deeply personal, so much so she felt herself blush as she realised his actions. Had it been anyone else, she was sure she would have felt strangely violated.

"Seiken, what exactly are we after, what are we doing here?" Her question did not receive an answer in the same tedious tone he had spoken to the others with.

"You mean you don't know?" His ageless brow wrinkled slightly as he paused as if to think over this strange occurrence. With all those who came before them, before the lands were so dangerous, they always knew what they quested for, they always knew the purpose of their pilgrimage, none of which had been the same. Why had the rules changed this time to leave them to wander aimlessly, were they expected to simply stumble upon the place which held the clues alone? Surely, that in itself was pointless and outside the boundaries of fair play. The other 'games' as they were called were slightly different to this one, almost as if they had been nothing more than a prelude. "From my understanding, scattered across our world there are five keys, sealed here from ages past.

"It's rumoured they link the worlds by some kind of gateway. Only once all the keys have been collected can the gateway be used, or something along those lines. We really don't know its true purpose, I only tell you what I've heard. The keys are said to dwell in five of the seven fixed locations of our world and this gateway is the only way to gain access to Night's tower where he keeps us imprisoned." Seiken began to look a little fatigued, he knew he needed to return soon to rest for a while. The unexpected confrontation had drained him more than he had anticipated.

"These fixed locations, what are they exactly?" Daniel questioned, as he made a quick note of everything Seiken had said in his journal, after all, some of this information may prove important.

"They are locations of our world which have been bound to yours by an eminent enchanter, or perhaps even a god. As for the keys, I have been unsuccessful in discovering their nature, the only assistance I could give you was that map."

Zo, suddenly realising what he spoke of, pulled the parchment from her pocket. Elly swiftly removed it from her hands to study it closely. Daniel moved closer to look, with difficulty, over her shoulder, he glanced around as he did so, taking in their surroundings.

"I think this is the closest." He pointed to a small area on the map. He glanced around again as he compared the landmarks he had seen to those documented, if there was one thing he could do really well, it was navigate, with or without a sextant. Of course, had he thought it would have done them any good, he would have taken readings, but since they were in an unfamiliar land it seemed rather pointless. As Daniel's finger traced the paper he noticed a strange symbol, there were five similar ones upon the map's surface. As he touched the one closest to their perceived location, the ink seemed to take on a life of its own as it scurried and scratched across the parchment to create a new image. The ink settled to reveal a closer, more detailed, map of their locality, on the far side of the image some words became visible.

'I am hidden by trees yet once stood taller, my disguise hides my purpose and my purpose came from my disguise, I was built for hope, now bring despair.'

"Well at least we know it's in the woods somewhere." Daniel stated unenthusiastically as he looked at the vast forests which stretched before them. With no known destination, finding something within this great expanse could prove challenging, then again, perhaps that was the point.

"Well, maybe we could find someone to ask, you did say the dreamers would be able to help us." Acha looked to Seiken for confirmation, only to realise he was no longer amongst them.

"I don't think we should wander around aimlessly, we know this world adapts to people's thoughts." Zo stated much to Elly's relief, at least someone else understood what she had been thinking. Although Daniel may have seen several landmarks which were also on the map, they were ones she too had noticed, however, there was no guarantee they weren't just created from their mind. As they had discovered on their first visit, some of the scenery was taken straight from their memories.

"Maybe our Elementalist can make things easier and locate the nearest town." Elly raised her eyebrow expectantly at Eiji, who met her gaze with a blank expression. She gave a sigh as she wondered why she had expected anything different. "Did your master teach you anything?" she questioned. "Humans, villages, towns, they all are alien in the natural environment. They destroy and pollute things around them, the natural world suffers as people bend it to their will. Mankind destroys the natural world so they may live." Still no reaction. "As an Elementalist you are in tune with the elements, with nature, correct?" She sighed again as she wondered why she even bothered, she should have known from his first blank stare that further explanations were pointless. "You should be able to locate areas nearby where the elements are dying, you know, a disruption in the natural aura." Was she really going to be his teacher? It seemed she knew more about his powers and abilities than he did.

"Oh." Eiji lowered his head in shame, he felt as if he was not only being a disappointment to his travelling companions but his master also. He had studied hard, there was no denying that, but for some reason, it seemed he always failed to meet Elly's expectations of what he should be able to do. "I've never..."

"I can help keep you grounded if you like, I used to..." Acha trailed off as she moved to take Eiji's hand but pulled away moments before they touched to back away cautiously. "I..." she looked from him to Daniel, a look with a meaning only her friends would understand, after all, she had not spoken of her curse to anyone.

Daniel gave her a reassuring smile before being nudged in the ribs by Zo, he looked at her blankly for a moment before he realised what she had meant. As Elly talked Eiji through the process, he took Acha to one side and passed her a small pair of gloves. Daniel had meant to give them to her last night, but somehow, the time had just never seemed right. She pulled them on and smiled. Once in place on her hands they seemed to vanish, much to her amazement. Daniel reached out, taking her hand, both of them were relieved when nothing happened.

"They're called thieves gloves, we picked them up from Collateral. The idea is you don't leave a fingerprint, but they're not as obvious as someone sneaking about in visible ones. We thought they may come in handy. I meant to give them to you earlier." He watched as Acha examined her hands, he had wondered how exactly she would take this gesture, whether she would be offended or hurt, but her expression alone reassured him it was a gesture she greatly appreciated.

"They're so light, it's like I'm not even wearing them." She smiled moving away from them to take Eiji's hand, he now looked rather pale after finishing his talk with Elly. "I can keep you grounded," she stated again, but this time with confidence.

"Why'd I need t'be grounded?" his voice trembled slightly, as he looked between them nervously, he wasn't sure he could do what was being asked of him. Surely there was another way, maybe if they walked a little further, they would find a signpost or something.

"The first time, it's disorientating, it's difficult to remember where you are. It helps to be able to feel someone holding onto your physical body, to remind you where you are so you don't get lost." There was a long silence as Eiji began to look increasingly less comfortable. He was just about to give in when he heard Daniel's voice saying the words which made him heave a sigh of relief.

"Or, we could just follow the sign." Daniel stated, brushing some shrubs from a nearby post to reveal a name carved on a piece of wood, it appeared they were not too far from the town at all.

"Was that there before?" Zo questioned, moving to stand beside him to examine the moss-ridden post. Eiji gave a sigh of relief as the attention moved to focus on something other than himself.

"I'm not sure, it just caught my eye while you were talking."

"I vote for followin' the sign." Eiji skilfully added his suggestion onto the end of Daniel's sentence, before marching off in the direction of the arrow, an act which left no chance for objections.

* * *

The seemingly endless forest stretched before them, its luscious green trees created a perfect canopy overhead, the area they searched for lay somewhere within its endless sea. As they got closer, through an area of thinning trees it was possible to see the silhouette of a town just before them. Daniel glanced up from the map, which he had skilfully managed to take from Elly's possession and looked to Zo.

"I've been monitoring our progress and we are here. This town, according to the map, appears to be called Abaddon. It's one of the seven fixed points Seiken spoke about, but I don't recall hearing of such a place in our world. The only thing here in ours is the Forest of Lost Souls." He looked towards the clearing, the pure white brick houses offset the perceived darkness which sheltered the town. The interlocking canopies of the mighty trees stretched across with their stifling arms, yet the very centre seemed beyond their grasp, a place where the only true, untainted light shone down from the sky above to illuminate the circular, central stone paving. It was upon this area that those of the town would have performed the annual dance in honour of Hades, under the light of the full moon which marked the end of the year.

It was a picturesque town. Its houses were built in a large circle lining the edge of the clearing, and each house possessed a uniform look. Carefully crafted picket fences lined each border. There was something eerie about the symmetry of each garden. Each one seemed to possess the same flowers in the same quantities. To those who paid little attention to things such as these, it looked warm, welcoming, and that was precisely how both Marise and Elly had perceived it on their first visit here, but now Elly knew better. Now she could see this place for what it truly was.

Not many knew about the town Abaddon which lay hidden deep within the Forest of Lost Souls, the fewer people who knew of this place, the better.

Nothing stirred within the town's boundaries, it gave the impression of a long-deserted ghost town with one difference, the houses and gardens were still as new and well-kept as the day they had been built.

"I don't like this," Acha whispered as they entered, their eyes scanned for any movement no matter how small, for some time now they had felt as if they were being watched.

"I'm sure I know this place." Zo kept her voice to the low tone that seemed to be demanded by the silence of the area. "It looks so familiar." She looked to Elly in hope to gain some confirmation. As always, Elly made no attempt to confirm or deny it. She did, however, give some information.

"Its counterpart, that is to say 'Abaddon' in our world, was once home to one of the Grimoire I told you about." Elly stated much to their surprise. None of them had heard of this town. The only reason Daniel had known its name here was because it had been printed on the map.

"What happened to this place? It's so quiet." Daniel looked to Elly who once again seemed to possess all the answers.

"There are many rumours as to what may have happened here years ago. One of which is that the Grimoire sustained the life of the people here, on the day it was removed, a terrible fate befell the people of this town. That is what most who know of its existence choose to believe anyway, but the truth is always a little more sinister." Elly paused as if for dramatic effect. "From what I understand—"

"It was placed under the darkest of enchantments." Zo walked slowly between the houses, her voice soft like the expression of gentle confusion she now wore. She felt the magic in the surrounding area, worse still, for some reason it felt familiar. "I know this story."

Zo closed her eyes in concentration, her hand rested on a wooden gate post as she tried to pull the memory from the tip of her mind. Unseen by anyone, concern crossed Elly's brow. It had been a long time coming, but a few hours ago news had reached her of Annabel's death, which meant as the enchantment faded some of her memories, under just the right circumstances, could be reclaimed. She could only hope she would not recall too much.

Annabel had been with her for a very long time, whilst everything possible had been done for her, there came a time when age won over even the most sophisticated methods.

"A curse was bestowed upon this village," Zo continued finally. "As a punishment for an unforgivable act. Due to their nature, death was too complex for those who resided here, thus, they were sentenced to an eternal sleep. Conscious of all that transpired around them, awaiting a death never to come, they are being eternally punished for a crime they committed." She looked to Elly once more for confirmation, but again she gave away nothing. Elly relaxed slightly, she had to admit, the punishment of these townsfolk had been an all too familiar one. There were times she almost felt sorry for them, almost, but then she remembered what they had done.

"They must have done something unspeakable to earn such a judgement." Acha placed her hand on Zo's shoulder, startling her slightly. Zo studied the web of magic which surrounded the town, it was so thick, so complex, that it almost passed into the boundaries of the visible.

"How come no one has heard of this town? It has no place in history or legend." Daniel looked from Zo to Elly, wondering which one would answer, but it was Elly who finally spoke, looking to Zo before beginning her explanation.

"The reason is, that once the spell was completed, Mari summoned a monster to guard the town and the surrounding area. Its mere presence alone repels intruders. Only those who know of this place are able to see it, that was part of the magic. When the spell was complete, the town vanished from any map and texts, thus was soon forgotten, but rumours of the forest still continue to this day. They now call it the Forest of Lost Souls, any said to enter never return alive."

"What kinda monster?" Eiji had grabbed the most important word in the sentence, the one which affected them immediately. As he asked, he glanced around as if expecting it to be lurking behind them.

"It was remarkable. I have heard only the tales Mari told me, this creature not only guards the town, but feeds upon those trapped in its induced sleep. It was truly an extraordinary conjuring." She smiled, remembering Marise's excitement when she had revelled in explaining what had been accomplished. The kind of magic she had called upon would have been no simple feat, even for a master of the artes, that night she had truly surpassed herself.

"Not to tempt providence, but, if such a creature exists within our world, surely it's only logical it exists here also." Daniel glanced around the quiet

village as Eiji had just moments ago, watching carefully for any signs of movement. Even the trees moving in the wind now seemed like a threat.

"No, it can't enter the town, it was imprisoned within the temple. As for
the town's people, it sustains them by hunting those who wander too far into
its territory, and it is limited to the time it is permitted to leave to find its prey.
Until its creator releases it, it will remain this way." Zo stated autonomously,
still reading the waves and links of the magic to gain a deeper understanding of
its purpose. Whoever had done this certainly hadn't wanted anyone to be able
to reverse their handiwork, it was far more complex than it had needed to be.

"Is this temple in the woods?" A sudden realisation dawned upon them,
but strangely, Eiji was the first to question its location. When he had glanced
around the village he had found no temple, just the houses and mile upon mile
of trees met his vision. He paused as another thought had entered his mind.
Without considering his actions, he approached one of the houses to open the
door. All fell silent to watch him cautiously peer inside. "If the town people
are meant t'be inside the village, where are they?" Eiji, satisfied the house was
empty, entered. He quickly took in the details of the seemingly unused house,
everything seemed new and fresh, untouched by the hands of the intended
occupier. Having not found any signs of life, he opened the window to call
through to his friends. "Shouldn't they be sleepin', shouldn't they be here?"

"Well the townsfolk may not be here, but we do have a lead as to where our
clue takes us. Where's this temple?" Zo shook her head as Daniel looked to
her. When she failed to provide him with an answer he turned his attention
to Elly.

"How should I know? I was not the mastermind behind it, maybe you
should ask Mari!" she snapped, she didn't understand it, why hadn't she been
told about the temple? Mari had told her everything, why had she chosen to
keep something like this a secret?

"Since she is not here..." Daniel said, his tone seemed somewhat relieved.
"The only other lead we have is..." he looked to Zo again.

"Why are you looking at me? I don't know anything." Her voice trembled
defensively as she felt the pressure of their eyes upon her. The more she fought
to remember, the more her head pounded. The town on the whole made her
feel uneasy and confused. The magic in the area seemed almost stifling, all
these things combined in addition to her own frustration and questions about
her knowledge of the town, she felt helpless and trapped, with no way to

escape. The anxiety and panic rose within her so quickly she thought it would explode, she glanced around searching for an escape from the claustrophobia which quickly threatened to consume her.

"But, you did mention it in the first place," Acha volunteered almost timidly. She hadn't noticed the strange panic in her friend's eyes, perhaps if she had she wouldn't have been so quick to speak.

"I don't know anything!" she snapped surrendering to the raw emotions and panic which built inside her, "maybe you can find something in the town to help us. Just don't ask me!" She turned her back to them, seeing a chance of escape. She needed to get out of here, the aura of the magic had become so thick it threatened to ensnare her as it crushed the breath from her body. Daniel moved to pursue but was stopped by Elly as she raised her arm before him.

"I will go. You stay and look for information," she stated in a well-practised authoritarian tone, before he was given the chance to argue, she had already left.

"That was strange," Daniel commented as he stared in the direction both Elly and Zo had vanished in. "I guess she's—"

"Think about it." Eiji came out of the house. In his hand he held a piece of parchment he had taken from the table. It was the one thing out of place, which was what had convinced him to remove it. "'Y' chose t'involve y'self in this matter, she didn't. One day she was just taken from everythin' she knew and loved." Eiji, unlike the rest of them, had clearly seen the rising panic within her, he saw her posture alter as she appeared suffocated. He and Elly both understood that, on some level, it was unsurprising she felt this way, she was walking in the steps of her alternate persona.

"Shouldn't we be looking for information?" Acha decided to change the subject, she wasn't feeling too great. Something about this area made her feel very strange, the sooner they could get out of here the better. A wave of dizziness passed over her.

"No need, I got this from inside." Eiji lifted the piece of parchment to their attention, he unfolded it to show them a small map.

"Why didn't you—"

"I guess, I thought it wise t'let them talk a while, there seems t'be some things they need t'discuss, besides it's no different t'the one we were given earlier." Daniel opened the map Seiken had given Zo and compared them.

"They're identical." he sighed, looking at them. "Even down to the writing."

"Almost, but not quite." Eiji turned the parchment over. Acha, who didn't look so well, moved to sit herself on a small mound under a nearby tree. Upon the back of the parchment was yet another unusual symbol, this was the only difference between the two.

"How exactly does this help us?" Daniel stifled a yawn as he looked over the two almost identical parchments. His fingers passing over the five symbols, each one, just like the map Seiken had given them, expanded their view on that area, each of the points had a similar riddle to that found in the place they were now. Daniel saw the lines blur before his gaze as he gave yet another yawn.

"I'm not sure, the symbol looks a little like the Apollo Favour." Eiji mirrored his actions as they moved to join Acha in the shade of the autumn tree. "So I guess we are protected durin' our daylight hours, just as Seiken said." He took a second look at the tree, he was certain just moments before it had thrived with life.

"This place is odd, I swear this tree was in full bloom just moments ago," Daniel observed, as if reading Eiji's mind. He gave another yawn. "I wonder where Zo and Elly are." He leaned back against the tree, he couldn't understand why he felt so tired all of a sudden. Giving a stretch he made himself comfortable as he awaited their return.

✳ ✳ ✳

Elly paced the village to look for Zo, her thoughts were on their last visit here. The last time they had been here she had nearly lost Marise to the dark-forces which had resided within this village. Those who lived here had schemed and planned very hard to get everything to fall into place, and unknowingly, Elly had left her in great danger. The effects of this place had taken their toll on Marise, and had followed her for some time afterwards.

Marise had been amazing that night, she had been surrounded by the nightmarish creatures, but alien to her normal thoughts, she did not fight. Instead she had summoned a being to feed on them as they had tried to feed on her; although she had never mentioned the sealing of this creature into a temple, or forbidding it from preying on those it wished. It was an action which did not seem like her at all.

As Marise had not spoken of it, it left her to wonder if perhaps the other persona, Zoella, had been responsible for this feat. It wouldn't have been the first time the two of them had briefly exchanged places.

Zo sat on the very outskirts of the town where the stifling magic was weakest, and the air seemed cooler. She had calmed down now, the headache had left her and all that remained was the heavy feeling from the magic around them. Having reflected on her childish outburst, she now felt rather embarrassed about her performance. When she saw Elly approaching, she acknowledged her wordlessly with a nod, stood, and followed her back in silence, but without objection.

Elly stood for a moment with her hands on her hips as she looked at Daniel, Eiji, and Acha all asleep against a tree. Zo followed at some distance behind. She still felt ashamed at being unable to control her emotions. The more fragments she recalled, the more frustrated she grew trying to grasp more than her mind offered. The harder she tried, the more difficult it became. It didn't help when they had pressured her to recall more, something she would have gladly obliged, were it within her ability, then her emotions had taken control.

"There is no time to delay, we should begin our search." As Elly approached her long shadow cast over them, but not one of them moved as they sat under the blackened tree. She didn't recall seeing this lifeless feature when they had first approached. A strange feeling descended upon her, as she watched the apparently sleeping figures she quickly came to understand what had happened, but the words she heard next confirmed her theory.

"They are not delaying Lee, my Abi did this." Elly turned in surprise as she heard the familiar dialect; there was only one person who called her by that name. She was unable to conceal the concern on her features as she turned to face Zo, nor the surprise when the blue-eyed figure was still the one who met her gaze. It left her to question whether she had really heard what she believed she had. The concern reflected in Zo's body language deepened as she saw Elly's expression. Something was very wrong. She warily approached her friends as Elly still stood in bewilderment questioning exactly what had just happened.

"I'm sorry about earlier, I shouldn't have snapped, it just got a little too much, I'm sorry." Despite her addressing them, there was not even the slightest stir of movement. "Did you manage to find anything?" Her voice grew nervous as they still failed to respond to her. Her panicked gaze shifted quickly to Elly in hope of some aid or explanation. Noticing Zo looked to her for assistance Elly approached, extending her foot to shove Daniel a little harder than was perhaps necessary, his body made no response other than sliding sideways from the tree.

"I think we need to get them out of here," she stated grabbing Eiji manoeuvring him expertly into a fireman's lift. Despite being thrown over her shoulder, he still failed to respond. Without another word, Elly carried him off towards the town's border.

"Zo." Acha whispered weakly as Zo had pulled her to her feet in a similar action to the one Elly had expertly used, she wasn't exactly sure how she was going to manage to carry both of them from this place, Elly had made it seem so effortless.

"Acha," the relief in her voice was obvious, Zo hooked her arm under Acha's shoulder as she managed to support some of her own weight. "What happened?"

"I don't know." Zo glanced back at Daniel, she was not comfortable with the thought of leaving him alone. This place gave her a sense of foreboding, the magic which permeated the air did little to still her nerves, just then, Elly returned to carry him in the same manner she had Eiji just a moment before. "I felt a little off so I sat down, then we started to get tired. The next thing I knew they were asleep, then you came for us." Zo steadied her as they made their way slowly towards the boundaries, exiting the opposite side to that which they had entered.

"Maybe it has something to do with the magic here." Zo stated. Speaking with Acha, voicing her thoughts helped her to focus on something other than the heaviness in the air. "After all, its inhabitants were forced into eternal slumber, maybe those who enter are also subjected to its power. There may be no one in the town but, from what Seiken told us, every dreamer has a home. So they must be somewhere in this world." It was the only logical explanation Zo could conceive, there was no reason to believe those who were forced into sleep weren't somewhere within Darrienia, dreaming.

Daniel and Eiji lay upon a small clearing where wild flowers fought their way through the grassy terrain. The forest itself was inhospitable to such things, given the density of the undergrowth and the poor lighting. It seemed these flowers sought every possible opportunity to thrive where this land would allow. Zo helped Acha to sit within the shade of a nearby tree as Elly tried desperately to rouse Eiji, but to no avail.

The surroundings were filled with a deadly silence, the only sound coming from the gentle wind which teased through the trees as it passed.

"It is no use." Elly sighed as she moved away from Eiji. She had tried all known methods of waking someone, even a splash of water followed by a firm slap across the face, which she enjoyed perhaps a little more than she should have. His skin now burnt with the angry red imprint of her hand. "It seems the creature's sleep enchantment even embraces this area, what we need is some negating magic," she looked to Zo. "Perhaps a magical ward."

"I got it the first time, you don't have to keep on." She touched Acha's face gently to check her temperature and health. She seemed fine, a little tired and anaemic perhaps, she never did seem to eat a great deal. "I wonder why we weren't affected?" Zo questioned aloud, not expecting to receive an answer.

"I would think it was quite obvious," Elly paused for a moment, she knew full well why she and Zo hadn't been affected by the creature's sleep, but to explain would compromise the situation. "We were just lucky." She cringed ever so slightly as she answered, was that really the best she could muster? Well, she always thought it was better to be vague than weave a complicated web of lies, which became all the more difficult to be freed from.

"Yeah, maybe." Zo sighed quietly, it was clear Elly knew more than she was revealing, just once, she wondered, would it be too much to ask to get a straight answer?

It took a short time to prepare everything for her ward, but finally she was ready. She had read the surrounding environment and knew just what to ask. She took a deep breath before she began calling upon the magic, as she did so, by force of habit she spoke.

"Awake and alert we wish to keep, I set a ward to counter sleep." A silver light momentarily surrounded them before it faded to become transparent.

"Do you always do that?" Despite her best efforts, Elly could not hide the amusement within her voice.

"What?" Zo glanced up from Daniel's side as she checked him over.

"Rhyme, you never used to, it is annoying."

"So, how did I used to..." Zo trailed off. For a long time she had questioned the validity of speaking her desires, she felt it unnecessary, but having no memory of doing anything else she continued it by habit alone.

"Never mind," she smiled. At least now she understood why the initiators of this situation had said something so pointless when they invoked their magic. They had been mocking her. Well what had she expected? Marise no longer asked for magic, but since Zo's memories were incomplete. Her recollection of magic would come from her childhood, a time when such things were used as a means of focus, so it only stood to reason she may still feel them necessary. It wouldn't normally matter but it just sounded so ridiculous, they would have to talk, she couldn't stand it if she was to continue this through their journey, it was just so pointless and only proved to delay things.

Elly watched Eiji for a moment, his fingers twitched as the sleep began to dissipate. Daniel awoke with a start, gasping for breath. He only began to calm as he realised that he was sitting with his friends, in the middle of a strange forest. Elly, Zo, and Acha all stared at him, his reaction was not one expected of someone waking from a peaceful slumber. Seconds later Eiji awoke, clutching his chest with his trembling hands. He glanced around quickly before he relaxed slightly. Although neither Daniel nor Eiji had spoken, they seemed to be out of danger. Acha, however, still sat as pale as ever, her breathing shallow.

"Acha, are you okay?" Zo took her hand from Eiji's forehead, happy both he and Daniel were fine, physically anyway, the look of terror on their faces, however, gave indication they had a story to tell, one that no doubt was not a pleasant one.

"I think she—" Elly began but her words fell silent as the area around them grew darker. It was almost as if in an instant summer had turned to autumn, an effect only seen within the area touched by Zo's ward. The flowers withered and died to leave brown stems in place of those which just moments ago had been in full bloom. The trees shifted and changed to drop their once green leaves as if autumn had descended, the grass drooped and turned pale. In less than thirty seconds the entire area within the spell had first withered, then died, there was nothing they could do but watch the earthly sleep spread.

"Oh no." Zo whispered sadly as she saw what she had done, somehow her spell had ignored the preservation rules. She didn't understand how it was possible, even if she had asked for more energy than the place could give, with the magic she used there was no way she could do this harm. The very style meant she could harm nothing and take only that which was freely offered. "I'm sure I used the forces correctly." Acha pulled herself to her feet slowly and approached them, it seemed, although delayed, she too was now recovering from the strange sleep. Unlike the area around them, the colour once more returned to her face. She joined her friends just as the shifting autumn had turned to winter, not a single flower was left in bloom, and not a single green leaf hung on the trees.

Zo quickly localised the magic to follow each person, hopefully in such a small area it would not harm the world around them. If it did, at least this small area was far better than them walking within a life-destroying field.

"I guess this place doesn't like my magic," she sighed. As she placed her hand upon the bark of a nearby tree she couldn't suppress the shudder, it was almost as if her ward had forcefully torn the life from it.

"What happened? One minute you were fine the next we couldn't wake you." Zo offered Daniel a hand to his feet, he now seemed well enough and eager to stand.

"I'm not really sure. It was the strangest thing, one minute I was listening to Eiji, the next everything grew darker. I felt so tired, I'd go as far as to say I had fallen asleep, but I could hear small parts of the world around me, although try as I might I couldn't move, or talk. Eiji are you okay?" Daniel looked to Eiji, who still sat on the ground, his hand still touched his chest, his eyes still wide in terror.

"Didn't y' see it," he whispered. "The creature from the darkness? It pulled some kind of silver cord from us t'attach it t'itself. Then there came the screams, the tortured cries of those life-forces it feeds on, each beggin' for mercy over and over again." Elly grabbed his hand to pull him involuntarily to his feet, a motion which seemed to distract him from the memories of what he saw.

"I do not think we need to concern ourselves just yet." Elly began, knowing in due time they would indeed have to face the creature as this journey's destination seemed to guide them to its prison. "A ward has been erected to counter the enchantment, you should be all right, for now. What else can you tell us of it?"

"Nothin', just that it seemed really excited about somethin', and a name kept repeatin' in my mind, Aburamushi," Eiji shuddered at the mere sound of the name, "but what I don't understand is it saw us, but somehow y' evaded its vision. Why?"

"Lucky, I guess. Maybe it targeted a certain area." Elly answered again.

"Maybe, but then how come Acha was unaffected?"

"I would not say she was unaffected, she just did not seem as afflicted as you. Maybe it prefers males." Elly felt her foot land firmly on the proverbial shovel as she dug deeper. She would have hoped Eiji, of all people, would not have put her in this position. Knowing what he did meant he should know the truth and realise there was no way she could give them a straight answer.

"But surely this wasn't an all-male town." Daniel intervened.

"As I know its creator perhaps I received immunity." Any guilt she had felt seeing the bright red mark across Eiji's face had now vanished. Even if it was premature, it seemed he had been given just what he was due.

"What about Zo and Acha?" he questioned stubbornly.

"Acha has a different kind of life-force to most people so maybe it struggled to entrap her completely and Zo, well, she possesses a unique magic."

"But so does Eiji." Daniel was about to press the issue further when he heard Zo gasp. In that split second of silence it seemed to cut through the air like a knife. Elly studied her cautiously before trying to pinpoint what, in her line of vision, could have caused such a reaction. Whatever it was seemed to have momentarily paralysed her as she stood rooted to the spot, her vision blank almost trance like. Something was obviously wrong, but Elly knew just how to counteract it.

A loud crack rang through the air as she slapped her. She slapped her so hard it had not only startled the silent birds from their nests in the trees, but had almost forced Zo from her feet. Without even time to blink, Zo had slid her foot backwards to regain her balance and thrust her weight into a counter attack as she retaliated. Her clenched fist stopped barely an inch from Elly's face, Eiji unconsciously rubbed his throbbing cheek as he let out a sigh of relief, unseen by anyone Elly smiled.

"Lee." Zo's voice spoke quietly as she unclenched her hand to touch the side of Elly's face gently. "You see the problem here," she subtly glanced in the direction of the three unwanted guests.

"What problem?" Daniel, although unable to hear anything, had sharply picked up on the word problem. She turned to look at him, for a second he could have sworn there were remnants of something hidden within her eyes, something he couldn't quite place. As Zo touched the place Elly had struck her, she noticed Eiji almost mirrored her actions, he hadn't realised it until now, but his face really hurt.

"A problem?" Zo was aware she had spoken, but was unsure exactly what she had said. "Oh yes, I remember, we still need to find the temple and it's getting late." Elly gave her a puzzled look before a flicker of understanding crossed her mind.

'*Don't worry Mari.*' Elly thought to herself, she understood the problem perfectly.

* * *

"So my daughter has awoken," the cool voice stated, although quiet, it commanded total attention. Night paced around the cauldron, which he kept for sentimental reasons more than anything else, his dark hooded robe trailed behind him on the floor. Within his hand he held a small crystal, through which he watched the figures as they went about their business.

"Yes, my lord, only as yet the outcome is somewhat uncertain. It may take longer than anticipated to see the desired effects." It was impossible to tell who the voice could belong to, the style of communication distorted it beyond any possible recognition.

"And what of the old man, did he fulfil his side of the contract?" Night asked as a mere formality. There had been much preparation to ensure everything proceeded as planned.

"Yes."

"And the machine?" He lowered the crystal to place it into his pocket, watching the travellers no longer interested him. The answer to this question, unlike the others, was one he could not predict. What they had touched upon was an ancient technology which had been long forgotten, resurrected in a time which was not prepared for it. It was difficult to say how it would function now. To be recreated after such a vast time phase, who knew what the outcome would be? There were many aspects which were fallible, over time he had encountered, and rectified many of them, but the materials needed for repairs and modifications were becoming scarce. Even the Research Plexus encountered difficulties when creating the components from what was available.

"There are no problems," the voice from the cauldron responded with very little delay. "As for your daughter, I imagine that once Darrienia takes its toll..." the voice trailed off, there was a slight uncertainty in its words. "What if they should fail?" A sharp sound of realisation echoed through the voice, when this had been planned their failure was never an option, but now, things had taken unexpected twists, unpredictable influences now had to be taken into account.

"Then they will remain there forever, the boundaries of the worlds will vanish, and havoc shall be freed upon the earth." Night smiled at the thought, but this unique form of peril was not exactly what he had in mind, he had much greater aspirations.

"A lot is at stake, my lord, should they meet with misfortune."

"Then see to it they don't. The mind is a tricky thing, things forgotten can seem second nature. I believe they will be safe, all things considered. The Oneirois can only be released by my victory, there is no other way. I am not worried, or, do you forget exactly who it is we are dealing with? My daughter will be fine, the company she keeps will only add to the entertainment."

"Entertainment? My lord, I feel they are the ones who hinder our progress."

"As I said before, I am not concerned, I would not be surprised if they do not have their uses. Tell me, have you gained further information on the location of the final Grimoire?"

"No, but I promise it shall be delivered to you personally. Although I do believe the location which you initially believed is the most plausible, but as yet we remain without confirmation."

"Very well, continue as planned. This is a good opportunity for me to utilise the patience I have developed in my many years of waiting."

"Or you could remind people your true power, they seem to have grown more insolent."

"All in good time, besides, I do believe it is time to fulfil my contract with the old man."

"Are you going in person?"

"But of course, you know the Epiales cannot approach him, the blind have senses which repel them, forbidding them to draw near. It will be interesting to see how they react when his senses have faded. All those years of teasing them shall not go unpunished. I cannot stand a man whose favour can be so cheaply brought. At least I can gain enjoyment watching as my army draws closer when he is no longer protected by the unseeing eye. Besides, I believe I may have a further use for him yet, who knows, let my minions have their fun, and if he lives, then I will consider his options."

Chapter 8

The Lair of Aburamushi

The temple towered before them, the huge pillars, which would once have stood so spectacularly to guide the worshippers to its magnificent entrance, now stood crumbled like the outer buildings which surrounded it. The pathway was broken, cracked by the half dead weeds which fought their way to the surface in the foolish hope to find light. The air here seemed darker than the canopy of trees and cloud cover should have allowed, almost as if the once holy shrine now emitted an aura of darkness so powerful that even the plants around it withered and died, despite the strength shown through their escape.

"This, is it?" Eiji's voice was filled with disillusion as they walked the path of what once would have been a spectacular monument. "I expected somethin' a little less decrepit." He gave a disappointed sigh as they walked slowly to the large dark oak door. It seemed to be barely held in place by the wrought iron hinges. It was a magnificent piece of carving, or rather, it would have been. Around the outside of the door was a thick deep groove. The top half of the door was carved with an intricate design, its meaning or relevance lost as parts of the detail had, like the temple, decayed into ruin. Still visible on the bottom half of the door, even despite the moss and rot, was a picture carving. Although unclear, it seemed to be a picture of what the temple had looked like back in its prime. The stonework around the door was plain and lacked the creative touch of the person who had designed the door, it too was aged and would seemingly crumble at the slightest touch.

The door itself, although it would have once been strong enough to with-stand a small barrage, looked barely solid. Elly pushed at it and took a few backwards steps, almost as if expecting it to crack, fall, or even open, yet it didn't waver. Despite its unstable appearance, it stood as firm as ever.

"It's sealed by some form of magic." Zo extended her hand to touch its sur-face, but retracted at the last second. The magic present felt slightly different than that in Abaddon, it felt more innocent. As she read it unconsciously, she realised one type of magic had been combined with one completely alien to forge the seal. "If we could get inside it could probably be opened easily, it seems only the creature can open this side, which, I guess, would make sense as it would prevent people from entering while it hunts." Zo surmised, it wasn't that she remembered having erected such a thing, it was nothing more than an assumption based on what she had discovered in the tale of how the creature was sealed. She knew whoever sealed it would need to make sure no one accidentally entered its domain, at least, she reasoned, that is what she would have done had it been her who had created and sealed the beast.

"So we need t'look for another way in." Eiji stated, he had intended to say, 'so we'll just hafta leave then', but since he knew this was not an option, he feared another attack from Elly's hand should he voice his thoughts of self-preservation. He knew, regardless of what may lie in wait, they would have to enter, but that didn't mean the place unnerved him any less, in fact, knowing they had to enter, no matter the situation, made it more difficult. There was something sinister, almost evil about the time-eroded building.

Slowly, carefully watching their steps amongst the tangled debris of stone and decaying plant life, they walked the perimeter of the holy monument. Despite the decrepit condition of all which was built around it, this central building stood firm, there was not the slightest crack or window they could exploit to gain entrance. Finding themselves once more at the door, Elly tapped her foot impatiently.

"These buildings quite often possessed escape tunnels in case they came under siege, perhaps we could find—"

"Over here." Daniel called from the distance; they could just see his figure standing beside one of the crumbled outbuildings, leaving them to wonder when he had strayed. He gestured for them to join him, all the time glancing inside.

The small crumbled ruin was nothing more than an entrance to what would have been a sleeping bunker, perhaps for the guards who protected the shrines. Rotted pieces of blankets, thick with slime, formed from the exposure to the elements, were carefully spaced upon the stone floor. In the shadows of the far wall lay a mound of bricks, the rubble covering the floor outwardly, almost as if something had dug its way through. Not one of them, on seeing this, failed to consider that with such a clear escape route it was possible the hold on the creature was no longer in place.

Hesitantly Zo approached the gaping hole, the air smelt heavily of earth and decay. Inside was dark, in fact, dark was an understatement, as they looked in through the hole they could see nothing at all, not even a ray of light from outside seemed to penetrate the empty void.

They had deliberately avoided the mention of the creature as they had made their way here and still they spoke no word on the matter, but it was impossible not to consider it, especially now they made preparations to enter its domain. An uneasy air spread amongst them, none of them wished to voice their fears on what they may face, nor could they even imagine what lay in wait. This was the first part of what had been referred to as a game; this would be their first encounter, their first understanding, of what it meant to be a player. The silence stretched on.

"Well, I guess we go in?" Zo swallowed her rising fear as she stepped closer to the gaping mouth in the crumbled wall, she leaned forwards slowly, in an attempt to peer deeper inside. She tried to get an understanding of what they would face, however, the uniform darkness continued to conceal all. "But we don't even know if it will go inside the temple."

"It will, given the consistent design of such places, this crevice should lead down into one of the chambers." Elly stated confidently from the entrance. She had very carefully been estimating the distance, there was no doubt in her mind that this would prove to be the entrance into the creature's lair.

"Y' could fall forever." Eiji suddenly grabbed Zo, an act which nearly sent her tumbling through the fissure. She had been so focused on her attempt to see inside the belly of the beast, she had momentarily lost focus on everything else. "There's no way of knowin' how far it goes down, there may not even be a floor." He moved to stand beside her, as he too looked down into the eternal pit of darkness, unaware that by his actions he had very nearly made her test his theory a little sooner than she had planned. All the time he nervously passed a small pebble over his fingers as he thought of their options, or more specifically, his only choice, between death or death. If he were to leave now, Elly would strike him down for sure, he wasn't foolish enough to assume he would be safe simply because there were others present. This in mind he decided to continue and try to prolong his life a little further, and enter. It would be better than being killed here and now, although his mind warned him if his instincts were correct, there wouldn't be much difference between the two. He wondered if anyone else had noticed the strange scent of death which hung heavily in the air.

He took his hand from her shoulder as he continued to contemplate his non-existent options. Zo placed her hand on his to still the pebble, she smiled taking it from him.

"I didn't plan on jumping in," she stated, turning the small stone over once in her hand. "The sun's rays are full of might, bestow on this the gift of light," she whispered. She felt the warmth of the magic pass through her as she began to condense and change the power she had been granted by the surrounding environment. It felt different to normal, heavier, but she tried her best to control it. In the corner of her vision she saw Elly roll her eyes.

A small ball of light appeared, hovering in the air just before her. It was no bigger in size than a small plum, yet it shone brightly enough to illuminate the air around it as it pulsed in time with her quickened, nervous breathing. She glanced down to the rock in her hands and sighed.

Daniel, although he watched in awe as always, found a slight frown had crossed his brow to mirror the one on the face of his friend as she once more glanced down to the rock, then back to the ball of light.

"That's not what I meant to..." Zo's words were spoken with such a soft confusion they were barely audible. She couldn't understand why it hadn't worked as she expected, she had read the elements and requested the light to shine from within the rock, but instead, once again, her magic in this world had a consequence other than that expected, she couldn't understand where it had gone wrong. It almost felt like being an amateur again, unable to completely control even the most basic magic.

Stepping closer to the edge, until there was nothing left between her and the steep descent into the temple, she reached for the light, but instead of being able to take it in her hand to manipulate, her fingers passed smoothly through it. No matter how many times she tried she could not take it from its position before her, the weight of the stares from her comrades made her feel the need to excuse her mistake.

"I guess I'm feeling a little off." This was the only justification she could think of for the strange occurrence. When it came to magic, she normally had no problems commanding its total obedience, yet for some reason, this time, it had chosen to ignore her will for the light to enter the stone, and instead took a firm residence in front of her, perhaps it was something about this world. Since arriving here, it seemed very little of her magic worked as she had planned. She could only assume she had missed something, everything here felt so different to their own world, perhaps she was just a few degrees out in her calculation of requirements.

She supported herself against the crumbling wall as she once more leaned inside the building. The light shone with just enough power for her to make out the marble floor about fifteen feet below the opening, the floor seemed a little uneven, parts of it seemed to trap and twist strange shadows, but it appeared safe enough.

"The floor looks solid enough," she called back from inside the hole as she pulled herself out. There had been a moment when she wondered if the grey stones used to support herself would decide to crumble, but they seemed strangely sturdy despite the state of disrepair. Eiji moved to join her, in his hand he held one of the ropes they had brought earlier from Mr Venrent. Taking it from him she lowered it into the darkness, she leaned through just enough to be able to tell when it had reached the floor. It was too steep a drop for them to simply slide down and have any chance of returning, and if one thing was certain, they had to ensure they had an escape route, who knew what the darkness would hold.

Eiji took the remainder of the rope from her, moving to the left of the area he wrapped the rope around the sturdy, rusted iron gate which blocked their path to the next chamber. He rattled it before thrusting the force of his weight against it numerous times, to ensure it would not fall from the wall the second they made their descent. He wasn't about to leave their escape in the hands of a small metal peg nailed into the ground.

He used the remaining length to fasten it not only around one section, but around individual parts and larger sections until no more remained, just to be certain it would not unwind, that way, even if the seemingly sturdy gate was forced loose, its size alone would mean they could still scale the wall to freedom. His mind warned him that even with these precautions, once they stepped foot inside, none of them were going to be coming out again. His mind recalled the images he had seen in the paralytic sleep, he reasoned by ensuring their exit was secure, at least there was one less thing that could go wrong.

He gave it a few more tugs to ensure there was no chance of it unfastening itself, perhaps several more tugs than were actually necessary. By the time he had reached them, Zo had already started to descend into the unknown territory of Aburamushi's lair.

As she reached the bottom, a wave of tiredness swept over her, for a moment her legs became weak, forcing her to lean against the damp wall, her back and hands pressed against it firmly as she tried to obtain a better view of her new surroundings.

A strange pain radiated through her, it felt as if her entire body had been engulfed in flames. Every part of her flesh felt as if it were burning, during that fleeting moment, through the agony, she truly believed she had triggered a curse, perhaps an ancient magic which was sealed within the chamber to ward off intruders. She bit down on her lip to prevent herself from crying out. The last thing she wanted was for her friends to rush down before she knew what they would face, besides, to cry out would surely serve no purpose aside from alerting something unpleasant of their arrival.

The pain grew more intense as the coppery taste of blood filled her mouth, she feared her chances of restraining the agony any longer. She crossed her arms before her letting the wall take her weight as she tried to restrain the cries. Then, suddenly, it was as if someone had released her from the spell, as quickly as it came, it had vanished. As the tension drained from her body she almost slid to the floor, had it not been for the wall at her back, she knew she would have no longer been standing.

After taking a few moments to regain her strength, she quickly scanned the area for curses, whatever it was, it had felt like it had targeted her life-force and magic, but aside from the heavy incantations and wards which surrounded the building, there was nothing she could feel that would affect anyone who entered. Perhaps, had there been more light, she would have understood the pain better, then maybe, she would not have been so quick to signal safe passage to her friends.

One by one they entered, she was relieved none of them had seemed to suffer the strange affliction she had, perhaps, she reasoned, it was a warning meant only for people with Hectarian powers, after all, the magic which surrounded the temple seemed to feel as if it came from a Hectarian source.

Daniel moved to position himself next to Zo, which was not difficult since she was the only source of light in the area. They all stood near to her, barely daring to take a step into the darkness. Through the pale light all colour was lost, only shadows of the paths before them were visible. Acha moved a little closer as Eiji finally finished his climb down.

They had emerged into an antechamber, to their immediate left, barely visible, stood the crumbled wastes of a passage. The stonework which once formed the entrance arches was now nothing more than an obstruction as the corridor had collapsed. Moving forwards, stepping through the dried, crumbled water feature, they could easily see their desired path, one which would lead them closer to the central building. Darkness enshrouded the area sealed by the huge cast iron gates. Approaching them, Elly searched for a lock or other means of access, but it seemed this path was one no longer open to them. There was just one other exit from this room, and that was down the crumbling passage to their right.

It was unbelievable how little difference the light made to the eerie darkness. It was almost like the glow of a small candle, only lighting objects in its close proximity, which made everything else seem darker. Daniel tried to calm his thought as he swore the twisted shadows just outside the light moved, from the corner of his eye he saw movement, he turned only to find another shadow flickering in the light. Something about this place made him feel uneasy. It was understandable, he reasoned, after all, they had just entered the monster's lair, they were in its territory now and it knew its home better than any outsider.

The central chamber was magnificent, the parts of it they could see through the shroud of darkness revealed it to be a large empty space. The few soft, rotted seats seemed to have melted into the floor from years of neglect. This room was as damp as the others, their footsteps slow and careful as the water on the floor made walking on the marbled surface treacherous.

At the rear of the temple stood a statue, the deity it honoured no longer distinguishable as the defining features and symbols had long crumbled. From the shape, it seemed to be a female, the only discernible feature a large shroud which wrapped around her. The altar before the statue where the priest or priestess would address the followers seemed prominent against the gentle sloping of the area either side. One side however, seemed to shrink deeper into the shadows than its twin.

"There's nothin' here." Eiji whispered, his eyes panning around the vast open space in which they found themselves, suddenly he started to feel extremely exposed. There was nothing untoward about this area, could they have been wrong? There were a few other explorable passages, but he had been certain whatever they sought would be found right in the heart of the temple. The stench of decay seemed to have been growing increasingly stronger the more they advanced towards the central point.

"I would not be so certain." Elly's footsteps echoed as she approached the altar. It was a few seconds before Zo realised everyone else had begun to move. She hurried to catch up with them, for some reason, she couldn't shake the overwhelming tiredness which seemed to stifle her. The infrequent drops of water, which dripped somewhere near them, seemed almost hypnotic as she tried to decide where they came from, they were too distant to be within this room.

The shadow from the light danced over the unearthed, cracked marble tiles, where something had burrowed deep into the bowels of the temple. The heavy stench of decay emanated from the piles of sodden earth which lined the area around them. As they stood examining yet another descent into a dark void, Elly secured her second rope to the statue. Often she was thought overly cautious, bringing multiple ropes, but she liked to be prepared for situations such as these. She lowered it into the depths and waited for Zo to descend. After a few moments had passed, and she still remained staring unseeingly into the hole, Elly gave her an encouraging nudge. An action which seemed to startle her, but it had the desired effect as she began her descent.

The area they encountered was as black as a moonless night, once more they found themselves huddled around Zo, the light so pale against the looming darkness. The solid marble floor stretched around them. They had expected some form of burrow, instead they found themselves in yet another room. It was from within these walls the infrequent sound of dripping had originated. Acha wiped a drop from her skin wondering how a place so far below ground could possibly be so damp.

"It seems like this temple has secrets of its own. If we could see more, I am certain a place like this would have a main light source." Elly stated, it was rare a temple would have its own hidden chamber, she could only guess its purpose. It could be anything from a solitary study to storage of unique or even dubious artefacts. Even with all her adventures she had rarely beheld places like these.

"Huh?" Zo shook her head, suddenly aware Elly had addressed her. She looked to her friends cautiously, could it be that the creature had somehow penetrated her magical ward? She stifled a yawn behind her hand, the rest of them seemed fine, but she felt as though she barely had the energy to take another step.

"I was saying, if we could see more then perhaps we could find a way to light the area," she repeated watching her carefully. She could read her well enough by now to know something wasn't quite right. Her skin seemed pale even in the limited light, she looked to her a moment longer as she waited for her words to register.

"Oh, yes, of course." Daniel also looked at her questioningly as she answered, she was clearly distracted, but by what he was unsure. He glanced around as he wondered if perhaps her senses had told her something they had missed, but from her actions, he had to wonder if she was even really in the same room, she seemed so distant. "A tiny flame can burn so bright, enhance us now this power of light," she muttered. No sooner had she finished her unenthusiastic words, a blinding flash encased the entire room, a light so bright it hid things almost as well as the darkness had. They moved quickly as Zo focused on maintaining the light, her body seemed rigid. As the light expanded and grew they spread out to make the best use of the moment. They groped around the damp walls as they tried to locate anything they could use as a permanent light source. Since Elly was certain there was one, not one of them doubted they would succeed in finding it.

The tension left her body, causing the light to fade as she fell to her knees gasping for breath. It receded quickly leaving her to watch as her friends were swallowed by the darkness. By the time it had vanished completely, they were too far away to notice their friend's distress.

With all illumination extinguished they could only trust their memory of what they had seen through that brief flash to guide them. The sound of something moving was heard through the darkness. Each one of them unwillingly froze, convincing themselves the footsteps that approached belonged to one of their group. Acha covered her mouth as what she could only assume to be a large drop of water fell down her back. It felt like something had traced its finger down her spine. A gentle breeze teased through her hair, she closed her eyes tightly, forcing herself to move on through the darkness. For a moment, she swore she had heard something behind her, she turned quickly towards the sound, despite knowing that, through this darkness, she had no chance of seeing it.

A breeze once more came from behind her, she began to panic. The noises of the room somehow seemed louder, closer than before. A rough scraping sound echoed around her and a strange hiss filled the air as the wind teased the hair around her ears. She let out an involuntary scream which she soon silenced as she became aware of the growing light in the room's central point. Elly stood near a large brazier which now roared and crackled with the freshly lit flames. The light was only faint but served its purpose.

This room, this secret place, had been used for unholy acts. Instruments of torture littered the floor and hung from the walls near raised marble slabs, but this was not the cause of their alarm, the cause of their shock came from something far more grotesque.

Acha stood in paralysed horror; the perfectly positioned light ensured they saw more than they had possibly wanted to. Looking around the chamber, the answer to one of the questions asked repeatedly had been revealed to everyone. Everyone, that is, except Zo, who was bent over on her hands and knees unable to catch her breath as she slid to the floor. Above them, the riddle of the missing town people had been solved.

"By the Gods it's some kind of..." Daniel stopped unsure exactly how to finish the sentence; another red droplet fell from above, it seemed to fall in slow motion to burst on impact with Acha's skin. The flickering firelight acted like an amplifier to the horror they saw, the lighting just perfect to create the most horrific scene they had ever set eyes upon.

Everywhere their vision turned was human flesh, ripped and torn to breaking point, forced to stretch beyond the realms of possibility by either the fine hooks or the strange webbing of silver saliva which seemed to support each of its victims. At least a hundred bodies hung suspended in grotesque, unnatural, positions, their bones disjointed, their flesh twisted where the hooks had penetrated. Despite the time which had passed since Aburamushi had taken them, not one of the bodies seemed to have decayed. They hung like fresh corpses, blood still dripping slowly from their open wounds.

Dark ringed, bloodshot eyes seemed to stare towards them accusingly with a piercing gaze which chilled them to the bone. It appeared as if these figures watched their every move from their twisted, disfigured, positions. In the flickering light, it seemed almost as if the congealed walls bled. In contrast the stone floor seemed almost dry, as if it had soaked the fluids into it like a sponge, leaving only the stains that were evident under each body. The figures watched them closely with what appeared to be a look of anticipation.

The red droplets of rain had started to fall more frequently, almost as if their presence had excited them, it fell now like a gentle shower. It was easy to convince themselves the movements they thought they saw were caused by the flames as they danced, but then, something happened which completely destroyed their comforting logic, they heard the first chain move.

It was a slow sound, it rang through the temple like the toll of a bell. It was only seconds before another joined the chilling chorus. The noise was quiet at first, perhaps a trick of the wind they reasoned, trying to ignore the rational side of their mind which told them, that down here, there was none. Then all fell silent once more, everything grew calm as the silence returned to reassure them what they heard, had indeed, only been a trick.

They walked the room carefully as they looked for whatever it could be that had brought them here, searching for a symbol, a key, anything they could be here to collect. They had to find it, they knew time grew short and not one of them wanted to join the ceiling artwork.

A hand reached down suddenly to swipe at the air before Acha, with this single attack, the room once again sprang into life. The chains above them began to shake as those held suspended started to fight and struggle, the death-like moans and screams of the tormented choir, echoed through the temple as they fought with quick unnatural movements, which stretched their skin further and further.

Acha became aware of another strange noise, a noise which did not belong to those suspended within this place, a noise which was neither chains, the dead, nor the crackling of the fire. A noise she should know but couldn't place.

A loud crack echoed through the air as Elly struck her, the action itself causing strange sparks to briefly appear in the air around them. It was only then, when the noise stopped, Acha realised it had come from her. Everything once more descended into an uneasy silence, but for how long, was a question none of them wished to ask.

"Do you want to join them," Elly hissed, nodding towards the ceiling. Acha's eyes were wide in terror as she shook her head slowly in reply. "Keep that up and you will be, or are you forgetting, there is a monster in the vicinity. It probably already knows we are here. Let us just get what we came for and go, before it decides to add us to its collection."

"We can't just leave them here, right?" Eiji looked between his friends for support. The screams they had released, those tortured cries, were the same as those he had heard when Aburamushi had come for him. He knew to leave them here would be wrong, inhumane.

To him, there was nothing more horrific than the thought of leaving those bodies to hang from the ceiling forever. His senses alone told him they weren't dead, not really, perhaps they were intended to appear that way, but there was no room in the realm of dreamers for beings who belonged with Hades. It was clear they were simply displayed this way, perhaps as a secondary punishment for their crimes.

There was no doubt in his mind at all, the people here were the residents of Abaddon, those ensnared by Marise Shi, surely this was their only chance to free them, to return them to their normal life, undoing the horror which had been forced upon them. "Right?" he questioned again with a little more power behind his voice as Daniel and Acha turned to look at Elly, after all she seemed to be the one with all the answers. It was clear it wouldn't be as easy as needing to find a way to unhook the victims. Not that scaling these smooth tiled walls wouldn't prove a challenge, but if this was truly Marise's doing, things would be far more complicated.

"Do you think Mari would just let anyone free her prisoners?" Elly looked straight at him in an attempt to ignore the urge to look again at the people above her. It reminded her of a twisted rendition of a famous cathedral she had seen as a child, but it, like most things, had been destroyed when the Old Gods' Era came to an end. If she were to make a reference to it, not one of them would understand, but she knew the placement of these bodies had to be more than just a coincidence, they were dealing with something very old.

"But she's not here, she wouldn't know," he protested as he looked again at the mothers, children, and families suspended above them in their gruesome positions, certain now they really did watch him.

"Although *she* may not be here, her magic is. It will not be as simple as just releasing them, her work is always secure. Any who try to tamper with her workings would be certain to regret it. Besides, this place is just a limbo, if you truly wanted to help them you could not do it here, it would have to be attempted at the origin of the spell, correct?" Elly turned to look at Zo, suddenly realising she had been very quiet since their descent. It was only then, as her eyes fell on her slumped figure, she realised why. Acha was at her side instantly, she touched her shoulder as she lay on the floor, at Acha's touch, much to their relief, she moved slightly.

It seemed she had been there some time, the blood from the earlier rain covered her hair and back, she seemed to have lacked the strength to move. It had been as if her body had failed her, she hadn't been sleeping, but nor could she claim to have been aware of anything which had transpired around her. Acha helped her into a sitting position.

"Zo," she gasped. "Are you okay?"

"I think, I overdid it," she whispered as she felt the familiar pain washing over her, similar to that she felt before but only on smaller parts of her body, parts which had been touched by the fresh blood as it had fallen. She managed to move her legs around to pull herself into a kneeling position. Acha helped her to her feet. It was a helping hand she had desperately needed, despite her previous efforts, she had lacked the strength to sit, let alone stand. The small orb shone dimly, following her every move as Acha helped her to regain her balance.

Daniel knew better than to crowd her, instead he carefully examined a figure which had caught his attention. She appeared so life-like, yet unlike the others she clearly was not. She had made no attempt to move or struggle like those above them had previously, this figure had stayed motionless the entire time.

The girl looked somehow familiar, her long golden-brown curls fell just short of her chest, her eyes, although filled with blood, still had within them the slightest hints of baby blue. He knew without a doubt she wasn't a native of Abaddon.

In the few seconds of laying eyes on her, the image had robbed him of all those years he had believed it would be peaceful to die during sleep. He had not yet come to realise that which Eiji had previously. Had he, he may have executed a little more caution. Suddenly, her name left his lips, plucked from the air as he concentrated on her image, he knew it was her name, he remembered her.

"Liza." As he heard himself speak, he realised why she looked so familiar, she had been on the missing poster board for perhaps two weeks now. A place he regularly checked in case, one day, it held a picture of his friend. She was the daughter of a well-known family, it was thought her disappearance may have been due to kidnappers, although there had been rumours she had run away to escape her world and live with the one she wished to marry.

Her body was suspended like the others from above by barbed hooks, but she was strung more like a marionette. Her feet dangled barely inches from the floor as she hung in a crucifix position, although the horror of the painful demise did not stop there, moments before her death, her stomach had been split, forcing all which rested within it to fall with gravity. The blood was fresh, Daniel was willing to wager her flesh was barely cold, but he lacked the stomach and courage to test his theory.

"I think, maybe that's what we're after." Daniel pointed into the cavity created by what used to be the girl's stomach. Within it was a small, circular, blood-soaked object. Even from a few feet away, Daniel could make out the symbol on the stone rune. "Sacrifice." He looked to Zo as he spoke the words. "This whole place exists because of Marise, it makes me wonder if this Darrienia situation is her doing as well. It's certainly twisted enough." Daniel stepped back to give her some room as she motioned for him to step aside. It seemed she had now regained her composure.

"No, I don't think so." Zo responded in a quiet whisper as she moved within reaching distance of the corpse. Something about the symbol called to her, she knew she had to be the one to take it. Everything fell silent except for the pounding of her heart within her mind. It beat so loudly, seeming to increase in both rhythm and volume with each step she took.

Slowly she extended her arm towards the figure, the light before her ensured she saw more details, more pieces of the human anatomy, than she cared to. She closed her eyes tightly as her fingers sealed around the object, Zo cried out in pain as the girl's blood dripped on her flesh, it felt like something restrained her while it tore open her stomach with its bare hands. She tried to will her body to move, but the pain rooted her in place. Something moved inside the girl causing a fresh flood of pain as more blood spilt upon her. With this movement, the figure's head shifted, to turn sharply, unnaturally, to look at her, try as she might she could not move.

Eiji grabbed the back of her cloak pulling her back sharply, at least five of the hooks which suspended the bodies shot from somewhere to one side of them. It was only thanks to his quick reflexes, brought on by his understanding of this place, that only one had actually pierced her. They looked to its source as they heard the sounds of moving chains, unaware they had barely missed a glimpse of the shadow as it moved.

The girl's arms swiped violently but due to the restraints holding her she lacked the mobility needed to strike, her hand passing just inches away from Zo's horrified face.

"Stay still." Eiji whispered as he looked at the blood running from Zo's arm. The wire seemed to tighten as if it tried to pull her somewhere, he bent slowly to unfasten the knife from his boot, watching for any tell-tale signs of movement.

There was a sharp pang with an unsettling undertone of something soft and organic as the wire he cut recoiled. Elly took the rune from Zo, wiping the blood from her in one clean motion. No sooner had she stepped aside, the pain stopped. It was something Elly had done with such autonomy it made Zo question again the nature of their previous relationship. The sympathetic touch was something she kept private, most people, even those with a basic knowledge of magic, didn't realise its existence.

"It has got to come out." Eiji squeezed the flesh around the hook hard enough to increase the flow of blood. For the first time he felt genuine sympathy for her, he hadn't realised it until then, but she had the healer's curse. It made him wonder how Marise could have taken so many lives. The sympathetic touch would have surely made such acts unbearable. He looked at Zo, who was still trembling. The skill was powerful, but it never normally affected people in this manner. From what he was led to believe, they would be aware of the discomfort, but still be able to move and function in order to treat the sufferer. Perhaps, for some reason, this place interfered with her magic on a level they couldn't understand.

"Erm, guys?" Daniel almost whispered, unheard by any.

"It'll hafta go right through." Eiji stated examining the serrated edge. He knew this was the only choice, it reminded him of the many times he had caught himself on a fishing hook. He would now do for her, what his master had done for him. There was something disturbing, organic, about its structure, almost as if each tiny spike was a tooth or claw from a greater creature.

"Guys?" Daniel repeated a little louder, but again it seemed no one heard him, perhaps if they had seen the horrified look on his face, or his ghastly pallor, they would have paid more attention.

"Ready?" Zo nodded closing her eyes tightly as Eiji began to push and turn the hook, she bit her lip as the pain exploded through her arm, a pain with no comparison to that she had felt when she had taken the rune from the girl's body, or unknowingly pressed her hands against a blood drenched wall, but it hurt none-the-less.

When the hook was removed he dropped it to the floor, unaware Elly had quickly collected it and slid it into her pocket. She was not so foolish as to leave something which could be used for enchantments in a place belonging to such a beast. Especially considering that if the beast's summoner was to die in just the right way, it was possible it would be granted immortality, who knew what such a thing born from Hades would be capable of.

"Guys!" Daniel's voice echoed around the temple as it bounced off the walls several times, by the time it had faded he had their full attention. He pointed towards the one detail which had gone unnoticed against the camouflage of blood. The fresh dripping trail, left by the inhabitant of this twisted nest, that had moved across the floor to mount the wall beside the hole, had never actually passed through it. "The creature never left the chamber." His tone once more dropped to a lowered whisper, the same kind of tone expected from a child who was afraid of being caught doing something it shouldn't. Not that his lowered tones really mattered, all of them had made so much noise it was impossible to believe they had been unheard.

A single drop of blood fell from above to smear Acha's cheek. They knew the area they stood to be free from the suspended corpses. Their relocation had been a deliberate attempt to avoid further attacks. This single drop meant they could no longer deceive themselves into believing the attack on Zo had been nothing more than a trap triggered by her movements. Knowing this, all but Acha stared fearfully into the darkness above.

Although masked by the shadows, the pair of eyes looking down upon them from the ceiling were clearly visible. It was then they ran. Eiji jumped up and down as he tried desperately to scale the hole from which their rope had not only been removed, but kindly wrapped into a coil on the floor. Elly grabbed his arm pulling him towards a dead end, her hand striking down on a stone. Above them the grinding sound of moving rock echoed as Eiji's waving arms beckoned the others towards them. Elly shoved him up the appearing staircase as the stone wall slid to one side, revealing a spiral ascent. One by one she hurried them through to emerge beneath where the temple's deity had stood.

Eiji fled to the door banging on it in the hope that it would open, yet, just like before, it stood firm. He rattled the handle several times, after all, hadn't Zo said it could be opened from the inside? Meanwhile as they saw this path was blocked, Elly and Acha ran to the passage they had first walked to gain entrance to this central area, only to discover the same style of bars, which had blocked their way from the first chamber, now sealed all their exits.

Elly grabbed Zo, who had stayed completely still near the hole since their ascent, waiting for the creature to emerge, ensuring it was unable to make a move towards any of her friends while they searched for the exit. As Elly pulled her away, the creature simply sat and watched them, its eyes just visible through the depths of the hole. It followed their movements like a cat hunting a mouse. Elly pushed her towards the doorway, none of them could penetrate the bars, however, there was one of them who could breach the threshold.

"Sword, now," she commanded shoving Zo ahead of them with a force which nearly made her lose her already fragile balance. Despite stumbling a few steps, the sword was drawn on command. A strange light filled the air momentarily as its blade of darkness and light formed, the glowing orb before her appeared to fade slightly as the blade was summoned.

The door seemed to shatter even before the sword had touched it, although she was sure this was just a figment of her imagination, something about it disturbed her. It hadn't felt as if contact had been made with it at all. She had a very bad feeling about what had just happened, one which started deep in the pit of her stomach. As the strike followed through the sword faded into a fine wisp to leave her holding the drawn hilt.

"I would keep it drawn, just in case." Elly stated as she hurried them out of the temple.

"It's not like I had a choice." Zo gasped as she started to run. As always, Daniel grabbed her hand, but she started to fall behind. He glanced towards her, wondering if this was really the same girl who could easily run for miles, for her, this level of exhaustion was unnatural. It was almost as if every step she took was an enormous effort, he seemed to be literally dragging her along after him, his lead forcing her steps.

He didn't need to glance behind to confirm his fears, yet for some reason he still did, the creature had followed them. There was still a good distance between them, but this gap was closing quickly. Its movements were as unnatural as the tangled mass of bones and muscle which constructed it. Despite its awkward build, it moved swiftly in pursuit. It was not a creature of their world, but they already knew that, they knew it was a creature pulled from the very centre of the underworld, a summoning. But knowing the thing that chased them should never be, knowing the very principal of it, scientifically speaking, was impossible, did not comfort them at all. The creature was neither human nor beast, and they were in Darrienia, the very place monstrosities like this could freely roam.

From the brief glimpses they caught as they ran, they saw it held the appearance of a skinned creature, and no matter how illogical or unreal the creature was, it did not change the fact it pursued them. As it gave chase its organs moved, trembling with its every step. There was something playful in its movements, and despite its awkwardness it gained, yet then, as if toying with them it slowed, allowing them to increase the gap between them.

The twisted form of man merged with beast pursued on its hind legs, running with a canine gait, baring its enormous, jagged fangs in a wicked snarl. With the imbalance of the strange limbs it seemed at times its rear would overtake the human hands used for forwards balance. An alteration of its unnatural stride quickly amended this, despite the apparent clumsiness of its sprint, its speed was remarkable.

"How come it left the temple? I thought it was restrained." Eiji gasped as he put in a little extra effort to stop himself from falling behind. It seemed last place in this race for life belonged to Zo as Daniel pulled her along desperately. Eiji reflected on how they seemed to have done nothing but run since they had first arrived; first from that dragon and now this.

"It seems its creator released it." Elly answered, avoiding the urge to glance behind them. She had known by having Zo break the door, any restraints which bound it would have been broken, but she hadn't expected it to pursue them with such intent. She had thought on gaining its freedom, in an attempt to avoid being banished, it would have simply retreated. "I warned you Mari encrypted things, or maybe it is hunting, after all, it is free to hunt." Eiji knowing what he did, already knew more than he wanted to. He turned his vision forwards and suddenly noticed there seemed to be a sixth member to their group, a figure who seemed to lead their escape through the forest barely a few paces ahead of them.

The creature remained in pursuit as they ran. When they had entered the forest earlier, they had only seemed to have walked for minutes, yet now it seemed to stretch endlessly before them. It was clear, not only were they lost somewhere deep within the forest, but the creature merely toyed with them, allowing them to think they had a chance of escape when clearly there was none.

It knew eventually it would have them, it was the same thought that raced through each of their minds as the gap began to close. How could you fight such a creation? It should be dead, yet it lived. As a being summoned from the underworld, it would live until its creator banished it, it discovered a way to become immortal, or the binds of the spell which summoned it were severed, or decayed.

The distance between them began to close, a gap this time they found difficult to widen as the creature drew closer by the second. It seemed it had stopped playing.

"There's no way we can outrun it." Daniel gasped. The energy he expended as he tried to keep Zo with him had begun to take its toll. Her hand suddenly jerked from his as she tripped and fell. He skidded to a halt, as did those who ran before him. Zo sat up quickly, turning her body to face the creature. "Zo!" He turned back towards her, hoping he could reach her before the creature did, but before he could even move it was upon her.

* * *

Night appeared before Eryx Venrent, who immediately rose from the old beaten chair which stood before the recently lit log fire. Eryx had been wondering how long it would take for one of his minions to pay him a visit, but for Night himself to arrive was something he had not expected. He ran his hand around the back of the chair, willing his old bones to move to face the area he felt the unmistakable power radiate from. A tired smile crossed his wrinkled brow as he faced the direction he knew the god stood.

"You truly are a man of your word. I thought maybe you would have had your minions descend upon me, after all, they've been watching me for some time now, ever since I..." The elderly man paused deciding it was better not to proceed with the direction of the conversation. "Yet, you stand before me smelling of promise." The old man gave a slight respectful bow.

Night did not speak, he simply watched for a moment. Time had not been kind to the man who stood before him. He and Eryx had once been great friends, until the day he had betrayed him, an act he would never forgive. For this, Eryx had paid a heavy price, Night had taken his vision and had vowed to complete his revenge when the time suited him. Although this did not mean when they were in each other's company things were unpleasant between them, in fact, Night was quite civil. He addressed the business at hand politely, but one day, Eryx knew he would make true his threat, it was a day he awaited.

"I have to wonder, what a mighty power such as yourself could want with a child like our Zo." Eryx asked the question, he knew but part of the answer, he knew part of the reason Night would seek her, but even without his sight, he could see there was something more to this than he knew.

"All in good time old friend, first I have to deliver that which I promised in exchange for your service." Night was beside him before Eryx had even felt him move, he felt the draught of air pass before him as the god gestured his hand before his sightless eyes. As he did so something changed, he felt it start deep within him, then all at once the darkness became a little lighter. "Do not strain yourself, to see after such a long time is a shock to the system."

The old man felt his way back to sit in his chair. He could almost make out the flickering light of the fire before him, this was more than he had seen for over twenty years. Anticipation filled the air around him, he could already distinguish colours, shapes, everything was coming back far quicker than he first expected.

"Tell me, what are your plans for Zoella?"

"I'm sure all will become clear in time, first a drink." He touched the old man's hand guiding his fingers around the tall glass. "Your promised youth will be found at the bottom of this, the process may take an hour or so, maybe less.

"As for sweet Kezia's child, she was born for one true purpose, to serve me. It has been some time since you have seen her, correct?" Night smiled, passing a picture to the old man. Eryx squinted finding a slight amount of focus on the parchment. As it became a little clearer, he stared at the drawing open mouthed. She was almost the reflection of her mother, her long brown hair held the same warm red glow reflecting the warmth and kindness of her heart, it was tied back loosely, the shorter layers fell to frame her face. Her eyes however, unlike Kezia's, were a stunning blue, a trait that without a doubt came from her father.

She knelt by a cabin, a trowel in her hand, she smiled brightly as she tended to the garden. She had her mother's smile, a smile so warm and friendly it reflected in her eyes. No matter how you felt, whenever Kezia had smiled there was nothing to do but return it, just seeing it would brighten the darkest day.

"I was surprised by how quickly she had matured, I never thought a year's training would have been adequate, but something happened which proved me wrong." The old man passed the picture back to him and smiled, maybe a girl of such pure heart and soul could bring a softness back to his eye. It was clear how much he cared for her, maybe she could ease his temper and calm his rage.

"Gods rest my heart, she looks just like her mother, how Kezia would smile to see." He took another mouthful of the sweet tasting liquid, it reminded him of a fine mead he had once sampled in his younger days.

"The resemblance is remarkable, this was done six months ago when we were looking for her. You see, she somehow vanished from Blackwood's care and ended up in Crowley, no memory of her reign."

"Reign? What a strange word you choose to use."

"Indeed. Anyway, I must depart, I have many things to attend to old sir."

"Forgive me for asking, but for this favour is my debt cleared?" The old man shuddered as he heard Night laugh, it was a deep haunting laugh which could drain the life from his very body if that was his desire.

"Cleared? I have paid you for your favour, this is no more than an exchange of goods for a service. Surely a trader such as yourself should recognise this. The Epiales have watched you for some time plotting how to carry out my revenge. Of course, they could not approach since you could sense them. You'll find with your sight restored that sixth sense of yours will quickly vanish. With your new-found youth, who knows, maybe we will have another lifetime to continue our games."

With those final words Night vanished, leaving the old man with a sinking feeling in the pit of his stomach. He knew one day he would have to answer to Night's judgement and he had just been deceiving himself in believing this single act would atone for what he had done. He had fooled himself into believing their friendship of old may offer some redemption, but considering what he had done, he knew he deserved whatever he was dealt.

The old man sat back on his chair, his mind wandering back over the day. Before he knew what was happening, voices ran through his mind, he had no choice but to listen.

'*I have about a ten-year gap... I awoke in an unfamiliar place.*' Her voice echoed in his head as images of the past began to race through his mind. He travelled back eleven years. It was Zo's twelfth birthday but she wasn't to have a celebration, no one wanted to be acquainted with her kind. Instead she left for the Blackwood academy. How her mother had shone with pride.

'*She somehow vanished from Blackwood's care and ended up in Crowley.*'

'*No memory of her reign.*'

'*No memory at all of the last ten years.*'

'*I never thought a year's training would have been adequate.*'

Just over ten years ago Marise Shi had first appeared, she had been a child of thirteen and deadly beyond her years, it was rumoured she worked for a lord by the name of Blackwood, although those who uttered the accusation only spoke it once.

He awoke in a cold sweat unaware of when his consciousness had left him. As he lay on the floor in front of the extinguished embers, his entire body shook. He was unsure where those dreams had come from, but they had brought with them a deep terror, one which gave birth to a feeling of dread as he realised what he had been too foolish to see before. Night didn't care about Zo for the reasons he had first thought, he cared about her because of her power. If he manipulated events carefully he could not only obtain the Grimoire, he could use her to train his armies as a commander to his reign. Was this really the truth behind why he sought her?

"By the Gods, what have I done?" He raised his once wrinkled hand to cover his face, a face which now possessed the texture of youth, but even youth was of little comfort to him now he knew the price of his actions.

"Why didn't I see it before?" he questioned. "The dates were there, but this old fool was blind in many ways. Too blind to see the awful truth that lay before me so clearly, what curse have I bestowed upon Zo, upon our world?"

In his hand he still held Night's elixir. Standing at a speed his old bones would have defied he cursed, smashing the glass which had housed the poisonous temptation into the fire. Had he realised this before, he would never have agreed to the proposition, he now knew the true terrors he had helped to release. He had but one choice, and that was to try to stop her before anything happened. He wondered if perhaps she would listen to reason, the Zo he knew would, if it wasn't already too late, he had to tell her everything.

From the distance he felt them, Night's minions still watched, he had to rectify the situation before the sense repelling them faded. Mere hours had passed and already his senses had become so much weaker, then again, knowing Night as he did, he doubted his revenge would be instantaneous, after all, as Night himself had stated, he could have another lifetime of waiting.

* * *

Zo felt its sickening breath upon her face as it sniffed the air around her, its hands resting on her shoulders as it pinned her down with the weight of its body, its hind legs straddled her. It glanced up towards her companions baring its teeth as it snarled viciously, warning them away.

"What should we do?" an unfamiliar voice whispered. They turned to look at the stranger, his short brown hair dishevelled from their retreat, yet somehow still looked styled in its chaotic form. His questioning eyes seemed so dark against his pale complexion. He stood amongst them almost as if he had been there all along. "We have to kill it before it harms her." Eiji stepped forwards to the challenge, as he began to focus a light breeze began to rise around them.

"No!" Elly commanded grabbing his arm in order to break his concentration. "Wait." As much as she feared what this could mean, she had to trust in the creature, trust it would know its creator and consequently still its aggression. They knew for certain Zo lacked the energy to repel it, her poor attempt at their escape had proven that. She lay now, eyes wide in terror as she struggled for breath, yet there seemed to be a certain calmness to her. A single tear left the corner of her eye as she looked upon it. It was almost as if they shared a silent understanding, a conversation hidden amidst the chaos.

Obeying Elly was their only option, her guidance was respected as her decisions and reasoning so often proved infallible, they could only hope this remained true. The creature snarled and growled as it repeatedly sniffed the air. Eiji shifted uncomfortably as he waited for a signal, for a command which meant he could do something, anything, to get the horrific creature away from them, away from her. Despite who she was, at this moment he felt the need to protect her. The girl who lay restrained was not the murderer Marise Shi, regardless of the things he didn't understand, she was not that assassin.

The creature looked at Zo as it tilted its head to one side to study her carefully. Its white eyes seeming to absorb every detail, her copper low-lighted hair, her fearful blue eyes spilling with tears. It took in everything to the smear of blood on her right cheek which she had, unknown to her, wiped from her hands to her face. It was the blood from inside the temple, the blood which had caused her the immense pain as she first entered, but it had dried now, as had effects of the sympathetic touch.

Without warning its tongue stretched out to lick her cheek, leaving behind a trail of saliva and blood, but Zo did not move, she did not make a sound. Her eyes simply gazed up in awestruck horror as her body trembled.

Then, for no apparent reason, it quickly dismounted moving to stand beside where she lay. It gave her arm a gentle nudge with its muzzle. She lay unmoving, simply staring up into the green foliage. She lay there long after the creature's weight had moved, long after it had nudged her to prompt a response. She lay there until finally she found the strength to move. Her eyes stared blankly ahead, the creature seemed to watch over her as she pulled herself to her knees. There was something almost protective about the way it now behaved, it seemed eager for her to stand, refusing to stray from her side. All the time it continued to look towards the group, growling with murderous intent. It stood beside her for a moment longer as she regained her balance, her vision now fixed on the blood-stained grass, as she supported her weight against a nearby tree.

It glanced to her before quickly returning to its pursuit of her friends, who, for whatever reason, remained rooted to the spot as the creature advanced towards them. For a second, Zo could only stare at the place the creature had been, but then, all of a sudden, like coming out of a trance something inside her snapped.

"Enough!" she screamed, the echo of her voice ricocheted around the deserted forest. The creature stopped on command and simply stared at the place its prey stood. She looked to her friends before seeing the newcomer amongst them, the stranger's eyes locked coldly with Zo's. She found her hand rested on her sword's hilt instinctively as the stranger glanced to the creature and back to her again. The creature padded the ground uncertainly and like the stranger, looked between her and them as if waiting for a command. Zo swayed slightly despite the tree's support, the ball of light before her chest illuminated her ghastly pallor, her pale skin now further enhanced by the dark streaks of blood left by the creature.

Eiji seized the moment of confusion and completed what he had started, the air grew dense, darker, as a pale ash descended around them. It thickened the air until nothing could be seen. Zo felt an arm grab her, she tried to fight it, but she was too weak to resist.

Eiji led the way, parting the ash around them as they walked, finally they emerged from the forest near a deep, crystal clear stream. It made a soothing sound as the shallower parts of the water washed over the protruding rocks. Through the crystal waters, making their homes near the central most point, small, fragile looking fish darted frantically beneath the surface. They were fortunate the creature had not forced their retreat into these waters, for even the smallest creatures within this world could prove deadly.

"Who are you?" Acha was the first to ask what the others had been desperate to know since the stranger's appearance. This was the first time, since he had mysteriously joined them, that they had a chance to breathe, and it was the first matter to be addressed.

"My name's Abi." Elly's posture seemed to stiffen slightly at his words. He looked around the group, almost as if he expected to be met with recognition, he gave a boyish smile when he received none.

"Abi? That's an unusual name for a boy." Acha commented before she could stop herself, there was a moment of silence before he answered.

"It's short for Gabriel, I never liked it much." He ruffled his hair uncomfortably as he flashed her a charming smile. "I really ought to thank you for what you did back there, you saved me from that creature."

"How?" Elly questioned suspiciously, her narrowed eyes clearly reflecting the emotion she felt. She wasn't going to let him get what he wanted so easily, but at the same time, she wanted to see how this developed.

"You didn't see me? I... I was hiding. You see, I got trapped in the temple. While the creature was on the prowl, I thought I could save some of the people, but I couldn't get back out. It knew I was there, but it couldn't find me." He looked to Zo, squinting at the light which still shone before her. "He was so close to finding me when you appeared, if not for you and your distraction I never would have escaped."

He moved to join Acha as she knelt by the riverbank, he watched her for a moment as she washed the blood stains from her skin. As Zo approached him, he shifted uncomfortably.

"I'm sorry to ask, but can't you do something about that light, after being in the dark so long, it hurts my eyes." He gave them a quick rub as if to enforce his words, turning her back to him she shook her head gently. Daniel looked to her, she didn't quite seem like herself, she seemed troubled. He approached, placing his hand on her shoulder, she gave him a weary smile, which soon turned into a yawn as Elly spoke.

"We need to cross the river, who knows how long it will take for that creature to track us down again." They followed her downstream, the sounds of the water as it raced over the rocky riverbed seemed to lull them. So much so they hadn't noticed the distance they had travelled, or the time which had passed.

An old bridge arched over the river in the distance. It was the kind of bridge seen in children's drawings, the perfect semicircle stretching from one side to the other. When they reached it, Elly was the first to cross, the stranger looked at it hesitantly a frown crinkling his brow.

"I can't cross this," he stated sadly looking to Acha, something about him seemed so young, so scared.

"What do you mean, is there something you need to do?" she questioned, hesitating just before the bridge.

"No, nothing like that, it's just..." he gave a sigh. "How do I explain this? I know I'm asleep, that this is all within my dream, and somehow, since you turned up I have been lucid dreaming, but unlike you, I can't walk into the boundaries of other people's dreams.

"Yet I fear if you leave me, it will find me again. It will never let me escape, and I will never wake from my coma. I'm sure my family must be worried, I have been sealed in this area for what seems like years." He wrapped his arms around himself as if the thought of the creature chilled him.

"For years, were you sheltering in there all this time?" Acha questioned with sympathy.

"No, I was hiding, running from that creature as it hunted, it's like I have been trapped in a nightmare and unless my family can find the cure, the only way for me to wake is to break the seal of this dream, to cross from this boundary into a normal dream from which I can wake. But to do that I need the mark."

"The mark?" Acha tilted her head to one side before she realised what he meant. "How... well what would you need to do to be able to come along with us?"

"I'm sorry, I bet this sounds silly, I mean I doubt you are trapped here, I've had a lot of time to think about what's happened. Only those bearing the mark, like you, may pass it on to others so they can aid them in their adventures. I can be useful, won't you take me with you? I mean I may wake once I cross the boundary, but what's to say we can't meet again in this world, or ours? Perhaps I can repay you then." He begged. Without warning he took Acha's hand in his, with no time to react she was once more grateful for the gloves.

"What do I need to do?" Something about the request made her feel uncomfortable. It reminded her of a story she had once been told, about a troll who had been sealed within a cave. The only way it could leave was if someone were to take its place. After much planning it had tricked a young boy into doing so. Leaving him sealed inside the cave while the troll took his freedom.

"That's simple," he smiled, giving her a small knife, "you just need to give me the symbol, then we can all cross the bridge, together," he said as if reading her fears. Acha smiled at his answer, the blood had already begun to drip from his arm when Zo spoke.

"No." Her voice seemed so weak, so distant, and despite her words, she was unsure the reasoning behind them. Her reaction had been one of tired fear. She was still trying to understand the events involving the strange creature. It seemed almost surreal and she was still having problems organising her thoughts. "I mean, do you think it's such a—" By the time she had spoken it was already too late, they had started to cross the bridge.

"I don't know how to thank you!" he exclaimed as he reached the other side. He ruffled his hair again and looked at Zo, who had just joined them on the other side of the running water. "I know." He stepped towards her, as he did so she unconsciously mirrored his step in the opposite direction to his advance. She didn't know why, but she felt extremely threatened by this stranger. "I know a few tricks. I'm sure I can put that light of yours out, if you wish." He took another step, again she felt herself retreat. "It won't hurt. It's just a quick reversal. Please, it's the least I can do after all you've done for me, and it seems to be causing you some problems." His hands reached out to position themselves either side of the glowing orb. Zo frowned, wondering exactly when he had managed to gain ground on her. For some unknown reason, the idea of this light being removed did not appeal to her. Regardless how ill this particular magic made her feel. Despite the fact she was tired, weak, and unable to remove it herself, she didn't trust him.

"Thea." Seiken stepped from the shadows of forest beside her, she stepped back just before Abi's hands closed around the orb. "Your magic here is very different to that in your world. It is connected to you. As the possessor of the sacrifice rune, every piece of magic you do affects you from the moment you entered this world. Although you did not possess it at the time, it is the rune you are here to receive, your key, you each have one.

"Take this illumination you created for example, it is not simply a collection of particles that emit light as it would be in your world. It is a light projected from your soul. If it were to be extinguished, you in turn would die. To destroy your magic, is to destroy you.

"Another thing you should be cautious of, it takes a lot more effort to sustain magic here. To use it for any length of time is potentially deadly. To be honest, I am surprised you have the tolerance to use it in this environment at all. Not many can outside their dreams so it didn't occur to me to warn you." Zo stepped further back, her hands moved to protectively shield the light.

"But Abi knew that," she whispered as she looked accusingly at the figure, suddenly her mind seemed to clear. "You!" she snarled; he laughed seeing the recognition in her eyes. "That creature wasn't after us, it was after you. It was the guardian, the being summoned to protect the innocent, to keep you in order," Zo snapped, pointing her finger towards him. Her friends turned to look at the stranger in surprise.

"Pity it can't cross boundaries isn't it? I guess the great summoner never thought I would be released." He took a swipe at the orb once more, his hand barely missed, thanks only to Seiken's quick reflexes as he swept his legs from beneath him. Quickly rising to his feet, he looked to each of them in turn as if committing them to his memory, still smiling as he did so. "Again, I thank you for your help," he laughed, dusting himself down. "In return, I shall spare you, this time."

With those words he vanished like a dreamer waking from their sleep. Somehow, they knew this part of his life-force was being reunited with its ties to their world.

Acha, realising what she had done, felt the bloody knife slip from her hand. As it struck the ground, it vanished.

"I don't understand what just happened?" Acha turned to look at Zo, her face seemed to show the reminiscence of a smile. She knew it was nothing more a trick of the light, that horrible light which, it turned out, was projected from her life-force. It was little wonder sustaining it had made her so tired.

"That creature wasn't after us, it was after Abi. Aburamushi is a shape shifter. It can assume the form of most life-forms. Although Marise was cruel there was also another side to her. To ensure the summoning only posed a threat to a certain area a guardian was created. One which could scare even the bravest of men, because of this only the ignorant and foolish would venture into its lair," Zo stated suddenly to the confusion of her friends. Elly and Eiji both turned to look at her sharply.

"Why didn't you say anything before, when we were at the temple, or before I gave him passage through the boundaries?" Acha demanded, the guilt in her voice ringing clear.

"I didn't know. The guardian told me its story. It tried to warn me, but I couldn't understand what it was saying. It spoke in an ancient tongue. It's taken me this long to translate," she lied slightly as she glanced across to Elly. She had understood all too well every word it had spoken and considering the circumstances, why wouldn't she have? "Maybe Elly should have told you about it." As if meeting Zo's accusation they all turned to look at her.

"I did not know." She lowered her vision slightly to look at the ground as she spoke. "*She* never told me!" she snapped, turning away from them as she made her way back to the central point of the bridge. If what Zo had just revealed about the guardian was true, it was an action unlike the Marise she knew, it left her wondering what other secrets the guardian could have whispered. Elly glanced towards the sky, it had already grown late. Staying on the bridge would be the safest option, especially considering the area.

"But why was it sealed away in the first place?" Acha questioned.

"You saw for yourself how manipulative it is. Unrestrained it could pose a great threat. To have something like that without boundaries would not be a good thing. It needs to be banished, or at least the original spell reversed to reduce its power." Elly looked towards Zo who now sat on the edge of the bridge looking very tired. She turned a small rune over in her hands, staring at it unseeingly. Strangely, Elly couldn't remember returning it to her. She felt in her pocket confirming both it and the small pouch she had stored it in had been removed.

"I think maybe we have done enough damage. It's getting late." Zo spoke wearily as she placed the rune into a small empty pouch which now hung around her neck. "I'm feeling quite tired."

"My thoughts exactly. We should stop here tonight, and when we get home we should head for Abaddon," Elly stated.

"And besides," added Daniel as he moved to sit beside Zo. "If what Seiken said about magic is correct, the sooner we get back the better." He smiled at her as they made themselves comfortable, each swallowing the berry offered to them.

Chapter 9

The Truth

"How dare you? What in the name of Hades were you thinking?" Zo challenged the moment Elly's figure appeared in the bed. She did not even pause to consider how strange it was to watch a person materialise from thin air. It wasn't important, not now. There was only one thing on her mind and she wanted answers. Elly sat up, involuntarily squinting against the light which radiated from the angry looking silhouette standing at the bottom of her bed.

Zo, her aura alone indicating her white hot rage, banished the magic without a word. With the light removed, Elly could now clearly see her fierce figure standing with her fists clenched at her side, her eyes filled with anger as she awaited her response.

"What—" Elly rubbed her eyes swinging her legs from the bed. Before she could speak any further Zo interrupted.

"Don't you realise how dangerous it was? Do you think if I would have known..." she lowered her voice as her friends sneaked past the door. They *had* been on the way to meet them but, having heard the angry tones, they knew better than to disturb them.

"What are you talking about?" Elly stretched, glancing around the room as she seized this opportunity of silence to finish her earlier question. She asked despite knowing this outburst clearly had something to do with what that creature had told her. With Annabel's death, there was no way to tell exactly what she knew.

"I should have known," Zo continued as if she had not heard the question, ignoring Elly's look of complete bewilderment as she further lowered her tone to ensure her friends would not hear. Harshly, yet quietly, she continued.

"The first day we met, you called me Mari!" She turned her back to Elly to hide the tears. Saying it had been more difficult than she expected. Even the rage didn't cushion the blow from hearing the words spoken aloud. "Did you really think you could keep something like that from me, did you think I wouldn't find out?"

Elly stared at her in disbelief, hardly able to believe the words she had spoken. Given the change in plans it was too soon for her to know. When they had found her and there hadn't been a trace of Marise present, the entire plan had been revised. When the time came for her to discover the truth, it should have already been too late to make a difference. The potion she had taken from Venrent was to ensure a controlled release of the memories. This complicated matters.

"Mari, I... how *did* you find out?" The only thing she could be thankful for was the discovery seemed detached from her memories. Zo seemed to grieve the discovery, but had no real memories of that time. At least that was one thing still in their favour.

"The guardian told me. You know the one *I* created. Although it spoke in its ancient tongue, I understood its every word. Over and over it called me master. It was then I realised, the places I knew, the information I recalled, it could only mean one thing.

"I'm a fool for not realising sooner. Then again, who would want discover they are, now how did Daniel put it? Oh yes, a bloodthirsty murderer!" she spat. Although her words were only quiet, the anger behind them made even Elly flinch. She had known at the time those words would come back to haunt them. "Why was it you came to me really, was I even in any real danger, or was it all just staged to get my cooperation, you came to take me back didn't you? You came so you could hand me over to your father."

Zo didn't understand anything, her mind raced with doubts and fears. How could she, the person who had dedicated her life to healing, become a ruthless assassin, just what had happened during those years of darkness, what had she become?

It was confusing. She wanted to believe it to be nothing more than a lie, but she knew the truth, and no amount of denial could change it. All those times she had asked to remember something of her past, all the time she had spent trying to recall the simplest thing, she had also been afraid of what the darkness concealed. Now she knew the name of the monster who lurked there she feared, more than anything, that she would become the very thing she despised the most. If that was who she was back then, who she had really become, what could she do to stop it? Surely it was only a matter of time before her old self returned, then what would happen to her friends, would she even remember them, or would they be erased like her memories of her time as that killer?

"Not you—" Elly covered her mouth realising what she had said. She had been caught off guard. She cursed her idiocy as Zo's posture stiffened, those two words had revealed Elly's true purpose, she turned to leave. "No, wait, you do not understand," she called after her.

Elly cursed under her breath, she hadn't been prepared for this. Initially she had expected, as had been planned, that Marise would awaken and return the Zo persona only when her services were required. She knew it was going to be tricky to keep her plans a secret, especially since Zo's friends had accompanied them, but there had been no reason for her to learn the truth, not yet. She was going to vanish again soon anyway, things couldn't have gone worse.

"Oh, I understand perfectly." Zo spoke quietly, not looking back as she stopped briefly at the door.

"I was not—" The slamming door halted the need for further words. She waited, listening to the hurried steps down the stairs. Once she was certain of her privacy her hand gripped her gossip crystal. Time was short. Zo's next actions were unpredictable, but there was something she needed to do before she could smooth this over.

There was a very real danger her reaction to this discovery could rush her own extinction. There was possibly still an option open to them. She just had to confirm its viability.

Zo stormed down the stairs, a strange hollow feeling rising in the pit of her stomach. She just wanted to get away, to leave it all behind. Back then, during the time she had forgotten, she had taken the lives of countless people. As she thought about the dark void of her past, for the first time, she was glad she couldn't remember it, glad she still recalled no more than before. She questioned how it could it have happened. Despite her difficulties, she had led a good life. She had even been accepted into a renowned school of the artes, although, from what she could remember, she *had* been the only student there.

She frowned intently willing herself to remember more, how could she possibly be a bloodthirsty murderer? No, it was wrong, it had to be a mistake, but even she couldn't bring herself to accept this wishful lie. Just what was going on, and what was this strange feeling in the back of her mind since discovering the truth? Something hidden in the darkest recess of her mind stirred. It seemed to offer to take her away from the pain, and all she had to do was surrender.

"Zo are you okay, what's happened?" Daniel stepped before her, placing his hands on her shoulders. Suddenly she became aware of her friends, aware that since she had joined them, she had simply paced back and forth along the side of the table, trying to make sense of the new thoughts and questions which stampeded through her mind.

They were thoughts which made her feel physically sick, in fact, she wasn't sure how she had managed to remain calm. Then again, she was certain she didn't seem calm to anyone else, but this was as composed as she could force herself to be as she realised the true meaning behind this revelation. Just how many people had she killed? Eiji had said an entire town, and before that, after that? She felt the room closing in around her as icy cold waves washed over her and stole her breath. She needed to get out of there.

She looked up to Daniel, his firm grip on her preventing her retreat. Until then her sole focus had been on her hands as she paced, wondering how many lives they had taken, questioning how many lives she was responsible for destroying. She felt like she needed him more than ever, but he couldn't make the truth any less real.

This discovery meant her friends were in danger, not just from the journey, but from her. They had to leave. Regardless of what their absence would mean for her, *they* had to be safe. She needed to distance herself from them, while she still thought about them as her friends, and not as her next target. Already her mind overflowed with repulsive thoughts about what Marise—no she—would do to them. She loved them more than anything. They gave her strength, courage, and their safety was all that mattered.

"I want you both to go back home. I'm leaving now, and you do *not* want to follow me." Her voice had failed her the first time she had tried to speak, stopped by the constriction in her throat which made it hard to swallow let alone breathe. When her voice finally came it was cold, her vision already focusing on the door which led to her escape.

She needed to leave immediately, to get away from them all and ensure they couldn't follow. She was a danger, a menace, but where could she run? Through her panic there was still one clear, calm, thought which demanded her attention. A voice impossible to ignore as it offered her the solution. It would take away her distress, her problems, all she needed to do was stop fighting.

"But Zo." As he looked at her, the turmoil which shadowed her eyes sent a shiver down his spine, but that was not all he saw. She looked terrified beyond anything he had seen. This was clearly serious, he questioned why she no longer felt she could confide in him. He challenged her gaze in the hope she would surrender some information. It normally worked, she felt uncomfortable being confronted, but he knew something about this time was different. She could barely breathe, barely hold herself together, but she did not break his stare.

"What's goin' on?" Eiji walked in from the kitchen to see them locked in eye contact, both breaking their gaze as he approached to place some toast, along with a jug of water, on the table. Moving away he caught a closer look at her, his stomach sank. She was drained of colour except for her red flushed cheeks. From her expression alone it was painfully clear what was happening. She looked so delicate, afraid, and confused. Somehow, she had discovered the truth.

"Maybe you should ask your partner, or better yet split company before she betrays you too." As Zo spoke, she slung her satchel over her shoulder, her backpack already resting on the other as she hurried towards the door. It was strange, she thought as she felt the cool metal of the door handle in her grasp, she didn't even remember picking them up. The world around her seemed to move in and out of focus with each, she needed air, solitude. She had to leave, now.

"You can't just leave. What about Darrienia?" That wasn't exactly what Acha had wanted to say. She wanted to ask why, to ask what had happened, anything to prevent her from leaving, but given her state of mind this seemed like the only thing that may have delayed her. Her only response was the sound of the door as it closed behind her. Daniel moved in pursuit, but was stopped once more by Elly; she always seemed to get in the way.

* * *

A hand grabbed her as she walked towards the exit she had chosen. It fastened around her arm, pulling her gently into a side street. The owner was lucky to still be in possession of it. Something about her had changed since she left the inn. Her hair shone a vivid red reflecting the anger within her soul, her eyes bore menacingly into the stranger.

"Zoella," the young man whispered, but he knew immediately she was not the person he addressed. She was different from the image he had seen, this was not his Zo. Her aura, her posture, everything about her was different to the girl he had welcomed into his home. She glanced down at the hand which still gripped her arm, before looking at the brown-haired youth it belonged to.

He was older than her, yet now, it seemed only by a few years. He possessed a build suitable for a soldier within Blackwood's army. It was his old grey eyes which betrayed his age, within them there was so much knowledge. The eyes never lied and at this moment they showed this man was afraid, she could see it clearly. She smiled at him feeling his hand begin to tremble upon her arm. Nearby the cheers from a tavern could be heard, it seemed something was happening there which gripped the attention of all who passed by.

"I know who you are," he whispered, suddenly realising his actions had been foolish. What had he truly hoped to achieve by confronting her? It was clearly already too late.

"Then, might I suggest you remove that hand before I take the liberty myself?" His hand moved at a lightning speed as she gave her warning. Hearing her speak he knew there was no resemblance to the girl he had addressed before, or the gentle nature of the young lady who had been portrayed in the picture Night had shown him. Not only did this girl's hair shine a brilliant red, her brown lowlights were nearly lost in the vibrant shades. Her eyes were not the blue the image had portrayed, but a deep sea-green, they reflected the very nature of her essence, beautiful but deadly, and right now they were filled with hate and bloodlust. "Now old man, tell me where to find Night?"

"What makes you think—" before he could finish his question, her sword was drawn and pressed against his throat, pinning him against the wall with a speed even the Gods would be challenged to meet.

"You reek of his magic old man, just as your house did when *she* stopped by. Now tell me where to find him, or you will not have time to enjoy your bargained youth." He felt the sword's pressure increase as a warm trickle of blood ran down his neck.

"I don't know. I swear. He approached from the shadows. He contacted me, I do not know." Her posture stiffened slightly, aware someone watched them. She knew if she were to look she would see a person in brightly dressed attire standing at the edge of the side street, paralysed as he watched. She knew this man, and thus knew exactly where his next point of call would be. He would report to Elly, someone she did not care to face at this moment. The man found the courage to move and, despite his size, he did so very quickly.

"You are lucky this time." She glanced to the street where the figure had stood. "Breathe a word of this to anyone and you will wish I *had* killed you. I am sure Night has his own plan for you. Can you feel them?" she taunted, a wicked smile turned up the corners of her almost pouting lips. "They are watching you, old man," she stated coldly, removing her sword as she threw him to the floor, smiling as he scrabbled in the dirt to retreat at speed.

She turned her back on him. The man who had seen her posed no threat to her, neither of them did, but she did not want to confront Elly, not until she had collected her thoughts. She had to decide how exactly they would meet, as friends, or as enemies, but even still, she would keep their promise. There would be no death within these walls.

* * *

"I thought you said there would be no trouble!" The inn door flew open as their time within expired. Elly welcomed him with a smile as the door slammed closed behind him. His bright clothes were drenched with sweat as he gasped for breath, his rounded face was almost as bright as his top.

"Whatever do you mean?" Elly asked; her tone alone implied she had more of an idea than she wished to let on, again a smile crossed her lips. She looked towards the dining room. Although the door was tightly closed, she knew just on the other side sat two people oblivious to the identity of their friend. She couldn't help but wonder when they too would connect the pieces of the puzzle like Zo had this very morning.

"I just saw her outside, her sword to some poor youth's throat! We agreed this place would remain free from her deeds, that while she was here no harm would come to those within these walls," he spat.

Daniel, knowing something was wrong, stood cautiously by the door listening to the hushed tones of conversations. He glanced across at Acha and Eiji, they seemed unaware the event was even transpiring as they began to eat the toast which had been prepared just moments ago. As he caught snippets of the hushed conversation, he grew more concerned. The scene he had just described did not sound like his friend at all. She was always so calm, so pleasant. She never lost her temper even when things were at their worst, although recently there was no denying there had been a change. It was true, it seemed she was quicker to anger, but even so, to threaten another's life was definitely not something she would do, not unless it was in her own, or someone else's, defence. Even then, he had serious doubts she would have the conviction to make true her threat.

"Is he dead?" The question alone made Daniel's stomach churn, why would she ask something like that so calmly? As if that wasn't disturbing enough, what she said next really alarmed him.

"No, but—"

"Then count your blessings." Daniel, unable to just stand and listen any longer opened the door, the conversation fell silent as he did so. Without a pause, he walked to Elly, determination filled his eyes as he stood just inches away from her. If this was his friend they talked about, it was time he was told exactly what this was all about.

"*What* is going on Elaineor?" He demanded. Although his words had been perfectly clear they ignored him completely, Elly simply sidestepped around him.

"I can't believe I let you bring her here."

"Which way did she go?" Elly handed him a roll of additional funds. As the comforting weight of notes fell firmly in his hand, the concern instantly left his face to be replaced by the mercenary smile he was known for.

"It looked like she was heading towards Tran-gin Street." He flicked the money past his ear before he breathed in its scent; all signs of his previous distress had now vanished.

"Thank you." Elly walked towards the exit, it seemed she too would leave them behind. Acha and Eiji now stood at the dining room entrance with the distinct feeling they had missed the crucial points of an important conversation. "Daniel, Acha, do you not have some place to be?" She had heard all too well exactly what Zo had requested of them. At least now Zo had decided to travel without them she no longer had to design a method for their departure.

"Exactly what did you two argue about?" Daniel walked a little closer to Elly and managed to position himself between her and the door to seal her escape. This was not a subject he was about to drop at her request.

"I believe she told you to go home, and that is all *you* need to know." She glanced at Eiji, "I shall meet with you later." She quickly scrawled something on a piece of paper from the inn's desk, before handing it to him. It contained a street name and directions. "I will meet you there."

"But even if they do go home, there's Darrienia t'contend with." Daniel and Acha looked at Elly hopefully as Eiji fought for them, but her reluctance to travel with them initially meant, without Zo, it was hopeless. The only reason they had been allowed to accompany them had been because it was what Zo had wanted. Now she had requested them to leave, there was no reason for Elly to entertain the notion of allowing them to continue this adventure further.

"No. They need to go home. It is far too dangerous for them to come any further." As Elly opened the door, she glanced back at them, Daniel suddenly wondered how she had moved past him without his noticing. "The rune branding which allows you to access Darrienia only works if the symbol is accurate, draw on it. You are no longer my concern."

"Then I suppose I'll accompany them," Eiji stated as he looked again at the paper, he felt almost envious of them, they were being offered an escape, something he so desperately desired. He wondered if this was his chance to leave it all behind, to escape, but he knew such fortune was not within his foreseeable future. The looks they already directed towards him betrayed that much. She nodded in response to his query as she left. Even with his eyes still fixed on the door he was painfully aware of the growing intensity of their stares. He didn't want to turn to face them.

"So where exactly is Tran-gin Street?" Acha crossed her arms as she moved to stand between him and the door.

"All y' need t'know is y' not goin' that way, anythin' else is not y' concern." He sighed, he knew there was no way they would go willingly, nor was there any way he could force them to do so, he gave another pained sigh. "I'd give anything t'be offered a way out, if y' knew what I do, y'd understand and accept this chance while y' can," he stated. He had to at least try to get them to return.

"Is Zo in some kind of danger?" Daniel questioned from behind him, as Eiji turned to face him Acha subtly removed one of her gloves.

"Y' could put it that way." He wanted to tell them everything, to explain what was going on. It was clear these people cared for her, but it was not something his honour would permit. He knew that if he could explain, perhaps they would not be so quick to follow. Perhaps they would take the chance of escape which had been offered to them. Then again, he found he too had begun to grow fond of the former assassin. It was a realisation which surprised even him. Perhaps he wasn't as intent on leaving them as he believed. The person he had been so afraid of was human, just like him, and it seemed she wanted nothing more than to walk the path of light. She would rather heal than harm. He couldn't understand it, but he knew the situation was complicated, and he feared what the self-ordered solitude from her friends would mean.

"And you're taking us home?" Daniel nodded to Acha, who reached out to touch him. There was no way he was going to stop them finding their friend.

"I never said that." He turned quickly to grab her sleeved arm. She looked to him in surprise as he gave her a cautionary stare before thrusting her arm away. Regaining her footing, she watched him carefully, shock lining her features. He had always seemed so clumsy and awkward, she was amazed he had seen through their ploy, but what had startled her more, is that somehow he seemed to be aware of her unique capabilities. "I said y' not goin' that way, not why don't y' try t'kill me! I know a shortcut, remember?" He waved the piece of paper at them in annoyance before placing the keys on the innkeeper's counter, watching as he meticulously counted them. "But y' hafta be sure y' want t'come, y' hafta be committed t'saving her, t'being there for her, regardless of what happens. If y' not, then y' may as well leave right now.

"This will be the only chance y' have of turnin' back, if y' come with me, y' may be in great danger, y' may get hurt, or worse." Eiji suddenly realised as he spoke, that at one point, despite his fear of death and his mind looking for an opportunity to escape, he was, in fact, determined to save her.

"All the more reason to go with you. Whatever is happening, we can't let Zo go through it alone. She needs her friends," Daniel stated.

* * *

"So what exactly is going on?" Daniel demanded. He had given Eiji a few seconds of peace as they had left the inn, but since they had stepped onto the streets of Collateral, he had bombarded him with questions. "Elly clearly knows more than she reveals, what's this danger, why does Zo need saving?" It seemed Elly would never give them any information. Since she was no longer with them, at least she would be to unable prevent any being relayed, so Daniel had decided to move his focus onto Eiji. It now seemed more vital than ever he was given some answers. It seemed Eiji didn't deliberately hide things from them, and since he had travelled with Elly before meeting them, he believed he also held at least some of the information they needed.

"It's really not my place t'say." Eiji glanced at the street names before matching one with the name on the scrap of paper. He had successfully sidestepped this conversation for some time now, but they were persistent. Despite his many obvious attempts to avoid the subject, they continued their interrogation.

"Is it something to do with what they were fighting about earlier?" Daniel was certain he could be of more help if he understood the situation better.

"Possibly, it was bound t'happen sooner or later." Eiji paused; he had to give them something, if only to give himself a few minutes of relief, something which told them nothing they didn't already know. "After all, Elly knows about her past, it must be frustratin'. There's bound t'be some tension between them, especially when Zo discovers somethin' she feels it was her right t'know all along." Eiji cursed silently; he had done so well, but he had just gone one step too far.

"And what's that?" Daniel prompted before experiencing the strange feeling of displacement as they passed through Collateral's boundaries.

Their footing became instantly impaired as they found themselves knee-deep in brambly undergrowth. They fought their way from the forest's boundaries towards the unknown terrain which stretched before them. Eiji glanced around, surprisingly, he knew exactly where they were. Large thickets obstructed their view of all which lay before them. Now, more than ever, he felt the need for caution.

"Be careful here, follow my steps exactly. We will soon be enterin' the Quakin' Bog, it's the home t'many a wild beast. My master told me great tales of the creatures he encountered in the peat burial grounds." Eiji had hoped Daniel would show interest in the distraction he offered, he was sorely disappointed.

The land underfoot began to moisten as the thickets gave way to the scenic view of the marshlands. Some of the waters appeared clear, the surrounding areas were filled with an array of coloured heather. Other areas were awash with greenery, a shade which concealed other bodies of water covered with sphagnum moss. Fortunately, the more dangerous areas of the terrain had carefully placed board-walks to guide those walking these grounds. Eiji hesitantly led the way, carefully feeling for any movement of the sodden terrain beneath his feet.

"You know as well, don't you?" Acha ignored Eiji's blatant attempt at distracting them, and, with a Daniel-like persistence, pushed it further. Eiji's response was delayed as he focused his attention on the dangers of the environment. He was certain they should have reached the planking by now. He glanced around before looking to his compass, they were still on the correct bearings.

"Please don't ask me anymore. I won't betray her trust." Too much relied on him keeping this secret. He knew it would destroy her if they found out before she was ready.

"You're referring to Elly?" Daniel scoffed, although he admired Eiji's virtues, he wished for once he would be given a clear answer. He knew they would get no further information from him, not deliberately anyway, but they had to try. They needed to understand more about the situation, and with each passing minute their concerns only grew about the danger they had found themselves in. Annoyingly, Eiji remained true to his word, which was just one of the many things which made him so honourable, but at present it was such an annoying virtue.

"That's all I'm sayin'. Just because I know what's happenin' doesn't give me the right t'tell you. It's not my place," he enforced as they continued walking. For a moment there was silence; it was short lived as Daniel spoke again. Eiji froze, feeling the earth beside him trembling, he adjusted his course carefully.

"Yet you found out about it from Elly, right?" Daniel couldn't help but feel infuriated. A complete stranger knew more about his best friend than he, or she herself knew. He had to know, he had to understand. He needed to be there for her when she needed him, to offer her comfort. At the inn she had needed his support, but she refused to confide in him. Her need to distance herself from them showed the extent of her concern, her desire to protect them from whatever it was she had discovered, from something she thought could endanger them.

"I didn't ask, I was told. Then I was given a choice, t'live or t'die." He gave a sigh before he quickly glanced around the area, something about this didn't feel quite right. First there were the missing board-walks, then the quaking of the ground. The route chosen had been specifically planned to avoid such dangers. It should have led them through the firmest, safest, parts, to the open plain. Something about this wasn't right at all. He looked before him seeing the trembling movements of the trees which should have marked the start of the plain, how could this land have altered so drastically? He closed his eyes for a second, his mind's eye remapping the safest path before he began to lead them once more.

"And yet you refuse to tell us? She threatened your life, yet you still protect her!" But his frustration met only with silence, it was a silence which stilled the need for questions as Eiji's posture stiffened before them. His concerned gaze looked out across the expanse of water which stretched before them. They were almost free from the confines of the bog, but his guiding steps had not stopped in relief. As he surveyed the area before him, he knew his initial concerns had been founded. There should have been board-walks. They were not lost, they were exactly on course, if not for the constant barrage of questions, perhaps he would have noticed sooner.

Small broken fragments of rotten wood lay embedded in the muddy terrain as the twisted clawed foothold told tales of being forcefully removed. Someone, or something, had wanted to ensure the route was no longer welcoming to travellers.

There was little choice but to wade through the putrid waters, and they were already tired from the difficulty of the walk. The water looked anything but inviting. Its dark, stagnant, scum-covered surface broken by numerous patches of debris. Thick rotting wood, vines, and moss all intertwined as if part of some enormous natural tapestry crafted by the hands of the Gods themselves. Somehow there seemed a strange order to the mangled chaos. The protruding footholds snagged the debris, allowing the water, where the walkway would have once stood, a small release from its stifling embrace.

"What's wrong?" Daniel whispered, adhering to the new atmosphere brought on by Eiji's alarmed halt.

"There should'a been board-walks," his voice trembled slightly. "Whatever did this surely can't be natural." He motioned across the tangled waters, bringing their attention to the shredded footings which once would have supported the path across to the plain.

"We're going through, aren't we?" Acha questioned fearfully looking across the water. She wasn't quite sure how to broach the topic of her being unable to swim. It was a skill she had never learnt, one she had never needed during her youth.

"It should be relatively safe," Eiji advised reassuringly, his eyes closed as if in concentration. "The board-walk crossed the shallowest terrain, from what I can tell, it'll be tirin', but we shouldn't need t'swim. I'll go first, stay close, off the walkway the waters are deep." Without further delay Eiji slowly began the gradual descent.

It was as he predicted, each step took its toll as the sucking mud restricted their every movement. Looking back, he saw Acha, her steps cautious, fearful, as her hands went from foothold to foothold as if to guide her steps. It was a slow, tedious journey filled with not only the reeking odours from the decaying waters, but the stifling air of silence. Acha found she gripped each wooden lifeline harder than the last as the tepid waters rose to her waist. They weren't even half way across yet, if it rose much deeper, she would find walking in these conditions impossible. Her breath shallowed as panic began to rise like the surrounding waters.

"It won't get any deeper now." Eiji finally spoke as they almost reached the midway point. Audible to all, Acha let out a sigh of relief, her death-like grip on the splintered wood released ever so slightly.

For a moment she felt the pull of a current in what had been otherwise stagnant water. Her stomach lurched as she gripped against its pull mere moments before the bog rose. Water exploded around her filling her calming breath with the familiar gasps of panic as a rush of fluid from behind threatened to pull her under. She screamed as Eiji turned to see Daniel disappearing into the stagnant depths. Lunging forwards Eiji grabbed her arm as she reached out towards the vanishing figure.

"Stay here!" he commanded, diving into the waters from their path.

Acha stood alone. The stillness of the lake was almost eerie as not a single wave disrupted its surface. She stood in paralysed horror. There was nothing she could do but watch over the vast expanse.

* * *

The town of Kerõs was a private place, an area which enjoyed its seclusion. Given its unique heritage it did not welcome outsiders, nor did they approve of having an access point to Collateral within such close proximity to their carefully concealed town. There were all manner of wards and deterrents erected to prevent those emerging from the portal, as Elly had just moments ago, from locating them through the forest's maze. Fortunately, for those who would like to believe their wards repelled all, Elly had no interest in visiting the ancient town.

She navigated the forest with ease. Her stride, although filled with purpose, showed signs of hesitation. She had been anticipating this moment for so long, she had envisioned all manner of scenarios which would result from their meeting. Scenarios ranging from the rekindling of kinship to a confrontation of epic proportions. Even she could not predict how her actions would tempt Marise's mood. Her pace slowed further as she neared her destination, the place where the assassin sat awaiting her.

"I knew you would come, Lee." Elly heard the familiar mannerisms before the figure even came into view. Elly took a moment to look upon her. Despite being aware of her presence, Marise did not turn to face her, she simply continued to stare out over the rise and fall of the hilly plain which stretched before her from the edge of the small forest. This did not bode well. Marise's vivid red hair blew wildly, free from its constraints as she sat on the grass, leaning back on her arms.

"Mari." Seeing her so clearly once more spurred her step as she hastened to approach. As she neared her, Marise turned slightly, her green eyes piercing her with a fierce resentment as they met for the first time in over a year. The gaze was enough to once more bring caution to Elly's approach. Her advance faltered. If possible, she did not want to engage her. There would be no victors in such conflict. They remained steadfast, neither averting their gaze until finally Marise's eyes softened before she once more turned to take in the lay of the land.

"Has much changed since I was banished?" she questioned bitterly, she leaned back further, tilting her vision skyward. It had been so long since she had seen light or felt the warmth of the sun.

"Very little." Moving to sit beside her, Elly found herself casting repeated glances in her direction. Despite the uncertainty of the situation, she was relieved to see her once more.

"Of all the people to betray me, I did not think it would be you. I would cut you down here, if I thought I could win. It is always unpredictable with you." Marise fingered the hilt of her sword gently while she contemplated her next move. Normally, she would not hesitate to strike down those who betrayed her, but this was Elly, it was different.

"Why do you say that?" Elly touched the pocket of her trousers, it was a gesture Marise was familiar with. She was ensuring she had the means to defend herself.

"Zoella. You assisted her return did you not? It took so long for me to completely seal her away and then you brought her back. Well over a year has passed since then. I want to believe you had the best intentions. Well?" she questioned harshly.

"Mari, you have to understand, there are so many reasons I did what I did. I saw her shadow within your eyes, she would cause you to hesitate. Because of her that boy lived, because of her the Elementalist walked. Aburamushi, who you created, was sealed by a guardian to protect the innocent. Blackwood noticed these things too, action was required."

"And the real reason?" Elly smiled giving a shrug. She had hoped the need for an explanation wouldn't be required, it was unclear how much information Zo would subconsciously retain.

"The initial order came from much higher. I think it was part of his plan, to seize the final Grimoire, remember only one pure of heart and such. Things needed to fall into place, but my previous comment still holds true." She extended her hand, touching Marise's hair affectionately. "I was concerned for you." She moved slightly closer as she continued to talk. "I followed Night's instruction. I knew nothing of the methods, nor how it had affected you until I met her.

"Once administered, I was committed to the act. I was forbidden from even observing you until the time came for us to meet once more." She spoke softly, regret clear in her normally controlled tones. "I am sorry, I understand your anger. My betrayal was on the deepest level imaginable." Marise looked to her in surprise. Elly was not one to offer apologies. Her actions were always well considered, making such regrets unwarranted. "Are you aware of all that transpires?"

"In some respects. Zoella still uses me to repress her fears, in her heart she knows something terrible has happened." Marise gave a wicked grin. "Her sleep is plagued with nightmares. Sometimes she will see something which reminds her of events from the past, although before she can recall them, her need for self-preservation prevents it. I see much through such a window.

"But Daniel, that boy to me is a complete mystery. He is protected from my view, and while they are together, even in distress, she knows comfort. I know his name but little more. He is what makes my return so difficult. Her friendship with him is strong. I feel her within me now, thinking of the harsh words she spoke, unaware I am even here, unaware I have taken control.

"I am not truly sure what happens to me when I am not in control, but during my reign it was as if she was never there. I could not feel her as I can now."

"That will be rectified when we find the final tome. It seems Night provided us with a distraction, ultimately I think it will serve some purpose in his quest, or else he would not have gone to such lengths. Do you know that she released Aburamushi?"

"*I* let him leave. I also felt him grow in power. Tell me are you going there now to undo what I did?" As they had fled from the guardian in Aburamushi's lair, for just a brief second, as Zo had drawn the sword, Marise had managed to release the weakened seal, shattering the door before Zo had been given chance to strike. It was the second time she had managed to influence her actions without her knowledge, both times had been when she had drawn her weapon.

"It would break one of the seals, I feel that is his plan, to weaken that which our ancestors constructed." A long time ago the magic Marise had cast there had fortified that which had created one of the ancient seals. By reversing her actions, now the rune had been removed, one of the seals would fail as the remaining magic was banished.

"Speaking of troublesome obstacles." Marise raised an eyebrow meaningfully. "I am thinking it would be better to remove three annoying ones."

"That is a little premature, besides, Eiji is under my protection." She was certain even now Eiji brought the ones who challenged her patience towards this very location. She would be surprised if somehow he had managed to convince them to abandon their friend, but she had needed time with Marise to resolve matters. "I am sure they will have their uses, if only to ensure things stay on course."

"When this is over..."

"You have my word you may do whatever you wish to them." Elly took Marise's hand in hers for the briefest moment, certain the lies she had spoken remained undetected. "It is a fitting reward for the sacrifices you have made."

* * *

Eiji's form broke the water's surface, once more bringing chaos to the surroundings. Dragged with him, securely trapped within his grasp, flailed Daniel's gasping figure.

"Go!" Eiji screamed in Acha's direction as he began desperately to swim towards the plains, pulling Daniel behind him. The waters around them swelled and bulged as the surface debris began to rise in pursuit. The entangled flotsam pulsed and lurched, as from beneath it emerged the fleshless skull of a creature so foul it could still the breath. Its hooked nose acting as sight to hone in on its targeted prey. The water-weathered muscle, intermingled with bone, was covered in the bog's scum and moss as the beast within wore the coating of its nest like a skin. Its long fingers and refined claws easily spanned the length of its forearm, visible only as its long limbs broke through the water. The balding chunks of white hair, which splayed from the creature's skull, moved quickly with its rapid movements as it traversed the thick water with ease, unhindered by the masses of moving detritus attached to its back. It was unclear if this tangled mass was a living extension of the hag-like creature, or something animated by her touch.

Acha's panicked steps seemed to sink deeper, her pace restricted by the surrounding water as she fought desperately to follow the footholds. Concerns of drowning were no longer at the forefront of her mind, pushed aside by the horror they now faced.

Eiji gasped for breath, his gaze fixed firmly on the pursuing monstrosity, glancing only towards the land to ensure he remained on course. More movement swelled from beneath the surface as Eiji called upon the tangled bramble below to ensnare it, slowing its pace, if just for a moment. The water between him and the shore began to part. He turned, swinging Daniel to rest upon his back as he found his footing on the sodden terrain. Water crashed behind him as he focused all his energy, all his skills, on manipulating the creature's natural environment to aid his escape. The ground became firm, heated, beneath his steps.

The creature, accepting their imminent escape, turned its focus to the one remaining still within its domain. Eiji, reaching the land, dropped Daniel to the ground as the creature sped across the waters towards the former boardwalk. Acha's steps froze as the blur of rapid movement sped towards her, she released a scream. A wave of water rose up slamming the creature to one side.

"Move!" Eiji yelled forcing another crashing wave before the creature's path. It howled as the jagged splints of wood pierced its unyielding form. More bramble rose trying to restrain it as wave upon wave of water disrupted its path. Roots broke through the surface, weaving a solid path beneath Acha's feet as she sprinted, clawing her way to the safety of the solid plain.

She collapsed on the grassy fields as Eiji sunk to his knees gasping for breath, his vision once more focused over the bog. The now still water reflected just the smallest glint of light as the soothing spread of coloured heather painted the landscape. The scene was so still, so tranquil they could have been simply observing a freshly painted canvas, still standing upon the artist's easel.

"Daniel, are you all right?" Acha now crouched over him, examining his injuries. It was as she had feared, they were serious. The events of just moments ago seemed surreal against the calmness of their surroundings. Daniel gasped in pain as he lay on his back, paralysed, as the growing patch of blood quickly began to stain his torn linen shirt.

"The town of Kerõs isn't far. I was t'meet Elly near there. Keep an eye on him, I'll get help." The urgency in Eiji's voice was unmistakable as he looked at the three enormous, gaping slash marks across Daniel's chest. The wounds seemed to pulsate as they bled heavily. If they didn't stop the bleeding soon it would be fatal. The double-edged blade of shock was their only ally, if not for it slowing his blood flow things would already be far worse. "Keep pressure on it," he called as he began to sprint. He hesitated for a moment removing his dagger from his boot and throwing it in Acha's direction. Although it seemed the danger had passed, it was not wise to leave them unarmed. She grabbed it quickly, tucking it into her belt carefully.

"Please hurry," Acha whispered, pressing the cleaner parts of her cloak against Daniel's wounds.

* * *

Marise gasped, her hand shooting to her chest and freezing her words. As she blinked, her eyes changed before Elly's concerned vision.

"Daniel," Zo gasped in shock, glancing around like a startled animal as she tried to take in her unfamiliar surroundings. Although her link to Acha had all but faded, she felt her distress clearly. "Where's Daniel?" she almost shouted. Her hand gripped Elly's arm tightly, any concerns about her where-abouts slipping from her mind as if they had never even arisen. She didn't care where they sat, she just knew her friends were in danger.

"What—" Elly began to question. She had been in mid-conversation with Marise then suddenly, out of nowhere, *she* appeared and took control. To say she was surprised was not an understatement. Elly didn't have time to finish her sentence before Eiji's desperate tones attracted their attention.

"Elly... thank the Gods," he gasped, barely able to speak between breaths. "It's Daniel... he's hurt." He leaned over, placing his hands on his knees, gasping for breath as Elly looked to Zo.

"How did you—" Elly stopped as she realised to question things would only raise suspicion on the situation. Marise was right, the group were trouble. The bond they shared challenged her ability to retain control.

"Eiji, tell me what happened?" Zo demanded, her voice filled with fear. When he didn't answer she pressed further, not realising his desperate gasps for breath hindered his ability to speak. "Where is he, where's Daniel?" Eiji sucked in another deep breath, each one becoming slightly more controlled until finally he could force the words.

"Over the brow... need a healer... there isn't much time," he panted, as he had answered Zo sprinted off in the direction he had appeared from, putting trust in her senses to lead her.

"How peculiar," Elly mused as she watched her figure vanish over the hill. "What?"

"Never mind, we should go after her." She glanced over Eiji's sodden figure, sliding her fingernail down his flesh to remove a few of the leeches which had attached themselves to him before she began to walk away. Unlike Zo, there was nothing rushed about her pace.

"We need t'get a healer! Kerõs is close," Eiji protested. Daniel's injuries were severe. Even if Zo reached him in time, perhaps she could ease his suffering, but Hectarians could only use one type of magic or the other, remedial or damaging, and from what he knew of Marise he knew where her affinity would lie. To treat Daniel, they would need someone of remarkable talent, even then, they would have to trust his fate to the compassion of the Gods.

"There is no point," Elly stated coldly. The town of Kerõs, although close, would not welcome outsiders, besides, she had no intention of wasting her time helping him to find his way there.

"If we hurry, we could make it back before..." Eiji pleaded realising Elly had no intention of turning back. He stared after her, his posture clearly displaying his disbelief. Elly turned back clicking her fingers.

"Follow."

Chapter 10

The Releasing of the Seal

"Zo, over here!" She heard Acha's desperate cries before she could even see them silhouetted against the marshland. They lay a short distance from the water's edge, the ground beneath Daniel stained with both mud and blood as he lay motionless before her.

Glancing around frantically, Zo surveyed the landscape in search of their assailant. The land was calm, still. Her feet slid on the damp grass as she dropped to her knees beside him, her hand resting on his forehead as she probed both his body and mind to make her diagnosis. His wounds were clear to any who looked upon him, she was more concerned about what poisons or inhibitors may have been introduced through the creature's claws. She would have liked to have caught a glimpse of the attacker, although all things considered, perhaps it was better she did not.

Her heart raced as she tried to locate the means to heal him quickly. The woodland was the only answer. Trees could heal themselves over great periods of time, she just needed to accelerate the process through herself. If they would permit her to call upon them, she could use their method of recovery to aid him. She turned her attention away from the trees to focus fully on Daniel.

"What happened?" Although she had covered much ground to reach them, she showed nearly no signs of fatigue. If it hadn't been for her slight shortness of breath, Acha would have believed she had been just steps away.

"The creature, it came from nowhere," she sobbed uncontrollably as her panic and adrenaline heightened her already delicate state. Zo had no time to offer comfort, her only thoughts were of saving Daniel.

"His pulse is faint. Acha watch for the others. When they arrive *don't* let them interrupt me." She kept her voice steady, despite the pain which flooded through her as she touched him. It was a white-hot pain that made her want to remove her hand, but she couldn't, not if she wished him to live. Acha nodded, turning her back on them to nervously watch the horizon.

Being healed by magic was a unique experience. You saw and felt things which the average person would not; you were opened to different paths and possibilities, and forced to see things which should remain invisible to the mortal eye. It was important that, regardless of what he may behold, Daniel remained calm. So when she spoke to him, she did so not with her voice, but with her mind, opening a method of communication that was almost exclusively available to healers. A means to offer comfort to people who may otherwise be unreachable.

'*Now listen to me,*' Zo whispered mentally, even her inner voice was not as calm as she had intended. She was plagued by so many doubts. Even if the forces offered her their aid, there was no guarantee she could still perform the rites required. It had been such a long time since she had even attempted healing on such a grand scale. It was a complex process, one most would not undertake. If it had been anyone other than herself who sat before him now, there was no doubt they would do all they could to make him comfortable, and nothing more. But she was not willing to surrender. She would not let him die; not here, not like this. It was this attachment to him which made the process more dangerous.

Hectarians, she had been taught, rarely attempted magic on those they were close to. The results of doing so were uncertain because emotions could cloud both magic and judgement, but now there was no other choice. The alternative was too unbearable. She knew she needed to concentrate, ensuring her emotions remained suppressed. A single change in her calling on nature could result in a shift or adaptation of the given power into something she could not control, into something dangerous. She had to act quickly, she could already feel Hades' messenger awaiting the outcome. It really was going to be close.

The severity of his injuries meant, if she were to heal him, she needed to keep him focused on her. If he slipped much further, she would have to battle Hermes for his life. For now, he simply observed from the distance, but even she could feel his presence growing stronger. She knew Daniel would see him too. He would be aware of all manner of things previously shrouded from his gaze. She only hoped she could stop his attention from wandering too far, in order to prevent his curiosity from directing him slowly towards his own death.

'*Concentrate on my voice, focus,*' she commanded as she felt his mind weaken further. She touched her finger from his forehead to hers to seal the bond between their minds before she tore the remaining shirt tatters from around the wound. It had looked bad through the shirt, but that was nothing compared to the damage which lay beneath. Seeing the torn pulsating tear marks made her all the more aware of the ever approaching footsteps of death. He was already closer than she had expected.

'*How do you get into these messes?*' she thought suddenly after a moment of prolonged silence, she realised she had been quiet for too long as she had focused on the first part of the enchantment. If the silence remained unbroken it could prove fatal.

She pressed her hand firmly down on the first wound, hesitating as a strange feeling crept over her, almost like déjà vu, a feeling she had done something very similar to someone close to her before, someone she cared deeply for. She shrugged it off, this was not the time to be distracted, even by the promise of a memory. The claw marks were almost twice the size of her hand in length and stretched diagonally across almost the entirety of his chest.

'*First that armoured guy, now this, you'd think I'd know better by now than to leave you on your own.*' She gasped as the cold force of nature flowed into her body. She felt the silver threads pierce her like small pins as the life around them connected itself to her. '*I'm so sorry.*' She clenched her teeth, forcing these tiny threads to combine within her in order to be released from her hand in a large intertwined string of pure energy. As it touched him, she felt it once again separate into tiny vines, the flesh beneath her hand becoming coated in a fine sap-like substance generated by the threads as they weaved themselves around the sides of the wound and began to pull it closed. But despite this, Hermes crept ever closer. She had hoped by now, at the very least, his pace would have slowed. Such was normally the case when successful healing had been initiated, yet his advance remained steady, constant. What was she missing, was there something else, or did things really hang so close in the balance? The tiny threads became thicker where they penetrated her as her needs became more demanding, she felt the pain of both nature and Daniel's wounds fill her body with agony.

Once the first wound was completely coated in the sap, she moved her hand to the next, allowing the painful spike of combined life to continue its purpose as it bound the wound together. She concentrated, seeing with her mind the plants and trees as they offered her a fraction of their eternal life. Her magic mirrored the way they would heal themselves in nature, a protective sap which encapsulated the wound while it repaired.

'Just one more Daniel.' She found her mind almost screamed at him as his pulse grew weaker. She found it difficult to keep his mind attentive, worse still, she could almost feel Hermes breath upon her. She knew if she turned to look, he would be as visible as Acha. It was for this reason alone she did not look, in the hope that if she failed to acknowledge him, he would halt his approach. He did not. Each passing second things were becoming more desperate.

Daniel's focus on her was waning. It was impossible now for her to concentrate on keeping his wandering attention and healing him physically. Normally she would have to choose one or the other, but this time there was no choice. To keep him here she needed his mind to stay focused on her, but she also needed her full concentration to heal the wounds.

It was a battle she could not afford to lose; a battle she would not lose, no matter what.

No matter how hard she tried, she could not do both simultaneously, and there was no way she could maintain this indefinitely. It was impossible, but if she couldn't, she would lose him.

Hesitation delayed her actions, there was but one thing she could do, but by doing it she would risk losing him forever, but at least he would live. It was a technique which filled her with dread, but his life was more valuable than the cost of her actions. She had vowed to protect him and so she did the only thing she could, the only choice which was open to her. She offered a piece of herself to him, her childhood, her thoughts, her memories. She just had to pray his curiosity would not see him venture beyond what was intended, that he would not somehow find the memories which even she did not recall, or perhaps find something even worse, waiting for him in the darkness.

As she opened her mind to him, the crisp steps of Hermes halted as Daniel's attention was torn from him. He knew now, this moment was not yet the time for this person. The claim had been lost, for now. Her memories held his attention fully where she herself had failed. She released him into her mind, into her memories, knowing this was the only way she could focus on healing, and finally, the last wound began to close.

Echoing somewhere outside her concentration, she could hear Acha shouting something, but it seemed so far away. She had to ignore it, keep her focus. Time was growing short, soon the pain of those tiny threads piercing her skin would become unbearable, and despite her will, when the pain reached her body's limit, the magic would stop. It was a natural inbuilt defence to preserve a magic user's life. They were never given more than they could handle.

It was ironic, everyone thought healing was a painless task. Unless they had actually done it, no one could ever imagine the distress it caused. The threads of energy burnt as their jagged composition pulsed through her. The longer she remained joined to this raw force, the more severe the ordeal, and that was only the beginning. Then she had to combine the tiny splinters of light within her body to form an intertwined force which felt as if it tore and ripped at all it touched, hurting more than the entry of all the threads combined. Healing was, by no means, a pain free magic. It was a trade. The pain she would feel was three times greater than that of the forces which aided her, and the injuries of the one who received her magic.

Whatever was happening would have to wait. She had already exhausted her reserves for this kind of magic on the second wound. As she worked on the third, she was aware of the damage she caused herself but she refused to stop. If she broke her concentration now, she could not attempt to heal him again for some time, her body would not permit it. The pain she felt now was nothing compared to the thought of losing her best friend, it was for this reason alone the magic continued to flow. It knew that, for him, she could handle just a little bit more.

After what seemed like an eternity, the last gash was sealed. Her eyes shot open as the awareness of her surroundings returned. Although she was never actually aware of having closed them it was always the case. Everything she saw was not through the eyes of her body, but through her mind's eye, Amelia had called it healing lore.

"Zo!" Acha cried pointing to her top, looking down she saw the spreading blood stain, mirroring Daniel's old wounds. For a brief second, as it ripped across her flesh, the injury felt very real. Whilst it faded quickly, she knew it to be a warning, one she would not receive a second time. Her skin began to relax as the threads faded, despite the process being complete, pain still coursed through her body. She coughed violently for a second as she tried to swallow. Looking to her hand she saw the taint of blood on her skin, she quickly wiped it away before anyone could see. Looking up at a nearby tree she gave her thanks, watching as it shed a single leaf in autumn shades.

She looked to Daniel, his life signs were becoming stronger. She touched her forehead, placing her other hand on his, she kept it there for a moment until she was satisfied he would be safe. Only then did her trembling hands sever the link into her memories. She lay back on the grass beside him, breathing heavily as exhaustion washed over her.

"That was amazin'!" Eiji exclaimed, moving to sit beside her. He hadn't even considered she would possess such aptitude in healing, given Marise's destructive nature, it did, however, explain why Zo possessed the sympathetic touch. He briefly wondered if Marise too possessed the healers' curse, or if there was a more vivid divide separating the two. As an Elementalist he had been able to see everything, Hermes, the silver threads joining her to the life around her, and the things the rest of them could see too, such as the sap coating and closing the wounds. She was unsure exactly how long they had been there. She had to wonder if perhaps the approaching steps she heard had been theirs, but she knew otherwise. The thought it had been so close had scared her beyond belief. She lay breathlessly, barely finding the energy to wipe the beads of sweat from her face.

"He's still very weak," she gasped, crossing her arms over herself in an attempt to still the tremors. "He's lost a lot of blood, but he should be all right." For a brief moment, as she turned her head to look at them, her eyes locked onto a figure on the horizon, it seemed to make a polite gesture before vanishing into nothing more than a fine wisp of mist. She glanced at Daniel to ensure he was still breathing, and hadn't changed his mind about his recovery.

She lay embracing herself for several more minutes. When she finally caught her breath, she asked something which had been bothering her for some time.

"How did I end up here anyway? I don't remember leaving."

"You mean you cannot remember? I suppose you *were* acting somewhat irrationally," Elly asserted. "After you left, I followed you, you were already on your way there. I was barely with you seconds when Eiji appeared." She smiled inwardly. She was beginning to understand more of the situation she was facing, it was more ideal than she had first thought. Zo hadn't remembered a thing.

'*Oh my head.*' Zo looked to Daniel sharply, unable to hide the concern as she heard his thoughts before his eyes had even opened. She looked away quickly, forcing herself to sit as she heard him recapping the most recent events in a disjointed order.

"We woke in Collateral?" he muttered aloud, as he slowly raised himself up slightly using his forearms for support. He glanced down at his chest finding the scars left by his injury. He opened his mouth to continue, yet for a second words escaped him. Zo placed her finger to his lips to silence him.

"Rest," she whispered, forcing him to lie back down, placing the autumn leaf within his hand.

'*I just wanted to thank you.*' She was certain this time it was not her imagination. She bit her lip, trying to keep the concern from her expression as the realisation of what had happened increased the burden she already bore. Now she had to protect her mind from him as well. Everything was becoming so complicated.

'*I was afraid something like this might happen.*' She silently scolded herself for being so careless, then again, it was a small price to pay in exchange for his life.

"Like what?" Daniel asked seemingly out of nowhere, earning himself strange looks.

"Collateral is beyond all common laws. It exists everywhere yet nowhere." Elly finally broke the silence as she decided to share a piece of her knowledge with them. She could humour them a little, after all, it *was* his first question, and besides, it was the perfect opportunity to avoid the previous topic of conversation. "Given these unique traits, there is nowhere we could have been returned to which we were not already near."

They rested in silence for some time; as the sun moved across the sky, colour began to return to Daniel's face. Elly had started to pack away their supplies, indicating it was almost time to be on their way.

"So why was I heading to Abaddon?" Zo questioned, her own thoughts now looping around. She couldn't help her timid glances towards Daniel. He was still trying to make sense of things. She could only hope he knew better than to broach the topic in their current company. As if catching the thought, he lifted his head to meet her gaze.

"It was your intention to release the magic, and see if anything had altered since Aburamushi's release."

"Oh." Her answer was short, she couldn't remember saying any such thing, the last thing she recalled, before the feeling of fear for Daniel's life, was telling them to go home. Everything after that was blank. A void in which she felt only her own burning anger. Maybe Elly was right, maybe she had been blinded by some form of emotion. That was the only explanation, at least she hoped it was.

"If the magic in the town were reversed, would Aburamushi vanish?" Acha joined the conversation, already knowing the answer she would receive was unlikely to be the one she hoped for.

"Doubtful," Elly replied flatly. Seeing the disappointment in her face, she decided to give her a little hope, and Zo a little motivation, "but it would greatly weaken it and stop it from feeding on people's life-force," she smiled reassuringly.

Elly knew full well their intervention would not make things difficult for Aburamushi and at the same time, it would release one of the seals which had already been partly destroyed when Marise had taken the Grimoire. She knew if they released these seals it would prove to be useful in the future. With each seal they removed, a fixed location in Darrienia would be released. Among other things, their journey would restore Darrienia to its intended form.

"But wouldn't Marise need to release the spell herself, after all it is her magic?" Acha questioned, her hope to reduce the damage soon faded as she realised the obvious. Even in her own time—when the number of people who could use magic had been limited—she had always been told the caster was the only one who could remove their magic, by death or design.

"Although that is technically true, we have someone here adept in the manipulation of magic." Elly placed her hand on Zo's shoulder as if to prove her point. "Such rules only apply to those of lesser abilities. Lacking the power to release an enchantment would result in the substitution of their life essence at the instance their magic failed to be powerful enough."

"I—" Zo began uncertainly.

"Nonsense, it's worth a try," Eiji interrupted before she had the chance to protest. "I mean don't y' wanna help all those innocent people Marise imprisoned, Zo?" Eiji added her name to the end for impact. Elly smiled, for Eiji, this push was a clever tactic, a subtle reminder which meant nothing, except to those who knew her recently discovered secret. A reminder which ensured she would do what was expected of her.

He began to walk away followed by Elly and Acha, he knew in his heart they would follow, after all, she, in a manner of speaking, was not Marise. He had faith she would do what her former self would not, the right thing.

Zo extended her hand to Daniel, helping him to his feet. In his hand he still clutched the leaf she had given him. Shivering against the wind, he looked at the tattered remains of his garment. Just as he had been wondering when the next opportunity would present itself to obtain another one, Zo held her arm out to present him with the shirt she had only moments ago been wearing.

Daniel took it from her gratefully, turning his back politely as she pulled a top she had just removed from her satchel over her head. As he turned back to face her, he froze, staring at her new clothing for a moment. It was a top that enhanced her feminine frame, and he had seen it once before. He remembered the low, front-laced top with its tight full-length arms. He remembered it and its owner all too clearly. That did not change the fact it was stunning, but to see her wearing it brought back a gut-wrenching memory. He pushed the thoughts back into the darkest recess of his mind, where he willed them to stay. As he pulled her shirt over his head, his nostrils flared with the comforting smell of her scent. He inhaled deeply before pulling his cloak around him.

Zo forced a smile as she looked at him. From the wall he had just constructed around his mind, it seemed he already knew the principal of shielding his thoughts. He was not perfect at it, she had felt something she could only describe as fear and sadness. As she studied him for a moment, she was relieved he seemed none too worse for wear, but she couldn't help wondering when the unexpected side effect would fade. She heard his voice in her mind seconds before he spoke.

"Zo, there's something—" He altered, hearing her thoughts as clearly as if they were his own, despite this he continued. He knew exactly what his recent revelation meant. There was no longer room for doubt, their paths had crossed once before, but he didn't know quite how to tell her. "Zo, when you, well," he started awkwardly. "You know." He touched his forehead, taking a deep breath before continuing. He had to tell her, at least some of it, there were some things which he would never speak of, to her or anyone. He couldn't believe he was able to stand here with her now and feel as if nothing had changed, as if nothing had to. "Well—"

"Come on you two, you're falling behind," Acha called waving to them, she waited while Elly and Eiji carried on ahead. Zo motioned for her to continue without them. Seeing this she nodded, quickening her pace to allow them a moment.

Acha knew they were always going to walk behind them at their own pace. It was clear Zo would want to monitor his injuries, ensure he didn't push himself too hard, after all it was only hours since he had been healed. He had slept a dreamless sleep before waking. A time spent in silence by all. She had been glad when he woke. They started talking, and he had even managed to eat some of the food Elly had prepared. She was glad to see he still had an appetite, she just hoped he had rested long enough to continue this journey. Seeing her continue on her way, Zo responded, using their new link to make her point.

'*You can read my mind, I know. I don't know how, it just—*' She stopped, feeling his anxiousness.

'*No, not that.*' He sounded almost timid, as if he didn't want to burden her. She looked at him curiously, her heart pounding as he looked away in a deliberate attempt to avoid her gaze.

"Then what?" she asked aloud as the others vanished over the hill. They had made no attempt to slow their pace, just as she and Daniel made no attempt to quicken theirs. The situation alone dictated that, eventually, they would have to give up and wait for them, after all, they needed her.

"I don't know, they think just because my injuries have faded," he grumbled. As he glanced towards her a serious look crossed his tired features. "About that, thanks. I had no idea you could..." He shivered, pulling his cloak even tighter around himself, he didn't feel so well, his deteriorating health clearly reflected in their slowing pace.

Zo stopped, placing her satchel on the ground to check through its contents. He waited silently, his back turned towards her as he spoke. Perhaps if he didn't look at her it would make this easier. He took a breath, yet despite the opportunity, he couldn't bring himself to say it, and so, he continued with his previous sentence.

"I mean it was incredible." He wrapped his arms even tighter around himself against the penetrating cold. He thought back to the welcoming voice, it had been so quiet at first. It drew him towards it pulling him from the darkness into a small speck of light. It pulled him away from another voice, a far stronger one. Despite his best efforts to concentrate on her, it began to stifle her tiny cries. Without reason he was standing behind her, his eyes understanding things that no mortal would normally see. A giant web of energy encompassed the area around him, stemming from the trees and ground making her the focal point of the strange entanglement.

In the distance he saw a figure, the owner of the voice beckoning him. It lured him closer. Suddenly he was no longer watching himself be healed, he moved towards the figure, but still he fought. He fought to hang on to the tired words of his friend who was so desperately trying to save him. He tried to stay standing beside her, yet still, against his best efforts, he moved towards the stranger.

He was close enough to see his features, close enough to reach out and take the hand he had extended. A hand, which despite his attempts to hold back, he reached for. He could smell the underworld on this figure, their hands were barely a moment apart. He knew if their skin touched it would be the end.

A resonating crack was heard only by his ears, disorientation and confusion were his companions as he inexplicably found himself drawn away from the figure of Hermes by one of the silver threads which pierced his friend. It forced him backwards into his injured form. But it was not content to allow him to slumber, it was not satisfied with merely having pulled him back. It continued its battle almost like taut elastic which now recoiled back to its original location as it pulled him beyond the confines of his body towards Zo, and into her mind. He heard the sound of ancient songs sung as a lullaby through the dark patches of her mind, the whisper of childhood dreams, her first spell, her studies, her home.

Then the light took him deeper into her mind, past the light and into the darkness.

"Daniel," she repeated again. As he looked at her, she fastened his fingers around a small phial containing a green tinted liquid. "You're going into shock, drink this." Normally fluids were ill-advised for someone in shock, but this was entirely different to the shock from a normal injury. This was the aftermath of his body realising something which was wrong had now vanished. It was a moment of confusion that could prove deadly if not treated with this special concoction, but if it were administered before he was ready, it would have been detrimental.

He drank the bitter tasting liquid quickly, pulling a repulsed face as he swallowed the last mouthful, wondering if the taste was her revenge for his intrusion on her private thoughts. Medicine, more often than not, was bitter, yet for some reason, whenever she had prepared it, the harsh tastes were expertly disguised, but not this time.

Zo pushed a root, which he now held in his hand, towards his mouth. Unaware he was doing so, he obeyed her and began to chew on it, as Zo carefully replaced the contents of her satchel.

"I'm sorry for the taste I have no Sweet Cicely, that's what I use to sweeten the flavour." She smiled slightly, but like most of her smiles recently it didn't quite reach her eyes. "Of course, it's not my way of punishing you." He blushed realising his thoughts were as clear to her, as hers were to him. "Besides, it's so bad it's made you forget about your symptoms," she teased; it was only as she said this that Daniel realised he had stopped shaking.

"So how long does this link last then?" he asked in a very Eiji like manner as he directed attention away from his embarrassment. He moved to stand near her as she made another batch of the bitter liquid, once finished she almost completely emptied her water skin over the grass before tipping the concoction into it.

"I don't know, it has never happened before." She shook the leather skin gently managing to avoid looking at him as she did so.

"What about with Acha? I mean, you knew she was in danger."

"That was different, because I forced her to wake, a trace of the magic remained on the tip of her consciousness. I was only aware of any powerful emotions. It was nothing like this." She placed the satchel back over her shoulder as they started moving again.

"Oh." He smiled slightly.

"I think it's best if no one learns of this." She held eye contact with him as if to enforce her words.

"Is this the reason you've never used your magic on me?" He thought back over all the times he had injured himself. She had always seemed to want to do something for him, but he was never sure what. Until now he had never realised her powers of healing passed beyond the skills of botany and assessment, although he'd had his suspicions.

"Kind of, it's dangerous to be emotionally attached to the people they are used on, it has side effects. That's why healers tend to keep to themselves, if they get too invested, they let their emotions rule their magic and things like this happen." Zo stared out over the horizon, her mind weighed down with worry. All of a sudden, Daniel felt her spirit lift. "Not to worry hey?" she smiled. "It's not like I can't tell what you're thinking anyway. It's easy enough to block. I mean I don't really want to know what I'm getting for my birthday, so I'll tell you how." Daniel suddenly got the impression she wasn't quite as cheerful as she tried to imply but, as yet, he lacked the skill to read her innermost emotions. Then again, she had become quite proficient at shielding them recently, even with this new link, he wasn't reading anything more than he would normally.

"Hey, who says you're getting anything?" He shoved her playfully as they approached the others, who had finally decided to wait. They knew Daniel had not fully recovered, but the longer they spent reaching Abaddon, the less time they would have before they needed to move on, and Elly for one wanted to be as far away as possible. Especially once the magic had been removed and the sun started to set.

"Daniel, are you all right to continue?" she questioned, as they approached. He took a mouthful of water from the leather skin Eiji offered him. Anything was better than the horrible tasting fluid he was being forced to drink.

"Thanks," he smiled, relieved at the freshness of the cool water. He returned it to him as he looked towards Elly, only to discover she hadn't waited for his response and had already pressed onward. "Come on," Daniel sighed. "We're falling behind, again." He placed his hand on his chest his breathing becoming slightly laboured as his chest began to sting.

"Are y' sure y' okay?" Eiji questioned concern flickered through his eyes.

"Just stings a little." Zo forced him to drink more of his medicine as she lifted it to his mouth. When he obeyed, she released her grip, turning to look at Eiji and Acha.

"You go on ahead," she encouraged as the two of them as they hung back, both had an air of concern about them. "We'll catch up, we just need to take it slow and steady."

"We don't mind, really." Acha smiled.

"It's okay, really, go," she seemed quite insistent, so they surrendered to her wishes. Daniel looked at her questioningly waiting for the others to leave before he asked.

"The perfect time for what?" In answer to his question, Zo simply smiled, placing her hand inside her satchel. Having had time to assess the unexpected side effect she knew now exactly how to feed him thoughts, whilst shielding everything else. Now she knew how deep their connection went, she no longer needed to worry about him discovering something accidentally, not as long as she remained calm.

"I should have given it to you before." She moved her hand through the contents of her satchel, her face filled with concentration as she searched for something. "I wanted to save it for your birthday, but I think you may need it now." She looked up and smiled as she found it, she could feel his intrigue and anticipation which was fuelled by her own. "But before you can have it, you have to drink at least half of that," she pointed to the leather skin in his hand, he let out a groan before drinking more of the medicine until she was satisfied.

"Happy?" he asked almost bitterly, although he had to admit, the pain had almost gone now. He began to chew on the root, which eased it even more.

She delayed for a moment longer before pulling six poles, bound together by a piece of twine, from her bag. Staring at it, he wondered how something so large could have fit so effortlessly into such a small satchel. Given its size he wondered if it had even been in there at all. Each section was exactly one foot in length, and contained unique symbols and carvings etched into the wood. As she undid the twine, he saw a faint ray of light pass from the end of each stick into the next.

"What is it?" As he took the mahogany coloured wood from her, he expected it to be heavy, yet he found himself surprised by its lack of weight as he passed it between his hands.

"It's a weapon, here." She took it from him, passing him a small notebook to study. As he flicked through it, he saw it was filled with text and sketches for various techniques and uses for the weapon in the various forms, all of which had been written in Zo's hand. "Let me show you." She flicked it together into its most natural form, a solid staff.

She spun it rapidly. The wooden composition a blur at the speed of her movements as she passed it from one hand to another in ways which told of a deep-rooted skill. The sections, by her will, released to be manipulated with ease, as they obeyed her every whim to attach or separate despite her never slowing pace as she retained perfect control of the various combinations. "I made it myself. When I was younger, I saw one just like it in a dream," she advised, returning it to Daniel. "I think you will find it's perfect for you. It's joined together by a very old magic. The links between them will grow and shrink as you wish, creating a weapon for any situation. It has an excellent defence against magic, maybe later I can show you."

Zo smiled as she watched him flick the stick into a few of its most basic forms, much to his surprise. He had never been able to control a weapon, despite his father trying to teach him on many occasions. But this weapon was different, even now, he skilfully executed moves he had only just read. It was clear this weapon worked on theory, not on skill.

"It's incredible! It's like it knows exactly what I want it to do, then does it." He grinned, panting. Even from such a short burst of activity he was clearly tired, but this time, even the unpleasant medicine she forced him to drink didn't dampen his spirits. Splitting it into sections he looped it over his belt, he seemed almost surprised that it held its position.

"It does, it's magical. I made it just for you." He glanced down at it again, clearly wanting to play with it some more, but now was not the time. They began to walk again as they spoke.

"What are these symbols? I don't recognise any of them." He fingered them as he stopped again, he noticed his name was carved on one of the sections, this was the only part of a long-forgotten language Zo had managed to teach him to read. "It must have taken you ages, the carvings alone are so detailed."

"Three months, while you were at college," she answered with minimal delay. She had plenty of time to do things like this without Daniel's knowledge. The college he attended was in the Eastern province of Albeth, it was both a boat and horse ride away. His subjects of study ran three days, from the day of Hermes to the day of Helios, which meant he would generally leave the night before, stay at the student housing, and return after his final lesson. She had more than enough time between helping Angela with her patients, and tending the garden, to do things without his knowledge. She was, however, surprised she had managed to keep it a secret for so long. "I intended to leave it for you to discover after I left. Just don't tell anyone where you got it, okay?"

This statement was easier than explaining to him exactly how she had managed to get it here. She had used a very old magic, like that used to bind it, one she had encountered only through her dreams. In her dream she had been witness to a story, but also privy to some lessons, almost as if the dream was a message passed through time, to ensure she could create it. It could be stored between boundaries and retrieved by its master from anywhere. Now it bore Daniel's name she would have to remember to try to teach him the technique, to see if even someone with no talent in magic could summon it.

"Especially Elaineor, right?" Daniel said as he caught a slight glimpse of a buried thought.

"Yes, you see, this weapon…" She took a deep breath as she realised what she was going to say. She was going to tell him, she had to. She steadied her breath and calmed her racing heart before she continued. "May be the only thing that will protect you from…" She paused lowering her head in shame. The darkened mood which descended upon her had been impossible to hide. She had to tell him, but the final word just wouldn't come.

"You?" Daniel queried softly, taking her hand in his. She looked away from him, blinking away the tears quickly before he could see.

"How did you…" she whispered, her voice failing as her vision fixed anywhere but on him. He knew her secret, he knew and yet he had chosen to stay. Part of her had hoped he would hate her and leave, at least then she knew he would be safe, but she hadn't realised just how much his choice to stay would mean to her. She fought back against the tears.

"I saw all the clues, but I wasn't certain until—"

"I healed you," she whispered closing her eyes, remembering how she had opened her mind to him. She had known there was a danger of him venturing beyond what she offered, beyond the memories of her childhood, but it was either that or lose him forever. "I didn't know I swear," her tone became defensive, "I have only just found out myself. That's why I sent you away. I didn't want to put you in any danger. I swear I will protect you, I promise."

This was the second time she had made this promise to him, but repeating it now held with it a promise of strength.

"Don't worry." He smiled reassuringly as they approached their waiting friends. His smile alone comforted her more than he would know. The reaction she had expected when he learnt the truth had been far different from the one she had received. As she glanced to him, she felt it again, the same feeling clouding his mind as when he had looked at her earlier. He was keeping something from her.

"Are you ready?" Elly walked up to meet them as they approached. Eiji and Acha sat on the outskirts of Abaddon. In this world it was found hidden deep within the forest, despite the dense trees, they had located them with ease.

"What exactly am I meant to be doing?" Uncertainty gripped her as she stood before the town. She glanced to Daniel, there was so much to discuss, but now the situation dictated their conversation needed to end prematurely.

"Just release the spell. It is fairly simple. While I am in these parts I have an errand to run, so if you will excuse me, I should not be gone too long," Elly advised.

"You mean, you're not coming in with me? But this was your idea," Zo asked, questioning the sudden change in Elly. Less than an hour ago she was determined to be here, yet now it seemed she didn't intend to stay.

"We do not have time to waste. It is quicker for me to do this now, rather than take you all with me later. Do not worry, you will be fine." Without any more room for argument, Elly walked away.

Hesitantly, Zo entered the town, followed by her friends who matched her slow pace. Acha approached one of the houses where the curtains had been left slightly askew. Straining her vision through this gap she could see the strands of light filtering through the artificial night within to illuminate a figure lying peacefully upon the bed. The fire had long been extinguished, and the windows shut, as if to protect the inhabitants from the elements.

"I guess I work my way from end to start then," she spoke to herself, feeling the complicated webs which were weaved into the spell. Each thread of magic looped and crossed with the others. She had to be careful not to damage the composition if she wished everyone to get out of this alive. "Can you stand over there?" She pointed to the edge of town, to a place void of any threads. "You need to stay there, okay?" Nodding, they made their way to the place she had indicated. Removing them from the magic's webbing not only gave her the room she would need to work, it also meant that, no matter what happened, they would not be linked in any way to the spell, should anything go wrong.

As she began, even they could see the faint sea-green aura which began to shine around her to illuminate the air, a colour which slowly changed to become an electric blue. This was the colour of her magic, whereas green was the colour of Marise's. Even as she thought this, she had no idea how she knew it to be true. She understood that the magic she felt at this location both here and in Darrienia was Marise's. But at the temple it had been hers, mingled with that of another person. It made her wonder who this second person could have been.

She felt the pull of the earth as she seized the first thread of the green magic, within her mind she crossed and curved it under and around those which came before it, forcing her blue magic into it to dissolve the thread. As she dispelled the threads, ancient poetry gently fell from her lips. Her body seemed to follow the threads she unwound. It was an amazing sight to behold. It was almost as if the ancient words had become a gentle song she, and the world around her, danced to. The flowers in the nearby gardens aged and died, before life came from new seeds once again. But as with any exertion it soon began to take its toll, and her pace began to slow as she grew tired.

She followed the threads as best she could, but with each twist, more energy left her. She pulled against the weave as it became harder to unravel. Even though the threads vanished as she unravelled the design of the enchantment, it began to feel as if they bound her, restricting her movements as she became entangled in the thread's web.

The force became so great, her pace stopped completely, the weight of her body covered in the tangled thread reduced her to her knees. She concentrated harder. She had found it far easier to follow the threads with her body than unravelling them with just her mind. She felt the energy of her own basic magic begin to fade, the colour alternating from blue to the faint silver shimmer of her life's thread. She knew then she had started something she could not finish.

Despite this seamless shift in the source of energy supplied, her resolve did not waver. To leave the damaged threads would be more dangerous than had she not begun at all. She could only hope she had enough life to offer as a substitute energy for that her own abilities lacked.

Daniel, watching her fall, moved to intervene, his sudden steps prevented as Eiji moved to stop him quickly.

"Y' can't interfere. What she's doing's delicate, if a non-magic user were t'interfere it could damage the threads she unwinds. It may kill her."

"What do you mean may? Barely a few hours ago she exhausted herself to bring me back from the brink of death, and now she needs to unwind a spell that's equal to her full power when she isn't in possession of it." He couldn't say any more without revealing her secret to Acha, but he was certain this was the secret Eiji had protected so honourably. Now he understood why, it wasn't something she should hear from anyone else. "If we don't do something it will kill her slowly, substituting her life-force for the magic she lacks when she has no power left."

There was a fatal difference between casting and reversing a spell, one created by the difference between taking and giving magical energy. When a magic user cast something, the energy they called upon was from an external source and would be disconnected as soon as it became dangerous to the caster's health. However, for the reversing of a spell, the energy came directly from them, the flow was completely different. Instead of the caster taking energy to give it, the magic being unravelled took it from the caster, once started there was no way to sever the linking of energy. The dissipation of magic would continue to pull the energy from the source, until there was nothing left to offer.

Eiji agreed with Daniel. It wasn't one of the greatest ideas to face her with such a challenge before she was given the chance to fully recover. But if what Elly had said earlier was correct, once Aburamushi was released within Darrienia there was only a limited time in which to release this spell before the people here would be trapped forever.

Each one restrained within his enchantment would only serve to multiply his power. If they released the spell, however, they would sever the final ties of his imprisonment. In this case, the risk outweighed the damage Aburamushi could do if left bonded to this town. By freeing the town, his power would weaken and he would pose far less of a threat than if things were to remain as they were. Eiji felt awful for the role he played in convincing Zo to accept this task, but the needs of the many were chosen over the needs of the few, the few in this case, however, was her. It was harder to make the obvious choice when it was a friend who would suffer the consequences. Now he just had to put his trust in Elly.

"Daniel." Eiji's lowered voice was filled with apprehension as Zo became more fatigued. By his calculations, the spell was halfway unravelled. There was no way she alone would possess the power to release it. Even now he feared for her, although Elly had assured him everything would be fine, and given the circumstances he trusted her word, it seemed it would be close. Eiji knew he was unable to help, not only because by his very nature he was clumsy and would no doubt damage the threads, but his magic was incompatible being from a completely different source than hers. To combine the two to undo this magic would probably not only fail to remove the curse but kill both them and those trapped by it in the process. Elly had warned him not to interfere, regardless of what happened.

As things seemed more desperate, Eiji sought for a method to aid her. Perhaps if he could calculate it exactly, he could sever the weave ahead of her complex workings in order to terminate her attachment. It would leave the enchantment only half broken, but she could take the time to rest before continuing. He just couldn't decide whether to intervene or heed Elly's warning.

A strange distortion filled the air, paralysing them under the sheer pressure which seemed to originate from somewhere before them. Through the shimmering shroud stepped a figure, his steps light as he traversed the complex weave of magic with ease to reach down to offer Zo his hand. There was something distinguished about his mannerisms, like a prince asking a lady for the honour of a dance. She reached up wearily accepting his hand, his touch bringing a weightlessness to her body. With just that light touch he moved forward to embrace her gently, and their dance began.

Lifting her head, Zo's tired gaze met with his intense blue eyes as she took in the stranger's appearance through her blurred vision. His long black hair was fastened neatly into a long ponytail. Somehow, he seemed familiar and his magic seemed to have shared the same colour as hers.

The figure shared the same glow which connected them to the earth. Although tired, she remained standing with his aid, he seemed to sway gently as if rocking her. She found the motion soothing, she rested her head on his chest, the sound of his heart echoed comfortingly as they followed the final thread. They stood in silence until the final ray of the magic's light had faded. She pulled away from his comfort to speak, but before the words could leave her, she felt her remaining strength vanish, as if his touch had been the source of her residual energy. As she fell forwards, she was once more caught in his embrace.

He held her close for just a moment before picking her up in his arms. Her friends hovered uncertainly as they questioned if it was now safe to approach. Before they had decided it was, he had walked past them, into the forest from the place they had first entered. When they were clear of the trees, he lowered her to the ground before touching her pale skin gently.

"You should know by now," he whispered in a tone so quiet none of them could hear his words. "I could never let anything harm you." He looked to her friends raising his voice so they could hear. "It was careless of you to have her take on such a task given the circumstances. You *must* be more careful." He brushed a stray piece of hair from her face with a tenderness and concern which made Daniel uneasy.

"Will she be all right?" Daniel stepped forwards; he was the first to address him, taking his attention away from his friend, and putting an end to that gentle caress.

"I believe so." He looked back to her, as he did so he waved one hand over the other, within it appeared five amulets. "I believe these will aid you on your travels." He passed them to Daniel before lifting Zo slightly. When a small phial appeared in his hand, he placed it to her lips, ensuring she swallowed its contents. "This will help speed up the recovery," he answered the question although no one yet had asked. They hadn't needed to. Daniel had looked ready to interrupt, he couldn't say he blamed him, how was he to know he meant her no harm?

"Why are you helping us?" Acha stepped forwards; the figure cast his gaze over her critically before answering her question.

"Darrienia is a place filled with unimaginable danger. To fail would be to condemn the world, yet, there is something even more valuable at stake." He glanced down at Zo as she stirred, the concoction he had given was already working to restore her strength. Although she slept a dreamless sleep, she was aware of all which transpired, and a part of her feared that rejuvenation was not the potion's only intention. There was a momentary silence while people exchanged questioning glances, before Zo's eyes opened.

As she lay in silence, she studied the stranger intently, convinced she recognised him. His raven black hair captured the spectrum as the light danced across it. He turned to look at her and smiled. The smile reached all the way to his eyes in a way that seemed so comforting she truly believed she could trust him.

"There is one thing which does concern me. Am I correct in understanding you have help from a force of their world? I was led to understand the entirety of the Oneiroi race are captives. Is it not your quest to free them?" The stranger looked between them, wondering if any would be so kind as to answer.

"Seiken?" Eiji questioned without delay, for a second he cringed, remembering how often Elly had scolded him for opening his mouth without due thought. Surely his words here could do no harm, after all, this person had just saved Zo's life, and aided in the release of a powerful enchantment. It made him wonder if this was an intervention Elly had anticipated. If so, perhaps he should have shown more caution.

"Ah, I see, an Oneiroi has come to your aid, interesting." He slowly began to walk away satisfied his work was somehow completed.

"Wait." Zo called after him. As if on her command he stopped, turning to face her. Her voice, although barely a whisper, had not gone unheard. She began to cough. Once more she saw the tiny splatters of blood on her hand, she was thankful they still went unnoticed. She had to be more careful, she was causing herself some serious damage. "Who are you?" she questioned having finally caught her breath.

"Who am I?" He smiled sadly almost as if he had expected her to know. "My name is not important. Perhaps we shall have time for introductions when next we meet, but I am afraid my time is limited. I must be on my way." The same paralysing pressure, which had marked his appearance, weighted the surroundings. The transparency of the air before him became opaque, almost liquid as it distorted to grant him access.

Daniel stared at the place the figure had disappeared to, his hand tightly clutching the five amulets as he questioned how he knew there was another person within their group. But this was not the query on the forefront of his mind. There was an unsettling aura, a discomfort which surrounded him as he questioned how this figure could possibly have aided in the release of a Hectarian spell when Zo was the last of wielder of these artes. He had seemed wounded when she asked his identity, so how exactly had the two come to cross paths prior to his appearance here? There was clearly more to this meeting than a stranger's concern. It was as if he had known she was in danger, and the way he touched her had sung of a deep bond. It made him question exactly who this figure was.

Chapter 11

Night's Desire

Night paced the length of the ebony table. His scowl was as dark as the heavy drapes which obstructed the view of the outside world. His steps were long, impatient strides as he paced back and forth, mentally checking everything was prepared to ensure occurrences such as these would not transpire. Having confirmed all the precautions and safeguards remained unbreached, unaltered, he was brought back to the one question which frustrated him more than anything else at this time, a question for which answer eluded him.

"How is it possible?" he questioned aloud as he paced back down the other side of the table. He paused for a moment once more in silent reflection before, in an attempt to break his continuous pattern in both thought and stride, he stepped away from the table to follow the wall's curve and approach the enormous cast iron cauldron that stood, as always, atop a never fading flame. He peered inside it at the jumble of magical essences and threads which stirred beneath its turbulent surface before he spoke again. "We have detained all the Oneirois," he stated flicking his gossip crystal idly between his fingers as he once more began to pace.

"Yes sire, according to our best estimation, their forms make certainty somewhat tricky." A dark shadow flickered across the wall, almost as if it followed his movements as he paced.

"Yet one is helping them. One in our possession no less. Tell me, have there been any fluctuations anywhere, have any of the guards noticed anything out of the ordinary?" As he once more reached the table, he raised the glass which stood upon it to the light in order to examine the ruby fluid contained within.

He did not wait for an answer, it was one he knew already. "Although I *am* surprised, I am not concerned. This may just work to our advantage." He mused, although this was an unexpected twist, it had the potential to work to his advantage. In fact, this was even better than what he had planned. He walked back towards the iron vessel, carefully adding the fluid from the glass. As he did so, a purple haze rose briefly from its surface as the contents within began to alter. He looked towards his visitor as they spoke.

"That one may have escaped you?" the shadow questioned uncertainly, approaching his vicinity once more.

"That one within our possession has found a way to assist them." Seiken's image flashed briefly upon the surface of the liquid. He appeared to be resting with the other Oneirois in the area they were being detained. "Go, bring me the one we call Seiken." He phrased the sentence carefully. He knew much of the Oneiroi race, after all, it could be said they were his children or—if one was to be really literal, given the circumstances surrounding his being—siblings at the least.

Night was no stranger to their lands and knew about their ever changing nature, but he also knew one thing which would never change within their realm. Each Oneiroi, like all living things, possessed two names, a social name, the name given to them by their parents or the ones responsible for their training, and their real name, their true name, a name kept secret from all. One which reflected the true power of their being, a name so powerful it should never be uttered by a creature from either world. This name could only be discovered by those who could look deep into the very being of another person, and the only reason someone would look at another thing in this manner was if they wished to control it.

In any world but Darrienia, to know a thing's true name would grant a person some control over that life or element. It was part of the fundamental practice of magic, but in Darrienia things worked differently for the Oneirois' own protection. Night knew Seiken's true name just by looking at him. He was, after all, once a god. A god, who was once part of a greater being, one who had assisted with creation itself.

In the past, some had even referred to the Oneiroi as his children, well Nyx's, whereas others hypothesised they were Gaea's. In reality, both were right. The first Oneiroi was something they brought into creation together, but they could only take credit for the first. Everything after that was left in its control, thus negating any divine influence. The Oneiroi became a race of their own making. Had it not been for this, he may have made the mistake of trying to place the Oneirois within his control, but fortunately, he was familiar with their world and its secrets. To know an Oneiroi's true name was dangerous, he would never utter it. The repercussions, even to one such as himself, would be great.

"And security?" The figure lingered as it awaited his command. Night hesitated for but a moment before his answer.

"I see no concerns, bring me the Oneiroi, and have somebody find Aburamushi." The new design was already developed within his mind. This was going to turn out far better than he had anticipated.

When Marise had summoned that creature from Hades all those years ago, he never imagined he would find a purpose for him. The guardian was no longer a concern. Since Aburamushi had been released, it had no further purpose, and so it had returned home once more.

Night knew Aburamushi would be difficult to locate, especially since it was now free from the restrictions of boundaries. It would no doubt be after the one thing it wanted more than anything, life. A life that was not based around the survival of Marise or Zoella. Whilst Marise had summoned Aburamushi, she had used Zoella's power to summon it, even if she had not realised it herself. Once one persona gained full dominance and destroyed the other, the spell which summoned him and the link between the summon and the summoner would be broken, as a result Aburamushi would return to Hades.

There were only two ways to prevent his ultimate demise, by his own hand he needed to kill those who created him in a way which took their life-force and sealed it within him, or find a way to break his ties to them and obtain a life of his own. In order to execute the first, Aburamushi would need to learn the manipulation magic, to do so would be a lengthy process; for the second, he would need to find that which most mortal sought, a means to gain immortality, thus freeing himself from the burden of death. Aburamushi was not foolish, quite the opposite in fact, he knew should either of his creators vanish, he would become nothing more than a memory. Night knew this being's desire well enough to know it would not idly await its fate, and hopefully, he knew it well enough to predict its next move.

"Yes sire, consider it done." The figure melted backwards into the shadow. Before fading completely, it moved slightly as if to bow.

It was only a few moments later that Seiken was thrown from the darkness to his feet. His hands were securely fastened before him with a strange cord which shifted through all the colours of the spectrum. The ones which bound his hands were the only restraints which seemed to serve a purpose. The others, which he wore one on each ankle and another around his neck, did not appear to restrict his movements in any way.

"My lord, the Oneiroi known as Seiken." The voice from the shadow introduced the figure it had deposited, although it knew there was no need. Night knew all too well who lay before him.

"Very good." He walked around the Oneiroi taking in his appearance carefully. He looked over his auburn hair and his gentle features before crouching to meet his eyes. There was fear within the delicate brown shades, yet there was something else too. Despite the fact Night knew he was not an Oneiroi of the last cycle, his eyes were old. Nyx had known each Oneiroi from the last cycle, thus Night did too, and *he* had not been among them. He would have remembered.

Although Oneirois were immortal, there were those who chose to become mortal, to cross over into 'Gaea's star' as they called it. When this occurred, a new Oneiroi was born by ritual, one who would possess the same wisdom and knowledge as their predecessor. The knowledge of Darrienia was removed and used to create the new being, allowing the retired figure to enter the mortal world in a form of their choosing. Thus, as they entered the mortal life cycle, everything they knew, everything they remembered, vanished with their final step through the boundaries as the new life was formed by that which they left behind.

A smile crossed Night's lips but only for a second.

"You're Eryx's successor," he observed, knowing he was the only figure this young man could have replaced. "Why am I not surprised?" He watched Seiken's eyes widen in shock, no doubt as he wondered how this god could have known his predecessor.

Night shook his head in mild amusement before looking back into the shadows. This Oneiroi also had a fascination with people he couldn't have, but in Eryx's case one person in particular had sealed his fate. Eryx had crossed into the mortal world to obtain her, yet somehow he had retained his knowledge of Darrienia. That was the first time he and Night competed for anything, although the word competition would imply there was a challenge where truly, there was none. Ironically, his successor had the same infatuation for one of their kind. It was through this weakness for the human world he saw his way to exploit them. Night did not need to speak for the shadow to know what was being asked of them.

"With his new-found freedom he is proving very difficult to locate, although I estimate his retrieval within the hour," it answered without the need for the question to be posed.

"Very good, then you are excused." There was hesitation from the shadow, almost as if they had expected a different response. Seeing this, Night spoke again. "These restraints are infallible, correct?"

"Yes sire." The bonds which held Seiken were one of a kind. They had been handcrafted to adapt to the life-force of the person they touched, drain them of energy, and seal their magic to render them helpless. The more someone resisted, the more energy they took. In fact, if someone struggled enough, they would certainly lose consciousness, perhaps even die.

"Escape from such a wonderful creation is impossible, correct?" The shadow moved as if to nod its confirmation. "Then I see no reason why you should remain. Even without them I am certain I possess the necessary means to control this child."

"I did not mean to imply—" Night raised his hand to silence the shadow.

"Now if you will excuse us, I have a proposition for my young friend, and you have work to attend to." Night waved a hand dismissively and the shadow vanished.

"I am no friend of yours!" Seiken spat, the words themselves hanging bitterly in his mouth. He struggled against the strange bonds, but with every movement he found himself growing weaker. To pull himself to his knees was an effort he swore had almost killed him, but he knew there had to be a way to escape.

"It's no use struggling, those bonds are a highly developed genetic seal. Here." A chair dragged itself across the floor from the nearby table to rest beside the struggling Oneiroi. Night watched him critically as he refused the gesture which had been offered. A frustrated sigh left him. He had hoped to keep this amicable, but it seemed this boy was as stubborn as his predecessor. With a flick of his wrist, Seiken found himself reluctantly placed upon the chair.

"I know who you are. I have no interest in anything you have to say." Sprays of his auburn hair had freed themselves during his struggle, the loose strands moved rapidly back and forth in time with his laboured breathing. He had heard rumours of such a restraint existing, he could only hope if he preserved his energy, he could regain enough reserves to disable them in a quick, unexpected, desperate attempt. Perhaps he could even find the strength to alter the vibration of his life-force, an act which would surely give him the time he needed to execute such a plan.

"Well, if nothing else it spares me the introductions." He stepped backwards slightly in order to fully take in Seiken's appearance once more. Visually, he seemed no older than his daughter, although his uniquely brown eyes held more knowledge than any one person could expect to learn in the entirety of their life. Night's knowledge of Eryx placed Seiken as an Oneiroi for almost twenty-seven years, yet the knowledge he possessed dated far before his appearance on Darrienia. He questioned his calculations, but knew that, had he been there previously, he would have known this boy. The power and knowledge he saw, had to be that passed from his predecessor, yet it seemed impossible.

There was something different about him, an age about his presence no passed wisdom could create. However, despite these doubts, this boy had a very Eryx presence about him, from his reaction alone it was clear he had succeeded his role. Night studied him harder for a moment, certain this child was older than he first thought. When he considered his hidden heritage, he had to be, but he could not fathom how they could have kept a being of his obvious standing hidden.

Seiken, was an unusual Oneiroi, his appearance, although similar to those of Gaea's world, was different to any other of his race which took that form. There were those who looked mortal, human, but something about his appearance, about the look in his eyes proved he was different. Each Oneiroi had a never changing form, unique to them and this was his, human, yet slightly different. Build wise he was slender, it would be easy to fall into the deception that he possessed no strength, any foolish enough to believe this would soon learn the error of their thinking. His build disguised his strength well.

"As for you choosing sides, it doesn't really matter. The outcome will be my victory." Night smiled deciding it was time to resume their conversation.

"Clearly to contain such arrogance you do not know your challenger." Seiken glared at him as he once more tried to release the bonds. If he could just escape, he would only need to dodge the guards, navigate the tower, find an exit, *and* free his people without any of them being seen. Realising the futility, he gave a frustrated sigh, leaning back into the chair. Even if he *did* break free of the bonds, there was little chance he could do much more. He had no choice but to listen to what Night had to say. Just then the reality of the situation became clear. Their only hope *really* was the success of this 'game'.

"On the contrary." Night smiled to himself as Seiken finally stopped fighting. "I know them very well."

"Tell me, what do you wish to gain from destroying both our worlds?" Ultimately, this would happen if things continued to progress along their current course. Should his kind not return to defend the barrier there was a very real chance both worlds would be forced into havoc and self-destruction as it tried to right the wrongs which had occurred. Maybe, if he could discover his ultimate goal, he could warn Thea. Perhaps, armed with this knowledge, they could stop his plan before it was set into motion.

"Destroy them?" Night questioned. "You misunderstand. I don't wish the destruction of the world, I plan its redemption." He walked across to the enormous window which stretched from floor to ceiling. With a wave of his hands the drapes opened.

As the heavy curtains parted, Seiken squinted against the light as his vision adjusted. After so long spent in the dark confines of the prison, even the light of this room had, at first, been too bright to bear. The time he spent out of his body to aid The Chosen, did not change his body's reaction to light, after all, he still remained confined within the dark prison. Those he aided simply saw a solid projection of his life-force.

This omnipresence was normally easier to achieve in his own world, here he had to bring his body to a near-death state, lowering his life-signs to the minimum, by doing so he could appear anywhere in Darrienia. It was a talent only those of the royal house shared and, occasionally, he could even do it without the need to stop his real body from moving. He could control them both, but only for easy tasks.

"Tell me, what do you see?" Night questioned as Seiken blinked several times. When finally his eyes adjusted he realised they were incredibly high. Despite the vision of what lay before him, he did not answer. He merely looked down on a world which was nothing like his own, a world man had destroyed to create a life for themselves. Unlike his own world, the damage caused here was permanent. "Can't you see it? The deceit, the treachery, the greed. That is the way of the world now. It's not only the corruption, it is the disregard for Gaea as they slowly sentence her to death with their selfishness. People need to learn their place, they have become too arrogant. Everything is not theirs to take as they wish." Night's voice was calm, yet undertones of outrage and disgust lined his words.

"So, you want to destroy them?" Seiken wasn't sure he quite understood the situation. If Night wanted to destroy them, he clearly possessed the power to do so. It made him wonder why all this was necessary. What was there to gain by this method when just a wave of his hand could see all he despised, destroyed?

"Not all of them, but a majority, yes." Night did not want to eradicate all of humanity, just the unworthy. After all, originally even Zeus himself did not want man upon this world's surface. He had wanted them to die out having never evolved, yet he seemed fond of them now, but still Night couldn't help but think by eradicating them he would win the favour of someone whom he was intent on destroying. "But once my plan is complete, the world will not tremble to man, but man to the world as it was millennia ago.

"The world's magic has all but been extinguished. Although we can thank the Hoi Hepta Sophoi for their role in this, even they cannot take the brunt of the blame. It is down to them." He gestured through the window in disgust, a burning hatred reflected in his eyes. "Things need to change. Those people exploiting the poor to line their pockets with gold, those who take yet never return, the predators and persecutors of this so-called society, I call for their eradication. An end to the arrogance even in blatant stupidity, the moral righteousness amongst the worst sinners, the apathy in the face of absolute manipulation, the unfulfilled promises, the sheer lack of will for the betterment of self and others. Out there they are nothing more than self-serving hypocrites and those who would do good, those who would sacrifice to bring others joy, are those mocked the most.

"Those remaining will serve the land once more. It will be Gaea who is their mistress. I shall simply take back that which was taken from me so long ago. The goddess has waited long enough for the final sign of the prophecy, and now it is upon us, I *shall* fulfil it."

"But then, are you not showing them the same persecution you just spoke of." Seiken was unsure how much he could say, but for the moment he knew there was something Night wanted from him, some reason why he was summoned to his presence. He knew, true to his word, Night would not harm him, or his people, at least not yet. It was a truth he planned to exploit whenever possible, especially if it could give him some information which could be used to their advantage.

"When the world was born, like animals, humans too would hunt and were hunted. It was a world where to survive was to live, and failure cost the ultimate price. Magic ran rampant 'across the earth and none could tame it. It moulded things in the way they should have stayed, but eventually, they were permitted a way to seal it. Since then, they have grown arrogant, self-absorbed, but soon they shall be re-educated. They shall learn their place in this world, or be torn from it as things revert back to the natural order."

"You're talking about unleashing the Severaine! To do such a thing, to unleash such a power, is reckless. You know it can't be controlled now." Seiken could barely believe what he had heard. In past millennia it took generations to finally devise a way to seal its power. This world had long forgotten its ancestors and their old knowledge.

When the world was young and Nyx had not long given life to Hemera, the wild energy born of Chaos and Gaea coursed across the planet in the rawest form. An energy so pure, so absolute that all trembled before it. Its approach was marked by chaos and disasters, tame to that it reaped on its arrival. Its sole purpose was to bring balance, to keep Gaea thriving and replenish that which had been destroyed. It pursued those who failed to heed its warnings until their threat was no more.

It was such a fearsome force, the Gods had eventually shown mercy, sealing it in order to allow mankind time to adapt, trusting they would adhere to the lessons taught by the fearful beast. Their trust had been ill placed. This had been the only time the Gods had assisted mankind with the Severaine, but their periods of development had seen them advance beyond the need for their guidance. As the ruler of the Throne of Eternity was overthrown, the power restraining the Severaine diminished, and once more this mighty force ran rampant.

It levelled all it approached, reshaping the very fabric of the world. But some people survived, as did their knowledge, and in time they too found a way to restrain this threat. But sealing it once brought only a slight reprieve until the throne of the Gods was seized once more by another. Being bound in the beginning to those claiming reign meant with the falling of each ruler, the cycle repeated and has done so times beyond count. But this cycle, and the people within it, were still young. If this fearsome force was to be released now, there would be little chance of any finding a means in which to once again seal it.

It was for this very reason Night believed now was the perfect time for him to act. Once released, they would never be able to evolve to a level which would permit them to restrain its power, and its release would reduce the population of the world. It was the perfect plan, their numbers would be reduced, and Gaea could be given a chance to heal and revitalise.

"Perhaps, but any further details on this matter do not concern you. Now down to business, the reason I brought you here." Night had wanted to re-cruit this young man's aid if possible, but no matter, if he were unwilling to lend his support to his desire, there *were* other means to obtain his full compliance.

"Whatever your plan, I will not help you." Seiken stated, he had wondered the reason he had been summoned and was relieved to find they were about to discuss it. The sooner he knew, the sooner he could refuse and be returned to his people. There was nothing Night could say, nothing he could offer, which would make him betray his people or his home. There was only one hope for freedom, and he would trust her to keep her word.

"We shall see. It seems you have little option other than to listen." Seiken still gazed out of the window when Night decided once again to draw the heavy drapes. He could see Seiken had understood what he had said, to a certain extent. He could feel Gaea's pain as he looked out across their world. However, what he was going to say was important, the young Oneiroi's dis-traction was not an option. It was vital he absorbed his every word.

"How is it that I am in your world?" This question had been bothering Seiken for some time, and although eager to leave, he realised the answer may provide him with insight on how to get his people home. "Is this place—"

"This place, neither exists here, nor in any other reality, although, it is accessible from all, like most gods' homes. Now, as I was saying, I know you are helping our travellers." Seiken felt himself turn pale at his words, his stomach churned under his stare as he wondered how it was possible for him to know such things. He had been careful, he was certain his motions had not been detected, and his time outside the prison in his astral form had most certainly been unobserved. He looked to Night in awestruck horror. If he knew this much, there was no telling what fate may await him, after all, it was in Night's best interests for The Chosen to lose. "You may now find my proposition, difficult to refuse."

* * *

"Are you sure you're all right?" Daniel placed his hand on Zo's shoulder, worry crossed his already wrinkled brow, further increasing the lines in his forehead. Glancing up at him she smiled, nodding, yet this did little to convince him.

He glanced back down at a book he had brought along for the trip, he was not *really* looking at it. The timeworn pages curled to meet his fingers as he flicked absent-mindedly through the content. He knew exactly where to find the information he sought, but he was utilising this pause for other things, such as trying to decipher what she was thinking about.

Since the stranger had left, she had been focusing her efforts on remembering him. Perhaps finding the answer could solve some of the riddles concerning her past. Looking to Daniel she pushed the thoughts from her mind, as if spurred by the realisation he stalled for time.

"Well?" She didn't need to read his mind to know he already knew the answer. It seemed he wasn't quite as good at concealing his thoughts as she had first thought.

"Well..." Placing his book on the ground for all to see, he tried his best to conceal his frustration, but even with this new advantage, he still found himself unable to gain insight into things she wished to remain buried. He had hoped if a new memory had tried to surface he would have the chance to retrieve it, after all, knowing what she did, it was doubtful Zo would really want to pull on the threads of memory. It was more likely she would force it back, in fear of what may be seen. "These amulets are somewhat of a rarity, they are similar to those used in astral travel, but the designs are more ancient in origin. I think what he said was correct."

"It is. My father possessed an identical charm," Acha confirmed, her tone showing her reluctance at having revealed so much. She knew well the markings upon its surface, her father had spent weeks carefully crafting one, and she had been the one asked to acquire some of the more unique ingredients. She had never thought to query why it differed to the one the local shaman used, but now she understood the reasoning all too well.

"Y' father used magic?" Eiji questioned, although Acha had now spoken much about her life as they travelled, she had only spoken of the time she lived in. When it came to more personal matters, she barely uttered a word. She had never mentioned anything of her family, and had avoided the topic whenever possible. She spoke only of the flowing fields and the way of life.

"In a manner of speaking, yes. My father once used an identical charm for just that purpose, but things were different during my time. Those with immense power were gods, with the power Zo and Eiji possess, perhaps they too would have been worshipped. The magic was very limited and only those of certain families developed the gift of healing, blessings, or astral travel."

There was a long period of silence before Eiji spoke, taking one of the amulets from the ground.

"I wonder how he knew there's five of us?" he wondered aloud as he flicked the charm over, it was a question which had previously crossed Daniel's mind when he had first received them. "And our names," Eiji continued, turning the others over to find the one with his name. Carved on the back, next to his name, was also a symbol. The symbol on Zo's was identical to the rune they had obtained from the church, each charm differed only by the name and symbol. Were they to assume these symbols represented the keys meant for each of them?

"Well, he knew about Darrienia, and the Oneirois, I guess it only stands to reason he knows who we are. Of course, I'm more concerned about how he knew where to find us, who he is, why he possesses Hectarian artes, and more importantly, whose side he is on." Daniel took a breath after he had reeled out the questions which had been plaguing his mind.

"Surely ours," Eiji answered. "I mean, he assisted Zo, and he gave us these charms t'help us on our way." Eiji placed the charm over his head tucking it securely under his shirt.

"True, but why did he choose to help us? And what brought him here in the first place?" Daniel closed his book, placing it back into the backpack Zo had brought. He *had* brought a bag of his own, yet it had been insisted they just kept the one, which now seemed to take permanent residence in Elly's possession. He wondered why she had left it with them this time, and where exactly she was.

"Maybe it's just like he said, there's somethin' more valuable at stake." Eiji wasn't sure who the figure was, but he was sure he had been genuine in his attempts to help.

"Like what?" Daniel glanced briefly at Zo, still searching for some indication of where she may have come across the stranger. If she could just remember something, anything, the slightest detail would make him easier to trust. Perhaps had he not discovered what he had about the life previously led by his friend he would have been more trusting, and just been thankful for his intervention, but the recognition between them was unnerving. Who exactly had his acquaintance been with? He hadn't realised he was staring at her until she looked up at him and smiled. "Another thing, why did he leave so quickly?" Daniel questioned when no one volunteered a suggestion to his previous enquiries.

"The people in Abaddon are different to you and me, I just can't remember how." Zo silently scolded herself, unsure if, when the people began to wake, they would truly be in the danger she felt. But for now there was little they could do. "Besides, it is not like we can leave until Elly returns anyway. I bet she could tell us what they are." The fact she had just used the word 'what' unnerved her almost as much as Elly's sudden appearance.

"They are children of Hades." Elly seemed to appear with such perfect timing that it seemed as if she had been waiting for her name to be mentioned. "Abaddon, it is another word for the devil, Hades. The town was not called such without reason.

"All who reside within it are cursed by the Gods, destined to live forever as the creatures your parents frightened you with when you were young. They may look human now, and they will even try to convince you they are, but when the sun sets we should ensure we are nowhere near here, they undergo a transformation."

"Into what?" Acha questioned, aware sunset, although a number of hours away, drew ever closer. She glanced nervously towards the forest.

"Banshee, gorgon, harpies, lamia, need I continue? First, they trick people into spending the night, feed them, make them welcome. Those who stay never see the light of another sun. Of course, if no one stays they hunt. Why do you think we once had so many missing people?" Elly smiled to herself thinking how different things were now. The first time she visited here was over five years ago. Back then, Marise knew no fear.

"There's not been many in the last five years." Daniel felt he had to add his part to the conversation. When he was younger his parents told him all the time about groups of missing children and adults. It did seem as if he didn't hear as much about that kind of thing anymore.

"Well, do you not think that is about right? They have been trapped, until now, and I warn you, tonight they *will* hunt." She smiled to herself, knowing not only would they hunt, but they would also find a new ally. When the sun set tonight the world would make a powerful enemy. "I suggest we try to put as much distance as possible between ourselves and the town." This place was dangerous. The town held many memories for Elly, it was the second time Marise had almost lost her life. It was not a place to be taken lightly. Although Elly blamed her own carelessness for what had happened here that night.

"Agreed." Daniel stood moving to offer Zo a hand, only to find she was already standing and seemed to have been about to do the same to him. "Are you sure you're up to it?" he questioned, noticing she still looked rather pale.

"Shouldn't I be the one asking you that? You are the one who was trying to infiltrate the underworld," she teased, but she was touched by his concern.

'*And you came unbelievably close yourself,*' he whispered to her mind. She was a little alarmed to discover how proficient he had become at projecting his thoughts.

"So where have you been anyway?" Eiji questioned as Elly grabbed the backpack.

"Well, it would not have been fitting to leave Liza in the town, especially tonight, then she truly would be dead. I took her home."

"Liza is alive?" Daniel questioned suddenly.

"Of course, she was in Darrienia. Dead people do not dream. She was simply subjected to Aburamushi's form of suspended animation," Elly advised, deciding not to tell them his unique torture had slowly been stripping her life-force from her. All that was important was they had found her before she had passed into the underworld and vanished from Darrienia.

They began to walk, the sun was barely a few hours from setting and, having discovered the dangers, getting away seemed more urgent than they had first believed. They stayed on the track, unsure really where they were going as Elly guided them, they were just relieved it was in the right direction, away from Abaddon.

"Hey where you kids headin'?" An elderly farmer slowed his wagon to a trot as he pulled on the horses' reins to keep pace with them. He had gentle features, although tired, his dusty coloured eyes sparkled as he offered them a warm smile. They turned to Elly for the answer, after all, it was her idea to head down this track, and she had given none of them the slightest clue where they were heading.

"We are heading to the Ring of Fire," she answered with a smile.

"My word, I haven't heard that name since I was a boy. It's a good hike, I'm headin' to a town close by if you wanna hop on."

"We couldn't just accept a lift. Can't we be of some assistance t'you in return?" Eiji asked, noticing the wagon was filled with fruit and vegetables. Perhaps they could help him to unload, it seemed a lot for one person to take on alone.

"All I ask is for the pleasant conversation of your companion." He looked to Elly and smiled, "it is, after all, a long and lonely road. Besides I am headin' your way, a few extra heads will only liven up the journey." Elly nodded, agreeing to his terms she climbed in the front of the wooden wagon, while the rest of them climbed into the rear to sit amongst the home-grown fruit and vegetables which were spread out in carefully packed boxes. They instantly felt the drop in temperature, caused by the huge lumps of slowly melting ice used to keep the produce fresh for as long as possible.

"So where are you heading sir?" Elly asked as she made herself comfortable. When he was satisfied everyone was safe, he picked up the reins and commanded the two horses back into motion.

"Headin'? Oh yes, Kalá Port, you see there's a new master of the castle on Therascia, I am takin' some of my crop for the banquet. That's my contribution back there with your friends." He motioned, unconsciously gesturing before he turned to look at them. "I wouldn't miss some if you're hungry. I should just make the ship, maybe with an hour to spare to catch up with some old friends at the tavern," he smiled. "And you, what takes you to the Ring of Fire?" He used the name she had given despite few ever knowing it as such. It was a name it had not been called for a very long time, only those who frequented Collateral, or possessed old cartography would even be aware of its former title.

"My companions and I are on a quest, we seek a safe place to sleep," she answered simply, looking at him suspiciously as he gave a wry smile.

"Ah I understand," he glanced back towards Zo, "the young witch is in trouble." Zo frowned slightly as she heard his words. While it was true Elementalists had a certain look and feel about them, an aura of power which betrayed them, but Hectarians didn't, not as far as she knew.

"What exactly is this circle of fire?" Zo questioned, feeling slightly embarrassed. From the moment Elly had mentioned it, she felt as if it was something she should have known.

"The Ring of Fire," Elly corrected, "is a circle of ancient volcanoes dating back to before Zeus." Not satisfied with Elly's short reply, the elderly man continued.

"They're on the furthest western peninsula. Though I've heard rumours of a land beyond, if it exists it's accessible by neither man nor beast. The rumours say it's the origin of the Phoenix, and there are those who would have you believe they bore witness to the creature's emergence." He paused, giving a slight smile, "I haven't heard it referred to as the Ring of Fire since I was a buddin' young adventurer. It's said there is no safer place for travellers than the forest before it. The volcanoes are said to stifle any location magic or technology. It's the ideal place to hide, especially if attempting to conceal someone who still has the gift." He glanced towards Zo. "I'm not such an old fool to think it was extinguished completely, your friend here proves that. Anyway, to stay in such a place is the safest haven in the world. No man, or god, could ever find you there, you could disappear, so to speak.

"Of course because of this, there are a few bounty hunters roamin' the area, and many unsavoury characters as you would imagine. In fact, last I heard Viriatus, the Highwayman Commander, had set up operations in those parts, but they tend to work at night so there should be no concerns as long as you've left by the time they return at daybreak." He turned back to look at Zo once more before he addressed Elly. "Your friend looks awfully familiar, is she from around these parts?" he asked quietly, Zo leaned forwards in hope to hear the response.

"She has led a somewhat eventful life when it comes to travelling these lands. There is a possibility you have laid eyes upon her at some point." Elly replied vaguely much to Zo's disappointment.

The steep, treacherous rise of the volcanoes appeared on the horizon, their jagged slopes descending down the sheer cliffs to submerge into the waters below. Their presence, even from a distance, was awe inspiring. They didn't appear as the ring their name had implied, but it was easy to imagine the giant crater which lay between them to form this apparent ring. Mountains seemed to span endlessly beyond the closest peaks, standing proudly, making them appear to fill the horizon.

They were old, perhaps even ancient, the peaks rounded by the journey of the swirling winds as they whipped around their now dull summits, making what once would have been the ferocious points seem calm and gentle. Concealing the base of the volcanoes stood woodland, which climbed the frontmost peaks, the green carpet stopping only when the lands became unfit for life to thrive or climb. The grey shades of the bare rocks and crags sat against the almost slate coloured volcanoes which stretched into the sky.

They had made better time than she had anticipated. If they remained in the wagon any longer, it would just increase the distance they had to walk.

"Anyway, I believe this is where we shall part company. I thank you again for your assistance." The old man nodded as he pulled on the reins bringing the horses to a stop. "Oh sir, our quest is of a secret nature, I trust you will tell no one of what you saw and heard." She placed some coins on his seat.

"I was young once too, quests are fun, but it wouldn't do to have groups of people after the same goal." He pushed the money back towards her. "Since I never had travellers, I dunno what this is for," he smiled mischievously as he spoke, "I don't require payment for a service I've not provided," he reinforced still smiling. She returned the gesture, there were rare few who would refuse such gratuity.

"You have saved us a great deal of time and effort, for that we are most grateful and insist you take it."

"I've a better idea." He secured the reins before stepping down from the cart, his hand grabbing a twine bag as he did so. Climbing into the back he placed some fruit and vegetables inside before passing them to her. "If you wish to pay me, then you'll do it for my food, not my favours." He was young and proud once too. Elly thanked him as she took the produce from him, as long as he accepted the coins there would be no issues.

"Thank you," she stated extending her hand. He shook it before remounting his wagon. "Although you are lucky to have any produce left with those four in the back," she added to bring a lighter mood to the air as she removed a small piece of apple pulp from Zo's chin.

They crossed the plains, their hastened pace saw them reach the dense green woodland within thirty minutes. To the north of the forest's border, a small town could just be seen. Its modest dwellings almost hidden within the foliage, but at this distance, none would see them gain passage into the forest.

It was clearly not a place often walked, there were few tracks leading through. Shrubs and bushes made the undergrowth thick, but would also prove to be a bandit's enemy should a skilled tracker be in pursuit. It made them question whether the bandits would indeed choose such an unforgiving terrain in which to centre their operations. Elly guided them carefully through the area, choosing the easiest routes to avoid leaving a trail, although with Eiji accompanying them, she was unsure why she took such precautions. He could probably leave tracks in running water. As a small clearing opened before them, Elly dropped the bag to the ground, signalling for them to stop.

"We shall make camp here, I shall secure the perimeter," she stated before disappearing into the woodlands, leaving them to make the necessary preparations.

Zo busied herself getting a few twigs and nearby sticks to create a small fire, but it was clear they would need more than the immediate area could provide. She glanced around, she disliked the feeling of numbness. Her senses—which were normally so tuned with her surroundings—were now dead to the world. It made sense when she thought about it. Her senses were nothing more than a location spell to keep her aware of her surroundings.

"I shall get the firewood," Acha volunteered, almost as if reading Zo's mind. As she walked past Eiji, she grabbed his arm. "It will be quicker with the two of us." She gave him an encouraging glance before releasing him. Eiji followed her into the woods. They had walked for about ten minutes before they found an area with ample fallen branches. Not long after they had started to collect them, Eiji broke the silence. It was clear there was more to this than safety in numbers.

"What's goin' on?" he asked, his voice nothing more than a whisper. He glanced around the area, only now did he realise how far from the camp they actually were. Given the old man's stories, he felt it was better if they kept their tones low so not as to attract unwanted attention.

"That's what I wanted to ask you," she paused as she felt the heat rise to her face. "First Elly vanished in Abaddon. Then that stranger appeared . We had barely been there a minute and she vanished again." She retrieved another piece of wood from the ground to avoid having to look at him, hoping he wouldn't see the redness in her face confronting him brought.

"Wait, you think—" Eiji seemed baffled, although in fairness he understood, after all, he had arrived with Elly. It made sense she would think he knew her motives, and to a certain extent, she was correct.

"That you know, don't you?" Eiji shook his head. "Then, exactly what is this deal you have with her?" A sudden realisation dawned on him as she asked.

"No, y' have it all wrong." He stopped so they could talk. It was clear she was just trying to protect her friends. Since he had first met her, she had become so much more confident, to the point now she would challenge someone to protect those she cared for. He didn't want to see this new-found confidence destroyed. He needed to give her some form of answer, but if he could avoid doing so politely, he would.

"Do I?" she questioned, looking away from him.

"Yes, Elly, that's t'say, she..." How could he get out of this one? He couldn't really explain the truth of the situation. He could not tell Zo's friend that, from what he could understand, Elly wanted to reawaken Marise Shi and, at first, he was only helping her in fear of his own life. He knew when Zo was ready to tell her, she would, and only she had the right to do so.

"She is trying to find Marise right? And you're helping her, what will happen when you find her, what were you promised?" Acha prompted, after a long drawn out silence.

"Nothin', the only reason I'm with her is because I know t'much. I told y' before, if I leave, I die, until she releases me that is." Eiji sighed as he thought back to how this all started with the best of intentions, then somehow he had become entangled in this situation, not that he minded as much anymore, he had even started to enjoy the company of the people he was with, he was just too careless. Besides, he had realised a little while ago, for some reason, perhaps because of his master's thoughts on Marise, he wanted to save Zo from the fate it seemed awaited her.

"What do you know that is so valuable?" she questioned, moving to sit on a nearby log. This seemed like it would be a long conversation. He joined her, although never moving his focus from the pile of wood he placed at his feet. It was a good thing, in her embarrassment, she couldn't look at him either, finding the gathered wood also held her attention.

"Marise Shi's whereabouts, and her weakness," he answered truthfully. He hoped this snippet of information would keep her satisfied. He saw her look up to him in surprise.

"So, she does live," Acha gasped as Eiji confirmed what she and Daniel both believed, Marise Shi was still alive. She had to wonder, if Eiji knew such a thing, had he shared it with Elly, was that where they were heading, to retrieve her? "And what about Zo, what role does she have to play in all this, why does Elly want her? I know something big is happening and I know Zo has a part to play, whether or not she wishes it. If we are in danger, don't we have a right to know what that danger is?"

"I dunno what she has planned. The only thing I know is Elly wants t'protect Zo, as much as y' may doubt it, it's what I know t'be the truth. She cares deeply for her."

"For her, or for the role she has to play?" she asked coldly. She knew this was another question he couldn't answer, in truth, she realised a lot of his answers were based on assumptions. He had no idea of what her plans may be.

"Only Elly can answer that," he sighed moving to pick up the firewood. Something told him it was about time they moved on.

"You said you know Marise's whereabouts, are you leading us to her?" Acha questioned, realising as she did so Eiji had made no attempt to lead them anywhere. He, like them, was being led by Elly.

"I don't need t'," he stated. A silence descended upon them, an uneasy silence which stretched on for some time. They collected more branches in an attempt to make the silence a little less harsh, both wondering why they would need so much to build a fire, yet still they continued to collect it until both of their arms were full. It was Acha who finally spoke.

"If it makes any difference, I believe you," she said after some thought. She really believed he was worthy of her trust. "And I believe in you. Eiji, there's something I need to tell you, but it can go no further." Acha knew she had to tell someone. It had been gnawing at her since Collateral, yet at the same time she feared what speaking the truth would mean. She knew she could trust him, time after time he had proved to be honest and defend his word. Even if he did know Marise Shi's whereabouts, or the situation that surrounded Zo, she knew no one would learn of it from him. It would be far easier to tell him than her friends. She took a breath readying herself to continue, but before she spoke, she was interrupted.

"It is fortunate I am not the enemy or you would both be dead." Elly appeared from the darkness to stand beside them. "Sorry I was so long, I had some business I also needed to attend to."

"What business?" Acha enquired, shifting the firewood uncomfortably.

"None of yours," she answered firmly.

"Well, we really should get this back t'the others." Eiji glanced down at the wood in his arms and began to walk away. He already knew he would not get very far, he had the feeling Elly had been around far longer than she implied with her sudden appearance.

"Before you do." The pure chill in her voice froze him to the spot. "I do not appreciate being the topic of other people's conversations." She looked at both of them meaningfully, all at once Acha was glad her confession had gone no further.

"Y'know what they say, listeners never hear the best of themselves." Eiji smiled, but his attempt to lighten the mood had failed miserably as she glared at him in warning.

"Eiji, a word," Elly commanded; she looked at Acha meaningfully. Acha didn't need to be told twice that this was a conversation she was not welcome to hear, and so, she decided to leave them to it and head back towards the camp alone, regardless of how tempting it was to try to listen in.

Once Elly was sure Acha would be unable to overhear she continued, but the topic of conversation was not what Eiji had expected.

"We need to be on our guard." Her voice had now lost its earlier chill. "I have it on good authority that there is a bounty order on our comrade, and a few in the vicinity with the ambition to pursue it."

"Y'mean Marise right?" As he thought about it, he wondered why Elly would mention such a thing now. Marise had *always* had a price on her head. Perhaps the old man's warning of hunters in these parts had stirred some concern. He moved, shifting the wood, it wasn't that it was heavy, just awkward, a little like their conversation. Elly didn't seem to trust any of them, he couldn't help but wonder why she was so willing to disclose information to him. He could only reason it was because he was the only one who knew the truth about Zo, and he knew exactly where he stood with her, his betrayal would mean his death.

"No, I mean Zoella," Elly declared. He couldn't help but feel shocked by this, after all, there were but a limited few who knew her true identity. To everyone else she was simply Zo, a young woman who assisted the physician on Crowley, if they knew of her at all.

"Ah." Was all he managed to say, no matter how hard he tried he could not think of anything more to say.

"Ah, is right. You know what this me—" she began to question, her voice dropped slightly.

"Wait a minute." Finally, he had found the words to follow his surprise, the words rolling from his tongue without a thought to the fact Elly was still talking. "What's Zo done that could possibly warrant a bounty?" Normally anyone with a price on their head had committed some form of crime, but what could she have done? Elly answered his question with a look of disbelief.

"Since when does that have any relevance? It is a basic process. You write a request, go to a Plexus, and offer a price. There are no questions asked." She wondered if he had believed it worked in some other way. The truth of the matter was, if you had money, you could do anything. Money was the only law bounty hunters respected. It was not about right and wrong, they were simply hired assassins who paraded under the cloak of justice.

"I think we best hurry back." He began to run as he realised what danger could await them on their return. Images of death and slaughter crossed his mind, but the one thing that wasn't clear in these horrific images, was whose blood it was that filled his mind. He knew to face Zo with such confrontation would not be a good thing, not considering her past and what she had just discovered. She had already briefly lost control to Marise once. He knew when she left the inn why she had been so desperate to leave. Discovering the truth had released her, and Zo had known she could not longer restrain her. If events pressured her into confrontation there was no guarantee she wouldn't lose to her again. "We need t'warn—" before Eiji could finish the sentence he heard Acha scream.

"It looks like we are too late," Elly stated.

* * *

"Look, it *is* her." Two men hid deep within the undergrowth of the trees and watched as the figure they targeted arranged some firewood into a circle. "The one from the bounty, just like we were told." He passed a small notice to the other man, who examined it quickly looking from it, to the girl, a number of times.

Within the undergrowth, a game of roshambo was quickly played. When the tall, dark man won, with scissors, he took the notice back from his brother, who was of a smaller frame and build. He rolled the paper as his brother quietly circled around to the rear of their camp to listen for his cue. This was the way they had planned it. It was fool proof.

"Zoella Althea I believe." The tall man emerged from the bushes with a smile that added a sparkle to his hazel eyes. At his hail, her hand had shifted to rest on her sword. Her partner, unknown by name, stopped unpacking what appeared to be food rations to look at him questioningly.

"Yes, and you are?" Her hand relaxed from her sword, suggesting she was still unaware of his brother, who hid nearby. As he saw her relax, his smile broadened. It was clear this child did not know she was hunted yet, nor would she have time to share that information with anyone else. He glanced her over and wondered what a child such as this could do to warrant such a bounty, but his was not the place to ask, such was the beauty of being a hunter.

"I'm Ben," he smiled. It was clearly a well-practised smile, it seemed friendly and comforting. She returned the gesture but it soon faded when she heard his next words. "We don't want any trouble, so I think you should come with us," he cursed silently as her posture straightened. Although she didn't move, she glanced towards her partner questioningly, a silent message seemed to pass between them. For a brief moment he stopped unpacking. He hadn't considered the implications of using the word 'us', it was something they would have to correct for the future.

After a quick glance of the immediate area, she returned her attention to him. It seemed her mind was on other things, something which would work to their advantage.

"Why would I want to do that?" As he reached inside his long, battered coat, her hand instinctively found her hilt once more. Something inside her commanded her to draw. A wild force called to her, she had only felt it once before, back when she fought with the enormous figure. It was something she feared, something which scared her more than anything else. The power called to her life-force and she knew now that this power, this temptation, had a name.

"It's like I said, you're Zoella Althea." From his coat he pulled a small parchment, he flicked it open to reveal a sketch of her. That was the signal, his brother moved with grace and speed to place the jagged edge of his knife at her partner's throat.

Daniel heard the anger in her mind as she scolded herself for being so careless, for having dropped her guard, and for not detecting the lurking life-force. Searching magic was useless here, a fact she had been reminded of when the stranger had emerged from the undergrowth without prior warning, but still, she had been careless.

Anger sparked in her fragile eyes, memories of blood and violence danced on the surface of her mind trying to remind her of who she was, trying to warn her what may happen should she choose to fight. It was a powerful hatred she felt, but worse still, was the desire to kill them.

Ben smiled at her, introducing his brother, Simon, although his words never met her ears, they were drowned out by someone no one else could hear. A female's voice who screamed her name over as it told her to run. It was a voice that seemed so familiar, a voice from a memory. Its words from the past begged for her to leave now, as they had back then, but she knew she could not obey. She could not abandon Daniel. The sound of the warning dissolved into the air as she heard Ben's mocking tones.

"I know what you're thinking," he sneered as his brother tightened the ropes around his prisoner. "But compared to us, a child like you does not know the first principle of fighting."

'Zo.' She heard Daniel's voice filled with desperation. He too had heard the cries which had echoed through her mind. As he fought against the ropes which now bound him to the tree. He heard the strange voice fill her thoughts again. It cried her name as it begged for her to leave while she could. It was a voice he didn't know, a memory he knew she couldn't find. Then there came another, a voice telling her to stay.

Daniel knew that voice, the voice of temptation telling her it would be all right to surrender control. It offered her a promise of stopping those who pursued her. It told her the price was worth it, and if she didn't pay it willingly, she would take what she wanted by force, and destroy more than just her attackers.

Daniel watched as she slowly drew her sword. He understood what was going to happen, and knew exactly what he was going to see. His eyes closed, forcing free a tear. He didn't want to see this, he didn't want to see her.

"I know a few tricks." She tried to sound threatening, only it sounded more fearful than she had hoped. Her best friend lay at the mercy of bounty hunters. There was only one way to save him and that was to fight. She couldn't fail, his life, his safety, depended on her. A silver flame formed at her fingertips as Simon moved to join his brother. From their expressions alone, it was clear they were already satisfied they would earn their money today. The boy was useless to them, there was no need for him to share her fate, in fact he had the honour of bearing witness to the justice they would deliver.

The ground absorbed the flame as it fell from her hand, seeing this they snorted, believing it to be nothing more than a parlour trick to intimidate them. Before they could voice their derogatory comments, flames shot upwards from the ground. The fire circled the three of them as the heat from the silver flames made the air shimmer, yet the ground remained unscorched by the flames' heat.

"Daniel, get everyone out of here." A spark flew from the fire to perish the ropes which bound him. He could not tell if this was a deliberate action, but he knew one thing for certain, what she had instructed him to do, and her actual thoughts were two different things. Her initial thought was only for his safety and that of the bounty hunters who advanced. Something frightened her, so much so she felt the only way to be safe was to distance herself from him, and he had a very good idea of what that something was. He opened his eyes as he felt the isolation, knowing all too well what it meant.

Trying to claw his way through the mental walls she had erected he attempted to force just one thought through, for her not to allow her past to control her. But now she had acknowledged it, it already had power. She had to be strong enough to keep its temptation buried, to find the strength to overcome things with her own will, not that of a murderer, of bloodlust. She had to fight it. He knew it hadn't reached her, the level of blocking she had constructed around her mind far surpassed anything she had done before. Then, through the silence, he heard Acha scream.

The sword tilted in her hand as she looked to those who opposed her. She had known from the beginning this moment would come, the moment that fear and need took over and all rationality was lost. This was the time *she* thrived. Zoella had feared this moment with all her heart. She felt the aggression within her grow, trying to force its way through the cracks created by her weakness, she felt its hunger, its power. It grew in power as if aware she knew it was stronger, that there was no choice but to give in to its desire. She wasn't strong enough, she couldn't restrain it any longer.

"A barrier, very clever," Ben snorted moving to stand beside his brother after having examined the silver flames. It appeared they were all trapped within its fiery wall until their battle was over.

"I suppose that is what common sense would seem like to those who have none," she sneered. She could still feel Zoella's shadow on the edge of her mind, but that would soon be over. Zoella had lost, surrendered. Nothing was going to interfere now, she was exactly where she belonged.

Not waiting for the first strike, she chose to make it. Her thrust barely dodged by Simon as his brother pulled him away. Half a second later and the sword would have been stained with his blood. For someone to dodge her sword was an achievement, then again, she wasn't exactly trying. She was more focussed on her attempts to permanently suppress the other persona, this engagement was just something happening in the background.

"I see you *do* know a few moves." Ben smiled giving his brother some kind of hand gesture. Marise smiled to herself, the people before her had claimed the title of bounty hunters, but she seriously doubted they had completed a single job request. They were clearly such amateurs.

"Oh, I know a lot more than that." The bone chilling tones of her voice made it difficult to suppress a shudder.

Her posture was different now, she seemed confident, alert. A ball of flames formed in her left hand, it was an action which startled them. There was no mention in the Plexus about her being some kind of Elementalist. They looked to each other in surprise as she stood with her sword held poised and ready to strike in one hand, and the unexpected magic burning fiercely in the other.

"I do hope you prove to be more than an easy kill." She drew her tongue playfully across her top teeth. The two men made their move, their short swords drawn.

It was an attack she had anticipated from such amateurs. One attacked high, the other low. The ball of flames engulfed Simon, leaving Ben with a poor hearted excuse for a charge attack whilst his brother rolled on the ground, trying desperately to extinguish the fire.

"I guess not," she sighed in disappointment. A spray of blood erupted from Ben's back as her blade followed through. He hadn't even realised she had moved to strike him until seconds after her sword had impaled him. Unable to free himself from her blade, he desperately struck out towards her. By making only the smallest of movements she dodged his wild slashing with ease. "What a disappointment," she yawned, using her foot to push his weakening body from her sword. He fell before her to the ground, lying at her feet where he belonged.

Simon screamed, seeing his brother's figure slump to the ground. He had barely extinguished the flames when his brother had fallen to her attack. Rushing to his side he took his hand, blood trickled from his mouth as he breathed his last breath. He looked up to her, his eyes filled with venom and pain.

"Come on then boy." A wicked sneer crossed her lips, she raised her eyebrow as if in challenge. It was a challenge he foolishly accepted. He moved with an unexpected speed. She didn't move as he struck out. She was unprepared, she hadn't expected him to strike, he was going to do it. He drew his concealed blade; she would pay with her life for the loss of his brother, she would die and it would be by his hand. The blades cut through the air at great speed their target locked, he would kill her. He would avenge his brother.

The sound of ricocheting metal rung through the air as his blades met with resistance, both blows were blocked, one by her sword, the other against the sword's scabbard which she now held in her hand. Their eyes met briefly, as he gazed within them he saw the gates of Hades as they opened behind him. He, like the many who had faced her before, now looked upon his own death.

She moved with grace and speed, grabbing his right sword by the hilt, she turned it sharply forcing it into his neck. She smiled as he gasped for breath, a strange gargling sound coming from his throat until he finally fell. She looked at them, at the fallen excuses for hunters, a look of satisfaction crossed her face. It had been a long time since she had smelt the scent of blood, by the Gods how she had missed it. Fishing in her pocket, she removed two coins and flicked them upon the bodies, being her calibre of assassin was costly, but she would never cheat Kharon of his fare.

"Zo," Daniel gasped as he stared in disbelief through the flames. Although she had ordered him to leave, he had stayed. Despite wanting to obey her request, he could not. The figure who stood before him had the same paralysing effect on him now, as she'd had all those years ago. He had been unable to move, unable to run, from the moment he had laid eyes on her.

He couldn't believe he stood before her again, but this time things were different. He knew somewhere, sealed away inside her, was his friend. He hoped by simply saying her name the demon he saw would vanish, but the red-haired devil still stood in the place of his friend. Her green eyes seemed to mock him as their vision met across the fire.

The silver flames vanished instantly. She flicked the blood from her sword as she looked at him.

"Daniel." Marise smiled running her tongue across her top lip.

Chapter 12

The Minefields

The emptiness was filtering through now. It was clear to Night he had to make the change soon. The effect of the abandoned library upon his ally posed a threat, it jeopardised her role. The longer she was without a watcher, the colder she would become, and she had already shown signs of indifference towards the survival of The Chosen. So much planning had been required and now each one within the group had a very carefully weaved role to execute. He could not afford for her to endanger them.

The library served as a source of information; a source which assisted with the recollection of information once possessed and now forgotten. But if there was no one there to access it, it became ineffective.

The death of the watcher had come as no surprise, and the atmosphere of friendship and mutual dependence had now been replaced by emptiness, allowing resentment and bitterness to grow. That was the problem with her existence. So many watchers came and went, yet she would remember them all, and as much as she would loathe to admit it, she depended on their presence, she needed them. For the watcher's brief life they would become part of her, a voice in her ear, a guiding light.

The replacement had already been selected, but this would be the first time since her rebirth that she would not be present for the initiation. They both had to be mindful of the side-effects such an invasive and personal connection would create. He would need to watch them carefully.

* * *

"Acha!" Eiji cried out as he saw her frozen against the darkened wood of a nearby tree. All colour seemed to have drained from her as she stood seemingly terrified of the empty surroundings. "What's wrong?"

"I didn't mean to," she whispered. Her legs shook so much she found herself involuntarily shrinking down against the tree, she moved to hug her knees tightly. Although his vision was fixed on her, she refused to look at him and simply continued to stare blankly before her.

"Didn't mean t'what?" He crouched to her level, her answer came only in the form of a sidewards glance. Following her line of vision, he looked across at the fallen tree that obstructed his line of sight. He was quick to understand the source of her distress lay just beyond it, and even quicker to investigate. His eyes fell upon a crumpled heap of clothing. As he moved to examine the figure, he heard Acha speak again.

"It was an accident, he came out of nowhere," she whispered desperately as Eiji looked down to the dishevelled looking bandit, who lay motionless on the forest floor. He was no more than a child, judging by his appearance alone he had been living the life of an outlaw for some time. He couldn't help feeling a twang of sympathy. The boy he looked at now could have easily been him, had his master not saved him.

It was not uncommon for bandits to take in and train children. They were after all the face of innocence, and often attracted far less suspicion. Many abandoned or orphaned children, if not taken into the temples, would ultimately lead one of two lives, the life of a bandit or that of a beggar. It was difficult to guess which of the two would be the harshest, each had so many different adversities and both had an equally high mortality rate.

There were but a few people who would look beyond circumstances when searching for an employee. Even servants these days needed to have a checkable history or references. It was the start of a downward spiral which meant children, like this boy, would be forced into a life of thievery, and a premature death. Eiji had been lucky, he had been rescued from such a choice and became his master's apprentice. If not for that he could have been the one who lay here instead.

Swinging his legs over the tree he bent down to check the young man's neck for a pulse, glancing towards Acha as he did so. His pulse was weak, yet as he quickly cast his vision over the body, he could not locate a single injury upon him. He couldn't help but wonder how she had done such a thing so cleanly. The only abrasions on him seemed to be those from a fall and the odd faded bruise where, no doubt, his master had disciplined him.

He found himself thinking on the past in that moment, or more specifically back to the inn when she had moved to attack him whilst Daniel had held his attention. He had thought she had been about to strike him with a concealed weapon, it seemed he had been wrong.

Despite the clear repercussions of her attack, his senses told him, given time to rest he would make a full recovery. Eiji was no healer, he did not possess a sympathetic touch or the ability to heal, his talents stopped at basic medicinal compounds, and a few speciality mixtures which could be passed only between Elementalists. Even so, he knew whatever she had done had somehow shortened his life span. The best thing they could do, for all their sakes, was to leave him where he lay. They could not risk taking him to camp. Where there was one bandit, more were never too far behind.

"What happened?" As Eiji looked at her questioningly, she found herself unable to hold his gaze. Even when he moved to once more crouch beside her, she could not bring herself to meet his eyes.

"I killed him," she whispered. Her stomach churned from the shock and repulsion of what she had done. She forced the pictures of the boy from her mind. She knew so much about him, his upbringing and abandonment, she had witnessed his every beating, his every deed. "I was heading back, then the next thing I knew he grabbed me, I screamed but he placed his hand over my mouth and I, I killed him."

"Y' didn't kill him," Eiji revealed calmly, trying to keep his tones as low as possible. He saw relief reflected in her eyes as he delivered this news, it gave her the strength to look at him for the first time.

"He's alive?" she gasped in relief, tears welled in her eyes as he nodded. He believed her when she said she hadn't meant to hurt him, but he also couldn't understand how it was possible to nearly kill someone by accident. Surely, she knew what she was doing, she had to. For the first time, they became aware of Elly, who glanced dismissively over the unconscious figure as she spoke.

"Why did you scream?" she questioned, rolling the boy onto his side with her foot. It was clear he had not had the chance to lay more than a hand on her.

"He surprised me." That wasn't exactly true, she had known he was going to touch her, she had feared what may happen if he did and so she screamed, hoping to scare him away, but her actions did nothing more than quicken his contact with her.

"But you feel better now, you have some energy?" Acha looked up at Elly horrified, although she had revealed many things to them, *that* was not something she discussed. It was her shameful secret, a secret she had worked so hard to conceal.

"How..." Acha whispered in disbelief. She had been so careful, it begged the question of how she had discovered her secret. Fortunately, she didn't have to wait long before Elly replied.

"It was obvious, especially in Darrienia before we encountered Aburamushi. I suggested the creature did not see you because you are a displaced life-force, you have told us that much yourself, but the true reason was because you had used your surroundings to revitalise your body. For that split second, you shared the same pattern of life-force, thus were invisible so to speak.

"If that was not enough, within the ward everything died almost instantly. It was obviously not a result of Zo's magic. You were the last to be encompassed by the field, it was almost at that instant it occurred. Your life-force is anaemic and must take life from other sources to sustain you. That is why Daniel gave you those gloves, so you could touch organic matter without any adverse effects." Acha gasped as Elly made this revelation, she was surprised at just how much she had learnt just by watching subtle actions and gestures.

Elly didn't mention the true betrayal had come when she had struck Acha in Aburamushi's lair. As she had struck her, small sparks had flown through the air. It was this alone which made her certain of her theory; nothing else would have created such a reaction with her.

"They don't know, at least not all of it," she whispered, brushing the dirt and debris from her clothes in an attempt to focus her attention elsewhere. Although her friends were aware, she could drain the life-force of things with a mere touch, she had worked hard to keep secret her dependency on taking life from things in order to live. Eiji opened his mouth as if to say something, but thankfully he was quickly cut short by Elly's interruption.

"Now is not the time for questions. We should return to the camp." She waited, allowing Eiji to collect the scattered wood before requesting he lead the way back whilst she kept watch of their surroundings for any danger. Although he knew it was only a short distance away, he glanced back to ensure Acha was still following him. She seemed quite unnerved by the whole experience, and perhaps a little relieved. He wondered if this was what she had been about to confide in him.

His senses warned him of an immediate danger, which was strange since, within this place, his sense of such things was numbed. Perhaps, given his clumsy nature, it was more of a proximity warning, but he was convinced something solid stood in his path. He stopped in mid-stride as he turned sharply. His instincts still warning of imminent danger, yet nothing stood before him, just the trodden path through the trees. He smiled slightly, thinking how this served as a reminder of how much he still had to learn, surely only fools convinced themselves the air was a danger.

He didn't realise what he had felt was not nature, but the aura of magic, a feeling which certainly wasn't deadened here, not when he was so close to it. He had barely taken another step when something knocked him from his feet. He looked up just in time to see a blue distortion shimmer across the air to reveal a large dome. From its curve, it was large, perhaps even large enough to imprison their camp.

"Mari." Elly placed her hand to the invisible field. In a similar manner to when Eiji had collided with it, the area she made contact with rippled for but a second against the touch, but unlike with Eiji, after this distortion had faded, she was permitted entry.

"Mari?" Acha fearfully glanced between them, they both wore an identical expression of concern. "But Zo and Daniel are in there, we need to warn them!" Acha exclaimed. Elly stepped through the field. Without looking back she calmly walked in the direction of the camp, much to Acha's distress there was nothing rushed about her movements. In the hope to hurry her along, Acha moved to follow only to find the same solid barrier, which had moments before struck Eiji, greeted her. "How did she..." Acha began but decided not to continue a question which neither of them could answer.

* * *

Daniel backed away slowly, his arm already bled from where her blade had struck. He was being slowly driven backwards away from the camp, away from sight should anyone return. Her movements had been so quick, he hadn't had time to dodge, although had he tried, he would now be dead instead of only wounded. She had expected him to at least *try* to avoid her strike.

Looking upon him now she was certain that she had clearly overestimated his abilities. Had he tried to evade, the sword would not merely have cut his arm, the battle would be over. It was a tactic which had been used many times before, only idiots, or the most skilled fighters would not dodge, and he was definitely not the latter.

"You have stood in my way far too long." She advanced towards him, normally she could have cut him down in a second, but she knew from her past experience that the bond of friendship between him and Zoella made it difficult for her to retain control. The strength of her promise to him lent her strength. This fight had to be addressed carefully should she wish the end result to be her victory. The longer it took, the more difficult it would become. Zoella was a limitation she had to be constantly aware of, a reason why she could not perform at her peak, but she was not worried, it was not as if someone of this calibre would ever really taste the full extent of her skill. Each step she took he matched in the opposite direction, but even that action would soon be prevented. He moved his hand from his wound to take his weapon, he had no other choice.

"I don't want to fight you." His voice trembled as she advanced ever closer. It was clear he would be no opposition for her. He knew all too well that the paralysing fear, rooting him in place as she had moved to strike, was the sole reason he still lived.

"Funny," she smiled. "I want to kill you." Daniel flicked together his weapon, amazed he had managed to move at all. He could see the staff's subtle movements, it trembled in his grasp as he crossed it defensively before him. "I have cut through the finest armour with this sword." She sneered at his attempt to defend himself. "Do you really think your little stick can stop me?" She pulled the tie from her hair, using it to fasten the sword's hilt to her wrist, an action that had become second nature to her.

She came at him, he saw himself as he moved away from her attack, despite his mind visualising the movement he once more stood paralysed, rooted to the spot with fear. Her sword moved at a speed he couldn't follow. He stood unable to do anything but watch, and could only wonder what it was about this person that inflicted this paralysis upon him. This was not the first time he had stood before her like this, but he knew it would be the last.

As before, he could only watch as her sword gleamed. It shone brightly as it arced towards him, slicing through the air with the sound of his death. Behind the blade he could see her smile, it wasn't Zo's warm smile, it was that of a demon with a lust for blood, an evil, malevolent, smile.

Something inside him screamed for him to move, commanded him to obey, but he simply waited for the end, despite knowing that if he were to die now, Zo would never forgive herself. She would lose herself to the darkness knowing she had hurt him. The death of the one she had promised to protect would be just the thing Marise needed to ensure control. He could not let that happen.

Just before the blow landed, his body turned slightly as his arms moved of their own accord to raise the staff. He had lost sight of her completely until the sword ricocheted from the block he had raised. He felt his legs begin to tremble as he gave a sigh of relief. Somehow the adrenaline which coursed through his body as he pushed against her blow, was enough to stop her strike and force her away from him.

As she landed, she turned to look at him, an ecstatic glimmer twinkled in her eyes as the sword's light intensified. A blue fire formed in her left hand as she moved to face him. He found the room to take one more single step backwards, but further retreat was blocked as he felt the solid pressure of a tree behind him, preventing his further escape. He found himself leaning back on it slightly for support as his trembling legs threatened to buckle beneath his weight. He knew if she were to strike again there was little chance of him evading the blow, no matter how enchanted the staff was. Without warning, Marise released the fire, the blue light streaking the distance between them like lightning. The fire crackled as it leapt from point to point engulfing the unseen magic in the air surrounding it, consuming its fuel to intensify its power as it was driven towards him.

"Mari, No!" Daniel never thought he would be glad to hear her voice, but as Elly appeared, positioning herself slightly before him in a protective manner, he couldn't have been more relieved. She stretched her left arm before him as her other hand opened to drop what appeared to be six dice to the ground. The small numbered cubes vanished as they struck the ground just seconds before a sword appeared in her hand. She moved effortlessly to intercept the magic. For a moment Daniel thought the fire was a mere after effect as it danced over the weapon, but when the sword she held erupted into flames he realised the truth. The weapon she held had been made from wood, and burnt rapidly. She dropped it, the weapon vanished before contact was made. "You will not harm him," she commanded, her fist clasped around the dice as they reappeared in her grasp, but her vision remained fixed calmly on Marise as she gave this order.

"And you would oppose me, you would fight me, for him?" Marise tilted her head to one side questioningly as her best friend stood protecting the enemy.

"I shall," she stated as she and Marise stood locked in eye contact.

"Your weapon has always been one of chance, my friend. What would happen should you obtain another like the one you just did, do you think then you could pose any threat?" Elly placed the dice inside her pocket as she stepped away from Daniel.

"If you had wanted him dead, I could not have stopped you. Nor would I have reached you in time," she added. Marise had been incorrect about the threat she would pose, but her perception was important. It was Elly herself who had trained her in the art of combat. Marise thought she knew everything about her, and her style, but she was wrong. Even the most dedicated master knew it was foolish to fight or train a student at their full strength, but she would prefer it if Marise remained under this misconception.

Elly momentarily broke eye contact to glance at Daniel. All in all, he seemed to have fared quite well, there was a single slash on his upper arm which he gripped tightly and his weapon, a carved staff, was still clutched in the injured arm. She didn't recall seeing him with it before so she studied it for a moment, there was something unusual about it, something which seemed almost familiar, but there was no possibility it could be what she considered, it was impossible, *that* weapon had been destroyed long ago. Elly tore her vision from it, reminding herself of the task at hand.

"That is where you are wrong." As Marise spoke, another flame appeared in her hand, highlighting the sinister smile that played upon her lips. "Let us pretend that you did not make it. Give me a while before you return." From the corner of her eye, Elly saw Daniel stiffen slightly. She knew he did not trust her, but did he really think she would step aside and let him be killed? It was only on considering this she realised she herself had not known the answer until now, so perhaps his fear was justified. This time she had chosen to protect him. Next time, he may not be so lucky.

"I cannot do that." Elly changed her stance ready for battle. "If you insist on fighting for this, I will meet your challenge. But if I win, you must swear not to harm him while he is involved in this situation." Elly's fingers hovered uncertainly near her pocket as she waited for the verdict. Marise was not naive, if she agreed to this battle and lost, she knew she would never have the chance to attempt it again. She would be bound to her word by defeat, but if by some strange fortune she should win—Elly paused for a moment as she considered this, there was no possibility Marise could defeat her. She could not use the magic required.

"You would truly oppose me?" she questioned again, her voice seemed to waver slightly with the tones of betrayal. "For him?" She sheathed her sword. Her green eyes locked onto Daniel, the promise of threat hung in the air as she crushed the flame, compacting the magic within her hand. "Lee will not always be around to protect you." A sadistic smile crossed her lips as she turned away. "You have company," she warned, and with those words she turned and strolled casually away into the forest.

The other persona would soon regain control, she had done well to even scratch him, let alone engage in battle as Zo fought to restrain her. All the time she faced him, Zo had fought with an unbelievable power, one which threatened her dominance, but it was an encounter she had learnt much from. Next time he would not be so fortunate, and as for Zoella, she would not be as resistant. She had learnt much indeed, she knew now how to counteract Zo's attempts to assert control, even so, her time here was fading, such things would have to wait until next time, even now, she was unsure whether it was herself, or Zoella, who took them deep within the forest away from their camp.

Within moments, she had faded from sight. The electricity in the air seemed to dissipate as his friends arrived. Daniel released his breath, sliding down the tree as his legs kept their earlier promise to collapse beneath him.

"By the Gods Daniel, you're hurt!" He had barely touched the ground before Acha had rushed to his side, she had noticed his ghastly pallor before anything else. In fact, from where she stood, there was nothing further her vision would permit her to see. The scene which lay before them was disguised by the terrain, as Daniel's retreat had forced him beyond the edge of the clearing. "What happened?" she questioned, removing his hand from the wounds to reveal the slice across his arm, she looked to him questioningly, her eyes almost tearful.

"Are y' all right?" Eiji enquired, his tone etched with concern as he moved beyond the shelter of the trees. If Daniel had responded it had fallen on deaf ears as he walked past him to see the true horror left in her wake, imagery Acha had been spared by being too preoccupied with her concerns of Daniel to notice anything of the surrounding area.

The kills had been effortless, flawless with little time wasted in their execution, and that was precisely what this act had been, an execution. A horrible realisation of exactly what had transpired here before their arrival filled him. Zo—no Marise—had drawn first blood. He had really hoped he would not see this day, he had recently come to acknowledge her as an ally and a friend. She was a strong person, he had truly believed if anyone's will could triumph it would be hers. But it seemed she did not possess the strength needed to suppress her darkness. The killer had now surfaced and a battle of time and wills had begun. It was as his master had foretold, it had been a warning he had failed to understand all those years ago.

He looked over to Elly as she busied herself removing the bodies from the vicinity. The manner in which she undertook the task told tales of the countless times she had been faced with such a scenario before. She was completely unphased, making such a task seem effortless.

"Where's Zo?" Eiji's voice was filled with concern. He had withheld his question until the final corpse had been removed from sight. Given the speed in which she undertook this task, he could only imagine she had left the bodies somewhere on the borders to their camp. He was unable to suppress a shudder as he lifted Zo's satchel from the floor to reveal the crimson grass beneath.

"I am sure she is safe," Elly answered promptly, her voice betraying nothing of the act she had just committed. She lifted the bag from his seemingly frozen grasp, walking the length of the camp to pass it to Acha. She was relieved her earlier comment about Marise had now been forgotten, had it not, perhaps she would have not been so quick in the clearing of the camp, such a sight was bound to have made Acha forget the careless words. "You treat Daniel's wounds, no doubt there is some purée already prepared. I shall start the fire." Acha took the bag from her, she found herself surprised at the sheer weight of a collection of herbs.

"But you can't just leave her! What about the bounty hunters?" she protested, she couldn't help but be struck by Elly's cruelty. She looked between her and Eiji, how could she want to just leave Zo out there alone? Eiji simply shrugged in response.

"I don't think," Daniel paused aware of the nervous tones in his voice, he took a few breaths as he tried to steady both his hands and his breathing before he continued. "They'll be bothering us again too soon." He was relieved that Acha at least had been spared the vision Marise had created. He had been concerned about his ability to hold her attention, he hadn't wanted her to see, he was grateful for Elly's quick actions. He flinched against the sting of the purée as Acha rubbed it across his wound, it was only superficial.

"They were here? Are they the ones..." she glanced to Daniel who quickly looked away to avoid eye contact, seeing this she turned her attention to bandaging his arm. She glanced up occasionally to see Elly and Eiji deeply engaged in hushed conversation, their voices little more than an inaudible mumble. Once she had finished, she decided to press the issues which had been bothering her, first she addressed Daniel.

"So what happened? I mean this clearly isn't the cut of a normal sword." Although he didn't answer, his silence said more than any words could have, it was just as she had suspected. She turned to lean against the tree as she sat beside him.

Acha had pieced it all together now. It was clear this wound had been inflicted by Zo. While they were away gathering the firewood, some hunters must have attacked. Daniel was not proficient in any form of combat so it would be up to her to protect him. Despite the skill she had shown in that earlier fight, she was no warrior, she had simply been lucky. The colossus figure had underestimated her and thus fallen, but, she couldn't fight really, people from her upbringing knew little more than basic defensive techniques. Besides, someone who could use magic had no need for weapons. She wasn't sure exactly how she had ended up wounding Daniel, from the look of it, it had been a passing blow, grazing him perhaps as she lunged at someone behind him. The sheer guilt must have driven her to leave, it would have devastated her to the point she felt unable to face him. She wouldn't have seen it as an accident, she wouldn't have realised perhaps without her intervention it would have been much worse. If she hadn't tried to protect him, what would they have returned to then?

Just as she finished her scenario she realised that no matter how she felt, she would not have left Daniel injured and unprotected, which meant she had to have pursued the attackers, no doubt to drive them away from their group, who at the time had still been within the forest. After all, Zo would have been aware they had yet to return, she would have wanted to ensure their safety. That had to be it, she reasoned, yet still found herself surprised she had left him.

"Daniel, I'm sorry, I shouldn't have taken Eiji with me, if he had been here—"

"Nonsense, it was just a matter of time before..." he paused before continuing. "Maybe if you hadn't have taken him, he would have been hurt too, or maybe worse, they would have found you instead," Daniel answered despite his obvious distraction.

"Do you think she'll come back?" she questioned following his vision as he stared beyond the clearing of their camp, deep into the trees. Whatever was wrong she knew that beyond the boundaries of their camp was not a safe place to be. Especially since now, as she had heard from Eiji, there was a bounty on Zo's head. If she had pursued the bandits then surely she was putting herself in worse danger. Maybe once she had chased them far enough away without falling prey to any trap laid, or ambush planned, she would return, but hopefully it would not be too long, it was nearly sunset.

"I don't know," he sighed sadly. The alarm in her eyes was clear. This had not been the response she had expected, not from him. She had to wonder if any of her assumptions about what had happened were correct. From his expression alone it was clearly serious and for whatever reason, none of them seemed to want to pursue her. She couldn't help but feel she had overlooked something very important.

"Okay, we've decided t'go t'Darrienia without her." Although Eiji had approached, he couldn't bring himself to look at them as he delivered the news. He stabbed the ground with his foot in an attempt to avoid the looks he had become recipient to. This action alone showing *he* was not happy with the decision either.

"You mean Elaineor decided," Daniel spat bitterly, despite her good intentions earlier, he couldn't help but feel this entire situation was her fault. They had been fine without her, none of this would ever have happened if only she'd left them alone. He resented her and all she represented. She had appeared from nowhere and turned their lives upside down. Why couldn't she have just stayed away? Well he knew the truth behind that now too, and now he knew what it was she really wanted, it made him hate her all the more.

"Wait a minute." Acha stood slowly, dusting her trousers down as she moved to challenge them. "This doesn't make sense. You claim to have travelled countless provinces in search of her, insist she leaves her home, her friends, and then you leave her out here where she's in more danger. Why bother finding her in the first place?" Acha glanced from Eiji to Elly as she demanded an explanation. Daniel looked to her in surprise, she really had changed, she was no longer the timid girl they had first met.

It had taken Acha some time for her to be comfortable in his company, and longer for her to open up. The first days around the table in Zo's home had been strained. He had made every effort to make her comfortable and keep her entertained. This was the reason Zo had invited him to keep her company in her absence, to help her to gain confidence. Soon she began to add to his tales, then finally share some of her own. It had been a difficult path, their first meeting had failed to betray her shyness, but now it seemed she had little pause for expressing her opinion.

"Darrienia is different from here. The chances are we won't be near any woods at all, accordin' t'what I can make out." Eiji pulled the map from his pocket. "It'll be easier t'find her there, than in this undergrowth, and if we hurry, we may just find her before she vanishes from sight." He paused, lowering his tone a little before he spoke again. "I don't like it any more than you." He looked at Daniel, there seemed to be something more to that sentence, but Acha couldn't quite determine what.

* * *

"So you have returned." Seiken walked into view behind Zo's reflection in the stream. She sat about a mile from the place she had arrived, and stared resentfully at the figure looking back at her from the water's surface as she considered her options. She glanced at his reflection before bringing herself to look at him. Something about him seemed different, then again at the moment everything did. "Where are your companions?" He glanced around slowly as if to check they hadn't suddenly appeared in the vicinity.

"I've left them," she sighed, turning away to once more stare into the stream. The stranger in the water still looked back at her. "It's for the best.

She, I, tried to kill Daniel." She wrapped her arms around herself protectively watching her image further distort as the wind whipped around the stream and shook the nearby trees before it died down to a soft whisper. She reached out, slapping the unfamiliar reflection angrily. Marise had somehow ensured that during her control she would bear witness to everything ensuring, despite being trapped powerless to change the events, she was permitted to observe. She turned her back to the stream, hoping that looking upon Seiken would ease her conscience, but it didn't.

"I see." He glanced around again. "They know your secret, yet they venture here to find you all the same." He smiled to himself as he looked behind them over the horizon. When he turned back to face her just concern crossed his brow.

"Is everything okay, has something happened?" she asked, Seiken did not look at her, he simply stared past her into the distance, as she followed his vision it seemed he focused on the top of a small incline.

"Why do you ask?"

"You seem troubled." She glanced at him, although she addressed him he never looked to her. It was clear something weighed heavily on his mind. At this moment in time it was almost as if they were complete strangers. She felt nothing when she looked at him, the warmth, the familiarity, their connection, all of it was gone.

"I'm sorry. I'm aware how little time there is, it's not your concern. Tell me, now you are here, what are your plans?" He looked at her briefly before fixing his gaze once more on the horizon.

"If you mean, am I going to find them?" she sighed. "I cannot. I shall continue alone. I doubt they can get too far without this." She pulled a piece of parchment from her pocket. "They'll have no choice but to return home." Elly had previously advised them how to stop their nightly trip into Darrienia. Without any indication as to where they are or where they should be heading, they would have no choice but to turn back. Things will be how they should have been all along, she would be alone.

The only problem would arise if they remained in the forest after waking, since the charms ensured they would return to the same place they slept. This meant, on her return, she would need to leave the area undetected, which, when she considered that it blocked all location spells and senses, would prove to be a simple task. She could not go back to them, just as she hoped they would not come to her. Things had become too dangerous.

"What's that?" Seiken looked to the parchment she held in her hand.

"It's the map you gave us, remember?" Zo frowned slightly before scolding herself. He was trying to help her, to save his race, and all she could think about was he seemed a little distracted. She scolded herself again for pursuing this feeling, situations reversed she would no doubt feel as he did now, and after what had just happened, she was more than a little distracted herself.

"Ah yes, so much has happened since then, I must have forgotten. Anyway, to what brings me here, your next target. Some on your travels will say you should pass only through the minefields, these are those under his influence, do not listen, although most know the true dangers of that place and will no doubt instruct you accordingly. I feel it is best I tell you now to avoid confusion. You must follow the path through the Contour Plains. It is the safest way to balance, the next rune.

"Once you get through, continue until you see a town. Speak with the villagers, they will know where you need to go from there. Since your friends have arrived, I shall warn them also." He began to walk away. She had wondered if they would follow her to Darrienia and it seemed that, as she had both expected and feared, they had.

"Seiken," she called after him, although he didn't stop she knew he had heard her. "Please don't mention our meeting." He raised a hand to acknowledge her words.

"Head west," he called back, and although he pointed in the direction, he never turned back as he continued on his way. She frowned slightly as she realised the sheer volume of information he had just provided her with. Was time really so short that he needed to push them? She glanced back one last time to see he had now reached the top of the rise. She hurried in the direction he had pointed, she had to maintain a good lead if she were to ensure they had no choice but to turn back.

* * *

"Seiken!" Acha waved frantically as he appeared on the rise just before them, as he joined them, she spoke again. "Seiken have you seen Zo? We became separated."

"She is..." he groaned, looking to each of them in turn. "I cannot lie, she wished me not to tell you, she is in great danger. Even now she makes her way to the court. While it is true the next rune is located there, it is not her hands which must remove it. The court is not a friendly place, all who pass through its doors are judged by the most terrifying adjudicator. Few survive the punishment they bestow upon themselves. She told me what happened, I tried to warn her, but..."

"She went anyway." Daniel sighed as he finished Seiken's sentence. "Well, she has a head start, we'd better push on." Daniel looked to the place Seiken had stood, and was surprised to find he was still amongst them. Normally, once he had bestowed his latest wisdom, he departed, yet now he seemed to hover uncertainly. "Which way is it?" he asked not expecting to receive an answer.

"West. Although I must warn you, there are two routes which you may take. Many will say you should head through the Contour Plains. The inhabitants of these parts always send people in that direction, it is by far the longest route.

"I would suggest you cross the minefields. If you tread carefully there should be no problems. West." He pointed, before casually departing.

"Well I never expected a straight answer, he never normally gives us any information at all." Daniel watched for a second as he walked away before turning his attention back to his friends.

"He never normally walks either." Acha pointed out. "Maybe he has a dream nearby, who knows, we know so little of him," she added noticing he had now completely vanished from view. Without another word, they started on their way. Eiji pulled the map from his pocket, thinking how fortunate it was Zo had retained possession of the other. Come to think of it, he could not remember even showing this one to her. He shrugged to himself as he studied it and the landscape before them carefully. He scratched his head in confusion, looking at the lines on the parchment and the area which surrounded them. He was grateful when Daniel took it from his possession, he never had been much of a navigator.

"There's no court on here t'the west," Eiji stated. He wasn't convinced he had read it correctly, there were too many wiggly lines and pictures, but there were no buildings marked upon it, other than the single ones he assumed would represent a town or settlement.

"Well it won't be shown as a court will it? It'll be a fixed point with a symbol and a riddle we now don't need to solve." Acha pointed to the strange symbol which was west of their location as Daniel held it before them. In their world it would take them beyond Phoenix Landing, but here it seemed the terrain was, as had been predicted, different to that of their land. She looked up at Eiji and smiled before following Elly, who had already started to walk in the direction Seiken had pointed.

"Might I recommend whilst we try to gain lost ground, you all attempt to make peace with anything from your past you feel you should be judged for," she called back. She knew much of the theory behind the workings of this mythical building. It was a place dreamers would visit in order to seek redemption. Exactly how this was achieved was knowledge even she could not invoke, not at present anyway. She disliked going into such situations blind, therefore making peace with their past was the only advice she could offer. But there was something, a knowledge sealed within the recess of her mind that told her that, since they were physically present within this world, this court could pose more of a threat than if they were merely dreaming. It had something to do with how dreamers were relieved of their guilt, but with Annabel's passing, until someone took her place, there was no way for her to recall the forgotten knowledge.

* * *

Zo glanced at the road ahead, true to Seiken's words, the few people she encountered warned her to avoid the minefields, encouraging her in the direction of the Contour Plains. As she stood near the fork which separated the two paths, she felt Daniel was close. Somewhere, in the back of her mind, she heard his thoughts and with every second she hesitated they grew louder. The thought of facing them again after what had happened became more and more difficult with each step she took. She couldn't face them, she was ashamed, ashamed and frightened.

She knew what Marise had done, she couldn't bear to have Daniel look at her that way. She was meant to protect him from being scared, protect him from harm, not be the one who inflicted it. He had been terrified of her. There was something about the way he had looked at Marise, something which told her it was perhaps not the first time they had met.

Looking at the fork she knew her decision must be made quickly, she had to keep moving.

"Either way I'm heading west," she muttered to herself. There was no way to know which path led where. She felt her heart lift as she caught sight of a young pedlar who approached from one of the paths. "Excuse me, I am looking for the Contour Plains."

"You're heading that way? And I thought you were crazy when you were just talking to yourself." The pedlar began to continue on his way stopped only by the desperation in her voice.

"No please, I need something from just beyond, lives depend on my getting there, please." He turned to look at her, glancing her over suspiciously.

"The only place past there 'til the ends of the earth is a small mining village. There is nothing of great worth there." He gestured down the left fork.

"A mining village?" Zo questioned as she wondered how balance could fit into that scenario.

"Are you not familiar with the lay of the land? I myself am on a quest of great importance but even the most stu— brave adventurers, will not venture that way, it is far too dangerous. It may be safer for you to head through those minefields." The pedlar glanced behind him to take in the surroundings. Her chances of surviving either way were slim, but at least the minefields route was shorter. "Look, there's a port three days walk from here. You could take a boat and sail around. If you truly must get there, that would be the wiser choice." He extended his arm to point Zo in the direction of the aforementioned port.

"My instructions are clear, I must head through the plains. I don't have time to—"

"Fine, but it would be safer if you travelled in numbers. When you find someone willing to travel beside you into death, take the northwest path, it will lead you to the minefields. You must be wary, such a path is not to be taken lightly. Unseen to the eye, the fields are littered with vertical mines, though some say this network of underground passages allow the dead within to climb and seize their prey. Of course, if you wish to live, the port is southeast from here." He paused, glancing towards the overcast sky as he scratched his head. "I have said enough, my time is also short." He began to walk away.

"Thank you, I hope your quest goes well."

"I have to rely on more than hope. I have wasted enough time already," he chuntered to himself. It took a few more minutes for her to bring herself to start walking. Trees, marked both paths, for this she was grateful. She knew her friends were already catching up, and this shelter may just conceal her from them. Maybe if they didn't see her, they would turn back when they reached this fork. She took the opposite path to that she had been advised, knowing by his words this would lead to her destination. She did so at a quickened pace, in fear Daniel may be able to sense her at such close proximity. She had to get a greater lead, one large enough that he couldn't feel her through their bond.

* * *

"Excuse me, sorry to bother you I can see you are in a hurry." Daniel stopped a young pedlar who walked in the opposite direction to them, unaware not too long ago Zo had done exactly the same thing. "Have you seen a young lady on this path, brown hair?" Daniel waited in anticipation for the answer.

"I've just seen one person on my travel, she was heading west. I told her to head to the port this way, but she was insistent she had to continue on. I told her if she had to go that way, the northwest path to the minefields was the shorter of the two, but I wish she would have taken the port route. The ghosts of the damned are still seen through the mists of those lands, stalking those who would cross their path. Some say they are there to warn away travellers, others say in their despair they try to tempt those crossing to share their fate, so that none may claim the ore they lost their lives in search of. Since she is not likely to return this way, it would be my guess that you will find her amongst the mists, but be careful not to be lured from your path."

"Many thanks." Acha smiled. "If we can ever return the favour." The pedlar nodded.

"I doubt we shall meet again my lady, but the sentiment is appreciated. I would hurry if you hope to catch up, we crossed paths about fifteen minutes ago." With these words the pedlar continued on his way.

"Right you heard him, we must hurry if we wish to catch up to her."

When they finally reached the fork there was no sign of her. Daniel had hoped she may have waited long enough for them to at least catch a glimpse of her, or at least for him to know where she was. When they were approaching, he had felt her on the tip of his mind. He had hoped by the time they got here the feeling would have been stronger, it wasn't. He had lost any trace of her altogether. They paused at the path before taking the route advised by the pedlar, the opposite one to that their friend had taken just moments before.

* * *

The entrance to the fields were surrounded by a low wooden fence, time-worn and battered in a state of disrepair which told tales of the few travellers who walked these roads. Daniel knew well the story of their world's counterpart, and inaccurately assumed this was one of Darrienia's fixed locations. It was clear from their map there was nothing here for them to retrieve, but it was still an omen of the care they must take in crossing it.

Straining his vision against the heavy mist he searched the open plain for signs of movement, the wind proving no ally as it pushed heavy areas of mist across the fields creating shadows through the haze, shadows that moved with an unnatural gait. If they were to believe the tales of the pedlar, this phenomenon would be that which preyed upon the minds of those approaching to create the illusion of echoes or ghosts. It was impossible to tell if any of these shadows could be a distant trace of his friend's movements.

"We'll have to take this slowly," Daniel advised quietly as they regrouped at the battered fence. "If memory serves, in our world this is a place of untold dangers." Elly looked to him, waiting for him to continue, an act which struck him as uncharacteristic for someone who seemed to possess knowledge on all the tales of this world. She gave a slight sigh, Annabel's absence was becoming an inconvenience. She was aware of this place, she could feel the information relating to its history playing on the tip of her mind, but it was a knowledge she just couldn't recall, not unassisted at least. The only thing she could remember for certain, as she explored the fragments of her mind, was there was more to this place than the tales would tell, more than could be perceived. Perhaps if Daniel were to share his knowledge it would trigger the memory of an area she had most certainly visited, but with so much history behind her, so many countless years and memories, she failed to find the one she searched for.

"What type of dangers?" Acha questioned from the base of a blackened tree where she had taken a moment to rest. It was clear given the warnings they would not simply rush through. Time was short should they wish to make ground, but to enter without a plan was to tempt providence.

"As long as we tread lightly, we should be all right," he answered. "If memory serves, I believe this is the Hollowed Field. It was the site of the largest recorded anthropogenic disaster ever documented. It was said someone camping outside the field awoke one morning to find the field littered with gold. Taking all they could carry and staking a claim, this prospector sought authentication for the gold he gathered. Word soon spread, it had been a season of heavy rain and it was believed the waters had driven the ore to the surface, people flocked from all over to mine these fields, but dwarves or gnomes they were not.

"The fields were filled by fools who, on hearing a rumour that the greatest yield was the deepest, set out to burrow the land. Not concerning themselves with a means to exit, they raced downward digging their vertical shafts, for whoever struck the gold first could claim the entire vein as their own. Day and night they dug, fashioning all manner of devices so they could continue their descent without being buried by the earth they moved. The further they dug, the harder the composition.

"Cheers had filled the air as a pick finally broke through the seemingly impenetrable surface, but the celebration soon turned to screams as the crack widened and all which supported the land fell away. It is a wonder this grassland still exists, few will dare to step foot upon it, after all, it should not even be plausible. If you believe the rumours, there is little beneath the land you see to suspend it. The whole area should have become a crater, yet this field still exists." Elly recalled this story as he told it, but it was still not the information she had wanted. There was something more. She stepped over the fence carefully and began to walk in silence. They had already wasted enough time, perhaps walking this ground again would surface the knowledge she sought.

The mist was heavy, sticky, and soaked all it touched. Their clothes stuck to them like a film as they walked in a steady single file. The obscuring fog made visibility so poor that the person before them was nothing more than a silhouette, despite the closeness. The shifting currents of wind through the mist created further illusions of movement. There were no signs of tracks before them. The heaviness of the low cloud's moisture, coupled with the powerful winds, removed all trace of footsteps of anyone who may have walked this land previously.

Acha shivered against the cold, carefully following the shadow of the person before her. She stopped suddenly hearing the unmistakable sound of movement behind her, the mists deafening her allies to the warning given as she stopped. Her vision panned the area as she searched for the source. It had to be Zo. Perhaps, since there were no paths or markers, she had become lost in this terrain, but she could hear her. There was the unmistakable sound of muffled footsteps close by. She called to her friends again as she failed to find evidence of the person she had heard, but as she turned back she realised the mist had grown denser, her friends were no longer visible. She looked to the ground desperately, relief filling her as she saw a set of tracks. She quickened her pace following them before the harsh conditions could erase the trail.

The mist began to lighten, the colours returned to the world. Elly halted, her vision scanning the area for any trace of Zo. The winds were lighter here, the mists finer, presenting the opportune time to check for tracks. Her vision panned the surroundings for footprints, but there was nothing. The airborne water particles still muffled the sounds around them, but Daniel's question pierced the air alerting them to his concern.

"Where's Acha?" His vision turned backwards into the blanket of fog behind them, questioning how they could have become separated.

※ ※ ※

'*What happened?*' Acha thought as she rose steadily to her feet from her sprawled position across a cold unknown surface. '*One second I was following the tracks, and now?*' Her vision met with nothing but darkness. She outstretched her arms as she began to move slowly forwards, her hand connecting with something moist. Moving herself closer she navigated her way through the darkness, using the walls as a guide, only to find she walked within an enclosed circle.

Damp mud and stone stuck to her hands as she tried, once more, to find any means of escape. Without warning, a bright light shone from above. For a second, she thought it may have been *the* light, the one her mother told her guided the dead to the gates of the Underworld. From being imprisoned in complete darkness, to now standing in an upward facing tunnel filled with light, it could only mean one thing.

A panic rose within her, to get this far only to die, surely that was wrong. She took a breath to calm herself. Had this been the light, then that meant her amulet would have been destroyed. Her hand gripped the charm, which still hung around her neck, to restore some calmness. Her mind, soothed by its presence, began to reason with her. If the place she found herself in now was the tunnel then she would not be surrounded by mud and stones. Once she realised this, her eyes began to adjust to her surroundings. She was not in the tunnel, she had simply fallen into a very deep hole, and by some miracle had been unhurt. It had to be one of the shafts Daniel had mentioned.

She dug her fingers in the dirt as she tried to climb its heights, but each time she did, she slipped against the damp walls. It was only seconds after the light appeared when she heard someone call to her.

"Are you all right?" *all right?* Daniel's voice echoed around the confines of the shaft as his silhouette appeared in the light above, much to her relief. For a moment she had feared they hadn't noticed, feared that when they did, they would be unable to find her, and a small part of her was afraid that even should they notice, they wouldn't turn back at all.

"I think so," *think so,* she called back. "I'm in a hole," *a hole,* she called, even as she said it she wondered why she had stated the obvious, surely everyone knew exactly where she was, after all, it was they who had moved whatever had obstructed the light to find her.

"The ground seems to have just given," *just given,* Daniel called back. They were lucky to have found her. If not for having Eiji with them, it would have been impossible to find the soft, grass covered shaft in which she had fallen.

"Elly has gone back to get some vines," *some vines.*

Listening to Daniel's voice flooded her with relief. She had feared they would not even have noticed her missing until it was already too late. Her nerves saw her hands once more tracing the edge of the shaft ensuring her confines had not become smaller. She took a deep breath trying to calm herself, certain the last time she stood with her arms outstretched that they had not touched both sides. She forced herself to believe it was only her fear which made it seem as if the walls were closing in around her.

A sick, nagging sensation tugged at her stomach. She was afraid, and the silence seemed to stretch forever, making her nervous. It played tricks on her mind making her believe she could hear the sound of breathing echoing almost inaudibly around her. It had to be the wind from above. It *was* the wind and nothing more. She extended her arms again, they were slightly bent as she touched the sides. A few small pebbles fell to echo quietly about her, the dampened noise sounding almost like something trying to claw its way through.

The silence quickened her heart as every sound she heard became twisted by her fears to make her believe she was not alone. The sounds seemed to grow closer, she knew it had to be the ghosts of the miners. Those poor people who fell to their deaths, seemed to now be clawing their way up to meet her. They were going to tunnel up until she met the same fate as they had, they were going to kill her. She glanced around frantically, convincing herself she could feel the trembling of the earth beneath her feet, she had to focus on something else before hysteria took her.

"Has she gone alone?" *alone?* she called up, her voice broke in fear. At least his silhouette still covered part of the light from the hole, as long as she could see this, she knew she wasn't alone. Daniel leaned up as if he was looking for something before he answered.

"No Eiji went with her," *with her,* "but I can't see them now," *them now,* his voice echoed before he spoke again. "Did you hurt yourself, are you all right?" *all right?*

"Don't worry, I'll be all right," *no, you won't.* The conversation fell dead as they both heard the final echo, the words unbelievably clear.

* * *

Zo stopped at the fork where the minefields joined the Contour Plains, to become one westward road again. Something was wrong. She felt fear and desperation on the edge of Daniel's mind. As soon as she acknowledged he was there, she heard his thoughts clearly. He was begging silently for help, for Elly and Eiji to hurry. She tried her best to ignore it, and forcing her gaze to the grass she even managed to take another step away.

"Damn it," she cursed. "Who am I kidding?" She turned towards the mine-fields and ran in the direction of his thoughts, in the direction she sensed his life-force. Now and again, as she felt soft earth tremble beneath her feet, she cringed, each time expecting to fall to her death. She questioned over and over why they had taken such a dangerous path. She knew the answer, it was her fault. The minefields were the quicker route, they had they gone this way to ensure they would find her. She had put them in danger again.

* * *

"Daniel!" Acha screamed, but fear transformed the words to an inaudible whisper, the hole had closed further. She called his name over and over, yet there was no reply, his silhouette had vanished. She gasped for breath in the darkness. The walls, now more than ever, felt as if they were caving in around her. From somewhere below her she heard the clawing sound from the wall resume. She reassured herself, she had touched each wall in turn, they were solid, except for the fact they seemed to be closing in around her, but there was no way something shared this space with her. Then again, there had been that strange echo. She clearly wasn't alone, inside the darkness something waited.

She could just about hear Daniel as he shouted for Elly and Eiji to hurry, he knew there was no way he could reach her. He feared there was no way they could reach him in time either, he wondered if they could even hear his cries as the heavy mist seemed to deaden all sound, that was, after all, why none of them had heard Acha fall.

The ground vibrated beneath her feet, each second the tremors deepening as the clawing sound grew louder. The tiny vibrations sent small shock waves through her already trembling body as she looked desperately for a means to escape. The sound of picks sinking into the wall were clear now from below. Click, click, click, closer and closer, with each echo the vibrations grew stronger. The ground began to break and crumble beneath her feet. Something crawled across her shoulder, she let out a scream before realising it was a rope, which had descended from above. Her hands seized it, securing it quickly around herself as the floor below crumbled into nothingness. The movement below barely visible through the darkened void. She dared not look, dared not strain her eyes against the darkness, lest the horrors she beheld cause her grip to fail as they pulled her towards the surface in short, jerking motions.

She cried out as something pierced her leg just an instant before a coarse calloused hand wrapped itself around her ankle and began to tug. She kicked out frantically trying desperately to shake the figure loose, to fend off the assailant who was determined to condemn her to an eternity within the hollow. It refused to release her, clinging to her desperately as she swung from side to side. All upwards movement halted under the strain of the extra weight. Unknown to her assailant, touching her was not without its consequences, even to a ghost.

It wasn't a ghost, she realised. It wasn't a monster, or a creature belonging to any kingdom but their own. The figure who grabbed her was a man, a living, breathing, man, yet in this world he was more.

The longer he remained in contact with her, the more she began to understand. There were indeed piles of bones somewhere beneath the surface, but these people were not the threat they had thought. The person here wanted to escape, but to do so, she had to take his place.

* * *

"Bandits." Elly clicked her fingers, recalling that which had previously escaped her as they began to work their way back through the mists with the vines. "A city of bandits built in the hollow." Eiji realised almost instantly that she wasn't addressing him. She shook her head in amusement, how could she have forgotten? She had spent a long time within the underground city. One of the fighting rings she frequented, in order to earn funds for her travels, had been there. The area, of course, had looked much different then. Mother Nature, or more accurately the Severaine, had made easy work of concealing the access tunnels which led deep into the bowels of this city. It had survived well, and still harboured those who would seek shelter from hunters.

Sertorious, the bandit leader many generations before Viriatus took charge, had claimed it as his centre of operations, in fact, she had been the one to make such a suggestion to him.

She shook her head, to think she could have difficulty recalling such a thing. The legend of miners was true, but only to an extent. The city had been constructed before the new gods took reign, in a time where technology was paramount. The underground city had better defences than anywhere else of that time, and, in this time, she had shown Sertorious how to operate them. The technologies used to create such a construct were the reason that locational magic, or items, were rendered useless. It wasn't certain how Darrienia would assimilate, adapt, and portray such a place, but given its ancient lore, it was doubtful much adaptation was needed. There were multiple stories and legends, enough to keep even a dreamer's imagination sated. She gave a slight chuckle.

* * *

The price of contact being satisfied saw her attacker plummeting into the darkness below; a darkness no doubt filled with countless more who would gladly take his place in an attempt to succeed where he had failed. The light above her grew ever brighter until she felt the welcoming hands of her friends pulling her forcefully from the trap, as her own hands clawed to find the safety of solid ground. She lay gasping on the sodden ground, her hand now finding her wound, returning her mind to the dark confines of the tunnel, almost as if she was the one plummeting below. The shaft opened into something so large her mind failed to comprehend, and below, hidden deep within the darkness, something waited, something hungry. Daniel's voice returned her to the openness, to the white glare of light across the misted plain.

"Zo!" Daniel gasped, finally able to think. When she appeared, he had no chance to say anything. There were more pressing issues. Now he could finally express how glad he was to see her, relief filled his voice as he spoke. "You came back." He pulled her satchel from his shoulder, throughout the entire ordeal it had never moved away from him, he offered it to her. When she didn't take it from him, he lowered his arm slowly. Acha felt the uneasy tension pass through the air.

"Thank the Gods Zo, if it weren't for you I would have been..." Acha stopped her expression of gratitude as she turned to look at Zo. It was painfully clear how uncomfortable she was around them, she wore an expression similar to that which she herself had worn when first finding herself in their company, before they had become friends.

"It was foolish of me to take the rope, I apologise," she stated quietly, although she was unsure exactly *when* she had obtained possession of it. It was only on the outskirts of the field she realised it was wrapped diagonally across her, shoulder to hip. They had lost the other one as they fled from Aburamushi. She extended her arm to offer the coiled rope, for a moment it hung loosely in her hand. Daniel took it from her, unsure what else he could do. He looked from her to it, as he tried to find the words which would make her stay, for that matter any words would have done, but he failed and so they stood there in an uncomfortable silence.

"How did you find us, this mist is like soup," Acha enquired as she clutched the slice in her leg. It didn't seem to be bleeding too badly, yet it stung and throbbed as if it was ten times its size and depth. That was not the only thing, she felt peculiar, as if more than just the memories of the bandit had been transferred to her, but she couldn't understand what she was being shown. It was something magnificent, but without the knowledge to understand it, she could gain no insight. If she were to try, using the understanding she had gained from contact, it would translate as a structure built beneath the earth in the shelved descent into the unknown. An unknown which in this world was home to something, something which the bandits here were subservient to, something which kept close vigil of their numbers.

"I heard you screaming, I couldn't leave you in danger. But you're safe now." She gave a quick, strained smile trying to portray warmth despite the monotone of her voice. She glanced down to Acha's bleeding leg. It was not as bad as she had expected, it would be simple to treat. Hugging herself, Zo turned slowly to walk away.

'*You are more than skilled enough to treat this wound.*' She projected the words into Daniel's mind, as she glanced back sadness crossed her face. Daniel couldn't hide the shock from her words, this was not what he had expected. For a moment he stood staring at her, he still held her bag loosely in one hand the rope in his other. She really was going to just walk away.

'*You're not staying?*' he questioned. The hurt in his eyes was something she didn't wish anyone to suffer. It would be easier if she left, easier, safer, and perhaps a little selfish. She knew she couldn't stand to see him look at her in that way again.

'*How can I?*'

Acha sat on the ground, looking between the two of them with a feeling she was missing something, something important.

'*We're your friends, nothing will change that,*' Daniel answered. He knew this conversation was not one for Acha to be included in. It was something personal between the two of them, something they needed to resolve before things could progress.

'*I tried to kill you.*' She felt his shock as she argued. It was almost as if he hadn't expected her to remember, or at least to be so blunt about what she knew. '*She let me remember.*' She lowered her gaze, crossing her right arm across her body protectively. Even thinking the words hurt. She knew this probably wasn't the best course of action, but it would be safer for everyone if she stayed away.

'*But it wasn't you.*' He knew then she had every intention of leaving them there, he couldn't blame her for this panicked reaction. This discovery had been a surprise for him too, but none of it had made any difference, why couldn't she see that?

'*It was, that's what you don't understand. What if next time—*'

'*What ifs spoil everything. I won't turn my back on you for things out of your control. I just don't understand, why me?*' Daniel had a theory, but it was simply that. He would have known by now if such things had come to light. He had been lucky to escape Marise before, if not for the help of a stranger, his life would have been hers, and she had *not* been happy to let him go. He wondered how much Zo knew, and if there was another reason to her wanting him dead. There had seemed something deeply personal about her desire to harm him. He glanced away from her to look at Acha. She seemed to feel increasingly more uncomfortable as the silence stretched on, unaware of their secret conversation. She glanced between them, waiting for either of them to talk, for one of them to say something, anything.

'*She feels our bond is a threat. You're something I've kept from her, that makes you dangerous. That's what puts you in danger, and that's why I can't stay.*' Daniel took a determined step towards her.

'*I can fight my own battles, even against you. I don't need you to protect me.*' He had to convince her, he needed her to stay. She was in more danger than she cared to realise, especially now she knew the truth, it gave Marise more power. A part of him warned that her only chance to suppress the killer, was to rely on her friends, to let the bonds of friendship carry some of the burden, to use them to bind Marise. He was certain if they remained united, drawing on each other's strength, then there was nothing they couldn't do.

'*Would you be prepared to kill me, would you?*' she pushed already knowing the answer. It was one he needed to accept, an answer that ensured she could not stay. '*Would you be able to take a weapon and drive it through my heart, to kill her when you knew it would also kill me?*'

'*I...*' Daniel glanced to the floor.

'*She wouldn't hesitate to kill you. It won't be like last time, I feel it.*' Zo fought back the blurring of tears which distorted her vision.

"Please somebody say something," Acha pleaded, the tense silence had become too much for her to bear. Zo looked at her apologetically.

"I'm sorry, goodbye." She had only walked a few more steps when Daniel stopped her again.

"Zo, if you go to that court alone, how do you expect to survive if you can't forgive yourself?" He was unsure exactly what Acha knew about this situation, but he knew enough from her questions when she treated him, that there was no doubt in her mind that his injury had been somehow caused by Zo. He wasn't going to say anything which would give her more information than was needed.

"Court?" Zo stopped as she turned back to face him.

"Didn't Seiken tell you? He said he warned you," Daniel questioned, surprise reflecting in his eyes.

"Tell me what?" She didn't look him in the eyes, she couldn't bring herself to do it, but she knew there was something to what he tried to tell her. It was at that precise moment she realised she had been looking for an excuse to stay and with this realisation came another one, she needed to say whatever it took to make them abandon the quest. She had to do this alone. She could not endanger them just because she felt comforted by their presence, it was selfish.

"The Court of Divine Judgement, it's where the next rune lies. Please, don't go there alone," he begged, lowering his gaze to hide the pain in his eyes. He knew without a doubt there was no way for her to overcome such a place, not alone. She needed them, and she knew it.

'*Daniel I can't risk—*'

'*I will just follow you. I mean it!*' he threatened. She shook her head. This was not good. She had just resolved herself to ensuring they abandoned the quest, but instead of trying to force her decision on him, she found she nodded. '*I will follow no matter the danger. I will not lose another person.*' Zo remained silent, knowing his last thought was one she was not meant to have heard. His words had swayed her. Even though she knew it was the worst thing she could have done, she wanted to stay with them just a little longer.

She began to treat Acha's wound with the pre-mixed paste which was kept in the satchel. There was just enough for one more application, how she prayed she wouldn't find cause to use it again. She began to wrap the bandage gently around Acha's leg. The bleeding had already subsided, with the paste applied, it would soon become less inflamed. She suddenly felt extremely guilty about having left Acha sitting there injured while she and Daniel had their discussion.

"Thank the Gods you found us." Acha once more spoke to break the strained silence. "If you hadn't have come, I would be dead." All three of them at that moment shared the same concern, Elly and Eiji had yet to return, if they weren't back soon, they would need to search for them.

"Acha, you do realise I can't heal this like I did for Daniel." She nodded, it was something she was fully aware of.

"Why is that?" Daniel asked as his curiosity took over; it made Zo smile slightly, he was being just like his old self, always questioning everything, even if it was a little forced.

"It's hard to explain," Zo stated, not really wanting to answer, but she continued, realising she needed to make the effort. "This body, although it was adapted to take on her original appearance, wasn't originally hers. If I used nature to try to heal this, it would not aid me, as far as it is concerned the life-force of the occupier has already departed. Her body needs to heal naturally. I guess the simplest way to put it is, I can't heal her body because it's not, in a manner of speaking, her body," she explained as she finished wrapping the bandages.

"I thought as much," Acha smiled. "But, if it involves you tapping into consciousness, it belongs to me so you can, right?" She remembered how she had felt Zo on the tip of her mind before she had woken in Daniel's house. She had somehow provided her with the strength she had needed to take charge of this body. It was something she would never forget, without Zo she would never have awoken. She had tried so hard to re-establish control on the body after her initial entrance, but her efforts had been in vain. The energy she had taken had not been enough. The energy she had stored did nothing more than go towards maintaining the basic bodily functions.

"That's right, that's how I roused you the first time we met. All done." Zo forced a smile as she pulled down Acha's trouser leg.

As she placed the remaining items back into the bag, she became aware of how depleted her medical supplies and basic essentials had become. Its absence from her possession had not even been considered as she had fled from them. It was a relief he had brought it, as old and battered as it may be it was hers, and she loved it.

"Zo!" Eiji exclaimed; his figure appeared through the mist. "Y' found her!" As he came clearly into view, they saw the enormous vine gripped within his hands.

"Well, she found us." Acha smiled. "Good job too, a moment longer and I dread to think what may have happened." She pointed to her leg as Zo and

Daniel helped her to her feet. At first the pain of the wound made her cringe as she applied a little weight onto the sore area, but it was already easing as she took energy from the life around her to speed up the body's natural process of healing. Taking the vine from Eiji, Elly secured it around herself suggesting they did the same. It was a wise consideration, at least this would ensure they would know should anyone be led astray again.

"As soon as we are out of here, I'll make you something for the pain." The boundaries of this field were but a short distance now, but even such a trek could prove hazardous. The field's natural camouflage was an ally to those who would wish them harm. It was best to make haste to the safety of the main track, before delaying further.

"Y'stayin' with us, right?" Eiji questioned. The silence seemed to stretch forever until finally she answered.

"For now." She glanced across at Daniel with regret, knowing the time would soon be upon them when their paths would have to part. Even now she could feel Marise's intention towards him.

Chapter 13

Trial of the Heart

Soot-stained wooden scaffolds, constructed with care and precision, slowly twisted up the side of the mountain. Built between the steep slopes and wooden platforms, resting on both lumber and rock, were small wooden dwellings, no doubt belonging to the miners who lived within. The platforms snaked back and forth, slowly gaining height to stop their ascension near a gaping tunnel in the side of the mountain. A cave visible to all, almost like an icon looking out across its followers, watched over them. A large man-driven conveyor belt descended from the source of the miners' livelihood. The conveyor belt still weighted with coal and minerals, from when their work abruptly stopped to accommodate the debate which seemed to be occurring at its base.

"I don't think these people will know anything of what we seek." Acha walked behind Daniel and Zo as they glanced around for anything which resembled the promised court, yet they saw nothing but the humble houses and workstations.

"Even so, I think it would be wise not to reveal the entire situation," Elly whispered as they approached the crowd who, as they had previously noted, were in heated conversation. A discussion which instantly fell silent as someone within the group noticed the appearance of the strangers. The masses parted allowing a single figure to walk through and advance towards them, the pathway closing behind him as they all turned to hear what would be said.

"And what brings *you* here?" The young man rubbed his soot-stained hands down his equally discoloured linen shirt. It was clear until recently the men and women had been hard at work. Flecks of rock and dust still clung to their hair. There had been an obvious, abrupt stop in the labour, but the reason was unclear.

"Please forgive the intrusion." Daniel stepped forwards, surprised Elly had not intervened. "My friends and I are travellers. We are seeking an ancient court and were told perhaps you would know of it." There was a long stretch of silence before the young village chief finally decided to answer. He passed his hand through his brown-blond hair, shaking free some of the loose debris. He opened his mouth, but before he could speak he was interrupted.

"What interest do yer have in such a place?" The chief glanced to the elderly figure who had intervened to draw their attention from his son. Although how they knew they were related in this world was beyond their understanding, they simply knew.

"A friend of ours spoke of it once. We are seeking something that was left inside." Daniel answered after a small pause for thought. Something told him he should be as vague as possible about what it was they wanted, and why.

"Must be mighty important for yer to come all this way." The old man stepped forwards, dusting his arms as he looked at each of them curiously.

"Then you know of it?" Daniel recognised something within the old man's eyes, he nodded as he looked to his son. "I believe these may be the ones who can help us." His son frowned, but despite his harsh expression, he still nodded in agreement.

"We know of it," the young chief admitted, there was a slight resentment in his voice. "It blocks our path. We seek something just beyond it. I have lost a dozen or more men to that place. We even tried to tunnel around but the ground will not allow it. The only way past is through. I shall grant you passage through my caves, although you must go alone without a guide, and the price is one ruebluebyal crystal." Daniel sighed, he knew this had seemed too easy.

"I'm afraid we carry no such thing." He glanced at Elly hopefully, she shook her head to confirm his statement. The village chief laughed bitterly, the villagers around him did not share his amusement.

"Of course not, it can only be found deep within the centre of the mine." Daniel glanced across to Zo, defeat showing in his eyes. A short silence passed before the chief began to walk away.

"Well, what now?" Daniel whispered, wondering if perhaps there was a way to infiltrate the mines, but with so many people around, they would have to wait until nightfall, and by then, they would be in worse danger.

"Come, that is if you care to hear my proposition." The village chief glanced back to them as they stood talking amongst themselves. On hearing his words, they followed quickly as he guided them upwards along the solid platforms of the town, and into a small cabin.

It was a simple structure, and as the one belonging to the chief no doubt, the grandest. It consisted of five first floor rooms made up of two bedrooms, a kitchen, bathroom, and the dining room, the place they stood now. The windows were simply holes carved into the wood split into four small sections. When they were all inside, he closed the door behind them, motioning them to a small table. The chief's father had also joined them as they sat around the small table patiently.

"As I said the ruebluebyal crystal is located just beyond the court, an ancient building from many millennia ago, or so it is thought. I heard a rumour, when I was a boy, that it is one of the buildings left standing from those that came before us. In exchange for granting you passage, while you are looking for your item, as payment for the use of our mines we request you bring this back for us, agreed?" Daniel glanced to the other group members. There seemed to be no objections amongst them, after all it was the only option open to them. If they were to refuse, they could never find what they sought. They either took this quest or failed their own.

"Agreed." The chief smiled at Daniel's acceptance, but it was a smile which lacked sincerity.

"Then please, allow me to guide you to the entrance. Follow me." As the young man stood, he gestured his guests outside. Once more they followed in his steps as he led them further up the twisting supports to the foot of the cave. It seemed they had wasted very little time in getting straight to the point and on to the matter at hand.

A large metal gate, imposingly suspended over the entrance to the mountain, was bound securely with rope. It seemed to be raised and lowered by a small pulley system which was constructed on the outside of the entrance. It made them wonder if there were things living within that the villagers didn't want to leave. The chief wound the crank handle to raise the portcullis. Once raised, he placed the catch on the handle and gestured for them to enter. But all hospitality seemed to finish there. As soon as they crossed the threshold, the gate came crashing down, sending a shock wave across the floor beneath their feet.

"Hey! We've already agreed to help you!" Daniel protested, his hands gripping the metal bars. Despite how easily the chief had raised the construct, it was far heavier than it had appeared. He was certain, even with their combined efforts, they would be unable to raise the metal gate. The young chief opened his mouth to speak but was interrupted by his father.

"Please, this is not as it seems, it's for yer own safety. When yer return yer may raise the barrier with the crank inside." He motioned across to the inside of the cave's wall. A few moments passed until he spoke again. "Yer really should know the truth about this situation."

"Father no!" the young chief protested, although he knew his words alone were not enough to stop him. "This concern belongs to our people."

"And they are aidin' us, they have a right to know. This gate'll offer yer some protection, should anythin' happen outside. As yer just felt first hand, yer'll know the instant this gate falls. The shock wave can be felt throughout the mines, but fear not, they are sturdy and'll not collapse." The old man patted the side of the cave entrance, as if to support his statement.

"But why would anything happen?" Acha questioned as she stepped towards the gate.

"Although time is short, I feel it best to tell yer." He gave a sigh before he began his story. "Thirteen days ago, a lord arrived. He rode a creature the size of a large horse, but never in my life have I seen such a beast. Its head was that of a snake, its body was covered in black feathers, and where a horse's hoof would finish it bore claws.

"Anyway, he approached us, clutchin' a strange device within his gold adorned fingers. Lookin' to the strange creature he gave a nod, as if it were to understand him. Of course, we didn't know his purpose, and he made no attempt to engage us. The village was distressed by his appearance, there was somethin' unnerving about him and his interest.

"We gathered the men at the gate, where yer now stand, in order to protect the livelihood of our town, havin' already sent our families to safety. It was a quick decision and although none of us could explain the loomin' oppression in the air, we knew any who remained would be in danger. They fled around the mountain and although they have not sent word, we trust they are safe.

"Once this stranger had finished examinin' the village he called for the Elder, my son. It was his first day as village chief, I had retired the title with the sinkin' of the last sun. We both met with him in our dwellin's. He spoke of a rare stone, the ruebluebyal crystal, he required it as an offerin' to the new King. He said he had been tasked to present the rarest of gems and he sought this stone within our mines. He demanded the crystal and gave us the means to track it, this device." He passed it through the bars to Acha who examined it closely as she waited for him to continue.

"Why couldn't he get it himself?" Daniel questioned.

"Well he could, he explained it to us very clearly. For him to obtain it he would use a method familiar to him, one which would mean the destruction of our home and the levellin' of our mines.

"Of course, we protested such actions and begged for the chance to retrieve it ourselves. He agreed to permit us fourteen days before he'd return, had we not obtained it by then he'd use his method. We have sent in groups of men. The first to return informed us that the giant structure, something we have always respectfully avoided, was impossible to pass. We have mined many tunnels but cannot penetrate the earth near to it.

"Three days ago, we sent someone through, they never returned. Since then, two more groups of our villagers have vanished. We can only assume they went the same way. Since yer headin' for the court, maybe yer know somethin' of its secrets, thus while yer there, if yer could bring us back this stone we would be in yer debt. Yer are our last hope, we cannot send any more of our men," he stated. There was something almost apologetic to his tone.

"We shall return before sunset." Acha smiled as she touched the former Elder's hand through the bar. "Although, maybe to be safe, you should evacuate." She looked at him meaningfully as she spoke. She knew the faith he claimed to have in them was genuine, but his next words enforced it.

"We'll wait for yer return"—a gentle smile crossed his wrinkled brow as he spoke—"until the last second," he added.

"I understand." She knew in her heart this would be the response. Those who would leave were already gone. A sinking feeling swelled in the pit of her stomach, they had to succeed. This town was wagering everything on their success, she could not disappoint them. She felt a strange kinship to these people, perhaps it was because the old man, in both mannerisms and profession, was so much like her grandfather. How she had loved that man. It had been he who had told her she could do anything she wished—even manage the affairs in her father's stead—when everyone else had tried to force her to become something more fitting to her gender. "We shall be back before sunset, with the crystal," she promised with sincerity.

"There are many other paths yer can take, that device has a map of our tunnels. If anythin' were to happen there's always another way out." With those words they began to head deep into the mines.

"They won't come back you know that, especially since you told them how they can leave without passing this way." The village chief placed his hand on his father's shoulder as he motioned for him to lead the way down. His father, however, refused to be led.

"Yer'll make a fine leader the day yer can put yer faith in people. I'll wait here for signs of their return." The chief glanced back at his father who had now moved to sit patiently beside the cave's entrance.

They had walked for almost an hour through the strangely lit complex of caves and tunnels. All the time they progressed they were unable to discover the source of light, yet still, the illumination was that of a rainy day.

They had discussed the town and the people there, and were of the opinion that it seemed they were all having the same dream, sharing the same threat. They wondered if perhaps each night this group of people dreamt of the same adventure, or if predetermined adventures enacted themselves through-out Darrienia, leaving the dreamers themselves to be interchangeable. Re-gardless of the process, they knew the dangers these people feared were very real. With the boundaries thinning, and no Oneirois to wake them, if death came for them in their dream it would take them. They knew they had to do everything within their power to ensure the lives of these people were not at risk.

* * *

Their eyes, their knowledge, their experience, failed to comprehend ex-actly what it was that towered before them. Within the mountain lay an open-ing of unrealistic proportions, but more than that, the monument within, which stretched to unparalleled heights, was beyond all understanding. The structure defied all logic, the dimensions alien. Somehow, gazing upon it failed to assist with the perception of its immense form. It seemed to both encompass all space and encroach upon it simultaneously.

The structure seemed to tower higher still as they drew closer. The craftsmanship of the heavy door was the only feature distinguishable upon its almost reflective surface. No windows appeared to intrude upon its smooth exterior, no insight could be gained as to what lay within. Two large stone walls, like appendages, stretched outward, tunnelling into the natural contours of the opening, as if they were enormous roots stabilising the prodigious structure.

"This buildin' must be old," Eiji gasped. He had stated the obvious as he tried to understand, to make sense of all he saw before him. The monumental door beckoned them inside. Although tall in dimensions it was narrow by design, allowing but a single person to enter unhindered at any one time. Daniel's hand fell upon the cool surface, the feelings from within flooding his now shaking frame as overwhelming fear encompassed his whole being from just the slightest contact. The door responded, gently gliding inward in a smooth, unhindered motion, as it welcomed them inside.

* * *

"Daniel wake up. This isn't funny, wake up!" Through the clouding darkness he felt two hands grasp his shoulders as his unknown assailant shook him roughly. As he opened his eyes a peculiar feeling washed over him. A boy, no older than seventeen, with short, messy black hair leaned over him. The boy's pale blue eyes filled with relief as Daniel looked at him curiously. "How many fingers am I holding up?" He waved his hand in front of Daniel's face, far too quickly for him to see, let alone count the fingers.

He vanished only to return moments later with a glass of water. Daniel pulled himself into a sitting position and rubbed his head. He felt strangely confused, disorientated, and as if he had forgotten something very, very important, such as how he had arrived here. As he sipped the water, his memory came flooding back to him. Everything became clearer as the haze began to pass.

"Stephen! You're all right!" Although as he expressed this relief, he was unsure why he felt the need to. Everything quickly began to make sense again.

He was sitting in Stephen's kitchen, a place he had spent most of his days planning his adventures and travels. Moments ago, they had been talking about college and then, the next thing he knew, Stephen had been shaking him.

"Of course I am. It's you who's on the floor." He offered Daniel a helping hand to his feet.

"What happened?" He watched as his friend walked across to the pantry, to remove what could only be a pitcher of his mother's lemonade. It was by far their favoured drink, and she always prepared more when he visited. It was said between the two of them they could drink the place dry. There had been many comments made, by Stephen's father, about the relief the village felt that they were too young to visit what passed as the tavern. After all it was only a small island and supplies *were* limited.

"Stress maybe? You were talking about how you'd finally convinced your parents to dismiss the tutor so you could attend college, instead of studying here. You were on a roll, listing the courses you still want to complete, I swear you were like a boy possessed. The next thing I knew, boom, you were sprawled out across the floor, but you know you've never really been right, not since..." His voice trailed off into silence as he placed the pitcher on the table, before grabbing an extra glass. On his return he filled both to the brim with the iced lemonade. "Are you sure you don't wanna go see your mam?"

"Nah, I'm fine, really." Turning to look at Stephen, he caught a glimpse of himself in the mirror. The strangest sensation washed over him, something seemed to be different. For a moment he looked at himself certain the person who now stared back was not someone he recognised. He tried to pinpoint the difference but couldn't. His brown hair hung, as always, just below of the top of his ears. His fringe neatly parted down the middle, his dark eyes shone brightly back at him. He knew then nothing was different, the mirror didn't lie, but for a few moments he thought he looked younger. He shrugged, it was probably down to something as simple as his pale complexion.

"If you're sure." Stephen watched his friend with uncertainty, but he knew better than to argue, besides, he was too excited about disclosing his most recently acquired treasure. "C'mon, I have something to show you." An obvious tone of excitement filled his friend's voice as he led the way to the staircase. Daniel hesitated as Stephen began taking the steps two at a time in anticipation. He was filled with the strangest feeling of déjà vu.

"A star fragment?" Daniel questioned, his hand resting on the bottom section of the banister, he still felt a little unsteady. Stephen turned to face him, unable to hide the amazement on his face.

"It's true! You really can read my mind just like me mam says," he laughed. When Daniel had caught up to him, Stephen already held a small black box in his hand. He could feel his friend's excitement as he stood waiting to show him.

He opened the box slowly for effect. That was, after he turned it to himself to glance quickly inside, ensuring his treasure was still where it should be. Once he was satisfied, he turned the box to Daniel, who heard himself gasp as he saw the small stone which shone brightly in the box. It twinkled almost as if it was a star plucked straight from the sky.

Daniel had always envisioned the stars as something beyond his reach, something no man would ever gaze upon but from afar. Never before had there been sightings of a star falling from the sky, meteors yes, but never a star. He wondered if this was the first. Gazing upon it he felt the strangest awe, wondering what events it had seen in its life, listening to its distant voice. He hadn't realised he had been daydreaming. Something about its presence here seemed sad, lonely, and for one moment, in his musings, it had asked him to complete it. He stood entranced until Stephen spoke again.

"Me dad thinks it's only a part of it. He watched it fall and retrieved it for me, he said once it fell it split into three. He thinks one didn't land too far from here. I thought maybe that could be today's adventure." He grinned as he lifted it from the box. As Daniel heard his request to find the other fragments, he honestly believed it was the star's plea being heard, but the thought of them going to find it filled him with such inexplicable terror that it made his chest tighten. He was filled with despair, as if no good could come from their expedition. The feelings were so strong, so powerful they surpassed his unquenchable thirst for adventure.

"No." His voice trembled with the terror reflected in his eyes. Alarmed by his tone Stephen looked from the star fragment, which now hung around his neck, to Daniel as he waited for an explanation for the uncharacteristic outburst. "Not today, I have a bad feeling..." It was the only response Daniel could give. Something about the idea of going on a jaunt today troubled him greatly.

"In the morning then? Stay tonight, we can plan our path. Besides, it's raining a little." Stephen glanced out of the window at the gentle spots of rain which fell. "Perhaps the water will unearth them," he stated, but the doubt in his voice was clear. If anything, the rain would further conceal them, but there was no question that they would postpone their journey, not after his reaction.

Daniel and Stephen both leaned over their map, after their hours of work it was now covered with small pencil lines and corrections where they had marked the potential places that, based on the first fragment's location and estimated entry point, the other two may have landed.

Various formulae, written against angled lines, covered the maps surface but now, by their final calculations, one landed close by. The other seemed to be lost, falling somewhere within the deepest regions of the sea, an unmapped area which no boats had sailed. Strangely enough it was a place they often dreamed of exploring, a dream that one day they would chart new lands. The map they knew possessed only Albeth, Therascia, Crowley, Drevera, Aimbria, and Living Stone, but this was surely but a fraction of the world documented by cartographers. There were whole new continents which awaited discovery. Countries which would be bathed in darkness while the sun shone on their part of the world, but as yet, none had survived the trip across the raging waters to discover them.

A huge clap of thunder echoed around the small island as the rain began to hammer down with such force it shook the glass panes in the windows. Unknown time passed until their focus was disrupted. Stephen's father stood in the doorway, his clothes sodden, his tense posture relaxing as his vision fell upon the two boys.

"Sure glad you two lads are here." He gave a heartfelt sigh of relief. "I thought you were heading down to the river, I looked everywhere for you while helping set the barricades. I'm so glad you're here especially since the river burst its banks. When I couldn't find you, I thought the worst! Daniel, I'll let your dad know when I head back. I'll tell him you're staying here tonight. This weather's not fit for man nor beast."

Daniel and Stephen exchanged meaningful glances as Stephen's father, clearly relieved, returned to the harsh conditions. Satisfied his family was safe he once again focused his attention on the task at hand. Every time Crowley had storms, the able men and women of the island would band together to line sandbags near the places the river swelled. The rivers would rise and flood, and so they worked hard to divert the flow from their town and crops.

As Daniel watched him leave a strange nagging sensation tugged at the back of his mind, something danced on the tip of his consciousness which he couldn't quite reach, he shrugged the feeling away. The relief he felt that he and Stephen had stayed home was far greater than the troubles of a fading dream.

* * *

Acha paused in surprise as she beheld their new surroundings. She knew this place and there was no possible way they could be here. She recognised the carefully sectioned fields, each dedicated to their own produce dependent on the time of year. In fact, she even recognised the figure who strip-tilled the fields with her trusty hoe ready to sow the crop. She had always been meticulous with the cultivation of land and crop rotation. Even the animals seemed to know her patterns as the seasons changed and their grazing areas cycled. Elly, Eiji, and Daniel stood before her. It was only then she noticed Zo was not amongst them.

"Where's Zo?" she questioned turning her attention towards a noise from the location they had just emerged, only to discover the sound she had just mistaken for someone's approach had, in fact, been small dislodged twigs striking the ground from a nest in the tree above. Noticing this brought with it a new realisation, the entrance was gone. Daniel turned in alarm, his vision searching the surroundings for any sign of their missing friend.

"I thought she was right behind me." His voice held the same panic that was displayed in his eyes, as he continued to scour the area for any indication of her presence.

"Despite how this appears, we *have* just entered The Courts, maybe she is already being judged. Perhaps we are in the waiting area, so to speak," Elly responded without hesitation, her vision calmly taking in the surroundings.

"But why take her? I entered first," Daniel challenged.

"Alphabetical reasoning perhaps, places such as these normally operate on a patronymic name basis." Although aware of the conversation occurring in the background, Acha's attention was focused on the young lady. If she was correct in her assumption, the when, of where they were now, was more important than anything they were discussing. If she was right, any moment now that girl would be led to her death. A death that, if prevented, would end all of their concerns.

"Please, we have to follow her." Acha gestured towards the silhouette, a figure who was now engaged in conversation with an older lady who motioned in the direction of the forest. Obediently the farming tools were set aside and the journey began.

"I do not—"

"Please, it's important." Acha stated interrupting Elly. She didn't wait for their response, instead she hurried after the figure as she journeyed deeper into the forest.

"Isn't this Crowley?" Daniel questioned suddenly, attempting to match pace with Acha's determined stride. It was clear she was following someone, but, as yet, not one of them had caught sight of this mysterious figure, thus none of them could understand the urgency which drove her every step.

"Yes," Acha responded. "And no. It's not the Crowley you know," she answered quickly. There was no time for questions, there would be only moments in which to prevent her father from doing the unspeakable.

"Then—"

"Yes, the young lady tending the fields was me. We must hurry, if I am right..." Acha paused in horror as she realised she couldn't lead her friends to her father, not now she knew the truth regarding who he had evolved to become. Surely, they would plainly see that which she had tried to conceal from them since she first discovered the truth in Collateral, and then what? Another thing her host had taught her through experience was that the sins of the father were inherited by the child, and Acha's father carried more sins than most. "It's best if you wait here." She knew she could attend to this alone. If they truly were here at this point in time, then she could prevent her death, and in doing so prevent Night from ever gaining power.

She didn't really understand what had happened that day, but one thing was certain, her sacrifice had been essential to his plan. There were too many things she didn't understand but something warned her they were approaching the very moment he had obtained his immortality. If she could prevent it, none of the perils he created could occur, she could make amends for her father's acts by preventing them from ever happening.

"But—" Eiji protested.

"Please, this is something I must do alone." She was relieved when they agreed. As she disappeared deeper into the trees towards the shaman's fairy circle, she could still feel their eyes upon her, but she was relieved when her backwards glances revealed they had respected her wishes.

The world around her became a little duller, perhaps as a cloud had moved before the sun to obscure some of its light. Like a timeworn parchment, the vividness of the colours slowly began to fade. Entering the clearing where her past self stood, she saw the brightness of the blue sky but never thought to question why the world around her was so much duller. A figure moved from the shadows, striking out at her younger self, a bloody branch now clutched within her father's hands. The bird song, previously unnoticed, fell silent.

"Acha, my daughter." The brown-haired man, wearing his time torn rags which told of their poverty, looked from the unconscious figure at his feet directly to her. "What are you doing?"

"Father, I have come to stop you."

"That much is obvious, but that was not my question." He gestured to the surroundings. The fading colours had been so gradual she hadn't realised what had been happening. Everything around them was dying. A greyness spread from her to stain all life with the colour of death. Only she and her father remained untouched by her curse.

"Acha." She recognised the weakened voice. As she turned, she saw her friends had not only failed to heed her warnings, but now lay trapped within the expanding desolation which she seemed to emit. Elly fought to remain on her knees. Unlike Daniel and Eiji, she had yet to succumb to unconsciousness. Her voice was barely above a whisper, if not for the stillness of all other sounds it would have been lost. "Stop..." She extended her arm towards her in a pleading motion, as her remaining energy vanished, she slid to the ground, where she, like her friends, lay motionless.

Acha did not dare approach them. The things closest to her seemed to suffer the most, and so she stepped away, putting more distance between them as she desperately attempted to regain control. A control she had been unaware had even been lost.

"I understand now." Her father spoke as he examined the unconscious figure of his daughter who still lay on the ground before him. He glanced back to Acha, they were identical in every detail but for their clothes. "You were able to survive because my spell was imperfect."

"What did you do to my friends?" she demanded, finding inside her a bravery she never knew existed whilst facing Night, but that was not how she had first known him. She had known him as her father, before he had become a god, and it was in the guise of this commonplace man he confronted her now.

"I am afraid I cannot take credit for what has transpired here. Although you have saved me much time."

"You, you're behind Darrienia, you're behind the abduction of the Oneirois. This, it's another trick, undo your magic!" she demanded desperately, taking a single step towards him, he smiled.

"I cannot undo the curse you create. I can only take it from you."

"What do you mean? This is not my doing. I am in control, this is one of your tricks!" Although filled with power, she couldn't help but doubt the words spoken. She had only lived with her curse a few months, and knew it could not be mastered in such a short period, but there was no possibility an entire area could be destroyed. She was so careful to ensure she never took life from a person, even when feeding on the energy around her.

"Have you forgotten already? Allow me to refresh your memory." With a wave of his arm the scenery around her shifted and changed. Although she knew it to be an illusion, a memory, she watched, not fighting his magic. "Tell me, are these the actions of someone in control?"

She watched as she was born again. An attacker grabbed her tightly to prevent her retreat, yet it was he who could not escape. She watched his face twist in agony as his life-force was ripped from him. At the very last second, she saw the tears in his eyes as he fell to the ground, never to rise again. She watched again as Daniel withdrew quickly from her touch, and as Zo helped her from Abaddon, a trail of subtle death had followed behind them. She had been mistaken when she thought Zo's ward had killed the life in the area it touched. It had been her. She continued to watch as the bandit seized her, barely managing to force him away in time. Even here, in Darrienia, as she leaned against the tree in Abaddon, it had withered and died at her touch before she had even realised, and the same had happened again near the minefields.

As the images faded, she found herself on her knees, tears streaming uncontrollably down her cheeks as the dying world around her came back into focus. It was as she feared, she wasn't in control. She didn't command her powers, they dominated her. They took what they needed, whenever they needed it. She had been certain she had some mastery over them, but these images from her own past had proven otherwise and convinced her far beyond the sway of any words.

"Did you not wonder why the area your town once stood lay almost barren, why everything around it thrived and grew whilst the area you were sealed within remained almost desecrated? You took the life of everything there to preserve yourself.

"That is how your power works, you take life so the body you retain holds true to the nature of those who live around you, and adapts visually to remain true to your original image, or as close as possible to how you once were." He circled her slowly looking down upon her as she knelt before him. "Everything a normal person's body does naturally, such as circulation, digestion, homeostasis, etcetera, you need to gather energy to achieve. You strip life from other sources to maintain its operation. That's why you become anaemic when your body needs more than you have provided. That is when your power becomes volatile."

"Does magic not work on that same principle?" Acha questioned, wiping the tears from her eyes. She had to regain control of the conversation, she had to find a way to stop the spreading death while she still had friends to save. If she could understand her powers a little more, perhaps it would give her the answer she needed.

"You refer to Zoella? Believe me, the powers you two possess are *very* different. Nature offers her what it can of its strength, but your curse is a force which rapes it, stripping its life against its will to maintain your own. Your magic destroys life, your friend's does not. The power I gave you is far too defiled to be called magic. It is little more than a curse." Acha still knelt at his feet, looking at her hands through blurred eyes, thinking of the truth he had just spoken.

"A curse, there is so much I don't..." she looked to him, realisation in her tearful eyes. There was only one place this conversation led and it was the only way she could think to spare her friends.

"I could take it from you." He said the words she had expected to hear. "I created it, I alone can remove it." His voice seemed filled with compassion, although Acha knew he stood to gain from this. Her curse was, after all, a mistake, and gods didn't make mistakes.

"Would my friends..." she paused as she glanced from her hands to her friends, aware that although there may be another way, at present she couldn't find it and time was scarce.

"They would recover, although their life would grow shorter. I cannot return what you have already taken. Tell me, don't you long to be free, to be at peace?" He extended his hand to her. "Take my hand, I can end your suffering. I assure you, there is only one destiny which awaits you here. Let us forge the correct one, for the sake of your friends." Acha looked from him to her friends, and slowly she reached towards him.

* * *

Daylight broke through the clouds as the sun rose. Daniel and Stephen were already on their journey. The marked map kept safely within their possession tucked into Stephen's belt, not that it was required for this area. They had explored every inch of this island, or at least believed they had. Although they had barely slept, neither felt tired, nor did they remember having seen the night sky, yet the sun rose now, so clearly night *had* passed. They had packed a small bag of supplies, and even now made their way towards the location where they estimated one of the fragments would have fallen, the river.

The location of the piece Stephen's father had recovered had been Albeth. It had landed quite close to where he had made camp during one of his many excursions, so they were fortunate their adventure meant little travel. It was doubtful their parents would have consented to the two boys leaving alone on such a quest.

'*Please stop!*' a female voice cried. It called out with such urgency it froze him in his tracks. Stephen stopped, a questioning expression on his face as he turned to look at his friend.

"Are you—" he began but was cut off as Daniel hushed him into silence. A few moments passed before Daniel spoke, yet his tone remained low.

"Did you hear that?" There was another extended moment of silence as the two friends stood listening, finally he dismissed the whisper as the lure of a playful Anemoi, gave a shrug, and began to move once more.

'*Please,*' the voice cried again. Daniel outstretched his arm before Stephen as they stopped once more. He was certain this time it was something more than the wind spirits teasing them.

320

"Didn't you hear that?" he questioned again as he wondered how his friend had missed the pleas twice. As he stood motionless, waiting for another cry, he wondered how he recognised the voice. It was no one of his home town, yet it seemed so familiar. Like a fading dream, remembrance played on the tip of his mind.

"You're daydreaming." Stephen smiled, there was another moment of silence before Stephen began to walk away. Daniel ran slightly to catch up.

'Daniel!' the voice cried. 'Please.' These were the last audible words he heard until a scream pierced his mind, sending white hot pain through his every fibre, reducing him to his knees. He gripped his head, begging for it to stop. As the cries grew silent the pain eased, and suddenly he knew everything he needed to.

"Zo," he whispered recalling all too well to whom the voice belonged. He wondered how he could have possibly forgotten something, someone, so important. How he could be here, not only reliving the past, but forging it into a better one, an act alone which was surely impossible. This had to be some kind of trap, but why, why suppress his memories of the past and place him here to change his future? He didn't understand anything, except for what he had to do. He had to find a way out of this memory. He could not change things, even if he wanted to. Stephen glanced at his friend in horror as the memories of that day resurfaced. Daniel could only watch as the events flashed through his mind...

..."Hey look I see it!" Stephen exclaimed climbing down the edge of the muddy cliff near the river. Below them, on a small ledge, a piece of star called out to them, twinkling brightly as if daring them to seize it.

"It's too dangerous," Daniel warned as his friend edged closer. The ground trembled slightly as some of the mud broke away falling into the unforgiving waters below. "Let's come back later when the river has calmed." He moved to seize his friend's hand to pull him back, yet instead of the targeted limb he found himself in possession of his backpack. Placing it to one side, he reached out again.

"No good, at this rate it'll be washed away. We'll lose it forever!" Stephen protested. He edged his way across the muddy ledge carefully, watching the raging water below which seemed to rise and swell before his eyes. He scrambled a little further down leaving Daniel no choice but to follow, despite his better judgement. Somewhere overhead, lightning flashed, followed immediately by the roar of thunder and, although it hadn't seemed possible at the time, the rain grew heavier. Daniel grabbed Stephen's wrist as he got closer. The winds rose, snatching the map from its secured location to send it billowing across the land.

"It's too dangerous, we have to go back." Daniel tried to pull his friend back, but Stephen's will was stronger than he was. He had no choice but to stay, it was clear he was not going to give up. The only thing he could do was try to keep a firm hold on him in case something should happen.

"I just need... just a little further." Stephen reached out his hand, his fingers barely scraped the star's surface. He edged forwards a little more, his reach now allowing him to grasp the fragment embedded in the muddy wall. The ground beneath him trembled with yet another roar of thunder, and the soft earth broke away under the extra strain of his weight as the small ledge collapsed. He gave out a yell as it tumbled down the face of the embankment into the water below. Daniel tightened his grip, but the rain made it nearly impossible to keep his grasp. He pulled as hard as he could whilst his friend begged him for help, but even then, he felt him slipping.

He swore over and over he wouldn't let go. With every ounce of strength he could muster, he pulled. The darkened sky illuminated with forks of lighting as thunder roared deafeningly around them. A blinding light shot through the air towards them, striking the ground above. The tree's root, which Daniel's other hand desperately clung to, pulled from the earth causing both of them to plunge into the raging currents below.

Daniel felt the burning pain in his lungs as he was forced beneath the water's surface, his hand still gripping Stephen's tightly. Had it not been for the tree which followed them, he would never have let go, but as it fell upon them he felt the currents pull at them as they tried to remove Stephen's hand from his grip. Muddy water filled his vision as he fought to find the surface through the tree's branches, but the tree had done more than try to separate them. His eyes blurred as his strength began to fade. Despite the numbing, icy water he could feel the throbbing pain from the wound inflicted. As the world around him faded into darkness, he felt his grip on Stephen slip. Before the silence took him, for but a second, he swore he saw a silver glimmer of light, and he was certain he was going to die...

..."I woke on the sands near the shrine. I remember it well because, although the sands showed evidence I had been dragged from the water, there were no tracks left by the one who had saved me. I ran for miles looking for you, hoping you had somehow fought your way to shore, maybe the same luck that had somehow saved me, had saved you. I looked for hours but I was so disorientated I wasn't even sure in which direction I was heading. I thought, maybe, if I got back to where we fell, I'd find you there, but I couldn't walk any further.

"My legs gave beneath me and my body refused to move. Despite everything I just sat there looking out over the river. The pain from my injuries numb as I stared blankly, willing myself to move. It was your dad who found me. I don't remember much of what happened, but I was told they had been searching for twelve hours, and he had sent patrols across the length of the island. All I can remember, before waking at home, was the questions in his eyes, why me and not you? The same question I asked myself so many times." Daniel glanced to Stephen, not sure what he expected now he had revealed the truth. A truth he had so easily seemed to alter by being here, but he just smiled as if to humour him.

"Don't be silly, you must'a dreamt it. We haven't even been to the river yet. Look if you are that worried, let's head back." He placed his hand on Daniel's shoulder as he slowly rose to his feet. "Maybe you hit your head harder than I thought yesterday. Let's get you home."

"You're right," he whispered, the lump still stinging his throat from the painful memory. It had been so long since that memory had haunted him with such clarity. It had taken a long time, but he had finally been able to forgive himself for that day. He no longer blamed himself, but the pain was still as raw as ever. Time had dulled it, but being here, seeing these ghosts, standing before his friend, had opened the healing wound. "I have to go back. This isn't real, as much as I want it to be, I cannot forge a better past, nor should I.

"You died years ago. I don't know how, maybe it's the magic of this world, but for a moment I forgot that, but it was good to see you again." Daniel slowly turned his back on Stephen, unsure exactly where it was he was heading. Whatever spell he was trapped in, surely had to be released, now he had discovered the truth.

"Stay." His friend's voice begged as he ran to catch up with him. "Please."

"This isn't real." Daniel silently scolded himself, not only for being so foolish, but for the part of him that wanted to stay.

"It can be, you don't have to remember this. It can go back to like before. I am your best friend, doesn't that mean anything to you?" he pleaded. "I am offering you everything we lost. Please don't choose her over me."

"Stephen, not a day goes by that I don't regret what happened. I've filled the best part of the last years with possibilities. I blamed myself for what happened completely. I promised I'd never become close to anyone again. I withdrew from everything to immerse myself in studies. I thought life was a meaningless sham that mocked me by taking those I cared for one after another, within the space of a year I lost both my brother and my best friend.

"I was convinced that anyone who befriended me would suffer. But, when I met her, I finally began to forgive myself. She saved me Stephen and, although I could not save you, she needs me now. Maybe I can succeed with her where I failed before. I wish things could have been different, perhaps that's why the court offered me this chance, but if I don't leave now... I don't want to fill the rest of my life with more doubts. I don't think I can do it again, I'm not strong enough." Daniel looked meaningfully at him glad that, for whatever the reason, he had been given this chance to see him once more.

"It could be different this time."

"After I lost you I stopped fighting, stopped living. I gave up on everything and just retreated into my studies. Only since meeting her did the battle start again. Please, I have to go, surely you understand." Daniel moved to place his hand on Stephen's shoulder, but hesitation caused him to pull away.

"You would forget me?" he questioned sadly, barely a moment before Daniel wrapped his arms around him.

"No, I could never. You are one of the reasons I am who I am. One of the reasons I now fight on against all odds, but she is the other, and she yet lives." Stephen returned the embrace patting him on the back as he did so. The scenery around them began to change.

"You will not change your mind?" Daniel pulled away to find himself in a large, grey, stone room, his friend still stood before him.

"I can't." Stephen grasped his hand and placed within it a small object, before closing Daniel's fingers around the glowing light. "That makes two. This one was destined to be in this world. When I lost consciousness, for some reason I didn't completely die. I passed into Darrienia and remained trapped within a death dream. It is unusual for items to cross into this world, but both myself and the star fragment have remained here waiting for someone to claim it. I am glad it was you," he explained with a slight smile. Daniel hesitated before the door which would lead him from this chamber. "I am glad to see you do not blame yourself any longer, or this would have turned out much differently. This place is only as unforgiving as you are to yourself. Once here you are either judged for your sins, or offered a way to change them and by doing so receive forgiveness from within your heart and earn your peace when you wake. There is more at stake in this world than you care to realise. I am sorry," Stephen whispered as his image began to fade.

"Sorry, why?" Daniel questioned.

"Because this will be the third ti—" but before the final words could be spoken, he had faded. Daniel stood for a moment staring in disbelief at the place his friend had stood. He opened his hand slowly to look at his parting gift. The star fragment they had found that day shone back at him. He smiled sadly as he slipped it into his money pouch. He was certain the boy, who had stood before him, was in fact Stephen, and he hoped their meeting here meant they would both finally find some measure of peace. His hand rested on the door, he had not expected it to move so easily, yet it swung open with minimal effort. Once he had stepped through, he began to call Zo's name.

Chapter 14

The Fearful Adjudicator

As she knelt before the one who promised to relieve the curse in exchange for her life, questions raced through her mind. Questions which she did not have time to answer if she wished to save her friends from the death she could not control.

"What will happen, to me I mean?" Acha pulled her hand back slightly before their fingers met. In her heart she knew the answer, in order for this curse to be removed, her father would make true his original intention, he would sacrifice her life-force to Hades. He glanced down at her before casting his gaze over the barely living bodies which lay behind her, as if to emphasise his next words.

"Isn't the question, what will become of them if you refuse, more appropriate?"

"How do I know this isn't a trick, like last time?"

"My dear daughter, the only person who should have died was you. Let us right that wrong together, let us rewrite history as it should have been. After all, now there is a lot more than just your life at stake, and each second you hesitate you steal years from theirs, years from the people who took you in and cared for you. Is there really a choice, do you know how painful it is to have your life torn from your body whilst you still live?"

Acha tore her pained vision from her friends to him, her hand still hovering just centimetres away. She took a deep breath committing herself to eternal slumber for the sake of those she cared for. Her posture became more certain as she made her peace, her hand about to make its final descent. It was then she heard it.

"Zo!" Even here, Acha heard his cry, it only took seconds to realise who it came from.

"Daniel?" she whispered questioningly as she turned to look at his motionless body, snatching her hand from the figure. There was no way that voice came from the body lying before her. "Daniel!" she called out, certain these urgent cries were no illusion. Glancing around the area she tried desperately to locate the source of the voice. It seemed the cries did not originate from this area, almost as if he was somehow beyond her field of vision. "This *is* a trick!" she snarled, no sooner had she done so, the scenery around her faded, unable to retain the form her belief had made true.

As the scenery shifted, she found she stood before a cynocephalus. For but a second her disbelief convinced her it, too, was an illusion, but the humanoid figure before her wore no mask as she had hoped. She could see clearly the movements of its jaw and ears, as its dog-like head stared her down in silent frustration, its dark fur was now clearly visible over any exposed flesh. Although the being before her was clearly not her father, she knew that had she surrendered her powers to him, the outcome would have been the same. The figure moved to approach her, a silver shimmer surrounding him. Within that aura she could still feel her father's powers.

"It is no trick, the images you saw could easily become reality, that is the reason you saw them. Think of it as a small glimpse into your future," he snarled. He had been so close, had he made this one surrender, he had been promised a reward beyond anything he could comprehend.

"Zo!" Daniel called again, each cry seemed more desperate than the last, and louder, as if he drew closer to her.

"Your friend really should not be shouting, who knows *what* might hear him." The creature recoiled slightly before lunging for her hand, but precious few seconds of his granted power remained. She had consented, if he could just touch her, he would be rewarded. As he pounced everything seemed to happen in slow motion. He was as close to her as he had been previously, so close he could feel the warmth from her skin. She moved slightly by reflex, his hand brushed across her skin gently. That touch would have been enough to take her life, but as they made contact, he lost the shimmer of power.

"If you want to feel my power so badly, I shall give you a taste," she snarled, removing one of her gloves to grab the arm which struck at her. She felt its life begin to absorb into her, the creature was reduced to the floor as her touch stripped just a fragment of his life before she released him.

Something about the way it felt seemed different, like the last time, when she had been attacked in the minefields, but this time it was more powerful. As she released him, she didn't feel refreshed, instead an unfamiliar sensation washed over her. Her ears began to sting and burn as if some invisible force pulled on them. She raised her hands to them, horror coursing through her as she felt their shape changing beneath her grip. They became wider, pointed, almost like those of the creature she had touched.

A wave of panic washed over her. She feared, given this alteration, that by coming into contact with one of their kind, she would become like them. Through her moment of dismay, as her eyes changed to greyscale and her body began to become covered in a fine almost invisible fur, she somehow gained a moment of clarity in which she remembered but one thing. Perhaps if she had remembered that the room took on her fears, she would have indeed become the creature, but fortunately that was not what she recalled, she remembered Seiken's warning about the magic in Darrienia being different to that they were accustomed to. It was this thought which restored some calmness. Zo's magic had, at least once, had effects other than those she had anticipated. This had to just be this world's interpretation on her unique talent.

Removing her hand, she brushed her hair forwards, concealing her newest feature before seizing the handle of the exit. With a new-found courage she stepped from the darkened room, her hurried steps halted as she crossed paths with Daniel.

"Acha?" he questioned in surprise. She grabbed his arm firmly, studying him intently to ensure he was real. Trusting her instincts, as she smelt the fear mingled with his perspiration, she knew that it was him and replaced her glove. She had been all too ready to use her ability again had the one who stood before her not been him, and given the insight she had gained into this place, it had been a very real possibility.

"Daniel, thank the Gods. I thought I'd killed you." She glanced backwards towards the closed door. "You are real, aren't you?" Her previous confidence diminished slightly, this could all be another trick. Despite what the new-found senses told her, it could be another impostor, or even an illusion like those within the room. Daniel looked into her eyes, unable to decide exactly what was different about her.

"Of course I'm real. We need to find Zo, she's in real danger." He pulled free from her grip and continued down the stone corridor, trusting she would follow.

"How do you know?" she questioned, remaining close. There was nothing nearby, no doors, and no sign of an exit. In fact, the only alteration in the area stretching before them seemed to be a large window just ahead, it seemed to look into another room instead of to the landscape outside.

"I just do," he answered, lowering his gaze, trying to focus on their connection, trying to find a way to use it to determine her whereabouts, but it was to no avail. Acha unexpectedly grabbed him, pulling him to the floor. Her warning had been unheard, her reaction too slow. He had already caught sight of what lay just beyond the window. The images he had seen had already burned into his mind, even as he blinked, he could see the scene projected onto the wall before him.

At the very centre of the room, four judges each tried their own cases. Separating the area into four equal sections ran large conduits brimming with blood. A small gallery consisting of stained wooden pews lined the first section, allowing all who desired to behold the deliverance of the verdict. The areas behind were filled with prisons, the cages full of blood-stained defendants, who had no doubt been subjected to some of the many instruments of torture which littered the blood-soaked room. Once this place may have indeed been a beacon of justice, but something had twisted its once unadulterated purpose.

Onlookers cheered as another person took the stand, ready to face the judgement of the court, dragged against their will to stand before the adjudicator, having already failed to convince their peers that they were either deserving, or not, of the punishment. The judge's role was to look into their heart and decide for themselves if the person before them deserved to live. If they did not, he became their executioner, their life's blood adding to the horrific water feature which now flowed through the room to places unknown.

There were a number of reasons a person would find themselves participating in what was referred to as 'the weighing of the heart'. Some sought absolution for acts they committed, undergoing judgement as a means to prove their worth. If they could pass the trial, they would be freed from the burden they carried, allowing the defendant to forgive themselves for their sins, real or perceived. Another reason one would find themselves within these walls was more of an intervention.

The inhabitants of the court would hunt down those it deemed necessary and force them to stand trial for their heinous acts. It would compel them to reflect on their deeds, and they would sentence them accordingly. Their retribution administered in the form of night terrors and hallucinations, eventually leading to insanity should their ways not be amended.

The judicators here had a similar gift to the Oneirois, one which allowed the defendant to wake moments before their death. But over time, as the Oneirois presence became depleted, their purpose became distorted, twisted, as the boundaries of justice became askew even to those who enforced it.

The Oneirois did more than any would ever realise. Their mere presence in Darrienia kept all things true to their form, be it good or evil. With their absence, those created to be redemption to those who deserved it, no longer understood their true purpose and sought only to punish those brought before them. As with many things in this world, with the Oneirois absence they had become tainted. Some however, were stronger than others, some still remembered their true objectives.

Daniel leaned against the wall, his eyes wide and his breath heavy, as his vision was fixed unseeingly before him. Acha did not push him on, his pallor was nearly as white as the wall his vision had fixed upon as he took gulps of air. He knew there was no time for this, no time for his body to betray him with this reaction. Even so, longer than he would have liked passed in paralysed horror, before his shaking limbs once more obeyed his commands to move. He slowly started to crawl beneath the window, trying desperately to push the disturbing images of death from his mind, but the more he focused on forgetting it, the more details he seemed to recall. He tried to think of other things, more important things, like finding Zo. Her screams, her thoughts, had been silent for a while, but still he felt her fear.

"We should work our way up," Acha said, catching the scent of something other than blood in the air. Although she was unable to identify it, it meant danger, to them at least. "There are no more doors on this level which lead anywhere but the judgement room." Daniel jumped as the sharp staccato tone of a gavel filled the air. Its tones were met with a rise of cheering almost loud enough to overpower the horrified cries of yet another defendant.

Acha carefully led him to the base of the nearby stairwell. From the lower levels, a cold draught rose to gently blow the hanging flags and wall scrolls which lined the walls at intervals. Slowly and quietly, they began their ascent.

"Daniel, something is coming." Acha's hushed tones were barely audible, matching the caution of their silent steps. A sickly scent, detectable only to her sensitive nose, hung in the air. Something approached them from above. There seemed little choice but to double back and hope they would not be seen, but the rapid footsteps of whatever approached had a luxury they could not afford, it had no fear of being detected.

Seeing her concern, Daniel grabbed her arm, pulling her gently into a small alcove covered by a strange unfamiliar flag. She motioned for his silence just seconds before the footsteps sounded from the stairs above. The pace of the walker seemed to slow ever so slightly as it passed them, almost as if to pay tribute to the flag, before it once more hurried on its way. Then, once more, everything was silent.

"How did you know about the nook?" Although she had caught the scent of something coming towards them, she had no thoughts as to how they could avoid detection.

"I saw behind the ones at the bottom as the breeze caught them. I'm just glad my theory was correct. Wait here." Daniel motioned for her to stay back as he crept forwards to where the staircase turned at a right angle. His hand resting upon his folded weapon as he peered around the corner. When he was sure all was clear, he signalled for her to join him.

* * *

Elly pressed her back against the wall. Someone, or something, was coming. It tried to be quiet in its approach, but the kind of people who could successfully ambush her were a rare breed indeed. In fact, she knew of just a few who could approach her undetected. Whatever came this way knew she was there, or its steps would not have been so guarded.

She listened intently as she stood with her back pressed firmly to the wall, allowing herself maximum time before becoming visible. She noted it was not one set of quiet footfalls but two, each of their steps almost perfectly synchronised. Whoever approached were clearly fools who had no idea who they were dealing with. She stood close to the opening which led to the staircase, a stone battle axe gripped firmly in her hands poised and ready to strike.

She had no time for games. She needed to find the others, who it seemed had decided to depart without waiting for her, or worse, been taken by something else. Either way she needed information and where better to obtain it than from those who tried to hunt her. It had been some time since she had been presented with the opportunity to use her ancient technique, it never failed to yield results. She would slay one of them on their approach, then the other, would find fear adequately loosened their tongue.

The movement came at the precise moment she had predicted, her body weight already behind the force of the swing as the pursuer stepped from the stairway. She swung her axe accurately, before even seeing what it was she struck out at. She paused in horror as she saw who stood before her. She pulled back on her weapon with all her strength as it crashed towards them. It was a strike no one could stop, the weight of the weapon alone carried the blow, but fortunately, she was not just anybody. The axe drew to a standstill barely a millimetre from Daniel's forehead. At the same time as the strike was prevented, just for good measure, she skilfully swept his legs from beneath him. She hauled the axe back releasing her grip from it as she moved quickly to cover Acha's scream. Daniel pushed himself forwards across the floor, reaching out in an attempt to grab the falling weapon. A few sparks ignited the air as Elly's hand clamped tightly across Acha's mouth. The weapon vanished into the air before even touching the ground.

As the scream silenced, Elly quickly released her, her arm already stinging from such a brief exposure. It would be a short time before she regained the full range of movement again. She flexed her fingers, carefully assessing the extent of the damage as she glanced around to ensure their movements had not been detected. Once satisfied, her fist closed around her dice as she slipped them carefully into her pocket. Daniel realised this was not only the second time her weapon had vanished, but that she seemed to possess a limitless arsenal. He made a logical, but incorrect, assumption that the force behind such an occurrence was magical.

"Where have you been?" she scolded in whispers as Daniel pulled himself to his feet. It was clear that for some reason she was *very* angry with them. "I have searched everywhere from the foyer to here!" She glanced around the corner expectantly, hoping to see Zo and Eiji following behind. Although she knew there had only been two sets of footsteps, she was still disappointed when they failed to appear.

"We... wait, you mean you walked straight into this building?" Acha positioned herself against a nearby wall. She was starting to feel somewhat exposed as they stood in the middle of the hallway.

"Yes, did you not?" She raised her eyebrow at them curiously, her vision watching Daniel carefully as his fingers rubbed his forehead. For a moment she second-guessed whether she had stopped the blow before causing him some harm. But the source of the pain was not the near miss of Elaineor's blow, it was that caused by his friend's distress.

"We need to get moving," Daniel insisted. "We still don't know where to find Zo or Eiji."

"Well they are not beneath us." Elly stated in a matter-of-fact tone. "There were two locked doors, the others led to the chamber of judgement." Elly hadn't been convinced they were locked, at least not by any means she was familiar with. She had tried all manner of picking technique without result, before finally continuing the search for them through the halls.

"Two doors?" Acha whispered, a theory behind their locations entering her mind, a conclusion which Elly had already assembled moments before. "Then we just need to find the next locked door." Her voice trailed off as she remembered what that cynocephalus had said about shouting. "Quietly," she added.

* * *

Zo glanced around in confusion knowing Daniel had entered before her, yet she couldn't locate him. Her vision panned her new surroundings, a morbid fear rising in her chest as she looked upon a place she was all too familiar with. She had stood here, in this very spot, more times than she could count. It was a place familiar to her dreams, or more accurately, nightmares. But how had she come to be here now, could it be her dreams had been warning her of things to come? She stepped backwards involuntarily as she recalled the fear this place represented, her hand fumbling through the air as she tried to seize the handle of the door she had, just moments ago, released. She didn't need to turn her vision back to know it was no longer there, yet she did so all the same.

She glanced around the darkened area in the hope to catch sight of anything but that which lay before her. She knew she did not want to be here.

"What is this place?" she asked herself. She knew the answer, it was obvious. The night lit landscape of an old run-down cemetery stood before her. Tombstones, which had weathered the ages, crumbled to meet the uneven rises in the overgrown grasses, the bulges almost indicative of something trying to force its way up from the depths. The raised stone coffins and broken mausoleums told similar stories of age, as weeds and rubble disguised further sunken monuments, in what seemed to be an endless shrine to the dead.

She knew the outside world was bathed in daylight, yet for some reason here stood always in the midnight hour. There was no way to know this for certain. There was no moon in the clear sky to use for guidance. Somehow, she just knew.

The only light came from the faint glow of the stars in the cloudless sky, and a small light which flickered near the edge of the cemetery. The shadows from the pale light twisted before her vision. Everything was silent. She shuddered despite the warmth of the night, wrapping her arms around herself comfortingly, hoping with all her heart her friends would come for her. But she knew they wouldn't. This was *her* nightmare, a nightmare no one else would share.

Two small flame torches suddenly ignited to light the start of a small winding dirt track, a track which curved its way through the centre of the graves. She seemed to know this place. It was the start of a nightmare. Since waking in Crowley, it had always started the same way, with her stepping into the cold shaded light of the torches that bid her welcome.

Even now, the flames waited for her to begin the first step of her uncertain journey. With no other choice, no other way to turn, she began to walk. The flames waited for her, flickering excitedly as she approached their orb of illumination. Just like in her dream, as she walked the flames lit before her, and extinguished all traces of the path behind. The world behind her seemed to vanish into the darkness, the world in front of her lit only by the small lights which guided her. She regretted stepping into their light, before doing so she could see so much more, but now, encased within the sphere, she could only see what she was meant to.

The flames danced, their light twisting the black trees into horrific shapes. The flickering shades giving the impression of movement where she hoped there was none. She held her breath turning down the path. She knew what came next; the small cabin with a single candle resting in its window, its tiny flame dancing against the wind as a beacon to all who found themselves upon this path. If she could make it to the cabin, she would be safe, but from what she was unsure. She had never walked beyond the next torch. As she approached, she hoped to wake from this dream. Her body began to tremble as her fear of the unknown grew more stifling. She never knew what was so frightening about this dream, she had seen far more horrific images in the dark recesses of her mind, but for some reason this silent landscape had always truly scared her. Passing the torch, she held her breath, closing her eyes as she took the next step. She didn't wake up, just as the deep-rooted fear had told her she wouldn't.

She quickened her pace, panic consuming her very being. She felt as if she needed to scream, to run as quickly as her legs would carry her and pray that she made it to the cabin. It was then she saw movement on the ground before her. The whole area seemed to pulsate as if something from below it was trying to break free. She glanced to the small light, although from her location she could no longer define its source. Everything seemed so much further away. She knew then she would not make it. Whatever it was that scared her, whatever it was she feared, it was here.

A shadow appeared before her, she stepped back in shock, her hands crossed her chest defensively as she gasped. It was only seconds before the light from the torches bathed the figure and her startled breath was released.

"Daniel." The relief pulsed through her body as she stepped forwards to embrace him, but he recoiled from her touch. As she looked at him questioningly, she saw the hatred and anger in his eyes. "Daniel, I..." She didn't know what to say, how to counteract his disgust. He moved forwards to wrap his hand around her arm tightly, a little too tightly. When he finally spoke, his tones were cold, heartless. He addressed her now in the way she had expected when he had first discovered the truth about her past.

She could only believe all the prior concern, the unaltered attitude, had been nothing more than a ruse for Acha's safety and the ease of travel, although she had hoped there was more to it than that. Looking upon him now, feeling the strength of the hatred which emanated from him, she wondered how she could have misjudged his feelings so drastically. She questioned if it could be related to all those times he had looked at her in that peculiar manner. It was clear he had been keeping something from her, and it seemed it was these feelings of hate which radiated from him now. She stood fixed in place, unable to move or say any more, the sheer force of his emotions robbing her of both words and strength.

"Come with me," he ordered, pulling her violently in the direction he moved. "There is something I *must* show you." Even had she wanted to resist, the force of his grip ensured she had no choice but to follow as he led them further and further away from safety. The light from the cabin become nothing more than a distant speck on the horizon as the glow from the lanterns extinguished with a sinister hiss.

He half dragged her across the soft soil of the graves. Regardless of her difficulties, he would not slow his pace, and just pulled her harder until they reached the highest point of the cemetery. As they stood there, he looked out over the mass of graves. In every direction, as far as the eye could see, lay the graves of thousands of people. "Every tomb, every grave within here has its own story," he began, he didn't look at her, just over the vast sea of crumbled stone and marble which lay before them.

"Daniel why are—" He tightened his grip, a warning for her to be silent and listen. With that single movement, he had almost reduced her to her knees. She never remembered him being so strong. He had always seemed so gentle, yet now, because of her actions he was filled with such anger and resentment, all the traits she had previously associated with him had vanished.

"Each life so different, yet they share one thing in common. Do you care to guess what it is?" Zo shook her head, tears spilling from her eyes. As she looked to him, the strength of his grip intensified, his voice snarled as he prompted her response. "Think harder, you know this one. Do you know what each one of these lives had in common?" His grip sent splinters of pain through her. She let out a cry as he twisted her arm forcing her to her knees before him. He maintained the pressure, keeping her where he wanted her, paralysed by the pain.

"Daniel please stop, you're hurting me." She tried to pull free of his grasp, despite the pain each movement she made caused. Normally it would be no effort to break free of his grip, yet he stood firm, unmovable, almost unaware that she even fought against him.

"Then I'll tell you, shall I? It's you. Each grave before you is a person *you* have killed, a life *you* have destroyed. Had I realised, I'd not have been so quick to forgive you. You slaughtered them like cattle, their cries for mercy falling on deaf ears.

"You never stopped to consider there were consequences to your actions, you thought you were untouchable. You made your final mistake when you turned on me." A gavel resounded through the night sky as he flung her from the mound to the ground below. Hands pushed through the soil, grabbing and scratching her in an attempt to hold her in place and, although she fought, she lacked the power to break their hold. There were too many, they were too strong.

Daniel stood looking down at her, never moving from the place he stood as he watched all that transpired before him. "You have been judged and found guilty. We the judge," he bowed, "jury"—he motioned his hand around the graves—"and executioner"—he produced a short sword from somewhere on his person—"will now begin your sentence." His face seemed to shine sinisterly in the midnight light. Her body began to tremble uncontrollably as she saw the demonic flames sparkling in his eyes.

"Please, no!" she whispered, her voice failing. She fought against the clawing hands as he descended the rise into the crowd of the dead. It wasn't that she didn't think she deserved to be punished. She did, but not by him, anyone but him. Her tears streamed uncontrollably as she fought for breath.

Through the sea of corpses, she caught the occasional glimpse of him as they dragged her towards the graves. Each time he looked upon her, his face wore a chilling smile, watching as they dug their rotting fingers into her flesh, each one demanding their pound. Their hungry vengeful cries silenced as he appeared almost next to her in the promise of giving them what they craved, the delivery of a justice which was long overdue. He tapped the short sword, which would become the very tool of justice, against his hand as he began to speak.

"They want you to suffer. They want you to feel the same despair they did, the hopelessness, the fear. They want to watch you bleed, dying slowly, aware of the pain caused by each breath, praying it will be your last only to find another one follows. They want to watch the life slowly fade, to see it extinguished. At the point when your body can take no more, and you are too weak to fight, when you lie unable to move, and darkness wraps around you like a stifling blanket, only then shall you know their pain. Only this way can you repent. It is less than you deserve." He stood almost upon her, smiling as he listened to her beg.

"Daniel, please," she cried, forcing back the tears. As their eyes met, she ceased to fight, perhaps she thought something had changed, or maybe she felt as if her life was the debt she owed. To die here, to give up, would be so easy. She saw in his eyes the murderous intent. If someone's hand was to take her life, perhaps it *was* better to be his. It was no less than she deserved. It seemed fitting she was to be destroyed by the person she loved the most. But as he looked upon her, fear, and perhaps her will to survive, took over, a will she thought she no longer possessed after everything she had discovered. She fought once more against her fate, desperately trying to break the grip of the dead.

"Did you think I'd ever truly forgive you? You tried to kill me. The magic of this place brings clarity. I see what I must do, I must do what's right. You tried to kill me, now I shall succeed with you, where you failed with me." He stepped closer to her again. With all her strength she pulled away, feeling her skin tear and bleed she screamed. Despite the energy and power behind her movements she failed to break their grasp. She called on everything within her, screaming in agony as an aura of flames erupted from her body. She scrambled to her feet as the dead recoiled. But even this final attempt was to no avail. More hands replaced those which had released her. The dead threw themselves upon her, once more forcing her to the ground. There were too many of them. Escape was impossible.

She looked up at Daniel tearfully as the sword rushed towards her.

* * *

Daniel gasped as her pain tore its way through his mind. He leaned against the wall to catch his breath. The agony driving him to the brink of madness as he was filled with such raw, terrifying emotions, without a moment of peace. He had been doing well to hide the discomfort he felt, and tried his best to settle the morbid dread which rose within him. He had, after all, promised to discuss their link with no one. It was a promise he would keep, but right now, it was becoming difficult. Her every emotion was heightened by her feelings of fear. Each moment had become so overbearing it was all he could do not to sink to his knees, clutching his head, as he begged for it to stop.

"Daniel are you all right?" Acha turned to look at him as he gasped for breath. Concern lay heavy on his brow. They were running out of time. Since he had first heard her, it seemed an age had passed. Her final words had begged him to stop and he could only imagine what she faced. She held so much guilt, a guilt this place would thrive on. Then, in addition to these feelings, there were the sins of her darker persona to answer for.

"I... yes, it's this headache." He shifted uncomfortably as he massaged his temple. The pure terror, the haunting feelings, stopped suddenly. Its abrupt end a relief until a single thought was passed to him. A thought about how the world would be better if she were to die; a thought to herself that she should just surrender. It was after this everything went silent. For the longest time he had felt her fear and torment, heard her screams. Whilst distressing, he knew that at least whilst she fought, she lived, but now there was nothing but silence.

"I am sure if it is required, Zo will make you a remedy. She has all manner of medicines in there." Elly pointed to Zo's satchel, which he still carried. "But of course, we have to find her first," she stressed as she began to walk away, wishing she knew exactly where to start.

* * *

"No please y' can't." The voice of a young woman begged as she caught hold of a stout man's arm trying to pull him back. Despite the strength of her conviction, she was no match for him. "Please no, I beg y'," she repeated. Her futile attempts to prevent her husband from approaching the ogre's lair were disregarded as he marched onward. He paused, turning back to face her before reaching the cave's mouth. In his arms he held a small child.

"Save y' concern for one worthy, do not waste it here on this monster," he snapped. "The priest has given us his instructions and we *will* comply, don't make me leave y' here too."

"I would rather suffer this fate than abandon our child." A hand struck her, knocking her to the ground.

"Still y' tongue Leda, enchantments are common with such beasts. Soon y' will see the truth, I pray before our next child is born." Leda looked up to him in terror, her hand nursing her cheek. "This creature is not our boy. He is the cause of our town's suffering and the one who causes such unrest amidst the people. The priest himself told us so, do y' doubt the words of

339

the holy man, the word of one who speaks for the Gods?" The young boy stirred from his sleep, roused by the raised tones of his parents.

"What's goin' on Daddy?" he questioned, softly stifling a yawn as he cuddled closer to the warmth of his father.

"It seems some scoundrels have planned an attack on our home. We are leaving y' here for y' own safety," he answered; his voice not betraying the lie he spoke. He had no concerns regarding what would happen to this boy. His lies were not to spare him, he was not their son. He only told such tales to ensure no harm befell him before his task was completed. Once trapped within the cave there was nothing, no power, this demon child could conjure that could ever hope to harm them.

"Please Jed, at least let me say goodbye." He looked towards her with disdain. His anger softening as he gazed upon his pregnant wife. He was a fool not to consider how difficult this would be, enchantment or not, he would allow her this request if only for the protection of their unborn child.

"Y' may say your farewell, but then y' must leave him in the cave. It's for his own safety." Leda nodded as her husband handed her the small child. She traced her fingers across his face lovingly as she held him close. She spoke to him softly, a promise to return lost on the winds to all but the child. She hugged him so tightly, held him so close, as tears flowed uncontrollably before she brought herself to place him down. She would return for him as soon as she was able. She embraced him one final time, sliding a sheathed knife inside the small sewn fold of his cloak. He was a wise boy. She could only hope the carvings on this knife would, as she had read, keep the ogres away, at least until she could return for him.

Despite the cave's alleged property for sealing people within, Jed still rolled the boulder across the opening, unaware his wife looked on with deep rooted hatred. The priest he spoke of was barely an apprentice and had initially ordered them to slay the child. It was only her intervention which saw his being trapped within the cave instead. She reasoned if the child was truly an evil spawn, as he claimed, killing him would invoke an act of vengeance, but sealing him would deny him this opportunity if he were to be imprisoned within a place that was sealed with magic. That way, by the time he realised what they had done, it would already be too late. The priest had agreed. Neither he nor her husband had seen through the deception. Had she not suggested such a thing she knew that she would wake one day to find him gone and their dark rite completed. At least this way she could find him.

"Is it done?" A young priest stood vigil on the border of the town as he awaited their return. When Leda erupted into inconsolable sobs, he had his answer. He smiled to himself, now the boy was gone, things would be far simpler. The priest had discovered his own gift as a child himself, he had been able to convince people to do his bidding by a simple request. The fates had gifted him with a silver tongue, yet there was something about that young boy which weakened his hold on those around him. It was better such obstacles were dealt with before things became too problematic. He had indeed been fortunate. He never believed the woman, Leda, to have been under his control, yet as she surrendered to his wishes, and even provided a more believable solution, he was reminded of his true strength. "It's okay, my daughter. The Gods understand your pain, surely they shall bless your next child."

"Blessed." Jed smiled as he repeated after the priest. "See Leda, all is as it should be."

The moon's image changed as time passed by, finally Leda escaped the clutches of her husband, only to discover her son had gone. She continued her travels, never looking back to the place she had once called home, swearing to raise this child as she saw fit. She had left in time to be spared, that very night the town was placed under siege.

"Why are y' showin' me this?" Eiji asked, as the scenery around him faded to darkness.

"Such reminiscing proves a welcome introduction, don't you agree, Eiji?" a voice from the darkness responded. He had known he was not alone, yet in his dream-like state he had felt compelled to watch the memories of a history he had not quite forgotten. "When the village was besieged, your father was thrown into the crossfire, to protect the very man who had him abandon you. But had you stayed, the same fate would have befallen them as your master's wife, the one you think of as your mother."

"Whaddya want from me?" he demanded, his tone stern as he challenged his unseen host.

"I come as a friend. I am here to remind you of your place, your responsibilities."

"And what would they be?"

"Solitude. It is required of your kind to walk alone with only the elements at your side. You know what befalls people who stay too long within your presence, you saw the truth in your mother's death. Your aura, the raw energy that surrounds you, is as a poison to them. The same fate will befall your comrades as did the woman who loved you. Everyone you become close to will die."

"That's a lie." Eiji was surprised at the force behind his own words.

"Really? I have been observing, shall we review? Zoella, her time is so limited it is barely worth notice. If not for your power rousing the boggart in the marsh, Daniel would not have been injured. Your presence will always rouse such forces from their slumber, and Acha, the one you seem to have the deepest concern for, is not quite of the living. And then there is Elaineor—"

"Acha's dead, whaddya mean? Explain y'self!" He knew that Acha was born a very long time ago, but he had never been clear on exactly how she came to be here in their time.

"You are no fool, you have felt it for yourself. Perhaps you need to take more notice of what happens around you."

"Why are y' tellin' me this?"

"I need you to realise the truth, if not now then in the future. I am not here to judge you, I belong not to these courts. There is nothing in your past you would change to weave a better future, nor crimes you must answer for, therefore I was permitted to petition your attention. I am known as the Dreamwalker, I ask only that you remember me, remember our meeting and the truths I have disclosed. Remember that I have not deceived you and then, when I approach you again, when I ask that you come with me, I ask that you do so willingly."

"Approach me again, when?"

"Time does not pass within these lands as it does in yours, despite how things may appear but, trust me, I shall find you once more. When this time comes, I pray you have realised the truth, and have embraced the solitude you were destined to reside within. But for now, you have a purpose, I shall keep you from it no longer." The darkness faded to reveal a small enclosed room. Eiji found himself lying upon the cold stone floor staring at the ceiling. He moved quickly, he knew the dream walker had told some truths at least. He had not been of this court, and it was best he left this room before this building had chance to further delay him.

He seized the door handle firmly, thrusting it open with an unnecessary force. As it sprung back powerfully, he was all too aware that its path had collided with something. He groaned internally, the impact had sounded almost soft. He hoped it was just the wall but, knowing his luck, it would be something worse, perhaps a creature belonging to the court. He stepped through, committing himself to the confrontation which would no doubt follow. It was only as he stepped past the door he could see the people it had obstructed from his view. It was Daniel. Eiji glanced around in surprise to see Elly standing behind him, her posture almost confrontational. As she looked upon him, she seemed to relax slightly. From the floor he heard a small whimper. There, pulling herself up into a sitting position whilst nursing her face, was Acha.

"Eiji." Relief filled Daniel's voice as he gazed upon him. It almost seemed as if they had expected something else to emerge from within.

"By the Gods, Acha. I'm *so* sorry, are y' all right?" He knelt on the floor next to her placing his hand on her shoulder. She nodded slowly moving her hands away from her face, pulling those strange facial expressions familiar only to someone who had been struck in the manner she had.

"Serves me right for not looking where I was going." She rubbed the sides of her nose gently. Despite the strength behind the impact being forceful enough to knock her from her feet, it appeared no real harm had been done.

"This place is so strange. It's like a hall of memories." He glanced around almost as if he expected something else to appear before them.

"You too?" Daniel asked as Eiji assisted Acha to her feet.

"Yeah, I was shown my parents." He turned to Acha. "Are y' sure y' okay?" She nodded wiping the tears from her eyes.

"Your parents?" she questioned, wondering what each person had seen whilst isolated within their temporary prison.

"When they... hey"—Eiji glanced around, a frown gripped his features as he made a mental note of who was present—"aren't we one short?" He smoothly changed the conversation. He liked his friends, and would even go so far as to say he trusted them, but there were certain things, private things, he did not wish to reveal. He had decided a long time ago not to live in the past, discussing it would only rekindle unwanted memories.

"Well at least it will prove easier to locate her now." Elly smiled. She had that strange look in her eyes again, an expectant gleam, as she looked at him. It was an expression he had come to dread, as he knew once more his knowledge and experience would fail to meet with her expectations. "You can pinpoint her life-force." It wasn't a question. She crossed her arms. As that look penetrated him, he desperately tried to recall all the things he had ever learnt, but in doing so he just found himself more confused.

"Sorry?" He couldn't help but feel maybe she was the one with the powers, especially since she always seemed to know exactly how to use them, and in ways he had never even considered.

"All right," she sighed. Many thoughts crossed her mind as she found herself once more disappointed by the extent of his knowledge, their main focus being on whether his master had taught him any theory at all. With no other option, she begrudgingly began to explain. "She is Hectarian, as such she utilises the energy from nature. Surely you have noticed a strange sensation you have when you are in close proximity to her?" Elly crossed her arms, again she gave him that look, the one that seemed to turn the sum of his knowledge into a meaningless drivel.

"I thought it was nerves, her bein'…" He paused looking at Acha, then to Daniel. "A stranger and all." Elly smiled with a slight amusement, even now she couldn't help but be amazed by his foolishness, but the fact he had managed to redeem himself fairly smoothly, at least meant he was improving, slightly.

"Nerves indeed." She cast a quick glance towards the ceiling in response to his comment. "What you feel is the life-force of another person who can manipulate the environment. A person who, like yourself, is attuned to nature. You should be able to isolate and locate that quality in order to pinpoint her whereabouts." Eiji looked at her, his expression blank then he smiled to himself.

"Actually, now that y' mention it." He paused as if for dramatic effect, yet for him it was a necessity to calm his rising frustrations. "No! Y' are mistakin' me for a master. I had only just been released t'learn all this when y' father abducted me. I've not had time t'become familiar with the spirits, nor t'commune with them," he snapped. Why did everyone expect so much? He had yet to even experience his first meeting with a nature spirit. As far as his powers were concerned, he was still a novice, although he held the powers of his master, he had not learnt to manipulate them fully. Nor had he learnt to define the different forces and feelings each element provided depending on the situations they were utilised in. That was, after all, what the journey after leaving his master was about, that is what he travelled to discover.

"I see, Acha?" Elly turned away from him to look at her.

"I can't do anything of that level. I am simply displaced," Acha advised. She truly wished she could help but she knew what powers her body held. What she asked was not something she was capable of.

"Then I guess we continue looking, one door at a time." Elly sighed again. It was an expression of frustration she was becoming all too familiar with of late. She was always filled with such fantastic ideas, but it seemed she was fated never to travel with those skilled enough to act on them. Only once had there been someone deserving of her ideas, and that journey had seen its forced conclusion over a year ago.

Chapter 15

The Verdict

Night glanced around the chamber, it had been empty for too long now. It had quickly become apparent that Lain missed the comfort of someone beside her, but the problematic emptiness would soon be resolved. Annabel's death had been untimely. The circumstances would be less than ideal but he could delay no longer. A young girl knocked gently on the door, her mouse-brown hair tied sensibly back into a neat ponytail. Night offered her a warm smile as she lingered uncertainly at the door.

"You requested my presence, my lord?" The young lady bowed slightly, her hair tumbling forwards over her shoulder as she did so. He acknowledged her presence, motioning for her to join him. She walked slowly, fearfully, to stand beside him. She stood in awe of him, her small frame almost trembling as she wondered for what purpose her master had called her here. Night had acquired several places such as the one he was about to reveal, each dedicated to a purpose of its own. All but this one were accessible through dreams to those the Gods deemed worthy. This one, however, was specifically designed to be of assistance to Lain.

"Elisha, welcome to the athenaeum." He moved, allowing her gaze to fall upon that which he had deliberately obstructed. She heard herself gasp, amazed at what stood before her. Through the second doorway stood a room, its size beyond all measure, lined with more tomes and manuscripts than she had ever seen, more than were held in the extensive library in which she had spent almost all of her waking hours. The room was filled with bookcases filled with tomes, carefully lined, expertly preserved. The domed circular room spanned upwards, walkways lining its outer edges as stairs and small walkways provided access to the vast information contained within. Gazing upon it, it almost seemed as if the room had been constructed from books, as if they themselves had been the building blocks as they filled its every inch so completely. She stood awestruck, never had she imagined such a place existed within this tower. It was clearly a sacred place, which led her to wonder why it was being revealed to her. As if in answer to her thoughts, Night addressed her in lowered tones.

"I would like to introduce you to someone." Elisha followed her master through the winding cases of books. She did not linger, but glanced over each row with excitement as they made their way to the central most point, an area devoid of any shelving, which was left empty, well almost.

Approaching this area, she saw, resting within its centre, what she could only describe as a coffin. The large case was constructed from what appeared to be ancient technology of the likes she had never even read about before. Small lights twinkled on and off around it as if communicating to each other in code. Despite its sarcophagus like appearance she found herself curious to learn more. She wanted to approach it, to feel the cool metal of the capsule against her skin, but fear suppressed her thirst for knowledge. She felt exposed in the large space, her reflection looking back at her from the surroundings of the vessel, where a number of mirrors had been placed.

"This is Elaineor." He invited her to approach.

She advanced slowly, almost fearfully, until she saw clearly the body that lay within. Once more she heard herself gasp. She hadn't been sure what to expect, many different ideas were conceived as she drew closer, some horrific, others fearful, yet within the case lay a delicate form. A young lady in her late twenties, her hip length hair a unique shade of blue, a colour she had never seen on any living creature before. She lay within the metal sarcophagus as if she were merely resting, sleeping. A strange black, almost skin textured clothing covered her, outlining the slender curves of her body, from this ran wires which connected her to the case in which she slept.

"Is she ill?" Elisha questioned. She was unsure how to interpret what she saw before her, but recalled reading something about regeneration chambers, back in the time of the ancients, used to heal those who were in poor health or incapacitated. She had read so much, after all, that was her role as one of Night's researchers.

Although she had accepted this position some time ago, Night had never called upon her until now. She had studied for hours, only to present information he already knew. She couldn't help but feel she was in some sort of training, but for what she was unsure. She studied hard, day and night, in hope to please him, in hope to show her gratitude for all he had done. Yet despite her many hours, many years, of study, she had never come across a description of anything like that which she saw before her now. Her assumption was based on the combined data she had read in several texts, but the chamber itself was lacking many of the key factors to be what she had considered.

"No," Night answered, motioning towards a chair. She sat obediently wondering what his plan for her would be. She was one of his most loyal mortal allies, and her talents were unquestionable. There was only a certain type of life-force which could undertake the role about to be requested, those with her talents were few and far between. He had plucked her from a life of misery, abandoned by society, and refused at the orphanage. Her limited years had made things easier, he preferred to find great powers whilst they were still young, before their essence became corrupted by the world around them. Children were quick to learn, quick to study, but unless nurtured, the talents of such individuals would slowly fade. He found collecting rare talents a much cherished pastime, one that had started with the figure who lay enshrined before them. "I shall tell you her story, then you will come to understand." He waved his hand before a mirror, colours swirled upon its surface before settling to display images of the tale he told.

"This is Elaineor, Lain, or Elly, whatever you wish to call her. She did not always harbour this appearance, she was, in the beginning at least, like any other mortal. Her story began a long time ago, before what you would refer to as the Titanomachy, before the time of Zeus." He spoke the name bitterly, as if the very mention of the name rekindled unpleasant memories. "As you know, that was many lifetimes ago now.

"She worked as a servant for what was a wealthy family. They had adopted her as a child, in an attempt to correct a terrible wrong. A mistake which had started a chain of events resulting in them feeling responsible for her. You see, times then were dangerous. Her father had been murdered for what little he possessed in his pocket, leaving her mother alone to support the two of them the best she could. She worked for what was called a multinational corporation, something, that fortunately, this world is without. She laboured all hours just to put food on the table, but one day there was an accident resulting in her death. The conditions surrounding it were suspicious, to say the least. In order to alleviate his guilt and regain some of his reputation, the family deemed responsible adopted the young girl vowed to raise her as their own, in an attempt to repay the debt.

"But Lain, even as a child, was intractable and would accept no such gesture. Although young, she cooked, cleaned, and assisted the other servants. In return, she was fed, clothed and given shelter." Night cleared his throat pulling himself a chair from a nearby table before he continued the story...

...Every waking moment, Lain knew there was something more to life, something that she was missing, something she needed to seize, but she lacked the power to do so. With every breath she took, she longed for more, but what it was evaded her constantly.

It wasn't that she disliked her life, in fact for the most part she loved her job. Those she worked for regarded her not as a servant, but as family. She was permitted to dine with them at the same table, even to address them by their first names, which, of course, she never did. She had been with them for almost as long as she could remember. This life was almost all she knew since she had become an orphan. She felt lucky to have been taken in by such kind people. Despite this great blessing, she found it hard to suppress the feelings of wanderlust. No matter how dedicated she convinced herself she was, no matter how much she knew she owed to this family, she longed for much more. She longed to be free. She stayed, stilling her desires, bound to these people with an unseen bond. A bond perhaps better known as fear, fear of the unknown.

She was a talented girl, quick to learn and enjoyable to engage in conversation. She was one of a few who could read in that time. Although the time of the ancients was technologically more advanced, it had become increasingly more expensive to live and be educated. Only the rich could afford the luxury of education, and since most of the menial jobs were performed by automated services, a high level of education was required to be considered for employment, and thus the rich became richer still.

There was a very big divide between the people. There were the very rich, people with the knowledge and funding to work as the automated service support teams, and the very poor. At one point, basic education had been free to all, but with rising costs, the greed of the government, and the replacement of low-level jobs with automated services, most, unskilled workers as they were referred to, were forced out of work and soon education became a luxury most could not afford.

It was not uncommon to see young children as servants, or working in any manual labour they could find. The only labour available now was unfit, or impossible, for the machines to do for them, the pay was poor, and the mortality rates high.

The reason Lain could read was not because she had attended school. No one of her class would ever have that particular luxury, but because it was a skill the master of the house had taught her. He knew that one day they would have a child of their own, and it would fall to her to assist with that child's education and so Lain, although a servant, was schooled. Their reasoning behind this was a façade. Even with the advancements of this age, those who were sterile remained barren. Then again, every rule had an exception, and it just so happened that this was it. Years had passed and they found themselves gifted with a boy, an heir to the empire they had built.

Once he was born, Lain's position within the household changed. She was no longer requested to see to such tasks as cooking and cleaning, instead she was to be nanny to the child, his caretaker. In the hours the child had no need of her she was to study, train, and learn skills in order to enhance her young master's learning. Even from his birth, she spent hour upon hour reading him stories of the great heroes and times past. As the child aged, he grew to love these stories as much as she did. Even the master of the household would, when possible, stand just outside the door to listen as she told the stories with such enthusiasm you would have thought it was she who had faced the beasts.

Lain brought the stories to life with her passion, but this was not something she did for the amusement of the child. Her enthusiasm came from the heartfelt desire that it *was* her out there who enjoyed the freedom of the adventures. As she read, she saw herself fighting her way past the Gods, and challenging great creatures. The extent of the child's stories had been vast, but as the years passed so did the time of unheard tales. It was only as they finished the final book, the final myth of heroes which had been left unread, that a new adventure appeared.

It was an old weathered book, one she had no doubt had been acquired by her master on one of his many business trips. Within its battered, timeworn, bindings was told the story of a great adventurer who had once gazed upon the knowledge of the Gods. It detailed his travels and great adventures, almost as if the story itself was guiding the reader, daring them to follow in his steps.

She read it to the child. The words she spoke, as always, breathing life into the stories, with the turning of each page she knew the feelings received through this tale were a sign. Within her mind formed a map, a guide to that which she longed for. As she read the stories, they seemed so familiar, almost as if she had been there, as if it called to her soul. At the end of the book she was filled with a great sadness, far beyond what she normally experienced as a story came to a close. But this time it was different, she felt empty.

It was that night she left. She gathered enough provisions for a short journey, taking less than she was owed. She never suspected she had done only what had been expected from her, walking into the trap *they* had laid. This moment, her departure, had been *their* plan all along. It was something she would fail to realise for many years, and long after it was too late.

She travelled for countless years, sharing great adventures both alone and with companions. Writing them in her journal in the hope the tales of her quests would also one day be read by starry eyed youngsters, and give them the encouragement to break the bonds of their life, and seize their freedom.

Freedom was harder than she thought. The world was expensive, and travelling was far from cheap. She would often tell young children the stories she had read, for just a morsel of food. On occasion she would take labour requests from the townsfolk for small payments, or a place to rest. When she needed to cross the seas, she would take a job which made it possible be it a cabin hand, harbour hand, or entertainment, whatever was needed to get her from one port to the next. Her payment in these cases was the trip across the ocean. It was a hard life, but never once did she regret her decision. She learnt many things from her work and travels, one of which was the different arts of fighting, far different to those she had been taught at her former household, which had been no more than techniques which had allowed her to be a sparring partner to the child she cared for. Some days she would join the fighting rings in the hope of making extra money. When she won, it made her journey easier, when she lost, it delayed her travels, eventually she stopped losing.

She had called herself Lain Exerevnitis, her real name, the one spoken from her mother's lips, long forgotten. She had never been given the brand that marked all those of low class. So when she sought work in order to travel, no one questioned her.

Many years had passed until she reached the land she quested for. Although when she arrived there, she found it to be a place she had travelled many times. When she first departed all those years ago, she had failed to see that which she had sought, but now the Gods deemed her ready, the markings stood clear for her to see. They had known this day would come, it was written, and they had prepared for it. Well Zeus had, for it was he who ensured the child would be in that family's care. It was he who insisted she was taught to read and fight, and for the story to be placed when the time came. He knew, once she found it, she would leave, and it would take many further years of travelling, and the mastery of different skills, before she could see what was concealed before her eyes.

During this time, Zeus had collected his allies. The Gods rejoiced, knowing the time would soon be upon them. Seeing her enter the final phase of her journey, they began a mighty war in Othrys. A war so powerful, so all-consuming that, as was planned, the Titans failed to notice the young lady who had entered a sacred area of their kingdom, until it was too late.

The knowledge of the Gods, at this time, was stored within a great mountain beyond a circle of ancient volcanoes known as the Ring of Fire. A place which could only be reached by traversing the labyrinth below. But armed with her memory of the labyrinth's tale, its perils were defeated and she proceeded into the valleys, past a small town and beyond a grand manor. There, once having traversed the incline, she found herself staring into the mouth of a beast. A dragon's head, carefully etched from stone, opened its jaws wide as if to grant her entrance to a cave which had long been sealed, and if not for the artefacts she had gathered on her quest, would have remained so.

Lain could not help but stare at it in disbelief. Never before had she seen such a sight. The entire mountain was hollow, the enormous steps which had guided her down, through the dragon's mouth, led her to its very centre. Strands of light, like a gentle silver rain, fell from a single opening in the cave above, to collect in a giant silver pool which seemed to also rise from the ground below. Circular steps, deep enough to be mistaken as mortal seats, encircled the glistening pool of knowledge. As she stood gazing upon her dream, her adventure complete, she was unsure what to do.

Although *she* was uncertain of her actions, the Gods knew she would never dream of missing this opportunity. It took only a few moments before, as they had predicted, she had made the slow descent towards the ancient well. Her face radiant with the bliss she felt at standing so close. Finally, all her hard work, all her sacrifices and trials, had yielded the desired result.

She hesitated for a moment. It was all too tempting. Could she really just settle for having gazed upon this wonder, or did she want more? It was then, as she gave into temptation and propelled herself towards the waters, she fulfilled their carefully planned expectations.

She felt the cool touch of the silver light from above as the pool's waters rose. She opened her eyes, her body had not broken its surface as she had expected, instead she seemed to be suspended above it, encased within the light she had once thought of as fluid. The silver glow from below touched her feet, the silver rain caressed her body, and as it did so, her awareness spread. She felt the tiny lines of the light's source stretch out like roots across the planet's surface, to return its stories here, to share its secrets, its powers, and knowledge, and now she was within it, it shared its wisdom with her.

Had Kronos not appeared when he did, she would have become one of them, a goddess, one who contained the knowledge of all the Earth. Zeus had felt Kronos weaken as the girl took their knowledge, and with a pre-planned precision, seized this opportunity to overthrow his father and take his rightful place on the Throne of Eternity, banishing his father forever.

Kronos moved quickly, there was but a short time until the power of the Gods abandoned him completely. When the Severaine broke free of its restraints, his power would be gone, sealed within the Star of Arshad, where the power of all fallen gods came to reside. Once stripped of his powers, he would be sealed within Tartarus for all eternity. He chose his final task as an act of vengeance. With his remaining powers he would ensure Lain suffered for her blasphemy.

He dragged the fragile form from the great waters of knowledge, but no longer possessing the strength for his planned vengeance. He did all he could with the remnants of his power. He placed upon her a curse, subjecting her to an eternal sleep, a suspended animation. Kronos had no intention of remaining forever bound within the deepest recesses of the underworld. No, he would be free, even if it took countless millennia he would return, and when he did, he wanted to take his time exacting his revenge. Now she would have to await his return, touched by the Gods, and aware of each passing second. Even if, for some reason, he could not return, such a fate would destroy the spirit of even the strongest warrior. Being touched by a god left a mark, a warning so any beholding the sleeping figure would know better than to interfere. His touch had altered her, changing the mousy shades of her dull hair to its vibrant tone. Her eyes, too, altered in colour, a curse ensuring she remained watchful of each passing second.

Zeus had learnt from his father's weakness, and saw it necessary to bestow the knowledge to the Gods themselves, so never again could a mortal approach and jeopardise all he had created...

...Night cleared his throat as the story approached its end.

"Nyx, Gaea, Hecate, and Selene, were the only old ones to survive who did not side with Zeus. They took no side." Night looked at the figure lying in the case before him, he smiled gently to himself. He knew the girl who stood before him would have many questions, just as he knew it was nearly time to take his leave so that Elisha could introduce herself to Lain. It was something simple to do from this side, but the same could not be said for the figure before them. Lain would not have a chance to engage with her while she travelled with The Chosen, so he had taken the liberty in her stead.

"Did the other gods perish?" Elisha questioned. Although she had read many a tale, none stated what happened to those who opposed their new ruler. Never had she found the answer to what became of a god who had lost their powers. The Star of Arshad was a myth shared between few, most mortals did not dream of its existence, and the last time one had taken it within their hands, it had resulted in the sealing of the dragons. None spoke of it, so it only fell to reason she was unaware of its lore. A lore that would answer many of her questions.

"Not as such. Zeus allowed them to serve him should they wish. As for those who chose to reject his offer..." he paused as if in contemplation. "A god is a strange being, people's belief is what gives them power. Those who are forgotten lose their powers and become mortal, those overthrown are stripped of all divine gifts and their heavenly bodies imprisoned." The powers lost by a god had a very special resting place, they were absorbed into the Star of Arshad once the mortal manifestation of that god died. But Night had been different. When Zeus had attempted to force Nyx into an earthly form, there was one thing he had failed to consider, as long as there was night, she would continue to exist. Zeus only managed to force mortality on but an aspect of her being. The god who stood before Elisha now, was but a fraction of a far greater, far larger being.

Night, the mortal, was in reality nothing more than a severed aspect of the goddess Nyx, but Zeus' actions had seen this fragment could never be re-joined with its original form. In his attempt to destroy an ancient deity, Zeus had unwittingly created a new one. He had never imagined his plan would fail, nor that the mortal aspect of Nyx, a being adept in magics far older than creation itself, would find the means to reclaim the severed power and become a god.

"So what of you and the other old ones, were you punished for remaining neutral?" Her eyes stared at him thirsty for knowledge. It seemed she had already realised that any questions she had about Lain could be answered within these walls.

"Of the old ones Nyx, Gaea, Hecate, Selene, and of course, Chaos are the oldest of our kind. The reactions Zeus had, varied for each of us. Gaea was allowed to live on due to a power only she can restrain, she is after all the very embodiment of the planet. Selene has always been a loner and possesses the power to create a key the future may require, so she was spared of judgement, and Hecate was the founder of Hectarian magic, without her, there is so much which would cease. As for Nyx, she always remained neutral when it came to such battles of power, for this, and his fear of her, Zeus attempted to destroy her, thus creating me. Nyx of course will continue to live on as long as there is darkness or life." He waited for her next question, knowing there would be many. He did not need to speak of Chaos, throughout history he had always been found beside the one who would be named victor. In this conflict he had, of course, sworn his allegiance to Zeus.

"You said you were created mortal from Nyx, yet I have only ever known you as a god, how is this possible?"

"I seized the severed power before it could be taken into the Star of Arshad. Even as a mortal, the powers I once possessed lay dormant within me. It would only have been on my death, normally spurred by an act of the Gods, which would have sealed them. It took years of training to even unlock the power, and an audacious covenant with Hades. Now, returning to the reason you are here." It was far too complex to explain his history, how he could have his own identity as the god Night, yet originally be a part of the goddess Nyx.

It was something only another god could truly understand. He knew there were many questions, but even he was limited as to what he could tell her, and this was all he cared to reveal for the moment. "Your duty here will be to sustain her knowledge. Around her you will find almost every tome ever written. Just ask a question and the most accurate answer will find you. It is focused on the intent rather than the question to make things easier, watch. Who is Lain?" A single book appeared before him, he plucked it from the air as he demonstrated the ease to Elisha. Her eyes lit up with excitement. He smiled slightly, releasing the tome, allowing it to file itself away once more. "Of course, there is certain information I do not permit her. These texts will not be located within this room, and references to it erased.

"Her last observer passed away not long ago. Emptiness within this chamber does not suit her, thus she grows colder to those we need alive. Your task, is to do what you love the most, read, read and watch." He waved his hand before the mirrors, images of a strange courtroom flickered before becoming steady. "There is but one condition to this role, you must never, under any circumstances, leave this room once you have accepted. It is dangerous, not to her but to yourself. Anything you require should be located within these walls. There is a kitchen stocked daily from an outside source, you can request anything you need or want. If there is something you lack, or require at any time simply leave a message for Matilda in the kitchen cupboards.

"Matilda, will see to all your needs without ever needing to approach. There are also sleeping quarters and any comforts you should require. Are there any questions?"

"No, my lord. It will be a great honour to serve you," she chimed excitedly, pausing briefly in consideration. "Well, there is one, how did she come to be here?" It was a question Night had expected to be asked far earlier than this, it was something his tale did not broach, nor, as she appeared to have realised, would she find reference to it within these, or any, walls.

"When I first regained my status, I sought her out, in a similar manner as I did you. After her encounter with Kronos, she became a unique essence, and so we made an agreement. I would use golemancy to create for her a vessel in which she could live, one linked to her consciousness by the device you see before you. In exchange she would assist me as I required.

"It was a challenge, but finally I recreated enough of the old world's technology and magic to achieve this. The result, however, did not look quite human, but as soon as Lain's consciousness entered it, it seemed to grow and develop. Just as I had hoped, it took on the guise of a human, but underneath it all the body out there is still nothing more than a machine. Her body here is now more like a link into her mind, after all her consciousness is now severed. It took her in the region of six months to learn control, after all the human body is operated by thought until it becomes a natural pattern. Lain had to create those patterns, those 'algorithms.

"Once she had mastered movement, we parted ways, and she went on to have many great adventures. More recently, within your lifetime that is, I have found another purpose for her, to protect and train someone for me. I have spent a long time improving the vessel, ensuring she would return at least once a century. The first was, after all, a prototype. There were many things I could do to improve it. For the task at hand she needed the best, and initially there were many limitations to the design. Nothing which would make the common mind suspicious, especially given their ignorance to the world around them, yet now, you would not even consider she was anything but human. She can feel and display the complete range of emotions, not capped by the marionette's limitations.

"There is only one problem we cannot fully overcome. Thunderstorms can temporarily damage her. In just the last three years we have resolved the problem with water, although she'll still find it a challenge to stay afloat, exposure won't damage the vessel any longer. Now if there are no further questions." Elisha shook her head, eager to begin her new role. She thanked him once more before he left.

* * *

"Wait," Daniel panted, as an overwhelming feeling engulfed him. He alone felt Zo's panic. It restricted his movements as if it were his own. No sooner had he fought its stifling embrace when a barrier—like the ones she had taught him to guard his mind with—surrounded her thoughts. "She's in here." As he placed his hand to the door, an electric current raced through his flesh. The force of the contact propelled him backwards with a loud crack, leaving him winded, sprawled across the floor.

"What gives y' that idea?" Eiji smiled helping him to his feet. "I guess we break the door down?" he questioned, not waiting for a response as he began to gather his energy, an action stopped prematurely as Acha stepped before him shaking her head, he looked at her questioningly.

"That barrier, it's not from this building." She moved to touch it, but changed her mind before her fingers made contact. "Zo uses magic, it's quite similar to the field we found back at our camp. Zo must have used it to keep people away when you were attacked. She probably didn't even realise she was doing it. It's something people with magic use to drive people away from dangerous situations, it's part of her. She probably isn't even aware that it's here." She glanced to Eiji meaningfully. She couldn't explain how she knew what it was, she had only seen something like it twice before, once at the camp, and once a long time ago, used by the village shaman to keep his conjuring within a set area and to keep others from around it safe from any ill intentions.

"Then I guess we just wait. I will keep a look out," Elly announced before disappearing around the corner, giving no one a chance to protest. She was glad for this opportunity to leave, in the last few moments something had changed. The empty feeling which had followed her since her last watcher's death had suddenly been replaced by something different. She glanced back at them briefly as she turned the corner.

'Zo?' Daniel called with his mind as he tried desperately to reach her on some level. He could still feel fractions of her emotions, hopefully it worked both ways. He moved to lean against the wall just short of the field's reach. *'It's Daniel, are you listening?'* He sat down with his back to the wall as he watched the others pace as they tried to think of a way to break through without hurting her, or themselves, in the process.

* * *

Zo felt the air part as the blade rushed towards her. She closed her eyes expecting the final blow to come, when it didn't, she opened them slightly. Daniel had stopped, the sword resting just inches before her throat.

"Please, don't do this," she begged as he stood over her. He smiled down triumphantly at her tearful face. She had stopped resisting now. He seriously doubted she would fight, even if the creatures did not hold her so tightly. He could see it in her eyes, she was broken and ready to accept her punishment.

"Tears?" he snorted. "Monsters don't cry, save your trickery."

"Daniel, whatever this place has done to you, fight it. I'm not saying I don't deserve whatever—" her words were silenced by her gasp for breath as he placed his left hand on the sword's pommel to apply pressure to her throat, not quite enough to break the skin, but enough to silence her.

"You really don't get it at all do you? Not everything is about you, just as this isn't about me. It's about the needs of many." He removed his hand from the pommel, motioning towards the rotting corpses that watched in anticipation. There was silence amongst them as each one watched, each head turning to look at them. In their eyes she could see the hunger.

'*—are you listening?*'

"I am listening, I'm sorry, I'm so sorry," she sobbed as she met Daniel's hateful gaze.

"Do you think the moment of fleeting regret before your death is enough, do you think that will satisfy *their* needs, do you think it will save you? Just as they suffer for the desire of revenge, you shall suffer in Tartarus." He looked over his sea of followers as they stood waiting impatiently. Zo realised that, not only was she going to die if she didn't do something, but she wasn't ready to, not yet. There were still answers she had to find.

He moved slightly to survey those around him, easing the pressure of the blade as he did so. Her quick movements, as she tried to slide from beneath, vibrated through the blade's deadly tip, with a look of satisfaction he thrust the blade down relishing in her cries of agony as it pierced her left shoulder pinning her to the ground before him.

"You can't escape your punishment," he warned, twisting the blade in her shoulder intensifying her screams. The dead around her revelled in the sound, rejoicing in her torment as the white-hot pain seared through the entirety of her trembling body. He looked down upon her in satisfaction, tears streamed down her face as she begged for him to stop. She was trapped, at his mercy yet, just like Marise, he had none to offer. The blade twisted again, but this time there came no agonised cry, only an explosion of bright light as her left hand, by some unnerving instinct, found the hilt of her sword pulling it free in a motion that, had it been any other weapon, would have been otherwise impossible. She flicked her wrist, the blade's magic severing the sword which imprisoned her. It was a movement she had been unaware of until the pressure lifted, a movement spurred by her will to live.

The shard itself remained firmly embedded within her shoulder, but there was no pressure now, nothing to prevent her movement. Placing his hand to his side where a sheath was now fastened. Daniel gripped nothingness as if to seize a hilt, its form materialising as his finger's wrapped firmly around the place it would rest. The motion of drawing summoning a new blade into existence.

"Now are you fighting me as Zoella, or Marise? Not that it matters, since you're both the same," he sneered, his sword poised in an offensive stance. He watched her challengingly. The *real* trial had finally begun, at the end of this, they would have their verdict.

'*Fight it Zo.*'

"I don't want to fight you." She took the sword into her right hand feeling the warmth of blood spreading gradually down her left arm. But that wasn't the only thing she felt. Deep in the forgotten recess of her mind, something stirred. She knew exactly what it meant. She didn't just fight against Daniel anymore, she fought against her darkness. It was a battle she feared to fight, a battle she did not have the strength to win.

"That's funny, I want to kill you," Daniel proclaimed, smiling at the irony of his words. "Wasn't that what you said to me? It seems the tables have turned."

'—*whatever you see, it's not real.*' The voice came again. For the first time she realised it was not the Daniel before her who spoke, but a voice which touched her mind. She raised her hand to her shoulder, the warmth of sticky blood stained her fingers as the pain erupted at her touch. She doubted the words, questioning how such pain could not be real.

Thoughts raced through her mind during that second of realisation, the truth now nothing but a blur. She knew there was only one thing to do, only one way to discover the truth, yet at the same time she feared the answer she would find.

"I... will fight you." But before she had even finished the sentence Daniel had attacked. He charged towards her to carry out an almost flawless impaling move, almost flawless because somehow it had missed. She had managed to lift her sword in time to deflect the strike. She knew why this move came to her so easily. It was the same reason as last time when she had faced that colossal figure back home. Marise had dramatically improved on her initial training. If it came second nature to Marise, it would to her as well. Despite this she knew Marise would always make the better adversary, after all, she had only a shadow of her skills and aptitude. She lacked the thought processes and strategy required for the fight, she simply moved by instinct. Zo sidestepped another strike, just able to duck in time to miss the sweep of the sword. He was skilled, yet still he had failed to land a blow. She had her answer.

"Daniel can't handle a weapon, not even a sword." She looked at him as he came at her again.

"Wrong." Their swords crossed. "I wanted you to think that. You know it's me. You're just finding a reason now to kill me, giving yourself an excuse, a justification. Just like Marise was your excuse for everything you did. I *am* Daniel, can you really stain your sword with my blood?"

Zo glanced around, relieved that his army of the dead stayed about four feet away from them. It appeared the sword's light was enough to repel them. From their reactions it seemed almost as if it burned them, for this small thing she was grateful.

"I can stain this with Daniel's blood, no more than you can now stain yours with mine." Zo cringed as that strange feeling clawed its way close to the surface. Those words were almost not hers. "Daniel cannot hold a sword, let alone use one," she repeated. As their swords crossed again, she felt Marise's strength begin to surface. She knew if she didn't concentrate, she would lose more than the battle. In an attempt to avoid further swordplay, she released a scalding magic as their swords struck once more. Her hand burnt as if she had been its target. She briefly pushed the pain aside, and with another strike his sword flew from his hand landing on the ground behind her. The fight was over, but to her, it was as if the real fight had just begun.

She stood, her blade pressed to his throat forcing him against a nearby cenotaph. The weapon trembled in her hands as her heart and mind gave conflicting signals. It was just like before, it took all she had not to force it through his throat. She fought against the driving compulsion that willed the blade forwards, yet she lacked the strength to pull away.

"Why do you hesitate murderer, why fight your nature?" Daniel's eyes locked with hers, within them he saw the fear, not only in his own eyes which reflected back at him, but in hers. The sword pushed a little harder against his throat. No matter how hard she tried she couldn't seem to lower it.

Time seemed to stretch for an eternity, so many thoughts and fears raced through her mind as they stood in deadlock, thoughts which were not entirely her own. Just as she could not move in fear of the outcome, Daniel could not move in fear of death. Suddenly the force she fought surrendered, releasing her so unexpectedly she stumbled backwards a few steps, before falling to the floor. Relief coursed through her. In that moment she had doubted her strength to walk away, doubted her ability to win the fight. Somehow, she had found the strength, but that didn't mean the danger had passed.

Mustering the strength to stand, she noticed Daniel still stood pressed firmly against the cenotaph, as if still scared to make even a single move. She turned her back to him.

"You owe me..." Her voice could manage nothing more than a whisper. Bile rose in her throat. It had been close, a paper-thin line in fact. She didn't look back to the figure, her vision focused only on the small cabin surrounded by the dead who craved her blood. "Now go!" she whispered hoarsely as her gaze washed over the sea of the dead, each still awaiting their pound of flesh.

Daniel looked at her. His posture relaxed slightly as his hand moved slowly to his throat where her sword had pressed. A realisation reflected in his eyes.

"The inability to land the final blow. That is what separates you from her, you will not to take a life." She turned back to look at him but he had vanished. His words just then had given her a new-found strength, a strength from deep within.

"I'm not a killer," she whispered. "I have never taken a life. I am *not* Marise. I am not a killer." She repeated the words over and over in a soft whisper, a mantra which brought with it strength. Marise had killed countless people, but she, Zoella, had never taken the life of another person. The creature had given her hope, a line of comfort she could use to distinguish herself from Marise, and as long as that line remained intact, she would remember who she was. She was Zoella Althea, a healer, a person who valued life and would never take it. "I am not a killer," she whispered again, surprised such simple words could give her so much strength.

Although the dead kept their distance, she didn't wish to be there a second longer. What just happened had scared her more than the creatures which lay in wait. Try as she had to lower the sword, she could not. She was certain she would have killed him, especially considering the sheer strength it had taken to stop the blade from taking his life. It had been as if she had been playing a game of tug-of-war against a stronger foe. Should she have not found the strength from somewhere inside, the situation now would be very different. It was close. Worse still she knew now, as long as she continued to draw her sword, it was always going to be.

She ran towards the small flickering light of the cabin, her sword still drawn to keep the dead at bay. Only when her shaking hand had gripped and turned the door handle, did she sheathe it.

Daniel stood suddenly, moving towards the door nervously. For the last fifteen minutes he had not heard a single thought from her. He had barely reached the door when it flung open and Zo stumbled into his open arms.

"Zo, thank the Gods," he whispered in her ear as she threw her arms around him despite the pain it caused. They both sank to the floor. As they sat, he held her tightly. He could feel the fear and desperation that forced the tears from her eyes as she held onto him for dear life. Not a word passed between them as they held each other, neither wishing to let go.

"Daniel, I..." She pulled herself away from him finally. The pain from her movements sending spasms through her body. "Thank you." She wiped her eyes in a quick embarrassed movement, before taking her bag from his shoulder and placing it next to her.

Acha and Eiji had remained silent. They had watched with concern and curiosity as Zo had sat there sobbing in Daniel's firm embrace. She looked far worse for wear than any of them had when they emerged from their door. Only Acha did not understand why a place of judgement was so harsh on her.

Zo noticed that Daniel's vision now followed the trail of pooling blood from her fingertips, up her arm, to her shoulder. He blanched slightly in horror as she untied her top, pulling it from her shoulder, to reveal the wound. He closed what little distance there was between them, to kneel beside her in an attempt to help. But he wasn't sure exactly what he could do. She placed her hand to the back of her shoulder before realising the fragment of the blade was too far embedded in her wound for her to reach it unassisted.

No sooner had she finished this thought when she felt a cool hand on her shoulder push at the wound, sending shooting pains through her body. She leaned forwards as she involuntarily cowered from the touch. Elly looked to her and smiled.

"Rough time?" As she met Zo's eyes, she saw within them a new determination. Whatever had happened in there had given her some hope and, from the looks of her wounds, she had paid a high price to find it, or perhaps, the cost had been equal to what she had gained.

Without warning Elly squeezed the wound so the metal tip protruded from the back, she pushed it gently forwards. Zo, somehow through the sickening pain, managed to grab the bloody shard.

Zo seemed to freeze as her fingers found the smooth edge of the severed blade. It wasn't until Elly leaned forwards to take her hand that she pulled. Fire exploded around her shoulder as she gasped for breath. Blood soaked the patch of floor below her as she leaned forwards to breathe through the pain.

Elly had already started to put into place the best temporary measure they had available. Zo had been lucky, had the blade stuck higher or lower it would have struck either her auxiliary artery or pierced her lung. Elly smeared a gum-textured liquid over the wound in an attempt to hold it together, before she added some dressings held in place by tightly wound bandages.

Daniel passed Zo some herbs he knew she could mix into an effective painkiller, all the time he kept hearing a phrase repeated over and over in her mind. The very phrase gave a small shimmer of hope to her otherwise saddened eyes. He smiled gently to himself, relieved she found some comfort in the words she thought. The words themselves were true. It was something he had wanted to say, but to simply hear them would have been meaningless. It was something she had to realise for herself. Now she had it gave her hope, and a new determination not to become what history dictated she had once been.

"It's okay." Zo gently pushed his hand away. It was easy to hear the concern and questions of his thoughts as he looked from her, to the bloody section of sword which rested under her hand surrounded by a pool of blood. He opened his mouth to object. "We don't have time." Elly pushed her fingers under the dressing, smearing more gum on the front of the wound as Zo bit down on a small root she had removed from the bag. The pain relief of the root was nowhere near as potent as what Daniel had in mind, but even the slight relief was better than nothing. Elly started to help her back into her top which had become thick and sticky with blood, unfortunately this action made all her other minor scrapes visible until she was covered.

"But your arm... and..." He stopped as his vision found the numerous bleeding scratches across her back. He shuddered to think what she had gone through in there.

"It's okay," she said again in a tone of calmness she did not feel. At that moment, it felt like it was taking all of her effort not to collapse. She felt so weak, so tired, but they had to keep moving. She touched Daniel's shoulder lightly as she stood to enforce her words, before placing her hand over the wound to press it lightly. Even doing so sent bolts of pain through her. Daniel simply sighed as he watched, she was so stubborn.

"I have located where we need to go." Elly stepped forwards offering to take the satchel from Zo, who, shaking her head, placed it across herself to rest on her right shoulder, the bag itself hanging the same side as her sword which may prove problematic should she need to use it. On the other hand, it showed her intent on not drawing it. "It is heavily guarded so we are going to need a distraction." Elly whispered as she moved to walk beside Zo, who nodded. Never once, while they walked, did she move her hand from the bandaged area, Elly was unsure if she was protecting it, or trying to stop the bleeding with light pressure. Even with the gum in place, the wound still bled around it, but it had reduced the blood loss dramatically.

"I'll take care of that," she added for the benefit of her friends. Her statement did little more than earn her injured looks as they wondered what she could possibly do without giving their position away to the enemy.

Elly motioned for silence as they reached the top of the stairs. Already they could hear the growls and pacing of the creatures which resided on the floor they were about to enter. The next floor up would be the roof, and consequently had an entirely different staircase to the one they had just climbed. It would have been so much easier should they have been able to continue all the way to the top.

"What's y' plan?" Eiji whispered approaching her, without a thought he touched her shoulder. Seeing her retraction, he removed his hand quickly as he realised what he had done. He saw the pain reflected not only in her features but her posture as well. He knew as a Hectarian, if the wound had been inflicted anywhere but here, given her demonstrated skill, she would have had no difficulty in healing herself. Sure, the smaller scratches she would be able to heal when she got home, but the larger injury, from what he could tell as he felt her calling on the forces around her for aid, it seemed no magic could heal. He could see the power enter her body, he felt the blockage in the channelling which prohibited her healing artes. He only wished there was something he could do.

She looked to Eiji and took a slow breath. It had been a long time since she had tried this, she could not afford to fail. The sound of footsteps echoed very faintly down the hall followed, almost instantly, by a loud noise. All but Elly and Zo retreated a few steps as the guards jumped to attention, most of them took off towards the sudden disturbance to investigate.

"What was that?" Acha whispered fearfully as she glanced around. Were there other people here who tried to find a way out, could it be the noise came from one of those people the village chief said had come exploring?

"An illusion?" Eiji questioned realising why neither Zo nor Elly had reacted at the sounds, they had expected them. Zo dipped her head in a slight nod. She was the first Hectarian he had met, and he couldn't help wonder what else she was capable of; but a small part, deep in the back of his mind, warned him he never wanted to find out.

"There are still a few guards, let us hurry before the rest of them return." Elly was already clutching a marble staff tightly in her hands, ready for battle, although not one of them had noticed its appearance. She moved to step into view but Eiji stopped her.

"Let me," he stated, stepping out where the guards could see him. It was about time he proved he was not completely useless again. He adopted a sturdy stance, a faint aura of silver shimmered around him. The guards already charged, their weapons drawn. Daniel and Acha began to worry, they had almost reached striking distance. Elly stood ready to intervene, should his plan fail. The guards raised their weapons and let out a battle cry, but before they could strike, an enormous eruption of water appeared from the wall, turning as if guided by an invisible force to make impact with the enemy, sending them rushing backwards under the force, leaving them pinned momentarily to the adjacent wall.

They seized the opportunity and ran through the door to the stairwell. Eiji found himself somehow amazed that Elly had known exactly which door led to the desired route, especially since the presence of the guards would not have allowed her the opportunity to investigate.

They reached the roof, relieved to find the door already open, it was almost as if they had been expected. Elly lowered the large wooden crossbar once they had passed through. She paused for a moment to consider how strange it was that the door should lock on the outside.

"Why are there no guards up here?" Daniel questioned suspiciously, as he glanced around the roof. With the exception of the statue in the centre of the building and the door they had gained access through, there was not a single thing, living or otherwise, on the flat stone roof.

"That's why." Acha glanced over the low wall which surrounded the edge of the building. Numerous guards and creatures fled through the very door they had first used to gain entrance. "I don't understand," she commented as all but Daniel came to look. He was busy with his examination of the central statue, it seemed to call to him. He paced around it cautiously. It seemed it was his turn to remove a rune.

"The rune here is balance right?" he asked, examining the base of the statue carefully.

"Yeah, why?" Eiji moved from the edge of the building to join him as he tried to locate what it was that had caught his friend's attention. He glanced to Daniel in request for an explanation, in response he motioned to the statue. As Eiji looked upon it for the first time, he understood.

"This statue is made from the same composition as the court. I'm willing to bet, it runs all through the centre of the building." He looked carefully at the scales held within Justice's hand as he thought back, wondering if, when he gazed into the court room, he had seen a central pillar. As the burned images resurfaced, he tried to see beyond the bloodshed, beyond the creatures. He thought back amazed at the detail his single glance could recall; the audiences, the galleries facing towards the centre of the room, then finally he saw it, the thick stone pillar behind the place the four judges and their sentencing boxes had stood. Four sections, four judges, four rulings.

"What do you mean?" Zo questioned as she joined them.

"This statue is a balancing rod, like those rumoured to have been used in large buildings in the time of the ancients. They were used to stop the tall buildings from falling over. It is perfectly balanced, so if we were to remove the rune from the left-hand part of the scale, I'm willing to bet the building would collapse." He stared at the statue again, and the rune which sat within. The rune was shaped almost like the small weights used by the greengrocer back home. He walked around it once more.

"So if we take it, we die?" Acha's question did not need an answer, it was clear what was being said. "Can't we just replace the rune straight away with something of equal weight?"

"The laws are different here. I'm guessing the second it's removed, the building will fall from under our feet, not like what would happen in our world." Daniel answered, unable to divine any other reason for such a hurried evacuation.

There was a long moment of silence while they weighed their options, they knew they had to take the rune. Zo and Eiji had stepped to one side to have their own private conversation in a lowered tone.

"I'm not sure it would work that way." She paused as she considered the likelihood of their plan succeeding. "I'll try my best." She offered him a weak smile as they moved away from each other. She moved to link Daniel's and Acha's arms. Eiji in turn linked Elly's, and Elly, who seemed to have already anticipated their actions, took Acha's. She had a very good idea of what they were going to try and was less than fifty percent convinced of the success rate, but, as Daniel had pointed out, the rules here were different. This was the only viable option, should the building crumble beneath their feet, and if it didn't, then they could just take their chances with the stairs.

"When I say go, grab the rune." Eiji moved to stand near Daniel, a movement ensuring that they now stood in a tight, broken circle. Daniel nodded, his hand barely a centimetre from his grasp. Eiji nodded at Zo. A silver ball of light began to form over them, and before it reached Daniel, he heard Eiji's command. He grabbed the rune just as Eiji grabbed his arm. As the circle completed, the ground below them began to shake and the building crumbled. Daniel and Acha closed their eyes as a light green mist enveloped Eiji.

They braced themselves to fall as they felt the ground disappear from beneath their feet, but the rapid descent did not come as expected. Cautiously, Daniel and Acha opened their eyes to see the pressure of spiralling wind pushing against the silver barrier. As the tornado's energy began to fade, they slowly drifted down. Beads of sweat formed on both Eiji and Zo's brow as they concentrated. From her posture alone it was apparent Zo was having difficulty. Pain splintered through her shoulder demanding her attention. She felt weak, nauseous, and as a result, the shield began to flicker. Holes began to appear and spread, she focused on retaining it, on visualising the sphere containing them, but it was no use, she was too weak to hold her focus any longer. The barrier flickered as the holes grew to consume it.

It was a short fall but one which felt further than it was. Zo and Eiji lay sprawled across the floor, breathing heavily. When her magic had finally failed, they had been just four feet above the ground. Their plan had consisted of so many assumptions both were surprised to have achieved this much. As their fatigue began to lessen, they were reminded of the imminent danger. Daniel and Acha were watching the area protectively, wondering where the guards and creatures of this place had retreated to. It was then they noticed Elly was no longer amongst them. She was not the only thing absent, taking in the surroundings fully, it became apparent that the area they had fallen to was void of any debris, void of the shattered remains of the court which should have filled the area. The enormous opening still towered above them, yet all traces of the monument had, for that moment at least, been erased.

"Time to head back," Elly announced, returning from a distant opening. Within her hand she grasped a small crystal.

"Easier said than done," Daniel commented, looking at the eight separate tunnels expanding from the area in which they found themselves. "Which way did we come in?" Elly had already started to walk away.

"It is this one," she stated. They followed her unquestioningly, simply because she always seemed to know exactly where their destination lay.

Chapter 16

Escape from the Furnace

"I don't believe it!" the village chief exclaimed as he rubbed his sooty hands down his stained white linen shirt. He paused for a moment to look at his father as if to confirm he had heard correctly. "Are you sure?" The old man nodded as he glanced up to the sealed cave at the top of their village.

"It crumbled just over thirty minutes ago, that was the tremor yer felt." The miners all gathered around to listen to their conversation intently. If the monstrosity that threatened their livelihood had truly fallen, then it was not a moment too soon. Although hours from the designated time there had been reports of the beast approaching. It seemed impatience had gotten the better of their tyrant. He was coming early.

"Shall I raise the gate?" The chief glanced up the terrain and slowly shook his head. There was no way they could allow them to leave the caves, not now.

"No, I will go to meet them," he insisted, as he began back up the slopes his father had only moments ago descended from. The chief could not help but wonder how it were possible that the group of strangers had succeeded where his own men had failed, but he had no intention of questioning them. If they had brought the promised goods, he had no need for knowledge beyond that.

When he reached the gate, he stood for a moment in disbelief as he discovered not only had they succeeded in their task, but they now waited at the gate, having already tried the faulty lever. They did not look happy.

"Is that it?" His eyes locked on the stone clutched in Acha's hand. It truly was the item they sought, it was everything that man had described. Elly smiled at him with hidden meaning, it was a smile which sent shivers down his spine and drove fear into his heart. "May I?" He extended his hand without passing it through the gate in a request for the stone. Acha stepped forwards, stopped quickly by Elly's arm.

"Raise the gate," she ordered. The village chief took a step back to make way for his father, who approached. He stood breathlessly for a moment yet still offered them a warm smile as he paused to catch his breath. They waited, Elly did so impatiently.

"Please forgive us." His voice seemed older than before, it trembled slightly with the tones of betrayal as he looked at the tired looking group through the sealed gate.

"Forgive you, for what? You need only raise the barrier to make this amicable." Elly's hand still stretched before Acha to prevent her further advancement.

"It'd be more dangerous to raise it, than it would for yer to navigate to another exit, yer see," the old man glanced around before he continued in lowered tones, "*he* has returned. He will be here within minutes. True, he will spare the villagers, but strangers..." He looked away from them towards the commotion which had already begun at the foot of the town. "He is powerful, even if yer stood a chance of defeating him before, yer tired from yer ordeal." He looked to Zo, who still clutched her shoulder tightly, then to the rest of them as he wondered what they could have faced which left them so exhausted.

It wasn't surprising one of them had been injured. He had expected to see far more casualties, if they had returned at all, after all, The Courts were guarded by those creatures, and although it was true that they had never hurt his men, those who entered had never returned.

"He will know we did not mine the rock ourselves, legends told of the appearance of someone who could make the great building crumble, he will know yer here. It is said yer worth a great treasure. He will surely wish to present yer to the new heir. That device I gave yer, it will lead yer to the nearest exit. Forgive us, we did not know it would end this way." He bowed slightly in apology, holding his lowered position until Elly broke the silence.

"So, correct me if I am wrong, but you enlist our aid, and once we fulfil your request you—" Acha stepped around Elly cutting her sentence short.

"I understand." She placed her hand through the gate to offer him the stone. The old man's cool grey eyes met with hers for a moment before he smiled, taking it from her. "Can you give us an idea of which tunnel to take first?" He nodded, it was the least he could do, especially since things had panned out as they had. Personally, he had wanted to share a drink with them and give them a mighty feast to celebrate their victory, but it seemed it was not to be.

"From where yer emerge take the third tunnel to the left, follow it through to the end. However, the creatures from the court shall be regrouping, yer must be quick with your escape. They are no longer as they should be, they have become tainted." Behind him, on the horizon, they saw the mighty creature making its approach. "Go, we shall detain him. Please, be safe." He glanced back to them with desperation, his son was already on the way down to meet with their visitor.

Once again, they found themselves at the tunnel mouth, looking at the crumbled remains of the court which now seemed to fill the previously empty area. They were all so weary now that they had hoped for a simple passage through the village. It was still hours before sunset, but since time moved at an unforgiving pace, they had to find somewhere safe to sleep, and to do that they needed to be clear of the mines.

The creatures which had once lived within the building's walls, were beginning to regroup. Just as the old man had said, yet somehow, they looked different now, more like an army than a group of adjudicators. An explosion of snarls and foreign words argued across the air until finally one voice silenced them all.

"We should—" Elly began but was soon cut short.

"Shh," Acha hissed, lifting her hand to silence them. "Listen." She leaned forwards slightly in hope to improve her hearing, wondering why they weren't paying attention and why she had become the recipient of such strange looks.

"I can't hear anythin' but growlin'," Eiji whispered. Acha glanced back at them realising why they were not paying attention. She raised a hand subtly to her ear, without another word she began to translate.

"They said something like, the thieves have taken the rune, now we hunt, they are close," she whispered, she paused again to listen, aware she had missed some of the conversation as she translated for their benefit. "They are separating into seven teams, one for each tunnel." Acha glanced around the room but counted eight, inclusive of the one they took shelter in. The snarls of many filled the air again as they began to choose their leaders and comrades.

"Y' can understand them, how?" Eiji questioned.

"I touched one of them in my trial. It was my father at first, but as I left it became one of those things. It seems in this world, I take on some attributes of those I touch." She shifted her hair to briefly reveal her pointy ears before quickly covering them in embarrassment as she became the recipient of their stares. "I can understand them, I have their sight and smell too. I don't know how long— wait." She stopped when she caught their next sentence. "They're going to get weapons from the far chamber." They watched and waited as the demon dog-like creatures began to move further away, it was then they made their move.

They had scarcely reached the entrance of the desired tunnel when the first group emerged with their weapons in hand. As they saw each other, they both stood immobilised for but a few seconds. They were those strange kind of seconds, the ones which seemed to last forever, as if time had stopped. More joined them, and together the creatures began to chant. With no other option, they turned and ran.

"What are they saying?" Daniel questioned, as they ran down the tunnel. As he noticed Acha's pallor, he wondered if it was better not to know.

"Just run," she whispered, and they did. They ran as fast as they could, following the twists and turns of the tunnel, never once daring to look behind. They continued their escape, their pace never faltering until the tunnel split into two before them.

"Which way?" There was never any question of them separating. Elly had been looking at the device the old man had given them for some time as she ran. She knocked it against her hand a few times.

"It does not work," she announced, discarding it. Removed from her touch it faded into nothingness, reminding them all it was but a figment of a dream. They paused considering their options, both waiting for a decision to be made and trying to make one. It seemed that despite the creatures' appearance, their movements lacked speed, or perhaps they were simply waiting for the remainder of their pack to ready themselves before they pursued.

As they stood considering the paths, they knew they were at the disadvantage. The creatures knew this terrain, these tunnels were their home. They would know every shortcut, every nook and cranny, they tried to listened for signs of water, a breeze, anything that would lead them out, but there were no such indications. The tunnels were identical with only one difference; one would lead them out, the other would lead them deeper into the heart of the mines.

It seemed like they would just have to throw caution to the wind and take a chance. As they stood, Zo removed the blood-soaked bandage from her shoulder. She looked at it for a moment before focusing her mind on the situation at hand. Her feet begged her to move, to choose a tunnel. But somehow she knew she must wait. She knew, given time, there would be a definitive, accurate decision made. The chants began to grow louder until finally Elly made a decision.

"Left," she asserted positively. With her instruction they began to run, all but Eiji and Zo who remained rooted to the spot.

"What y' doin'?" he snarled suspiciously, watching her drop the blood soaked bandage at the start of the passage. He couldn't imagine what she was thinking. If she did that, the trail would lead those creatures right to them.

"Throwing them off," she answered, her hand clutching her injury tightly. She only hoped since the wound itself was still bleeding the scent would be lost by that of the bandage. She pushed her hand into her bag removing a small phial, and rubbed its contents on her top and shoulder. Her eyes watered as she bit down on her lip against the pain, at least it should cover the scent, if only a little.

"Shouldn't it be on the one we're *not* usin' then?" he demanded.

"Exactly, trust me." Eiji nodded with a sudden realisation as he understood exactly what it was she was attempting. It was foolish to assume they would take the bait, it was an old hunter's trick used to mark the path not taken with an item identifiable as the target's to fool their pursuers into taking the wrong path. It was a gamble, one which not only assumed these creatures were good hunters of fair intellect, but also relied on them erasing all possible traces of them moving in this direction. They ran to catch up with the rest of the party, covering any hints of their presence they may have left. The darkness of the tunnel made it difficult to see what lay in the distance before them, something which would work in their favour as the pursuers approached.

They ran as quickly as they could, whilst trying to make as little noise as possible. The sound of gentle flowing water masked their steps as it echoed from a small waterway below the floor. At regular intervals they noticed the appearance of holes in the wall that provided a perfect place for gathering water, not that they had time for that, or would trust the water.

Acha stopped as snarls erupted around the tunnel in echoes. They were far closer than any of them would have liked.

"They have found the bandage?" she repeated unsure of what this meant, until Zo and Eiji, caught up. "They think it's a trick." Zo looked at Eiji meaningfully, but there was also relief hidden within the quick gesture. "A small search team, about two, maybe three, are coming this way just to make sure. If they find us they could let them know we are here before we even have a chance to run," Acha advised, their heavy footsteps already approaching, echoing through the cave walls as they advanced.

Eiji touched Acha on her shoulder lightly, pointing her towards a small hole in the brickwork. It was too small by far for those stocky built hunters to enter, but it would meet their needs perfectly. He could only hope they would overlook the fact they could fit in with ease.

It was impossible to see inside the darkened area, which made it a perfect hiding place. It was almost as if luck was on their side. Despite not knowing what lay within, Eiji pushed himself through. Their only choice was to try to conceal themselves here, or be caught. The water was surprisingly warm. From the current of the water it seemed this tunnel led somewhere, perhaps even to an exit. There was a slight undercurrent which ran in the opposite direction to that they were heading.

Without hesitation they followed him inside as he silently indicated the ample room. The inside of this waterway was quite unusual, it was by no means man-made, it seemed the water's current had worn away at the stone work to create the underground canals which seemed to stretch into the distance. The overhead wall also shared the same watermarks. Seeing this unnerved him, it meant at some point the water had risen far above any areas, such as the one they had used to gain entry. He reassured himself that the hole would surely make it impossible for the water to rise that high again.

His friends had all entered slowly, just as he had moments before. Moving to grip the stones, which made up the walls of this tunnel, they positioned themselves in an area away from direct sight, just in case their pursuers thought to peer inside.

Acha pushed herself across the floor awkwardly as she manoeuvred backwards with difficulty to lower herself inside. It was an action which allowed her to continue holding the stone walkway once she had been submerged into the water. Waves of fear washed over her as her feet failed to find a solid surface, slowly, carefully she felt for handholds in the rocks, using them to pull herself to the side.

As the footsteps approached, they all unconsciously held their breath. Outside, was slightly lighter than the place they were hiding in, so when the creatures arrived, they could clearly see the giant boots as they stopped just outside. The creatures sniffed the air around them in search of any signs they had passed this way.

Acha cringed, biting down on her lip to prevent any sound leaving her as she felt the creatures which swam around them in the water. A slight colour had returned to her vision, but she could still see the movement below the surface. She gripped the wall harder as something the size of a large water snake brushed past. She knew in this world, there was little chance it was something so harmless. Her heart pounded so loudly she feared their pursuers would hear. Her grip tightened further, knowing if she were to slip, she would be unable to suppress her panic. She would not only drown, but give away their location. Stilling her breath, she tried to calm her nerves. She could not afford to panic, not now.

An icy silence froze the air, even the slightest movement would betray them.

Everything was still, everything was silent, so quiet in fact that when the creatures resumed their conversation, the sudden sound had startled them. Had it been the tones of speech instead of the low growls, perhaps this sudden outburst of sound would have startled them into revealing their location. The boots vanished from view to return down the path. The sound of footsteps gradually faded into the distance. They looked at Acha as if to check it was safe. She held herself pressed against the wall, her eyes closed tightly, yet still she felt the weight of their stares.

"He was right," she whispered, it was all she could do to keep her voice steady. Her knuckles had long turned white from the intensity of her grip. All she could focus on was getting out of the watery grave, but she knew not to hurry their departure. "Nothing lies ahead but the furnace. No one has passed this way, the door remains unopened. We must head back quickly and report." Acha spoke slowly, as she had listened to them speak, she had realised her vision was not the only stolen ability which had begun to fade. Her capacity to understand their language had become strained. She only hoped the translation she had given was accurate.

Much to Acha's distress, they waited silently in the water a while longer before they moved, a precaution needed to ensure their movements would not be detected. It was at this point, as they pulled themselves from the water, that they first became aware of the heat in the tunnel. The small trails of water they left soon evaporated in the heat of the stone tunnel. Despite this warmth, Eiji shivered rubbing his arms and legs as he glanced around.

"Is everyone okay?" he whispered, his hands still violently rubbing his legs, almost as if he tried to rub out a cramp. They all nodded, and in silence continued towards the place the creatures had referred to as the furnace. They could only hope there was a way out, after all, continuing along this path was now the only option open to them.

The vibrations of the ground as it rumbled underfoot reminded them of the old man's words. Their slow pace quickened as they realised the meaning behind the tremor. The gate had been breached, now there were more than just the tainted judges to consider. Another hunter had joined the pack, a person who, for reasons unknown, also sought them.

Each step became more difficult as the dramatic rise in air temperature saw their every breath burning as the heaviness of the scalding air stifling. The moisture from their clothes had now evaporated, even the beads of sweat formed by the intense heat were short lived in these conditions.

The enormous metal constructs of the doors sealing the furnace stood before them. Its carefully crafted metal design caused waves of nauseating heat to be emitted from it. It stood before them as a barricade, a door, yet with no apparent means to open it. To touch such a thing would result in serious burns. Two lit torches either side of the doors added to the heat which already stemmed from this apparent dead end. It was additional heat quickly removed as Elly extinguished them. Daniel mentally traced his hands down the perfectly crafted seal of the double doors as he tried to decipher the means of opening them. To touch such a thing was impossible, but even if the heat could be withstood, the implied weight alone would see them fail to move the blockade.

Elly looked between the worried faces in amusement as they realised all their trekking had been in vain. They stood before the metal partition, knowing that going back was not an option. No matter where they ran someone, or something, would be waiting for them. She couldn't believe they could have overlooked something so simple, she had even provided the only indication they should have needed. She allowed herself a further moment, her hand resting on one of the extinguished torches. When she felt they had suffered enough, she pulled down on it.

The first rule of treasure hunting, in her mind anyway, was to always pay attention to your surroundings. If something seemed impossible, too heavy or sealed, there was normally something in the vicinity designed to be of aid. In this instance, as the door possessed no handles and was clearly heavy, she would have automatically expected them to look for something resembling a pulley system to allow them to gain access. A system which would easily support the weight and make the task of moving such a heavy object simple. On this realisation, they then should have looked for the one thing that seemed out of place in the area, the two torches. It wasn't difficult, but to believe themselves trapped without investing any time to take note of their surroundings truly was the height of idiocy.

As the torch locked into its new position it revealed, as she had expected, a small wheel which, if you looked closely enough, was linked to several other cogs. The torch itself became the handle needed to operate the pulleys. No doubt when they entered the room, they would see a set of heavy chains attached to the door which would be pulled into the wall as the door opened.

Zo hesitated before mirroring Elly's actions on the other side of the door, slowly they began to turn the handles. Zo, however, found the handle almost impossible to move as her shoulder complained against the pressure needed to push it forwards. Eiji, seeing her struggle, took over. The sound of moving metal echoed through the air as the giant doors finally began to open. When there was a crack big enough for them to pass through, Eiji stopped, he maintained pressure on the handle as he gasped for breath. Elly rotated her torch with ease until her side of the door was almost fully open, ensuring they would have ample time to pass through.

Hot, stagnant air raced from the room, the pressure behind it forcing them back a few paces as its contact stole their breath, turning the once clear air into a sickly haze. They fought against the immense heat as they stepped quickly through the doors which slowly started to closed behind them.

The creatures had referred to this enormous room as the furnace, and it was clear why, although not entirely practical in its design in their world, the rules here were different. It seemed this 'furnace' as they called it would provide heating to anywhere the carefully positioned pipes led. Just below the crumbled path they stood on bubbled molten lava. It stretched from wall to wall throughout the entire room, blatantly ignoring most of the fundamental laws of lava, such as the fact that it could melt rock.

Should these rules have been followed, however, the area they stood on would not have existed, nor in fact, would the mines. The air pockets, which slowly oozed through the lava, hissed and spat on the surface, occasionally splashing uncomfortably close to where they stood, and there was no question that, even if this lava did disobey some laws, should it touch them it would show no mercy.

Throughout the room, huge titanium pipes were suspended from the tall ceiling, but some larger ones also started an upward journey against the walls around the room. The path, at one time, would have crossed from one end of the room to the other, but the entire middle part of it had long crumbled to vanish into the sea of lava. Across the distance of the room, through the sticky haze of the air, they could just see the exit. Another ledge stood opposite them, but of course with no path there was no chance of them reaching it. None of the pipes were close enough that they could consider trying to use one to bridge the gap.

"What do we do now? There's no way we can turn back, they will know the door has been opened." Acha paced alongside the door. She had noticed that unlike the hidden levers on the other side of the door, there seemed to be no device to open it from the inside. It seemed once in this room, the architect assumed whoever entered would be passing over the collapsed walkway. Perhaps the beings here did not fear the lava's heat, or could leap the distance between the paths. Whatever the reason, with the area being left in this state of disrepair, they were trapped. It seemed their only choice was to wait for the creatures to open the gates to this prison, only to release them into another.

"This is a furnace, that means the heat has to be going somewhere." Daniel observed. He knew this obvious information didn't help the situation, but he refused to accept the fact that there was no hope of escape. He looked briefly to Elly who stood examining one of the large pipes which ran up the walls both sides of the path.

"These two pipes lead out of here, they emerge fairly close to the surface," she advised after a moment of silence. "We can edge across the maintenance ledge. It is fairly steep to start but it levels out further up."

"Well what's our other option, go back out and face them?" Zo asked rhetorically. The only real choice was the one Elly had suggested, unless of course they wanted to sit here and wait for death. She doubted the creatures would be content in just taking them prisoner, they hunted for blood.

Zo moved to join Acha at the edge of the path, who seemed to be watching something with a look of horror on her face. On approaching she could hear a strange scuttling noise coming from one of the pipes, followed by a popping sound. As she watched the place her friend's attention was focused, she saw something the size of an apple drop from the pipe, exploding as it made contact with the lava.

"What are they?" Acha rubbed her arms as the hairs rose to send tiny prickling sensations all over her body.

"Baby spiders, just hatched from the look of them." Daniel moved to stand by Zo, placing his hand on her good shoulder momentarily before he wiped his sweating brow. They had to get moving soon. He was sure they had been weighing the options between the pipes and the creatures, but if they didn't decide quickly, dehydration would weaken them, making them more vulnerable regardless of the choice they made.

"Babies? They're the size of my hand!" Eiji exclaimed, joining the conversation.

"True, but you can still see part of the substance they've hatched from." Daniel pointed as another one fell into the bubbling lava. A silvery thread was attached to it, it shimmered in the heat as it fell to its death.

"I'd hate t'meet their parents." He shivered at the thought. "All in favour of the left pipe?" He raised his hand and hurried towards Elly, who had started to impatiently wonder when a decision would be made. She could wait far longer in this heat than any of them, but then the task of seeing them all to safety would be more of a burden than if they simply made a decision quickly.

"Do you really need to ask?" Elly intervened. Unlike the rest of them she lacked the rapid progression of fatigue brought on by the heat. "I seriously doubt we could fit in there with them as well. Then again, it may just prove to quicken your pace." A small smile tickled the edge of her lips as she mulled over the possibility. "Besides, the left one is more structurally sound." As they looked between the two pipes the right one did seem to bend out slightly, almost as if it could fall from the wall at the slightest movement, but the other not only sat flush but didn't seem to climb as high either, it stopped halfway up to enter the wall. It would be a difficult climb, but definitely better than the alternative options.

"I'll go first." Eiji gently moved Zo from the side so he could get a clear view of what needed to be done. He instantly regretted volunteering, but there was no other choice. His worried gaze turned to the tiny ledge fearfully, it would not even be wide enough to support his entire foot.

"My thoughts exactly." Elly confirmed. Although Eiji had offered out of chivalry, he would always have been the first choice. His elemental nature should sense any approaching obstacles, and his powers meant he could utilise his skills before anything dangerous grew too close. At least this was her reasoning, although with his past efforts of such tasks, she hoped her theory would not be tested. She did, however, have concerns regarding his clumsiness. It could prove problematic, but it was either him or Zo who had to take the first step into danger and, although she had vowed to protect him, she had no real connection to him.

She watched as he gripped the wall tightly to slowly sidestep across the small ledge. He pressed himself firmly against the wall, afraid to look down, while attempting to ignore the feeling of the heat from the lava burning his legs as he edged across. On reaching the pipe, he hesitated for a moment, not daring to look back in fear he may be reminded of what lay below him. The only way he had made it so far was denial, denial of the death which awaited if he fell. To look now may be just the spur to tip him off balance and fulfil the self-made prophecy.

"There seem to be some holes, it should help with climbing." His voice trembled as he ducked into the pipe. He stood there for a good few seconds as he caught his breath. At least inside the pipe he reasoned he could not fall backwards, then again if his footing slipped, a vertical descent would prove just as fatal. Spurred by the visions of his death he began to climb, using the holes in the pipe to aid his struggle.

Elly sent Daniel across next. He couldn't help but wonder if this had been planned more than she had implied. She seemed to know exactly how she wanted to proceed and, if he recalled correctly, she *had* been studying this pipe whilst the rest of them had been more concerned with the broken pathway. Once he was safely inside, she motioned for Acha to follow, she did so without hesitation. Elly looked at Zo almost fearfully, she had some concerns about her ability to climb with her injury. She had been watching her closely, it was not nearly as painless as she tried to imply, but there was no other choice. The creatures were advancing and in greater numbers than they had initially seen. Soon they would be outside. There really was no time to waste and with the skills of their kind almost faded completely from Acha, it was getting more difficult to estimate their location by sound. Fortunately, Elly now had other methods of tracking them. Acha glanced back, before entering the tunnel to see Elly motion for Zo to proceed.

"After you." Zo smiled politely, although her tone seemed to lack any courtesy as she motioned for her to take the lead.

"There is no cause for concern," she responded. Marise always preferred to take the lead, and Elly had been the only person she had trusted to accompany her, the only person she would show her back to. It seemed Zo did not yet possess this trust for her.

"But still." She motioned again, her voice holding a little more insistence than before. Time being short there was little spare to debate, so Elly reluctantly made her way across the narrow ledge with ease. The footsteps of the guards echoed down the corridor for all to hear, it would only be moments before they entered the chamber. She stopped just outside the pipe, turning back to look at Zo.

"I have stood at your back more times than you can count, perhaps you should trust me more," she stated, even as she did so, she realised this may be the exact reason that Zo refused to offer her such trust. As she entered the pipe, she felt the sickening heat rising from the lava pools below. The metal pipe was not as hot to touch as she, or the others, had anticipated, in fact, it was barely warm. Despite this, the air flowing through it restricted their breath. They could hear Eiji's footing scrape across the metal as the footholds began to fade near the top of the pipe.

"It levels off here," he whispered; his voice echoed through the structure. "I bet y' could—" A loud ringing resonated through the pipe sending vibrations through the entire structure. "No, never mind. It's big enough t'crawl through." He winced, rubbing his head as he moved deeper into the pipe. He stopped, waiting for them all to reach level footing.

"Is there any light up there?" Elly questioned, aware of the scraping sound from below them. The creatures had already begun to operate the door. She wondered if maybe she should have replaced the torches, or even cut the chains, but doing so would only have served to delay them further. Since the creatures knew this territory, it would have been of no real benefit, there was bound to be at least one other entrance.

Elly felt the curve in the pipe approach, it would be better if they had all made it to the level platform before they entered the room. It would be obvious to the creatures which way they had gone, after all, there was only one real path of escape. Since they were familiar with dreamers, she could only hope the creatures would believe them to have woken, even so, there was a lot left to chance. At least if they were all on level footing the worst they could do would be to rip the pipe from the wall. The creatures' builds were by far too large to allow access to such a narrow space.

"None. We could get lost in here forever, goin' 'round in circles, lost," he stressed. All fell silent as the doors below opened, the snarls and growls of their conversation carried through the metal pipe. They froze not daring to move, or even breathe, in fear they would give away their position.

Countless minutes passed in the darkened space, seconds filled with fear as sounds from unknown sources moved and scraped around them. The darkness and heat were all-consuming, and the only thing to focus on until finally the footsteps retreated. They remained quiet longer still, until the snarls were inaudible to Acha. It was only then they continued.

"We need to get out of here as soon as we can," Acha commented. "They were not too concerned about the chance we had escaped, in fact, for some reason they found it quite amusing. They said something about creatures called Catspidres living within the tunnels of the furnace. They were certain we would not escape."

"Catspidres?" Elly questioned, her movements paused for a moment. "Then I suggest we increase the pace. I very much doubt any of you would want to encounter one of those."

"What are they?" Eiji called back, now more than ever he felt the pressure of his role to lead them to safety.

"They are creatures very much like baby spiders, only much larger, like the ones you saw back in the furnace room come to think of it. Once they bite a victim, they are cursed to become a living egg sac, the chemicals in their saliva race through the body until it twists and deforms the host, splitting their flesh so new limbs and features form.

"It is a very painful process. On infection, the human dreamer becomes comatose, their dreaming form trapped within Darrienia. The whole process takes about six hours to complete, by which point the victim has been engulfed by pain-induced insanity to become a creature of this world. They hunt and kill those who stumble into its territory, they are truly a deadly predator.

"During their incubation period, each life-force the living egg sac consumes creates additional eggs, which wait just under the skin to be hatched. When their race is low in numbers the body will die, and from it will crawl numerous Catspidres. As the eggs are grown within this mutated adult creature, they not only consume the body but devour its life-force too. Unfortunately for their race, only ten percent of any born actually survive then out of those only a small number will find a human dreamer suitable to become an egg sac to continue their race. A strange race really, dreamers are the only way they can continue to breed.

"The lifespan of the Catspidres and the egg sac is one moon cycle, a month. The Catspidres only have this time to locate and infect a suitable host to bear their next generation. Catspidres themselves can never evolve to become a creature capable of birth and so their strange cycle will continue." Elly smiled to herself in amusement, aware that her tale had motivated a very sharp increase in pace.

"The passage takes a sharp left," Eiji whispered nervously as they began to catch up. "Only left," he added as if to answer their silent question. He had now mastered the art of feel crawling through the dark and now somewhat slime-coated tunnel, but was relieved as a dim area of light came into focus in the distance. His heart leapt, in the hope of it being an exit, he was certain, now more than ever, that they were not alone in this tunnel. Something was approaching. He glanced up uncertainly just before he reached the circle of light, he could just about see the top of the pipe. He cautiously rose to his feet as he entered into the light to stand at full height. The pipe here was far taller than the rest of it. He could hear the faint sounds of scuttling from further down the tunnel, but the light acted as a trap, forbidding him from seeing what lay beyond.

Above him, just out of reach, was a circular vent. No life stirred above, at least, not as far as he could tell. He knew they would have to get out of this tunnel quickly. Whatever he felt hidden by the darkness was getting ever closer.

"I need a foot up, I'm sure this will come loose." Eiji didn't want to say anything about the noises, about the presence he felt, but he knew they had to get out of there. Whatever shared the space with them was not friendly, he could feel its hunger.

Daniel knelt on the floor below him to give a large enough boost to reach the vent, with Elly's hand he steadied himself. With this extra height he found he could just fit his fingers through the holes. He looked at the grooves in the grid's seal before he turned the vent, lining the hole and the prong together, he gave it a hard push. It lifted easily. Eiji grabbed the edges and, with Elly's help, he pulled himself into the room above. Painfully dry, hot air rushed down the tunnel as he turned to help his friends into the room.

Zo waited until everyone was safe before she glanced up the hole. She stood for a moment trapped in the light as she heard something breathing. It was coming towards her, its pace quickened. She reached up grabbing Elly's arms, intense pain creating patches of darkness through her vision as she was yanked upwards. As soon as he could, Daniel grabbed her midriff pulling her the rest of the way.

Elly slid the grid quickly back into place as something passed beneath them. Before she had time to secure it, she felt something strike it. As it flew into the air, fleshy suckered tendrils fought their way into the room. She moved with speed and grace, her hands seizing the in-flight grate, her leg sweeping the climbing suckered tentacles from the floor in a smooth, skilled motion as she thrust the seal down once more over the opening. The creature below released an inhuman howl as it withdrew quickly. Throwing her coat across the grid, she locked it quickly into place before sitting firmly upon its surface. The thrusts of the creature's attempts to once more break through, making her body jerk with each powerful strike.

"What was that?" Acha questioned as everything began to calm. She had never seen such horrors, she had heard many tales of sea dwelling creatures with appendages such as those, but nothing which roamed the lands, then again, these weren't ordinary lands.

"Does it matter?" Elly responded, her tones quiet as she listened for any signs of further movement from below. "I would rather not know than to share this room with it, how about you?" Acha nodded.

"I can't believe this hole came out in a sauna," Daniel stated. With the danger passed he had taken a moment to examine their new surroundings. They found themselves sealed within a large tiled room. Everything, with the exception of the small circular midway tiles, was white or grey. The room itself had some tiled seats which formed a semicircle. Placed carefully above another grate, like the one they had used to gain entrance, stood a pile of heated rocks. Somehow it seemed hotter here than in the pipes they had crawled through. It wasn't until he looked around for the second time he noticed something was amiss, there didn't appear to be a door. Remembering the furnace entrance he began to walk the outer wall in search of something that didn't belong, his hands leaving a slimy residue on the clean walls as he traced his fingers across its surface.

"Ancient baths. This is a dry room," Elly observed, walking to the wall. She touched one of the small blue circular tiles which marked the halfway point around the room. It did not seem any different to the others, yet in response to her touch a faint glow illuminated the wall for just a second, before the tiled door gave a hiss and swung outward. For a moment, as the refreshingly cooler air rushed inside, Daniel stood in disbelief, wondering how she had located it with such ease. It had been well concealed, invisible to the eye.

"By the Gods," Acha gasped, wiping her grimy hands down her equally soiled clothes. It was an action which did not have the desired effects as more slime from the tunnels found its way onto her hands from her clothing. For the last few minutes of their journey the tunnel had been filled with the strange slime, somehow, it seemed to have covered her completely, even places she was certain had never touched the metal piping. Acha glanced to everyone in turn, relieved to notice that they too were also covered in this substance. "It's fit for a king," she added, stepping out into the cool air of the magnificent baths.

The area was dimly lit, even so there was no way to not appreciate the splendour. Like the room they had just vacated, everything was covered with tiles. Impressive mosaics decorated the walls with imagery of the Titans and vast scenes depicting the ancient stories of forgotten gods and heroes. Directly in the centre, surrounded by numerous heated tile benches, stood an enormous bath, built in such a manner that it descended into the floor itself rather than standing upon it. Like themselves, the waters within were thick with green sludge and slime, the occasional bubble fought its way to the surface, struggling to break free from the treacle-like water.

"An emperor, Acha," Elly corrected softly as she took in their new surroundings. "These ancient baths were constructed for the emperors, well almost, they are not quite accurate," she added noticing the imperfections as she glanced around, pausing as she wondered how long it had been since the title of emperor had been abolished.

When Daniel spoke, she realised that none yet within this cycle had claimed such a title. This was the only concern with having a new watcher, until she settled more into the role, the information they shared would be a little erratic. Clearly this new girl, Elisha, was well read, but as yet, she lacked some essential discipline. It was almost as if her every thought was passed on, and sometimes the result was that Elly would speak out of turn. The calibration wouldn't take long, but until then she needed to be more mindful of her words. She smiled slightly, it didn't seem that long ago when she had given a similar warning to Eiji. This was the reason she had always been present when a new watcher had been initiated. It sped up the bonding process and thought calibration, ensuring these kind of things did not occur. This time, however, her presence had not been an option.

"By the Gods, I didn't believe any culture from that age still existed. I've only heard about such rulers from ancient times, but I've never found anything which indicated they lived like this. It's fascinating, even in Darrienia such untouched relics are left behind, think what we could learn it's—" Daniel was cut short before his monologue could reach full rhythm. It was an interruption Elly was pleased to receive. If not for Seiken's appearance, once he had finished, he would no doubt have followed his expression of awe with a barrage of ceaseless questions.

"Disused. It's located just below the surface, contained within a secret tunnel." Seiken approached a small pedestal near the bath to push a small lever on the side in a downward direction. As he triggered it, a large section of the tiled base rose, allowing the water to drain. Once empty, high-powered jets of water blasted the bath from all angles. Some sprays came from carefully concealed nozzles within the bath, others from the ceiling. It continued in this manner until the bath looked new and all trace of grime had been removed. "And safe," he added, looking approvingly into the feature before returning the lever to its original position. As he did so, steaming water erupted from the edges of the bath to fill the air with strange and wonderful fragrances, until it was full once more. A light steam rose to dance across the water's surface.

He moved in silence to a nearby wall where he manipulated another small lever to bathe the dimly lit room with light. It was a strange light, it shone through numerous pieces of square, almost transparent glass that were mounted in the ceilings. It was a style of lighting which none but Elly had seen before. One that didn't belong to this time. "Not a creature of this world knows of this location but us. With nightfall approaching it will be the safest place for you. You can get clean, shower, bathe, freshen up," he listed, almost as if he thought the grime covered life-forms standing before him were in need of a good wash. "You will find this place will cater to your every need." He turned to Elly. "There are two or so hours until sunset. Clean yourselves up, relax and wash away the grime. It's not like you could achieve anything in that time anyway." He gave a slight shrug before leaving through the door.

"I guess we could do with freshening up a little." Despite the heat of the room, Zo shivered, thinking back to the rancid touch of all those creatures as they clawed at her. Diverting her attention from such images, her vision met with Eiji. He looked somewhat distressed as he sat on one of the heated, tiled benches. She approached, placing her hand on his shoulder. A seething pain radiated through her leg, so unexpected, so intense, it forced her to move quickly. He turned to her in alarm, he knew she had felt it.

"Oh, it's nothing. I caught myself in the tunnel," he answered quickly, before she had the chance to ask. He couldn't tell her the truth, not after what Elly had said, he couldn't force this burden on them.

Since he had travelled with Elly it seemed her constant expectations, and explanations of the things he should be able to do, had actually helped him to become more accustomed to his talents. He felt himself becoming more familiar with Zo's magic since Elly had explained what the feelings he had around her, actually were. He wondered if this was how two magic users, ready for battle, assessed the threat of their opponents. He knew just from the feel of her aura she was powerful, but through it could also feel her fatigue. From the understanding he gained, it seemed every person she touched was subjected to an assessment of health and injuries, such was the curse and blessing of being a true healer.

"I can make you something for it," she whispered matching his lowered tone. It was clear he wanted to keep his injury from the others, a wish she respected.

"When we get back, sure." He smiled nervously before, in an attempt to politely finish the conversation, he walked towards the showers that stood at the far end of the room. Each shower was segregated into a small room of its own. He entered the first one, it was the best place to take a look at the damage in private.

The room itself was enormous. It was easily the size of his bedroom when he had lived with his adoptive mother, his master's wife. The air in the room was filled with the different scents of the shampoos and gels which were expertly placed in alphabetical order of fragrance and spread across two shelves.

A full-length mirror stood just next to a large cupboard. He opened it slowly, like a child not wanting to be caught doing something they shouldn't, and since nothing in this place belonged to them, it seemed like stealing. Inside hung a luxurious dressing gown, enormous towels, and several assortments of swim wear, no doubt for use in the bath. On a small shelf there stood both medical and bathing supplies. He slipped the lock across the door before moving to sit on the small seat just outside of the shower, he wrapped a towel around himself before carefully examining his leg.

The bite didn't look anywhere near as large as it felt. It was hard to believe that the two tiny pin holes were responsible for the strange shooting pain which extended through his leg. He studied it for a moment longer before placing his clothes and a small amount of liquid from one of the bottles from the shelf in to a small, but deep, bowl next to the seat. This place was like nothing he had seen before, yet things were similar enough for its operation to be fairly intuitive.

He was just looking for a valve of some kind to fill the strange basin with water when it made a strange clicking sound. The water, as if by his desire, began to fill the small bowl. A strange substance bubbled through the water onto the clothes, he could see the grime lifting from them as they rose to the surface. As the water drained, he readied himself to remove them. As he went to take them several jets of water started to spray, almost as if they had waited for him to place his hand inside. They bounced from his hand spraying his surroundings, he recoiled in shock from the surprisingly powerful force. For a moment he had images of it being a trap, one where whatever was placed within it could never be removed. Of course, he knew he was just being silly, or at least he hoped he was. There was a small part at the back of his mind that still wasn't convinced about the possessed washing bowl.

He decided to stop watching it as it beat and spun his clothes, and shower while he waited for them to be released from their watery prison. He took the items he wanted and got into the shower pulling the sliding partition closed. As if sensing his presence, the powerful jets sprung into life startling him. He grabbed for the door fearing he would too be imprisoned just like his clothes had been. He was relieved to find it still opened, but just to be safe, he placed one of the small bottles between the partition and the wall, ensuring it couldn't seal him within.

After the shower, he slipped on the gown before opening the first aid kit to use some of its contents to bandage his leg, happy in the knowledge that the length of the gown meant his injury would remain hidden. He gave a yawn as he rose to his feet, surprised at how much his body hurt and ached as waves of tiredness swept over him. It was all he could do to keep his eyes open. He felt a growing need to lie down as a feeling of foreboding washed over him.

When he finally emerged from the shower room, Elly took his wet clothes from him placing them with the others she held in her arms. He looked around to see it seemed that everyone else, having finished their showers, now sat together talking in the large bath.

It wasn't until he saw this, he realised its true size. It could easily seat about twenty people. It was clear Elly, like Eiji, had no intention of joining them. Instead she busied herself with other things such as pacing back and forth to gather up the remaining wet clothes, which their owners had spread across the hot tiles upon finishing their showers.

"Come on, you could both do with a rest." Zo patted the side of the bath inviting them in. Being here now felt like their first real moment of serenity, a rare opportunity to recuperate, if only for a short time. It was something they all greatly needed.

"No thank you, the shower was quite sufficient. I will put the clothes in the dry room, at least then they will be ready for when we leave," Elly answered walking away.

Eiji shook his head before making his way to the heated tiles, he needed time to think, to rest. Besides if he were to join them, it would only invite questions about his injury. He had already seen the way they looked at the marks on Zo's skin, and had caught both Daniel and Acha glancing to her when they thought she wasn't looking. It would only be moments before one of them had to ask and he wanted to avoid such attention. He too had been guilty of examining their wounds, Daniel's scars from the marshland attack, Zo's injuries, it seemed little by little they were being worn down. It was only natural that he too would suffer. He touched the inflammation around the bite mark before settling down on one of the many heated platforms. The heat warmed and soothed his tired muscles, despite this, he still felt a slight chill. He closed his eyes, resting.

"Zo." Daniel's voice became serious, a drastic change in the tones of their last conversation about the strange washbowl. His smile faded. He had tried his best to ignore it, to respect her privacy, but he couldn't delay any longer. He had wanted to ask, more so since the continued effort he had made in politely trying to ignore the raw looking marks which covered her body. But he couldn't ignore them any longer, he had to know. "What happened?" He saw her shift uncomfortably for a second.

"What do you mean?" she asked, as she rubbed water up her arms before cradling the elbow of her injured shoulder. She had known he would ask at some point, but him actually doing so made her feel all the more self-conscious. Both he and Acha had noticed the injuries, and now, despite her trying her best to hide them under the water's surface, they had still asked.

She was glad the room had possessed medical supplies. If they were alarmed by the scratches which were less visible now the small streaks of dried blood and dirt had been washed away, they would have been even more distressed to see the bloody hole through her shoulder which still bled. Each time she moved, she felt the pain and the warmth of blood as it seeped through the gum seal, and was grateful the bleeding had not yet penetrated the fresh dressings.

When they returned, she knew she would need to cauterise and stitch the injury but this world was not the place for such actions. Injuries needed to be attended to in their own world, after all, dream items rarely passed into the waking world. Treating it here would probably only result in further injury on waking. This wound would scar. It would leave the mark of those who tried to kill her, physical proof of the lesson she had learnt. Whenever she was unsure of herself, she knew she could take strength from the wound to remind herself of the line between her and Marise. *'I am not a killer.'* She thought to herself as she touched her dressing. She would need to leave the bath soon, before the wound bled through, but she hadn't wanted to miss this opportunity. It seemed like so long ago since they had last been able to bathe.

"In that room, what happened?" he asked again. He felt her desire for him to refrain from pressing her further, but now he had mentioned it there was little choice. She could not simply ignore him.

"It's not important," she whispered, turning away from him, his words rekindling images of the rotting corpses as they grabbed at her. She rubbed more water up her arms. Although she had said it wasn't important, it was. What had happened in there was more significant than she could explain. Her experience had given her a new strength, a strength to fight on.

"Okay, you'll tell me when you're ready." He touched her gently in what he hoped was a comforting gesture. "Since we have some time before we need to return, you could always heal them." Her defensive posture had caused him to realise it was better to leave it until she was ready. He was certain he would be the first person she spoke to, but this did not stop his desire to discover the truth about what happened. He knew whatever she had faced had somehow involved him. The way he had heard her scream his name still haunted him. If she would just talk to him about it, he could at least offer her some comfort, some reassurance.

"I can't," she whispered, realising she had never really explained the stigma attached to her rune to any of them. She wasn't exactly sure how his would affect him, but hers had a specific purpose, and that was to make things more difficult.

"How come? Surely you don't want to be in pain," he pressed, wondering if this was somehow another way she could torture herself for things beyond her control.

"No, Daniel, I mean I *can't.*" She raised her voice slightly. "My rune is sacrifice. I can heal others, but not myself. When I get home maybe I can do something about the superficial wounds, but this"—she motioned to her shoulder—"it has been made clear there is nothing to be done, not with magic anyway."

She knew her rune was the reason why she could not heal it. She could heal others, but with her actions would come a cost, one they didn't need to know. To heal another would be to take their injury as her own. An injury she would not be able to resolve, or there would have been no reason for this world to set such limitations. It was just like her magic, when she used it to inflict pain on others, she too felt the same. Each time she used it, she sacrificed her own body in return. To heal she took the wound, to hurt she too felt the pain and effects just as the recipient did.

She thought back to the time she had healed Daniel, she remembered how his injuries had momentarily transferred to her. Perhaps, somewhere in the unwritten rules of this game, this response was intended to serve as a warning of things to come should she act again. On the more positive side of things, since she could not heal the wound, it would serve as a good reminder. With it came an understanding of herself and in years to come, she could look upon the scar and remind herself of the truth. She only hoped she would still have those years, and her injury would not hinder their progress. She knew she would have to rely on botany to relieve the pain. Unfortunately, there was nothing she could really use which wouldn't seriously affect her senses and concentration. It was not possible to take such potent medicine on this journey.

Daniel opened his mouth as if to speak but was silenced by Elly.

"Come on, get dressed." They looked up to find her and Eiji already dressed in their now clean and dry clothes. "The two hours have nearly passed." Zo and Acha sighed, as always, she was right. They took their clothes from her arms and disappeared to change.

Zo smiled as she looked at her top. There was a fine, almost invisible thread that closed up the damage from her trial, so fine, it was difficult to see against the normal weave of the material unless you knew exactly where to look. Elly had always repaired her clothes with such expertise. Zo hesitated for a second, it unnerved her when she recalled such things or felt nostalgic. Elly had not repaired any of *her* clothes before. That feeling, that thought, did not belong to her.

Once dressed, they all chose to follow Eiji's example and rest on the heated tile seats as they settled down to return home.

"Well, Seiken did say it was safe." Zo smiled comfortably, wondering why every safe place couldn't be this relaxing. With that, they each in turn took their berry and closed their eyes.

* * *

When Zo awoke in the pre-dawn light, the first sensation to strike her was isolation. As she opened her eyes, she felt no one in the proximity. It took her a few moments for her to understand why. Before she had passed into Darrienia, she had left everyone behind, and this area sealed all the senses she could have used to locate them. All this was realised in the sleepy haze as she woke. Then, as she fully became aware of her surroundings, the second sensation she felt was the almost crippling pain which radiated from her shoulder. It was just as Seiken had warned at the journey's start, her injuries had returned with her. She nursed her wound as it throbbed with pain. Although her wound had remained, its dressings had not. It seemed, as she had suspected, items other than the runes would not return with them.

As she walked through the dense forest in an attempt to locate her friends, she focused her energy and concentrated on her wounds. She knew her minor ailments were unimportant, that the stigma attached to her rune wouldn't care for things which caused only superficial damage. As she expected these tiny cuts and scrapes began to fade. But the shoulder wound remained as prominent as ever, for this nothing could be done. She would need to redress it as soon as possible. That was if she could find Daniel, who had once again taken possession of her satchel before they had returned.

"Zo, there you are!" Acha rushed towards her as she arrived on the boundaries of their camp. "Have you seen Eiji?" she questioned urgently; Zo glanced around the camp quickly as if to confirm he wasn't there.

"No, why?" she queried, despite the reason being obvious.

"Well, we don't think he woke. We were hoping he'd gone to find you, but Elly was the first back."

"What?" Zo felt the heat rise to her face, a sick feeling filled her stomach as she recalled the injury he had sustained. Mingled with her own pain, it had been impossible to pinpoint the problem, but thinking back, it seemed like more than just the scrape he had implied.

"Have you noticed something else?" Daniel motioned towards the rising sun, his stomach churned as he brought himself to say the next words. "It's dawn."

"And?" Zo questioned. She didn't quite understand why it being dawn posed such a big issue, until Daniel opened his journal and explained.

"Every time we've crossed back it's taken at least two hours between our sleeping there and waking here. We sleep at sundown there but when we wake it has always been two hours after sunrise, meaning we should never see dawn.

"Zo, Seiken lied. It wasn't two hours to sunset, it must have been at least four," he stated as she looked again at the rising sun. The amber light spilt over the horizon as if the sky itself was on fire. It burned angrily igniting the small clouds which had tried to conceal its appearance. An angry sunrise that seemed to burn with the fuel of betrayal.

"But why?" The pain in her shoulder seemed to increase, her hand moved instinctively to grasp the wound tightly. She found pressure against it somehow relieved some of the deeper pain with a different type of pain, a numb one. "Why would he lie to us about something like that? He's never led us wrong before, has he?" she questioned unsure now of the truth herself. Just seconds ago, she had trusted Seiken with her life, now she was no longer sure he was worthy of that trust.

Chapter 17

Deception

Agony coursed through Eiji's stomach as he keeled over in pain. Any moment now he expected another limb to come piercing through his trembling body. The pain was like none he had experienced before. How he wished he had told his friends of the bite, perhaps they could have done something, even if it had only been to spare his suffering.

Their bodies had vanished now, but it would still be some time before they noticed his absence. By the time they realised he had not returned with them, it would be too late, his transformation would be complete. He had to get out of here, the darkness of Darrienia may be fatal, but if he were to remain here he would no doubt inflict the same agony, the same fate, upon his friends on their return to this world. He would rather walk amongst nightmares than be responsible for the death of his allies.

He painfully fought his way to his feet, his body writhing and trembling as he dragged himself across the walls towards the door. His hand reached out, fumbling through the air as he tried to decide which of the three handles before him he needed to seize to make his escape. The numbness had started to spread from his fingers, making it impossible to tell by touch alone if his hand had made contact or not. The door opened.

"Ah, Eiji, I see you have yet to wake." His eyes took a moment to focus on the figure standing within the darkened hole. As Seiken stepped through into the light, he hooked his arm under Eiji's protesting figure to lead him back inside to be seated. "It's an unfortunate side effect of the Snarson's bite, it is quite toxic." Seiken ruffled his hand through his hair as he spoke. "You just need to hope your friends acquire the antidote."

"Snarson? Y' knew about—" Eiji questioned, the wave of relief assisted the spread of numbness through his body. His chest began to tingle, his focus became more difficult as his chest tightened. Every breath seemed to assist the spreading numbness as it spanned across his body, the pain had almost completely gone.

"The fish? Of course, this is my world, you are simply visiting. Tell me, have the others woken?" Seiken glanced around, inspecting the area for signs of his friends. It was an action which, even through the descending numbness, alarmed him. He glanced upon the figure, his focus failing. If Seiken had known about the bite, why had he not thought to mention it sooner? Then perhaps Zo could have made an antidote. He gave a laboured sigh, it was his own fault. How was Seiken to know he wouldn't mention it? But after the tales Elly had shared in the pipes about the Catspidres, even he had begun to believe he would transform into a horrific living egg sac.

"Yes," he answered through shallowed breaths, "is it dark, am I safe?" His voice contained the urgency created by his panic. He had watched his comrades' bodies as they faded into nothing, but despite growing tired he could not join them in slumber. He had wondered if it had been because the pain prevented him from sleeping, or if it was because his body was about to transform into a creature of this world, that certain laws would prevent his return. But now it seemed although the bite was the cause, it was not because he was in any danger of a slow painful death and mutation. So why did the symptoms persist? He opened and closed his mouth a few times as his tongue started to become numb.

"As I said, no creature of this world knows of this place, then again, since Night's minions are not technically of this world, it would stand to reason they would, but as you say, you are safe after dusk." Seiken smiled seeing the slight relaxation in Eiji's posture.

"Then I'm lucky it's after dusk." His words slurred slightly as his tongue moved in ways other than those expected. "They can't touch me after dusk, can they?" Even through the spreading numbness he had the strangest sensation he was no longer alone. He turned his head slowly, nothing but shadows met his gaze. Despite his failing vision he was certain just moments ago the baths had been far lighter.

"No, they can't, but it seems I was mistaken, it's still an hour until sunset." Eiji gasped in horror as a mass of shadows spewed through the open doorway.

"But y' said..." Eiji gasped as the black masses descended upon him. He fought to the best of his abilities, but it was impossible to injure a shadow. They wrapped around him to restrict his movement with their icy lifeless grip. He knew his struggle would only serve to quicken the poison's path, but he would fight until he had to surrender to it, or them. He flung himself around in hope to break free of the darkness which seemed to bind him.

"I say a lot of things, like the minefields are the safest way. I didn't think you all would have survived. That was fortune bordering on the divine." Seiken smiled, watching Eiji's desperate struggle. It was good that he fought so hard, if he used the rest of his energy here, there would be nothing left by the time he reached Night.

"Y' lied!" Eiji spat, trying to force himself away from the shadows and towards Seiken, the creatures held him back. "Y' knew about the bite, y' knew I couldn't wake! Y' planned this all along, why?" Eiji felt his body go limp as it ignored his desperate attempts at movement. No matter how hard he tried, it refused to do his bidding any longer.

"I was made a proposition I could not refuse." He motioned for the creatures to follow him as he led the way into a dark portal. "As you may have discovered, it's no use fighting, the poison is already affecting your nervous system. In about five minutes you'll be as good as paralysed, until the antidote is administered, or you die. Either way suits me really." Eiji felt himself surrender as the icy grip of the shadows began to drag him into the darkness. In the last few moments, the poison had become so potent he could barely force himself to breathe. It was almost as if his acknowledging it, combined with his struggle, had quickened the effects of its attack.

Darkness surrounded his vision as he lost the battle. As his eyes closed, he heard Seiken's voice echo through the shadows.

"What do you know? It is still thirty minutes to sunset." Eiji could hear the triumph in his voice. As the world around him faded, he once more found himself thinking that which he thought so often.

'*Why me?*'

* * *

"You have returned." Night placed down the text which he had been reading as he rose to greet his company. "And I see you have brought the boy." Eiji was barely conscious. Through the darkness, he tried to move his limbs. He put so much energy into the effort, only to discover the desired action had not occurred. His mind willed his body to respond, yet through the darkness and the numbness he was no longer even sure he had a body to move. He felt like just a mind, a consciousness which had just awoken from a thrilling dream to return to the nothingness of the large empty void.

He tried to call out for help. But the problem with becoming a being of pure thought, he discovered, was there was no voice for him to cry out with. There was nothing, just the emptiness and his thoughts. For a moment there was a disturbance in the darkness, it seemed to tremble and distort as if his position had moved. Through the silence he heard something faint, muffled. It seemed something else shared this space with him. But how could he get its attention when he was incapable of making a sound?

"Yes, my liege."

"Good, now be sure they hear of the antidote." As Night spoke, Seiken stopped as if to question the words he had heard.

"As you wish, what should I do with him?" He glanced down at Eiji who seemed now to be almost under the full effect of the poison. Soon he would slip into a lapse of consciousness, a sleep which existed in this realm as well as their own, but this was unlike an ordinary sleep. It did not mean he would wake in another world, he would be confined to the one he resided in. Outside of Darrienia, when a dreamer was affected and made unable to return, it was called a coma.

"Take him to the new heir and have him do as he see fit. There is now a bounty on their head in that area. I am sure there is much information they wish to extract, and if they should happen on some knowledge that proves useful... I'm sure you understand." Night smiled to himself, so far all had proceeded as planned, but the next steps were the most important ones. They were the ones that would determine how events would progress. There were certain things which had to fall into place soon, perhaps he should spur such matters along a little and leave less in the hands of fate.

"Yes, my liege. Is it safe to leave him there while no one sleeps?" he questioned as he considered the small possibility for the chance of escape, or the likelihood he would somehow find himself in life threatening danger before time.

"Of course, the Epiales will take good care of him until light comes and that area's dreamers arrive. The shadows of this world care little for them and do well to leave them alone. He shall not be in any danger even if it is nightfall there, do not fear, all shall be put into place. You could always stay with him if you wish, but I believe you have more important things to attend to." With those final words Seiken vanished, taking Eiji's limp body into the shadows with him.

* * *

"We have to go back!" Acha pleaded as she paced back and forth across the clearing. The charred ash remains of their fire blew across the surrounding area in the rising winds. "He could be in danger." She stopped pacing briefly to look at the others, to plead for their support, wondering why it took so long for them to make such an obvious choice. Something had to have happened between them sleeping in Darrienia and waking here, and whatever that something was had prevented Eiji's return. It was clear they needed to go back before it was too late.

"But Seiken said it was safe." Zo lowered her head slightly as she wondered if she could trust his words. It could have been a simple mistake, a trick by one of Night's minions to make him believe the time was as he said. She knew what the others would be thinking, they would wonder why she trusted him so unconditionally. Although she couldn't explain it herself, she knew deep inside, in the very core of her being, that she could rely on him. This solid foundation of trust made this truth all the harder to accept. No matter how she reflected upon it, even if Night's minions *had* tried to trick him, Seiken belonged to Darrienia. He was part of that world, he would know something as simple as the sun's position as second nature, even if it were not visible. That of course, led her back to the only option, he had indeed betrayed them.

"Seiken also said when the sun would set, but that did not make it so," Acha snapped before resuming her restless pacing.

"He wouldn't betray us." It seemed to be more of a question than a statement. She looked to her friends in the hope they would agree, yet each one had the same sceptical look. Even she herself had to admit something had changed. The last time they had met he hadn't seemed like himself, he had seemed colder, less like the person she thought she remembered.

"Zo, what do you really know about this guy?" Daniel questioned softly, he had chosen his words so carefully. It was clear Zo had some kind of connection to this person. For some reason she believed him to be very important. Each time she saw him, Daniel felt the familiarity wash over her, feelings so strong that even he had begun to believe that Seiken had played some important role in her past, and would maybe play it again in the future. But just like Zo, he could not place what this connection was, or where it had originated from. This led to the question, if he was important, if they *had* created an irreplaceable bond of friendship, one which she felt so strong even through her amnesia, why would he betray her?

"I know he saved us from the dragon, from Aburamushi, and he gave us an advantage with the map." She began to list the things she recalled, but there was something else, something he had done a long time ago. She felt as if she owed him a great debt, as if their paths had crossed many times during the darkness.

"Did he really?" Elly joined the conversation, still no one answered Acha's own pleas relating to the safety of their friend. "He ran with us from the dragon and utilised your magic to shield us from sight. He merely warned you of Aburamushi's intentions, and although he *did* give us a map, it proved of no use until we found the first location where one awaited us anyway." She tapped a finger with each point she made as if to enforce them.

"How do you know about the map?" Zo questioned suddenly realising Elly had not been in the village when the others found it, she had been with her. She herself had only just found out about it as she and Daniel had both pulled one out for inspection. Elly couldn't have known about it, the existence of a second map had never even been mentioned until now.

"I was there," she stated confidently. "Now if we can get back to the matter at—"

"No, you weren't," Zo interrupted. She couldn't quite place why, but something about her having this knowledge unnerved her a little. "You were with me when the others found it."

"Then someone must have told me about it, what difference does it really make? We used it to navigate the minefields, it probably came up then, but we are losing focus, what is important now is the location of our..." she paused a moment as if to rethink her sentence. "Eiji," she finished.

"We should head back." Acha repeated her previous suggestion, her tone pleading for them to listen. Even now he could be in serious danger, they couldn't just abandon him.

"We should not." Elly was aware that her stating this would not be sufficient to keep any of them happy. "It is nightfall there, it is too dangerous." Elly's posture stiffened as something moved in the undergrowth behind them. Both she and Zo turned simultaneously as the presence appeared, but it was Zo who issued the challenge.

"Who's there?" she demanded, seeing her reaction Daniel moved swiftly to her side placing his hand on hers. She was surprised to find she had already grasped the hilt of her sword. She removed it quickly, pulling it from his as she did so. She glanced to him gratefully just a moment before another Daniel appeared from the bushes. Zo couldn't help watch as the Daniel beside her saw his mirror image, as it approached, confusion crossed his wrinkled brow as he tried to make sense of the situation, but for some reason, he didn't seem threatened. For a moment he thought it may have been some form of reflection. It was like looking into a mirror, the figure had the same ear length brown hair, the same dark eyes. He found himself moving slightly to see if the reflection would do the same, it did not. "Oh, it's you." Zo sighed once more releasing her sword, she couldn't help but wonder when exactly she had seized it for the second time.

"Forgive the intrusion." Daniel moved again, the image still did not follow his movement. The figure spoke again in his voice, instead of listening to its words he wondered if he truly sounded like the person who now spoke. "Your friend is in danger, please forgive my intrusion." Zo glanced at him, he seemed to act far more timidly than when they had first met and he was trying to kill her. Acha stepped forwards, her eyes carefully studying the figure.

"You know where he is?" she questioned eagerly, interested to hear what this living reflection had to say about the danger their friend found himself in.

"Yes, he was detained. The one you know as Seiken planned it to be so." Daniel shot a meaningful glance towards Zo who, in an attempt to ignore him, focused her vision on the new arrival, although this did little to block his thoughts. She did not like what she heard, but it did not make it any less true.

"Detained how?" Elly questioned, trying to keep her tone unemotional, but it seemed she had indeed developed a strange bond with these people. The hint of concern lining her voice was proof of this. She had, until this point, been silent in order to watch their reactions, to watch the creature, to analyse it. It was clear it was a shape shifter, although very limited in the forms it could actually take. The faint smell of blood around it made her believe it had followed them, or had been sent, from the court, and if this was the case, it was very probably a trap.

"Before you reached the furnace, you took shelter from some of my race, ones which have been tainted by the Epiales, although unlike me now they showed you their true appearance. I use magic to seem less... disturbing to your view." Daniel looked at the creature with an amused smile, wondering how disturbed it would feel, coming face to face with *its* living reflection. "Anyway, the Snarson's, they are creatures in the water where you hid..." he trailed off for a moment as if he had lost his train of thought. He shifted uncomfortably before continuing. "They are deadly to dreamers. People in your world bitten by them, their minds seem to be trapped in our reality, unable to return to their bodies. The effect of the bite on the mind is that the body is forced into a permanent sleep, a coma, that's what you call it yes? Their minds are left to wander our world until they stumble on the antidote, or the ones they love give up hope.

"But it's different for you, since you completely cross over, it's not just your mind you lose but your body too. Since it is his physical form which took the bite, he would not simply be trapped in our world, but also suffer the coma within it. He will lose most, if not all, of his consciousness. It's just like any poison, after so long the person dies, it can be hours, days, even months, but eventually..." he paused to look at them as if to ensure they understood the words he had spoken.

"Are you saying he was bit?" Acha screeched in a pitch that surprised even her. "Why didn't he say anything?" She clenched her fists in frustration, why had he not thought to mention it? Perhaps they could have made the antidote before they had returned. She couldn't explain why she felt so angry at his foolishness, but when they found him, she was certainly going to give him a piece of her mind. *'Of all the foolish things to do'* she thought angrily to herself.

"Yes, although I am afraid I cannot answer your second question, I do not know your friend as you do. I must leave now before your gateway seals."

"Wait!" Zo commanded, the creature stopped instantly. "You mentioned an antidote, what does it look like, where do we find it?" The creature turned back slightly and nodded.

"Of course, I knew I had forgotten something. The Narca berry originates from Pirates' Isle. The next land from there is where your friend will wait in the presence of the new heir, in our world of course, not yours, but it won't be easy to retrieve him, they have many guards. Is my debt to you satisfied?" There was something unnerving about the look he gave her. It was not the kind of expression she was accustomed to seeing on her friend.

"Yes, thank you." The creature then vanished as he turned away from them, it seemed as if he had turned to enter a non-visible realm.

"There is a town just through Phoenix Landing, we should rest. We have had little time to do so over the last few days." Elly did not wait for them to agree, she had simply started walking. Daniel was about to protest, remembering what the old man from the cart had said about the area being uninhabited, but he thought better of it, after all, it seemed Elly was always right. Acha heard her stomach rumble, she placed her hand to it gently.

"Well, I am kind of hungry," she admitted. It seemed, although her body took the energy she needed from the world around her, it had also become accustomed to eating.

"And we will get a chance to think about how we locate Eiji." Zo added. As she followed Elly's lead, she couldn't help but think she had walked this path before.

* * *

"You Elementalists are more resilient than I thought." A strange voice oozed through Eiji's darkened mind. Small bubbles of light rose through his vision, momentarily lighting the darkness before popping. Through these brief moments, he tried to imagine what lay in wait beyond the veil of darkness he had grown accustomed to. "I guess your key skill must lie within water. No matter, you will still only retain a little of your consciousness, you are of no threat. Your magical base will do little more than dilute the effect." The voice seemed to grow more distant as if the figure was leaving, a few moments later, the darkness faded. The lighting and shapes which he had seen through the bubbles were not in the least bit similar to the place he now lay. The darkness had lifted, but still he could barely see. He was sprawled out across a cold, dirty floor, in a dank, musty-smelling prison. He slowly moved in the hope to get a better grasp of his surroundings, perhaps even an idea of how to escape.

He knew he was not alone, he had the feeling someone near had been trying to reach him, to rouse him from the stifling darkness. It seemed they had succeeded.

He could see waves of colours as they pulsed across the dimly lit cell. He moved again, this time finding the strength to pull himself to kneel. His vision swam and reality began to twist in protest to his movements. The bubbles of light came again to distort his thoughts and vision, bringing with it the inaudible mumble of a conversation being held somewhere far away. He tried to ignore it, fighting to retain his view of the dark cell with the strange multicoloured light which alternated gently as if it were breathing.

All at once the bubbles faded again, the pressure felt from his weight upon the cold damp floor aiding him to retain his presence here. He felt the floor give beneath him as the pockets of reality contorted. His arms gave beneath him. He felt as if he would fall forever into the darkened void that opened before him.

Once again, he began to hear the strange rhythmic beeping noise of that white place, the darkness now only a quickly fading bubble as if *it* had been the illusion. He was sure his eyes were open, how else could he see the light? But other than this light he could see nothing more. He focused on the beeping sound, it was an unfamiliar noise, a noise so quiet it was almost drowned out by a conversation between two people.

A gentle voice spoke to him, it sounded so close. As his eyes slowly began to make sense of the different shades of white to create shapes, he tried to speak but the words would not come.

"Try not to move," it whispered weakly, suddenly the light was gone, replaced instantly with the darkness without the strange bubbles of change. The voice was so weak that it seemed even the whisper had taken so much effort from its source. As the shadow had spoken the light seemed to have grown brighter, as if feeding on the energy of the person it seemed to coil around.

"Who are y', why are y' helpin' me?" he whispered, vaguely remembering the same voice pulling him back from the darkness a few times since his arrival. It comforted him from a distance as it called him back to reality. There came no reply, just laboured breathing from the corner of the tiny cell. Eiji once more fought to kneel, it felt as if his body defied him. Every move he tried to make resulted in waves of pain and exhaustion coursing through him as punishment.

An age seemed to pass as he once more fought slowly to his knees. Occasionally, the light and chatter would beckon him, but he focused. He had to fight the illusion or else he would have to go through this pain again when he next returned. Eventually, with much effort, he pulled himself to his knees. He moved slightly, finding some support against the damp, mossy, brick wall, he turned slowly to find the source of the glowing light.

A boy sat in the corner, limp and listless, fighting for each for breath, it seemed as if every one was such an effort that another may not follow. As the light intensified, Eiji could see the red shimmer of his long hair. Suddenly he realised who it was he shared his prison with.

"You!" he snarled venomously, trying to find the strength to strike out at the figure. He raised his hand but fell against the wall, his body void of all the angry energy he felt. "Traitor!" he hissed, moving his knees to sit with his back against the wall. Seiken opened his eyes, the light shone brighter, his breath became more laboured.

"I... am... many... things..." he barely whispered through strained breath. Had there been any noise, even a light breeze, it would have drowned out his weak words completely. "But a... traitor... I am not." As Eiji looked upon him he could not help but feel a twinge of sympathy, but only for moment.

As an Elementalist he could feel the bonds pulling at his life-force. It was a cruel and painful torture but, Eiji reasoned, he deserved it. He only had himself to blame for the situation he was in. He had betrayed them and then in turn had been betrayed himself. It was a classic story the betrayer reaps what he sows.

"You led them right to me!" Eiji tried to raise his voice but found an exhausted whisper was all he could manage. "We trusted you, but it seems your arrangement... made you no better off... than me." Eiji gasped as he finished his sentence with difficulty. His body exploded in pain, as it did so, he could hear the chatter from the other place in the back of his mind.

"I... do not know... what you talk of... I am *not* for sale," he answered after a short period had passed, long enough for Eiji to catch his breath.

"You sold yourself to Night! I hope he paid well. You betrayed me, *and* you betrayed Zo." The anger which coursed through his veins returned a little of his strength.

"What?" Seiken's voice rang with an unnatural power, his voice echoed through the prison, as it did so the light from the bindings exploded in an array of colours.

Through the intense light Eiji saw the shock and questions in his face, the confusion, the fear. Seiken cried in pain, slumping against the wall, the bright light fading. That outburst had cost him most of what little energy he had left to feed whatever bound him.

The glow from his bonds exploded again as Seiken reached out to grab his arm. His grip was weak, his hands trembling under the strain of maintain the grasp. The movement of his mouth suggested an unheard protest, until finally his thoughts were forced to be heard.

"I could never betray... my Thea."

"But I saw you," Eiji whispered, he was now not as certain as he had been just moments before. Seiken gasped, his hand falling from Eiji's arm. Those were the last words Seiken heard for a while, his eyes closed and his breathing became inaudible. Eiji reached out to grab him as he fell towards the floor. He could feel the shallow rise and fall of his chest. It took all his strength to rest Seiken back against the wall, his skin was so cold, the feats of his laboured breathing making him clammy to the touch.

As Eiji sat in silence he tried to make sense of things. Seiken had been genuinely shocked, a shock beyond that of mere deception. It even made him question the validity of what he had seen, but that was the problem, he *had* seen him. Seiken had come for him, like death to the aged. But there was no denying his current, weakened condition suggested he had been trapped for some time. He needed answers, answers it seemed he could only get from Seiken. He was certain now there was more to the situation than he first believed. There was no way someone could deteriorate this quickly. It seemed like barely an hour had passed since Seiken had delivered him to Night, but the weak voice had been calling him from the moment he first entered the darkness, at a time when, technically, Seiken was with Night. It just didn't make sense.

Eiji's lungs began to hurt, each breath burning with intense pain. Although Seiken had only been unconscious for around five minutes, the hallucinations had encroached upon Eiji many times. Sometimes he just heard the low murmur of voices, other times he would see a blinding light and hazy images. He continually needed to force himself back to reality, back to Seiken. Thoughts raced through his mind, questions and fears circled on a constant loop. He knew, whatever his captors had planned, he would be in no condition to defend himself.

As he leaned against the cold wall, he tried in vain to gather his strength, all the time listening for the change in Seiken's now audible breathing, an alteration which would mean he was awake. When that change came, it seemed they would have much to discuss.

* * *

Just as Elly had promised, after working their way through the winding maze beneath Phoenix Landing, they had emerged just outside a town.

The town itself was a wonder to behold. It stood proudly just outside the ring of volcanoes, in the midst of an enormous valley which housed a number of smaller vantage points and rises, which concealed anything beyond the settlement from view. There seemed to be a strange aura of power surrounding the whole area.

The town itself had a single storey inn. At most it consisted of seven separate rooms, which would include the eating and social areas. An unknown town such as this, away from the eyes of travellers, would never need to worry about overcrowding. Even should people know of its existence, the journey here was nearly impossible. It made the need for an inn such as this somewhat questionable.

The tavern of this town doubled as a restaurant. A sliding partition, with an embedded door, divided the two places. It had a few well-kept wooden tables outside and huge front windows. The smell of exotic foods filled the air to make all who passed by realise the extent of their hunger.

There were several agricultural barns and storage sheds littered throughout the town. It seemed almost everyone here would lend a hand to cultivate the well-farmed slopes and fields. Since they grew all their own food, it made travel beyond Phoenix Landing unnecessary. Despite the obvious occupation of the town, the area seemed strangely quiet.

"Is it just me, or does this place give you the creeps?" Daniel walked beside Zo down the path which led into the village. The children who weren't currently assisting with the responsibility of the area sat quietly, they didn't play, nor make a sound. They just sat perfectly still, completely silent as they watched them.

"What do you mean?" Acha whispered, slowing her pace to join the hushed conversation.

"A town like this should be filled with noise, the sound of life, even the children are quiet. My home town is easily twice as loud with the noise of life. This is like walking into a ghost town. I suppose it could be our arrival. I guess visitors here would be unsettling considering..." Daniel found he also whispered to adhere to the town's forced atmosphere. "Hey, where's Elaineor?" he questioned noticing she was no longer amongst them. For one horrible moment he thought she may have deliberately stranded them here, knowing they would be unable to navigate the labyrinth acting as a passage beneath Phoenix Landing. He soon realised this would have been pointless. Once night fell, they would be free and anyway. If she was trying to separate herself from them, she would have taken Zo with her.

He cast his vision across the area in an attempt to locate her, as he did so he noticed something peculiar. The land they walked on, and that around them, was very dry and sandy. It should have been impossible to grow anything within these barren soils, yet the area around them thrived with fruit and vegetables, despite the fact that it should have been impossible to nurture life under such conditions.

"She was here a moment ago." Acha also glanced around as she too searched the area for their missing companion. Zo was the only person not to have noticed her absence, and that was mainly because she stood almost paralysed, trying to seize the thread connecting to the memory of this area.

Zo, for a long time now, had found herself referring to her missing memories as threads. They came in three forms, the feeling of déjà vu was a basic thread. Should she seize it and follow it to the memory, it would be something trivial, like remembering she had previously had a drink in the tavern of this town. A recollection of being in this place before, a thread with no real emotional attachment. The second was silver in colour, this was a bond thread. A special memory, if she took that one within her hand, she would remember an important person and some of the details of their time together. Then there was the third type which she classed as a true memory. This would grant her a glimpse into the past, so instead of remembering having had a drink in the tavern, she would know why she was there, and recall the events which transpired.

There were too many to count, the first and third were in abundance, but somewhere in the back of her mind she saw the silver one. These were the ones she treasured most. Her mother's face had been at the end of such a thread when she had first awoken in Crowley. It seemed someone special had been here too, a friend who longed to be remembered, that was the one she reached for as she stared out across the stables to the grazing horses.

"You're travellers aren't you? We don't get many in these parts on account of the labyrinth beneath the Ring of Fire. How did you—" The voice of a young man behind Zo startled her. She turned to look at him as he continued to question how they had come to be here. Not one of them realised this gentleman had referred to Phoenix Landing under the old name, the one Elly had previously used and had since corrected in their presence.

As she took in his appearance, a strange feeling of familiarity washed over her. His hair was short, scruffy, and kept swept back, small flakes of debris from his field clung to it. His skin tone was considerably darker than her own, he looked familiar, but even more frustrating than her own feelings, was the recognition in his eyes. To both be recognised, and see a silver thread, she reasoned it was a location she must have visited a few times in her past. She was certain she had stayed here but, frustratingly, each thread evaded her grasp. It was then he confirmed her fears.

"Ah, Miss Shi, that explains it. Welcome back. I see you have brought some companions. I thought I had seen Lady Elly a moment ago. She was on her way to the inn to book your normal room then I guess." He looked away from her to glance her companions up and down critically, as if making a mental note of them. "As Miss Shi's guests I doubt I need to warn you, but still. As newcomers to this town, and me being the first to approach, it is my duty to inform you that this town is under the control of the Twilight Empire. No form of disturbance will be tolerated. Should you, at any time, disrespect our laws, you shall find yourself facing the judgement of the high court." He glanced towards the highest of the rises as if to suggest that if they travelled beyond it, they would find the place he spoke of. He looked back to Zo and smiled. "Please enjoy your peaceful stay, and sample our fine fruits." He passed both Daniel and Acha a peach coloured, apple-like fruit. After finishing his clearly scripted welcome, he bid them farewell and returned to the fields.

Zo felt her stomach sink. Despite the fact she repeated her words of comfort, the words that gave her strength, she seemed panicked. It was as she had feared, they did know her here, but as someone else. She could barely force herself to turn around to look at her friends as she waited for Acha's reaction. She hadn't wanted her to find out this way, but she hadn't been ready to tell her, not yet. She had needed more time to understand everything before she could approach Acha. Her upbringing alone would cause this revelation to be a shock. It was possible she wouldn't understand. She had wanted time to find the best approach, to break the news to her gently in a way she could understand, without threatening their friendship, but it was too late now. It seemed the farmer had introduced her to Acha without having realised the complications he had caused.

"I've never had a greeting like that before." Acha smiled, looking at the strange fruit within her hand. It had an unusual feel to it, one which could easily be mistaken for a life. She was just about to take a bite when Elly appeared to pluck it straight from her fingers, and place it quickly within her own pocket. Acha stared at her in disbelief for a moment before wrapping her arm around Zo's shoulder. "So, it seems you've been here before, Missy, do you remember anything about this place at all?" Acha smiled, at first she had wondered how it was they addressed Elly by name and title, but referred to Zo as something so unusual. But there were still many strange traditions and cultures she didn't understand. Normally something like that was a sign of respect, or perhaps endearment, either way, it seemed their friend had been here at least a few times, especially to have acquired a 'regular room' at the inn, perhaps their stay here would prove beneficial.

"Huh?" Zo questioned before realising what Acha had said. A few of the worries lifted from her brow. Because of the accent here Acha hadn't really understood what he had said, how he had addressed her. For this she was grateful. It was one less thing to worry about. Once Eiji was safe and they were reunited, she would find a way to tell her. "Oh, yes. I am well-travelled, I think," she responded with a slight shrug. Daniel withheld a sigh of relief. She had already spoken to him about her plans to tell Acha. He was relieved she would get the opportunity to do so on her own terms. It wasn't the kind of subject which could be broached in casual conversation, they needed to approach this delicately. Even now he could still recall the fear in her voice when she had discovered Zo possessed magic, and this would be even more difficult for her to accept, especially given the opinions the two of them had shared on Marise at the table in Zo's cabin. It would be better to try to avoid too much contact with people here, just in case there was a less fortunate repeat of the recent conversation.

Daniel watched Zo carefully as he heard her remind herself of the lesson she had learnt, remind herself she wasn't who people here thought. She was smiling. How he hated that smile. Each time he saw it his heart ached. She wore it as a mask to avoid giving anyone cause for concern, to cover her worries and fears, to disguise her pain. It was empty and he was not fooled by it, unlike those who accepted it without question. He saw the torment reflected in her eyes, he couldn't help but wonder why no one else did. She didn't really smile, not any more.

"I have booked our regular lodgings for tonight. Shall we go to the restaurant?" Elly broke the silence reminding them once more of her presence, only to depart once more at their recognition. They watched as she walked away without even waiting for their answer. By the time they reached her, she had already procured a table and made herself comfortable.

Daniel eagerly grabbed a menu and began to study it intently, his vision panning down the names of the unfamiliar dishes. He had just about shortened his list to five possible choices when Elly plucked it from his hands.

"I have already taken the liberty." She placed the menus to one side just outside their reach. It wasn't long before the waitress appeared. She wore an ankle length black dress with a white apron, similar to those worn by the servants in the house of a lord. In her hands she carried a large tray of food in their direction. Daniel rubbed his hands together in excitement, it had been a long time since he had been given the chance to try foreign cuisine. His mouth watered in anticipation of being one of the first people he knew to sample food from this hidden paradise. He was sure that, given the luscious greenery of the town, the strange fruit and vegetables unknown to the land beyond its borders, he would not be disappointed.

"I can't wait to try the foreign cuisine. It really must be something spe—" His words were cut short as she placed the food before him.

"I thought you would be missing your mother's home cooking, all the products are specially imported." She smiled as he looked to his food in disappointment. "I thought it best to leave the culture to a time when there is not a rescue required. We would not want you to get ill now, would we?" He wasn't sure if she was genuine in her concern. A look of amusement crossed her face as he looked from her to the plate a number of times, before letting out a large disappointed sigh. Resigning himself to the bland looking meal before him, he looked at the strange apple in his hand, at least he still had something to try from this land. He had barely finished the thought when Elly's quick thieving fingers removed it from his grasp, he stared at her in disbelief.

"I suppose you're right," he sighed again, unable to hide his disappointment as he looked back down at the plate of steamed vegetables and meat. He couldn't help but think the dishes being served to the other tables looked and smelt far more inviting.

The waitress hurried back to serve Acha and Zo. As she placed the same meal before Acha, she brushed her blonde hair from her face with the back of her hand, offering a friendly smile before pouring water into the empty glasses on the table. Elly had already started to eat the food she had been given, a mixture of meat and vegetables in a small bowl. It was the same thing she had cooked when they first made camp at the start of this adventure. The waitress placed the same thing before Zo and filled her glass.

"Stew, just like Mum used to make, isn't that right miss?" Her ruby red lips formed a gentle smile. "Would you care to sample some of our local wine, on the house of course." She looked at Daniel and winked, he moved to take the menu once more.

"That would be—" Again Daniel found himself cut off by Elly's interruption.

"No thank you, besides you know we do not accept this kind of compliment, but you could bring us some of your imported Machica." Daniel looked to her in surprise at her choice of words. It was clear she was comfortable here, but to speak so carelessly in front of Acha and himself almost suggested she wanted them to realise something was amiss. Although he knew the farmer had recognised her as Marise, this was the second time Elly had implied they had spent a great deal of time here. First the regular room at the inn, and now implying they knew enough to offer them complimentary items, it made him wonder exactly how much time they had spent here. The use of the word we and our was far too obvious for them to think she had been here alone.

"Yes, Lady Elly, although I must warn you the price has risen considerably since your last visit. Import is becoming increasingly more difficult," she apologised.

"Shipping trouble is it?" She remembered how challenging it had been to negotiate the first shipping contract for this secluded area. Normal export was out of the question. They had to find someone who would keep their secret, someone whose silence could be easily brought by coin and the suggestion of underhanded dealings rather than a secret.

"No, miss, it has just become more difficult since the pirates increased their rates. Of course, we always keep some just in case you should stop by, and since you let us know in advance, we were able to get the meals ready too. You know we can't have anything we import, we only get it for the lord and those in his employ. Now our exported wine is selling well, the handlers are demanding more of the profit, so there isn't much—"

"Sara, kitchen!" A voice commanded, she gave a small bow before hurrying away. As she entered the kitchen, she gave a bottle of wine to a passing waitress who brought it to their table in her place. Elly examined the bottle curiously as she poured the glass. She preferred it when wines had labels, but in this town it was uncommon. The only wine with insignias here were those to be exported. The pirates, who brought items to a nearby, hidden inlet using a merchant boat, dragged the wine and produce in a net, that way they could comply to any searches the authorities demanded. Elly was glad they had accepted her suggestion of using a standard trading vessel. It would have been far harder to keep this place a secret, had a pirate ship been seen to make regular stops here.

"They aren't allowed to try the external produce themselves?" Acha questioned in disbelief. The way Sara had spoken of the imported food had been with such longing that she couldn't help but wonder why it seemed to be taboo. She had been so focused on this she had overlooked the implication that Elly had, somehow, already alerted them to the fact that they would be visiting.

"You have to understand, this town has a very delicate ecosystem. The food here is funded by the exports, they eat what they sow, and their local wine sells well outside. The food they grow is for their own use, the fruit is mainly for the wine.

"The people here, because of the lack of rain and fertile soil, have a completely different genetic make-up," she paused, realising genetics and epigenesis had not yet been discovered outside this town. Being here, combined with the side effects of having a new watcher, had made her less cautious. She had spent too long within this town not to be lulled into a certain sense of security. "That is to say their bodies have adapted to live in these harsh conditions. Some of our food would be poisonous to them." She spoke in a lowered tone. "They have regular import of external foods for those who once lived beyond The Ri—Phoenix Landing."

As they ate, Elly noticed the small restaurant had become quite empty. Out of the ten tables inside, only the furthest two still had people sitting at them. The other diners seemed to have left through the door which led in to the tavern. It was an expected reaction, despite the fact neither of them would cause harm to this place or its people.

"Still, if the wine is expensive, surely the profits should be returned to support the economy here, but this town doesn't look wealthy," Daniel observed, glancing around. Unlike Elaineor, he was not noticing the lack of people, he was focused on the small cracks in the ceiling, and the splits in the wooden walls and doors. Although it was a charming little restaurant, it had seen better days. The interior was more unforgiving in revealing its need of repairs.

"Well I am sure you know the saying, the rich get richer? All profits are utilised by the prison court and areas such as scientific research."

"Prison court?" Acha questioned, unsure if she had heard correctly. She pushed her plate to one side having eaten more than her fill. She had to admit the food had been cooked to perfection, just the way she liked it. It had reminded her of the simple meals she would prepare for her mother and father after her long day labouring the fields. She glanced around, it seemed everyone else was just as satisfied, except for Zo, who seemed to be pushing the food around in her bowl as she sat, deep in thought. Only occasionally would some find its way to her mouth.

"Yes, it is a court that doubles as a prison. Once seized by the Twilight soldiers, criminals are tried and sentenced there, although outside these volcanoes, most people think them a myth." She rolled her eyes as she wondered what about the words, prison court, had the need for further explanation. How more of a concise description could she have given? "It's also a hospital. Come to think of it, the research labs are there too, everything governed by the Twilight Empires," she added. Acha stood and stretched slightly as she listened. Elly knew all too well exactly what was found within the walls, she had spent much time within them. The special facilities here were one of the reasons she had been assigned to this area in the first place. She frequently monitored, even assisted, their progress over the centuries, although once Blackwood became the figure head, she gave this area a wide berth. She had never liked that man much.

"If you don't mind, it's a little stuffy in here, I think I shall go for a walk while you finish up." Acha gave another stretch before making her way to the door. Daniel rushed after her, leaving Elly to continue examining the bottle of open wine which Zo had just poured.

"Are you all right?" He touched her arm gently as she reached the exit.

"Uh-huh," she nodded. "It's been a long time since I've seen a working harvest, it reminds me of home." That was true, but there was another reason she needed to be outside, she could feel the need for energy rising within her. It was better to be as far as possible from any living person when it took what she required. She would hate to be responsible for stealing years from them. After the insight gained in The Courts, she was certain she had gained greater control, and could take just enough from large areas so not to have the same impact she had previously. Her trial in the court had alerted her to how careless she had been and, for some reason, in Eiji's absence, restraint seemed to have become more difficult.

"Do you want some company?" Daniel questioned already knowing what her answer would be.

"No that's all right, but thanks." Daniel nodded, returning to the table where Zo nursed a glass of wine with the same attention she had previously given her food. She had been trying to decide whether or not drinking it would be a good idea, but when met by Elly's stare, she returned it to the table. She disliked knowing that it didn't smell like what they had ordered. The glass had been set down for less than a second when the table jerked to send it, and the bottle, crashing to the floor.

"Oh dear, how clumsy of me," Elly stated without apology. Daniel reached out in an attempt to catch the bottle, but it was too late. It, like Zo's glass, shattered on impact. There was a moment of silence before someone peered around the kitchen door. Seeing what had happened they hurried out to clean up the mess.

* * *

"So what you're saying is, although you have no water, the food you grow is never treated?" Acha rested her chin on her knees as she sat watching the farmer as he worked on the area near her. He had proven to be good conversation. They did everything here a lot like they had in her own time. It was strange to think that she looked back on those days fondly. With all she had seen, all she had experienced, there was still a part of her which remained trapped in the past, a part of her that belonged to that simple time where each day was an effort to ensure the future of those who depended on her. She knew, even despite the experience she had inherited from the person whose body she now possessed, and from the people she touched, that her morals, her beliefs, would always stem from that time, from a time where there was a clear line which divided right from wrong, and shades of grey were non-existent.

"That's right young miss. We just plant them and protect them, after that they take care of themselves." He mopped his brow with the back of his hand before continuing with his work.

"Forgive the questions, but your soil is like sand, and from the climate it's clear you don't get much rainfall."

"True young miss, but beneath that soil life thrives." Their conversation was cut short as what sounded like an argument erupted from the area behind the restaurant. Although the tones themselves weren't very loud, it cut through the silence like a knife. "Oh dear," the farmer sighed, lowering his head to concentrate on his work.

Without a thought Acha jumped to her feet to run towards the restaurant, unaware she had even done so until she stopped around the back, near the kitchen exit. Once there, she heard the voices again.

"I'm sorry it was an accident." Acha recognised the girl's voice instantly it was the one who had served them moments ago, her voice trembled as it filled with fear. Acha pressed her back to the wall as she listened. The streets, even the fields had emptied quickly, only she now stood in the open.

"Don't you realise who she is, what were you thinking?" The voice, which belonged to the man who had summoned her to the kitchen, previously now scolded her quietly. "You could have done some serious harm if they hadn't—"

"I know, I'm sorry, I didn't know it was *that* bottle, truly I didn't," she cried. Acha heard the sound of footsteps as someone paced back and forth as if in rushed contemplation. A short silence passed until the chef spoke once more.

"Run, with any luck you can make it out before they arrive. Don't ask me how, but they'll know and will be on their way. Go, I'll stall them all I can." The girl nodded, her hurried footsteps growing louder until she turned the corner with such speed she could not stop herself from colliding with Acha. She fell from her feet trembling, her eyes filled with fear as she looked up to her.

"Are you in some kind of trouble?" She offered the girl a hand to her feet, a hand which she gratefully took. Even through her gloves she could feel the dormant life which slept within her.

"Please I meant no harm, please don't let them take me," she begged, her brown eyes welling with tears as she glanced around fearfully.

"Who?" Acha questioned, unsure who this girl was so terrified of, so desperate to escape from.

"The Twilight Empire," she whispered almost afraid to speak their name. "I meant no harm to your friends, honest I didn't."

"My friends?" Acha questioned "What's wrong with them?" She resisted the urge to run into the restaurant, from the conversation she had overheard, *they* were fine.

"Nothing, they're fine," the girl confirmed, "I just gave them the wrong wine. It could have poisoned them had they drunk it."

"But they didn't so no harm done right?" Acha couldn't understand why such a simple mistake was being blown so far out of proportion. Surely an apology was more than enough to right the wrong here.

"They won't see it like that," she whispered as she glanced fearfully over the area. It was clear she felt exposed, standing in the open like this.

"Quickly, I know a place you can hide until we smooth this over." Acha smiled reassuringly, placing her cloak over the young lady's trembling body before leading her towards the inn.

When they reached the building, she left her by the window to one of the rooms. It was the only chance they had of finding out exactly what was going on in this town, perhaps this girl could offer some answers about the strained atmosphere. Something was clearly very wrong here, the tension was palpable.

The inn itself was quite large, especially if you were to consider the lack of guests to this area. It was a lot like all the other buildings, built mainly from wood. As Acha had noted previously, this inn possessed windows which would slide open and closed, although this meant there wasn't a full seal around the edge of the window, as they had no rain there was no cause for concern.

Acha took a deep breath before she entered the foyer. It was a small area with a semi-circular wooden-built counter. There was only one route she could take to get to any of the bedrooms, the other seemed to lead to a sitting room and a dining room. She approached the desk, aware that time was short. The girl seemed convinced *they* would be here soon to take her away. The elderly lady sat at the desk, she never looked to Acha, only to the wooden surface before her.

"Elaineor's room please." As she spoke, the lady placed a key on the desk and slid it towards her before pointing her to the left. Acha picked it up, leaving quickly, but not so quick as to cause suspicion. As she entered the room, before doing anything else, she switched the shower on, a precautionary measure to drown out any noise they may cause. It was times like this she was glad that, unlike normal houses, most inns had automatic pumping showers. If it hadn't, then pumping the water pressure for the shower would have taken much more time than they had. She slid the window open and signalled to the waitress.

"They're already here," she whispered, just before a knock came on the door. Acha glanced around the room quickly. When her vision rested on the bed, she knew what she had to do. She tiptoed around to lift the sheets, finding their construction was as she suspected. Material had been sewn over the wooden frame, but the beds themselves were hollow, she signalled for Sara to help her, she tilted the bed to make a slit with Eiji's knife in the bottom of it. Another knock came at the door. It was firmer, louder this time, making them both jump.

"Just a minute," she called as she motioned for Sara to move underneath.

Acha carefully lowered the frame over her before sliding the mattress back into place and straightening the covers. Removing her clothes, she stood in the shower, she took the shower hose from the clasps on the wall off to douse herself with water. As she grabbed the towel, she heard another knock. She had barely reached the door when it came again. She opened it cautiously to reveal two burly men standing in the hallway, one's hand rested upon the wooden surface as if he were about to push it open further, an action he continued with despite her presence there. She felt the heat rise to her face as the two invited themselves in.

"Is there something I can help you with?" Acha tried her best annoyed voice, after all they *had* just dragged her from the shower, and it wasn't exactly comfortable standing before two men in nothing more than a short towel.

"You took your time." Acha looked to the man who spoke, his short black hair was gelled back, and not a single hair was out of place. She looked to the other man, if not for a few subtle differences they could have been mistaken as twins. They both wore a deep purple uniform, although the one who had just spoken was slightly taller than the one now snooping around the room.

"Well, I *was* in the shower," she responded, both men stopped to look at her. It was as if they hadn't noticed until this point that she had been standing before them not only wet, but in nothing more than a towel. They looked from her to the trail of wet footprints. The taller man nodded before his partner vanished into the bathroom.

"Do you often shower with the window open?" The taller man asked, as Acha went to follow his partner, hearing his question she stopped and turned to look at him.

"It stops the glass from steaming, keeps the room dry too," she answered, trying to see what the other man was doing, whilst also attempting to keep watch on his partner who paced the room as if searching for something.

"All is in order sir." The shorter man came to stand by his partner.

"Is there a problem, who exactly are you?" she demanded, her patience had begun to wane.

"Sorry ma'am, we're from the Court of Twilight, a dangerous criminal is at large," the tall one answered. He opened the door to the cupboard, he seemed somewhat disappointed to find it empty.

"We're conducting a search," added the shorter one.

"Please excuse me if I sound rude, but is there anything I can do to hurry this along?" she glanced down at the towel, all too aware that they were now doing the same, their vision lingering far longer than she thought necessary.

"Forgive us, with you being new to the area, we thought she may approach you. It's not very often we get visitors, in fact, I would say it was somewhat of a rarity." The smaller man began to walk around the room again, he seemed to hesitate around the area Sara lay concealed. He studied the cloak which lay sprawled across the bed, his finger shifting it aside to reveal the backpack beneath, as he stepped away Acha couldn't help feel a little relieved. "She's fairly new too you see, you never know with her type."

"Although I am new, I *am* with Elaineor and—"

"Lady Elly?" The smaller man interrupted, on hearing this he instantly stopped his search of the room to look at her again. "Forgive us, we did not realise you accompanied her. Please, forgive the intrusion." He made his way towards the door. "Oh, by the way, have you sampled our fruit?" His hand gripped the door handle tightly as he turned to look back at her slyly.

"Not yet, but I do have two pieces for after the shower." She cringed, hoping someone would not get scolded for their generosity. This town seemed very highly-strung, especially when she considered the trouble Sara seemed to be in for simply serving the wrong type of wine. "Well of course, one belongs to my friend, they're not both mine," she added nervously.

"I see." One of them answered, his tone filled with suspicion.

"Sorry?" she questioned.

"We'll leave you to it, let us know if you see her." They exchanged glances and walked out of the door, stopping only when she called them back.

"See who?" She knew all too well this conversation bore none of the innocence the topic implied, she knew their game very well.

"Ah, did we not say?" The two men smiled turning back to face her.

"No," she answered flatly. It was obvious that this was more than a simple search. They were interrogating her, in a very subtle manner, whilst trying to pinpoint the additional life-forces they felt within the room.

"Oh never mind, I'm sure she would not bother you. She would be a fool to approach Lady Elly's guests, but if you do see her, please advise one of the officials posted here. She's your age, short blonde hair, brown eyes, she worked at the restaurant, I think her name was Sarah, Sara, something like that." He scratched his head as if trying to remember the name. Acha knew this was still part of their scheme.

"Sara?" She pretended to mull the name over. "Oh yes, I think she was the one who waited on us. What did she do?"

"That does not concern you. Please go back to your business." The guards turned and began to walk away. Acha closed the door, she knew all too well they would now stand within hearing range. They were still checking on her despite what they had said, despite her satisfying their questions. She flicked the lock on the door closed as she muttered to herself.

"Damn, I hope there's still water or Zo will kill me." She walked back into the bathroom. Stepping back into the shower she washed her hair. Knowing they were still listening she began to hum. A further five minutes had passed before she emerged from the shower, she dried her hair on the towel before slowly starting to dress. Finally, she heard them leave. She let out a sigh as she closed the window, that had been close. "Sorry about that, they were listening in," Acha whispered pulling the mattress from the bed, she tilted it to allow Sara back out through the split at the bottom.

"Thanks, how did you know about the fruit?" she whispered. "You don't have any do you?"

"Something a farmer said, besides, it was clear they were counting life-forces, and I noticed myself the unusual feel to it, perhaps enough to fool someone's senses. Since they were here so quickly, I assumed they tracked the unusual number of life-forces." Acha smiled.

"But why did you say two, how did you know?" Sara dusted herself down before helping to pull the mattress back onto the bed.

"Well, you're pregnant right?" Acha blushed, the look on Sara's face told her she was wrong, but there was no mistaking what she felt. There was definitely another life within her.

"Ah, no, I will explain later, but not here. Did you say this was Elly's room?" Sara glanced around.

"Yes why?"

"Perfect, there's an exit here to The Courts, it's where I'm heading. She and Marise used it all the time to avoid the climb."

"How do you know that?" Acha questioned amazed at this girl's local knowledge, from her accent it was clear she was not from these parts and from what the men had said, she was new here.

"When I was younger, I heard a rumour Marise Shi was staying here. I wanted to see, after all she and I are the same age, yet she has done so much. The men always spoke of her. I watched them, through the very window you used to grant me entry, as they vanished into the bathroom floor. There's clearly a trapdoor or something." She felt along the floor, her fingers traced over the wooden surface before she pulled one of the planks up, as she did so a whole section lifted with it.

"I shall join you until you're safe," Acha insisted, following the girl down the darkened tunnel. She wondered if perhaps she should leave a message for her friends so they knew where to find her, but she hoped they wouldn't be gone too long. Surely, she would return before anyone had the chance to miss her.

"No need, I am heading to The Courts. I doubt I'll ever be safe." She turned to face Acha who had already lowered the trapdoor above them. "Please, you have already helped enough."

"The Courts?" Acha questioned wondering why she would head to the very place which she was trying to avoid. Then again, going there of her own will was far different to being escorted there as a prisoner, still, she had to wonder what business she could have there, and why she had decided that now was the time to pursue it.

She glanced around the cold stone passage, the layout reminding her of the stories her mother had told when she was a child. Adventurers would always seem to find themselves within a large stone walled tunnel, questing for something to save the world. The tunnels in her mother's stories were always lit by some form of torch, these were not. Instead it seemed the light came from some strange stones which were embedded into the wall every few feet. They emitted an orange glow to keep the lighting just above complete darkness. It seemed to be a straight path and, luckily, Sara seemed to know exactly where they were going.

"I believe they are responsible for my brother's disappearance." She sighed quietly as she continued walking. Acha looked to her in surprise. This had to be the reason she was desperate to go there now, being identified would place her brother in further danger. There had to be more to this situation than a simple mistake with the wine, perhaps she was their intended target. It seemed as if they had been looking for an excuse to apprehend her.

"Then I shall help you. We can find him together, I'm sure of it." She turned to Acha smiling with an obvious relief.

"I never would'a thought..." Sara shook her head gently in disbelief as her sentence trailed off, she quickened her pace, knowing time was short.

"What's that?"

"Oh, nothing," she smiled again.

There was a long silence. The only sound to be heard was their footsteps as they echoed through the stone corridor until Acha finally spoke. There was much she wanted to ask the young lady, so much about this area she didn't understand, but she didn't want to intrude too much, so she chose to return to the conversation they had started earlier.

"What were you saying earlier about the life-forces?" There was no denying what she had felt, it had been playing on her mind for some time. There was no reason she should have felt such a thing through her gloves, perhaps the answer lay in the type of life she carried.

"Ah yes." Sara placed a hand on her stomach. "This land has always been barren, there is no water except for that taken from the sea, and that is only suitable for bathing. It's kind of hard to explain.

"The food here is grown with thanks to parasites that live beneath our ground. They feed on the rich chemicals produced by the volcanoes, and in turn they excrete a nutrient which somehow hydrates the area, allowing things to grow in our sand." She paused a moment in both step and speech as she glanced around as if to ensure they were still alone. When she started walking once more, she continued her story. "For as long as anyone can remember, dating back to the first records, when a child is born, it is taken to The Courts and a young parasite is implanted into the baby. It sleeps inside the body, feeding on the electric impulses of the nerves.

"The nutrients from the food grown here keep both it and the host healthy, that's why our people can only eat food grown from this soil." She paused again, this time it seemed she was in two minds whether to continue her tale or not, eventually she did. "But lately, something strange has happened, the laws have been tightened and people are being taken to the court for no reason and are never returning.

"Three days ago, I received a message from my brother, he was frightened. He wrote about an amazing discovery he had made, a way to wake the parasite. They found while it was awake, the hosts became susceptible to suggestion and control as they fell under the influence of the parasite. It's all a bit confusing really. I don't understand half of what he wrote.

"He went on to write about how only three of his team remained. The bodies of the other three had turned up brutally killed. I knew then I had to come home. When I got here, all I could find of him was his journal. I soon discovered his other team members had also vanished not long before he had, each one of them had turned up mutilated beyond recognition. I only hope we're not too late." Her eyes filled with tears which she quickly rubbed away with the back of her hand.

"You think someone from the Twilight Empire took him?" Acha placed her hand comfortingly on the girl's shoulder as they stopped for a moment in the darkened tunnel.

"I think so. I fear what they may do, they are always more intense when *she's* around. That's the reason I left in the first place, no one is safe when she's here." Sara rubbed her hands up and down her arms. Despite the heat outside, in the depths of these strange tunnels there was a definite chill in the air.

"Who?" Acha had a good idea exactly who this figure referred to. It seemed people had gone out of their way to be nice to her since they had arrived here, but she needed to hear it for herself.

"Your friend," she confirmed.

"Elaineor," Acha sighed, confirming her fears. She had wondered why Elly had been so insistent on coming here. It had seemed they were expected, she vaguely remembered someone saying something earlier which had given her that very impression, and from Sara's story it seemed news of their impending arrival had clearly initiated the events which had transpired with this girl's brother. Even though they hadn't arrived until today, she was certain it had something to do with Elly. It would have been better to stay at another place, somewhere which had someone of skill who could treat Zo's injury. "Why is it wherever she arrives, there's always trouble?" The whole situation in which they now found themselves had started with her arrival. It seemed trouble would greet them wherever they stayed, as long as they travelled together.

"Maybe it's because she travels with that monster, Marise Shi." Sara covered her mouth as soon as the words had escaped. Her eyes shone in fear as she looked apprehensively to Acha.

"What?" Shock lined her voice. It was true she knew Elly had known her. She had referred to their relationship as friends, but to discover she had travelled with her suddenly made her a lot more dangerous than when it appeared she was simply looking for her. What exactly did she plan on doing when they found her? She was certain no one in their group would consent to travelling with that monster. It was all starting to make a little more sense. She had almost pieced together the motive, but there was still something missing, something that prevented her from seeing the situation in its entirety.

"I'm sorry, I meant no harm. She's always been nice to us, she even got my brother the job at the court. Please I beg you, please don't say anything. What was I thinking? She's your friend, I'm sorry." She bowed her head in apology to Acha, who couldn't understand what had triggered this reaction.

"I don't travel with her, just Elly, for the moment anyway. Although, even if what you say is true, as you have seen Marise not with us..." Acha trailed off as a thought crossed her mind. It was something which she had not even considered until Sara had mentioned it. It was a simple case of mistaken identity. Now she thought about it, she could see a few vague similarities to the picture which had been circulated on the bounty. That was one of the problems with sketches, they left a lot open to interpretation. "You mean Zo? According to the bounty details Marise is far taller, her hair is red, and her eyes are green. Although now I think about it, I can see why you were worried, but..." Acha smiled to herself, the thought of Zo being that murderer was just too unreal, but at a glance, it was an easy mistake for this young lady to make.

"Sure as the sky is blue, you travel with none other," Sara enforced, from her wary facial expression it was clear she thought that she was being deceived.

"I see the resemblance now you have said it, but believe me, Zo is kind and gentle," she answered with a mild tone of amusement in her voice.

"Zoella Shi?" As Sara questioned this, Acha suddenly realised that, despite all the time they have been together, she had never asked what her family name was. She vaguely remembered an introduction when they first met, but even then she couldn't recall if it was a formal one. At the time she was more concerned with other things.

"I'm not sure of her family name," she admitted shamefully. The amusement had now faded, especially when she took into account the fear in Sara's voice, a person who had not only lived in this town, but had claimed to have seen Marise with her own eyes. Seeing the uncertainty in Acha's face Sara continued.

"Look, this town..." she started, unsure of how exactly to make Acha see the truth. "Just before the second rise is Blackwood's mansion. It's not common knowledge, I understand that, but they *are* one and the same.

"Years ago, Zoella arrived at Blackwood's mansion. She was about twelve, I think. Marise Shi is her alias. It is the name she uses to cleanse her conscience so she doesn't have to face up to what she's done!"

"If that were true, how come you know this and no one else does?" *'Blackwood.'* Acha thought to herself as she heard the name. *'That's the name of Elly's father, the one who she said Zo served under, the one who wanted her returned. Could it really just be a coincidence he lives here?'*

"Aside from Elaineor and, Zo, as you call her? Well, it's quite simple really, when Zo first arrived here, my brother was at an age where he sought adventure. As a dare he decided to sneak into Blackwood's mansion. I thought I would never see him again after he climbed that wall, but when he returned, I expected to hear all about his adventure, but instead he said nothing.

"After that I heard him sneaking from the house at night. About a month of this occurred before I followed him. I watched as he climbed the balcony and crept through the open window. I followed him, watching as he talked to a girl about my age. She was clearly an outsider, you don't get any with such fair skin tones in these parts, besides Elaineor that is, but she too is an outsider. She's been here so long that people seem to have forgotten this.

"I couldn't understand what this girl was doing there. It was said only his warriors and Elaineor could gain access to the property, from her build it was clear she was neither. Other than Elaineor, there were no other women permitted in the building at that point, even the food was prepared in a separate section. Yet, sure enough I saw her, it seemed she and my brother had become friends.

"I saw the panic in her face as she saw me at the window, but as you said, she was so gentle. My brother introduced us, she seemed happy at the thought of having another friend.

"One day we went to meet her as planned but found not her, but Elaineor. She warned us away. After that, I was scared, for him especially after what Elaineor had said. Six months passed until we saw her again, but something had changed, she seemed so sad and alone. She approached Michael, vowing to protect him no matter what. After this promise, she left for a while, but every night Michael would still sneak out to the first rise, the place we call

Ipsili Thesi. It is the highest point in Phoenix Landing that is not part of the volcanic ring, it is where they would meet.

"One evening I saw her return, knowing where she could find my brother, I rushed to her. As I touched her arm, she drew her weapon as if to strike me, her green eyes greeting me coldly. I knew then it was not the same person who now stood before me. I put the rumour about Marise together with this information and discovered the truth. I tried to warn Michael, but he wouldn't listen.

"A few days later, I found them at Ipsili Thesi, talking as if nothing had happened. I confronted her about Marise, it was clear her denial was nothing but lies. After that, my brother only met with her a few more times. Then she warned him away. She told him it was getting too dangerous, she couldn't trust herself, she was scared, but as long as he was safe, she knew she could find the strength.

"None of it made any sense but he promised to stay away. People from our background don't have many friends, the people of this area have little to do with us. You see after Mother died, she had been his only friend, the only one other than myself that did not avoid him. Our mother was very sick, a mind sickness the physicians said. Those who knew her, feared her family may have contracted it also. It was hard on him when she left, but it was for the best, and now, the same day she returns, he goes missing. Not only that, but she never even asked of him."

They walked in silence for a while, small coincidences leaping to Acha's mind. If all this was true then it explained more than she cared to imagine. It would explain why she had to leave with Elly, and why she could handle a sword. It explained everything, even the difficulty of her trial at the court. It was all starting to make sense, and she did not like what the facts were suggesting.

"This is where we will part." Sara broke the silence as they approached a flight of dimly lit stairs that stretched upwards to ascend into more darkness. It was clear this was the very base of The Courts, she could only imagine what lay above.

"Part?" Acha questioned surprised by this sudden decision. "I said I would help you, didn't I?" Acha heard the distress in her own voice as she spoke. She thought about Zo's lies, and about her own concern about her friends finding out who she really was, especially after hearing Elly's story of the

Grimoire. She had never thought the real threat had been standing beside her all the time.

She had to warn Daniel, but first she had a promise to keep. *'The last Grimoire.'* Acha thought suddenly to herself as the final pieces fell into place. *'That's what this is about. All this time she must have known I was his daughter. She planned it from the very beginning. All of this is her plan to get the final book. Elly said she was cunning, but I didn't even realise. I trusted her without question, I had no reason to doubt her. I let my friendship cloud my judgement, she bewitched me.'* Acha scolded herself silently as she grew angry about the truth she had just discovered, angry she had been so blind not to see it from the start. She was certain now Sara's words were true, everything had finally fit into place. Zo had retained Hectarian powers, they had been told plainly that only someone possessing these artes could retrieve the Grimoire. Then it had been revealed that Marise had been the one who retrieved them. Acha knew she should have realised the truth then.

She was shocked when she had discovered that Zo was a witch. She had taken to heart the tales of such creatures from her time. She knew they were beings of malice, yet due to their friendship, their bond, she had managed to overlook it, despite knowing such monstrosities could not be trusted. She could see now what a fool she had been, such things were masters in manipulation and she had certainly been deceived. After all, what use were her Hectarian artes if her hands could not retrieve the Grimoire, had this been the intention all along, had she been deceived from the time of their first meeting, and what of Daniel? It was unlikely he knew the truth given the conversations they had shared in private regarding this murderer.

"I appreciate it." Sara smiled moving to sit on the steps to take a short break. It looked like her companion could use one.

"It's the least I can do. You have just helped me more than you could imagine." She sat on the steps beside Sara, worrying now not only about what lay ahead, but what she had left behind too. Daniel was alone with her, clueless. She could only pray he would be safe.

* * *

"I don't know about you but I feel really comfortable here," Zo expressed contently, leading Daniel to the peak of the rise where a huge tree grew. It stood proudly on the grass as if keeping vigil over the lands. She glanced in the direction of the town before taking a seat. Had she taken the time to truly take in her surroundings, comfort would not have been what she felt. It had been a steep climb, but this location had seemed so familiar that she felt compelled to come here. She sat in the shade of the tree watching the clouds. Her shoulder seemed to grow increasingly more painful, but Elly was going to attend to it after obtaining the necessary supplies. Until then, she had to rely on her medicine to suppress some of the discomfort.

'*Shall we count the stars?*' A voice whispered to her mind, for a brief second she thought it was Daniel. She was about to question him on his choice of words considering the hour, when she realised it had been a voice she couldn't quite place. This was the first time a thread had spoken to her to gain her attention. It called to her from her memories as it begged to be retrieved, yet the harder she tried to seize it, to remember, the more she lost of what she had caught. In the second it had whispered to her, she swore she had almost remembered something, someone important.

"Lying here in the shade of this tree, I feel like I could have done this a hundred times before." Zo sighed contently. For the first time since their journey had begun, she felt comfortable, even the pain seemed to dull slightly as she relaxed. She felt guilty, especially when she considered one of their friends found themselves facing such grave danger. Daniel walked the area slowly, he looked down on the mansion below, a mansion which was shielded from the town's view by this cliff. It was then he identified the gnawing sensation which had been following him for some time.

"Zo, the name of the lord Elly mentioned when you first met, her father, it's Blackwood, right?" Had she not been so focused on trying to find the silver thread, she would have detected the strange tones held within his voice, or even the effort he made to suppress his feelings. Despite the fear recalling parts of her past now held, this particular thread felt safe, comforting. Thus, as she lay watching the fine, brilliant white clouds drift overhead, she wasn't really paying much attention to Daniel at all. It was a few moments before she even realised he had spoken, and when she realised what he had asked of her he felt her defences fortify, as if to protect herself from the recollection of who she was.

"Yes, why?" She answered with a feigned calmness, but inside she felt the panic rise as she wondered what would make him ask such a thing. Why would he bring up a part of her past that he knew she did not wish to recall?

Turning her head, she took her gaze from the clouds to focus upon him. Seeing his expression, she sat up quickly, splinters of pain radiated from her injury, protesting against her sudden movement. This was more than just the passing curiosity his initial tone had implied.

"It appears he has a second home here." He pointed to an area enclosed by tall walls, within it stood several small buildings which surrounded the mansion. The main building itself stood three storeys high and was constructed from stone. It was clearly a relic from the old world, parts of it had been repaired by people possessing far less knowledge in such things as those who had initially constructed it. The material used for repairs didn't blend well with the original composition.

It appeared as if Blackwood had wanted any who looked upon it to acknowledge that this was his home. Outside, on one of the large walls, was an enormous plaque that clearly displayed his name for all to read.

Daniel had been suspicious for some time. He had overheard someone speaking of this Blackwood character earlier as they made their way here. Thankfully, Zo had been focused on other things. He had questioned whether or not he should tell her, he finally decided it was for the best. It was better to inform her now than have her discover the truth by other means. Besides, it wasn't as if his mansion could be easily overlooked from their position, he was surprised she hadn't noticed it herself during the climb.

"Don't you find it suspicious that Elly didn't happen to mention it," he added. Zo rose quickly to her feet, her injury, its obvious pain, forgotten, as she began a quickened descent in the direction of the buildings below. "Hey, wait up," he called after her, aware of exactly how much distance she had put between them, not only physically but mentally. He didn't need to be connected to her to know exactly where she was going and what she wanted. She wanted answers.

Chapter 18

Betrayal

It seemed a long time since Marise had lived within the confines of Blackwood's mansion, so since hearing news of Elly's approach he had been filled with the same excitement as all those years ago, when she had first brought him news of the mission's success. It had been an important milestone in the creation of his assassin, the release of her darkness. As Blackwood awaited her arrival, he found himself thinking back to the day he first received news that his ambitions had finally been realised. He had been granted power beyond imagining, and he had been the one to give Marise her name. In doing so he believed he had created a bond stronger than any other.

It had taken hard work and dedication to shift the balance, but Elly was never one to disappoint his expectations. His heart leapt as he saw the silhouette at his door. At last waiting would be over.

"So she *is* here." Blackwood rose to meet his guest. He had expected her visit for some time now and he had been growing impatient.

Elly could not help smiling to herself as she entered his domain. It was his throne room, or war room depending on his mood. To the far side was a jewel encrusted throne that he—as the self-appointed king of all he surveyed—would sit upon to relay his orders. Like his study, it had many hidden chambers, some covered by curtains and others simply hidden so well that they were impossible to detect. This was his favourite room, more often than not his next targets would be brought here, in secret, to be shown to his assassin, so she could hunt them should he not win their support.

"Yes," Elly replied, her tone short and to the point as always. She stared at him as she awaited his next question.

"Well, where is she?" he prompted after a short pause. He tried to look behind her despite knowing that she wouldn't be there.

"That is none of your concern." As she entered, she forced Blackwood back a few paces as she closed the door behind her. "It was unfortunate we had the need to travel this way, an unavoidable detour, but know this, she shall never be yours again." She smiled, even now she could feel his anger bubble under the surface of his cool exterior. He paced back and forth across the length of his table for a moment before losing the calm exterior he had tried to portray. He slammed his hands upon its surface, yelling as he did so.

"What! What are you talking about? Your job was to return her to me!" he screamed. The anger he had held so composed just moments ago, now released in force. "Are you forgetting who you work for?" he snarled. If he had the strength, she was certain he would have overturned the table. She watched him with a smile.

"No, but perhaps you are." She saw the dawning realisation fill his eyes. It had been so long since she had allied with him that the details of her origin had almost been forgotten.

Night had always been kind to him. He had granted him this mansion and control over the Twilight Empire, all this he received in gratitude for the tasks he would accomplish. Yet, had it not been for Elly, none of it would have been possible. It wasn't that she was jealous, she didn't want power or gratuity for her work. The appreciation she was given far surpassed that of material gain, but she could not understand why he employed such a weak, dirty little rodent like Blackwood. There were obviously far better choices, people far more qualified for the roles he had been given.

"Stay away. This is the only warning you will receive, and the reason for my presence. Now if you will excuse me, I have business to attend to." She slowly walked up the stairs aware of the defeated looks he gave her as he watched her leave.

Once the door had closed behind her, Blackwood smiled to himself. He had no intention of looking for her, she would come to him. Elly did not give him the credit he deserved. He had known that she would return without her. She thought him a fool unwise in the passions the two of them had shared, but Marise had done so in loyalty to him. He knew unquestioningly that Marise would seek to return. Such was clearly the reason for her absence. Elly was keeping them apart. He had spent many hours in preparation for his audience with Elaineor, but he held all the cards now, or more specifically the only one that mattered. All he needed to do was wait. After all, once Marise awoke, he was certain she would choose to be beside him, not only in light of Elly's betrayal, but because she had always favoured him. Each time he had insisted Elly journey with her, or they spent time in training, he had to convince her to leave his side. She would choose him, of that, he was certain.

✻ ✻ ✻

"Are you sure you know what you're doing?" Daniel rushed after her, although they were now on level footing, he still found it difficult to keep pace. Her stride remained steady and determined until she stood at the foot of the giant wall surrounding the mansion. It was only then she hesitated. "What do you plan on doing, what answers can he give you?" She turned to look at him with the same heart-breaking smile he had seen all too often. He touched her arm finally catching up to her. The mansion wall now towered intimidatingly above them.

"I don't know," she whispered. The smile faded a little and he felt her fear, even through the walls she had constructed. She was frightened for so many reasons, the main one being that this would prove, beyond a shadow of a doubt, the truth behind her identity. Even if it was something she now understood, this was the first time she would be confronted with the truth. For some reason she felt as if she needed to understand this persona better, as if by doing so, it would give her some power to control it. Daniel feared it would do just the opposite. The more she discovered, the worse things would become.

"Then why, why put yourself through all this?" Daniel already knew the reason. She needed answers, answers to questions she had not even considered yet. She wanted to know the how and why of what had happened, of how Marise was created. Only by understanding this could she hope to find a way to stop her, a way to protect her friends from the murderer within, to stop her being so afraid of being alone with him, with anyone, in case she tried to hurt them again. Despite trying to push the incident from her mind, it was something she saw each time she looked at him. "Okay, I understand, but what are you going to do?" His voice was so gentle it was almost a whisper.

She turned to lean against the mansion wall. It was easily four times their height, it would be nearly impossible to scale without help. Her only way of entry would be to walk right through the front gate, not that either of them anticipated there being any problems with that.

"I don't know," she sighed. She had come this far, so close to answers, yet now here she hesitated, afraid of what may be found just over these walls. It was so easy to get here, but getting through the gates would be the hardest step, and once they had been taken, there would be no turning back, whether the gates led to her freedom, or sought only to imprison her further.

"Did you hear?" An anxious voice called out; the voice grew louder as if its owner hurried towards them. No doubt he was on his way to join the other guards as they stood vigil at the guardhouse near the main entrance.

"No, what?" another questioned. Zo and Daniel stood in silence, listening carefully.

"Well, I heard it from Alfie, he just escorted Lady Elaineor to Lord Blackwood. It seems Miss Marise is in the village, but Lady Elaineor refuses to bring her home."

"That's hardly surprising." Spoke the same cool voice. It seemed he knew more on this topic than he had first indicated. "Nothing gets past her, he's a fool for even trying. She properly knows he imprisoned that friend of hers, and wishes to avoid unnecessary bloodshed. You know Lady Elly has always watched out for us." There were a few murmurs of agreement, Daniel and Zo exchanged silent concerns.

'*When did you last see Acha?*' Zo questioned silently as a sickening feeling rose to her throat. She did not like what was being implied by their excited gossip.

"Tell you what, I wouldn't like to be on duty when she finds out. I wouldn't even like to be on the island. It's not like she'll just walk in calmly, and it'll be us who are in her way," one of the guards stated.

'*Not since she left the restaurant,*' he answered remembering how he had offered to go with her. While he had been exploring with Zo, he had been too focused on the whispers about Blackwood to wonder where she had gone. It was only now he realised just how much time had passed.

Daniel cringed, he knew what she had planned even now. She dusted herself down, unfastened her hair, and began to march towards the source of the voices, anger and determination filled each step. Daniel heard the conversation die, no doubt as she stood before them. He began to follow, ensuring he remained out of view so he could move quickly to intervene if he was needed, although he wasn't exactly sure how much help he could be in this situation.

"Where is my friend?" she demanded. Even from around the corner, the anger in her voice made him shudder. Her voice was cold, heartless. There was no way they would dare not to answer. The mantra in her mind grew weaker and more desperate as she was faced once more with the undeniable truth. *'I am not a killer, I am not a murderer.'*

"A-at the courthouse, M...Miss, that's all we know. They were taken there today, please that's all we know." The guards fell to her feet, their heads to the ground as they bowed before her, hoping for forgiveness, hoping to live another day. She felt herself blush slightly, hesitating unsure what to say, or even how to react. She tried to push the panic away, repeating her magic words, words which eased the nausea brought by the truth of her past.

"I think it's best that no one knows you're here." Daniel turned the corner to stand beside Zo. There was an air of authority in the way he carried himself. He had to make them believe he was in charge, that Marise would do as he instructed. He tried to carry himself with the same aura of power as Elaineor. Zo seemed a little lost about what to do as she stood in silence with the figures grovelling before her. She was shocked at the fearful reaction portrayed by the guards. They were terrified of her. "I am sure the guards understand." Daniel gave them a meaningful look, they glanced up briefly to nod frantically. They understood, his words were an attempt to spare their lives. Zo nodded gratefully at Daniel.

"Tch. You are right as always." The disappointment in her tone was clearly evident. Since she stood before them, she may as well play the role. "They are fortunate you arrived when you did." She fingered the hilt of her sword meaningfully, an action she somehow knew was familiar to her alter-ego. Letting out an annoyed snort of breath, she turned and walked slowly away. Once they were certain she had left the vicinity, the guards once more rose to their feet, but not before offering silent thanks to the Gods that they had been granted such mercy. Once the higher powers had been thanked, they turned to thank the one before them, the one who had intervened in order to spare them.

For a moment, Zo hadn't been sure her shaking legs would carry her around the corner before they kept their promise of giving beneath her. But she had made it and now leaned back against the wall as she waited for Daniel. It seemed Eiji's was not the only rescue mission which needed planning. She could only guess what they had in store for Acha, it was clear Blackwood planned to use her to gain an advantage, but to what end?

Even from her position, she could hear the guards still thanking Daniel for sparing them. The question of who he was, not even a consideration, it was not relevant. The fact he had just saved their lives was the only important detail.

"You're lucky she listened this time, but if Blackwood were to discover—"

"No sir, I understand, she, nor you, were ever here. Thank you." They repeated their thanks and promised not to breathe a word several more times before he finally managed to separate himself from them.

"Very well," Daniel stated, finally able to walk away. For a moment he had concerns as to whether they would attempt to follow him, but their better judgement saw they remained at their post. As he turned the corner, he saw Zo supported only by the wall at her back. Until then he had thought the guards had looked scared. He had wondered what she had expected to encounter, did she not think the guards would be afraid of Marise? It had been a reaction which made the truth she had to bear heavier. Despite the fact they were meant to be allies working under the same man, they honestly believed that she would have killed them without a second thought. It made her question the kind of monster she truly was.

"I don't know what his plan is, but we need to save Acha." As she looked up to him, he saw her wipe the tears from her eyes in a subtle movement as she once more fastened her hair back.

"You know—" He placed his hand delicately on her arm, as if on cue Elly appeared to interrupt him.

"I thought I may find you here," she interrupted, as she saw Zo and Daniel dangerously close to the place she had once called home. "It was only a matter of time until you discovered where we were."

"Elly!" Zo's voice filled with relief. She never thought she would have been so glad to see her. It was everything she could do not to embrace her.

"Do you plan on finding some answers?"

"She's already found one," Daniel answered coldly. "It seems Blackwood has taken Acha."

"I knew there was something insincere about that tantrum of his. He must have orchestrated it, knowing I had no intention of returning you. Did you discover her whereabouts?" She had grown so very tired of Blackwood's childish games, but she had to applaud him, this was an action guaranteed to get their attention, but it wouldn't yield the results he had anticipated. There was no need for them to go within the walls of his mansion, she had a feeling they already possessed all the information they needed.

"The guards informed us they had taken her to the court." Zo joined the conversation, her voice sounding peculiar to her ears. She felt strange, almost as if she was watching everything from somewhere very far away. Somehow none of what was happening seemed real.

"He planned to use her as a means to see you returned. We must hurry, it is about time I told you the truth of this place." She knew from the silence of the guards they would remain true to their word. They wouldn't dare even whisper what had just transpired. They were lucky in that respect, their silence was the only chance they had of getting Acha back quickly. If Blackwood were to discover they knew, there was no doubt he would take drastic measures to stop them. If he thought things were not going his way, he would kill her without hesitation.

* * *

"So anyway, what's your name?" Sara leaned forwards from her place on the steps to take in her appearance. Acha's short dark hair framed her now pale complexion as she looked up to her. She was unable to bring herself to smile as she answered.

"Acha. Sorry, I didn't realise I hadn't introduced myself." She hesitated as she decided whether or not to offer her hand. She decided against it. The area where they now sat resting felt colder than when they had walked the stone hallways, she realised she was shivering.

"Acha?" Sara smiled as she repeated the name gently as if to commit it to memory. "That's an old name, from around 100 Z.E. if I'm not mistaken." Sara stated, glancing up the stairs impatiently.

"Close, 150. That's when I was born at least." Acha smiled, her vision followed Sara's timid gaze up the mountain of stairs which led the way to her brother. They seemed rested enough, yet both of them seemed hesitant.

"Your name you mean? That's when your name was born." Sara covered her mouth as she giggled, even so it seemed to be a display of nerves rather than amusement. Acha nodded, realising how strange her statement would sound to someone who did not know the circumstances surrounding her existence. She was accustomed to talking freely to her companions, she hadn't even considered the need for caution with a stranger. Honesty just came so naturally to her, of course, with recent events it was clear this was not the same for *everyone* she travelled with.

"Something like that, so what's your plan?" She was aware of Sara's increasing impatience, her face had grown serious and weighted with worry as she realised they must soon press on.

"Plan?" she questioned. It was clear she had been so concerned with getting here she hadn't even considered what to do once she arrived.

"Well, we can't just walk in and expect them to take us to your brother." Acha touched Sara's hand gently.

"I see." Her face seemed to drop as the glimmer of hope in her eyes began to fade. "I guess I didn't really think it through, maybe I should have told—"

"Nonsense, we don't need anyone's help, just a plan." Acha cut her sentence short. There was no way she would consider asking for *their* help, not after what she had just discovered. She smiled a weighted smile as she saw the hope rekindle in Sara's eyes.

"Well, we need to find out where he was taken," she volunteered. It was an obvious comment and Acha knew that if this place was anywhere near as large as the facsimile in Darrienia, they could be lost for hours. It was time—from her understanding of Sara's tale—that they did not have to waste. They needed to attend to matters before anyone could become suspicious.

"How about we walk around until we find him? We have to start somewhere." A sudden thought dawned on her. It was an unusual idea, and whether or not it would work was something she wouldn't know until she tried, but there was no other option. It wasn't as if someone would just give them a map and lead them to where they needed to be. "If we don't come across too many people, I can make sure they don't see us." She saw Sara's face light with joy.

"You possess the power of invisibility?" Awe filled her voice as she jumped to her feet, a new excitement filling the air around her.

"Well, no," Acha answered. "But I *think* I can influence people so they don't remember seeing us, I think," she repeated. "But for the most part let us hope they are too engrossed in other things to notice we don't belong." Sara nodded as Acha began the ascent into the darkness. Her stomach fluttered nervously, all of a sudden, she had more to do than she cared to think about. She had to help Sara rescue her brother, then she had to speak with Daniel, and rescue Eiji, '*one thing at a time,*' she told herself.

* * *

"You need to do this alone." Elly stopped without warning to stand at the start of the steep path which led towards the court. They gazed down upon it in awe. The Court of Twilight was almost identical to the one they had seen crumble in Darrienia, with two apparent differences, this one was above ground and its size, while immense, remained within the bounds of comprehension.

Zo stood in awe for a moment as she wondered how such a thing could still stand. Relics and buildings from the previous era were said to have been destroyed during the war between Zeus and Kronos. She wondered how many times she had stood here before, how many times had she looked at this very sight, and whether she was always filled with such awe. Elly spoke, intruding on her thoughts.

"If I am not mistaken, the guards will soon be approaching the village. He will have sent an escort for you. He will want to tell you in person of his deed, to bargain with you and assess your current worth. If we are not in the village, he will grow suspicious, which could have disastrous consequences for your friend.

"I shall try to occupy them, whereas you, Daniel," she turned to look at him, "you must hold the attention of the rest. Do so by having them truly believe she is with you somewhere in town. Hide, creep, and run as if to shield her for as long as you can avoid them." She looked back to Zo. "Now will be the best opportunity for you to go. Security will be light." Elly placed her hand on Zo's shoulder seeing the look of doubt and fear in her eyes. "Remember who you are. If you doubt for just one second, you will put us all in great danger. Acha's life depends on your ability to convince them, as does ours. You must return before Blackwood grows suspicious."

Elly reached forwards to make a few minor adjustments to her clothing. Little by little Zo had been adopting Marise's attire, need alone saw she now found herself wearing her complete wardrobe so, for the moment at least, she looked the very image of the assassin, well almost. There was still one detail in need of correction. Elly pulled the leather tie from Zo's hair to complete the illusion. It was enough to see no doubt would be raised, even so, everything relied on her ability to act like a person she so desperately wanted to escape from. She had to think and carry herself like someone who placed no value on other people's lives, who found joy in bringing suffering to others. Zo feared how well she could uphold this guise if she were confronted inside the walls of this prison. Then there was part of her which was concerned she would attune herself so perfectly that she would never retrieve what she would lose in the pretence. But none of that mattered now. For her friends she would become the very thing she feared and despised. She would be Marise.

Elly's sole concern was that there had been insufficient time to repair her shoulder. The temporary measures in place would have to be adequate, but it was less than ideal. The wound was clearly troublesome, just by watching her gait it was painfully obvious that she was injured. Marise was known for being untouchable. An injury on Marise was inconsistent with her image, even when they did occur, with how well Marise managed pain, and the manner in which she carried herself, no one was ever suspicious. No one ever saw any weakness from her, except for Elly.

"Zo, I will not fail you," Daniel asserted, placing a hand lightly on her shoulder before he turned to leave. It was clear she struggled with what awaited, not only had her fears been confirmed, now she had to become the embodiment of them. She had started to close her mind to him, to erect walls as she created the image of exactly who she had to become, and how she was expected to behave.

She did not answer, but simply looked at the great building before her with a feeling of foreboding. Its image distorted in her mind, her fears twisting it to become a horror beyond all perception. She pictured how Marise would act, piecing together the information she knew and had heard, her guise had to be perfect. So perfect that even she herself would believe it. Despite all the things which could go wrong, all the fear and concerns, she found putting one foot before the other was not quite as difficult as expected. After all what she was doing was far more important than anything she felt. She could not fail, but there was a part of her that warned the steps she now took marked the beginning of the end.

The court towered over her, the urge to stare at it in awe had long vanished. She just wanted to escape it as soon as possible.

Had the court been, or signified, anything else, it would have been a sight to behold. Its tall shadow stretched menacingly across the uneven landscape to reach as far as the mountains lining the land's edge. Its strange windows and the eerie light that shone from within were made from relics of a time long past, nothing like this existed anywhere in the world. It was breath-taking, frightening, and something she hoped to never see again.

As she approached, she threw her shoulders back to straighten her posture, ignoring the almost crippling pain to the best of her ability. With her head raised high she walked with confidence. It was harder than she thought to maintain this illusion, but she did suddenly have a clear understanding of why people said Marise was taller. Her confident posture alone had added inches to her height.

The door opened quickly before her, but despite this she gave not so much as a glance to the doorman, after all, he should be thanking her for allowing him to hold it for her, or at least that is how she would think. He stood to attention as she passed, his sigh of relief audible, even through the glass as the door closed behind her. She wondered if they had seen her coming or if there was always a person standing vigil here.

The entrance had taken her into a magnificent foyer which consisted of four possible paths. The room was filled by a large reception, with small wooden tables and chairs placed in seemingly random locations. Nothing within these walls seemed to belong, everything seemed more advanced. Even the lighting was different than that she knew, it was certainly not powered by flame or magic.

She walked straight into this area, hoping nothing would be determined from her quick glance around. She knew, having been here many times, hesitation would only prove to draw suspicion. She quickly chose a random door hoping that her choice would not see her in a storage cupboard. Surely, she would not need to justify her actions anyway. Marise was feared, and regardless of how stupid they were, surely no one would dare to question her actions.

She had decided within seconds her choice and committed to the decision. Despite her doubts and fears she showed no hesitation as she walked towards the double doors situated just past the reception area. She could only hope she had made the right choice. Time was of the essence, she could not afford to get lost in a building of this magnitude.

The receptionist glanced up with a friendly smile, a smile which soon faded when she saw who had entered. She looked away quickly, suddenly finding herself overwhelmed with imaginary work. Not that this pretence mattered, Zo had ignored her completely as she walked to her destination, all the while attempting to determine if she would need to push or pull. But it seemed even the doors here feared her, they opened as if by magic.

The corridor she had entered seemed to stretch on forever and, despite the many doors leading from it, all was still. Everything seemed so clean, from the sterile looking white tiled floor to the whitewashed walls. Her footsteps echoed sharply through the unnaturally cool air. The hairs on the back of her neck prickled, she could only hope this feeling was due to the coldness of the corridor. She repressed a shudder with difficulty and continued her steady pace as she listened intently for the sound of approaching footsteps.

As she walked through the winding hallways, it didn't take her long to realise she was completely lost. She wandered aimlessly, the beating of her heart grew louder and louder, racing in time with the approaching footsteps. She already knew what she had to do, she needed information and fast, she could not afford to waste any more time.

The footsteps were closer now, two people approached, they were so busy studying their paperwork they had yet to see her.

Just because she knew what must be done, didn't mean she felt confident she could execute it. She could only hope that she was convincing, after all too much was at stake for her to fail. She refused to lose the bonds of friendship which she had waited so long to form. It wasn't just being nervous about the act that was to follow which made her heart race. It was a combination of her feelings of insecurity, desperation and a silent part of herself answering her fears. It whispered to her an unnerving thought.

'*If they do realise, I would just have to kill them.*' Her heart skipped a beat. The thoughts of the murderer sometimes merged so seamlessly in with her own that even she couldn't distinguish one from the other. She concentrated on her words of comfort, reminding herself of the differences between them.

'*We are the same, you'll see.*' The thoughts taunted. Zo tried to ignore her growing concerns regarding how Marise had grown so strong so quickly.

'*I am not a killer.*' The more she repeated it the more comforting the words seemed. It was a technical truth, after all she had never stained her hands with another's blood. The day that happened would be the day Marise won, the day Zo would lose all she believed in. It was a small line between life and death, but this paper-thin line, no matter how fine, meant something so enormous it kept her sane. It reduced her fears, no matter how much she appeared like that murderer, they were not the same. '*I am not a killer,*' she thought again, the truth that gave her the strength to suppress the assassin.

Steadying her breath, she once more straightened her posture, preparing herself to approach one of the two men who walked towards her. They were dressed identically in long white laboratory coats. Their heads remained low, their pace steady, pretending they couldn't see her as they walked past. The papers one of them had been shuffling in an attempt to avoid her view, flew from his hands as she touched him. It was almost as if the touch itself had brought immense pain. His colleague watched in horror as she grabbed him from behind, his head snapped forwards under the force of her pull, his partner quickening his pace to leave him alone to face her wrath. There was no other choice, not after the warning glance he had received when he had hovered uncertainly.

"Where has Blackwood put my prisoner?" she growled, her voice filled with both anger and intolerance.

'*You should have killed the other to loosen his tongue.*' Marise's voice whispered to her. It was not really a whisper as such, it was just a thought which seemingly stemmed from nowhere. She had been getting them more frequently lately, thoughts that would simply appear, mingling with her own.

"P-P-Prisoner?" the man stammered. The colour drained from his face as she pulled him to one side, away from the room he had been about to enter. He was clearly petrified, in the hidden depths of her mind, she couldn't help feeling some sympathy for him. As she held him pinned to the wall, she was aware of the spreading damp patch down his trouser leg. Only her words of comfort allowed her to continue without fear, because even if they thought she was Marise, this was the line which divided them. A line Zo treasured with all of her heart and one which meant that when she had finished with him, this frightened man would live.

"Yes," she snapped in an impatient, authoritarian tone. The man had now begun to tremble uncontrollably, he raced his hand through his once neat black hair as he nervously shifted positions under the weight of her stare. His back pressed firmly against the wall, panic closed his throat and stole his words.

"Erm, I..." he swallowed finally forcing the words free. He tried to regain just a shred of his composure but failed. "The only person they brought in today, well the details are confidential." He shrank slightly as he met the intensity of her cold stare, he pulled at his collar as he swallowed. "Not to you of course," he laughed nervously, "I was just saying—" She grabbed his lapel pulling him closer, despite her being shorter than him, it had the desired effect. "Hospital ward, recovery room three." He slid to the floor when she released him, his legs failing to hold his weight. She stood over his trembling figure, looking down on him as if he were less than worthless, and with that final gesture she began to walk away.

"Erm. Miss," his voice broke. "They have updated the door systems, and erm... well, please take mine." His hand was shaking so badly, the small flexible pass vibrated in his fingers as he tried to force himself to stand. She waited for him to bring it to her before snatching it from his petrified grasp. He cowered back to make himself small against the white wall, a place he stayed until long after she had left.

* * *

The last door stood before her now, the pass had not proved useful. Looking at it, she wasn't even sure what it did, whenever she approached a door it had either opened or been opened for her by whoever was near. Those opening them for her seemed to possess similar pieces of this strange supple material, which they seemed to show the door before it opened.

She stood now within the medical area, a section larger than she had hoped, and more extensive than she would care to have imagined. She had been fortunate, her search had been assisted considerably simply because she had made a mistake, one that found her in a small windowless room. Standing to attention within this area was another person, one who after greeting her politely had asked where he could take her. She had ordered him to take her to the hospital section as the doors had closed behind her. She had watched him suspiciously, his nervous fingers causing a strange illumination to appear on the wall before him. She waited impatiently for him to lead the way, his inaction seeming to warrant further persuasion. She had been ready to challenge him when the doors behind her had opened once more and she found herself exactly where she had needed to be.

The lift operator, realising the predicament he was in, had sensibly disabled all other floor collection sensors, permitting a smooth and speedy trip to her desired location. He could see her growing impatience as she waited. He prayed for the machinery to pull them up through the walls at a faster pace. For a moment, just before the doors had opened, he had feared for his life.

She had saved so much time with this approach. As long as she kept sight of the truth, she did not fear people mistaking her for the cold-blooded murderer, nor did she fear she would lose herself in their belief. Stepping out into the large foyer, she continued on her way. Even without the need for contact, she could feel the pain of the people who resided in there, pre-death pains which were beyond her skill to relieve nor, as Marise, would she have attempted to. As she walked, she managed to ignore the pleas for death from the rooms. She had long lost count of the number of people she had passed.

On the approach to the courts Elly had prepared her for what she may encounter. She had explained how this place was used for human experimentation. She dared not linger, fearing that if she were to see what had become of some of those who begged for death, it would shatter her fragile disguise. She stood before the final door on the ward, waiting while a young nurse hastened to unlock it.

She stepped inside the dark room without hesitation. Her every instinct screamed for her to look but she knew Marise would not. As the door closed, she felt the chill of a call to Hermes upon her neck, her stomach sank as she felt the stigma of death within the room. She could only hope she was ready for the challenge of repelling Hades' collector.

There was a slow, rhythmic beeping from somewhere near the back of the room, the beeps chimed in time with the faint heartbeat she sensed. As her eyes adjusted to the dimness, she could see a single bed with padded metal guards, similar to those found on a child's bed. The entire room was filled with ancient technology, although she could not understand any of its purpose. Her back pressed against the soft padded door in fear of what she would find should she approach the bed. She could still hear Elly's words.

'*They use the ward for many kinds of human research experiments. Who knows truly what goes on within those walls, and for what purpose.*' There had been a cruel smile as she had told her this. Once again it was clear she knew more than she was willing to say, but this time, she had not wanted to know what secrets were being hidden. The fact Marise could walk around so freely showed she too had seen more of this place than she would like to have believed. She felt the padded wall around the door in an attempt to find some form of lighting, but she met with failure. Her eyes continued to adjust to the darkened room as she made her way to the bed.

"Acha?" she whispered almost afraid of being overheard, something which she knew was impossible if she believed the nurse's words about the room being insulated to ensure privacy.

Wiping her clammy hands across her top, she timidly approached the bed. Carefully and quietly she lowered the restraining bar which was attached to its side. But before she could touch the figure who lay before her, a voice startled her.

"Zoe." The figure sighed wistfully, "I'd know that voice anywhere. I knew you'd come back," it whispered weakly. She knew immediately that this was not Acha, although weak, the voice which spoke to her in whispers was male. It was a discovery which filled her with confusion and doubt. If this wasn't Acha, then where was she, and who was this person who spoke to her with such familiarity, who meant so much to her that Blackwood thought she would do anything to protect him. "If only it had been earlier, we could have run together from your guardian."

Zo leaned over the bed as the figure began to cough. She couldn't suppress the surprised gasp. She knew his face, she knew his dark eyes, and his light brown hair. He looked so much like Daniel. Had it not been for his darker skin tones, in this light she could easily have mistaken them. As she looked over him, she wondered if perhaps he was the reason she had felt so comfortable with Daniel from the time they first met. Now if she could just remember this person, she was sure things would become far clearer.

"By the Gods," she whispered, she could think of little else to say as she gazed upon him. A spreading dark patch appeared on the bed where his abdominal injury had begun to bleed out.

"Zoe, I don't have long. I've fought all I can. Now you are here I can rest. I can't tell you how happy I am that the last face I see, shall be that of my treasured friend." A weak smile crossed his lips, a small drop of dried blood marked the corner of his smile. "I tried to keep it secret. I have done a terrible thing. Please, will you hear my confession?" he whispered. A name came to her as he stretched his hand to touch hers. She sat on the side of the bed hesitantly. He smiled as she spoke his name.

"Michael," she whispered, squeezing his hand gently. As she did so, in addition to the seething pain, a rush of memories flooded back to her. They came in small fragments at first, flowers, running together, hiding from guards, laughing, but the more she saw, the more she remembered of this boy, of her first friend. He had been her window of sanity in those trying times.

"I always liked you better this way." He gasped in pain, his other hand clutching his stomach through the blood-stained sheets. "Will you listen?" As she nodded, he moved to rest his head closer to her arm, she touched his face gently, her touch allowing her to share and relieve just some of his pain, but there was so much. It was a pain she knew she could not heal. His was a life she knew she could not save, no matter how much she wanted to. She felt Hermes' presence, he lingered at a distance as if to allow him time to make his final confession.

She lifted her hand gently wiping a tear from the corner of his eye as she wondered how she could ever have left him. He had always been alone but for his father and younger brother, why hadn't she taken him with her when she left? But in her heart she knew the answer, it was the same reason that she would sneak away alone when the time came for the quest to end, and that reason was a prophecy. A prophecy that would only make things harder for those she travelled with, one she had to protect them from and so, when the time came, she would face the end alone.

"Forgive me, Zoe, I have failed. You trusted me with the task to protect them," he gasped through the weakness and pain as he told his story. "We accidentally stumbled on a way to wake the parasite. There are two breeds, the normal one found in most of our people, but there is another, an alpha one called the Hikoriti, which we discovered slept within me and other younger hosts.

"We swore not to reveal our findings, but one by one they slaughtered us, until they discovered the truth. Through the Hikoriti, I can control the people with parasites, as could the one who possesses the next alpha after my death. I fought as long as I could my friend, forgive me." Michael began to cough, more drops of blood tarnished his paling complexion.

"Hikoriti?" Zo moved closer to him, turning his head so it now rested upon her lap. She stroked his hair gently. Despite the pain touching him caused, she would hold his hand and offer him comfort for as long as she could, even if it only eased a fraction of his suffering. She owed him so much more than the small relief she could provide.

"Yes, a special parasite. They stole my journal, and discovered my parasite was different, my actions will bear a heavy price. Already they have placed it in its new host, but when I die..." he began to cough once more, moments passed until he could speak again. "You have to save them before it knows I am dead." He cried out in pain, the white sheets on his bed growing darker. She knew there was nothing she could do, the people here lived in harmony with the parasite in their body. If it was injured or removed the host always died. No matter how skilled she was in healing, no one from this village would respond to her healing touch.

"Michael, I'm so sorry. I promise I will do what I can," she whispered.

"How beautiful you were that day. You looked so sad and alone as you brushed your hair before the mirror, I knew you were different then." He raised his shaking arm to touch her cheek, she placed her hand over his, tears welling in her eyes. "You grew more beautiful with each passing hour. Elysium, should I see it, will pale against your kindness.

"The light shone so gently across the floor, your hair looked so warm I wanted to reach out and touch it, to take you in my arms and run away where we could both be free. That day, I remember you turned and smiled at me, you hid me in the cupboard as Lady Elly prowled. You weren't allowed friends, whatever would she think?

"Come, she's not looking, let's escape and count the stars together one last time my Zoe." His hand grew heavy in hers, his pulse slowed and his breathing stopped. The machine's rhythmic beeping fell silent.

She remembered him so vividly now. He had been the one who brought her escape from the four walls in which she had been imprisoned. He had been her first friend, her best friend, the one who had done so much for her and asked for nothing in return. Seeing him now brought back so many memories, the strongest of which was the last time they had been together, when he gave her back her freedom. She sat for a moment, still holding his hand as she thought about it...

...Zo released her grip on Michael as she dismounted the horse. He walked her slowly down the wooden pier. The pre-dawn light had already started to ignite the sky with the sun's crimson flames as they tainted the clouds a fiery red. She was certain her guardian would have noticed her absence by now, there was no time to waste. Once on the boat it would take some time to reach Drevera, but her heart leapt with the anticipation of seeing her mother again, she was finally going home.

"I can't thank you enough," she whispered, her eyes filling with tears as she hugged him tightly. For a moment she feared she would never let go. "Come with me?" she asked, but his expression only confirmed what she already knew. Even if he had wished it otherwise, his only choice was to return home.

He had been the best friend she had ever had, the only friend. He was the first person to offer her a bond of friendship, and she sworn she would never forget him, they had done everything together. He had saved her from the worst enemy of all, loneliness, and for this she would be forever in his debt.

When he heard how her training was progressing he had provided her with the means to return home, to leave it all behind, but it also meant leaving him. He would not be able to survive long away from his homeland.

Before leaving, she had taken steps to ensure he would know the level of her gratitude, giving him a chance to pursue his dream. Even this small act of helping him was insignificant in comparison to all he had done for her.

"Lord Blackwood spoke of needing a new scholar in The Courts." She spoke softly, wiping the tears away with the back of her hand. "A science researcher, he was too busy so gave me the profiles. I recommended you for the position, it's what you've always dreamed of." Blackwood often gave her menial tasks to perform, there was no reason for him to doubt her tale.

"There's something else," Michael stated. Even if they had only known each other for a short time he knew her well enough to know there was something more to this story. He searched her eyes for the answer, knowing she wasn't quite telling the whole truth.

"Yes," she sighed. "Remember I told you of the darkness I felt within me? I'm scared Michael, scared I'll lose control," she blurted it out quickly as the tears streamed down her face once more. If possible, she hadn't wanted to tell him. "You've been the greatest friend I could ever ask for, but if I don't do this..." Zo paused, there was more at stake than he could know. Last night, hours after the sun's rays had vanished, Elaineor had stood outside her door. As always, she had been pretending to sleep, waiting for her to leave so she could meet with Michael. It was just before Elaineor had entered that something unusual happened, something which gave Zo cause for concern. Their voices had been nothing more than low whispers, but being awake she heard them all too clearly. They spoke of her friendship with a person from outside the walls and how, if the guards were to see him again, they were to kill him on sight.

When Elaineor had entered her room to find her awake, she admitted everything. She confessed that they knew of her secret meetings with the boy and asked what it would take to stop her from seeing him. She asked for the one thing he wanted more than anything, a placement as a scholar at the court researching the new science. He had dreamt of a chance like this his whole life, he studied alone in the walls of his home. It was for exactly this reason he was always excluded from recruitment, especially since Blackwood would never employ anyone who had not been formally educated, even if that meant recruiting an outsider when someone locally possessed the knowledge.

Elaineor had agreed. She even gave her permission to see him one final time on the understanding that, if she were to see him again after this, both Michael, and what remained of his family, would pay the price. But that night was all Zo had needed, she was leaving and had no intention of ever returning.

"I understand." Michael sighed. *'Understand, how can I understand?'* he thought to himself as he heard his own words. After his mother had died, the people of the village had turned their backs on his family. They had justified it by saying the mind sickness his mother had suffered was surely passed on to her children. She had been the first person after his mother's death who would speak with him. "Why?" he asked, unable to silence the question. He knew she had her reasons, that was why he had helped her escape, but he had not considered the possibility of being forced back into that life of loneliness, and in that moment, for his own selfish reasons, he wanted her to stay.

"Because, aside from my mother and Amelia, you're the person I hold dearest in this world. I promise I'll protect you no matter what. Also, I've no intention of returning and becoming what they wish of me. If I stay there, they'll turn me into something terrible, I can feel it." The boat sounded its whistle, a warning of its approaching departure. With one final look she vanished into the shadows. He knew there was nothing he could say or do to change her mind, and realised that perhaps her leaving was for the best, especially for her...

...She was gripped with sorrow as the memories of their goodbye surfaced, she lowered his hand wiping the blood from his face and the tears from his closed eyes. She leaned forwards, kissing him gently on the forehead as she placed a coin under his tongue to cover his passage into the underworld. She could feel the presence of Hermes start to fade as he made his departure with her friend.

"I'm sorry," she whispered, pulling away. "I never did thank you." The door flung open suddenly, light spilt into the room stinging her eyes.

"Michael!" Sara screamed pushing Zo to one side to hold his lifeless hand tightly. "Michael, hold on, please." She turned to Zo with accusation in her eyes. "You!" she snarled. "You murderer, you promised to protect him. Why didn't you save him, why?" she demanded; Acha grabbed Sara tightly pulling her into an embrace as she glared at Zo.

"Acha, you're safe." She almost swallowed her words when she saw the look in her friend's eyes as she held the sobbing waitress.

"Oh yes, Hades forbid something should happen to me," she spat bitterly. After discovering the truth, even speaking to her made her feel nauseous, the very words seemed dirty. After everything Sara had told her, the truth had picked so many holes in all Zo's lies. How could she stand there now with such a convincing act of concern? "Careful, Marise, it almost sounds as if you care." She watched the colour drain from Zo's face, so her fears had been realised. Acha had discovered the truth after all.

"I... I can explain." Her voice was nothing more than a whisper as the shock stole her breath. Even the thoughts which had brought so much comfort before did little to calm her now.

"It *is* true?" Acha seemed more shocked by the immediate confirmation than having found the courage to confront her. Then again, given the fact she looked the very image of the assassin there was little point in denial. Acha had seen her in this attire before, how could she have been so blind to the truth? Her identity had been so obvious then, how could she have failed to see what was so plainly before her? "So you don't even bother to deny it! Well, I don't need your explanations, I understand all too well. How did you find out, did *he* tell you?" she snarled, tightening her grip on Sara, who sobbed heavily in her arms.

"What?" Zo's voice was full of questions that Acha almost believed she had no idea of what she spoke. It was no wonder she had so easily deceived them.

"My father, did he tell you who I was, that *was* your plan wasn't it?" she hissed. Zo looked to Sara who still sobbed against Acha's chest. She didn't have the strength for this discussion, and this was certainly not the time or place for it. Acha fell silent as if Zo's meaningful glance had forced her to remember herself. With regret, she looked at Michael's body on the bed.

"When you come to leave, no one will question you, it is all I can do," Zo whispered. She forced herself to hide the despair and sadness which fought its way to the surface, she could not afford to show emotion, especially if the people around here were to take her next command. She placed the pass on the bed, she had no need for it anyway. As she passed them to leave, she touched Sara's shoulder gently, suppressing a shudder as she did so. As Zo stared at her, Acha pulled her away from her touch protectively. With nothing left to say, she opened the door to leave.

"You really are heartless, you killed her brother and that's all you have to say for yourself?" Zo paused a moment, almost as if she wished to say something, but it seemed she could not bring herself to say the words. She walked away in silence, it took all her effort to keep the posture expected by those around. Sara pulled herself away once Zo had left to wipe her reddened eyes.

"I'd hoped it wouldn't end this way. It's all her fault, she did this to us. He was all I had left," she cried, placing the blood-stained sheet over his face. "I want her to suffer, she deserves to. I know she's your friend, but..." Sara erupted into tears once more.

"*Was* my friend, at least I had been tricked into believing so. How can she use people like that?" Acha pulled Sara close again. "But what can I do? I would help if I could, but..." Sara once more pulled away from Acha's embrace wiping the fresh tears from her face.

"Do you really mean that?" Acha nodded. "Then I know someone who can help you," she whispered. "Since you are already in her group, maybe we *can* do something. I want her to pay. I wanna avenge my brother..." she sniffled before once more breaking down into tears.

* * *

Daniel and Elly had parted ways, both entering the town from different sides in order to create the best opportunity to distract those who would be searching for Zo. But there had been no guards as Elly had predicted. It seemed their presence wasn't needed. Daniel was immediately met by the townsfolk as they emerged from their sheltered positions to surround him, and it was not a warm welcome he received.

He raised his hands slowly to indicate his immediate surrender as he met with the unruly group, their scythes and weapons poised as they moved to surround him ensuring escape was impossible. Their movements were jerky, almost disoriented. A figure lurched forwards, reaching out a dirt-encrusted hand to grasp Daniel, ensuring he could do little but obey the herding movements as they led him through the town.

Elly glanced over to him, she too had fallen victim to the ambush and stood now on the borders of the town, where it seemed he too was being carefully guided. Given the respect they had shown her earlier, it seemed too sudden of a change to have been uninfluenced by an external force. It seemed highly probable that they had already missed the encounter with the guards, whose sole purpose had been to spur the malice within the residents. Or perhaps there was more occurring than met the eye.

Night watched with a smile of amusement as the puppets obeyed their master. It seemed even Elly was confused about the current situation, and why wouldn't she be? She had no idea of the groundbreaking discovery which had been made. He would be very interested to see how this progressed, but it wasn't their involvement he was interested in. They, like the townsfolk, were mere puppets, and the true objective behind this experiment was about to unfold.

"Are you certain this boy understands?" Night observed the events upon the surface of the mirror. It was clear from his tones alone that Blackwood was particularly proud of himself, so much so that one would almost believe the results being witnessed here were his to claim credit for, they would of course be wrong. He had neither the skill, nor the intellect to even conceive such a plan, let alone put it into motion.

"Yes, sir, as you can see, although temporary, the operation was a success. Every living person with a parasite is now under our control." Blackwood grinned proudly as he puffed his chest forwards.

"You do realise what the outcome of this will be if things don't go to plan? I trust you have taken the necessary precautions." Night questioned, it would be inconvenient if everyone in the town was lost. They had been the result of careful selection and breeding over countless centuries. Their biology had been specifically selected and introduced to the environment for the sole purpose of these experiments. Then again, he could not imagine things concluding in any other manner than those he had so carefully orchestrated.

"Yes, my lord, the Hikoriti will be dead within an hour, as soon as its first host has completed his journey across the river Acheron and severed his link with this world." It was a well-known fact that the river Acheron formed a barrier between the mortal plane and the underworld. What most people didn't consider was that once the river Acheron had been crossed, all physical, spiritual and even magical ties were severed.

"Then what of the hosts?" He knew Blackwood would have thought of something. In fact, he didn't only know this, he knew exactly *what* he had thought of. He may not be the most intellectually gifted of subordinates, but he was learning. It would have been foolish to leave something so important to just one man in the hope that he would consider every eventuality. He had people there who watched over him and guided his actions from the shadows. They were the real rulers of the Twilight Empire, although Blackwood didn't realise this, his role was nothing more than that of a figurehead. Despite knowing all this Night needed to be certain he could trust him completely. If he passed his test on this little project, there was no reason why he couldn't be moved to more rewarding things, in fact, he already had something else in mind.

"The control is fairly easy, it's a mixture of different pitched notes only audible to the parasites. We have recordings of both the awaken and the sleep cries. Once this trial has ended, we should be able to control them without the Hikoriti. We have tested this on several small groups and found it most effective.

"That boy didn't know what to do when we brought his little brother before him. He as good as handed over the research and volunteered for the procedure just to save him. It is a shame he had no more family, maybe we could have manipulated him into doing it instead of this substitute. That, I believe, would have had a greater impact than what we are doing now." Night ran his finger around the glass, as he did so it sang in different pitched tones.

"Oh, I nearly forgot, it turns out there is more than one of these parasites, but only one at any time can be the alpha.

"I have already located the next host, so should things go awry, we can always use the child." Night smiled at Blackwood's words, he had not disappointed him. He had wondered if he would try to keep the boy a secret. Blackwood, however, had made a personal vow never to withhold information from Night. He was grateful for the power and positions he was given, and for the gift of Marise, who he had seen fit to bestow upon him, after all, the final act in the creation of Marise, had come at a very high cost. Since that time Blackwood had never stopped trying to make amends for his misjudgement. He blamed himself for the misfortune, but Night had eventually defined it as a learning experience, how could he have known what no one had told him? Besides, on that fateful day almost nothing went as intended. Even had Blackwood's plan been perfect, it still would have been foiled by those who, at the time, had posed the real danger.

"Very well, I believe she has arrived, let us begin. Let us destroy her resolve, let us show her what she truly is beneath her pretence." Despite the commitment of his words, something about the tone in his voice seemed almost regretful.

"And what of your daughter?" an undertone of concern rung through his voice, Blackwood knew all too well the ultimate price of these actions.

"I need Marise in order to release the final seals, everything else is irrelevant. My daughter too has a role she must conform to, and we will ensure it is one she accepts." Night paused, Marise would be a fantastic ally, the only person who could accomplish his objectives. The act he was about to witness would be the foundation to ensure things would proceed as required. It was a necessity, as were the results which would follow. All had been planned; all would be executed to perfection.

"I understand your predicament, my lord, after all that time when you finally see her again, she reminds you so of the woman you loved. It's a shame there must be a sacrifice." His daughter would be the final sacrifice, the one that would mark the return of his powers. There was no choice, it would have to be her. The Hoi Hepta Sophoi had ensured that this final role could be undertaken by no one else.

"All things worthwhile, have a sacrifice. Some sacrifices are greater than others, these are the things which are truly worth obtaining," he answered simply.

* * *

Zo gave a sigh of relief as she left the court. The doorman had suddenly found the need for his presence inside, allowing her solitude at the base of the enormous building. The pretence was finally over, and Acha would be able to leave without question. There was no longer any danger, but what a strange few hours it had been. She had to question Blackwood's true objective. Why would he take Michael only to ensure he would die just as she arrived? If she hadn't discovered his ruse by accident then she would have been too late. There was too much left to chance, what purpose was it meant to serve? Yes, she mourned his death, but surely his plan had more in mind than to cause her pain. She only knew one person who could even begin to understand the motives behind his schemes, and that was Elly.

The pretence of being Marise, had brought with it a strange numbness, but as she began to increase the distance between herself and the court, the barriers around her mind, like her tears, slowly began to fall. As she grew further away, she tried her best to silence the small sobs. Since she had parted with Daniel, she had built impenetrable barriers around her mind to avoid distraction; as they faded, she felt the intensity of the emotions she had suppressed. All the feelings which Marise would not have shown now flooded through her, as did an uneasy feeling of danger.

Her sobs stopped instantly as she realised the severity of these new feelings. It wasn't just danger, it was fear, and it was projected from Daniel. The emotions had struck her with all the power of a solid blow, taking her breath away. She climbed the slope as fast as she could, urgency driving her every step as she raced towards the town.

As she reached the top of Ipsili Thesi, the place where she had sat with Michael to count the stars and exchange stories, she stopped suddenly. The view from here was incredible. She could see everything, the courts, Blackwood's mansion, and the village, and therefore she could also see the danger, the cause of Daniel's panic.

As she looked down at the hordes of people, she was reminded all to clearly of her trial. There was something about the way the people moved that reminded her of the lurching steps of the dead which had seized her. This had to be another part of Blackwood's scheme. If he had wanted to hurt her friends he clearly could have done so, but instead they stood below, hostages to the townsfolk in what was too convenient a location to have been something which had occurred by mere chance. No, they had been driven there so that she would have no choice but to see them. What was his plan now that she was here, did he intend to make her watch them die as well?

The slope leading down towards the town started with a steep drop. It was not an easy path, even if she wanted to, she knew there was no way she could reach them before someone could hurt her friends, if that was what they had planned.

She tried to convince herself that everything was going to be okay, that somehow she would find a way for them all to emerge from this situation unscathed. If Blackwood wanted to negotiate with her, then fine. She believed she understood now. He had killed Michael to show her he was serious. Killing him sent a message. He had been a prized researcher and by proving he could murder someone he valued so easily, he suggested he would not hesitate to kill her friends, even his daughter. Now he had made clear his position, he would surely approach her, but the foreboding feeling in her stomach, and the scent of death in the air, warned her otherwise.

Daniel was frightened, even from this distance she could see it in his posture, even Elly seemed confused, but Zo knew she needn't worry for her safety. It was doubtful, even with their numbers, they could harm her. It was a confidence in Elly she knew did not stem from her, even so she hoped she wouldn't have to find out just how accurate her belief was. She was just about to start her descent when a voice stopped her, suddenly all the coincidences did not seem too unintentional at all.

"I knew you would come." She turned quickly to find its owner. He was a sickly-looking blond man, he seemed to have stepped from behind the tree which she and Michael had once sat beneath. She didn't even wonder why she had failed to notice him. Her vision had been fixed on just one thing since her arrival, and she had paid nothing else any attention at all. He leaned upon its bark for a moment for support as he clutched the bloody bandages which wrapped around his abdomen before continuing his laboured approach. When she turned to look at him his eyes fixed on hers, she had the feeling he would never so much as glance away.

At first, Zo foolishly believed she could help him. His voice was so weak that the hostility went unnoticed. She thought maybe he was also someone from her past, or perhaps one of Michael's colleagues, given the location of the injury. She had taken the first step towards him before the realisation of the situation struck her. She glanced down at her friends again, the memory of Michael's words, pieced together with the stranger's wounds, left just one horrible conclusion.

"You're using the Hikoriti, you're making them do this," she gasped, her advance towards him freezing instantly, before her stood the man Michael had asked her to stop.

"Well wha' d' ya know? You worked it out." He clapped his hands a few times before clutching his stomach. "Funny thing though," the man let out a painful gasp as his hazel eyes filled with immense pain, a pain which weakened his legs until he fell to his knees. Despite this, his eyes remained locked on her. He breathed deeply, when he could force himself to speak it was through clenched teeth. "This thing inside me, it'll only live until all electrical impulses have stopped in its host.

"If that happens b'fore I die, I lose control..." he gave a strained chuckle. "When I lose control, they'll kill everything, even themselves, you'll have a massacre on your hands." He knelt forwards, smiling to himself, thinking how soon the end would come.

He had his reasons for accepting this arrangement, reasons none but he, and the voices truly could understand. Soon he would know death's sweet embrace and the reward, if he was able to complete his task, would be all the more sweet.

"I don't understand." She tried to stall, desperately searching for the means to end this in any way but for the one that taunted her. Whilst she kept him talking, the townsfolk seemed less violent towards her friends, perhaps they could see their chance and escape while he was distracted. Maybe they could run, but even then, very little about the situation would change.

She glanced away in an attempt to avoid his heavy gaze, but no matter how hard she tried, she only seemed to be able to look at him. Worse still, she knew where this scenario would lead. This was another reason she wished she could avoid his eyes. There was very little chance she could talk him into releasing his control over the people below before he passed away. Beneath the pain she saw the suffering of one who was haunted by the voices of the damned.

"When the Hikoriti realises the impulses from its host have stopped, they'll all die." He couldn't understand why she had yet to strike him down, perhaps she didn't understand the situation fully. For his cooperation he had been promised a quick death. "You see the link they share is not only physical but psychic, if the host crosses the river Acheron and the body it's in still lives and exploits its control, it'll grow angry.

"Its death occurs just moments after its host crosses, it will use this time to eliminate those under its influence, any person, any creature, locked under its control will be annihilated. Even now the Hikoriti is preparing for its passing, I have ways of knowing such things, so know I speak the truth when I say within three minutes his journey will be complete." His voice seemed to challenge her insecurities. He knew she was afraid of what was to follow. It felt as if someone had looked inside her mind to find the words which brought her so much comfort, the words which gave her the power to fight back against Marise, and devised the means to strip them from her.

"Why, why are you doing this?" she begged. "What do you hope to gain?" She heard an explosion echo through the air. She turned sharply, his eyes still stared at her as she glanced down to the crowd in panic.

"A scratch, a warning, I never miss twice," he threatened. Daniel gripped his arm tightly as more figures poised their weapons. "Now you know I'm serious let's get down to business."

"What do you want from me!" she demanded, fearing it was an answer she already knew. His eyes smiled slightly through the pain.

"It's simple really, either you kill me, or them, it's an easy choice. After all you are Marise Shi, like the Gods you have the power of life and death within your hands, why do you hesitate to use it to save those you care for most? Could it be, is the fearless assassin frightened?" he sneered. Lord Blackwood had explained the situation to him fully, the only thing he would regret is that he would not live to see the fruits of his labour, but at least the voices would leave him too, those horrible little voices which screamed in his mind. There was nothing he wouldn't pay for a little silence, even his life.

Zo stared at him in horror, frightened was not even close to how she felt. She knew each time she used her sword, her alter ego grew stronger. The more she used it, the more danger she put her friends in. How could it come to this? If she were to kill him, she would lose herself, she would destroy the paper-thin line that divided her and Marise, a line that gave her strength. But if she didn't, she would be responsible for more than just one life. A cold realisation surfaced, reminding her that this was how things were meant to be. To win she had to lose everything, that's what the prophecy had promised.

She feared what would happen should she surrender to this stranger's will, yet, she was left with no choice. As she looked down at her friends, the count-down echoed through her mind, she felt the hairs on the back of her neck stand to attention and her stomach sink. Her hands trembled as she released the clasp forcing the hilt and scabbard to rattle as she slowly drew her sword. There was no choice, one life or many, the fates had intervened to deal her this losing hand. The battle she had fought to find her words of strength would soon be meaningless.

She did something then she had never knowingly done before, she called on Marise, on her strength. She had no desire to see this through, but Marise liked to kill. Zo begged for her to take control, to seal her away in the place of darkness. There was less than a minute remaining, and Zo would gladly surrender if it meant avoiding this, if it meant she could still hold dear those words.

The sword trembled at his throat, his eyes remained fixed on hers. He reminded her of an animal caught in a hunter's trap, his fate obvious. But the figure who knelt before her was not an animal, he was a person. She felt Marise's delight as she waited in the darkness, relishing in her torture. Zo knew then there was only one way for this to end. Marise would enjoy this more than the act itself. It would destroy her belief, one of the only things she had which prevented Marise's dominance.

Zo closed her eyes as she swung her sword, there was no choice. Nausea rose within her as she felt the resistance as it struck his flesh and followed through. Although her eyes remained closed, she seemed to see everything so clearly. His eyes somehow still seemed to be locked with hers, seeing for her, forcing her to watch his final seconds. As the sword's swing became free of all resistance, she dropped it loosely to her side still standing with her eyes firmly closed. The images faded with the stranger's life. She stood paralysed, unable to move as a warm light rain began to fall.

Time seemed to freeze as she stood in the rain fearing to open her eyes, the images of his death still burnt in the back of her mind as the body slumped to the ground. She stood immobilised, all too aware that what had fallen just moments ago was not rain. It never rained here. Through her own pain, that from her sympathetic touch seemed to be negated, perhaps because no amount of physical pain could even compare to that which she felt at this moment.

She stood unable to control her trembling body as nausea continued to rise within her to greet the empty feeling in her chest. She stepped backwards before even gathering the strength to open her eyes to look upon the result of her actions. She gazed in horror at the scene which lay before her, an image which would be forever burned into her mind. She stood staring, forcing back the urge to vomit. She took another step backwards, another step away from it, away from what she had done.

"Couldn't hide your true nature any more Marise?" Acha's voice startled her. Had she been able to move her fixed gaze from the horror before her, she would have seen all too clearly that both Acha, and Sara, were soaked in the same blood rain which stained the grass around them. Acha gave a disgusted snort turning her back on her to walk away. Tears flooded Zo's vision as she took yet another step back, her grief streaking her blood-stained face. She stifled a cry as the world around her began to lose focus. She felt the gentle arms of darkness embrace her, she felt the lightness in her stomach as she fell deeper into its grasp. Somewhere, from far away, she heard Daniel scream her name, but there was another voice too, a whisper which simply said.

'*Two more.*'

Chapter 19

The Breaking of Bonds

Zo opened her eyes; in that brief instance there was a fleeting moment of serenity. A moment owed to those few seconds of confusion as she found herself in a room at the inn. Her chest tightened, drawing breath became almost impossible, as the tears started to stream uncontrollably down her face as the memories of what she had done surfaced.

Her feet could barely carry her quickly enough to the bathroom where she emptied the acidic contents of her stomach. She sobbed between retches, barely able to breathe. Her body shaking violently as she saw the images of death play over and over in her mind. The bloody rain began to fall time and time again, burning her skin where it touched. Even through the memory, the agony she felt was real. She felt its sticky dampness on her skin, and the white-hot anguish of the person it had belonged to. From a single touch she could feel the afflictions of another, and his pain had fallen in thousands of tiny droplets to impale her like knives.

She clutched the toilet as the dry retching continued, she couldn't breathe, she couldn't stop, and she wished only for death. She would rather that, than live knowing what she had done.

She managed to gain some control over her stomach, but not the sobs and tears, they wouldn't stop. She moved, curling herself into a ball, even the pain of her shoulder, that Elly had stitched whilst she had lain unconscious, was dull compared to what she felt now.

"You're awake, that was quite a fall. We were worried." Zo didn't even move as she heard Daniel's voice, instead she just curled herself tighter as she wished the world would forget about her. She heard him close the door as he entered.

If not for the sound of her sobs, as his vision found her on the bathroom floor, he would have feared the worst. Grabbing a blanket, he wrapped it around her, carrying her to the bed before placing another cover around her trembling body. Her eyes were red, filled with fresh tears which seemed to fall in endless supply. He sat with her. He didn't know what to say. Anything he could tell her would just seem so empty, even seeing her like this hurt him deeply. He had to hold back his emotions, if she felt them, she would never understand his weakness.

"Daniel, I..." she spoke finally, it hurt to do so, as if each word leaving her was barbed, catching on the rawness of her throat. She swallowed in an attempt to prevent herself from retching again. She wondered if he knew exactly what had transpired up there, if he was aware of the outcome, if he knew what she had done. From his silence, she could only assume he did. After what she had done, she couldn't understand how he could bear to be in the same room as her.

She looked at her trembling hands sadly, although clean now, they seemed so sullied. It seemed Elly had gone to great lengths to ensure not a single drop of blood had remained on anything she would be in contact with. It appeared she understood all too well the suffering of a healer should they take the life of another.

"Daniel, I..." she said again but her words froze at the same point as before. She knew what she wanted to say. She wanted to tell him the horror of the act she had committed, to confide in him, and seek his comfort, but she couldn't. The sentence was too horrific even the thought of saying it made her nauseous. Daniel squeezed her hand gently before he moved to stand.

"I won't be a minute," he spoke suddenly. He couldn't bear to be there a moment longer. He couldn't do it, he couldn't tell her what she needed to hear. He offered her a short, comforting smile before he hurried from the room.

He closed the door quickly, unable to take another step. He wanted to be near her, but he couldn't, not like this, not while they remained connected. It was just too much to bear. Daniel leaned against the door, his own tears flowing uncontrollably. He wasn't strong enough. He wanted to be, but he wasn't.

He didn't know what he had expected, what he thought he would encounter, but to sit there with her had been far worse than he had imagined. She was heartbroken, he could feel the extent of her pain as if it were his own, and that was without the added burden of the link they shared. He knew she would have given anything for that man to live, even her own life if it meant the survival of everyone else. But he hadn't wanted her life, not in the way she would have offered it anyway.

Anger fought for dominance over the pain, but this feeling belonged to him alone. He couldn't understand why someone would do that. Once again it all seemed a little too timely to be random. Someone had orchestrated this, he was certain of it. They had arranged it so she would be given no choice but to take his life, no choice but to destroy the one thing which kept her able to continue since discovering who and what she had been. With their single act they had taken everything from her, leaving her with nothing, not even hope.

Even from outside the door he could feel the sorrow escaping her to encompass everything within its suffocating embrace. He felt responsible, by being so weak, by being unable to resolve the situation without her intervention, she had been forced to once more protect him. But worse than his own feelings of guilt, worse than listening silently as she suffered, was knowing that nothing he could do or say would make it any better.

More than anything he wanted to comfort her, to take her in his arms and tell her that everything would be all right, but he could not lie well enough to even convince himself of this, let alone her. He knew all too well what this meant, and he was certain whoever created this scenario did too.

Perhaps if their minds had not linked, if he had been unaware of the words of comfort she used to find courage and strength when things looked bleak, he may have attempted to console her. But instead he felt her pain through their bond, a pain so desperate and hollow it seemed even the smallest ray of hope would be devoured by the all-encompassing darkness.

It was a cruel thought, but he hoped she was so encompassed in the grief of what she had done, that she had failed to realise what it meant for her, otherwise, Marise would have gained a tremendous power, and power is not stripped away nearly as easily as it is created. Lost in his thoughts and fears he stood separated from her by a mere few inches of wood. He was unable to be in the same room, and yet was unwilling to leave her.

A hand touched his shoulder gently, it pulled him back from his concerns. He had been so overwhelmed by the never-ending circle of worry, he had failed to notice that Elly now stood beside him.

"How is she?" she whispered; she knew as long as they kept their tones quiet, they would not be overheard. Daniel wiped the dampness from his own face as he met Elly's concerned features. There were a lot of things about her he didn't trust, but at least a part of her seemed to genuinely care for Zo, which he found strange considering where her true loyalty lay.

"She's been like this since she woke," he whispered, matching her tone. As he spoke, he became aware of exactly how much time had passed since he had left her. He had intended to steel himself and return, but he felt so helpless, so lost, he feared he would only make things worse. He wished he could find a way to take away her pain, and for this he would have given anything.

"It is just like when—" Elly stopped suddenly, almost as if she believed herself to be talking out of turn. "Shall I talk to her?" Daniel was surprised she had even asked. Normally, she just did as she pleased without question, he found it even more unnerving that she now awaited his response. He couldn't help but notice how much she had changed since they had first met, but he couldn't quite decide if her question was simply her way of encouraging him to realise who it was that should be in there with her, or if she genuinely awaited his answer.

"No, I should... I just don't know what to say," he admitted shamefully. He realised now his foolish act of saying nothing, and leaving her alone with her grief, was surely worse than him being there with her sharing her pain.

"Sometimes, you do not need to say anything. It is not what you say that is—" Elly began her words of encouragement, only to be interrupted by Acha's harsh tones as she rushed towards them. It was easy to recognise where she had been at the time of the incident, her clothes showed the same blood splatter as Zo's had. But where she had retreated to afterwards remained uncertain.

"Why waste your time? You'll think differently when I tell you who she really is, right Elaineor?" Acha spat venomously. Her angered words echoed around the silent inn which had been deserted since they had returned. The townspeople were still confused as to why they had taken arms against their guests. They had scarcely lowered their weapons when they had seen who they knew to be Marise, falling from Ipsili Thesi. Understanding that their actions were responsible for this, they had made themselves scarce, not even daring to even utter a word as they quickly dispersed.

Until Acha's arrival, everything had been silent, even the conversation held outside Zo's door had been carried out in low inaudible tones. Acha however, was unconcerned who heard what she had to say. Elly simply met her accusing stare as if answering the challenge her voice had issued. It was, Acha who finally looked away.

"I will begin preparations for tonight. We still have much to do." Elly walked away leaving in the direction Acha had appeared from just moments before; she knew all too well what would happen now. She glanced back at Daniel before turning the corner. Despite not being able to see them anymore, she would listen to their every word. She knew exactly what this conversation would be about, and it was in her best interest to determine how this would affect their objective. As she stood in the shadows, she couldn't help but wonder how things would unfold, especially when she considered the complex fate the two of them seemed to share. She could not see how her friends would think to do anything but distance themselves from her. No friendship was that strong, Acha had already proven that.

"What do you mean?" Daniel questioned, his voice no longer a whisper. There was no point in trying to hide their presence further.

"That, that thing in there, the one pretending to be our friend, I wouldn't waste your concern on her. She wouldn't on you." Acha spat; he could see the anger and disgust in her face as she looked towards the door. She had always seemed so calm, so delicate, it appeared Elly was not the only person to have changed. It made him question what had turned her this way, the person he saw now barely resembled the friend he knew at all.

"What are you—" Daniel had a feeling he didn't need to ask what had ignited the vicious tones and dangerous attitude she now possessed. He feared the truth had found her, before Zo had been given the opportunity to reveal it herself.

"She killed someone up there, but that's not all, she's a good actress I'll give her that. I never would have guessed she had known all along," Acha snarled, pacing back and forth before him, searching for the appropriate manner in which to reveal the facts. She asked herself why she hesitated, after all it was only the truth, but even so, she had to find the right words. Daniel cared deeply for that monster, and despite the hate she had for her, she had to consider Daniel's feelings when she revealed the true nature of his supposed friend.

"Knew what?" Daniel questioned, he needed to find some way to diffuse the situation before someone did something they would regret, but it seemed there was more to this than he first thought. It seemed Zo's former identity wasn't the only issue here.

"That I'm Night's daughter." Daniel's posture held some relief. This revelation had not been what he had expected, Acha was Night's daughter? His reprieve was short lived as he realised things were far worse than he had first assessed. His relief had been very premature indeed. "She knew all this time, I'm his blood, don't you see? She planned it from the start. Pretending to care, befriending us, when really all she wanted is that book. The final Grimoire." Acha let out a sharp breath which seemed filled with tension.

"That's insane." Daniel replied after taking a moment to process all this new information. "Firstly, you don't share his blood, not now anyway, you could take that book no more than she could, or are you forgetting, that body is not yours? It's not your blood that flows through its veins, so nor is it his either!" Daniel snapped, suddenly everything had become far more complicated. "Secondly, it was me that brought Zo to your aid. She never even knew of your existence before she saved your life." Acha couldn't believe what she was hearing, she had discovered in the court that her life-force used energy to recreate her former body, which meant everything, inclusive of her blood, was as it had been originally. They had to know that, but perhaps she could pretend to entertain this idea for her own safety. Then again, just because he didn't realise it, didn't mean Marise hadn't.

"That's what she wants you to believe. Besides, don't you know who she is, are you too blind to see it? The person in there claiming to be your friend is Marise Shi!" Acha spat; he lowered his head to look towards the floor as he found support against the wooden panels of the door. The added complication of her paternity could only prove to worsen the already volatile situation, it was clear that Acha had already reached a decision about Zo. Her reaction had been the very one feared, the reason she had delayed revealing the truth.

"I know," he muttered quietly.

"Even if... you know?" she gasped as she heard the words he had spoken. It hadn't been an answer she had imagined in *any* of the scenarios she had rehearsed before she had found the courage to approach him. He watched Acha's face fill with betrayal and questions. How could he know, how could he not tell her? It didn't seem like he was involved in their deception, but had she been mistaken? No, she was certain he was simply under her enchantment. He had been very clear concerning his feelings towards Marise Shi. His hatred obvious when they had spoken about her in the past. So how could he stand before her, knowing the truth, and pretend that it didn't matter? She didn't understand.

"Yes," he admitted glancing towards the door as he pulled himself from its support.

"You know and yet you still..." All the energy had died from Acha's voice to be replaced with confusion. "I don't understand, didn't you see her true nature before, when you were fighting for your lives? She killed someone. She sliced his head clean off his body. That's all she's ever done. All she is capable of is fighting and killing. She's a murderer! A murderer who will do whatever it takes to get what she wants!"

"True nature you say?" Daniel asked quietly, his voice now filled with dormant anger. "If Zo had not done what she did, there would be more than just one person dead. We are talking a fatality rate of every person here who possesses a parasite along with myself, Elly, and possibly even you. Someone has shown their true colours today, but it wasn't her."

He turned away from her to place his hand on the door. He was so angry at this whole situation, he was angry at Acha for acting in the very way Zo had feared. He was angry at Elly for bringing them to this town in the first place. He was angry that once again Zo had been put in a position where she needed to protect him, to sacrifice her beliefs in order to keep him safe. But most of all, he was furious at himself for not being there for her when she needed him the most.

"What do you mean, more dead?"

"The man she killed he had some kind of alpha parasite implanted inside him. He was using it to control the actions of the people. If she hadn't killed him, once it realised its real host was dead..." Daniel stopped to look at her, it was clear from her expression she was already aware of more than he had believed. It seemed the tale of the parasite was one she was familiar with.

"The Hikoriti, I knew it had been separated from its host, but..." Acha sighed as she remembered where the information had come from. It had been deduced by Sara, poor Sara who now had nowhere left to turn. As soon as they had reached the village, they had parted ways and their paths had not crossed since. How could Daniel even try to justify what she had done? One life or many it was still murder all the same. Was she meant to understand, to forget everything she had learnt, because perhaps, this one time, Marise Shi had killed for the right reason? What about all those who came before, were the people of this time really so foolish as to overlook a past filled with sins for one act seemingly for the greater good? No, it had to be the enchantment. He was trapped in his belief, just like she had been, like all those who failed to see the truth. But they did not have Sofia to assist them. She owed Sara a debt for introducing them. She would have to try to make him see through the illusions, save him from whatever it was Marise had planned for him. "But that doesn't change a thing," Acha continued. "She's a heartless murderer!"

"Really, do you think so?" Daniel's voice still oozed with his dormant anger. "Then tell me, why have I been standing outside, for only the Gods know how long, listening to her cry, listening to her torture herself over what happened?"

"It's a trick," Acha hissed, why wasn't he listening? Perhaps words alone weren't enough, but what else could she do?

"If you really think so, maybe it's better for you to leave. You're no Astraea yourself. If I remember correctly, you killed someone before my father found you. Strangely I don't remember you harbouring a single regret, shedding a single tear." He turned the handle on the door. There was a place he was meant to be, a place he was needed, and as he looked back over the last few hours, he was disappointed in himself that he had not been there.

"That was different," she protested.

"Oh yes, that's right, unlike Zo, you did it to save your own life." He pushed the door open. Once he had stepped through, he closed and locked it, not only to finish the discussion but to ensure she would not try to continue this conversation in front of Zo, who once more sat slumped by the toilet, the tears still as fresh and raw as ever. He wrapped the sheets around her cold trembling body. "Hey." He moved to sit in the bathroom beside her. She looked so pale, so fragile. "How are you feeling? I'm sorry I was so long." He smiled gently as he looked into her reddened eyes as more tears fell from them.

"She's right," Zo cried; she never looked at Daniel she just sat on the cold floor looking to her hands. "I am a murderer." She looked away from the instruments of murder to stare out of the bathroom door and through the window to Ipsili Thesi. She could still feel the rain falling on her skin. In her mind it burnt her with its touch, forcing her to relive a pain unfelt at the time.

"You heard that?" Daniel pulled her towards him. She didn't protest, she just stared over his arms as he held her, her vision still fixed outside on the place of her nightmares. What she had learnt in Darrienia, about the difference between her and Marise being the ability to kill, was meaningless now. It was nothing but a fairytale, how she wished it had been true, but if it had been her actions would have killed all those who possessed the parasite. There was only one result to whichever choice she made, and that was to walk in the footsteps of her alter-ego. She now understood that there was no other path open to her. No matter the detours, it seemed she would always return to the road of a murderer.

"How could I not? But, I didn't know," Zo whispered. Daniel tightened his grip on her protectively. Regardless of what she had faced, she had always been strong enough to overcome her feelings, to do what needed to be done; but right now, despite his company, she seemed so isolated, so lost. Barely a shadow of her old self remained behind her pain filled eyes.

"Know what?" He pulled her closer, holding her so tightly he feared he would crush her. If only he could make the hurting stop, erase the last few weeks of her life, he would have done things so differently.

"That she is Night's daughter? Even if I had, it wouldn't matter. It wouldn't have made any difference."

"I know." He shushed her gently, rocking her slightly as he kissed the top of her head.

"I killed him Daniel," she said emptily. "With my own hands, I killed him." She covered her face with her trembling hands as she pulled away from his embrace. She could not accept comfort for her unforgivable act.

"Shh, but if you hadn't, neither I, nor most of this town would be here now. That one life saved so many."

"But... I am meant to be a healer, I give life, not take it. I am no better than her. No... why deny it any longer? I am her." Daniel grabbed her again, this time more firmly. For a moment she thought he would strike her, but instead he pulled her back to hold her tightly, both unaware that on the other side of the door, Acha was still listening.

"Did you hear anything worthwhile?" The voice startled Acha as she turned quickly to look at Elly, who was now leaning against the wall at the other side of the door. Acha was unsure how long she had been there, her approach had been silent. "You know, listeners never hear the best of themselves." With that simple comment she walked away. Acha watched her for a moment before hurrying after her. This was the opportunity she had needed. If she was correct, she would be able to assess the extent of the damage Marise's enchantments inflicted on those around her. Was Elly also a victim, or was she really her ally?

"Wait, Elly, I need to ask you something." Elly smiled to herself, slowing her pace, the reason she lingered so long was due to Daniel's response to Acha's revelation. He had claimed to have known that Zoella was Marise. This much was expected, after all, Marise had attacked him, making the truth clear. Considering that the two of them had crossed paths before, there would be no question to her identity. Events such as those were seldom forgotten. She had to wonder when exactly he had discovered the truth, she hadn't noticed any extra tension between them since the event outside Phoenix Landing, so it only stood to reason that his discovery must have preceded this. She had contemplated, as would any in her situation, whether his apparent acceptance of the facts had been a mere pretence to allow him to seek his revenge when it was least expected, but it seemed she was mistaken. Despite everything that had happened, despite their history, it appeared his unwavering friendship could, perhaps, compete with that shared between her and Marise. Such a powerful kinship could prove to be detrimental. Then again, it could also be exploited to her advantage.

* * *

When Daniel and Zo finally emerged, Elly and Acha were already waiting outside her room. If they had been much longer, there would have been the need to take the conversation inside. Daniel had helped her to dress, she had stared at her reflection in the mirror with a deep-rooted hatred, but the tears had finally stopped, for now anyway. She looked down to the floor, unable to stand the way they looked at her; Elly's looks of sympathy and concern, versus Acha's looks of hate and resentment. If the situation had been any different, she would have stayed hidden away forever. Then again, if the situation had been any different, she wouldn't have found herself here in the first place.

"I'm sorry, we have things to do. I should not have been so selfish. What plans do we have for Eiji's rescue?" Her vision remained focused on the ground. Stepping before her, Elly reached out, lifting her face to look her in the eyes. They looked empty, as if something irreplaceable had been lost. Zo averted her gaze. The pain Elly saw, reflected in Daniel, confirmed that he too had seen the emptiness which had engulfed his friend. It had happened as the tears had stopped, as if each tear drop had contained part of her soul, and now there was so little of her left that the emptiness was unmistakable.

"You needed time. Are you feeling better now?" As Zo's eyes filled with tears Elly removed her hand, with the release of Elly's firm yet gentle grip Zo moved quickly away. Better, how could she be feeling better? She had become that which she detested more than anything in the world.

"We don't have much time," Zo answered. Turning her back to both Elly and Acha she wrapped her arms across herself protectively. She had to see this through. It didn't matter what happened to her after, but she had to see Eiji safe.

"Very well, come. I will discuss my ideas. There is little we can really achieve until we see where he is being held, but we can still start looking for the antidote. Daniel, you do still possess the map?" He nodded, pulling the crumpled parchment from his pocket. He and Zo followed her into the dining room. Acha lingered behind as if trying to decide what she should do. "Right," she stated, as Daniel tossed the map on the table before them. Her tone professional as they began to formulate their plan. "What did that creature say about the Narca berries?" Elly glanced around. She remembered all too well what had been said, but wondered if anyone else would care to volunteer the information. The next few minutes would be crucial, although it was not the rescue that was important right now.

"The berry is on Pirates' Isle, the land next to there, with a new king, is where Eiji will be." Elly smiled as Acha appeared hesitantly at the doorway before moving to join them. It seemed she had reached a decision.

"Pirates' Isle it is then." Elly unfolded the map to spread it across the table for all to see.

"These fixed locations, each have a counterpart in our world, right?" Daniel crossed the church and the court locations off the map, deliberately not mentioning that the same places no longer showed on the map which Seiken had given to Zo. It was almost as if the map itself changed as they released the seals, each time they did so, another section disappeared. "Well, this one is Crowley, it would be little more than a village, so that's out of the question. But in our world, there is a castle that's recently lost their King, right?" He glanced between Zo and Acha.

"Therascia?" Zo questioned, in a low murmur as she joined the conversation. She remembered the elderly gentleman who had offered them a ride, telling them all about the death of the old monarch and the arrival of his successor. Although her tones were quiet, she knew she had to make an effort. Her own self-pity could not jeopardise Eiji's life, or she would be more of a monster than she already believed herself to be.

"Yes, he informed us of a new heir to the throne." Elly smiled, at least they could all be in the same room and still cooperate with each other. It was a start. Perhaps this tense atmosphere would have no effect on their mission at all. Elly had already formulated her own ideas about how this journey would pan out. If they were to get through this, friends or not, they needed to act like comrades, something it appeared they were willing to do, at least for the moment. It was a situation that was likely to change as soon as Eiji was safe, but for the moment, she was glad for the cooperation. "He was taking his finest stock as an offering, he said he was heading to the port, meaning..."

"We can exclude all the fixed points on Albeth, which leaves these two." Daniel pointed at the two small locations on the map. "But this is the only one with an island near it."

"It is also the only one in the vicinity of a castle." Elly smiled. "But we were after the antidote remember." Daniel glanced to her, he was certain she had arrived at this conclusion a long time before they had even started this discussion. He knew exactly what she was trying to do, and for this single act he was grateful. Perhaps she wasn't quite as indifferent as she liked them to believe.

"Well, we could always ask around for any legends of pirates." Acha stepped a little closer to the map as she cast her vision over it. "Wait a second, don't you think the shape of those islands is familiar?" Daniel turned the map a little as Acha pointed to a small cluster of islands between what would be Therascia and Albeth.

"You're right. Now that you mention it, it looks like the constellation of Tredious, the legendary pirate." Daniel added glancing across to Zo. He remembered how, when they were in Crowley, they would sit together with a picnic under the night sky. He would listen intently as she told him the stories behind the names of the stars. The more common ones he knew himself, but there were so many he had yet to learn, so many adventures he had never imagined. Every word she had spoken was like magic, her enthusiasm bringing the stories to life. Her eyes had been so alive as she told the tales, but now her empty gaze was fixed steadily upon the map. He had doubts she even saw it, let alone recalled the story of the pirate who pillaged the skies.

"Then that shall be our intended location, but we will need to utilise every resource, ask every dreamer. We cannot afford to be waylaid, after all, this is all assumption, it may not hold true in Darrienia. That said, I suggest we think about departing," Elly summarised, as she folded the map and secured it within her pocket.

"But it's still hours to sunset," Daniel commented having already relinquished the thought of having the map returned to him, not that it mattered, somehow he had come to possess both of them anyway.

"True, but by the time you have finished procrastinating it will be time." She winked at Zo who forced an empty smile. "Besides, this is a good opportunity to gather supplies, who knows what we will encounter."

"You're the most organised so we'll leave that to you," Daniel asserted; he knew exactly what she had in mind, for once it seemed they were thinking along similar lines and once again he appreciated the effort she made. She gave a nod as if to acknowledge his request, but they both knew there was more to that single gesture. "Acha and I have things we need to discuss."

"Me?" Acha's voice queried with surprise. She had hoped to have some time alone before they departed. It wasn't that she really wanted to go with them, but she had other things she needed to accomplish. Rescuing Eiji was just one of the reasons she couldn't be separated from them just yet, and she still had to save Daniel.

"Yes, you, me, and Zo," he answered. Elly turned her gaze briefly to the ceiling as she left the room. He could have at least tried to be subtle. It was very doubtful, given Acha's blatant hatred, that he would now manage to seat them in the same room, and had serious doubts there would be enough time for the situation to meet an understanding. The best that could be hoped for now was a momentary reprieve.

"I think I'll pass." She wrinkled her nose slightly in disgust. "I have nothing to say to the likes of her." Acha snapped as she too walked away.

"But—" Daniel was stopped by Zo's interruption.

"It's okay," she sighed. "I don't blame her." Daniel watched as Acha left the room. He couldn't help but wonder what had happened to the unspoken promise of truce which occurred earlier, had he just been fooling himself?

"Zo, can I meet you in Darrienia? I've a few things I need to do. Will you be all right?" Zo was not the problem here, although he knew she was suffering more than he could imagine. Unless he could somehow make Acha understand things as he did, the situation would never get any easier. If he could convince *her* what he knew to be the truth, maybe he could even convince Zo.

"Sure," she responded emptily. "Take all the time you need." As she watched him leave, a strange sense of foreboding washed over her.

* * *

"I hoped I'd find you here." Daniel stood in the doorway of the main lounge. Acha didn't turn to acknowledge him, she continued to stare through the enormous bay window. The farms and mountains stretched as far as the eye could see, no matter where you stood in this town, you would always be facing mountains. Right now, she gazed out over the ring of volcanoes which they had travelled beneath.

"Daniel, I don't understand," she sighed, finally turning to face him. Perhaps now was the opportunity she had been seeking, but somehow she knew that even this moment alone would not be enough to make him understand. If she couldn't save him, she would simply have to take matters into her own hands and liberate him in another way. "You know who she is, *what* she is. She is the very personification of evil, why do you defend her?" Daniel pulled one of the small wooden chairs close to her. This was going to be a long conversation. It was one he had hoped never to have.

"Acha, I, more than anyone have the right to hate her, to agree with you, but..." He gave a sigh, how could he possibly explain this to someone who was so content with despising her?

476

"You, hate her?" she spat venomously. "The way you feel about her is clear, how can you even begin to state such a claim?"

"Acha, I trust you, and I know that you would not betray *my* trust. What I am about to tell you must never, and I mean never, leave this room. It must never be mentioned again, understand?" There was a very real danger with what he was about to reveal, if she were so minded, she could use it to her advantage. He had weighed the options carefully, this was the only way to make her understand the truth.

"I..." Acha paused for a moment before nodding, after all, it wasn't Daniel who she was angry with. They were still friends and as such she would be true to her word, just as he, no doubt, had been true to his by not revealing the true identity of the monster who they travelled with. She would not betray his trust, even if it meant she had to pass the opportunity to injure Marise further, that was if her concern for Daniel was something more than a façade. From the grave expression Daniel now wore, it was clear whatever was to follow could be a powerful weapon, but one she was bound by her friendship not to wield.

"Okay." He took a deep breath releasing it quickly. "Just before my seventeenth birthday I received a letter from my brother, Adam," he started so simply, but it was a tale that did not come to him easily. He was relieved that he had never discussed this particular event with Zo. The repercussions would have been unimaginable. Acha was surprised, Daniel had never mentioned having a brother before. "Mail from my brother always came to my school, otherwise I'd never receive it. My parents never forgave him for becoming a mercenary. Anyway, as I said, I received a letter, my brother was writing to tell me he had some leave and invited me to stay with him for the duration. I was so excited, my brother had always been my hero.

"With the help of my tutor, who had always been close friends with him, we convinced my parents it was a field trip during the term holiday to study the festival of Albeth. Every year a group of students would go from the college to witness it. It wasn't difficult to convince them, despite me not being a student, I was studying their material. I worked every afternoon after school for a month, earning money any way I could until finally it was time to go. Adam met me at the harbour." Daniel gazed out of the window, but it was not the rise of the mountains he saw before him, it was a window to the past. "I remember the impatience as I was waiting for the boat to reach the dock.

It had been three years since I had last seen him. So many thoughts raced through my mind, would I know him, would he know me? At last I saw him, he was exactly the same as I had remembered.

"I had barely been there a few days when my visit was cut short. His home was a small village, built to be mobile so their homes could be moved easily should the need arise. I lay in bed one night looking at the stars through my window. As a mercenary camp it didn't really exist, so light was scarce, after all to illuminate it would be to invite travellers.

"The skies that night were exceptionally clear and there was a comforting warmth to the air." He paused, starting to wonder if he was doing the right thing by telling her this. With the exception of Stephen, he had spoken of these events to no one, but he had to make her see things the way he did. It was the only way to put an end to this uncomfortable situation. "It happened around midnight. I was filled with such excitement that I couldn't sleep, so the quiet knock at the door, followed by the low tones of hushed conversation, wasn't lost to me.

"I couldn't catch most of what was said, just the parts where the stranger's voice broke, something about a girl, who later I discovered to be Marise Shi, arriving at the nearby village. I heard my brother's footsteps pacing across the floor as if in silent contemplation." Daniel paused as the window of his past he had been staring into once again engulfed him...

..."I will head to the village. My little brother sleeps in there, should I not return, please see that he gets home safely." Daniel could hear the concern and fear concealed within his brother's voice as he spoke to the figure who had entered. From this alone he knew how dangerous the situation would be.

"Adam, with all due respect, you are on leave, I only bring you this news so you may watch the village in my absence. The men are almost ready to mobilise, I should not even ask, you are not here," the figure protested.

"I know." Daniel watched through the keyhole as his brother fastened his sword around his waist before pulling on his long coat. "But your wife is with child, it would be foolish for you to attend and deprive your family of a father." Although the tones of their conversation were urgent, the pitch never rose above a whisper. Daniel strained to make out the exchange of words, the more he heard, the more he was afraid of exactly what his brother was about to become involved in. He knew he had been in combat before, he was a hero even amongst his own men, he always protected them, kept them safe regardless of the danger to himself. He had lived through countless dangers, his body a canvas to the battles he had fought. Even so, the air was filled with foreboding.

"Sir?" This was the first time the conversation had sounded formal. When the stranger had addressed his brother as Sir, he had moved to position himself between Adam and the doorway in physical protest.

"Step aside lieutenant, you *will* stay here, protect this village. If you disobey me so help me there isn't a punishment I have thought of yet that would be fitting." This time his brother's tone rose slightly. "Relay my orders and request the mobilisation of the men once they are adequately prepared." Having made his position clear, Adam left, stepping past the blockade created by the one who had tried to stop him. The figure had been speechless, he had not expected this reaction, he had not expected for Adam to utilise his authority as he had. The camp had always possessed a very informal structure. There were ranks and hierarchy, and everyone within their group was respected. They knew their roles and positions, but there had never been any need for them to remind others of it. The fact Adam had done so, a man who had no attachment to his title or position, had been all the more shocking.

Daniel had rushed to his window, watching as his brother disappeared into the forest. As he forced the wooden pegs from the window, he was vaguely aware of the door opening behind him as he made his escape. Whatever danger his brother was going to face sounded serious. There was no way he was going to face it alone. He had to delay him, at least long enough for the other mercenaries to catch up.

He ran as fast as his legs would carry him as his brother hurried onward through the trees. He knew he had to stop him, he knew if he failed to intervene nothing good would come of this. Every instinct screamed for him to reach his brother and stop him in time. He had no idea why he felt so strongly, or what lay in wait. He just knew he had to stop him regardless of the cost.

The town itself was one they had passed near on their way to the mercenary base. Although not confident in this area, Daniel remembered the way well enough to keep himself on his brother's trail. He stopped suddenly, paralysed by the smell of death.

The corpses of the townsfolk littered the ground. Despite this unwelcoming scene, his brother did not hesitate. He had rushed onward into the town to confront its cause. Daniel stood cloaked by the forest's shadows, unable to call out after him, unable to shake the fear-induced paralysis.

He had wondered how it was possible for so much harm to be caused by just one person. It was during this unshakable paralysis that he first laid eyes upon her. She was not a person but a demon. Her hair was crimson red, it flew wildly in the breeze crafted by her swift movements. Daniel's heart leapt with both fear and amazement, with just one swing of her sword she had struck down three men with seemingly little effort. She was his age, yet she displayed such mastery in the art of murder.

She stood still for but a second, placing something within a pouch which hung upon her sword's belt, something which until this point she had held grasped within her hand as she fought. It was then Adam stepped forwards. Daniel cried out with his silent voice, he knew this would not end well. Before the stroke of his brother's attack had even finished, she was clear from the path of his blade. His brother had been an expert in swordsmanship, yet it was her sword that impaled him as she sidestepped around him to dodge his attack. She had made it look so easy.

Daniel screamed as the scene before him shook the paralysis. He ran from the undergrowth, somehow within his hand he found a weapon, even in that moment of haziness, he was amazed at its weight. Adrenaline coursed through his body as he charged forwards. With all his being he wanted to kill her, he wanted to drive this machete through her blackened heart and watch her die. The gap between them started to close, the heavy farming tool was lifted under the flag of vengeance and poised with the strength of his anger.

From nowhere he heard a voice. For that brief second everything seemed to turn white. Someone grabbed him with such force he lost both his breath and the machete in one swift movement as his body was wrenched backwards. He fought violently for freedom as the figure draped itself over him protectively, refusing to comply to his demands as he screamed after his brother.

Marise approached. With each of her advancing steps, the figure's grasp grew tighter. The wild energy and thoughts of vengeance which had once filled him were pushed aside by the fear of death, a death which now stood before him. She flicked his brother's blood from her sword, glaring at the one who held him. A figure whose tight, almost suffocating grip showed how much they were willing to risk in order to protect him.

"So, he is the one you choose?" Those were the words she had spoken. Although to Daniel they had held no meaning, he felt movement through the protector's grip, as if they had nodded in response. Satisfied with the answer, she turned her cold gaze to him. "It is pointless to continue. I have what I require." As she spoke, he realised the figure that had protected him had not only released him, but seemed to have disappeared. If not for the gift of his life he would have questioned their presence. He looked up to her from where he sat. He found himself paralysed, even the slightest movement impossible through his fear. He flinched as she thrust the hilt of a sword towards him. As he looked upon it, he realised almost instantly it was the one his brother had worn with pride, the one he had sworn would be used to protect those in need. Daniel reached out to take it within his trembling hand, as it left her grip he once more became aware of the weight created by a weapon which could be used to take another's life, the weight of the burden his brother had carried since he had first chosen to become a mercenary.

Sheathing her sword, she turned away, something about her posture changed slightly, and then she spoke once more. Her voice seemed somehow different, almost desperate, trapped.

"Take your revenge, be quick, take it now, I welcome it." She remained with her back to him for what seemed like forever as she tempted him to strike. When he failed to advance, she continued walking, her stride unhindered.

Words could not explain how much he had wanted to thrust the sword through her, to accept and answer her challenge, but, for all his anger and hatred, he found himself unable to. Her figure slowly faded from view. He had missed his opportunity for revenge.

He was unsure how long he had been sitting there, unable to control his helpless tears, as he stared after the murderer who had taken the life of his hero. A cold hand gently squeezed his shoulder, an act compelling him to break his gaze on the place she had long vanished.

"Do not be in such a hurry to die," the voice whispered, the touch the same as the one who had protected him. He had barely heard the words which had been spoken as everything became confused, his brother's sword slipped from his grasp.

"Daniel!" The familiar voice resounded through the trees as he felt a firm touch upon him. Someone else was here now, someone who seemed to be checking him for injuries. "Daniel, are you all right?" He felt the presence of his saviour recede through the descending numbness, wondering how it was that no one had acknowledged the presence of the one who had saved him...

...."I had tried so hard to speak, to answer his questions, but words failed me. I had simply knelt, once more staring at the place I had last seen her. I don't even remember how I arrived home, but when I finally regained consciousness I was told a week had passed.

"I remember, for a minute on waking I thought it was all a dream. No, that's a lie. I had wished it was so. The truth is, Marise Shi killed my brother," he summarised, amazed he had once more managed to speak of this time. His throat was sore from the pain his story had rekindled.

"Daniel, I had no idea. I'm so sorry." Acha's voice was shocked, so much so that the words she spoke were barely audible. For a moment she could think of nothing to say, but that brief instant soon passed. "Then surely you of all people should understand."

"You still don't understand, do you?" Daniel sighed; he had hoped his tale would provide her with the insight she needed, a point of comparison between the two personas. "Marise Shi is a cold-hearted murderer, Zoella is not that person, if she were"

"No, I think it is you who doesn't understand," Acha interrupted. "There is no Zoella and Marise. Marise is just a name she was given, an alias she used, an excuse to pass the blame to someone else. They aren't two separate people. Zoella just chooses to use that to her advantage, just as she chooses, or maybe simply pretends, not to remember."

"How can you even—"

"Zoella lived here from the age of twelve. At that time there *was* no Marise, which means if this whole facade is true, then she should remember being here, remember her old friends, like Sara the waitress. So how come she doesn't?" Acha gave a frustrated sigh why wasn't he listening, couldn't he see that she was right? Acha tuned sharply as the door opened behind them.

"The responsibility for that lies with me I am afraid." When Elly entered the room, neither Acha nor Daniel cared to imagine how long she had been listening to the exchange which had occurred between them. "Sorry to intrude," she stated dismissively. It had actually come as a surprise to her that Daniel, still recalling the details of his brother's death so vividly, did not see his murderer each time he looked upon Zo. It was unexpected. She had known of their history for some time, after all, she had witnessed it, observing the event in its entirety from the shadows. Her recollection, however, was slightly different to Daniel's.

"What do you mean your fault?" Daniel questioned suspiciously, their attention now focused upon her.

"It is true what you said, they are one and the same, but that phase only lasted through the first few months of her training. We pushed her beyond her limits knowing a divide would develop where Zo would stop, and Marise would begin.

"That had been the plan all along, after all, only Hectarians possess this unique darkness, and the darkness in this case was nurtured and made to take on its own identity through a series of... unfortunate events. That was how *he* had wanted it.

"Eventually, as time went by, Zo's light vanished entirely, she no longer regained control. After further weeks of training with Marise, we used various methods, compounds and opiates to ensure she had been fully sealed. Then one day, the restraints weakened, moments would filter through where Marise was no longer in control, like those both you, and Eiji's master witnessed.

"Blackwood saw a few of these, but luckily I had noticed it first. The night Marise vanished, I used an ancient lore to create a potion in order to seal her away, leaving Zo with no memories of what had transpired. It was my way of being merciful, after all, she had been Blackwood's assassin too long, she had become nothing more than a symbol of power. To this day, she remains unaware of anything which transpired after she left home at the start of her twelfth year, but even now, her memories of that time remain fractured. Initially I believe she would have been fortunate to recall anything of her past, but since the person who enforced the memory repression has been taken to Hades, I believe things are gradually becoming clearer."

"Why are you telling us this?" Daniel questioned.

"I do not claim to know Zo, my kinship and loyalty *is* with Marise, I serve her, and that is my sole purpose at this time. But one thing is blatantly clear, Zo holds you both very dear, more so than anything else in this world. Every time she is forced to draw her sword, she loses a part of herself to Marise.

"To some extent this was the symbolism behind the blade she forged, a blade to bind darkness and light. Each force will forever fight for domination, but when created in equal measures, the darkness will *always* win. Just as that blade will eventually turn to darkness, there will come a day when Zo too will disappear.

"Sometimes, you will not notice Marise just under her consciousness, it becomes more apparent when she fights. Each summoning of the blade weakens her resilience, this she understands all too well. One day when she draws her sword, there will be no return. Her time is measured, yet each time you are threatened concerns for herself are not even a consideration. She is willing to sacrifice herself for you, that is true friendship. It is a shame only one of you can see that." Elly wondered if they understood enough about magic to know that a Hectarian was born with equal parts of both light and darkness within their soul. Over time, a Hectarian would normally find a balance between the two, allowing them to be unaltered. But in some cases, when a Hectarian fully embraced one side, the other could be encouraged to take on an identity of its own. One reflecting the nature of the magic which was suppressed. That was why when Zo chose to walk the path of light, Marise was created when she failed to balance her darkness. One thing she did know for certain was, that despite the obvious contradictions in the explanation she had offered, they were both too absorbed in other matters to take note of them.

"But she killed someone. Murder is unforgivable," Acha protested pathetically. She could not deny Elly had explained more than was needed, but as she had said so herself her duty was to Marise, which also meant ensuring Marise's tasks progressed unhindered, therefore, her words could not be trusted.

"I believe, if you were listening, Daniel has already explained that. If I were you, I would be looking at the situation in its entirety, did the act of taking his life come easy to her? Did she just draw her sword and," Elly made a slicing motion across her neck with one of her fingers. "Or did she try everything else within her power first? Now, the hour grows late, I suggest that we prepare to depart." Elly approached the table, looking meaningfully at Acha before she spoke again. "Acha, as I have mentioned before, the rune on your arm will only pass through the boundaries if the symbol says it can do so. Do you understand?" She placed some ink and a quill on the table before walking away.

Chapter 20

The Roads of the Ampotanians

Despite Elly's disapproval, Zo arrived in Darrienia long before her friends, departing soon after Daniel had left in pursuit of Acha. Despite her warnings about premature travel being dangerous, Zo was insistent. Elly supposed she should have been grateful that she had been informed, but would have preferred for her warning to be heard. With nothing more to do, she had decided to keep a close vigil on Daniel and Acha, to see where the conversation took them with regards to their loyalties. So much already hung in the balance. She could not afford another unpredictable element.

Zo had lied about the reason why she had wished to depart so prematurely. She was certain Elly had realised this and was relieved when she wasn't questioned further. She had wanted the isolation, to sit in the place where Seiken, a person she would have given her life to protect, had betrayed them.

The events had made Zo question many things which she had believed to be true. She needed time away from her friends to think about the consequences of her actions and reflect as she tried to find a different path, but most of all, she needed time alone. She had so much she needed to consider.

She sat in the dimly lit baths. When they were last here things had seemed far easier. Eiji was still amongst them, Seiken was an ally, and she was not a cold-blooded murderer. She wondered what else could have been done, the answer, nothing, proved little comfort. Despite having acted in the only manner possible, given the situation, it was still an outcome which could not be forgiven. She knew this calmer, less hysterical thought pattern was just the result of the concoction she had forced herself to drink. Normally she wouldn't condone the use of medicine to calm her conscience, but when her friends arrived they would undertake an important task, and in her current state she would prove to be of little use. She could not be a hindrance, but despite the effectiveness of this particular drug, her feelings of sorrow were not completely masked.

She wondered if forgiveness could be considered for taking the life of another, given the circumstances. After all, by doing so she saved the lives of so many, but even with the aid of the medicine, she still could not bring herself to answer yes. There was another voice to her reason, a voice whose twisted logic seemed to mock what she felt. Unlike normally, through the haziness of the drugs, it took some time for her to realise it was not her own thought she had heard.

'*He would be dead by now anyway.*' This voice dismissed her act as irrelevant as it tried to sway her to accept its own belief that life was unimportant. She pushed it aside with less effort than expected.

She needed time to reflect on other things as well. The potion supplied by Venrent in Collateral had started to take effect. The small whispers she heard, the ones which told her how to think, what to say, and how to act, had grown stronger. She was doing things she would not normally consider as if by second nature. What were once but fragments of memories, now became small scenes which acted out before her. Scenes which made her stomach churn, and ask herself if she could be this person, a person who murdered and destroyed so much without a second thought. Perhaps, she thought for a moment, if she embraced this version of herself, she would be free of the pain. Should she surrender, she would never have to feel anything again.

She stared at her sword, not really taking in the details of the finely crafted hilt. It seemed to weigh nothing in her hands, although to her mind its weight had become immeasurable. Each life she had taken pulled on it, increasing the burden, and the more she remembered, the heavier it grew.

She clicked the hilt up and down, unaware she was doing so. It was a trait familiar to Marise, one she had done many times without noticing. To Marise that weapon was an extension of herself, as such her playful manipulation of it was no different to someone scratching their chin or twisting their hair. She felt now, more than ever, that her time was limited, it grew shorter with each passing second, but before she could surrender, she had to ensure Daniel and Acha's safety. She could not submit, not yet. She refused to allow herself to be further weighed down by her failure to keep them safe.

On reflection, she knew that despite everything, she preferred her life this way, she had friends. When she was younger her retention of Hectarian powers saw to it that no one would accept her. She was different, and people feared those who were aberrant. Even today, there were villages where people of unique lineage, such as Méros-Génos, would not be welcomed.

With all her heart she wished things could be different. She wished she did not have to return to the purpose for which she was trained, and that Marise would be the one to vanish along with her blood-stained history. But she felt it more often than she cared to admit, that dark desire to destroy those who opposed her, those who wronged her. She was not Marise, but there was no denying this dark persona *was* growing stronger. Her shadow was always present on the tip of her mind, projecting her thoughts and feelings towards her, trying to force her actions.

Lately, even Zo herself had begun to question if they were really not one. Such were the words Marise taunted her with, and since there was no longer a definable line between them, who was to say that she was not truly her but in a dormant state, a restful period, from which she had now begun to stir. Who was to say that now that line had vanished, they would not become one, after all, how could they be separate beings if there was nothing to differentiate them?

There was at least one part of Marise she envied, the complete disregard for the opinion of others. Marise would have felt nothing for Acha's betrayal, more than likely, she would simply have killed her. She had heard the whispers in the court, and again at Ipsili Thesi, the gentle tones promising her relief if she had simply struck down those who opposed her, thus far however, she had managed to ignore them. Yet now those thoughts grew in power and she could only hope they were not stronger than her.

When she had accepted the potion from Collateral, she had understood there would be consequences. There had been something different about that seemingly innocent remedy. She had intrinsically known that once consumed all that was forgotten would return to her. She had never imagined the horror of the truth, never considered there would be such undesired clarity in the memories which returned. The blood rain had brought back visions of more terror than she had imagined in her darkest nightmares, more so because the images she beheld were not illusions woven by the Epiales, but memories of events which had occurred, and it was she who had been the monster.

"A coin for your thoughts." Daniel's voice had startled her. She had been so absorbed in her thoughts she had not even noticed his appearance.

"You build your walls so high, Daniel Eliot." As she glanced towards him, she couldn't help wondering if the barricades he constructed were to shield his altered perspective of her It was a concern soon released as he relaxed, allowing her to feel the concern and worry he felt towards her. The flood of emotions made her falter slightly. "I didn't even sense your presence."

"I think you're just distracted." He smiled warmly; he had been watching her for some time as she fought with both her conscience and beliefs. He had been watching her for long enough to see the glaze of the sedative enter her eyes. "How much do you remember?" he asked suddenly and perhaps more indiscreetly than he had intended. He needed to understand the weight she carried, how else could he support her? "I don't mean how much you *want* to know, how much *do* you know? You've been very quiet since Collateral. I began thinking surely that potion had some result, but..." he trailed off catching a glimpse of the fear and sadness in her eyes. "I'm guessing you don't really want to talk about it." He decided not to press matters further, so when she started to answer, he found himself surprised.

"I have never deceived you about anything. But, lately, since Collateral, I remember fragments. It's because she's getting stronger again. Her memories filter through, but I have never lied to you."

"I've never said you did, I just don't think it's a burden you should bear alone." He had only recently realised how quiet she had been, the conversations between them almost strained, unrecognisable to those enjoyed in times past.

"Initially, there was a slow join between us, it seemed to develop as I was trained. She was my darkness, you see every Hectarian is born neutral, created from an equal balance of both light and dark. Should they choose to only embrace the altruistic forces, the malign are repressed, and the reverse also holds true. It was once said that evil is stronger, but good possesses greater numbers, thus those who embrace the darkness do not falter to the light, yet the light's recipiency to the darkness is endless.

"Marise was my darkness, nurtured by my trainers she became her own being. Near the beginning I started to suffer blackouts. I'm not sure what triggered them, but I began to wonder why no one noticed my absence, especially since, as time passed, it became longer phases.

"I began to think that surely they would notice I was not around. I mean, I wouldn't be in lessons or at the meal table. Surely someone would notice my absence, after all, I was the only student there. I couldn't exactly get lost in the crowd." She gave a sad, half-hearted laugh. "The day I realised why my absence was unnoticed was the day the darkness won. The next thing I knew, I woke in this strange land with nothing behind me but an empty void." She closed her eyes briefly, she felt like the sun's rays on the planet, darkness both pursued and awaited her no matter her path. It was only a matter of time until one of them finally ensnared her.

"And now?" he questioned, moving closer. He extended his hand as if to comfort her, but for some reason he couldn't quite bring himself to place it on her arm.

"Now it's sunset, and the final darkness is approaching. This time it will be eternal," she answered truthfully; she knew she fought a losing battle to outrun the wave of darkness that crept ever closer.

"I guess that makes this somewhat ironic, to be trapped in perpetual light, never seeing the darkness of either world." Daniel paused, he was not really sure what words of comfort he could offer and, just as Eiji would have, he said the first thing which came to mind in order to avoid a drawn out silence. "Zo, you'll get through this, you've said it yourself, something is different now, you have friends. Friends who will sacrifice themselves for you.

"We *will* protect you with every bit as much determination and commitment as you protect us. We will not let you lose yourself." He smiled as she looked up at him and he finally placed the hand of comfort he had been afraid to offer. "I promise." She looked to him meaningfully as he offered a warm smile. In that moment, as she saw it, she felt just a little better.

Elly cleared her throat, drawing their attention to her presence. Zo and Daniel moved across to join her as she made them aware of her presence.

"It seems at the moment the only real choice we have is to follow rumour and head to the coast. We are certain to encounter a town or settlement of some description before we arrive there," Elly stated walking towards the exit, stopped only by Zo's quiet protest.

"Aren't we waiting for Acha?" she asked gently.

"I do not think that necessary, do you really think it is wise to have someone so fickle accompanying us?" Elly didn't turn to look at Zo, she merely paused in the doorway as she answered.

"But what if something—" she protested, the rest of her sentence lost in Elly's harsh words.

"Did she concern herself over you? I think not," she spat.

"She had every right to be disappointed in me. I should have told her the truth when I first discovered it. I should have trusted her." Although she spoke the words, Zo couldn't help but wonder if her reaction would have altered even if it had been herself who had revealed the details of her blood-stained past.

"Like she does you?"

"Why should she? Although it's true I have never lied to her, nor have I been completely honest either, that is just as bad."

"But nor was she truthful with you." Elly sighed; her head slumped forwards slightly as she waited in the doorway still not turning back to face them. "Tell me, did you know she is Night's daughter, that she is related to the person responsible for all this, to the person who drove you from your home? Her deception is the same as yours, all but for one small detail, hers was deliberate."

"What does it matter? A person's past and bloodline do not dictate who they are, such things are meaningless. So what if Night is her father, what does that mean exactly? Nothing," she snapped, feeling her temper rise in that strange region at the back of her mind where the shadow waited. Daniel placed a hand upon her shoulder as he saw Acha standing behind her eclipsed in the shadow of the dimly lit room.

"You clearly differ in opinions there," Elly highlighted coldly; she too was aware of Acha's appearance, despite the fact she had not turned to confirm it.

"It means you can use her to obtain the last Grimoire, or at least that's what she thinks, right?" Daniel stated looking over Zo's shoulder to Acha as he spoke. Zo turned slowly to see her standing in the shadows.

"What else? There's no other reason for the pretence of kindness. In all honesty, who would even imagine taking a stranger into their home, let alone put their lives on the line to protect them? I should have seen it from the start. It was all just a deception, no one is that stupid, even priestesses would hesitate to do such things. I should have known." Although she didn't direct her words towards Zo, her voice was vicious. She had been informed all too clearly about the motivations behind the apparent acts of kindness. Now she had discovered Marise's agenda, she would never be fooled again.

"Is that what you think?" Zo whispered turning her back to her once more. Daniel was the only one to see the extent of the pain as her heavy lashes lowered to the floor. Despite this, she tried to keep her head held high. The only way she managed to do so was by not turning back to look at the one whose words had struck her a deadly blow. "We should go, Eiji is in trouble." Those were her only words, they were low, empty, and betrayed the pain she tried to conceal. As she pulled her satchel over her shoulder she winced against the discomfort. It was a feeling which just hours ago would have consoled her, but now it was nothing more than a reminder of a broken boundary. "Let's go, there is a lot of ground to cover." She glanced at Elly quickly as she stepped aside to permit her passage through the door before her.

"Mari, it has always been like this. Allies are a weakness." She ran her hand down Zo's arm gently as if to offer some comfort.

"And you, are you not an ally?" she questioned quietly in monotone as Elly followed her through the door.

"That is different, *we* are different," she confided truthfully. Marise was the only one to truly understand the reason behind her being. Zo knew they were more than just allies and Elly was certainly no weakness.

"True, but why, when you clearly surpass her skill, was she made to be the assassin, why was she the one to gather the Grimoire with such a clear superior? I still don't understand," Zo stated in lowered tones revealing some of what she had learnt from Marise's shadow and memories.

"As the darkness comes, you will understand more than I dare say you want to." This made Zo question how long Elly had been listening before she had made her presence known, or perhaps she too understood how this would end.

"But," she sighed resisting the temptation to look back and see if her companions followed. "The more I remember, the stronger she becomes. I feel her watching, I feel her desire to eliminate the weakness rising up within me. What if I can't stop her and one of my friends get hurt again?" It was strange,

Zo now felt so close to Elly, as if she could trust her completely. She couldn't help but think back to the furnace, then, she had not trusted her, but now she felt like there was no one she would rather have at her back. This served as a reminder of just how strong Marise grew.

"I will not lie to you, it is my duty to protect Mari, but she is the darkness created from you, so it is just as important that I protect you from harm. Do you understand what I am saying?" Elly glanced back to see Acha and Daniel following behind them just outside of hearing range, no doubt a subtle gesture enforced by Daniel. *'Besides,'* she thought to herself, *'he said they too have a role to fulfil.'* A subtle smile crossed her lips. *'I wonder if they would be so quick to protect her if they knew what she will do.'*

* * *

Eiji's vision was blinded by a bright sterile light. The colours which filled the room only added to the discomfort already felt by his gritty eyes. He was no longer in the dark confines of the damp prison with Seiken. This place seemed so much like the image that had beckoned him away all those times. Before now, it had appeared that here was the illusion brought on by the poison, but if he were wrong did that mean everything else had just been a dream or, since this was the world of dreams, a dream within a dream?

As his eyes became accustomed to the surroundings, he saw the cause for the room's brightness. A huge dome of light surrounded the area in which he lay. It arched over him allowing enough room for him to stand and move if he should wish, or more accurately given his weakened condition, be able to. The heavy numbness still pressed down on his body as he lay motionless on the floor. He tried to move his fingers, he couldn't, but he did find he could move his head slightly, but doing so achieved nothing, except making him tired and dizzy.

The dome's form seemed to be like the ward Zo had used in Abaddon, to protect them from the effects of Aburamushi's sleep, but it was not quite as stable. From his position he could look around enough to see it was created by several mirrors and prisms that worked together to bounce and fan the light, which shone down from what appeared to be a small opening above him. Across the entire field, an array of different colours danced, shimmering upon its surface in an attempt to mesmerise him.

From what he could tell, just beyond the near-transparent field there were several people. He strained his eyes trying to get a better focus on what happened just beyond the shimmering light. He tried to see the faces of his captors, it was certain from his situation he was not a welcome guest. Unless it was their custom to strip their guests of all personal belongings and leave them imprisoned on a cold concrete floor, with only their clothes to keep them warm. Part of him felt lucky that he was at least allowed to keep them.

He knew he needed to stay calm. The poison still spread through his body, and he could not explain why he had regained consciousness. The effects of the poison seemed to have diluted somewhat. The footsteps that echoed around the room drew closer, he closed his eyes quickly, if he could learn something by feigning sleep it could only help him to better understand his situation and what these people had to do with Night's minions. The distorted voices cleared as they grew closer to him.

"But that's what I am saying, there was some strange activity." The soft voice protested with a gentle annoyance, almost as if she had said it time and time again without it reaching the ears of the person she addressed.

"As I said before, it's impossible, this field, prevents all external contact. Enough of this nonsense, we have bigger things to worry about, like the fact he is a water-based Elementalist, his nature will be diluting the poison as we speak. No doubt he will regain consciousness soon." As if on cue, Eiji opened his eyes again, letting out an involuntary groan as pain exploded through his stomach.

He found it strange that before the figure had approached, aside from the disorientation and weakness, he had felt none of the expected pain. Then, in the moment when he had hoped to gain some information, the symptoms had struck him with force.

"Where, am I?" he whispered, surprised at the weakness in his own voice.

"This is castle Iris, you were brought here after you collapsed." A lady crouched before the field, her pale blonde hair falling forwards as she moved closer, allowing him to see her through the shimmering light field. Through the distortion of both the field and his vision, all he could discern was her long hair and her clothing, which seemed to be a white dress resembling the ones normally worn by a physician's aide. The dress itself bore the symbol of Karykeion on the front, a short rod intertwined by two snakes with a pair of wings at the top. It was a depiction of the staff held by Hermes, a symbol which had become associated with those in the healing profession.

"Who, are y'?" he groaned, wondering if this person would be kind enough to inform him of his current situation. He was in trouble, he knew that, but exactly how much he was unsure. One thing was certain, they needed him alive or they would have killed him by now.

"Me? My name's Julie. I've been monitoring you," she answered, softly.

"Julie, enough. Do not associate yourself with criminals." Eiji glanced up slowly to see a dark-haired, commonplace man standing beside her, his hand placed firmly on her shoulder.

"That doesn't mean he is any less entitled to my care," she snapped, just moments after she spoke, her hand tightly clasped over her mouth as she realised her words were out of line.

"Do as you're bid. Now he's conscious you're no longer needed. Don't waste our medicine on someone who'll soon be dead. I want you away from here, word has it there is a rescue party on its way. They're fools to think they can overpower the defence of these walls to save this murderer," he spat.

"Murderer?" Eiji, despite the numbness, managed to force his body to move. On his command, the alien limbs slowly pushed him into an upright position. He felt his head spin, were they talking about him, was this the hand he had been dealt in their reality, one of a criminal?

"You think we're so uneducated as not to recognise one of the marked bandits? Lord Seiken told us of you, once we've destroyed your rescuers you're to be drawn and quartered at sunset." Julie opened her mouth to voice her protest, but before she could speak the man had raised his hand to silence her. "Silence! I'll have no more of your objections. Lord Seiken spoke the truth, how dare you question him?"

"But—"

"To your room, I'll tolerate no more of your insubordination. You do-gooders are all the same, that's why you end up dead." Eiji gave a sigh hearing the man's words. It seemed his initial assumption about being needed alive had been wrong after all. He couldn't help but wonder why it seemed, no matter the path he took, someone always wanted his life.

"Yes sir." She lowered her head before she walked away. He listened until her footsteps had completely faded.

"The other marked bandits should be arriving soon, even in the unlikely event that they do make it this far, your whole cell is a trap. One way or another we'll be rid of your menace."

It was a fine trap, Eiji thought to himself, taking in its details while he still could. Its nature was not immediately apparent, but it was clear now he would be dead should he try to escape. Or equally, as things seemed to go in his life, he would meet the same fate should he be rescued. He could do nothing more than sit and wait for Hermes. He had to wonder, though, if this prison was so secure that it could neither be left nor entered, how did they plan on retrieving him to answer the death penalty?

"Marked bandits?" he muttered as the arms he used to support his weight grew weak.

"Is the poison affecting your brain, or is this one of your tricks?" As the man scolded him, he pointed to a large wanted notice on the sterile white walls. Strangely enough, it was the only thing he could see clearly. Despite the dream-like clarity of the picture, which was of him and his travelling companions, his vision grew dark and his eyes refused to focus. "This fortress is the best place to end your days, Lord Benjamin has become unstoppable since obtaining the rune of power." Eiji felt himself begin to sway as his captor's words became an incoherent jumble of sounds. His vision twisted the figure in the room until finally a swirling darkness took him once more. He was aware of falling, it seemed as if he was falling forever until he felt the strike dealt by the cold floor.

* * *

"Eiji pay attention!" His master's scolding voice echoed through the air, a few nearby birds took to flight, startled by the noise. Eiji looked up seeing his master standing over him as he sat in a small rocky stream.

"Sorry master, I—"

"It's fine, go on be off with y', y' no use t'me like this." Eiji nodded, his master's features softened into a smile as he gently shook his head in mild disapproval. He had barely been back a week and already his student had lost his focus.

Eiji jumped to his feet and disappeared into the woods where, only moments ago, he had seen the figure trying to attract his attention. A boy, no older than eight, sat on a fallen tree in the woods. As he waited for him to catch up, he swung his legs back and forth, his heels making a small thud each time they hit the bark. His legs only stopped swinging when Eiji came to sit with him.

"I have the information on the town y' wanted. Mind y', it wasn't easy. Marise Shi razed it to the ground not too long ago. Those who survived are thinly spread across the continent, if they do exist at all. It seems it never endured much fortune."

"Tell me Pip, what did y' discover?" Eiji's voice trembled with excitement. This town, the one which had been destroyed, was the one he knew to be his home and now, for the first time, he was to hear news of it. He had been interested in learning the truth since just after his adoptive mother's death. It was at this time his father became his master. The death of his wife had revealed the truth about the young boy. It was unusual for such power to manifest in one so young, and since their kind were fairly scarce, he had never thought to check to see if the one they had taken in as their son possessed the potential to become an Elementalist.

Now he was far older and had been training for some time, he felt the urge to learn about his roots. He reasoned that, if he knew where he came from, he could understand more about his future, more about the person he was and why his parents had felt the need to do what they did. A part of being a skilled Elementalist, his master had said, was to know yourself, of course Eiji hadn't quite realised his master had not meant his history, he was asking his student to learn about who he was as a person.

"Historically it's been the centre for all major disasters, earthquakes, floods, fires, droughts. Rumour has it, the area of land it was built on has a strong elemental link to the Severaine." The young boy began to swing his legs again as he smiled brightly. He had been desperate to reveal this information, so much so that he couldn't wait for Eiji's training session to finish. During this particular mission, it was the first time he had ever heard tales of the strange force referred to as the Severaine. The Severaine was a myth barely spoken of, only those who spent their time in the company of ancient texts could even have a chance of discovering its theoretical existence. Even so, for most it was a forbidden topic and the information was so limited that no one really knew what it was.

Pip had come to understand, that since so little information existed, many people would disagree on what it was. The scholars he approached had argued in his company about whether it was god, magic, or beast, but it made the task so much more exciting, to trace something back to a myth somehow made it seem bigger.

"Meaning?" Eiji knew a little about the Severaine, researching it through the elements was a favoured diversion of his master, but one he rarely spoke of. He had never heard of a place having a link to it, how was that even possible, how could they tell?

"Meaning its location, although beneficial to the people living there, stands on the border of all natural environments, water, forest, mountains and such, meaning it creates a problem as to which one will dominate the area of land deemed neutral. The elements fight over the right to the border. This has subjected the area to a high rate of natural disasters.

"It is thought to have been an important landmark in the sealing of the Severaine because of these boundaries, although it sounds a little fishy to me." He shook his head as if to imply Eiji should have known that much himself, especially given his profession. "Anyway many years ago now, it's said Night himself rose to attack the small village. Rumour has it, something of great importance was hidden there, for some reason he left empty-handed. Most of the townsfolk survived and continued on with their lives as normal.

"Then just two weeks ago, a warrior appeared there, demanding some form of literature. They had operated a different policy of mercy to Night. The entire village was destroyed, a reign of death and terror like nothing seen before continued until this book was handed over. I heard that as the priest handed the book over, he begged for the lives of the town people, y' see he swore to this warrior he would get it as long as the town people remained unharmed. When he returned, he found all but a few people had been wiped out. He surrendered the book, begging for the remaining lives of the small town, but the warrior laughed viciously before continuing the killing spree."

"Well, what was this book, why's it so important?"

"Well it seems when the Hoi Hepta Sophoi sealed Night's power, it was a location selected to hide one of the Grimoire. Because of the area's unique design, it was thought he would not be able to detect its power. At least that is what I was told."

"Grimoire?" Eiji rubbed the back of his head; he hadn't expected so much information, especially in all one go. He knew the story of the Grimoire, but he had always believed it to be nothing more than a legend, especially since it happened within his lifetime, yet no one spoke of it any more. He wanted to be completely sure about the implications of the tale told. When he had asked about his birth place he had expected a run-of-the-mill tale about when it was built, the population, and the industry. He had never expected such a wild and outlandish story.

"Y' know, the Grimoire, the seven books used to seal Night's power. It's rumoured that this was what Night was after, all those years ago." The boy gave a big sigh. "Only, what people seem to be forgetting is they hadn't even been created then, so why would he need to retrieve something not in existence? I am only seven and three quarters, and even *I* figured out it meant there was something else there he wanted, y' would think people four times my age would know better." Pip shook his head in disapproval. A few moments of silence passed between them. "Is it true, y' were born there?"

"Erm, well, sure that's what I'm told." When his master had first found him, he wore clothes made only in that town, and within the child's possession was a note, it was written in what they believed to be a man's handwriting. It told of how the village had found him guilty of crimes and wanted him to answer for his sins. It stated the infant was a spawn of Hades and any who looked upon him with favour would suffer unimaginable peril. It went on to recommend that if anyone should find him alive, they end his life. Of course, his master did no such thing. "Did anyone survive?"

"I'm not sure." The boy sighed. "The pieces of the story itself came from a traveller who was passing through at the time, an Elementalist like y'self. Only the Gods know how he made it out alive, that's why we know so much of the final events. Although in fairness, the only person who *really* knows what happened is that traveller, and no one can even remember what he looked like. Even I can tell the tale has been fabricated and twisted as it passed from one to another," the boy paused as if in thought. "Is there anyone y' wish me to try to locate?"

"Sorry?" Eiji asked suddenly as he realised the young boy was waiting for a response. He blinked several times as he tried to pry his unseeing gaze from the rich forest before him.

"Is there anyone y' wish me to locate?" The boy repeated, looking questioningly at him.

"No. No thanks." He smiled, passing the young boy a parcel which until now he had kept in his pouch. A pouch which fortunately he didn't wear for his training or the contents would have been ruined.

"Very well, if there is anything, y' know where to find me right?" The young boy jumped from the tree and began to run.

"I sure do, Pip, thanks. I hope it helps y' mum." Eiji called after him as the child ran deeper into the forest.

Eiji had been all too happy to give the boy as much medicine as he needed free of charge, but after Philip Ingred, or Pip as he was called due to his somewhat slight stature, saw how much the first dose helped his mother, he insisted he worked to pay off the debt. There was nothing Eiji could think of that he wanted, but he had always been this way. Once a week he would come to Eiji's master's home to place his order, and refuse to take it unless he could give something back. At first, he asked little things. Pip was skilled in information gathering. He was only seven—and three quarters as he kept reminding him—and already he had a huge network of contacts. If you wanted to know anything, all you had to do was find him.

Eiji asked for stories from the outside world. He wasn't interested in anything in particular, just helping the boy's mother was enough. As time went on, he began to ask for harder tasks saying that the tasks presented were not to the value of the medicine which was saving the life of his mother. So Eiji gave him one last task on the condition that from that point forwards he would take the medicine for as long as it was needed. Thrilled by the challenge, Pip agreed. It had only taken two weeks to obtain all the information he needed. Eiji had been surprised, even the most skilled researcher would struggle to uncover what he had in months, let alone weeks. The final package Eiji had presented to the boy contained enough medicine to cure the sickness, after that she just needed to take things slowly and she would be fighting fit again in no time.

Having heard the tales about his birth town, Eiji now had other things on his mind. Something Pip had said opened an entirely new possibility to him, one he had to follow through. He raced towards his master's tree top home already running his questions through his mind. Could it be that all the time since his return his master had been keeping something from him?

"Master!" As he opened the door he stood for a moment leaning against its frame. The leaves which shook and whispered in the breeze made enough sound to drown out the sounds of his breathless gasps as he tried to gather enough breath to speak. Seeing the exhausted, over-excited tremble of his student's body, not to mention the urgency reflected in his eyes, his master sprung to his feet ready for action.

"Where's the fire?" His master had made ready his weapon and bag as he started towards the door, his departure was stopped only by Eiji's next words.

"At Napier it seems." Eiji entered, closing the door gently behind him. His movements were slow, his vision simply staring ahead.

"Ah." His master dropped his bag and replaced his weapon on the small hook before moving to the table, he poured two small glasses of dew. It was a fine and rare drink, in fact, most people didn't even know about it. Living with the forest had its advantages, when he sensed the activity under the tree's roots, he would spread a waterproof canvas across the treetops to catch this uniquely flavoured water. It was said through dew, you could taste both the past and the future as water itself possessed the unique ability to bend light as time passes around it. As this type of dew is only available at a very precise time of day and year, its short life ensured the properties of time stay within it as long as it should exist. Uncollected, it would exist for a matter of minutes. Being so limited in its existence, it retained its memories of all that was and would be. It was for this reason that the fairies and other creatures would gather it, of that gathered, his master would keep but a small bottle. The rest he always presented to the raised tree roots of his home, for those who lived beneath it. It was something he partook of only in rare situations. He felt it was needed now in order to give his young apprentice all the information he required of the event he had tried so hard to push from his mind.

"So it *was* you!" Eiji knew this just from the look in his master's eyes, that, and the fact he had sat ready to discuss this topic further. "Why didn't y' tell me?"

"I'm sorry, what can I say? I know it was y' birthplace. Maybe y' parents even lived there, but I saw the place, if they had been there..." He shook his head sadly as his aged eyes met with Eiji's young ones, he was reminded of himself at that age. He and his wife had done well raising the boy, his essence was pure. He had accomplished many feats in his time, but Eiji was his triumph, his pride.

It was nearly time for him to leave this realm, when he had chosen to train another, he had accepted this price. Seeing the fire in the boy's spirit he knew everything would turn out for the best, even if he was still young for an Elementalist, he would be fine. Most his age would just have developed their potential, and although he was never very good at remembering the theory, or its relevance, his instincts were uncanny. When the time came for him to leave, his master knew he would be able to learn from the spirits. He had a potential of the likes he had never seen, which was why he had decided to train him. He had lived a long life, longer than any would imagine. Such was the blessing of an Elementalist, that which granted them power also gave them life until the gifts were relinquished to another. Unless of course they met with misfortune, it was only age which would not claim them.

"I've no ties t'that place or those people, but y' still should'a told me. It was my home, or so y' say, y've always been honest, why has that changed since you have returned?" His master shook his head once more before he lowered his gaze to the table's surface.

"Eiji," he sighed gently. "I would'a told y', I just wasn't ready. Yes, it was me. Back then, at the village, death herself looked me in the eyes and smiled." Eiji saw his master's hands tremble slightly before he moved them from view. Seeing this his anger died, leaving him to wonder what could have possibly happened that was so terrible the mere thought of it turned his master pale. The story from Pip was bound to be an embellishment.

"I heard Night sent a warrior t'the village, what was he like?" Eiji broke the silence as his master struggled to find a place to start.

"*She* was only a child, a mere adolescent, yet she bore the power of Ares himself. The scenes of death she created were so horrific even the mind fails t'comprehend their true terror. When I entered the town, everyone was already dead.

"I stood at the edge of the village having just witnessed the death of the priest. I was without a doubt the last person who was still alive. She walked slowly t'wards me, despite my greatest efforts I couldn't seem t'move. I thought then I'd meet my death. I remember the terror as her eyes met mine, they were so old for one so young, but as our gazes met something changed, they grew almost gentle. 'Next life, you save me.' I still don't understand it, but that was what she said, then she turned and slowly walked away, never looking back."

"What did she mean?" Eiji questioned intrigued by this new story. Why would a murderer, intent on erasing all life from a village, speak a line like that? Normally only healers say such things.

"It means, Eiji, we hafta train harder. Something's on the horizon, the elements grow restless."

"But, y' didn't answer my question." His master smiled.

* * *

The images changed on the screen before them as they dug deeper and further into his memories for evidence of his crimes. So far there was nothing to prove his guilt, his memories seemed pure.

"How odd." Another scientist dressed in a white coat ran his hand through his dark black hair. His hand had passed through it so many times during his shift it was no longer as neat as when he had first arrived. "Are you sure he's one of them?"

"Certain why?" The commonplace, dark-haired man, walked up to the rather tired, frail looking scientist. Power oozed from him to the extent the lanky figure retreated as he approached.

"All his memories, his life, none of it resembles anything they are accused of. Look, he grew up on Therascia. He was abandoned by his family and taken in by another. He was adopted, trained, and finally a few weeks ago made a deal with a Lord Blackwood which led him to meet the others, who, with one exception, also seem—"

"What trickery is this?" he roared interrupting the scientist's assessment. "Our lord said they were cunning, but to overpower modern science! That is all the proof you need." He pointed to Eiji, who lay unconscious on the floor. "That mark, that is all the proof you need." He repeated as he pointed out the symbol which was burned into Eiji's skin, visible only as his cloak fell from his shoulder as he tried to move. The mark he referred to was the rune branded upon his skin, boundaries reversed.

"We did, however, learn something of interest, sir." The scientist was almost afraid to address him again, it was clear his anger rested on the surface.

"And *what*, may I ask, is that?" he questioned through clenched teeth.

"The others seem to possess some runes themselves, sacrifice and balance."

"That is interesting," he muttered to himself. "Since their runes dictate their fate, and it has attached its symbol to their destiny, maybe we could claim their power without suffering its consequences. With the added power of their runes, we could be invincible." He paced eagerly back and forth, pleased at the thought of this new concept. "We could request all enemies slay themselves, the rune of power combined with that of sacrifice would mean the world could be ours. I must tell Lord Benjamin, I must brief him immediately on this new development."

* * *

Since appearing in Darrienia they had done nothing but walk. They walked through the open plains, traipsed through the forest lands, hiked the dirt tracks, and climbed the hilly terrain. All had been silent, not a dreamer or town was anywhere to be seen as they made their way towards a port shown on their map. A place which had no counterpart in their world, a place they hoped would be willing to aid them in their journey to Pirates' isle. As they trekked through the field, the uneasy silence was gradually replaced by the small whimpers of animals from all around.

"Sounds like a cat?" Daniel stopped momentarily to find the source of the tiny cries. He was certain they were close. "By the Gods," he whispered as they entered the field the noises originated from. Before them stretched a large field in which hundreds of kittens were buried to their necks in the ground. Zo rushed over to dig one out when a farmer approached.

"Admiring me crop are yer?" he questioned; his shadow blocked all the light from Zo. "Been a good 'un this time."

"What are you doing?" Daniel asked horrified, as he watched the kittens' heads turn to watch him sceptically as he approached. Their little mews and chats filled the air. Somewhere in the distance Daniel saw a bird land teasingly by one of them. The kitten chatted and snapped its tiny jaws, trying to catch its meal while the bird hopped around just outside its reach as if to taunt it. The farmer clapped his hands startling it away.

"Farmin' cats, who 'lse d' yer think keeps the roden' problem dan?" The farmer stooped to one of the kittens extending his hand. He didn't even flinch as it tried to bite him, he smiled petting it on the head, it looked annoyed by his touch as it continued to snap its tiny jaws. "This 'uns ripe." Grabbing it by the scruff of its neck he pulled it from the ground. It gave a small mew before it was completely free from the soil.

"Cat farming?" Daniel questioned in disbelief.

"Well sure, each year I plant the seed 'n wa'er 'em with milk, add fish t' soil, yer see. Every town yer go t' has cats, more thun likely it be me who farm the lil cri"ers, tis a fine business. I pluck the crop 'n pass them on t' towns t' control the rat problem, dun' tell me yer never 'eard of me." They shook their head much to the farmer's disappointment. "Well, where else do yer think cats come from?" He smiled pulling another from the ground and placing it in a box with several others, each sat with their heads on the edge looking out curiously.

"That one's got no tail, what happened?" Zo questioned starting to come to terms with the strange situation.

"That 'un be very special m'dear." He stroked the head of the small black and white cat, it raised its head to accept the fuss gratefully. "This 'un be a Manx, 'e'll 'ave a very special 'ome 'e will, somew'at of a rari'y, or more accurately a crop mutation. Now be there anything I can 'elp yer folks with or were yer just passing to admire this year's crop? Per'aps I can in'erest yer in one?"

"No thanks." Zo smiled. "Maybe when our adventure is over." The farmer placed another kitten in the box. "But maybe you can help us. We are after something called Pirates' isle. It's where we can obtain Narca berries I believe."

"Cudn't say much about an i'land, but I know where your berries be, in fact I'm on m' way there with this shipment. A fishing town be a great 'ome to these lil cri"ers." He fussed each of the heads of the eleven kittens. "Could do with someone riding in back, yer know t' keep an eye on 'em. They be quite curious after they be unearthed, lost many a ki"en, I have, as they go off to explore the territory. All seem t' find 'omes mind yer, so it dun hurt much. There's an old lady just dan the way, seem t' flock to 'er they do, perhaps it be saucers o' milk and fresh fish she leaves for the li'l 'uns." He smiled to himself attaching the last reins to the horse. "Besides there be plen'y of room in back since we be heading the same way."

Although it was a short journey, it would have taken much longer by foot. The trees flashed by them as they sat in the open backed carriage. Throughout the journey, the little kittens scrambled and climbed from the box. Daniel watched Zo intercepting their desperate attempts for freedom, to fuss them before returning them to the box. No sooner had one been returned to the wooden prison, another tried its daring escape. Sure enough, the journey passed quickly and Daniel swore to himself the first thing he would do when this was over would be to get her a kitten.

They hopped out at the edge of town outside an old house where the first of the kittens was about to be delivered. After thanking the farmer for his help, they went on their way.

On reaching the town they each followed their own path. An action which allowed them to cover more ground as they began their search for information on Pirates' Isle. The town was large considering it had been classed a fishing village, normally this gave the impression of a few small houses dotted around, but this town had no such appearance. The shops and sea front restaurants were built from brick and mortar, the small residential homes were constructed of wood from the nearby forests. Once they had each exhausted all avenues of enquiry, they regrouped to share information, as it happened, they were none the wiser than when they had first arrived.

The area was like a carefully designed maze of houses, the streets twisted around on themselves. In order to cover every area, to speak with every person, they had to loop around on themselves numerous times.

"It's no use." Acha sighed. "No one has even heard of these pirates, let alone know where they are based. I really thought we were on to something with this island thing." They had finished their search just moments before and regrouped at the dock-front restaurant's seating area. She positioned herself as far as possible from Zo yet still within the group. Daniel glanced over the menu curiously, they had discovered fairly quickly that the food in this world was unsatisfying, still it never hurt to look. Besides, for some reason, the water here was still refreshing. Acha glanced over his shoulder looking at the seafood delicacies which filled the pages.

"Narca berry pudding!" They stated in unison before Daniel continued. "Maybe we've been asking the wrong question, after all didn't the farmer say he knew about the berries but nothing of the pirates. I don't know why we didn't think of it before." As Daniel and Acha vanished into the restaurant, Zo moved from the table to sit on the concrete wall that lined the water's edge by the dock. Her legs hung over the side barely missing the water's surface, she leaned forwards on the lower bar, watching her own reflection with what could only be described as unfamiliarity. Elly moved to sit beside her, mirroring her posture.

"Are you all right, you have been unusually quiet." A long silence stretched out as she watched Zo stare deep into the water below.

"I'm surprised, I know I don't have long, yet I still sit here now," she muttered. A gentle breeze whipped around them teasing its misty fingers through their hair. Zo closed her eyes to feel the wind's gentle embrace, it seemed to almost call out to her.

"What do you mean?" Elly questioned not quite understanding her concerns.

"Well, Marise." Zo almost whispered her name, as if she feared saying it too loud would disturb her. "She's not been active since before, I could almost believe it wasn't real." She sighed. Her vision followed the rise and fall of a small bird as it flew across the water's surface, her mind wandered. She wondered if birds dreamed and, if so, was the one she observed now from their world, or just a figment of a dream? Or perhaps it was a person dreaming of flight and freedom. She watched its carefree movements and found herself a little envious.

"You need to keep things in perspective, why would she want to be here now?" Elly, of course, knew the real reason Marise had been quiet. Her last visit had taken a great deal of energy. She needed time to recover before she could force her way through again, but she was not about to reveal this to Zo. The last thing she wanted to do was give her hope.

She had been surprised when Marise had managed to injure Daniel, especially since the almost instantaneous switch between Zo and Marise the last time he was in danger. Fighting Zo's will was tiring, she needed tremendous strength and the right opening in Zo's defences to exploit. All the times she had appeared had been while Zo had been in a heightened emotional state. Forcing her way into control was not an easy task, and this was why she had remained quiet. She was saving her strength for the right opportunity. Besides, the potion which Zo had taken wouldn't allow the appropriate rise in her emotions. Marise would certainly be here if she could be. Of course, Elly wouldn't dream of telling Zo this, the more she doubted her own strength, doubted herself, the more power she gave to Marise.

"Yeah, I suppose," she whispered bringing her knees close to her chest to touch the bar she leaned against. "I'm scared." She was barely able to believe she had spoken these words aloud. "I am afraid of death, afraid of vanishing, but saying I don't want it will not change things. No matter how hard I fight,

I cannot change the course of my own destiny." Elly looked to her in surprise, for some reason she felt the rise of sympathy in her chest. She had wondered if the girl who sat beside her had always been this afraid. Until this moment she had hidden it well, locking her emotions under the surface where they would not burden anyone, but to look at her now it was clear to see she was terrified. No matter how hard she tried to hide it, no matter how powerful the sedatives, she could not hide the strength of this emotion.

In that one moment, Elly felt as close to Zo as she did to Marise, it was a feeling which surprised even her. Zo knew she was going to lose. She knew everything would end and that there was nothing she could do to prevent it. All this time Elly had thought perhaps it was the hope of triumph that kept her motivated, kept her strong and pushing forwards, but now she knew Zo understood there was no victory waiting for her at the end of this journey, only death. She knew she would lose everything, but instead of hiding away or refusing to progress with the journey, which had been a concern of Elly's, she faced her destiny unfalteringly, despite knowing what it would bring. Through her many years, Elly had known but a few with this courage.

"Marise is part of you. I think to a certain extent you misunderstand what she—"

"We found it! A small island to the east, it's where the berries originate!" Acha ran from the small restaurant followed by Daniel, who was buried in his map. For once, Elly was glad for the interruption. Maybe it had been the desperate look in her eyes, the sadness, or the still imperfect link between herself and Elisha, but for some unknown reason, after her previous thought about how her doubts served to increase Marise's strength, she had nearly followed through with something she was never to reveal to anyone, something Zo could use to her advantage. She turned ready to listen to what Daniel had to say.

"It seems that would put us due south of one of the fixed locations. On those islands which look like the constellation as we originally thought. There are no rumours of pirates, but there *is* a castle with a small town secured inside its walls. It's said it would be able to withstand a pirate attack, other than that..." Daniel stopped his excited chatter as he looked to Zo. In the instant she had looked to him, she had seemed truly afraid, but within seconds she had replaced her mask. A mask which shielded her emotions from those around her, almost flawless as she gave the smile which didn't quite reach her eyes. But this time it was different than before, even the smile itself seemed filled with sadness.

He knew her well enough to read her eyes. She maintained this front for their benefit and, should he address it, he feared she would recall her decision to leave them, and so, as much as it pained him, he left it unmentioned. He could only offer her support and again, it was her choice if she chose to accept it.

"There hasn't been a single boat departure since we got here." She gave a small sigh. He had tried so hard to get the information, yet even so, they still found themselves unable to proceed, in almost exactly the same situation they were in just moments ago.

"True, they don't sail until tomorrow, but, the restaurant owner said they were due a collection of berries and would take us over. As for getting the rest of the way, it seems there isn't a boat built which could sail the treacherous current of the sea across there. Even so, I say we get the berries first, then maybe we'll find someone who is willing to lend a helping hand. There's always someone with the courage to try." As he spoke, he led them towards a small rickety looking boat. He paused before climbing aboard. "Besides…" he looked back towards the restaurant but chose never to continue his sentence.

* * *

"What were you thinking!" A voice erupted from the restaurant just after the small boat had set sail. The raised tones were clearly aimed towards the elderly woman who, with a smile of triumph, watched the ship set sail.

"Did you not know who they were?" she hissed back into the building. "They are that gang, you know, the ones with the marks. I figure they're best out of our way, leave them there to rot," she replied as her well-built son emerged from the door to the restaurant. His shadow almost blocked all the light which would have shone through the doorway, a small white apron hung around his neck.

"But that's Narca berry isle, how will we make our pudding now?" His mother's hand slapped him across the back of his head, although she had needed to stand on her tiptoes to do it.

"And what do you think those are? Narca berry isle may have been the place they originated from, but it's not the only place you can get the damn things. Look around you, they're everywhere. Soon as the first seed came to shore, they spread like wildfire."

"Oh, you don't need a shipment at all then? You're just gonna strand them there. But what if they get off and want our heads. They were a member missing."

"Well, they'd have to escape first and it's a long swim. Funny thing though, they didn't seem much like the rumours. Actually, that young boy was quite nice, like the son I never had." She smiled as she watched the boat fade into the distance.

"Aw Mum." Her son pouted as he looked down to his mother sorrowfully.

* * *

They had arrived quite quickly at the island. It was comprised of mainly evergreen trees making up a solid forest. The trees had started on the edge of the land, close to the point the small rowing boat had stopped to allow them to scramble up the muddy banks with the aid of tree roots. Once to the top they thanked the rowers, who were already on their way back to get their collection crew from the main boat.

Underneath the trees, almost invisible at first glance, were small brown-red bushes, each containing berries of the same colour. The island itself seemed deserted, not a single animal track marked the soil.

"You sure this will be enough?" Daniel sighed as he dropped some more berries into Zo's bag, he seemed to be a little distracted. "Well let's take just a few more to be on the safe side," he answered himself, pulling another twig from a nearby bush and placing it into the bag. "Then again, if it's not enough we can get some more if we ever get back to the dock."

"What do you mean?" Acha stopped collecting the berries and turned to face him.

"Well, look at them." He gestured listlessly. "They're identical to the ones in the town, to the ones which grew by the road. They're everywhere we've been, they're not exactly a rarity."

"So why offer to take us here, are they more potent?" she asked, noticing the boat had vanished from their view.

"No one has been on this island for years, if at all. They simply wanted to ensure our departure, surely you realised that." Elly stated, pulling something from her pocket as she continued. "I would have thought it was clear when they returned to port shortly after we had entered this area."

"But why?" Acha questioned; there was a crack of paper being flipped open. "Marked bandits?" she read, staring in disbelief at the wanted notice in Elly's grasp. "But—"

"Well, think about it," Elly began begrudgingly as once again it seemed she had to explain things. "We violated a sacred temple, collapsed a court, and no doubt have committed crimes without even realising it along the way. It is only logical that this world would take action against such behaviour, and anyway—"

"You mean it won't simply be part of someone's dream?" Zo questioned, despite already knowing the answer. They were so focused on the paper none of them noticed Daniel had slipped off into the trees as the topic had turned to the marked bandits.

"Afraid not. It is very much like our own world, as such the concept of some kind of law enforcement is not too unreasonable, after all, this world has its own inhabitants, not to mention those creatures which brought us here. Since keeping the peace seems to be the Oneirois' role, in their absence I wouldn't be surprised if this was *their* doing." Elly took the poster back from Acha and folded it up. It was only then she noticed what had been missing for some time. "Where is Daniel?"

"He was here a second ago, he can't have gone far." Zo glanced around frantically. As she felt the rawness of the panic rise within her, she realised the potion she had taken had now all but worn off. He was doing this too often, didn't he realise how dangerous it was? He had been lucky until now, but how long could he truly do this for and expect to be safe? "I hope," she added. Who knew what they would find on the island, since their arrival there Zo had felt a pulling sensation. The whispers on the wind which had previously embraced her at the port had been growing louder, almost as if it had not been the wind at all, but a call carried by it.

"Well, we had better look for him." Elly began to walk into the undergrowth, Zo lingered behind, drawing an arrow in the ground towards the direction they were heading.

The island, although small, was quite sheltered. The tall trees blocked the view of anything and everything. The branches acting like a giant umbrella above them. The light in the area seemed green as if tinted by the colour of the leaves. Strands of sunlight broke through the canopies to create golden rays of light, in which pollen and dust could be seen to pass through.

A small shout echoed around them, the voice was one they knew in an instant, although it contained no urgency, there was something hidden in its depths, a secret lost as it echoed around the forest. Did he really expect them to be able to locate him by a call alone?

Against the odds, led by Elly, they found him quickly. He stood in a large clearing, as he saw them, he ran to greet them.

"Look it's an ancient shrine of some sort. I've never seen these markings before, it's incredible!" His voice clearly filled with awe as he glanced to each of them in turn, both Zo and Elly smiled.

"It is also our means of escape." Elly approached the sealed shrine to place her hand on the door. "Mar—" she looked to Zo, she was forgetting herself again. Lately the urge to call Zo Marise had increased. Perhaps it was the subtle changes in her she had become aware of. Her hair seemed redder than the journey's start, and there were times she even spoke like her, perhaps not in the things she said, but in the manner in which she spoke. Marise had, during their time together, adopted some of her own mannerisms of speech. "Would you do the honours?"

As Zo approached the door, she repeated the ancient words which called to her in the voice she had previously heard on the wind. She placed her hands upon two small engravings on one side of the door's stonework frame. As she did so the thin carvings began to glow a strange earthen brown as the roots of nearby trees began to intertwine in the indents of the door.

The roots climbed and wrapped around the whimsical carvings, as if tracing them. As the last section was completed a piercing shade of golden brown dazzled them as it illuminated the root lined engravings. The doors pulled apart as the roots receded. Zo still stood staring before her, unaware it had opened, her hands still in place as she listened to the quiet whispers in the back of her mind. Around her, all she could hear were the whispers, they were calling to her.

'*What?*' she questioned silently. '*What do you want me to do?*' The voices whispered again. She knew what it asked of her was wrong. '*If I release it then what?*' But she already knew the answer, she knew that no matter what, she could not do as the whispers asked, yet at the same time she felt the magic rise within her. She seemed powerless to control it. The whispers circled her. She felt the force of their movements as they swirled around her. Somewhere, far beneath the world it was waiting, waiting for its freedom. It had been doing so for aeons, cycles beyond count, sealed there by a strange force, a strange seal. She gasped as she felt the second of the three seals break, the silent words still leaving her, as her magic began to attempt to release the third.

"Zo?" Daniel questioned both mentally and aloud as she stood before the open door gasping for breath, beads of sweat clung to her forehead. Hearing his voice, she seemed to wrench from whatever trance she was in. Her body swayed slightly as the force of the whispers released her causing her to stagger back a few paces. "What is this place?"

"I thought you studied mythology." Elly smirked. "The Ampotanians were famous for their architecture, you may have heard brief tales, mostly they are long forgotten now, but for a few words of rumour, but one thing which no one seems to recall is that they were also famous for their mines." She looked at Zo and smiled. "In early history, before seafaring vessels were even a concept, they burrowed beneath great waters to join lands, linking them by carefully crafted tunnels and shrines to their deities." Elly looked at the strange carvings on the door, this shine had been erected to Geburah, a demon of destruction. The carvings told the story of how he turned on mankind, trying to destroy them all, and how he was sealed by the Mystics within an artefact known as the Goddess' tear and imprisoned in a shrine thought once to honour him. Elly knew nothing of this figure or his story, but she did not question that once he was a real being.

Three seals had been placed, hope, strength, and survival. The demon would have infinite chances to find a host to release the seals, within their life, events would remove them. Long ago the demon had chosen Marise in the hope she could break the bonds by demonstrating those three traits, but the demon had been mistaken. For so long it had been mistaken, for the seals could only be neutralised by their opposite. Geburah's understanding of his prison had been flawed. It was within the host the bonds that sealed him must be destroyed. He had only come to realise this since his chosen one had lost her hope, only then did he realise this was the key to his freedom. All the cycles, all the failed attempts, and now he finally understood what was needed.

On Ipsili Thesi, Zo had lost hope and the first seal had been broken. Just now, she had demonstrated weakness, losing her strength as she failed to fight the whispers which took control of her powers. Had Geburah been able to continue for another few moments the third would have been released. But there was no hurry now, he knew it was just a matter of time until he was free.

Elly was impressed Zo had found the strength to fight the hypnotic whispers at first, yet she also felt her surrender to their will to release the second seal. Had it not been for Daniel, perhaps things would have turned out differently. She was lucky really, this time there was something to distract her from the traps. Elly knew it would be safer if she led the way through the dark labyrinth that awaited below. She could not risk the demon's whispers hurrying along events.

"I've never heard of them." Daniel looked to Elly for more insight on this forgotten culture.

"It does not surprise me, few have. Their existence was all but erased by the Mesagen."

"The Mesagen? You're talking theory dating back to before the Titanomachy. How could you possibly know this?" Daniel questioned.

"It is not important *how* I know it, just that I do. Now hush, let us see where this leads. The people of the island said the waters were not fit to cross, so this is our only option." Not another word was spoken as they descended into the darkness.

Elly took the lead. She knew what would lie ahead. Whilst it would have been interesting to see how her fellow travellers would have dealt with the obstacles that lay in wait, time was not a luxury they could afford right now, therefore they remained unaware of the traps which stretched before them, after all Elly was a great adventurer, she knew every trick thus disarmed them on approach with ease. Through the tunnel she never let Zo fall from her side. If the whispers were to come again everything would be for naught, the demon would take their lives, and since even she could not complete this mission alone, she watched them intently.

Chapter 21

The Demon Awakens

"They found the tunnel? Then all proceeds as planned." Night smiled to himself as a voice from the shadows spoke softly. There was nothing particularly unusual about the shadow. It was a long shapeless form, it was only on closer examination of the room, that it became apparent, that unlike the others, this one had no source.

"A nice touch of mythology makes things all the more believable, even in a dream world," the shadow answered. The mythos provided had not been entirely correct, but it was the oldest source they could muster which Elaineor possessed some knowledge of. The real story of Geburah spanned back to the very first cycle, when Moirai and Daimons, now thought of as demons, had walked the surface, and the Mystics fought to retain the peace. The shrine of Geburah was a monument protected from time, in their world it was not a relic from the Ampotanians, as implied in Darrienia, although the information she had spoken was the truth, the gaps in her knowledge had provided an excellent means to guide them.

"Has everything been prepared at the castle?" he asked, as with most of his queries this was nothing more than a formality. He did not leave such things to chance. He would be a fool not to monitor such important events closely.

"Yes Sire, I must say using that girl to upset the balance was pure brilliance, none but you could compose such an insidious plan. In that split second I saw her heart shatter, her defences are weakening, she feels it."

"Yes, she does," Night confirmed, ending the conversation, he had other things in need of his attention. For a brief moment he looked deep into the gossip crystal. There were other things which required his intervention now, a location he needed to be, and thus, as he stepped through the silver portal which appeared before him, he focused his attentions there.

"Gaea, my dearest friend, I will revive you from your slavery, soon you shall be the mistress of this world once more." Night approached the figure who had awaited his arrival. Her long earth brown hair fanned across the floor from where she sat. Although rich in colour, over the cycles it had paled considerably as she had been slowly destroyed by those living upon the surface of the world that embodied her. She looked up to Night as he bowed in respect. Standing to greet him she placed her delicate hand upon his shoulder, he stood much taller than she.

"Night we have long been friends, why the formality? Pray tell what ails you?" The softness in her voice still surprised him even now, it was filled with all the gentleness of nature, but he also knew there was a darker, more savage side to her. One which he had only ever witnessed when she was free, when she was one with the untameable power of the earth itself.

"Nothing, the cause is far greater than the sacrifices. How lives the Severaine?" Gaea, taking his hand, led him to a large smooth surfaced crystal, so flawless, it could have been a mirror. Whenever she made contact with it, she could open a portal to anywhere, through it, Night now beheld the true form of the Severaine as it slept.

"There has been an alteration. Something is occurring which is rousing the sleeping power. When your powers were sealed, its sleep grew deeper and its manifestation became nothing more than a spark. It was almost as if the Grimoire reinforced the barriers which were erected, now you have once more reclaimed most of that which you lost the restraints weaken, and the Severaine begins to thrive.

"Soon it shall awaken, for reasons I do not understand it is now absorbing power, an action which was previously inhibited by the seals. The seven barriers restraining it are weakening, it seems a number of them have been destroyed, is this your doing?" she questioned gently as she looked from Night to the Severaine. She knew this was his design, he had spoken of his ambitions many times, but now something played on the tip of his conscience. If the prophecies had been correct, he would rise again, but there was something distracting him, something he hadn't been prepared for, his daughter. He had distanced himself from her, yet as he saw how she had grown, how much like her mother she was, doubt within him rose.

This situation was unpredictable, firstly he had suffered the loss of his loved one at the hands of another, but this time it would be he himself who orchestrated it. Since his emergence from Nyx it was rare for him to hold something dear to him, but in his doing so he became conflicted. To fulfil the prophecy, the final Grimoire had to be released, and there was but one person who could seize it. Gaea appreciated the sacrifices he made for her. The countless cycles had left her weary, she could only hope she still possessed the power to tame it. It would be a strenuous battle, one which would be very difficult indeed, but if she succeeded, the Severaine could restore the planet, returning what man had raped from its surface.

Once Marise rose this final time, there would be nothing left to interfere with his desires. With the final emergence of this darkness the Severaine would be free, but at the same time he would have to sacrifice the one who he wished more than anything to protect. Night knew her thoughts as if they were his own and smiled softly.

"Perhaps when I was not so tired, I could have controlled my pet, but now, now I fear the power we will unleash will be too great, people have stolen too much of my energy. Tell me, what will we do if I fail to create dominance? As gods, we cannot interfere with the destiny of man." She looked to him meaningfully as if to link the words to an unspoken conversation. Until Night regained his final powers, he could not truly be classed as a god. It was for this reason his interference with mortal affairs would go unnoticed.

"If that is what comes to pass, then we shall do what we have always done, inspire a quest amongst man to serve our needs." Night paused. "I understand, this is the way it has always been for us. Once my daughter returns with the final Grimoire, I shall be a god once more, and everything will proceed as planned. The Severaine will soon be free, prepare yourself, the day draws near." Even as he spoke, Night wished there was another way, a way he could both fulfil the prophecy and spare his daughter, but he could not let his feelings interfere, this was by far too important.

✳ ✳ ✳

"It is as I said, a straight path through." Elly smiled offering Zo assistance up the steep slope that had become the tunnel's mouth. Daniel had kept cautious vigil behind them, still amazed at how Elly had navigated through the near black tunnels only to find a door which once more opened to Zo's touch.

It was almost as if she had walked it before, something about her knowledge seemed unnerving. If he didn't know better, he would think her a skilled treasure hunter, rather than an aristocrat's daughter. It was said they had uncanny instincts for such things. When he was still young, he had envisioned himself following in the footsteps of the renowned treasure hunter Lain Exerevnitis, he had read so many of her exploits. She had adventured with the old heroes and retrieved artefacts thought impossible to seize. She had been a hero of both him and Stephen as they aged. Had it not been for his death, Daniel wondered if they would have pursued that life.

Zo reached down the sloped exit to offer Acha her hand, but the concept was dismissed entirely, she seemed offended by the gesture. She would rather struggle alone than take *her* hand. Daniel, seeing this, took it gratefully, it wasn't that he had needed aid up the slippery incline, he just hadn't wanted the gesture to go to waste.

"A castle?" Daniel questioned, his eyes adjusting to the pale light of the overcast island. Of all the places he had expected to emerge, within walking distance to an enormous castle was certainly not one of them. Yet they now stood before the magnificent structure known as Castlefort.

Castle Iris, which was found within the giant constructs, was barely visible, but inside the enormous fortification stood both the castle and a town. A heavy iron portcullis sealed all access to the entrance, its thick chains entering the higher walls to allow the enormous weight to be raised. Behind this stood an equally impressive wooden gateway, no doubt because of the sheer weight alone, operated by pulleys found inside the remarkable walls. Beside this, a smaller entrance was barely visible, blocked in a similar manner. One which would permit access to individuals without the need to open the main gate.

The fort itself stood in a strategically gifted location. Behind it rose then fell steep faced mountains which descended deep beneath the sea. To its front stretched a large open area of marshland, providing no shelter to those who would attempt a military advance.

"Of course, power, the riddle from before." Zo looked to Elly, who had been waiting impatiently for them to reach this realisation. She nodded at her gratefully, which made Zo think she had been waiting for this for some time, but also made her question why she had not thought to say anything herself.

"Let's hurry." Acha started her determined march towards the castle, stopped only by Daniel's intervention.

"We all want to get in there and rescue Eiji, but how do we plan to get inside? We're wanted, they're not exactly going to raise the portcullis and welcome us, let alone open the door, not now anyway," he stated. Acha rejoined the group, an action she clearly wasn't too pleased about.

"That is true," Elly began, still wearing the same expression. It was clear she already had everything planned. She simply waited for the others to reach the same conclusions she had, then again, she realised it was perhaps quicker to spur them along a little. She paused for a moment to ensure everyone was paying attention. "I believe Acha can move between life-forms. Maybe she could control a guard and cause a diversion while we sneak inside. We can take her body with us, so all she will need to do is return to the amulet once we are inside."

"Well, I..." Acha blushed slightly at the sudden attention. She had barely used her abilities, but a sudden thought gave her new confidence, something which had been discussed earlier. She had after all, found a tutor who was teaching her to use her powers. "Okay, I can create a diversion, just something to distract the guards, right?"

"Yes." Elly glanced towards Zo and Daniel, she hadn't expected this to be so easy, she had expected far more resistance. The traveller she had seen recently grew ever closer to the castle, he was the perfect target. If not him, then who knew how long they would have to wait for another to approach. "We will wait for you to send a signal." Elly motioned Acha in the traveller's direction, bringing him to their attention.

"Okay." Acha rushed off towards the young merchant. His dark hair, although short, had grown messy during his travels giving the impression he had been on a long and tiring journey for some time. His travelling cloak was ragged and beaten by the elements. His journey here had clearly not been an easy one. "Excuse me," she called, waving to him. He acknowledged her with a wave, stopping to allow her approach, she smiled gratefully. "I'm really sorry, I'm afraid I'm a little lost," she panted, her breathlessness distracting him from the motion of her removing her thieves gloves, as she did so they once more took on a leather appearance in her hand. "Can you tell me the name of this castle? Maybe then I can find my way," she asked, glancing meaningfully in its direction. She had become quite the actress recently. With the help of her secret tutor, Sofia, she was really gaining confidence in herself. She was doing things she had never imagined possible, and all was for the greater good. As long as she kept telling herself this, she knew she could do anything, even travel with that traitorous assassin.

"Surely milady knows that this is Castlefort, the castle within its walls is the castle Iris." He scratched his head as he thought how she must truly be a stranger to the lands not to know the castle or its location.

"Iris? Well, thank you." She gave him a charming smile as she extended her hand, no sooner had they touched, Acha's body fell limply to the ground. She looked down on it for a moment. She hadn't really noticed it before, but she did have a look of innocence about her. Sofia had implied this was why she had been so easily manipulated. She had been too ready to trust people, well not any more, she certainly wouldn't fall into that trap again.

Acha flexed the fingers of the traveller, amazed at how much control she had gained since her training. She watched through the merchant's eyes as Elly lifted her body. If it wasn't for seeing her own form before her, she wouldn't have known any difference. Everything felt exactly the same, well almost. There was a small awareness of a sleeping consciousness buried deep in the back of her mind, and then, when she started to walk, she noticed the body felt less graceful than her own, heavier.

"I shall not be long, you will know when it is safe to enter," the merchant's voice spoke. Already she knew his every thought, although he slept, while she possessed the host, his memories were hers to share. Once her friends had hidden themselves from sight, she advanced, her hand firmly striking the door in a bid for attention.

"Who goes there?" a voice boomed from the sealed gates.

"Tis I, Sir Catgar, I come bearing gifts as is customary." Acha was unsure how much information she had really needed to divulge. The stranger's voice who asked this of her seemed somewhat familiar, although she knew she herself would have never laid eyes upon him, she wondered if the same would be true for her host, and searched his memories for its owner.

"Hey Catgar, it's been a while." The portcullis raised, and the gate opened. A hand slapped the merchant on the back in a friendly gesture as he had entered. The figure who greeted him smiled warmly before shaking the extended hand heartily. The switch was almost instant. "Best you hurry along." The merchant rubbed the back of his head as questions appeared in his eyes, he stood for a few moments in a dazed confusion until he finally spoke.

"Y...yes, of course. Sir Robin, I am glad to see you are in better health." He nodded at the guard before hurrying on his way. Acha watched the figure rapidly take his leave before turning her attention back to the entrance. She searched the depths of her new host's mind for anything she could use to her advantage. The background story of this dreamer's character was a complex one. It seemed he had not long returned from a great adventure, it had been a trying quest issued by the King. During his journey, he had fallen prey to a violent curse as he accidentally triggered an ancient defence which protected the amulet he had sought. Although he had returned, he had not been in time to save his King, and he had brought with him some Keres. Had it not been for his wife, he was certain these death spirits would have descended to feast upon his blood. She had managed to banish the curse with the power of her love, the one true weakness of any curse. He had been in a fevered state for some time after this, today was his first day back on duty.

'*I can't believe it.*' Acha thought to herself. '*Even here in this world, the worries and fears of the dreamer hide within the shadows. It was just as I hoped, just as Sofia had implied.*'

"Knight Robin, whatever is the matter?" A stout man approached, clearly their commander by his dress and decoration. He had been keeping a very close eye on this man, he had been so proud when Robin had been selected to undertake the King's task. It was just unfortunate that he had passed away just after Robin's departure. They had tried to find him, to call him back from his quest, but he had been impossible to locate, almost as if the Gods themselves had shielded him from view. Robin had requested to be allowed to return to his duties, but in his opinion, it had been too soon. The young man's ghastly pallor, and the fact he had stood stationary staring into nothingness for the last few minutes, seemed to support his original decision.

"I wish not to alarm anyone sir," Acha whispered in Robin's voice. "But, I believe I just laid sights on an undesirable."

"I beg your pardon?" the commander questioned as he removed his gloves. He was all too aware Robin had not been fully free of fever when he had insisted on returning to work. It had been a terrible fever which had plagued him with illusions.

"No, no, I am certain, gather the men we are under attack." Robin's voice sounded desperate, distraught. The commander looked around, there was no possibility Robin had seen anyone. After allowing the merchant's entrance, his eyes had been fixed on the closed door in front of him.

"I feel no threat, I see no one. Are you feeling all right?" He touched Robin's forehead, as she passed between them she saw Robin shudder, she removed the commander's hand from Robin's forehead. She was surprised at how easy this seemed to be.

"My word!" The commander's voice boomed, at the outburst the guards all rushed forwards. "It's true, men, gather your troops, alert the perimeter, they are all to report here to me immediately." It was not long before his wishes were met, as the troops gathered they huddled together permitting him to speak in lowered tones. The hope was to spare the public any panic which would be induced by this report, but the gathering of the guards in such numbers alone was enough to see the streets emptied, as people barricaded themselves within their homes. "Listen closely men, we have an advantage, the enemy is unaware we are onto them. Ready your weapons and follow me." Acha immediately saw this comment had been pointless, the men had come armed and ready for battle. All that was left was for her, or more accurately the commander, to do was to open the gates and lead them. "We have to attack while we still have the upper hand. Our target—" She marched the guards from the base, despite their number their movements were silent but for the hushed tones of their commander. "—Is no less than..." There was a dramatic pause as they turned the corner, their eyes rested on the group of travellers. "Marise Shi." She drew the commander's sword to point it at the travellers. Some of the army faltered, yet all stood their ground as they looked upon the figures.

Had Acha looked behind her, she would have seen that very few of this army were in fact human, most were creatures, made only humanoid in appearance by the soldier attire they wore. She, the dreamer, had wanted a huge army and so this world had done all it could to accommodate her.

"By the Gods, look, that poor girl's already dead!" a soldier cried, his vision falling on Acha's body cradled within Elly's arms. To an onlooker, the scene was perfectly staged. The intended victims cowered from her advance. Their terrified figures huddled against the walls as she approached. Zo had, in fact, stood just moments before the sea of soldiers had turned the corner. She had known they were coming, despite the fact there had been no sound to warn of their approach, but it was not her they saw, it was the assassin who slept within her soul. They saw her now as Acha did, as a bloodthirsty murderer.

"Men attack!" the commander screamed, thrusting his sword forwards. His men let out a battle cry as they charged. "Buy some time for the innocent to flee to safety!"

Daniel grabbed Zo's arm pulling her gently as she moved to meet their accusation. Her trembling hand gripped the hilt of her sword, but she lacked the will to draw immediately. She had never wanted to draw this tainted sword again. She stood almost paralysed by the sea of men that washed towards her. She could see clearly most of those who charged towards her, were nothing more than the figures of dreams. Acha had wanted a large army, one big enough to destroy her. This world, by utilising the dreamer's desire, had provided her with such, but this didn't change the fact that, mingled amongst the not quite human faces, there were people, dreamers, ones in very real danger of never waking should she strike them here. People or dream figures, she knew it didn't matter, if even one of them struck her, or one of her friends, the injuries would be very real, maybe even deadly. She could only pray somehow, somewhere, there was at least one of the Oneirois watching over them. There was once again no choice concerning the action she needed to take. She had to delay them, she had to protect her friends. Acha's eyes shot open.

"Go," Zo commanded inexpressively. "Finish what we came for." Elly pulled Acha to her feet, for the first time ever she seemed surprised by what had occurred. She was unable to understand how such a simple request had turned out this way, how had Acha, as a merchant, managed to find herself in a position to mobilise an entire army. She knew how she felt about Zo, but what had she been thinking when she had led them here?

"Acha, what did you do?" she questioned, Acha was unable to hold her own weight. Now she had returned to her original body the exhaustion caused by her actions became apparent. Despite her behaviour, Elly assisted her pulling her from where Zo stood to protect them. Acha smiled, watching as the army descended only moments away from the attack.

"Go." Zo insisted again. "I will detain them, with them here the castle will be—" She pulled her arm free from Daniel.

"Zo, what will you do?" He went to touch her again but receded at the last second. She never turned back to answer him, her vision stayed fixed as the soldiers were nearly upon her. She would have to arm herself soon, the sinking in her stomach warned her of this. Elly was already helping Acha away, she just needed to ensure Daniel too reached safety. She didn't want him to see this, but she couldn't wait any longer, unlike during the event on Ipsili Thesi, this time the sleeping power begged for control.

"The only thing I can, they came here for Marise, they will get me." Zo's posture straightened, her shoulders pushed back as she raised her head to look confidently at the advancing enemy.

"It's dangerous to use her like that," Daniel protested; but he knew it was already too late. The sword was now drawn, although he could not remember having seen the movement which unsheathed it.

"Are you still here?" her voice was harsh, filled with threat, a warning he chose to ignore.

"I'll go, but understand this, I'm coming back for her." She turned to face him, smiling as she did so. It was a cold, bone chilling smile filled with sadistic pleasure.

"I am counting on it." As the first guard attacked Daniel reluctantly left to pursue Elly. Catching up to her was an easy thing to do, after all, she half carried Acha, who was still unable to take her own weight. He hated leaving her, he hated the thought of turning his back and running, but if he didn't, he knew Zo would never forgive him. She had once more sacrificed control to buy them time. It was an act he could not waste. They would save Eiji and then, he would do whatever it took to get her back.

Marise watched the army approach, she remembered the lay of this land well. She and Elly had visited it in their world. Although this was years ago it seemed like only yesterday. Elly had revealed many secrets about this place to her, the most surprising of which being that a temple of Gaea was sealed beneath it. With such little skill amongst those who opposed her she let her mind wander as she fought.

* * *

Daniel breathed heavily as they entered the cold stone walls of the castle. The town itself was quiet, not a person walked the streets, although this was hardly surprising given that the guards had just been called to battle. Elly walked slowly, supporting Acha, although as she did so, she wondered why she bothered, why it had seemed so important to bring her with them. It would have been more fitting to have left her where she was. Daniel leaned against the wall as he waited for them.

"What in *Tartarus* were you thinking," he challenged as soon as they had reached him. Although he never raised his voice, the words struck Acha as if he had. "You're not only endangering Zo but the dreamers too."

"I'm thinking," she stated slowly avoiding his angry gaze. "That we get Eiji and leave her to clean up her own mess."

"You just don't get it do you?" Daniel spoke through gritted teeth, every part of him screamed, how he wanted to grab hold of her in the hope of shaking some sense into her, to shout and scream. But despite this he stood firm, exercising a self-control he was surprised to find he had.

"Daniel, there is no time for this now," Elly interrupted. "We have to get Eiji and get out of here as soon as possible. We have to go back for her while there is still time."

"Elaineor, that's not Zo fighting," Daniel stated soberly.

"By now, I would say not." She cast a meaningful glance between him and Acha. Even she hadn't foreseen this. Acha had wanted so desperately to rescue Eiji that Elly had never even imagined she would jeopardise it all to act on some immature grudge. A grudge which could have killed them all.

"No, you misunderstand, back then, she knew she couldn't..." he trailed off slightly as his words failed him. "She wanted more than anything to protect us, she summoned Marise herself, before the sword was even drawn."

"Idiot," Elly hissed looking straight at Acha, although it *had* proven a fantastic diversion, it was not what she had in mind. This one act of stupidity could jeopardise the entire mission, the whole reason behind their appearance here would be destroyed if her control ended so prematurely. Zo *had* to retain control a while longer to force things into place, or everything would be for nothing. She looked to Daniel. "Does she not realise how serious that is? She is testing the Gods, she knows the consequences." She released Acha from her support, forcing her to stand on her own. "You stupid child! Do you even know what you have done?" Elly knew full well she couldn't even begin to comprehend the result of her actions.

"I brought judgement," Acha said defiantly. "You're just under her spell, you'll see."

"No, you may just have destroyed the only person who ever really gave a damn. Why in Tartarus do you think she stayed?" Elly could feel the rage building, were they truly about to lose everything, lose what the last twenty-four years had tried to accomplish, all because of one moment? All because of one unpredictable action from someone who should not even have been with them? If Marise was to be reborn now it was over, and given the fact Zo had *willingly* surrendered control to her it was very likely she would be lost. Elly had seen the weakness building since she had killed that man, the fractures in her will meant there was a very real possibility the next time Marise forced herself into control, that it would be almost impossible to bring her back. If Zo had voluntarily been suppressed, it was doubtful they could ever retrieve her. They would need an event of great magnitude to facilitate her return, and even that may not work. Perhaps Daniel was the key, if something really terrible happened to him, would it be enough to trigger the change if needed?

"She wants to fight! It's in her nature," she snapped.

"Again, you are wrong as always. She stayed because her place has always been between her friends and those who wish them harm." Elly thought back to all Zo had sacrificed for Michael. Her loyalty had been a part of the young girl she had admired. Especially when she had confronted her for his safety. "She stayed because, if she had run, they would have seen *us*. If even one had strayed their vision from her who do you think they would have seen, us, or the criminals with a bounty on their head which could keep a family comfortable for a lifetime?

"But let us for a moment say that she did take the chance and ran with us, hoping we survived, who would have brought up the rear, who did I carry here?" Elly questioned venomously; Acha gasped her eyes widened at the thought of a new possibility. "And even worse, for you, she became something she detests with all her soul, but she did not even think about it. The skills, the awareness, the reflexes, all of the things which made Mari great, can only come with her. She is the only one who knows the full potential of her abilities, any skills Zo possesses are weak compared to Mari's true power.

"If she could not be sure where each one of the army you brought were, we would all be in trouble now. You say it is in her nature to fight, maybe it is in Mari's to some extent, and yes, maybe Zo shares some of her skills, but is it in *her* nature? No, it is in *her* nature to protect those she cares for regardless of the cost to her. She is a healer, a nature's child, or have you not noticed? Her place is, and always has been, between you and those who wished you harm. It is a shame you are too stupid to see that!"

"I didn't ask her to fight for me." The righteousness faded from Acha's voice.

"You did not have to. I do not know Zoella as well as Mari, but she wants to protect you, this much was clear from the first time I met her, when she was risking her life for you, yet again."

"But that was her fault. They wanted her not me," she protested weakly.

"Regardless, she fought for you. She never thought for one second she would subdue her opponent, she just wanted to give *you* some time to escape. She protects those she loves, that is the kind of person she is. I hope you are truly satisfied with what you destroyed. I hope the look of betrayal she gave you, before turning to fight, haunts you forever. Which, if you are lucky, will not be too long with the irreparable damage you just did!" Elly took a breath to continue, she could not believe how angry she was.

"Hey, I know you." A small voice interrupted from a nearby room. It was followed almost immediately by a young girl, who was dressed as a physician's aid, emerging from a nearby door. Despite the fact their voices were raised, the girl pulled the door behind her closed carefully so not to make a sound. Her pale blonde hair fell just below her elbows, it swayed with each step she took as she approached them. "You're friends of Eiji." Elly, in a very Zo like reaction, took a defensive position between Daniel, Acha, and the stranger. "I saw you in his memories. Please, come this way, I can take you close to the chamber of his imprisonment," she whispered, almost fearful that the castle walls listened.

"How do we know we can trust you?" Daniel questioned.

"The same way I know that 'the marked bandits' will not kill me. Please quickly, my father called the knights to battle, now is your best chance." Julie glanced around quickly before she led the way.

＊ ＊ ＊

"You're fighting armies?" Marise looked to the source of the voice and smiled. Blood from the victims now smeared across her. Their deaths had been bloody and violent, what had they expected, going up against her?

"Indeed." She turned her back to him to impale the final standing soldier through his chest with little effort. Glancing around for movement she saw that most of the figures she fought had somehow vanished. This was an occurrence she had noted previously, when some of her targets, the human ones, had vanished before her blade had even struck, or at least, before the final blow had been dealt. No matter, the ones who had remained had been entertainment enough. "Now if you will excuse me." Marise began to walk away.

"Marise, you know it is not time, not yet." The voice stopped her movement. She turned slowly to look at the concealed figure, a figure who addressed her with such familiarity.

"If she is *foolish* enough to summon me, then she must suffer the consequences, and there will be consequences." She flashed him a seductive smile. Although very little of him could be seen due to the hooded cloak of darkness which shadowed his features, Marise knew, should it begin, this would be one battle she would not dominate. The being who stood before her was as a god, and for that matter, one she was familiar with. She placed one hand on her hip after sheathing her sword, it was a stance which accentuated her hourglass figure, with her other hand, she teased her fingers through her loose fiery red hair. It was so good to be free again.

"Your time will come shortly, for now there is a greater picture you must step back to see." As the figure waved his arm, the air before him seemed to shatter and reform until a door appeared. Marise looked at it, even her magic could not produce such a thing, a simple door, complete with handle, she knew it would be a portal to somewhere.

"My time is now!" Marise snapped; danger flashed through her sea-green eyes, this look alone would have seen many a warrior falter. "I refuse to be sealed away this time, there is at least one person whose blood I must taste." She traced her tongue across her full lips as if to emphasise the point.

"About your vendetta," the figure sighed. "It is in all of our best interests if you restrain yourself, for now at least. Zoella *will* be returned. Oh and one more thing." He looked to Marise who, having seen some movement as he talked, had worked her way across to the writhing soldier. She twisted her sword through him permanently stilling him. She was surprised he had even dared to move while she still stood before him, the hooded figure offered his hand to her. "The boy Daniel, despite what you may feel, you have no claim on him. Do you understand?"

"So, I am denied even the simplest pleasure?" As she took his hand, she suppressed a shudder, he possessed such tremendous power that even she was unworthy to challenge him, yet despite this, he was not complete. There was something missing in his aura, something perhaps he shielded from her. She had never really paid him much attention when last they met, for now she knew it was best not to anger him, but she refused to surrender that which she had earned.

"Not yet," he warned. "Now if you have quite finished," he glanced around the field littered with corpses, "your friends are through this door, I expect you to return her when you wake." He opened it, guiding her through by the hand leaving no room for objection.

"Z—" Daniel stopped, it was clear in an instant that the person who stood before them was *not* his dearest friend. Acha and Elly stopped their search around Eiji's light barrier prison and looked up to the figure who had appeared from nowhere.

"Lee." She smiled enticingly as she made her way towards them. Her hips swayed as she used her body with a confidence Zo had never shown. "It has been a while. And you." She looked to Acha, who, despite her best efforts, stepped back, letting out a slight whimper as their eyes met. Acha looked to her fearfully, the person who stood before her now was so different than the one they had left behind. Everything about her seemed to have altered, her stance, her aura, her whole presence seemed to breathe danger. "Acha yes?" She didn't wait for an answer, it was clear she had no real interest. "Very resourceful. In appreciation how about, just for now, I let you live." Marise smiled, winking at her as Acha grew increasingly pale. "So what have I missed?" She turned as Elly approached.

"Mari, still your bloodlust. There is little purpose to it here." She looked from Marise to Daniel as if to emphasis her point, for now, Daniel may be the only way to undo the damage Acha had caused. If Marise had realised this too there was no telling what his life expectancy would be.

"A Gordian knot." Marise smiled in a deliberate avoidance of the topic. "How tediously boring." She raised her eyebrow at Elly before approaching the field to touch it lightly. She walked a complete circle around the holding cell, her movement, steady, graceful, like a cat stalking its prey.

"It is unstable, the slightest imbalance in the light and the components will collapse it, causing an explosion with enough force to destroy most things in the vicinity. Disconnecting the sun beacon at the top would prove the safest method of disarming it, however, the time needed to complete such a feat is something we are not privileged to," Elly explained as Marise drew her sword.

"Sun beacon?" Marise questioned, she would never be too old for Elly's enlightenment.

"Yes, it is the device they use to gather the light energy from the sun. It is a large crystal which transports and stores the energy. In this case, half the energy travels to this location in a condensed beam, it is then divided through the initial prism and made to create a solid field of light. Due to the energy conversion it becomes highly unstable, so the slightest imbalance will result in an explosion. The power it stores throughout the day continues to support it at the same capacity overnight. It is quite a remarkable creation, yet at the same time..." Elly stopped aware of the others looking at her, she had forgotten herself for a moment.

"And you are certain you want him alive?" Marise spun her sword idly in a few circular movements with a flick of her wrist. Her piercing gaze passed over Eiji, who lay unconscious on the floor.

"Mari, he is under my protection." This was the only answer Marise had needed, and possibly the only one she would have accepted.

"How fortunate for him." She flipped her sword ensuring the lighter shades now illuminated the air above the blade. She walked around the barrier once more as if in silent contemplation. Elly, as if knowing what would follow had already made her way to the door. Yet both Daniel and Acha stood motionless, watching in either awe, or paralysed in fear, even they were unsure which. Marise gently inserted her sword into the barrier, the blade began to shine a brilliant white as a small section opened, a section more than large enough for a person to walk through. She retracted her sword without entering. Elly, who now stood at the door, knew she had not only solved the riddle of the retention cell, but the solution she had discovered was not the one she intended to use. Then came the words she had expected. "I suggest you run." She looked to Elly and smiled mischievously, the smile was returned.

Her sword struck the field, before it had even begun to collapse she had passed through, grabbed the scruff of Eiji's shirt, and shattered the other side in one smooth movement. Her 'friends' had reached the door by the time the explosion began. Elly rushed them through into the smoke-filled corridor as the heat from the blast pursued them angrily.

Black smoke billowed down the corridor as the air became thick with ash and debris. Marise and Eiji were not behind them. Even with her renowned speed, they were certain there was no possibility she could have avoided the explosion, they had been barely in front of it themselves.

The air around them began to settle. As the ringing in their ears receded, they became aware of the slowly approaching footsteps through the smoke, just moments before Marise's figure became visible through the settling haze. She and Eiji, unlike themselves, were both untouched by the smoke or debris. She dragged him behind her like a sack of refuse.

"Here is your plaything." The barrier surrounding her vanished as she flicked him towards Elly. Daniel and Acha stood open-mouthed staring in disbelief at what they had just witnessed. Daniel swallowed as Marise approached. She looked him over critically before touching her sword gently to his cheek, the blade's energy was strangely cool. She stared deep into his eyes for just a moment before he felt the burning sting of the blade's magic as it vanished. Daniel gasped feeling the warmth of blood on his face. She moved closer to him, leaning her body into his. She stood so close he could feel her warmth as she pressed against him. Raising her hand, she touched his face, he felt her fingers trace the wound she had inflicted. She leaned closer, drawing her tongue slowly across it before whispering something in his ear.

"Must you destroy everything?" Elly asked, drawing Marise's focus from Daniel. Turning her attention to Elly, Marise smiled, stepping away from Daniel as she licked his blood from her finger.

"Power is it?" she questioned, looking at the smouldering remains of the room and corridor.

"Well, if nothing else, the guards know we are here," Daniel whispered, finally finding his voice, he hadn't expected her to hear. A deep shiver passed through his spine as he heard her laugh.

"Guards, do you think I would let even one live? The only power to worry about here is me. Let us press on. Surely this castle has more entertainment to offer." Marise clicked her fingers, the door before them dissolving into flames as she stepped through. They found it impossible to keep up, but the path of destruction she left made her easy enough to follow. The only thing that concerned Elly at this point was how overly destructive she was being, although she was ruthless and violent there was normally at least a small amount of restraint to her actions. Something had annoyed her, this was about more than her excitement at being in control. It was almost as if she was trying to prove a point.

* * *

Marise finally reached the chamber of the heir. She glanced towards him with little interest before addressing him, he was nothing more than a child playing dress up as a would-be king.

"Surrender your rune now," she commanded. Although her voice was gentle something about the way she spoke oozed with threat. The young man shifted uncomfortably, trying to straighten his posture to appear more confident, attempting to portray that her presence failed to intimidate him, whilst reminding himself *he* held the rune of power, therefore no one could defeat him.

"W-Why, why would I give it to you? This rune gave me my army." He pulled the cord to the side of his throne, the deep toll of a bell filled the air, echoing down the halls and corridors to be heard by all.

"Look out of your window child and see what has become of your *great* warriors." He rose to his feet to meet her challenge. Even with the best pretence he could manage, his shock was evident. He turned back slowly to face her, fear now lining his eyes.

"Your comrades are quite impressive, but I am more than a match for any girl, if you want my rune you must take it from my cold, dead, body." Something about the way she smiled made him shudder. He drew his sword, he knew there was no possible way she could beat him. He had the rune of power, he was all powerful.

"Fine by me." She matched his stance as she waited for his first attack.

Acha and Daniel stopped to catch their breath. They had finally reached her, and were not relieved at having done so as their gaze met with battle. Already she was engaged in combat with a young man, the one who—in this world at least—seemed to want to possess the title of king.

"I guess she's not as skilled as they say," Acha mocked, the young man she fought with was not unskilled, but if the rumours were true Marise could have killed him with a single blow, yet instead, it seemed as if she had been forced to defend as she did nothing but block his advances. Elly took the satchel from Daniel and began searching through it.

"No, she is just playing with him, cat and mouse." Elly looked at Acha, her eyes pierced directly into her soul as she made sure she heard the next words she spoke. "She could kill him at any time, but that would be foolish without first taking the time to assess the guardian."

"Guardian?" Daniel questioned as Elly removed the berries from the bag and began to make a purée. She placed some of the excess into her coat pocket, who knew when they may find themselves in further need of them.

"There are two challenges to a rune. Let us say, like in his case, that the rune already belongs to someone. Once the rune holder is defeated the person wishing to claim it must prove their worth by wagering their life in battle with the protector of the rune. The guardian links itself to the one whom it is destined to be with, runes which are not in the possession of someone still contain the guardians, but they will only link to the one who is meant to retrieve them. Think about it, each time we have taken a rune, there was something to overcome, each time we may have died in the process." Elly glanced towards the battle. "It is over." Despite her warning, when Marise effortlessly switched to the offence to strike her first and final blow, Acha screamed. Blood sprayed from the body to paint the walls. She breathed a sigh of relief to see the young man still drew breath, his weak voice pleaded Marise for mercy.

"From your cold, dead, body was it not?" She smiled down at the young heir as he begged for his life. "It would be dishonourable not to adhere to our arrangement." She lifted him up to his knees by his hair, thrusting her sword through his throat. He grabbed the blade as he coughed and choked. Snatching the rune from its cord around his neck she pushed him from her sword with her foot.

The pendant began to bubble and ooze in protest against her touch as the force which slept within answered the challenge of its new master. Placing it in the centre of the room Marise backed away.

The dark tendrils of mist extended from the centre giving width to the height it gained. The wisp-like cloud growing thicker, textured, as the creature was spewed from its prison. The almost solid mass was torn aside by something within, a form which used the darkness as its means of escape. Giant hands reached out tearing the fabric between the worlds. Its finely crafted claws, flawless in their design, forced their way through into this new reality. Its forearm muscles pulsed as it further shredded the separating barrier, tearing its way from within. The creature's muzzle already snarled to bare its blood-stained fangs as it emerged further into their realm. The predatory eyes scanned the area for its target before it had even fully materialised. The torso pushed through, its appearance of solid muscle made its black hide seem all the more impenetrable. With the large horns upon its head, Marise had at first believed it to be a Minotaur, but then, before the gateway closed, its most powerful weapon passed through, an enormous, prehensile, barbed tail which grew thin into a razor sharp point, capable of impaling its prey with little effort.

Its four burning yellow eyes focused on Elly. Seeing this, Marise forced her open hand towards the doorway in which the others sat. Her movement creating a small impenetrable field, much like the one they had discovered at Phoenix Landing. This creature *would* face her. It was only distracted from its target by the blow she struck as she leapt over its side. As the creature turned, a dazzling bolt of lightning crackled within her grasp. Although a direct hit, it did little to penetrate the demon's thick hide. Marise felt the blisters from the burn across her side where the same heat thrown at the demon had somehow been reflected to her. She looked to Elly in annoyance.

"Lee, let me guess, my rune was sacrifice." She gave a frustrated sigh, shifting the sword in her hand. Daniel and Acha watched in shock, it was clear why she had a place in legend as the most dangerous warrior of all time. Such speed, grace, and accuracy went behind each movement. The creature, due to its size, should have been fairly slow, yet its attacks fell at a speed impossible to its body. Despite this, it was unable to connect a single blow. It was so unnatural watching her fight, it was a skill they imagined only a god could possess.

Then something happened, for a split second Marise looked away. Something else had caught her attention, something which made even her stop for a brief second. But that second was all it had needed, the creature turned to deal what would have been a final blow with its spear-like tail. It would have been fatal, had she not moved. Its razor sharp appendage pierced her already injured shoulder. Despite this, she didn't let out a single sound, she simply drew back as far as the barbed tail would allow, before slicing through its thick skin, severing the tail from its tip. She forced the remaining part through her shoulder whilst she dodged its next blow.

She moved quickly, in a blink of an eye she was on the creature's back. It charged forwards, turning to thrust the full force of its weight against the wall with a thunderous crash in an attempt to crush her. The wall cracked and buckled, unable to withstand the weight of the onslaught. Marise leapt upwards mere seconds before impact, taking advantage of the moment of confusion she readied her strike. Using gravity to gain momentum she brought her sword down on the beast's neck as it lowered its horns ready to attack, the strike not quite severing its head. Its charge was unhindered by its wound, it advanced the moment she touched the floor. Rolling to the side before impact, she drew her sword across the remaining flesh to deliver the final blow severing its head from its body.

Yet the creature continued to move, even headless it continued to fight, seemingly unhindered by its lack of vision. They could do nothing but watch in morbid fascination as the headless creature's relentless onslaught never ceased. It seemed almost as if Marise took flight as she attacked, putting as much force behind each blow as possible. Both hands now gripped the hilt to provide extra force, but she was injured, it was starting to slow her movements. She rested for a single moment, her own blood staining her weapon as she fought.

Elly, having now completed administering the potion to Eiji, began to watch. The battle grew more intense as the demon simply refused to die.

"That thing is an immortal, how can she win?" Acha whispered, as she did so, she wondered why she cared.

"It is not immortal as such, but it is one of the most powerful creatures of this time. It is created by fear, fear and power run in unison. When a ruler possesses this rune the fear generated by those he controls makes the rune stronger, thus the guardian grows and the power the rune provides does also. It is a never-ending cycle." Elly gave a sigh as Marise once more slowed to catch her breath. It was only a second, unnoticeable to the untrained eyes that watched, but Elly was all too familiar with her fighting patterns. "She is using up more energy than she has." Daniel glanced to Elly with concern, her vision was fixed firmly inside the room. "Even so she will not be defeated." It seemed she was not talking to them. He followed her vision, and swore for a second he saw a dark figure in the shadow of the room, near the exact place Marise had looked before being impaled. As Daniel blinked, the figure vanished.

Marise raised her sword, tearing the creature's chest apart with her blade. She dodged another strike once more placing herself on its back, manoeuvring herself to thrust her hand inside the cavity of its chest. The creature bucked, flinging her to the floor. She lay motionless as the creature approached, its giant claws poised over her to strike, moving quickly, her hand thrust once more into the gaping wound, this time seizing its beating heart. With her remaining strength she raised her legs thrusting them against the creature's torso as she ripped the organ from its cavity. The creature reared backwards giving an inhuman roar as it thrashed wildly, its movements slowing as its life's energy drained. Marise tore the still pulsing muscle apart with her bare hands, to seize the pendent from within. As she did so, the creature dissolved into the same mist from which it had emerged to once more be contained within the pendent.

Elly stepped through the field, Daniel moved as if to follow only to find his way still blocked for a second until it vanished.

"Lee." Marise reached out to take her hand, she turned it over placing the rune within it. "I believe this one is yours."

"Did you have to drag it out so? We have a deadline." She smiled playfully.

"True, but where is the fun in that? It has been a while since I have been able to test my mettle." Elly smiled at Marise and shook her head.

"You never change, but you do grow careless." Elly touched the open wound, despite the fact Elly's hand pressed firmly against it, Marise didn't even flinch.

"Blame my stupid half. I guess that is the trouble with this world, not to mention my rune, but it does prove to make things interesting." Marise looked at the body of the young heir. "This is one mess we will not have time to clean, shall we?" Marise motioned towards an exit in the back of the room in the same manner a gentleman would guide a lady to a dance floor before him. Until that moment none of them had noticed their means of escape.

"There they are, assassins! They murdered Lord Benjamin, they assassinated our heir!" Marise's hand fell to the hilt of her sword. Five guards rapidly approached, followed by demons in similar armour. Elly placed her hand on Marise's shoulder shaking her head.

"Now is not the time." Elly walked away, supporting Eiji's weight. Although he was not yet fully conscious, he had the awareness to be able to put one foot before the other as he was guided. Marise waited at the door as she saw the others through it. The guards hesitated by the entrance, watching as Marise turned and slowly walked away, their will to live let her.

* * *

Marise awoke to the sweet scents of home, the exotic fruits, the clean air. She took a moment to enjoy all the sounds and smells, it had been so long since she had last been here. She climbed from her bed, which was already stained with the spreading blood from her wound. She looked at the injury in annoyance, it would be troublesome to repair. A quick shower cleaned the blood from her. Once dry she wrapped the towel around herself and washed her wound in the alcohol that still sat on the shelves from her last visit. Despite the pain such an act brought, her posture remained unfaltering.

Wearing just a towel, and leaving her clothing to soak in the basin, she made her way to the dining room. Spread across the table was a map, it seemed Elly had been examining this since their return. The pale liquid in the small glass on the table was unmistakably her preferred beverage, it seemed she had just missed her.

Marise smiled, running her fingers through her quickly drying hair. She took the quill from the table, she had been just about to write on the map when something caught her attention.

"Lee?" Elly had barely approached the door when she heard her name. Marise continued, not needing to turn back to confirm her presence. "This place Darrienia, it is like a document of our adventures."

"Explain." Elly approached the table to look over the map. She held a needle already prepared to stitch Marise's wound. Elly knew that by design this was a difficult wound to treat, but fortunately, once again, Marise's skill had ensured the damage remained minimal.

"Okay, well each contained a Grimoire, Abaddon, the Grimoire of Darkness, Napier village, Light and Life-force, the Perpetual Forest, Air, Castlefort, Earth, The Courts of Twilight, Fire, the Mountain of the Spirits, Water. Each of the seven fixed locations must be a place a Grimoire was sealed." Marise traced her finger along the seven fixed points on the map of Darrienia. Her finger tapped the final location, the only one from which she had not retrieved a tome. "That means the final Grimoire lies here..." She pointed to a small almost deserted island. "Crowley."

"Well, you were there for some time, surely if it was there you would have known." Elly knew this wasn't strictly true, she was simply stalling for time while the others left the house. Luckily, Marise was oblivious to her deception. Elly moved to sit her facing away from the window as she began to cauterise the internal part of the injury before starting to stitch her shoulder as they spoke. Normally she would have closed the wound in the same manner, but for this injury she felt stitches would be safer, that way she could keep a vigil for signs of infection from within, and treat it before it became too serious. Once she was finished here, she would need to meet Eiji on the trail, or he would never find his path through Phoenix Landing.

"Maybe not, these seven locations are key magical points. Each one, before it became a home to the Grimoire, was thought to be one of the seals created to restrain the Severaine, and it was this magic that shrouded them from our detection. As both worlds are linked, when the seals were erected their magical residue flowed over to secure these points in Darrienia. The power of these seals is what prevented us from locating the final Grimoire, but as they passed into both worlds, they could only be released if both were accessible. If we were to destroy the barriers, the seventh book's location would, without a doubt, be revealed to us. It is not impossible that it would be located on Crowley."

"Then how do you plan on doing that?" Elly questioned, watching Daniel as he walked from the building. He seemed to be looking for something, he certainly seemed to have a purpose, she could tell from his stride alone. She was pleased to hear Marise's intellect had not dulled during her imprisonment. All she had just revealed had already been known and understood by Elly.

"Well, first we remove the barriers which can only be released in Darrienia, they happen to be part of the magical composition which creates the protectional beacon for the Grimoire. Then we destroy the counterparts in our world, that is if they still remain. This means we need to reverse anything I may have enforced along the way. Once this is done, the remaining barriers will be weak enough for us to pinpoint its location and then we can get the final Grimoire and rule beside Night," she stated.

"True as that may be, you know as well as I, it cannot be you who seizes the tome. We still need her cooperation, which, given the current situation, seems highly improbable." Elly finished treating the injury, she had taken great care in her actions knowing that neither Marise, nor Zo, would be able to use healing artes for their own aid, not that Marise's skills with healing would have been sufficient.

"Then what do you suggest?" Marise questioned, waiting for a response. She knew without a doubt Elly would already have the answer.

* * *

"Are you sure?" Acha asked timidly. "I did as you instructed before but..." She sat at the edge of her bed, swinging her legs gently as she looked towards the floor instead of her visitor.

"You doubt me?" A gentle voice questioned. A young lady stood before her, her long blonde hair fell in gentle ringlets to her waist. She tipped Acha's head to make her look into her beautiful blue eyes. Acha pulled away slowly. Still, after all this time, she found it hard to believe the one who stood before her was a Moirai. She was everything she had imagined, the innocent eyes, the soft voice, the large flowing white wings, yet still she had doubts about what she was being told.

"I... no, it's just." Acha sighed, she found this conversation their most strained yet. When Sofia had first visited her, it had been like the return of an old friend, one who trained her to use her powers. Everything she had spoken had made so much sense, it all seemed so right, but even now, the haunting look of betrayal played on her mind, not only that, but the clear difference between Zoella and Marise had left her doubtful.

"Acha, I understand." She smiled, gently locking eyes with her. "I feel your confusion, your pain. The pretence of old is bound to leave you somewhat confused about where her loyalties lie, but I assure you, everything she did that day was for her own selfish desires."

"I... I really thought she was my friend." Tears welled in Acha's eyes, things had become much more complicated since meeting Sofia, but, in the same way, everything was also clearer. Especially since Sofia had explained how even the simplest of gestures had concealed so many hidden schemes. It was all so clear, yet still she didn't want to believe it.

"You know that was her intention, to gain your trust, to win your friend-ship. If it hadn't been for Sara and myself you would still be ensnared by her magic. You're so innocent, so trusting, how could she not take advantage of the situation? Her only thought, her only desire was not your friendship, it was the Grimoire. You are her easiest path to it, her only way to seize it, can't you see? She used you, and as painful as it is, it is better you discover this now, from a true friend like me, than someone who would mislead you from the moment you met. Is it not better to win your trust and have you assist her willingly, than have to force you into submission and draw attention to herself in the process? I only wish to protect you, why else would I violate our laws of contact, and risk banishment, in order to speak with you? I could not let her actions go unopposed."

"It is true, I am his daughter, but when I was sealed away, all those years ago, I became no longer his flesh and blood. I am the flesh and blood of the body I take, so not his by anything but life-force. There is no way I could take the Grimoire." The Moirai paused once Acha had finished, almost as if in silent contemplation. She was indeed a bright young girl, but too innocent and trusting. Acha had almost convinced herself this was the truth, if she believed it, she was sure Marise would too. But given the words the Moirai spoke next, it seemed perhaps the truth was already known.

"But do you not now look like you used to? You have recreated your flesh of old, your energy has altered the body to be the very one which you lost all those years ago. One thing is painfully clear, if you don't act, everyone you care for, all those too involved to see through her spells, those whom I cannot reach, will all be destroyed. Everything you have fought to live for, to protect, will be lost. This is your destiny, you are the only one who can end this, it is the reason you were spared. Only you can save your friends." Acha looked to the Moirai as a new confidence filled her eyes.

"Tell me, what must I do?" The Moirai placed a gentle hand on her shoulder before perching herself on the edge of the bed.

* * *

Daniel had been searching for Zo since he first returned from Darrienia. He had scoured the area from the town to The Courts with little success. He approached the gates to Blackwood's mansion. It was the one place he had yet to try, the only remaining place he thought he might find her. Seeing his approach, the guards called out their greetings. They remembered him from the day before.

"I don't suppose Marise has come this way? She is evading her duties again." He groaned adopting the same air of authority he had done previously. He wasn't really sure what to expect, but they had already accepted him as their saviour previously, perhaps they could offer some insight on where she might go.

"Yours is a job I do not envy," replied one of them as Daniel moved to lean on the exterior of the small guard house, giving a hefty sigh.

"Tell me about it," he complained, "I've scoured from the town to the court."

"Have you tried the training area of the arena?" This was the one suggestion which stood out from all the others as they called out their thoughts. Daniel turned to the man who had spoken.

"Arena?" he queried.

"Yes, she spent a lot of time there training with Lady Elly, its due north of here. It's the place that grants us access to the hidden coves." Daniel gave the man a hearty pat on the back in thanks, before heading on his way.

A gravel incline stretched before him into the towering mountains to the north. As he followed the shallow slope, he became increasingly aware of the enormous area he approached. The gravel became stone, fashioned by hand into what were now age worn steps, steps which had been carefully carved from the mountain itself to guide him to the foot of a giant opening. The area before it had been levelled, the gaping mouth of the cave's entrance easily spanned the width of Blackwood's outer wall. What once would have been an entrance to a naturally occurring cave had been carved with consideration to appear as a dragon's open mouth, lined with teeth the entrance challenged even the bravest souls to enter. Through the giant mouth, steps descended the gullet to the belly of the structure. It was lit sparingly by torches, which were kept alight at all times due to the frequency of training sessions held within. Daniel walked into this enormous walkway.

Natural light began to filter through as the area opened. Stone pillars led him down as the area either side of this walkway expanded outward in a large oval, providing what would be seats to any spectators who cared to observe. Stalactites hung from the barely visible ceiling. In the centremost area, for all to see, was the training ground. It was larger than he had ever imagined. The western section was littered with training dummies and obstacles. Blackwood liked his men highly trained. It was essential both his guards and the enforcers belonging to The Courts of Twilight, were unstoppable. It was Elly who handled most of their training here. Although here long before her arrival, she had adapted this place to suit her every training need, thus it was expertly equipped for both individual and group sessions. It contained all manner of obstacles, and it was the perfect place to train an assassin who needed to be well-versed in using environmental features to their advantage.

The eastern area had been adapted to host various terrains from sand to water. Then in the centre of the two was the main part of the arena, the open training ground. Blackwood, when he could find no other way to alleviate his boredom, would announce a challenge to find the greatest warrior. It was generally an annual occurrence, the victor was rewarded heftily. It was a battle Marise was never permitted to participate in, it was assumed she would be unable to show enough restraint. After all, the aim was not to kill his men, but motivate their training and desire to be the best.

A figure stood bathed in the natural light which filtered from a large opening in the cave side to illuminate the area.

"Zo!" Daniel called, descending the steps to the level ground. She was practising her sword skills. It was clear she had sensed his presence, but she had chosen to ignore him until he approached. She glanced to him dismissively. Already he knew it was not the person he had sought. He had hoped the return to their world had somehow sealed away her monster, but was devastated to find he had been very much mistaken. "Zo," he said again, a little shakier than before, his hand unconsciously rising to the scratch on his face. While he had searched for her, he had thought of so many things to say, but now, as he was faced with this daunting figure, not one of the many sentences, carefully constructed to call to his friend, would even come to him. In her presence his mind had emptied. The look of annoyance in Marise's eyes made him falter, yet he continued forwards regardless of what his better judgement warned.

"Zo?" she mocked his words. He would certainly have to try a lot harder than that, especially with how deep and securely she had been repressed this time. It was unlikely even his death would summon her from the darkness. *She* was in control now. It was almost like before, she could barely feel the weakening presence in her mind. Regardless of what anyone had said, it was time to have some fun. "Is *that* the best you can do?" Marise's hand sheathed her sword. If he hadn't witnessed the injury himself, he would have been unaware she had taken any damage, her movements and posture were no different to when she had first attacked him. "I had expected so much more from you after your previous challenge. I guess this is your way of making it clear that I have, once more, overestimated you. You are a disappointment, you are about as much use as a rusted blade, well," she scoffed. "Less, if I were to be completely honest."

Daniel clenched his fists at her mocking words. Something about her infuriated him, more than he could possibly imagine. Maybe it was the sheer anger at her controlling his friend, maybe it was the complete lack of respect she had for anything and everyone. But more realistic than any of those reasons, he hated her, despised her, because she kept taking away the people he loved, first his brother and now his most treasured friend. He did not want to lose Zo, not to her, not to anyone. He would do anything, give anything, to protect her.

"I don't care if you are the renowned Marise Shi," Daniel was surprised at the force and venom behind his own voice, "you release my friend, now!"

"And if I do not, what can you do about it, boy?" A challenging smile crossed her lips before she continued. "In the interest of fairness, I have a little proposition for you. We will fight. If you defeat me, I shall give her back to you, for now." Her smile sent an ice-cold shiver through his very core. "However, if I win, you belong to me and I will do with you as I please." He stared at her for a moment in disbelief. He knew there was no way he could possibly win, but if he didn't try, he would lose Zo forever.

Daniel felt the sinking feeling in his stomach as he nodded in acceptance of her challenge. There was never really any choice. His dearest friend was being consumed, fading into a void dominated by Marise Shi. She had surrendered herself so that once again they would be safe. She had given everything she could, everything she was, to ensure their safety. He would do the same. He would bring her back, or die trying. To offer anything less would be unacceptable. He snapped his staff into its solid form, with this simple movement their battle began.

Daniel's fists clenched on his staff as Marise's first volley of attacks landed. He was unsure how he had managed to keep speed with the constant change in direction as his staff somehow span to barely block the advancing strikes which effortlessly seemed to bend the air around them as she thrust, feint, and parried. Marise dropped to her knee striking out at his leg, his weapon barely able to stop her. She moved quickly, striking upwards, throwing him off balance, thrusting her body forwards to strike his stomach. The weight of her strike knocked him to the floor. It was only then she unsheathed her weapon.

As the relentless strikes continued, Daniel somehow managed to force his own blows, although blocked, his confidence grew. His movements became more fluid as the sound of the weapons ricocheting sung tales of his own ability. The more they fought, the more he saw through her technique, almost as if the staff learnt through their battle how best to oppose her.

Daniel dropped to his knee striking at Marise's leg as her blade sailed above his head. She stepped over the staff with ease, spinning her body as she did so to add force to her next strike, targeting his throat. The tip of his staff barely reached it in time to block. She thrust her foot forwards knocking him to the floor. Following through, she moved to strike, stopped only by the force of his legs rising to push against her.

He was barely on his feet when her next attack thrust towards him. His balance only saved as his staff found the ground preventing the backwards tumble. He ducked, answering her advance with another low strike before once more being kicked to the dirt.

Panting for breath, he rose once more as her sword swung wildly down to meet his raised staff. It was a move clearly predicted. Her weight shifted to push the block sideways allowing her to step into him, her sword sliding behind his neck as her weight forced him to the floor. The sound of the staff skidding across stone as she struck, told tales of her victory as he lay pinned beneath her at her mercy.

"That was fun," she whispered tauntingly. "Shall we get serious now?" He felt the pressure lift as she released him. "Get up, I am not finished with you yet." He rose steadily to his feet as if by her command, knowing then he would get up as many times as it took, as long as his legs would hold him and a few more times after that. Her strikes had been playful at first, but as their fight raged on, they had become more serious. He now nursed a number of deep slashes, where the speed of his defence had not quite matched that of her strike. He took laboured breaths, his body protesting against this level of exertion.

"Your participation in this battle is finished. Pick it up." She motioned towards his staff. He knew at this point his life was over.

His trembling hands once more seized the weapon. Her sword bore down with a fearsome swing, as their weapons collided Daniel turned his body into the block, her blade sliding down the staff's surface. By the time he felt her hand upon his chest, it was already too late. She released a force of energy so great it propelled him backwards, blood erupted from his mouth as his body struck the floor.

"Marise, enough!" A figure appeared to stand between them as Daniel tried in vain to once more move his broken body. He barely saw the dark-haired figure before the arms which supported him collapsed.

"But…" she protested, her hand rose to her shoulder briefly, despite the repairs it once more bled through its gauze. She felt the warmth of her blood as she passed her fingers over one another. Daniel was aware of the distant conversation as the encroaching darkness rocked him to sleep.

"I believe I made myself perfectly clear about hurting my daughter's friends," he snapped.

"Even *you* have rules. He accepted my terms his life is forf—" As Marise spoke the figure glanced down at Daniel. It had become apparent as he had watched their struggle that his persistence in rising to fight her had started to annoy her. The flesh wounds, which had been playful at first, had slowly began to deepen. He was in need of medical aid, he shouldn't have allowed her to take things this far. There was no time to stand and argue. He snapped his fingers, the protests silenced as Marise fell to the floor, caught only by his swift movements. Daniel forced himself from the darkness just long enough to see the figure lowering her to the floor with such tenderness. It was almost as if he was afraid she may break. This was the last thing he saw before the darkness took him completely.

"Daniel?" Zo whispered, she opened her eyes to the strangest feeling of déjà vu as she gazed upon the stranger from Abaddon. He smiled at her reassuringly. She let out a cry as she became suddenly aware of the pain from her shoulder. It seemed the wound had been reopened. Estimating its size, she knew she was wrong. Something must have happened, something to injure her further, but she couldn't even begin to imagine what. It had not been like last time, she had been completely unaware of anything. The last thing she remembered was talking to Daniel as the army approached and letting herself go. Her next awareness was his suffering which she felt from the instant her eyes had opened, so much so that, in that moment, it had blinded her to her own pain. She began to cough, feeling the repercussion of the final blow Marise had dealt him. Blood covered her hand, had it not been a sight she had grown accustomed to she would have been more concerned.

"He'll be all right, well, after you have seen to him that is. They will bend the normal rules this once as this should not have occurred. As for your shoulder." The stranger passed his hand over her shoulder and chest, she felt the pain instantly relieve. "Although circumstances dictate, it cannot be healed by magic, this should help relieve the pain for a few hours at least." She lay perfectly still for a second as a strange feeling drifted over her.

"I remember you from the village, but also..." She stayed in his arms a moment longer while she fought for the memory. Within his embrace she felt safe, protected, but she had no time for such feelings. She pulled herself into a sitting position so she could see Daniel. She almost cried with horror when she saw the wounds which covered his body. "By the Gods what did I do?" she whispered, raising her hand to her mouth. "Daniel?" She moved around to place her hand on his chest. He opened his eyes slightly, and for some unknown reason, he smiled at her.

She closed her eyes, not for concentration, but because she couldn't bear to look at the injuries she had inflicted. She whispered inaudibly to the winds. Daniel watched through her mind as nature forced its way through the stone architecture to enter her body in fine silver threads. The threads joined and connected inside her to form a larger energy which left her hands through her fingers to join them. As he drifted away, he felt himself being pulled into her once more. She felt his presence in her mind, the shared images flashed before her, the blood, the violence, everything she hated about herself, on display for him to see. Without even a thought, the psychic walls were erected to keep him out, but he had already seen too much. She was losing her focus, this was the reason why Hectarians never formed bonds of friendship. The first time she had healed him they had become linked, now every time she used her magic on him, she would be on display, whether it was things she remembered, or not.

She continued to heal despite feeling tarnished and sick to the stomach from the images they had shared.

Daniel stood at the edge of her mind, now blocked by the walls she had summoned. She wanted to keep him from the memories, keep him from the truth, although she knew he had already witnessed it first-hand. She continued building the walls, as she did, a single image entered her mind, one he had offered her, an image she held on to.

'*Is this how he sees me?*' She moved her hands across his body as their link strengthened further. She watched his memories. It had been just weeks after they had first met, she watched as a beautiful girl smiled brightly, her electric blue eyes enchanting, making the beauty of nature pale in her presence. Her brown copper hair shimmered gently as she ran before him. Finally, they stopped, setting down the picnic; he had listened with such awe as she told him stories of the stars as they came into view. Zo remembered this day well, it was the first time she remembered having felt so comfortable with another person.

The moon had risen slowly, it had been such a perfect night. The image had soothed her, comforted her more than he could know, but then the violence started. She was near a village. Just through the trees behind her she could see the Caves of the Wind, she chased someone who had stolen something from her, something she had to get back. There was a town before her, and she was angry. She entered the village without discretion, she wanted the people to hear her, wanted them to come. Then it was over, she stood in a dark void with nothing around her but the bodies of the dead, corpses littered the field like grass, each of them grabbed and pointed at her accusingly, behind her flames lit the horizon. She tried to run, yet as she did, the dead grabbed at her as they tried to pull her down. She held back the horror, the desire to recoil from this recollection as she continued to fight the images. If she stopped now, she would not be able to try to heal him again for some time and by then, she was certain the rules would have reverted back to their original form.

She tried to suppress the imagery but despite her efforts, they grew stronger, more horrific, until finally, she removed her hand, pushing the images deep within the recess of her mind, although the sick haunting feeling they left followed her. She wiped the tears from her eyes as Daniel gasped, the scenes of death and violence still floating before his eyes. Were these the images that haunted her, the reason she called out in the night? For a moment there he had been concerned, he had offered her a single thought, a single memory, but he had recognised all too well the vision of the village. She had almost seen the truth about the secret he hid from her.

"Daniel I..." She looked away so he couldn't see the fresh tears forming in her eyes, yet in an attempt to avert her gaze, her vision met with the stranger from Abaddon.

"Zoella, your friend understands. He chose to fight and face the consequences. If he hadn't, I doubt you would be sitting here now." The figure smiled gently, crouching to wipe the tears from her eyes, his touch was so gentle, so tender. She closed her eyes as he wiped away the tears only for them to be replaced by fresh ones. Standing once more, he smiled at her gently, then, in the blink of an eye he was gone.

"Daniel." Zo sighed, still averting her gaze. She felt his hand rest on hers, when she turned to look at him, she saw he was smiling.

"For a moment there I thought I'd lost you." His trembling voice whispered as he pulled her into his embrace. He held her tightly, fearing to let her go. Zo opened her mouth as if to reply but changed her mind. She would never know if he heard the words she had intended to speak.

'*You almost had.*' She had felt it as she was sealed in the darkness, the touch of death upon her shoulder as she stood on the edge of obscurity. If not for the stranger's intervention, if not for him calling her back, she would have vanished forever.

"Ah, there y' are," Eiji called from the entrance to the area they sat. He blushed as he saw their embrace. "Sorry I..." he turned to leave, unsure exactly what to say. The day was still so young and he was already so tired. If it hadn't been for Elly meeting him along the track with a horse, he would be nowhere near the area yet. He had barely had a chance to eat when she had requested him to find the remainder of the group while she gathered supplies.

"No, it's okay." Zo pulled away, rising to her feet. Eiji watched as she tried to subtly wipe the tears from her eyes. Daniel was covered in blood, although he could not locate the source of his injuries. It left him to question exactly what had occurred prior to his arrival. "What's wrong?" Eiji somehow felt he should have been the one asking that question.

"Elly sent me t'look for y', she's ready t'leave," Eiji advised. Elly had sent him just moments ago, with very specific directions on where to find Zo and Daniel. It seemed there had been no question as to whom he would find and Eiji, having no memory of his rescue or return from Darrienia, had no reason to question this.

"Leave?" Daniel was unable to hide the surprise in his tones. He glanced to the openings above them as if to ensure the sun had not suddenly sped across the sky, it was still morning.

"For Collateral, it seems it's the quickest route t'our next destination," he answered.

"I see." Zo's voice seemed a little strained, as she answered she and Daniel dusted themselves down. "Eiji, I'm glad you're feeling better." She smiled, aware of him flinching slightly as she linked her arm through his, her other arm linking Daniel. She seemed to use the two of them to support just a little of her weight as they walked. "It wasn't the same without you." He looked to her in surprise, almost as if he hadn't expected any of them to think of him as part of their group.

"Erm, thanks." He blushed slightly.

"Eiji, there's something I've been meaning to ask you. How did you end up here, with us I mean?" There was something different about her, the way she talked seemed calmer, as if part of her had changed to allow her to accept her deeds and move forwards. This was the impression she intended to give, she didn't want them worrying anymore. She was going to do everything she could to keep them safe and see things through to the end.

"It's a long story." Eiji sighed, he knew at one point someone would have to ask, but he hadn't decided how much he was willing to tell, so far he had managed to satisfy them with his vague answers. It wasn't that he had anything to hide, apart from his own foolishness, but for some reason, he didn't really want to expand on what he had already told them. Perhaps it was the embarrassment of being tricked, not only by Blackwood, but by Elly.

"You really are quite the mystery." She smiled once more, looking back at the giant gaping mouth they had just exited.

"Not really, fate just led me here I guess."

"Maybe when this is all over, you can tell me everything." Eiji looked across to Zo. Daniel cringed, expecting him to state that which he feared to be the truth. Instead, to his surprise, he simply smiled back and said.

"Sure, why not."

Chapter 22

The Forest of Silence

They entered Collateral through an almost invisible portal to find themselves once more in the bustling metropolis. The streets were filled with the delicious aromas of late morning foods. The birds, fated to remain within this sealed town, flew across the streets, singing brightly as they hunted the discarded crumbs from the early morning patrons. Nothing was different, not that she had expected it to be. Zo somehow found it reassuring that, while her world twisted and distorted so dramatically, the world around her stayed true to its form. She too would continue to move forwards like the world around her, keeping her promises regardless of the cost, regardless of what poison life threw towards her. Even if only externally, there was the desire to remain strong right until the very end. Only those travelling with her would remember her once she was gone, and she needed to be remembered for the right reasons.

"Zo listen," Acha interrupted Zo's thoughts of determination, determination to spare her friends from the extra weight of her own suffering. She hadn't realised until now how deeply friendship hurt. Friends shared each other's pain by sharing the burden, but this burden, her fate, was hers alone to carry. She refused to force it onto their shoulders, even if they would carry it willingly. There were some things even they were better off not knowing. "About before," Acha slowed her pace to walk beside her. She still avoided looking directly at her as she spoke, almost as if she was ashamed of her actions.

Elly took Daniel and Eiji to one side so they could busy themselves examining the nearby storefront, despite this gesture of trust they never left hearing range. They were unsure exactly what was about to transpire, and stood ready to interject at any time. There were things these two needed to discuss, perhaps this conversation would be Acha's way of showing that she was willing to look beyond the facts and see the truth behind them. Maybe seeing the contrast between Zo and Marise had been beneficial, perhaps now she could understand what Daniel had been trying to explain all along.

It was better they resolved things sooner rather than later. Their conflict could not be afforded. Such behaviour would only jeopardise the mission, and they could not be placed in another position where Zo may lose herself trying to protect them. Despite knowing the importance of this apparent gesture, they felt uneasy about what would follow. A delicate bond of trust had been shattered and so, they remained close. There was no telling what may occur, especially since Acha had shown them the true extent of her hatred.

"In Darrienia?" she questioned, avoiding Acha's glance in the same manner. She wasn't sure exactly what had happened after Acha had brought the castle's guards to kill her, but when things involved Marise, there was no telling what else may have been done. Something about the way Acha spoke seemed almost sincere, regretful.

"Yes, I feel awful. I *think* I understand now." Acha sighed, as she stopped walking to stand in the middle of the thoroughfare, much to the annoyance of those busy patrons who found the need to walk impatiently around her. Zo turned to look at her, she found comfort in noticing her friends were nearby. She hadn't realised until just this second, but being alone with Acha made her feel vulnerable. "I want to resolve this, things can't go on as they are. Until I understand what happened we can't move beyond this. I don't want to feel this way, you're my friend, but with all the things Sara told me, it's hard to focus on anything else. I was hoping you would give me the chance to talk this through with you alone. Help me to understand." She lowered her eyes to the cobblestones. "That is, if you want to."

Daniel and Elly exchanged cautious glances as they heard this remark. They both had a very good idea where this conversation would lead, and as much as they didn't like to think ill of Acha, her recent actions dictated the need for caution. The last time they had trusted her, Zo had almost been lost forever. This time who knows what she would be capable of, especially if there was no one else around to keep watch on her. Seeing the concerned glances pass between them, Eiji was left to question what had happened to cause the air of tension which enveloped them. Seeing his confusion, and not wanting him to interrupt what could potentially be a chance to resolve conflicts, Elly pulled him to one side and began to quietly explain the events after his imprisonment. As Eiji listened to the tale, Zo began to answer the request.

"I think..." She paused as a sickening feeling rose in her throat, so many concerns and doubts crossed her mind. No, she did not want to, how could she? She could never look at Acha in the same manner again. The only thing which concerned *her* was the fact *she* wasn't dead. It was Zo's determination to move forwards which finally, and against her better judgement, answered. "Okay." She never looked to Acha when she answered, in fact she looked anywhere but in her direction. In her attempt to avoid her gaze, she was once again reminded everyone still remained close, unprepared to leave her vulnerable.

"We should go somewhere outside of Collateral. While we do, they can pick up the supplies we need." She smiled reassuringly at Zo, who had finally brought herself to look at her. Acha could already see the questions in her eyes, why did they have to talk outside, would she be led into another trap? Seeing these questions, she realised the extent of the damage caused by her actions. Zo no longer trusted her, but would she be willing to take one final chance? "A random road so no one can interrupt or eavesdrop," she continued.

"Understood," Elly interrupted, although she had to wonder why Acha seemed so eager to take this conversation outside the walls of Collateral, especially when there were so many places within the city that would prove just as private. But if Zo agreed, there was nothing she could do but respect the decision and hope it wouldn't end as badly as the incident outside Castlefort. "If you are *that* concerned, why not hire a horse? You would be certain to avoid us then." Elly moved to examine the contents of a nearby shop window, cursing her thoughtless response as Acha disappeared down one of the side streets quickly. Her sudden disappearance surprised them all, but at the same time it came as a relief. It offered them the opportunity to speak with Zo, who had yet to give her answer to this new proposal.

"I dunno if it's such a good idea. Are y' sure y' know what y' doin'?" Eiji was the first to approach. He always knew things would become difficult for her once she had discovered the truth. Given her nature, the implications would be difficult to ignore, but he hadn't expected for someone who knew her so well, someone who had called themselves a friend, to react in this manner. He valued Acha's friendship, he felt, given their forced isolation from others, they had a special connection, but at this moment he was more than just a little disappointed in her. "Elly's told me what happened," he added. Zo looked to Elly, it seemed she had told him everything, another person now carried some of her burdens. The only way to relieve their weight was to resolve the issue once and for all. This path was the only one left open to her.

"I know, but I have to take the chance and—" Before she could continue, Acha returned with two impressive looking steeds. The act of acquiring horses so quickly raised a few silent questions about how premeditated this had been. If it weren't for the fact she had never left their group, and making contact with Collateral was nearly impossible, they would have believed the events had been put into place before their arrival, and not allowed this to continue any further. However, there was no choice but to assume the availability of horses, and the ease of the transaction, was nothing more than the luck of having found a good and speedy stable hand. It wasn't outside the realm of possibility, but her recent actions had brought them to question her much more.

"I *was* only joking," Elly stated as Acha led the horses towards them. She didn't like this at all but she knew better than to interfere. Zo had to make her own decisions. She could only hope if things didn't work out, they could intervene. Of course, that would mean somehow knowing exactly where they had gone, but if it came to it, Elly was sure that all she would need to do was ask.

"True, but it wasn't a bad idea. The less time we spend looking for somewhere quiet, the sooner we can get to what's important, right Zo? Plus, I thought you would approve of the idea of her having a quick escape, in case I try anything," Acha said almost sarcastically as she met Elly's gaze.

'*I have to trust her.*' Zo thought freely, in answer to Daniel's concerned looks. She wondered if he had also heard all the doubts which echoed in her mind. Since she had last healed him, their connection had grown stronger. It was something she had to be constantly aware of, lest he discover the truth. A truth she fought so desperately to conceal from everyone. She had constructed her defences well in the hope he could gain access only to the thoughts and feelings which wouldn't concern him, but the reality was, she had no idea how deep he could probe. But just as there were thoughts of his she couldn't reach, she could only assume it was the same for him.

'But she's already betrayed you twice, yet now you plan to go riding with her to only the Gods know where, and we can't even check if you're all right. Does that really sound like a good plan to you?' Daniel protested, unsure if Acha's turning on her would, in Zo's eyes, be classed as a betrayal, in his it certainly was. She had betrayed Zo's friendship, then, she had endangered her life, who knew what she would try this time, especially if she succeeded in getting her alone.

'If I don't, then what?' Daniel knew from the feelings behind this thought she was already resigned to continue, regardless of the outcome of this conversation, and undeterred by her instincts, which he knew warned her against it, and despite what anyone had to say on the matter, she was going.

'But if you do and—'

'I can handle myself, besides I'll let you know as soon as we hit danger.' Zo shifted uncomfortably, aware they all stared at her as they waited for her response to Acha's question. As she became aware of the growing tension, the dull ache of her shoulder began to resurface. It seemed the suppressant magic used had started to wear off, she resisted the urge to raise her hand to the injury.

'As soon as?' Daniel questioned, immediately. This confirmed his fears, she was as sceptical as he was.

'I meant if, if we hit danger'

'It's not the we I'm worried about, are you sure—' Zo looked away from him to Acha.

'I have no choice, things can't continue as they are. It is better we settle this alone. One way, or another this has to end.' Zo was very concerned about exactly *how* this would end. If things escalated it was likely only one of them would return, and since Acha's ability posed no threat to her, if it came down to a confrontation between them, Zo knew she would have the upper hand. If there was no other way, she would end this, if possible without taking her life, but she also knew there may be no other option. She had to do whatever was needed to complete this journey, failing to do so would have terrible consequences to the world. She was resolved to see this through, to face the constant turmoil, but she would have given anything for just a little peace.

'*But...*' Zo couldn't help feeling the concern in his mind, but the feelings of resolve emanating from her stopped his further protests. '*Fine, but you better come back.*'

"Right," she said finally, as if to answer both of their questions. "Sorry." She added, becoming aware of how long had passed in silence during her conversation with Daniel. She would have attempted both, but with her current level of fatigue was concerned that the conversations would become confused, and that would have taken some explaining.

"Y' shoulder?" Eiji had noticed earlier that, although it was no longer bleeding, the pain she suffered was slowly returning. She hid it well, it showed as merely a shadow in the back of her eyes. He probably wouldn't have realised at all, if it had not been for his mother displaying the same traits as she suffered with the illness that eventually killed her.

"Yes, the suppressant magic is wearing off." She gave a half-hearted smile and mounted the horse, shifting uncomfortably. Still, everything about how this felt was so familiar, she could almost remember galloping around, the wind blowing through her hair on her quest for new adventures, just her and her best friend. She looked to Elly as she placed yet another memory that did not belong to her. She disliked such recollections.

"Suppressant magic, y' can do that too?" Eiji questioned in amazement, as she took her satchel from Daniel. She searched through its contents quickly, recovering a small spherical object wrapped in a square of white cloth.

"I can, but not since Darrienia."

"Then who?" Eiji questioned; Zo felt herself blush unsure if she should reveal the details of the strange encounter, finding herself grateful for Acha's almost stern sounding interruption.

"We really should be going." Zo threw the small wrapped ball to Daniel. It took him less than a second to realise it was the keepsake given to her from the merchant in this very place. As Daniel held it in his hands, no music played, he wondered why she would leave him with such a thing, but part of him feared he already knew, it was her most valued possession.

"Look after this for me will you." She turned the horse to follow Acha. They rode through the bustling city until finally Acha chose an exit. Unlike the area of town they were used to seeing, this area had been deserted for some time. The buildings, which had fallen into a state of disrepair, were being rebuilt, despite the hard work which seemed to be going into the repairs, there was not another person in the vicinity. Zo looked at the street name as they began towards the faint glow which marked the portal. '*Commerce Avenue,*' she thought, unsure if Daniel would have heard. She sent it, more than anything, to put his mind at ease. Even now from this distance she could still feel his concern.

As they passed through the portal, they emerged on a small island. There were no settlements to be seen, just miles of heavy woodland, and the small area of grassland before it on which they now stood. The scenery itself stood high above sea level, on this inaccessible plateau. Zo could not think of any location meeting this description, despite the time she had spent examining maps for places of familiarity. Through the silence, barely audible, were the sounds of the waves crashing on the cliff face below. It certainly was a peaceful environment, even so, as Zo looked upon the forest, she was unable to shake the foreboding feeling.

On the way, Acha had explained how she had come to hear of this deserted location. Apparently, this area had been recommended by the stable hand as a good place to clear the mind, an isolated island, untouched by man. It seemed to fit their requirements perfectly. Despite the explanation, Zo couldn't shake the strange feeling in the pit of her stomach, first the horses and now this, it all seemed just a little too convenient.

Whilst Zo had stopped to take in the view as she emerged from the portal, Acha had continued and now waited just outside the forest's entrance. Zo spurred her horse to a canter, but the closer she got, the more distressed it seemed to become. She spoke gently, calming it. Was it possible the horse could feel Acha's intentions, or were her own emotions causing it to react this way? She pulled gently on the reins trying to calm both herself and the aggravated creature, but despite her efforts it refused to settle, and grew more anxious. Trying to locate the source of its distress, she scanned the surrounding area. She pushed herself backwards on the saddle to examine it for any cause of the creature's discomfort. The horse let out a loud cry, stepping backwards before it reared in a desperate attempt to fling her from its back. It was only by a strange instinct of pushing her body weight forwards on the saddle she had managed to stay rooted. It took off, dashing towards the forest, snorting and crying frantically. Behind her, Zo heard Acha scream her name as her own horse started to pursue.

The horse continued to speed through the forest, ignoring its master's orders to stop. Although the forest was as black as night, the well-trained steed had no problems navigating the treacherous terrain, clearing all from its path. The trees flashed by in a dark haze. Zo turned quickly as she felt an unexpected pressure upon the saddle, the weight of someone behind her. Her hand reached for her sword as she turned unsure how her attacker planned to strike. As she laid eyes on the passenger, she gave a relieved sigh, it was Seiken, but with this realisation came a new fear.

"Thea, wake up." The voice, filled with elemental rhythm, eased her tension. His voice seemed strangely distant, despite his current closeness. The surrounding area seemed to grow darker, a strange feeling warned her to look around. It was then she saw the eyes. Somehow the light in these woods made their black pupils glow an eerie burning red. Only a few came into view at first as they watched her being carried deeper into the forest by the runaway horse. The longer they ran, the more appeared until finally, it was as if she was surrounded completely. They watched from the shadows of the trees, hidden in the branches as the horse sped on.

Heeding Seiken's warning, she closed her eyes tightly, willing herself awake, the weight from the saddle shifted and the eyes, along with Seiken, vanished. She glanced around just to be certain, even if they had disappeared from sight the feeling of being watched did not subside. She tightened her grip on the reins as she once more tried to gain control over the horse, all the time looking around cautiously. There was something about this place, about this forest, that unnerved her. Perhaps it was because, like the forest outside Phoenix Landing, she felt a complete numbness of all her senses.

* * *

Acha watched from just within the forest's boundaries as the horse sped deeper and deeper into the trees. A forest that even Marise Shi wouldn't return from. The Moirai held the reins of Acha's horse as she offered her other hand to aid her dismount.

"Acha Night," she whispered, softly helping her from the horse, whilst lulling the creature to a state of calmness. Acha looked to her gratefully, she hadn't expected her own horse to follow the other so desperately as it raced into the forest. If not for Sofia's intervention, she too would have been lost to it. "You did as promised." The Moirai smiled as the forest floor around them came to life. The tree roots crawled towards them as if attracted by the scent of the living. "Rest assured, the forest will take matters from here, you need not worry, your part is over."

Acha breathed a sigh of relief. There was a moment when she had doubted her ability to succeed, she had questioned her ability to be civil to that monster, but it had been worth it. She shook her foot as she felt something move over it, but instead of shaking it lose it seemed to grow heavier. Looking down, she saw the roots of the trees moving as they crawled across the ground to coil around her feet and legs. Even had she noticed sooner it would have been to no avail, this forest always caught its prey. The roots rose around her legs wrapping tighter, they snatched backwards, forcing her to the ground. She screamed for Sofia's aid, but the Moirai did nothing, only watch as the scaly stems slithered their way up her legs to her thighs. Sofia smiled as her calm eyes met Acha's terrified stare. The warmth of tears flowing uncontrollably as she cried out, but she knew no help would come. This place was deserted, sealed away from the world. That is why it had been the perfect place to bring her, the perfect place to finish what she had started.

As she begged Sofia for aid, the Moirai's image began to shift to take a new form. One Acha recognised in an instant, the person who stood before her was Aburamushi, seeing her recognition he laughed mockingly.

"You!" she cried, fighting desperately to free herself from the forest. Just one touch and perhaps things would turn to her advantage. She reached out for him, but before she could make contact, her hand was snatched backwards by the thick binding bark. "You tricked me!" She clawed at the ground as she tried desperately to free herself of the vines that now wrapped around her wrists to hold her firmly in place. Aburamushi leaned forwards to examine her closely. He inhaled deeply committing to memory everything about her, her looks, her clothes. He leaned closer still. She could feel his breath upon her as he reached out to touch her hair and face, unaffected by contact with her.

"I never tricked you," he spoke again, this time in a softer voice. A voice she knew all too well. The creature changed before her to take on the appearance of Sara, the waitress she had helped gain entry to The Courts of Twilight. The figure smiled at her sinisterly before her image changed again to that of Seiken. "It's just you chose to believe me over someone who has only tried to help you, to protect you." He changed once more, Acha screamed, crying out as she saw the perfect replica of herself. "And what's more, you just sealed the fate of all your friends. I believe I told you, only you *could* have saved them, it's just a shame you chose the wrong path." Acha's scream was met with the sound of her own mocking laughter as Aburamushi watched the vines drag her into the forest. With all her will, she called her powers to drain the life from these trees, but they failed to respond. All she could do was scream until the trees stopped her unwanted noise, coiling their roots tightly around her mouth. She felt them grow tighter around her ribs, forcing the breath from her body, until finally she could no longer fight.

* * *

The horse finally slowed to a stop, Zo leaned forwards to stroke its nose gently as she dismounted. She carefully unfastened the straps of the saddle, before hauling it off to discard it on the forest floor. She could see all too clearly the source of its distress, built within the saddle had been a spike, when she had shifted her weight to request the horse to gallop it had pierced its flesh. Then as she tried to find its source of discomfort her movements had aggravated the poor creature more. But that was not the only thing which had caused it to panic. There was a darkness to this island, something almost sinister which she had only been able to feel briefly as they emerged, something she was grateful for not being able to feel now. Then again, it wasn't just the darkness she couldn't feel, it was everything.

She stroked the horse, checking the area where the spike had pierced, it seemed no lasting damage had been inflicted. She spoke gently, her soft tones now calming the creature, a tone of pretence to convince both herself and the steed that no harm would come to them. Remounting, she sat stationary for a short time, in case it once more became uncomfortable. Once convinced it was now calm, she encouraged it to continue through the forest.

Despite Acha apparently pursuing, there was no sign of her. Even at a slow pace it was difficult to believe she would not yet have caught up. The trail left by her panicked horse would make tracking her easy, even to a novice. It seemed more likely her apparent pursuit was nothing more than a further deception, and if this were the case, it meant Acha had led her to this area deliberately, and nothing good could possibly come from such deceit. As she mulled over the possibilities, a scream pierced the air. Its direction lost as it ricocheted through the trees to surround her. A long time ago Amelia had taught her to track, she could only hope her estimation of the sound's source was accurate, and her skills had not deteriorated. Back then, as a child, the reason for learning to track without using her abilities had escaped her, but now after all these years, it was finally time to utilise that which she had learnt.

Zo carefully led the horse through the trees, soon realising just how much she had relied on her senses, even at a young age. It was one thing to *intend* to learn the skill without using her natural talents, but it was another to actually do it. No matter how hard she tried to concentrate, it seemed impossible to navigate the identical trees. Growing frustrated, the horse began to fuss again, stepping backwards as it protested against her request to advance. She glanced around cautiously, despite being surrounded by nature, she felt anything but calm. This would be the type of place normally sought for quiet reflection and comfort, but there was nothing comforting about this forest.

"Thea." Seiken's voice spoke in a gentle warning tone. "Wake up." He stood behind her just a few feet away from the horse, but even so, his voice, like before, seemed to come from so far away. Now she was able to see him clearly, she noticed how different the atmosphere felt compared to the last time they had met by the stream in Darrienia. Their eyes locked onto each other as he spoke, already she felt the heat rising to her face.

"I am awake, aren't I?" Zo forced herself to turn away from him to speak, even now, despite the situation, she could feel herself being drawn towards him. This was no time to allow herself to be distracted, not now, she had to find Acha.

"If you are awake, how can I be standing here?" His words caused a shift in her, it was like waking in that moment just before sleep, first came the sensation of falling, then she jumped awake. She turned to look at him, only to find he had vanished once more.

Acha's screams still resonated through the air as Zo tried to spur the horse once more into motion. It had barely moved several paces when once more it bucked but, unlike before, there was no hope of recovering her lost balance. Closing her eyes, she braced her body for impact, yet instead of the solidity of the ground rising to meet her, she found herself within Seiken's embrace, watching as the horse disappeared into the darkness of the forest. Before even having time to thank him, he had vanished, her fall to the ground far softer than that which had first been anticipated. Frustration rose within her as she questioned how it was possible to even tell the difference, awake, asleep, it all seemed the same, and regardless of her apparent state, her journey through this forest remained unaffected.

"How far have we come into this forest?" Zo questioned aloud, hearing her voice sent a sudden shiver up her spine as she hoped there was nothing around to answer. She had warned herself countless times to only ask questions to the silence should she want a response. Her only reply was the ever-fading sounds of Acha's muffled cries.

"Thea." Seiken once more stood before her, waiting for her to draw closer before he spoke again. "You are in great danger, this is no ordinary forest." Acha let out a desperate scream, the sound enough to once more rouse her. It was impossible to tell if it had been louder, or if she was getting closer. This place and its constant deceptions were tiring. Thinking on this, she paused for a moment, doubts now crossing her mind, how could she even be sure Acha was in danger? It could just be another trick to lure her further into the forest, or worse, an illusion created by this place to entrap her.

Regardless of her doubts, she found her pace quickening until it became a determined sprint. One way or another this had to end. This confrontation had grown tiresome, deception or not, she would discover the truth. The subdued cries seemed closer, yet every second they grew weaker. Straining her hearing, she listened intently, trying to determine their direction over the sounds of the crunching debris beneath her feet. Even stumbling upon the undergrowth did little to slow her pace. The dark, twisted shadows almost made her believe the trees roots rose from the earth to wrap around her ankles. The more she stumbled, the more this seemed plausible. Her pace froze as the air grew still, the world around her filled with a deadly stillness. Acha's screams had been silenced. With nothing to assist her, she could only hope venturing deeper into the forest would somehow lead her where she intended.

* * *

"Commerce Avenue, are you certain? That street has been inactive for, years at least." Elly couldn't hide the concern in her voice as they stood on the edge of the abandoned dirt track, which Daniel had apparently seen them disappear down. This area had been in a state of disrepair for some time and was currently under renovation after the smaller houses became unsafe. Most of them were still boarded up whilst the workmen focused on demolishing the smaller buildings first in order to allow the entire area to be rebuilt. The odd tool lay on the ground where it had been discarded, no doubt as they took a well-earned break.

"Positive, I saw her and Acha go down it not long after they left," Daniel answered. Strictly speaking it was a lie, but he knew without a doubt this was the way they had gone, and this lie was the only way to explain it. Hopefully they wouldn't think to question how he had arrived here around the same time as his mounted friends. Had they, he would be unable to explain. Elly looked from Daniel to an elderly man, whom Elly had insisted they brought along.

"But that's impossible, that portal has been out of service for what seems like forever. It's non-operational, Lady Elly, see for yourself." The elderly man had been a powerful Hectarian in his time and now found himself a member of the council who helped to control this settlement. There had been many concerns raised since Daniel first asked where it led over an hour ago. Elly had almost dragged them straight to this man when she had discovered the truth behind his query. He had clearly passed into his twilight years, but he possessed youth and dexterity of one half his age. When Elly had explained the situation to him, he too had seemed concerned about Daniel's observation. In fact, he had seemed positively alarmed at the thought that *anyone* could have exited down this particular street, so much so, he had agreed to accompany them in order to ensure the bind remained intact.

Elly paced the avenue to find only a solid field at the road's end and nothing more, no gateway and no signs of a frame left by a temporary portal, she walked back sighing. This did not bode well.

"Daniel, are you certain it was this street, could it have been another one?" Elly questioned, even as she did so it seemed as if she wasn't really expecting a different answer.

"Positive." Elly gave another sigh as she looked to the councilman who, in response, once again shook his head. But it wasn't disbelief behind it, it seemed far more serious.

"What's in Commerce Avenue?" Eiji questioned, seeing the grave expression. Sooner or later, either he or Daniel had been bound to ask. Elly had been surprised it had taken them this long, especially given her initial reaction to the query.

"It was condemned centuries ago now. It was rumoured to have led to the island that was home to none other than the Perpetual Forest." The old man failed to hide the excitement in his voice as he delivered the distressing news. "But to pass through now is..." Daniel looked to Elly, instantly realising the time-scale she had given was far shorter than the councilman had claimed. Could it be that she was wrong, or was she hiding something from them again? Maybe she knew something even this well-learned man did not, a way to activate the dormant portal. If that was the case, then why were they standing around here instead of pursuing them?

"You mean the Forest of Silence, the Forest of Sleep?" Daniel interrupted, the surprise enough to halt his pacing, an action which led him to wonder when he had started this movement. His interruption beat Eiji's by seconds, but both had wanted to ask the same thing. Daniel looked between Elly and the councilman as he waited for the much feared answer. If they *had* gone there, it would explain why Daniel felt nothing of her presence. It would also explain the feeling of sheer distance just before he lost his awareness of her completely. He wondered had it not been for her healing him again if he would have felt anything, but since then he had been so much more aware of her and her feelings, almost as if they were his own. Even if she shielded them from him, he could still feel her, feel that she was near without the need to look. He was constantly aware of her, regardless of where she was, that was until after she sent her message when their connection dissipated. Since then he hadn't felt her and knowing now what he did, he knew he had every reason to be worried.

"All of those yes," Elly answered. "It is rumoured to be as old as existence itself, a forest filled with traps and lures which even the Gods cannot claim immunity to. Within its boundaries, magic is useless as it is absorbed to nourish the surroundings, hence effectively silencing magic. The other aspect to this forest was that travellers began to lose the ability to define reality from dream. This is due to its existence between our world and Darrienia. When anyone enters, with the exception of certain creatures such as those summoned by magic, the forest will sense their presence and—"

"Eat them!" The old man exclaimed, unlike when Daniel interrupted, Elly did not give him a scornful look. "You see, the forest causes a sleep unlike anything known to these worlds. The trees lure their victim to its centre, feeding images into their mind, then, as they reach the beckoned place, they never wake again. The trees are said to absorb them into their bark, allowing them to devour their life-force, preserving their life artificially as they feed on them for centuries, until nothing remains. It was for this reason the path was sealed and no one has ventured to that accursed place since. The portal has been sealed for—" There was no time to finish his sentence, the sound of a galloping horse broke the conversation. From nowhere, appearing through the sealed portal, rode Acha, a panic stricken look on her face. She rode so hard that when she realised they were already before her, she nearly fell straight from the horse as she forced it to a quick stop.

"Come quickly," she panted, the tones of urgency clear in her breathless voice. "Something terrible has happened." She paused a moment to take in yet more laboured breaths. Daniel rushed to her side, he already knew Zo was not going to miraculously appear behind her. "I was riding with Zo, and we appeared on this island, her horse went galloping into the Forest of the Epiales! You have to hurry." Daniel offered his hand to help her down, unable to read the thoughts behind the suspicious glance which Elly gave her. Despite a nagging doubt at the back of his mind, he began to walk towards the place Acha had first appeared. Moving quickly Elly grabbed the back of this cloak, pulling him back forcefully.

"What are you doing!" he snapped, struggling to break free of her grip.

"I do not think it is wise to rush in. Let us go to the tavern. Miss Night can tell us exactly what happened." Elly stated firmly. She didn't question that Acha had led Zo there deliberately, what she hadn't anticipated was her return, it certainly warranted further investigation, fortunately there was just the place to conduct such a feat nearby.

"But Zo, she's in trouble," Daniel protested, aware Acha also made this protest. Elly, who now also held the reins of the horse, released him to brush some debris from the creature before giving it a slap to return to its owner.

"True," Elly said calmly, "but it would be pointless to rush and be trapped ourselves, besides we need as much information as possible regarding the Forest of the Epiales, I thought it was merely a legend." Had any further objections been spoken, she had not taken note of them as she grabbed Acha's arm, her hand pressed firmly on the small of her back as she forced her in the direction of the tavern. Elly's grip on her never yielded until they entered the small building which sat just outside the boundaries of the disused area.

Elly had no doubt that, if she knew what this place was, she never would have entered, but now she had stepped through the doors it was only a matter of time before the truth was revealed. This place was yet another one of Collateral's unique features, even she couldn't stay here too long. It decomposed any enchantments with the addition of its own very potent one, anyone walking through the door would be susceptible to it, but its manifestation time varied. Elly just had to keep her here long enough for the charm to take effect, then the truth would be revealed to all.

"But you just said—" Daniel finally found himself able to speak, something about the atmosphere as they marched here demanded silence; Elly shot a silencing look to him, this was the only warning he would need.

"Acha, how did you escape? Maybe you can give us some insight into how to assist her." Elly questioned, before thanking the waiter, who had brought them some water, despite the fact they had never ordered. It had probably gone unnoticed to her companions that she was very well known in these parts.

"I never entered," she answered, a tone of urgency in her voice as she glanced through the window in the general direction of the street.

"But your horse was covered in forest debris," Elly challenged. Already she could feel the tingle of her own enchantment breaking down, but she knew from experience she could withstand these premises a while longer before it became a danger to her. Worst case scenario, she would return to her dormant state until she was removed from the tavern, the truth enchantment which lined this place worked incredibly slowly on her, mainly because she wasn't really here in physical form. Things, however, would be different for Acha.

"Was it?" she questioned.

"Most definitely." She kept the same calm, unreadable tone which she had adopted since Daniel had helped Acha from the horse.

"Oh. Well, I can assure you I most definitely did not. I was a coward, I only watched as she vanished into the forest." Elly looked to Eiji, who in turn, turned his sight to Daniel.

"We're wasting time, surely she can tell us all this on the way." He sighed impatiently, as a sick nauseating feeling washed over him, why did they insist on lingering here? The longer they spent interrogating Acha as to whether she did or didn't enter the forest, the worse the situation would become, what relevance did it all have anyway? They had to go there.

"I have to agree, who knows what danger lurks there, what fate befalls her even now. Time is of the essence." Acha stood followed by Daniel, she slid a hand into one of her pockets as the nature of the place started to become apparent.

"Daniel, be patient," Elly scolded as she warned him to stop. It was a warning he did not give heed to. "To head into the Forest of the Epiales without a strategy is reckless. We need to plan this carefully or else we will end up trapped for eternity." More precisely, vessel or not, *she* would be trapped for eternity, they would only last a few centuries. Daniel ignored her warning and continued to follow Acha out of the tavern. Elly gave a heartfelt sigh, why were they always so impatient? If they had just waited a few more moments the reasoning behind this conversation would have been apparent and the true interrogation would have begun, but now that Daniel followed her, there was no way to prevent them from leaving. There had been a very specific reason she had brought Acha to this establishment, but it was meaningless now Daniel had given her the very thing she had needed, a way to leave.

Elly gave yet another sigh as she looked to Eiji who, although standing, had made no attempt to pursue them. At least he had the sense not to rush into this situation, he probably felt the same sense of alarm as she did. With no other choice they followed, but not before she asked Eiji a single question. He covered his mouth, his eyes wide in alarm as he gave an all too honest answer before hurrying from the tavern, Elly smiled to herself.

Acha and Daniel had already covered a lot of ground, but even should they arrive before her, they would be unable to go any further, after all the portal was sealed, and she highly doubted Acha could open it this time.

* * *

"Thea, you need to get out of here!" Zo stopped her aimless wandering as she turned to look at Seiken in surprise. She had been listening so intently for any indication that Acha was near that his sudden appearance had startled her.

"Why are you here?" she snapped, not intending to direct her frustration towards him. She had been walking around for what seemed like hours, unsure exactly how she was meant to find Acha in a place which not only neutralised her senses, but somehow seemed to make her walk in circles. She was no closer to finding her now than when the search had first begun. It appeared so much distance had been covered as she walked deeper and deeper into the darker parts of the forest, yet its centre somehow continued to elude her.

"You're asleep again." His gentle voice did not rise to meet her short tone.

"Sure just like you said the minefields were safe!" she spat suddenly. Her memories had played heavily on her mind during the walk. She found herself thinking back over events and betrayals, a train of thought reminding her of the need for caution, a reason to remain focused and not be distracted from things of importance when she found herself looking upon him. He had endangered them, deceived them. If not for his actions, Eiji wouldn't have been abducted. If she had been more cautious of him, Acha may never have discovered her secret, at least not in the manner she had. There would have been no reason to pass through Phoenix landing, no reason to find herself at the top of Ipsili Thesi, and no reason to now question if she and that murderer were in fact the same.

"What?" The utter bewilderment on his face made her doubt the words she had spoken.

"How can I trust you?" She turned away, trying to force herself to remain angry with him. Her arms crossed firmly, her gaze burning into the forest debris as she pushed onward. Inexplicably, she felt the anger soften. It was useless to try to pass the blame, it fell neatly on her shoulders. Besides, something about the way he had acted since Abaddon had raised doubts, warnings that she hadn't listened to, warnings which were no longer roused when she was near him.

"Thea, you have to believe me, I knew nothing of that. Think back, was it really me who stood before you and endangered your life?" He tried to maintain his calm composure, yet as he spoke he failed to hide the underlying sadness her doubt had caused. He wasn't really sure exactly what had happened, but from his brief conversation with Eiji it had seemed serious. He moved quickly to stand before her, meeting her eyes before continuing. "Night discovered I was helping you. He imprisoned me, ask Eiji if you doubt my words. It could not have been me," he stressed as his voice rose to meet her accusation.

"You're here now, did you by some miracle escape?" How could he claim imprisonment yet stand before her now? She wanted to believe him, after all her own mind had told her something had been different the last few times they had met. There had been none of the electricity or the feeling of history which seemed to flow between them when they were together.

"This place is different. We don't have time for this now, Thea, you have to wake up they know you are here." He glanced around nervously, there was a reason his people never entered this domain, it was filled with the only creatures the Oneirois feared, the Epiales. The Epiales were not beings of Darrienia, they resided within this forest, yet still despite this, they walked Darrienia's surface. They frequented the darkness, but also hunted the dreamers in hopes to lure them here to feed their master. They were the only enemy of the Oneirois, the only creatures which could do them harm within their own world. They had the power to turn nightmares into reality, and as such had taken control of the darkness of their world. "Please," he begged.

"Even if I am asleep as you say, it's day. They cannot touch me by their own rules, right?" Zo felt the unexplainable anger begin to fade, realising she had somehow known all along that he wouldn't betray her, but she still scolded herself for being swayed by but a few words. "Don't I only have to contend with the monsters after your nightfall?"

"You don't understand. In Darrienia this is the Forest of the Epiales, it is both in and parallel to our world as it is with all others. It remains the one place our people do not enter. The forest's master is known as Melas-Oneiros, the black dream, it is he who controls all within this domain. It is *always* night here, this is their territory. Those who step inside are fair game, regardless of what rules are set. Acha knew this. She knew and—"

"I know." Zo sighed, reluctantly. She had felt it even before they had left Collateral, the betrayal which hung in the air. She had hoped it was nothing more than a figment of her imagination, but upon their arrival, and seeing the forest, she had known. It had felt almost familiar, as if she had been here before, but even with her lingering doubts she had been so desperate to believe, to put her trust in Acha and their friendship one last time.

"Then why?" His voice seemed to plead for her to listen. He took her hand gently in his and sighed.

"This, this is the third time she has betrayed me. I was hoping things would be different, but as soon as I entered here, I knew." She felt Seiken squeeze her hand softly.

"What would you offer me for some peace, your life, your soul?" he questioned, gazing deeply into her eyes, his own reflecting such concern and pain as he looked upon her.

"Excuse me?" She snatched her hand from his. That voice had not seemed right. Seiken glanced around before grabbing her shoulders tightly, it seemed almost surreal but he began to shake her.

"I said wake up, they're coming!" He released his grip as Zo looked to him in confusion. "In this place both your sword and magic are useless. Please wake up, they're coming." He clapped his hands, for a second the scenery changed, but all too soon she was facing him once more. A wave of panic rose in her as, even without her senses, she could feel the darkness closing in. "Run then!" he exclaimed, pointing her in what she could only assume to be the direction of the exit. His voice seemed desperate, alien to its normal calm exterior. He knew if the darkness reached her she would be trapped forever within this forest. The same darkness that had taken Acha would seize her. "Whichever way your mind tells you to go, follow the other. You must leave this place," he called as she ran. Somehow, she knew he couldn't follow her, at that moment he was in as much danger as she was, and so she ran.

Her continual running finally yielded results as the familiar prickle of her slumbering powers began to stir. Looking around, there seemed to be nothing but the darkness which led deeper into the forest. Then, for but a second as she blinked, the exit had been visible. She desperately aimed towards the once more concealed escape, holding its image in her mind, until finally, to her relief, her vision now fell upon the area where they had first arrived. She hesitated on the forest's edge. Now she knew its secret. As long as she walked towards what appeared to be the denser trees, she would always be able to locate the exit.

"Not without Acha." Once more she spoke aloud, but this time, as she ran, she received a response. The smaller trees reached down, their branches grasping and tearing at her clothes. Their attack yielded little result but relieved her of the satchel as she ran through the tangling undergrowth. She slowed her pace for but a moment, questioning if she should return to retrieve it. She knew time was of the essence, she could always find it later, but for Acha every second was critical. She continued her determined run, all the time making sure her path continued in the direction her mind convinced her led to the exit.

"But she betrayed you!" Seiken shouted from just outside the forest. Eight more steps, eight more steps and she would have been safe. She had known how close she was to the exit, Seiken was sure of it, yet she turned back.

"I know," she called out, only to find Seiken had appeared in front of her once more. He seemed tired, almost as if his presence within the forest drained him. She realised that each time she had seen him he had looked more and more fatigued. On the forest's boundaries, she had felt the forest eating away at her magic, she could only imagine what effect it would have on someone like Seiken, whose entire form was composed mainly of magic.

"Three times she deliberately turned on you, endangered your life. Why must you risk yours to save hers?" He could have understood her actions if it had been Daniel, or nearly anyone else, but for her to risk her life for someone who wanted to destroy her, it didn't make sense. He appeared again before her. His presence here had not gone unnoticed, his time was now limited. The Epiales knew part of him encroached on their land, and it was taking every effort, every skill he could muster, to distract them from his location. It was a feat he could no longer maintain, yet he had to try to stop her.

"If I don't, all her thoughts of me become true, but despite that, she only acted on what her heart believes to be true." Acha had always been somewhat naive. There were times which her innocence, nurtured by the belief from the time she was raised, shone through. When she had first discovered Zo was a 'witch', she had been almost panicked, and how someone had easily convinced her she was Michael's sister. She hadn't said anything at the time, she hadn't realised the harm one little lie could do, besides, she was unaware of any events which occurred after she had been sealed. This person could have been close to her friend, but she doubted it. It took very little for Acha to believe someone, she never seemed to question anyone's word, unless of course it was hers.

"She *will* do it again." Seiken called after her, although he could travel here in astral form easily due to its nature, this place mirrored the effects of the bonds that still bound him. Now both fed off the very source of his energy he knew he couldn't last much longer.

"I'll be ready. I need to address this one thing at a time. I must find her. To the centre first," she called back.

"No, wake up first!" he shouted with all his power to ensure it reached her. He could only hope for the next few moments she would be safe.

* * *

Acha stared up at the gentle green shaded canopies of the surrounding trees from the small grassy clearing in which she lay. The rays of sun penetrated the gentle foliage to highlight the small insects and pollen drifting within the area. In that moment she felt truly at peace. So this was the underworld.

Given what she had discovered, it seemed unlikely she would be welcomed into Elysium, so where exactly was she? She pushed herself to sit, she could hear the sounds of a nearby river as it raced through the forest. It truly seemed like paradise, she didn't deserve to be here.

A young girl skipped merrily in the area just to her right. Acha turned her vision, watching the dark-haired child pick the nearby wildflowers. She sang gently to herself, her face growing strangely serious as she blew the white seeds from a dandelion clock.

"One," she whispered taking another deep breath, "two," she looked to Acha with concern, "three." With a final blow the final seeds scattered through the air, chased away by the gentle breeze. "Whatcha waiting for? If you don't follow me, you'll never escape," the girl called, vanishing into the trees. Rising to her feet a wave of dizziness encompassed her. The air seemed heavy with the sense of foreboding. She had felt this presence once before. Her vague recollection of it suggested it had fought to seize her, moments before she had been confined to the amulet.

"Wait!" she cried, pursuing the child quickly into the forest. As she did, three shadows passed over the clearing. She could hear the child's hurried steps from just ahead. The occasional glance of her hair, or clothing, caught her eye as she fought her way through the tangled undergrowth. The sounds of the river grew ever closer. The child's movements stopped abruptly, her hesitation allowing Acha the chance needed to place her hand upon the girl's shoulder.

"We shouldn't be here," the girl whispered, her eyes wide with fear as she gazed upon the meeting of two great rivers to their left. Their very structure was unnatural, giant waves crashed across their surface, twisting and grabbing towards the strange creatures that flew above. The black winged monsters delivered the bodies of people into the raging waters or fires below as the rivers rose hungrily to snatch their meals. She backed away slowly. "Quickly before they see you. There's still a chance you can escape."

"Escape?" Acha questioned in surprise. There was no escape from death.

"It's too late for me, I have been here for too long. But you, you still have a chance. You must purify yourself before Melas-Oneiros or his creatures find you," the girl whispered desperately, backing further into the protection of the trees. She had done well to avoid the creatures all these years, but she had already lost the most important thing.

"Melas-Oneiros?" Acha questioned, wondering if this strange entity had any connection to the Oneirois.

"The ruler of the forest, the dark rider, he feeds on the life-force of dreamers. You entered the Perpetual Forest, your being here represents your struggle to reject the reality he presented you with, but it also shows how close you are to losing the link to your body. You must fight. There's still time, as long as those creatures don't seize you there's still hope for escape. You can still get back." The young girl looked to Acha, she spoke now with a maturity which defied her youth.

"What about you?"

"It is too late for me. I no longer recall my own name, he owns it now."

"What do you mean?"

"Centuries ago I came to the forest, like you I was taken by it. I rejected his reality but was tricked into drinking from Lethe. I forgot my name, and I am resigned to walking these lands until the creatures submerge me in Lethe and return me to sustain him, or the last of my essence fades. My body has long been devoured, even if I found the path I could never return. Soon all I was will be forgotten." She placed something within Acha's hand. "Please guard this. It has brought me luck in evading them for so long, perhaps it will do the same for you."

"What is it?" Acha questioned, examining the strange looking flower.

"It is all that remains of what I once was." Acha inserted the flower carefully through the buttonhole of her shirt. She knew she would need all the fortune possible to avoid the patrolling creatures.

"But how do I escape?" Acha heard tormented screams as a creature dropped another humanoid figure into the waters. If the clear waters that rose to catch them were, as the girl implied, Lethe, did this mean the river which seemed to be composed of fire was Phlegethon? These two seemed the only ones the winged atrocities seemed inclined to deposit the humanoid prey within. Was there some significance to the one they were taken to? Perhaps some meaning in the reality they would experience as they lay trapped within the forest.

"You must purify your essence. Cleanse yourself of your wrongdoings by drinking from Styx and Acheron, but I warn you, do not so much as touch the river Lethe, or you too will lose your name and be trapped within this facsimile of the underworld, walking its fields until either you are returned to him or are no more. Once you have succeeded in your inward purification, you may pass through the ivory gate and return to your body. Then you need only stay strong until your friend rescues you. Listen to your instincts, they will warn you if you are about to partake from the wrong source. Your failure to respect them is why you are here in the first place. You would never have betrayed your friend had you listened to your intuition instead of the words of strangers."

"How do you know about that?" Acha questioned, the shame ringing clearly through her tones of surprise.

"All within this realm are connected." The girl gestured towards the great marsh where the five rivers met, as if to imply they were symbolic of how all things within this world were joined.

"Is there nothing I can do for you?"

"Yes, make it out no matter what. Time is short, I cannot follow you, they have my scent already. It is only by the grace of this forest I stay protected from them, now go." As she spoke, Acha became aware of another dandelion clock appearing near the girl. "Go," she repeated, and once more began to blow the seeds counting as she did so.

Acha reluctantly left, her steps cautious as she sought the means to take cover from the skyward predators. Inhuman screeching filled the air as the creatures circled and dove through the skies. They stalked the figures which scurried below, seizing them, only to deposit them within the waters, returning them to the dream-reality which had been expertly crafted just for them. Her path would not be an easy one, the best course of action would be to approach the marsh and drink near the confluence, but the surrounding area was open, she would be exposed. Only the occasional tree, found scattered across the meadow, would provide cover on the approach to the first river. She cast her gaze skyward, dashing frantically from tree to tree hiding herself beneath their branches in hope that their protection would be enough to conceal her from view. The river was close now. There was no cover between her and the riverbank and she could already smell the heavy decaying odour which seemed to permeate the waters.

The water was foul. The dirty, muddy liquid seemed almost solid as the rising stench of decay made her heave. Her hands hesitated above the polluted surface of the river Styx, also known as the river of hatred. It had been hatred that had spurred her actions, there was no denying the need to partake in fluid from this source, yet as she watched the thick bubbles struggle to the surface, she gagged. Within the matte surface she saw images from her past, spanning back to the earliest recollection of this feeling, the moment her father had taken her life, and progressing to her discovery of Zo's secret. She thrust her hand through the image, seizing an almost solid lump of the congealed liquid. Retching and heaving, she forced the chewy substance into her mouth. For a moment she feared she could not swallow. The rubbery texture clung to her throat as her body used all the means available in an attempt to expel the contaminant from her body, until finally, the lump forced its way down her throat. The foul taste lingered, and every breath seemed ripe with the vile odour as she was forced to taste it again and again.

Acheron was the next she approached, it had been no small feat passing through the swamp. With each slow step, she seemed to sink a little further into the squelching bog as it threatened to consume her, each step was an effort to pull her footing from the thick muddy terrain. By the time she stood, knee deep in the boggy waste, which brought her to the edge of the stream, she was exhausted.

Without hesitation, she plunged her hands through the clear surface. She had no fear of the taste of this seemingly pure water, nothing could taste as bad as what she had previously swallowed. She released a cry of agony as contact with the waters caused insufferable pain to course through her. As her hands instinctively recoiled, she cupped a mouthful of fluid within her palm, forcing it to her mouth not only to consume it, but to silence the sounds of her screams before she attracted any unwanted attention.

As she waded through the shallow stream, the riverbank seemed beyond reach as every second within the waters inflicted unimaginable torments upon her. Her energy was being drawn from her by the water's trial until she feared she could no longer take another step. Looking back, she knew it would be easier to return to the shore she had left. Despite what her mind told her, she had travelled but a few steps, had been in the water for but a few seconds, yet each one felt almost like a lifetime, but she knew she could not turn back. Eternities seemed to fade and surface. The distant horizon of sanctuary was her only focus through the eras, until finally she reached the shore, collapsing onto what she assumed to be the pathway leading to the fields of punishment. Her body curled in agony as the river of pain demonstrated its unyielding power. Her vision grew black as she began to crawl her way across the broken shards of the wasteland in the direction of the ivory gate. Her body screamed in distress as she lay exhausted, unable to force another movement as the darkness descended upon her.

Acha became aware of a faint breeze. It seemed refreshing as it flowed around her body. The gentle swaying of movement seemed so comforting as it gently roused her. It reminded her of being on a ship, sailing upon a calm sea. She had frequently travelled in this manner during her youth, after all, it was a necessity to make frequent excursions to Albeth castle. She had not been what most would call a normal child in her time. Most young girls relocated to Albeth in hope to take work within the castle, instead she tended to her parents' land and as such, she took their percentage of the crops' yield to them. It was not common for females to work such tasks, but her father had been attending to other things, thus it was left for her to reap and sow their livelihood.

She shifted slightly, returning from her brief memory as a familiar sensation of pain washed over her. Suddenly, recalling her predicament, her eyes shot open. For a moment everything had been so calm and peaceful, these were feelings soon forgotten as she gazed once more upon the underworld. Feeling the talons of the creature that carried her, a scream escaped through her panicked breaths as she kicked and fought at the air in an attempt to free herself from its vice-like grip. The black feathered wings hummed as they beat heavily to carry her with ease, its flight unaltered as it seemed unaware of her desperate struggle. From her elevated position she could see every twist and turn of the rivers, she could see each contour of Styx as it circled below. Her panicked vision panned from left to right as she sought a means of escape, but such a feat was impossible. Even should she escape the creatures grasp, it would only serve to hasten her death. Despite her aerial view, she knew all too well that only Lethe was beneath her, forgetting was the only escape that awaited her.

The river below rose as if in greeting while the creature swept down towards it. Her mind became blank as her fearful gaze beheld the surface of Lethe. She turned slightly, attempting to grasp the creature as its grip began to loosen. Pain exploded as her arms desperately reached up, the panicked grasp missing its enormous claws by mere inches as it released her to the forces of gravity that propelled her towards an inescapable demise. Just one drop of water from this river would seal her fate. She would lose her name along with any hope of escape, but being a slave to her momentum meant she could only watch in fear as the waters approached to welcome her.

"My name is Acha Night," she whispered to herself in hope this mantra would somehow nullify the water's cleansing.

A sudden force hit her with such impact her trajectory changed, sending her sliding across the raised bank of the river. She watched in horror as the body of the young girl vanished beneath the surface of the wave. The creatures above shrieked, diving rapidly as they saw their intended victim escape. Acha knew there was nothing she could do for her except take advantage of the chance she had been given. She struggled to her feet, propelling her body forwards, fearing to look back and see the closeness of those whose cries seemed mere feet away. She could see the smooth texture of the gate before her, her pace increased to beyond her limit. She stumbled to the left feeling the rush of air as the blackened figure's claws failed to find their target. Realising its prey had evaded capture, it circled around once more preparing itself to attack. She ran quickly, she was nearly there.

* * *

Roots wrapped around Zo's legs as she kicked and fought her way to the centre of the forest. It seemed the closer she got, the more resistance she met. As she approached the circle of trees, she noticed the area all around her led into the darkness, from this alone she knew she had found what she sought.

Walking into this dark clearing, she saw a small cottage. The sweet aroma of roses, and various other flowers found planted carefully around it, filled the air. It was the image of the house she had called home, the place where her mother still awaited her. Zo closed her eyes tightly, telling herself it wasn't real, but even with her eyes closed, she could still smell the enticing fragrance from the garden.

She shook her head, dislodging the thoughts, as the world around her twisted back to its true nature, a circle of enormous towering trees. In the very centre, like a knight watching over all it surveyed, stood an enormous tree. Just under the skin of the bark, she saw Acha. She was suspended within the tree's sap, deadly still beneath the transparent bark, not a breath left her body.

Zo rushed towards her, falling several times as her feet tangled in the roots that spanned the undergrowth. She touched the bark near where Acha rested.

From what she could see, despite there being no air bubbles, there was the unmistakable rise and fall of her chest as if she was breathing, or was somehow being forced to.

Giving thanks to the Gods she drew her sword, swinging it with all her might. Her footing slipped as the blade failed to appear. It was only then she recalled Seiken's warning, neither her magic nor her sword would work within this forest. With no other means to aid her, she did the only thing she could. Fastening the hilt back to the scabbard, she used its pommel to chip away at the surface, calling Acha's name as she did so, in the hope she could reach her. Small scratches began to appear on the surface of the bark, but even still it wasn't enough. She continued her forceful blows, she could only hope that repeated strikes to the same place would weaken it enough to allow her to penetrate the tree's defences.

A different noise echoed with the sound of her strikes. The bark cracked slightly, a sound made inaudible by a sickening thud. She hadn't even realised she had been struck until she was trying to stand. An explosion of lights pulsed behind her eyes. Once to her feet her balance failed, toppling her once more to the ground in a dazed confusion.

It was then she saw her attacker, the giant root coiled itself across the ground as it slithered closer in its continued effort to restrain her. She retreated backwards, her legs pushing frantically across the forest's floor trying desperately to gain the speed needed to escape its advance, unaware her actions were expected, unaware more lay in wait just behind her awaiting their opportunity to strike. Something seized her, wrapping its coarse flesh around her waist. She struck out wildly as the advancing root poised itself ready to strike. Blocking its advance with her sheathed weapon had caused an opening for another adversary, one it hastened to use. The sword fell from her grasp as, seeing the vulnerability, another root secured her wrist to wrench her towards the ground. Her free hand reached out desperately in an attempt to grasp the fallen weapon, her body twisting almost unnaturally, trying to evade the continuing barrage of roots which fought to seize her. Her legs kicked in hope to shake loose the coiled tendrils, whilst she fought with all the strength she could muster against the ones that slithered up her arms.

She understood now why Acha had screamed. With her legs now bound together, it was already too late. The living appendages worked in unison to drag her across the undergrowth, coiling higher and higher, strengthening their vice-like grip as they pulled her towards what it appeared would be her final destination. The giant mouth of a mighty tree stretched before her, the bark splitting to create its teeth as the roots guided her gently inside. Her feet grew damp, then her legs, the thick sap, combined with the roots, making movement impossible. She fought to breathe as the fluid began to thicken around her. She held her breath frozen within her while she fought to escape. Tiny green mossy roots, suspended in the fluid, forced their way down her nose making her heave, forcing her to release some of the breath she desperately held. Hope began to fade as escape became impossible. Through the watery prison, her blurred vision saw the bark of the tree sealing behind her, the roots receded slowly as something secured her midriff in a lethal embrace, forcing the remaining air from her lungs.

* * *

Zo pulled away from the gentle embrace, her heart leapt as she saw who stood before her. It was almost impossible to believe she was here, she was finally home again. The figure took a step backwards, the two of them shared so many features that it was impossible not to realise their relationship. The older woman smiled in admiration at the young woman her daughter had grown to become. Zo felt the shock tremble through her body, her hands turning cold as she advanced once more into the embrace. Her tears fell uncontrollably as she clung to her mother, the insuppressible rise in her emotions seeing her grief pour from her as she finally released everything she had held back for so long.

"Shh," Kezia whispered softly. "Shh, shh, shh." It was some time until Zo calmed her tears, and longer still before she could bring herself to release her mother. Within her arms she had felt safe, at peace, things she had not felt for so very long. Kezia gently took her daughter's hand, leading her towards their home and up the wooden stairs into the modest cabin. Each second she remained near her mother she felt herself relaxing, becoming at ease as the tension drained away.

"Thea, you can't block me out." Zo glanced back in alarm as she heard his voice, Seiken stood just outside the cabin. Seeing him, those feelings she had fought so desperately to forget, began to surface once more. "Do you even know..." His image vanished by the sheer power of her will, and within seconds she had forgotten he had even been there. She pushed the door closed, smiling brightly as she joined her mother.

Chapter 23

Exposed

Elly and the elderly man stood patiently at the end of Commerce Avenue awaiting the arrival of Daniel and Acha. They may have left ahead of them, but she had spent more time within the city than any would care to realise, as such she not only knew most of its secrets, but all of its shortcuts too.

The town, despite being accessible from many locations, could never be entered or exited through anything but one of the portals. It was said that this city had stood through countless cycles and disasters, but most dismissed this rumour, stating that this place had been constructed in order to create a safe haven for scholars and those seeking knowledge of the artes, both were in fact correct. The land outside this city was unknown to anyone. Marise had once informed her that the barrier surrounding this city acted as an atmosphere stabiliser, creating an artificial atmosphere by drawing on the presence of the people within it to adapt to their requirements. It was an observation Zo too had made on their arrival here. This alone made Elly wonder where this strange town could be. She was certain it was not on their planet, or regardless of any wards or magic she would have found it.

"It's like I said before—" The elderly man began, Elly interrupted to finish his statement.

"It is sealed." She smiled at him dismissively in quiet contemplation. She knew all too well that, despite his assurances, he too had seen someone emerge through it on horseback. She placed two small, circular, metal objects on the ground. Without a word she glanced first to the councilman who gave a nod, then to Eiji. It was at this point Daniel and Acha arrived, they were somewhat surprised to see them already there and waiting.

"Water?" For once, to her surprise, it seemed Eiji had understood her perfectly which, when she considered that this was an advanced technique in water manipulation, was very impressive indeed. Especially since he seemed unable to grasp the more basic concepts of his abilities.

He approached the markers, outstretching his hands, his face filling with concentration as he called upon the power of the elements. Slowly, an almost invisible layer of water began to rise. Once it was high enough, he let out a sigh of relief, lowering his trembling hands. It had been a long time since he had practised this particular control. Despite his base element being water, creating a barrier just a few molecules thick was both physically and mentally exhausting. It was fortunate he didn't need to map a route, the ancient technology, which Elly had placed, had completed the task as the secrets of the forgotten ancestors tracked and mapped the path last travelled. He was glad for this, without knowing the coordinates of his destination this ancient travel lore would have been virtually impossible to create accurately. There were many times in his training that he had taken himself, and his master, to strange lands just at the slightest mathematical error in calculation. He never even thought to question how she had come to be in possession of such things, let alone how they could be in a working condition. He was simply grateful for their presence.

Elly hesitated for a second, it was but a brief pause, one which probably went unnoticed. She felt the tingle of an old memory across her skin as she was reminded why she feared this substance so much. It was a fault which had been corrected, a problem that had not since reoccurred, yet still, even now, it caused her to hesitate.

Daniel watched in bewilderment as Elly stepped into the fine skin of water. He could still see her clouded image through the surface, yet she no longer stood amongst them. He followed her cautiously into the unknown, followed closely by Eiji and finally Acha. The councilman, who had been with them, did not join them, it was not his place. He knew what was needed from him already. After the water creating the portal had released to become little more than a puddle, he collected the spheres and returned to his business about the town.

"How..." Daniel began to question in amazement as he tried, through his disorientation, to absorb the new surroundings. He glanced around the small island, other than the small area of open plain they stood on, everything before them was covered with dense woodland.

It was incredible to look at the forest from where they stood. It almost appeared the trees had united to create an impenetrable wall, an impassable barricade that made entrance seem impossible, but as he walked closer, he saw this was just an illusion created by their sheer numbers.

"Basic science. Light travels in a straight line and this is said t'be the quickest way between two points. Distance is measured by the speed light travels, water bends light, so by creatin' a container in which t'bend it, combined with the correct elemental manipulations, y' can create a portal between two points. As y' cross through it, the light bends between us and the point of exit, which means instead of hours it takes just over half a second t'travel half the distance of the world. Y' studied magic I thought y' would'a known this." Eiji smiled, he was glad he remembered so much of what his master had taught him. It was the kind of explanation they would have expected from Elly, not from him, and this was clearly reflected in their faces. As both his and his master's key element had been water, it was only natural he knew its intricacies to the highest level of mastery. He knew his lower level skills were somewhat lacking, he still needed to return to some of the basics, but the advanced water magic, and the calculations accompanying it, came almost second nature to him.

"No, but logically it makes sense, I suppose." Daniel rubbed his head taking a mental note of the information he had been given. He committed it to memory, ready to be added to his journal at a more appropriate time. He did this with anything he found of interest.

"Luckily, it was used as a portal previously, so the foundation magic remained, otherwise it would'a taken much longer t'map its path." Eiji smiled at Daniel, he was secretly relieved that Elly had not questioned their location. Still feeling proud of his accomplishment, he glanced around in an attempt to locate Acha. He had seen her emerge from the gateway just seconds before it had closed, but now, she was nowhere to be seen.

"But how do we get back?" Daniel questioned as any trace of the portal completely faded, leaving only a small patch of damp grass where they had emerged.

"The same way, did you get everything I requested?" As Elly turned to Eiji, she too noticed Acha was not amongst them. She had a strange feeling about the events that would follow, any second now she expected to be faced with an Oneiroi.

"Yes, I don't—" Eiji began, but he was soon interrupted as, just like Elly had predicted, Seiken stood before them.

"You came?" Seiken seemed almost surprised by their appearance, he glanced over them quickly before he continued. "Thank the stars, Acha and Thea have been trapped." Only seconds after he spoke, did Acha seem to appear within the group. She stood amongst them almost as if she had been there all along.

"Why should we believe you? You led us astray before. Besides, as you can clearly see Acha is here." Daniel pointed to her, wondering how she could have previously escaped his notice.

"As you wish." He shook his head as the words left him and turned to walk away. If not for the severity of the situation he would have. "But tell me, where is her talisman?" he questioned, his back still turned to them. Seiken knew if there was one thing Aburamushi would be unable to do it was replicate items of magical potential, just like he could not have predicted that straight after emerging from the portal, Seiken would summon them to this plane. This action had consumed most of his energy, meaning he could not appear before them instantly. This summoning was the reason why Acha's facsimile had only just arrived. When the one impersonating her realised what must have happened, he followed them into Darrienia's version of this area. It was a transfer, which, given this area's unique properties, was instantaneous.

"I lost it back in the forest," she stated flippantly, shifting uncomfortably under the weight of their stares. She quickly moved her vision to Seiken who had now once more turned to face them. He could not walk away from this, no matter how much he wanted to, what was at stake was far too important.

"As I recall, you said you never entered," Elly stated, her tone was filled with self-satisfaction.

"Does it matter? What's important is Zo is trapped in there and yet again, the son of Crystenia is causing problems. He did this before remember, when he nearly got me killed?" she snapped.

"Wait a minute," Eiji interrupted, his tone holding the pained realisation of an important fact long forgotten. He looked from Acha to Seiken. "Back in Darrienia it wasn't Seiken, his abilities have been sealed in Night's tower. I remember seeing him there while I was captive. He came to help me, there was something glowing around him, restraints of some kind." Eiji couldn't think why he had failed to mention this before. So much had happened that, much to his shame, it had slipped his mind. Then again, until this point, he wasn't even sure the images he had seen during his imprisonment were real. He had seen so many strange things, why would he believe it to be anything more than another illusion? Of course, the fact that Seiken had been sealed in such a manner begged the question as to how he could be before them now. Acha seemed about to speak when Seiken interrupted.

"Magic inhibitors," he admitted bluntly. He looked almost ashamed as the details of his capture were revealed. "They prevent the use of my abilities, inclusive of my omnipresence."

"So how come you're here now?" Acha questioned sceptically, turning their focus back to him. There were too many things left to doubt, this situation may still be salvageable if she could cast the suspicion back onto him. It should be straightforward enough, after all, both Eiji and Seiken had admitted that he shouldn't be able to even be here.

"You know more than anyone, this place is exempt from the rules, even ours," Seiken revealed. The Perpetual Forest was a place which existed between both realms, one that was always accessible, an exception to the rules, and the only place the Oneirois feared to tread.

"The son of Crystenia?" Daniel questioned, as there was a brief pause in the conversation. He saw Acha's posture stiffen, almost as if she hadn't realised the betrayal her words had revealed.

"Crystenia is my home, the capital of our world, but no one here would know that. It is not information I have disclosed, correct?" Seiken knew there was only one person who knew the name of his homeland, and although she couldn't remember doing so, she had visited there once before.

"You told me," Aburamushi protested. Although he still held Acha's form he knew his deception was about to be revealed. His appearance had started to falter slightly, as it had in the tavern. At that time he had been given an escape, now he would not be so lucky.

"Very well then, tell me, Acha, what is my name?" Acha hesitated as if contemplating her answer. Seiken knew the impostor had already revealed himself, just as he knew that, even if its very existence depended on it, he could never speak his name. That was one of the wonderful things about summoned creatures, and a reason why any, brought to life in their world, were not long of existence. A summon had the ability to look deep into the minds of others, but when talking to an Oneiroi, they could only find their true name. This was why one of the Oneirois' responsibilities was to hunt and banish the more dangerous of these creatures, after all, speaking the true name of an Oneiroi brought with it disastrous consequences. It was quite the opposite in Gaea's star, where knowing the true name of a being gave a person power over it. In his world, for his people at least, the reverse was true. He knew, as did Aburamushi, that if he spoke his name, he would banish him forever, and so, Seiken waited patiently.

He was trapped, although he knew that the people he stood with had addressed him previously as Seiken, if he was to attempt to say it, this would not be the name leaving his lips. It was a flaw in their creation, a flaw that allowed the Oneirois to protect humans from things that should not be by asking a simple question. Most creatures would answer having learnt the Oneiroi's alias, but as the name was spoken, it became the one which lay hidden. Most summons were compelled to answer. Aburamushi, however, was not.

The reason this particular creature had survived in their world so long was because his summoner, along with this Oneiroi, had sealed him within one of the seven fixed locations. As long as he was sealed, no real harm could be done. Aburamushi had been different to other summons, he possessed a great intelligence and, in the act of sealing it, they had fractured his life-force into two parts. One part resided in Darrienia, the other in Gaea's star. It had been a desperate measure to control a critical situation with the only means available at that time. But it was also this action that had created their inability to destroy it. As long as he existed in both worlds, he could be banished in neither.

The situation had changed when he had been released from the seal. It had restored his life-force and he now lived on borrowed time. All summoned creatures existed for a predetermined span of time, due to something known as a magic trace, an unseen link which joins the creature to its creator, determining how long the summoned being would survive in their world before being returned. Aburamushi's immortality had come from the split between Darrienia and Gaea's star, therefore his trace could not decay. But now he was free, and his life would slowly trickle away as the magic sustaining him eroded. That was, unless a way was found to overcome this mortality. One of the methods which would accomplish this, a method the Gods had devised to ensure the summons guarding the forest remained protected, was to bring the one who summoned them to sleep within the Forest of the Epiales. Those trapped within the forest's sleep were granted frozen longevity until the day the forest devoured their life-force completely. On average this took in the region of two centuries, which he was certain would be more than enough time for him to find a more permanent solution to his problem.

"I thought your life-force was contained within the amulet," Daniel added when Acha failed to answer Seiken. He was surprised by her refusal to answer such a simple question. Now the seed of doubt had been planted, the strange gnawing feeling had returned. It all began to make sense. Something had changed about her, it was so blatantly obvious he was unsure how he had failed to see it before. The one thing he had discussed at length with Acha was her amulet, it was always with her, yet since she had returned, he hadn't seen this familiar object. He had noticed something was out of place, but it wasn't until now he had realised what.

Acha's form distorted. It was a sight to behold as the contours of her body twisted and altered to become something else. There was a moment where the figure seemed almost liquid before the shape was reforged, settling to become a form they all recognised, the form previously identified as Aburamushi. The dark-haired figure smiled at them playfully, his steady retreat towards the portal unnoticed as the shifting of his form held their full attention. By the time they realised exactly where he stood, not one of them could have moved quickly enough to prevent his escape. As his figure passed through it, the distortion shimmered, collapsing in on itself until nothing remained.

"He will have completely sealed the path now." Seiken unconsciously glanced towards the area where Aburamushi had made his exit. When the time came for them to leave, they would have to set up the foundations and chart the path using the magical residue left behind. It would take them far longer than the reactivating of the sealed portal, but he was certain they could manage it. If not, they could simply wait until nightfall, enter Darrienia, and remove their pendants before they returned, that way, they would at least wake somewhere else, even if it did mean losing the charms.

"Then how will we return?" The situation had changed since the last time Daniel had asked, they were now stranded.

"Let us concentrate on returning from there first." Elly motioned towards the forest aware of how much time had already been wasted since their arrival. She felt a sickening realisation, this had been Aburamushi's plan all along. This being was intelligent, he was trying to disable, or kill, his creator in a way that would not threaten his existence. He had known she would not accept the imperfect copy of Acha, and delay their departure in order to challenge him. All the time she had spent trying to expose him, Zoella fought for her life. If her body and life-force become severed, it would be too late. "Seiken, how are they?" She questioned desperately; questions ran through her mind without end, what if she had just followed Aburamushi, would that have been so bad, what if now, because of her delays, they failed to make it in time to save them?

"Well." He bit back a scathing reply, they were the ones responsible for this after all. "Acha's still fighting, it bodes well given the time that has passed since her arrival, but Thea, Zoella," he said sadly. "She gave up long ago. Even I can't reach her now." He felt as if he had failed her by not being stronger. A long time ago he made a vow to protect her. There had been times, when she had travelled with Elly, that he had succeeded in pulling her from the darkness which restrained her, drawing her away from Marise's seals, if only for a few moments. He had always been able to reach her even if it was for just a second, but now, for the first time ever, it truly seemed she had ventured beyond his reach.

"That brings me to my next question, why are we here?" Elly crossed her arms as she looked at him accusingly.

"Apologies, I had little choice if I were to speak with you. Although Night's chains bind me in your world and mine, the power of this place sits in neither, but my time here is still limited, both Night's bonds and this area inhibit me now." He looked towards the forest, there wasn't time to explain this, he had to try to get back to her. Even if it was meaningless, he had to try to reach her, he had to make her see the truth behind this reality.

"Y' mean we're asleep?" Eiji questioned in disbelief.

"Yes, but you can wake up now." Seiken appeared to fade as they switched between the worlds.

"So how do we get them out without losing the way ourselves?" Daniel looked towards the silent forest with a sinking feeling in the pit of his stomach. Somewhere among those trees, Zo had surrendered, something he never thought she would do. It made him fear that which lay within, what could it do that would cause even her will to surrender? Even he had felt her new-found determination, it had given him hope.

"If you had not been in such a hurry to leave, I was hoping for some answers from the impostor. Why else do you think I would take you to a tavern?" Elly clarified her earlier actions. Although what she said was true, she knew this delay may also be mean they would be too late. She regretted not killing the impostor on the spot. It would have saved time.

"You mean you knew?" Daniel questioned sharply.

"Of course, only the inhabitants of Darrienia call this place the Forest of the Epiales, we call it the Perpetual Forest. Think about it, it is the same name that appeared on the map of the fixed locations." As Elly explained, she knocked a large peg into the ground and began to fasten a thin, shiny cord to it. She gave it a few hard tugs before she spoke again. "We will find our way out the same way treasure hunters do when they navigate complex caves."

Without further hesitation, the three of them ventured into the forest. They had barely walked a few paces when they found Zo's satchel clutched on the branch of a nearby tree. Eiji reached up retrieving it. It had hung directly in their line of vision, impossible to overlook. It *was* possible that Zo had left it there as a marker, but it was unlikely, it seemed the forest was baiting them.

"She was nearly out, by here she'd surely feel her magic. She'd see the truth as we still can. The forest's magic is at its weakest here, but she still turned back, is this the power of the forest?" Eiji questioned, noticing the oldest set of footprints led away from the forest rather than into it. She had been just a few steps from safety when she had turned around.

Daniel took the satchel from him, slinging it over his shoulder. He held it tightly against himself as he glanced around cautiously. Just ahead, the forest was submerged in darkness, minimal light filtered through the heavy canopies, but this was not the only thing he noticed. As Eiji had seen, there had been a single trail of footsteps leaving the forest, imprints which he instinctively knew had been left by Zo. The answer to why she had almost made it out was clear from these alone. She had turned back for one reason and one reason only, and it had not been the power of the forest.

"There's only one set of tracks," he stated firmly. "She went back in for Acha." Although she had predicted Acha's betrayal, she had still returned into the forest for her, unable to leave her behind to face the consequences of her actions. This did not sound like the action of someone who was ready to surrender. These were the thoughts of someone who wanted to desperately push on, to protect those dear to them. Despite his reasoning he knew without a doubt Seiken's words were true, he saw, reflected in his eyes, the same fear and sadness he now displayed at the thought of losing her.

They pressed on, barely a space between them as they trekked through the forest. The overhead canopies were knit so tightly together that they blocked all the light to create an artificial night, which was why the forest had been given its name. They blindly navigated deeper and deeper through the twilight trees. Everything was deadly silent, the only sound was that of the trees moving in the breeze. Little did they realise there was no wind in this forest, just like the sunlight it failed to penetrate the trees' barricade.

Elly stopped quickly, Daniel and Eiji were forced to a halt as she stretched her arm out before them. For a brief second she had seen the eyes watching them from the shadows, but as quickly as they appeared, they had vanished back into the darkness. She knew well the secrets of this place, she had been here once before.

"Be careful," she warned lowering her arm. "They know we are here." She glanced around, her vision searching the darkness for danger. The last time she had been here even she had fallen prey to its tricks.

"Who?" Neither he nor Daniel had seen the eyes for that fleeting moment, then again neither of them were close to her calibre in observational skills. She had been doing this for so long now that she saw almost everything.

"Our esteemed hosts. It seems we are already under the spell of the forest, we are asleep," she whispered.

"You are." Seiken did not whisper, his voice was so loud against the eerie silence it startled them. "Not to spoil the mystery, but those who enter these woods soon realise its terror and find themselves looking for the exit, may I suggest you do the same?" A branch swiped at him from nowhere, as it struck him, he vanished, it was by this alone they realised they were now awake. There was no discernible way to distinguish one state from the other. Whether they were asleep or awake, it all seemed to look the same.

"Why the exit?" Eiji once more reduced his tone to a whisper to fit the silence of the surrounding environment. He looked to Elly, her gaze tracked backwards to look over the way they had come. As he followed her line of sight, he too noticed that it seemed to lead deeper into the wooded area. The shadows and density of the trees seemed far thicker than those they remembered walking through. It was then he understood Seiken's words. "The councilman said somethin' about this place leadin' travellers seekin' its exit towards its centre." Eiji was the first to continue walking, leading them confidently towards the lighter area ahead of them.

"I am *not* going to keep wasting my energy warning you when I could be trying to reach her." Seiken stood at a nearby tree nursing his side, as they looked at him several other small injuries became apparent. "Wake up," he commanded, "if you don't, you'll die." He turned his back to them, hiding both his frustration and fatigue. "I can't believe I have to trust Thea's life to such amateurs." In the instant he faded from sight, Elly had already thrown her dice, a weapon, like the one used by Hephaestus to aid Zeus in the birth of Athene, appeared in her hand. The large labrys, a double headed axe easily her own height, was comprised of a strange black metal. The blades shone for a moment as what little light there was glinted across their razor sharp surfaces. It was a metal which Elly recognised instantly, it was similar in composition to that of Marise's hilt, by this alone she knew they were close.

It seemed confrontation was not what they faced. Their paces stilled instantly as the world altered dramatically, barely a moment ago they had been walking through the dense path of the forest, and now before them stretched an enormous gorge. Seiken had been correct, and much to Elly's annoyance, his assessment of them had been accurate. She had made an amateur mistake. She of all people should have known better. Small debris crumbled from their rapidly halted steps, ricocheting down the tangled webs of roots which wove themselves within the dirt of the sheer cliff face they stood upon. Even another single step would have seen them plummet to their deaths, Seiken's intervention had been timely indeed.

Eiji took the first step backwards, his vision met by a seemingly impassable wall of dense brier. The thick thorny stems coiled upwards to weave within one another sealing their only exit.

"Oh great," Eiji muttered; the sky seemed to darken as the roots rose. "I don't suppose we needed t'head down?" He glanced to Elly, who seemed to pause in a moment of consideration.

"Unlikely, wherever this forest chooses to guide us, you can be assured it will not be where we intended to go."

"What do you mean, the forest lead us?" Daniel glanced around cautiously.

"Surely you did not believe there was nothing more to the enchantment than the bridging of dream and reality, were you not listening?" Daniel thought back a moment, back to the conversation outside the portal.

"The trees are sentient?"

"They hunt, and I am afraid they have led us exactly where they wanted us."

The ground beneath them began to tremble. Slowly, Elly and Daniel both began to back away. More insects than they could count, more than any of them had ever hoped to see, emerged from the chasm, the tiny sounds, made by their movements, amplified by their sheer numbers, as the roots broke free from the chasm in pursuit. Tendrils filled the air gaining length and height as they struck out towards them.

Eiji rolled to the side of a strike, his hand passing quickly over the scabbard fastened on the inside of his left ankle and concealed within his boot. He cursed silently, his grip catching only air where a hilt should have been. On his feet once more, he focused his attention on the roots, it wasn't that he needed his dagger, it was doubtful its blade would even damage the large thick earthy attacker, but he always felt so much better with it in his possession. Just having it near him somehow helped him to focus. Elly gave a shout, throwing something in his direction. His vision fell upon a small knife, which he hastened to scramble towards, his hand seizing around the somewhat crudely fashioned hilt with relief.

"Daniel, stay back, your stick is useless here," Elly warned as he snapped his weapon together. She had been surprised that it had even managed to hold itself together, given the nature of this forest. Perhaps there was more to it than she had first assumed, even so, there were better things he could be doing than getting in their way. This confrontation was going to be challenging enough, without having to keep watch on him as well. "Try to make a path through the bramble," she commanded. Now the forest had roused from its sleep staying and fighting would serve no benefit but to delay them.

Eiji shoved him from the path of an incoming strike, missing being injured himself by mere inches as the root caught his shirt, tearing it slightly. As Daniel made his way towards the barricade, Eiji focused his attention on detaining the roots. The blade in his hand began to stretch and glow as he channelled small blades of wind through it, sharpening and extending its reach as the tiny threads of energy wove themselves together. Eiji used his hand, manipulating the wind energy, bending it slightly. Raising his arm to his shoulder, he threw it forwards, the wind-blade spun through the air like a boomerang, its return severing numerous roots from the edge of the chasm. He caught it with a grace that seemed alien to him, the energy vanishing as it made contact with his hand once more. Or at least this was how he had envisioned it as he focused on what he wanted to do. It was only when none of his imaginings came to fruition he was reminded why this place was called the Forest of Silence. His magic was useless here. He was useless here. The knife had left his hand before he had even realised the magic had not responded. It was normally such a quick process for him, visualisation and result, he hadn't even realised the elements had failed to manifest themselves.

Elly fought back the vines with a speed the labrys should not have allowed, power building from the continuous momentum she kept. The weapon within her hands never stilled as it sliced through their attackers. Her movements seemed almost fluid as she dodged and struck with ease, using the weight of the weapon to aid her movements, as it used hers to deepen the blows, they fought as one.

"Eiji, go," she panted; she could feel it now, the strain, the pressure on her body, but she dared not slow her pace. "Follow Daniel. Get to them, I will be right behind you." It had been a long time since she had exerted herself so much, and this forest was not without consequences on her. She blocked a strike aimed towards Eiji as he dove into the thicket.

"Where's Elly?" Daniel questioned as Eiji appeared behind him. It was but moments before they broke through the remaining bramble to exit into the forest.

"She told us t'go, she will catch up t'us."

* * *

Elly felt it begin, the lightness in her body that meant the connection was weakening. She had not anticipated such exertion, fatigue was virtually unknown to her, except for within the boundaries of this forest. She took another swing at the endless barrage of roots, all the time trying to gain ground towards the thicket. But it knew her thoughts almost as if they were of one mind, her every step of retreat, blocked. She could only hope Daniel and Eiji had made it to Zo in time. Her weapon faltered for a second before dissipating, moments before she could block. The root struck her with such force it threw her backwards, even in her weakened state she secured the dice, sacrificing a graceful landing for their safety. This did not bode well. Her body was starting to become heavy, she needed to rest, but before that she had to stand, or better yet move.

Two hands grabbed her from the thicket, pulling her sharply backwards. She felt her weight land upon someone as they both fell to the ground. Daniel winced against the pain, but it was not her weight upon him which caused him to stifle a cry, it was the thorns on the undergrowth he had, until now, been so careful to avoid.

After a few moments of respite, protected in the shelter of the thicket, Elly finally found the strength to move. This time it was Daniel who was in need of assistance. He could feel the spreading numbness from the thorns, it seemed they had penetrated deeper than he had anticipated. As Elly took his hand, he felt the vines rise with him, almost as if they tried to pull him back down. He heard the straining of the stems as the thorns snapped, remaining firmly rooted in his flesh.

It seemed Daniel was not the only one to disobey her request, Eiji stood uncertainly outside the thicket's edge. He moved as if to assist Elly who, with a quick gesture, had him focus his attention on Daniel. Everything was still, it was a moment Elly desperately needed to regain some of the energy she had expended. It also presented a perfect opportunity to assess the damage that her rescue had caused to Daniel.

Eiji began to remove the thorns, hoping they were safe in the place they sought sanctuary, which was nothing more than a small clearing. Now they understood the will of the forest a little more, the further they were from the trees the better, at least while they rested. She knew all too soon they would once more walk the deadly terrain. Silent words passed between herself and Eiji as she glanced over Daniel. In a subtle movement she brushed a few smaller thorns from her own leg, they would never know that she too had been touched by the poison. It had no doubt been the forest's intention to administer this infliction upon them all, but like most things of this nature, it would have no consequences for her.

"Eiji, how is he?" She looked over his shoulder to observe the damage more closely, already the redness lining the inflammation had started to spread.

"*He* is fine," Daniel growled through gritted teeth as Eiji continued to remove the small thorns.

"I've already removed seven," he responded. Looking at Daniel's back there were still a number left embedded in his quickly swelling flesh. He said no more, if there was one thing he had learnt well from travelling with this group it was that, when Elly gave him the look she did now, he was to be quiet. For now, they wouldn't breathe a word of this to Daniel, not until it was absolutely necessary. The less he knew, the better he would be.

"We must hurry," she warned, resisting the urge to sigh, it would have been better had he not involved himself. He had reached her before she had gathered the strength needed for her retreat. She was quite certain she would have made it, if not in time to dodge the next strike, then the one after. Although she had to admit, she was flattered that he seemed to care enough to put himself in immediate danger without a thought to the consequences. It was an action that reminded her very much of Zo. She would have done exactly the same thing in his position. "We have come too far to turn back, pushing on is our best option."

"I said I am fine, they're just scratches, I've had worse, they don't even hurt," he lied. Of course they hurt, but no more than the injuries he had sustained when his father had tried to teach him archery. In fact, since the last of the thorns had been removed, the pain was already beginning to subside. He rose to his feet, aware that Elly and Eiji exchanged concerned glances, ignoring them he walked on.

They walked in silence for some time, knowing they were awake without the need for confirmation. The roots still seemed to twist beneath their feet as they walked carefully. Daniel's pace had slowed slightly, which meant as he tripped, both Elly and Eiji extended their arms to grab him. His head swam for a moment whilst he regained his footing. The scenery around him seemed duller, darker than before, causing him to wonder if his mind was playing tricks on him. It had been so dull since they entered, it seemed almost impossible it could grow any darker.

They pulled him to his feet, supporting him as he steadied himself before continuing. They had barely taken ten steps when he tripped again, this time he landed on his knees as his vision began to blur. A strange wave of nausea passed over him as Elly and Eiji once more pulled him to his feet.

"Okay," he sighed his tone lined with defeat. "Tell me about the poison." He had known, since he had first seen the thorns, the danger they would pose. He knew all too well the consequences of his actions, and had hoped ignoring this fact would help them push on quicker. His only comfort was in the initial thought that they didn't know, but it soon became apparent he was mistaken. What *did* surprise him however, was the shock which now registered on their faces when they realised he had known about it all along.

"Those thorns, as you say, introduced a fast-acting poison into your system, if you do not get medical attention soon you will die," Elly confirmed, stopping briefly to allow him to rest as she mulled over their chances of success factoring in the accelerated pace of this poison. Although fast acting it should have permitted them enough time to reach Zo, and make an antidote, before it became critical. She was all too aware that things did not always proceed as desired within the boundaries of this forest. She estimated the maximum time they had after its introduction was three hours, of which just over two remained, and already the poison had excelled beyond expectation. "Eiji, follow the lifeline back, take him to Collateral and ask for The Medic. The poison is accelerating at a rate I had not anticipated," she commanded; she was confident she could make this journey alone, she could only hope Eiji possessed the skill to create the portal without her guidance.

"No." Daniel pulled himself away from Eiji to stumble forwards into the trees. "We must... find Zo," he gasped. Having his fears confirmed did little to suppress the continuing spreading pains that ailed him.

"Daniel," Elly smiled. "You are right, it would be quicker." She would have been lying if she had said she was not impressed at his commitment to his friend, regardless of the personal cost. It was a sacrifice she herself understood completely. They let him walk ahead a little, subtly allowing him to set the pace.

"Look, Acha!" His words slurred and his head span as his legs once more gave into the fatigue. As he fell to his knees his hand, by some strange grace, fell upon the cold metal of Zo's sword. Elly took it from him, placing it in her belt before hoisting him up into a fireman's lift. "Weren't you affected too?" he asked quietly as he thought back to the incident, Elly shook her head.

"No," she reassured. She was surprised, given everything that had occurred, he had noticed. Eiji was already examining the tree where he could see Acha's body suspended under the transparent bark.

"It seemed Zo tried t'get t'her." He ran his fingers over the indentations on the tree's knotted skin. The semi-circular marks had clearly been left by the pommel of her sword. He removed Elly's knife from the holder in his boot, he had been quite surprised when she had handed it to him as they left the briar. He made several cuts through the transparent bark before the force of the escaping fluid split the remaining fragments of the wood. Moving quickly, he reached out, catching her as she fell forwards. For some reason, it seemed the forest wasn't retaliating, perhaps it was because it knew they would never escape.

He held Acha near the ground for a moment. Her eyes shot open as she coughed the fluid from her lungs, along with several long strands of a green plant. Acha continued heaving uncontrollably until the last of the strange vegetation had been expelled. It was an unusual substance, one which fixed itself into its prey's respiratory system, sealing the tree's sap within the target and converting it to oxygen as needed. It ensured the body lived long enough for the life-force to become severed.

"Where's Zo?" she whispered hoarsely. "I... she tried, to save me," she panted, gasping for air. Elly passed Daniel across to Eiji. She knew exactly where Zo could be found, given her ties to this place there was only one who would seek to claim her. Without a word, she left them. Her vision cautiously flitted from tree to tree whilst watching every shadow. The last time she had found herself in these woods she had fallen prey to the Epiales, the shapeless forms which could manifest themselves into a person's worst fears. It had been in this forest that Marise had faced her most challenging opponent. They had been fortunate to escape this forest once, it seemed it was not willing to relinquish its prey a second time.

Elly moved with a speed and grace the interfering forest should not have permitted, her feet seeming to predict the movement of the undergrowth whilst her body pivoted avoiding its attempts to slow her.

Looking upon the King of the forest, she recognised its gnarled matted form, but knew it was also a doorway to another prison within this land.

The tree towered taller than the others, she was certain, should the need arise for her to cut it down, it's bark would possess rings beyond counting, rings surpassing each of the others found within these enchanted boundaries.

The air fell still, nothing moved, nothing stirred as she approached the giant. It was as she suspected. The trunk was already darkening where the body of Zo lay suspended beneath. Unlike Acha, who had been taken by the forest, Zo was both within and separate from the forest simultaneously. The magic of this world had worked faster on her than on Acha, it did not bode well. Placing her hand upon the tree's surface she gave a very quiet, very specific warning. To her surprise, her words were heeded. The tree groaned its bark splintering, cracking, before the limp figure was released into Elly's waiting arms. For but a brief moment, she caught sight of him, the black dream, the one most knew as the Melas-Oneiros. The shrouded figure watched them from the darkness, seeming to smile beneath his cloak before vanishing back into the shadows of his forest.

Daniel felt his heart lighten as Elly appeared from the darkness of the forest, within her arms lay Zo, like Acha she was soaked, but there were no signs of movement, she simply hung limply in her arms. For the first time his eyes left the body of his friend to search Elly for some answers, for some hope, but the expression she wore scared him. She had always masked her feelings so well, but now she looked truly terrified.

The trees began to stir once more, Eiji took Zo from Elly whilst Daniel fought to stand. Elly hooked his arm around her shoulder helping him to walk. Even now she could see the concern for his friend was more consuming than that for himself, this would help them to move forwards. She was surprised by his silence. She couldn't help but wonder why he had failed to ask why they weren't helping her, maybe the reason was clear. They had to get out of the forest quickly, for all of their sakes. While they remained in the forest, its grip on Zo would only strengthen, although she may no longer reside within the tree, it still controlled her. At least once out of the forest she would be stronger. They could only hope once they were clear of the trees, she could find the strength to wake.

"Acha, are you—" Elly offered her a hand to her feet.

"I'm unhurt," she whispered quietly, looking at Zo's motionless body cradled in Eiji's arms. It was strange to think that just hours ago this was exactly what she had wanted, but now, as she looked upon the result of her actions, she couldn't find the words to describe the shame and regret. She could not understand how any part of her could have possibly desired this. "Will she be okay?" Eiji gave a little shrug in response. Acha looked at the ghastly ashen shade of the figure he carried. Now she was outside of the tree it would only be a matter of time before the plants blocking her airways depleted their supply of oxygen. Time was of the essence.

"None of us will be if we do not make haste." Elly pulled the string, only to find it had been severed just a few feet from the place she stood.

"Great," Eiji sighed, "how do we get out now?"

* * *

"So, Seiken, I see you have *still* found a way to warn our friends." Seiken was thrown before Night's feet. "I never expected anything less from you. You truly are a strong willed youngster. It's clear you have a—"

"Enough, you didn't bring me here for idle chatter, make me your offer, so I may refuse." Seiken forced himself to stand. Although the restraints made it difficult, his pride alone made him fight. He would not kneel before this fallen god, before the one who had tricked his Thea into believing he had betrayed her. Whilst he was here, he could no longer focus his efforts on reaching her. He needed to get back, he had to keep trying.

"Very well, but I think you will find this proposition more to your liking than my last."

"What do you mean?" Seiken questioned as the magic inhibitors vanished. He rubbed the places they had touched, the red welts began to slowly fade. He felt his strength begin to return, by this alone he knew Night was certain of his cooperation.

Night watched as Seiken adjusted to being free by stretching a few times. Despite the fact they did not restrict movement as such, the bonds were a heavy, draining burden for any movement he should make. Night was not concerned about giving him this moment of freedom, even should he try to escape, he could summon the inhibitors back before he had even taken a few steps, but this time, he did not believe it would be necessary. He predicted his full cooperation.

"This time, Seiken, I am offering you everything you desire. Your world, your people, your freedom."

"My world, my people, *our* freedom?" Night nodded. "Things would go back to the way they were before?" he questioned in disbelief at what Night seemed to be proposing.

"Well, not exactly. I'm sure there will be some damage here and there. The fixed locations that have been liberated will remain destroyed, so it will be as close to before as possible."

"How do I know you will be true to your word?" Seiken studied Night cautiously before moving to sit at the chair he had been motioned towards.

"If nothing else, have I not proven myself to be noble and honourable? I promised not a single one of your race would be hurt, as a god I am bound by my word."

"True, but you are no longer a god, you lack some power still." Seiken said, as he contemplated this information. "You were renowned for being an honourable deity. I cannot see why one such as yourself would fall so far from grace, now you take hostages, and for what?"

"My daughter, but I would be lying if I were to say this would be my only motive. Can't you hear it Seiken? The cry of this world as the beings upon it drive it closer and closer to extinction. Can't you hear the laboured breath of Gaea? I want to liberate her, return her to her former glory.

"Surely you of all people understand, would you not do the same for your world if you were in my place? While you use the beings of this planet, their dreams and imagination, to keep your world alive, using their thought patterns to replenish your world's resources, I too, must use my methods to accomplish the same task." There was a long pause where neither of them spoke. It stretched on for minutes as Seiken clearly wrestled with an all too difficult decision. He looked up at Night, it couldn't hurt to ask.

"What is it I must do in order to free my world, to liberate my people from your control?" Night smiled gently as he leaned forwards to speak softly.

"You must first choose between those you love, and those your loyalty binds you to." He produced a small mirror from the air, upon its surface it displayed the image of Zoella, not at this present point, but at the moment they had first met in Darrienia. There was something about her presence in his world that made her more radiant. The image faded, overpowered by another, one of his friends and allies, his race, all those who relied on him. They looked to him and his father for guidance and, despite their earlier objections, they willed for him to guide The Chosen. They had faith that he could lead them to victory. "Of course, I don't expect you to make your decision straight away, first eat. I believe the food the guards provided was not to your taste." In an instant an enticing feast lay on the table before him, the room filled with the aroma of delicacies from his homeland.

'*To choose between loyalty and love, will my choice make that much differ-ence?*' he thought to himself unable to eat. He simply stared at the food before him as he reasoned with himself. '*I have known Thea for a blink of an eye in the time of my people, although I have watched and adored her, aided her unseen by fate's eye, compared to my people, to those who have faith in me, who believe in me, and look to me for guidance...*' He looked to Night having not touched a morsel of food which had been placed before him.

"Tell me of this proposition," he asked, his voice listless as a wave of nausea washed over him. What Night had offered was unexpected, it was almost as if he was surrendering his advantage to gain an alternative one. To relinquish the prize of the game in exchange for his cooperation seemed surreal. What could he possibly offer that would be of more value than the hostages he had already taken, the peril he had already set into motion?

"All in good time, first eat, build up your strength. Let us toast to our new arrangement." Night raised a glass and drank from it. Seiken followed his motion with an empty feeling building in his chest.

Chapter 24

Between Life and Death

"There's no way t'navigate these trees now." Eiji groaned, turning his body sharply as he dodged the swiping motion of yet another tree branch. He looked desperately at the broken string, which hung loosely in Elly's hand, as he begged for it to be nothing more than an illusion brought about by the forest. However, the harsh reality was that the trees had done their best to ensure they could never leave. When their first attack had failed, they had managed to sever their lifeline to keep them there forever. Even if they knew the secret of leaving the forest, they were certain the rules would now change to ensure they remained here.

"You will never deceive me twice, have you learnt nothing?" Elly removed a small, intricately crafted metal box. As it opened, she removed the metal encased flint, drawing it across the rough inner workings of the opposing side until the sparks ignited the tinder. Eiji looked to her as she addressed the master of the forest, unsure if the next sentence was directed towards them or it. "When I was searching for the legendary treasure of Phliomese, I learnt the true meaning of allies. There were those who would do anything in the name of greed, even sever a lifeline.

"To counter their deception, I have my own artifice." She dropped the flame into the undergrowth where the severed twine had lay. The area ignited with a hiss as a small purple flame moved slowly, leading a path through the forest debris. "I always coat my rope in a special essence, one that, once lit, burns anything it has touched." Elly stood for a moment whilst she ensured the flame passed over the place the severed fibre had last lain. Even despite the loss of the twine, it seemed they still had a guiding line to their exit after all. The trees seemed to howl as the flame passed over them to reveal the path they had walked. Whether the trees had moved or not was irrelevant, the flame led on.

"Elaineor," Daniel gasped, quickening his pace as much as his fatigue would allow He had chosen to walk without aid and was grateful that the flame's speed seemed to be a steady, controlled one. "The treasure of Phliomese... was recovered... centuries ago, it's all documented... the treasure is kept by... the King of..." Daniel trailed off as breath escaped him, both talking and walking were too difficult. For a moment Elly had considered warning him he should only attempt one or the other, but feared he would stop in favour of talking. As she had looked to him to answer she noticed his increasingly ghastly pallor. Without giving him a chance to object, she once again picked him up, balancing him effortlessly over her shoulder without so much as losing pace.

She was now more concerned than ever about the rate in which this poison seemed to be accelerating, so much time had already passed since he had been exposed to the deadly thorns. Thus far, he had survived the impairing effects admirably. His desire to push forwards to find Zo was no doubt the driving force allowing him to counter its consequences with minimal symptoms. He had not fallen prey to its paralysis, instead he had managed to overcome the debilitating properties, suffering only weakness and impaired balance. However now, aside from the fatigue, there were no symptoms of this either which brought with it more serious concerns. This relief was nothing more than a momentary reprieve before the poison's final victory. A moment where, although fatigued, he noticed very little inhibition from the deadly toxin.

"That explains why I could not find it," she mused, quickening her pace now she had no concerns regarding leaving anyone behind. Acha, who walked steadily in front of her, seemed relatively unscathed. It appeared the effects of the trees were less severe on a mortal who possessed no magic. A few of the trees moved a little in their attempts to dodge the path of the wandering flame.

This was one forest that would regret its actions. Last time she had been here it had been lucky and caught her unaware, but this time she had a keen desire to reduce it to ashes. It knew her thoughts, it knew she was nothing if not sincere with her threats and so, on this occasion it decided to yield. A few escapees seemed a reasonable loss to ensure its own plans could come to fruition.

"I'm surprised you didn't know." Daniel resumed the conversation after a moment of silence, a moment he had used to draw his weary breath. Talking was tiring but it diverted his attention from the pains of the poison and the embarrassment of being carried. His words were laboured by his breath, yet still he continued. "It was found by a renowned female treasure hunter, Lain Exerevnitis. Rumour had it she also once found the hidden knowledge of the Gods just before the Titanomachy, of course, the time scale alone deems such things impossible." Elly smiled to herself as he spoke the name, it was one she hadn't heard for a *very* long time.

"Lain the explorer," she translated, the language she had used to invent that alias had long been forgotten. She had adapted it slightly to fit her needs, namely by spelling it phonetically for people unfamiliar with the dialect. She had many such aliases, but she had been particularly fond of this one, it had appeared in many stories spanning countless centuries.

They continued in silence as they followed the flame. Its slow path revealing the many unnoticed turns their journey had taken, until finally, the exit became visible. Their pace quickened as they emerged from the tree line, desperately attempting to place as much distance between themselves and the forest as the small island allowed. The wooden peg burnt fiercely as the flame traced the path of the remaining twine, burning unmercifully until nothing remained.

Elly quickly placed Daniel down, satisfied that they had not drifted into a trap caused by the forest's sleep. Eiji, upon seeing this, placed Zo gently on the ground next to him. He rummaged through her satchel until he found what he was looking for. Seconds seemed like minutes as he held the small mirror to her face. Despite her concerns, Elly had left him to attend to her for the moment, while she ensured Daniel was comfortable. It seemed he possessed barely enough strength to hold his own weight. By the time she reached Zo, she was hoping to have an answer, even now Elisha was searching the vast library for anything which could assist her. She already knew no matter how long Eiji held the mirror in place he would not see even the faintest sign of condensation upon its surface.

"What can we do?" Eiji stood and began to pace nervously as he glanced between the two friends. "Daniel needs a physician, maybe we could make it in time t'take her too?" He looked desperately at Zo, her pale features exaggerated the subtle appearance of the blue shading on her lips. Everything pointed to one thing, time was running out.

Daniel gasped, crawling painfully as he forced his heavy body to move until he came to rest beside Zo. He took her cold hand in his as she lay motionless. In her lifeless sleep there was a strange beauty to her gentle features, perhaps it was because she looked so peaceful, an attribute he had not seen in her for some time now. He whispered her name repeatedly in his mind in the hope that it would somehow reach her, and draw her back from wherever she resided.

"I do not think a physician could help either of them now," Elly acknowledged bluntly, before deciding to offer an explanation, all the time waiting on even the slightest glimmer of hope from Elisha. Even now, she could feel her resolve weaken as her emotions threatened to consume her. "Herbal poison needs herbal remedies. Since the appearance of chemical compounds in this last decade, pure botany is very much a forgotten art.

"Zo is a nature's child, a healer, and as such she possesses herbal lore. She would know exactly what, and how much to mix just by touching him." Elly paced, she could feel her normally calm exterior begin to falter. Her voice broke ever so slightly as the fear and panic began to take firm root. For the first time in as long as she could remember, she genuinely didn't know what to do. "Did you hear that?" She leaned towards Zo to whisper her words, so not to be overheard. "Without your help, Daniel *will* die." Her emotional walls began to crumble further, she stood up again to pace back and forth alongside Zo. "Elisha?" she begged aloud in a desperate low whisper. Acha and Eiji were deep in conversation, only Daniel, through hazy eyes, glanced to her curiously, but no answer came. "It is of no use," she admitted fearfully. "No one has ever survived this forest, no one knows how to counter its sleep." Sitting beside Zo, she silently called for aid, knowing that the one person who may be able to help them, who would want to ensure things progressed as required, could not enter this ancient sanctuary, and there was no time to recreate a gateway to somewhere he could approach.

She tried to weigh her options. She needed something, anything that would start her breathing. If not for the vines embedded in her lungs, she could have given the kiss of life, but their presence did one thing and one thing alone, they secured the water in place ensuring no air could be forced through. The fluid she had been suspended in was absorbed by these vines in order to ensure her body's needs were met, but, once released from the tree, they were nothing more than an obstruction that blocked her airways. Elly knew she couldn't simply pull them out, they would have attached themselves, which meant the removal by anything other than a natural body reflex, such as choking, would, very probably, result in her death.

"I-I could go into her mind, try to reach her. Or if I could just take control—" Acha approached them warily, she knew this whole situation was her fault. She had never intended any of this. It was true that her intention had been to destroy Marise, but looking back, and given the event she experienced whilst in the trees' sleep, she knew she had been wrong all along. She could only hope to be offered the chance to make amends.

"Hmm yes," Elly snapped. "Trust the one who betrayed you. I can see how *that* would work!" she spat bitterly. Even now, Elisha called upon every resource at her disposal, but despite the immense knowledge she had access to, with each text that was exhausted, each potential solution that was dismissed, just one word was clear across the distance, hopeless.

Elly leaned Zo forwards slapping her on the back with a sharp force. She didn't know what else to do, but it was evident she could not delay action any longer. If she could somehow loosen the blockage, even slightly, her body's reflexes might reject them. But it was no use, even gravity failed to dislodge the vines. She was getting desperate, her calm, rational thought process deteriorated as the rising panic finally took hold. If they couldn't do something soon, she had only one, very dangerous option. She looked to her trembling hands, unsure if she could she still them enough to do what was needed. Even if she could, the chances of Zo surviving through such a thing were astronomically low, and if by some sheer twist of fate she survived the odds, she would be immobilised for some time. They would lose months and the Oneirois did not have that long. Her solution *had* to be a last resort. She looked to Acha once more, despite her doubts there was no choice, but the idea of allowing someone like her, someone with her abilities, close to Zo did not inspire confidence. It could be just the opportunity she needed to destroy her once and for all. Indecision gripped her.

"Elly." Eiji placed his hand on her shoulder, he was surprised to feel her tremble beneath his touch. She always seemed so calm, so rational, regardless of the danger they faced, yet now, she was clearly afraid. He felt his stomach churn at the sheer hopelessness which radiated from her. He took a breath to compose himself before he continued. "It's the only choice. She's the only one who can do it." She finally nodded, conceding to the truth of his words. Acha had waited for her permission, once granted, she took a deep breath as she moved to kneel beside Zo, placing her hand on her cold, damp skin and waited. She waited and waited, but nothing happened.

Acha ran her hands over one another as if in an attempt to remove her gloves, forgetting in that instant that they had been lost when she had taken possession of the merchant in Darrienia. A sudden fear crossed her eyes, without being able to draw on her life-force there was no way to control her body, or enter her thoughts. She glanced from Zo to Daniel.

"It's not working!" her voice trembled in distress, how could it not work? Anything with a life-force was susceptible to her ability. This would have been the first time she had been able to use her curse for a positive outcome, to turn it into a gift, a means to reverse just a fraction of the damage she had caused, and now it chose to fail her.

"It never did on Zo." Daniel gasped as he interrupted Acha's panic. "Remember when you met?" his voice was barely a whisper, but the words had been enough for Acha to understand his meaning. "I have an idea" He took Acha's hand to place it on Zo's. He knew there was no time to explain. He remembered all too well the invocation she had used that day. There was no certainty it would work, but there was little else left to do but try. Even now he felt Acha's stifling touch. While he still possessed the strength, he slowly began to say the words Zo had whispered when she first healed Acha, the words she had needed to find and awaken her. He could only hope the forces would allow him to act as a medium between them; it seemed reasonable in theory, given his link with Zo. He felt dizzy as if he fell into the endless darkness that now clouded his gaze. He felt two hands pull him sharply away, even through his darkened vision he knew from the silence that Zo's eyes had not opened. Acha had been unable to possess her.

* * *

Zo smiled, pouring a small cup of tea from the beige teapot. She stirred it slowly as she looked to her mother and smiled. Words could not express how happy she was to be home again. A strange sensation of relief filled her, the endless fears vanished as if they never were. All the challenges, the trials which had burdened her, forced her beyond her limits, had simply faded. She felt no distress here, just peace.

The sun filtered gently through the window. It danced across the wooden flooring as its light passed through the leaves on the trees. Even from inside she could smell the comforting aroma of the freshly blooming roses, mingled with the fading scent of the plum blossom flower as its season approached its end. She passed a cup to her mother, moving to sit beside her.

Zo's heart was filled with such joy as she sat talking that the past years faded into oblivion, the turmoil nothing more than a faint whisper passing on the wind. Everything was calm and relaxed, so the knock at the door came as an unexpected interruption.

The cup fell from her hand as the knocking echoed through the house. It seemed almost as if it had fallen in slow motion, the contents spilling over the floor as the cup shattered beyond all repair.

"No, don't let them take me," she whispered; her mother smiled briefly before approaching the door to welcome the company.

A brown-haired young lady stood nervously on the threshold. Seeing the comforting smile of the figure who had responded to her desperate knocks, Acha returned one of her own. It was clear immediately who this figure represented, the similarities between them were striking.

"I was wondering if I might come in?" Acha questioned softly. The figure politely stepped to one side, permitting her entrance into the modest dwellings. Their home consisted of four rooms, two of which were bedrooms. The room she had entered into was the main room, it was lit warmly by the sun's rays which filtered through the large window near the cooking area. It was a small room given its multiple functions, and possessed little in the way of furnishings. Near the kitchen area, tucked up against the wall beneath the second window, stood a small age-worn table and chairs. The central part of the room possessed two wicker chairs, large enough to sit two. The rest of the room, aside from a few charms which hung upon the walls, was empty.

"Acha!" Zo frowned, in her peace such people had slipped from her mind, her deeds nothing more than a distant memory. The peace she had found here, the belonging, had made all that had happened seem unimportant, but now she stood before her, an unwelcome intrusion to an otherwise perfect death. "You are not invited." She made no attempt to greet her, in fact the only motion she made from one of the wicker chairs was adjusting her posture to remove Acha from her line of sight, almost as if in the belief that with this alteration her presence would also vanish.

"Zo you have to listen to me." Acha's voice desperately begged, her reaction was understandable all things considered, but she had to listen, she just had to.

"Get out of my house!" she snapped, rising to her feet, propelled under the force of her anger. She walked towards the door near the back of the room. If Acha would not leave, then she would. She opened the door, stopped only from passing its threshold by Acha's frightened tones.

"Zo, don't you understand?" she pleaded, even if it was for but a second, she was relieved Zo had stopped. She needed to make her understand, to enforce the urgency of the situation which brought her here. It would have been far simpler if she hadn't already destroyed the delicate bonds of trust between them, what reaction had she expected, given that she had done all things conceivable in an attempt to cause her harm. Zo turned back, the anger and distrust clear in her expression, but now, more than ever, Acha needed her trust, she had to believe her, there was too much at stake. "This, none of this is real," she warned, gesturing to the area around her symbolically. Already the outside world had become so much darker. It was doubtful that Zo herself had noticed, but not only had the scents of the garden vanished, the garden itself was no more.

"Am I missing something?" she snarled. "Why would you even care?"

"Please, Zo, I cannot ask for your forgiveness, but you must listen." Acha's desperation was clearly audible through the raised tones.

"Why must I?" she demanded, her voice matching the increased volume. "Get out. This is exactly where you wanted me, right? Leave me be." Zo slammed the open door, advancing towards Acha. If she wanted a fight, then she would get one. She had left Collateral knowing that things may have ended this way, and if facing her in battle was the only way for her to find peace once more, then so be it. Zo saw her falter as she glared coldly upon her, her gaze warning her to leave, yet challenging her to stay.

"I can't leave, not without you."

"Why not? It was you who brought me here in the first place." Zo knew she was happy here, it solved so many problems, but the longer Acha stayed, the weaker this reality became. She didn't care that it wasn't real, she was going to disappear anyway so why couldn't she be content until that time came? At least this way they would both be trapped, her *and* Marise. She couldn't take it anymore, she had tried her best and surely that was enough. Since fate seemed intent on erasing her, and recent events did nothing but hasten her disappearance, why couldn't she just stay here?

"It's true I betrayed you, but I would be betraying you further if I were to leave now." Acha moved as if to approach, but the warning look she received made her hesitate. She glanced to Kezia as if requesting support. Although fictitious, surely a mother would still wish the best for their child. It was dark outside the house now, before long this place too would fade.

"What's once more between friends?" Zo snapped bitterly. Her gaze too fell on her mother, the world around them seemed to distort slightly. Zo knew what it meant, but wasn't ready to accept it. If staying meant dying, it was a small price to pay for the peace she had found. She felt her barriers weaken as the reality faded a little more. She tried desperately to cling on to it, to force things back into their solid state as they grew transparent to reveal the emptiness beyond the walls. Seeing this, Acha spoke again.

"Please, Zo, it's Daniel." Zo looked to the doorway, it was there her eyes met with Seiken's. He had been attempting to reach her for so long that he had begun to lose hope. In that instant, as she saw him, her anger vanished.

"Daniel can take care of himself," she stated, but there was something in the way that Seiken shook his head. Although he had not spoken, he didn't need to. He had always held a power over her, she felt this truth deep in the core of all she was, and as they stood in silence his presence alone, the way he looked at her, was convincing her to leave. She tried her best to ignore him, this ending was better for everyone.

"Really? Then tell me, how do you expect him to survive this forest's poisonous thorns?" Acha watched Zo's expression change as she felt the danger seeping through their bond. "Thorns that impaled him as he tried to help Elly when they came looking for you. A poison he left untreated to find you. You can hate me all you want for what I did, the Gods know I deserve it, but please, please don't punish him because of my actions," she begged.

Acha could see how much this place, this illusion meant. But it had to end. She needed to release this fantasy before the darkness consumed them both.

Kezia moved, guiding Zo towards the door. She hesitated for but a moment, passing her a small frame which had been standing, unseen, upon the table. Inside the time-eroded mounting was a sketch of both her mother and father. It had been something she had seen many times as a child, an image she had long forgotten. She looked to her mother, unable to hide the surprise.

"I told you your father was handsome." Kezia embraced her tightly as she kissed her on the forehead. "It broke his heart to leave without ever having seen you, but if he hadn't, far worse things would have happened. Not to worry, I think you should go, you don't need me to remind you of the truth. Really my Zoella, how can you still be here, knowing what you do? You already knew I was not really her."

The house around them began to fade, as the last part of the reality began to crumble before the darkness could consume them. Zo looked to Seiken who smiled before he vanished, along with the illusion into nothingness. She forced herself to let go, to follow the one who betrayed her. She knew her words may be lies, that this could be the final betrayal, but she couldn't afford to doubt her, not this time. Kezia reached out, taking her daughter's hand and placing it in Acha's.

* * *

Elly's hand hovered uncertainly over Zo's throat, the sharp glint of metal reflecting the sun as her hand refused to steady. She had waited as long as she could, regardless of the risks it was better to attempt this and give her at least a chance of surviving. Taking a breath, this time her hand stilled in preparation to make an incision. The scalpel was barely an inch from her flesh when Zo's eyes opened, Elly discarded the instrument in the same manner she did all her weapons, her hands finding the dice quickly as she thrust Zo upright into a sitting position. She sat behind her, supporting her heavy body, the force of her gagging expelled the same green vines as Acha previously had. She had barely taken her first clear breath when she looked to Daniel. He welcomed her return with a smile, lying back as he threatened to lose consciousness.

"Daniel, pay attention." It was meant to sound so harsh, so commanding, but all that came out was a slight whisper as she gasped for air. Her throat and lungs burned with every breath as her limbs stung and felt heavy. Her reality spun and distorted around her as her body threatened to fail her. She leaned forwards to touch him gently. "I need..." She closed her eyes and began to reel off a list of herbs and quantities he was to mix between her pained and laboured breaths.

Eiji tipped her bag to spill its contents across the ground. He found himself surprised at the empty satchel's weight as he tossed it to one side. His hands rapidly spread the individually preserved herbs across the ground, his fingers tracing over each one as he tried to recognise the first ingredient she had requested. Opening her eyes, Zo looked to Elly in shock.

"Since exposure it has been—"

"Two hours twenty?" Zo interrupted, Elly nodded, confirming her assessment as Daniel's eyes flickered closed. "Eiji, can you mix?" Her voice, like her balance, threatened to fail her. Each of her breaths was desperate, laboured. Beads of sweat clung to her forehead as slowly, the signs of cyanosis began to grow faint on her pale skin. Daniel was the only person she had trusted to complete such tasks in her stead. Being as well trained as he was ensured he had great aptitude for such things. She needed him now, more than ever. There was no time to lose and she knew she lacked the energy required.

"I can't, not the way y' need it." He knew only enough about medicine to create basic compounds and a few more complex ones. It was an essential skill, but he couldn't yet recognise the ingredients by appearance, let alone estimate quantities. Acha grabbed a small bag as Eiji's hand passed over it.

"I'll do it," she interrupted before Eiji was given the opportunity to say he would try. She had picked up the mortar and pestle from the ground as Elly tossed her a thin pair of leather gloves. Acha moved to position herself by the herbs, lining them up carefully. "I know how to, I was raised in that time remember." She looked to Zo, but she did not return her gaze. Even now she still couldn't bring herself to look at her.

"Okay, Acha," she answered trying to steady her breath in hope to alleviate the dark shroud she felt within her mind. An attempt to use magic to relieve her symptoms of fatigue served only as a reminder that, although this place lay between worlds, her magic was still affected by the rune. She had hoped that, since this environment belonged to neither, it would be an exception to the rules. There was little choice but to accept her help. She barely had the strength to sit, let alone for what was to follow.

She closed her eyes to allow herself to concentrate. Once more she started to speak the herbs and quantities. She paused courteously after each one, allowing Acha the time to mix it, although it seemed it was barely needed.

Ten minutes later the compound was complete. Acha passed the bowl filled with the now ground powder to Zo, her shaking hand seizing a nearby leather skin to add what was needed. It was now she would truly be tested, she only hoped she had enough energy to complete this concoction.

Zo placed the bowl down before her and began to empower it with the spirits of the elements, along with those of light, spirit and darkness. It was a tiring endeavour. Calling on *one* spirit was exhausting, but to channel the energy from all of them, even those who had been lost, was a trial in its own right. She sat stationary, her hands cupped over the fluid forcing the energy of their invocations into the mixture. Time was running out. With the last of the blessings added, she raised her trembling hands pouring a small amount into Daniel's mouth as she lifted his head to rest on her knees. She had ensured an excess had been made, allowing for any mishaps during administration.

"Elly, time?" she questioned, fighting for breath, a slight panic edging her voice. It was clear from her movements she was tired, her entire body trembled uncontrollably as her energy neared depletion. To make it this far in her condition had been a feat in itself. Her body swayed back and forth with the effort to remain upright.

Elly was amazed she had done so much after the forest had been feeding on her power. Even after all this time her effort to continue breathing could not go unnoticed, beads of sweat ran down her face as she awaited the answer. Elly had to question if she would still be conscious to hear it. The expression seen now was a familiar one, one she had seen on Marise in the past. Zo was barely aware of her surroundings, her body was starting to shut itself down to allow it the time needed to recover.

"Twenty-five minutes exactly." She looked to Eiji before he could query the importance. "She made excellent time," she added for his benefit. The invocation of the spirits into compounds had become an almost forgotten art, even most physicians now excluded this ritual. It originated from the time when the seven spirits would take a maiden to unite them. Each spirit would choose a maiden to empower with its magic, and these seven would serve under the Mitéra, a maiden whom the seven saw worthy of their combined powers.

Even now, healers would ask for the spirits blessing in their medicines, invoking their power. As time and cycles passed, the spirits refused to take a Mitéra, but the invocation of their powers remained a constant in early medicine of all cycles, as if somehow, instinctively, the people knew of their existence. Even after three of the spirits had been lost, all were still called upon for their blessings. It had reached the time in the cycle where people had started to move away from such blessings, trusting the power of the items used rather than the spirits they could not see. But a true healer, one who used magic, would never turn their back on such an important rite. It made a significant difference to the end result.

Zo attempted desperately to get Daniel to swallow the mixture, but no matter what she tried, he coughed weakly forcing it to dribble from his mouth. In general, this kind of potion, including the invocation, usually required an excess of forty minutes to see through to completion. Despite their accomplishment, if he no longer possessed the ability to ingest it, all was for naught. There were mere minutes remaining before the poison would still his heart, despite implications, there was no time to spare.

"I had a good mixer," Zo answered autonomously as she tried to think of another way for him to swallow the concoction.

"Zo," Acha cried out, watching her fall forwards to lean on her hands as she gasped heavily for breath. More fluid spilt from Daniel's mouth as he failed once more to swallow.

"Damn it, Daniel, swallow," she pleaded, her voice, like her body, now trembled violently with her words.

"Zo you have done all you can." Elly placed her hand on Zo's shoulder, squeezing gently. It seemed, despite their best efforts, they had been too late. If he couldn't swallow the mixture, there was nothing that could be done.

"Elly, do you still have those sleep berries?" Zo demanded in a sharp whisper; Elly pulled them from her pocket, almost fearful of why she would ask.

"What are you thinking?" Zo somehow found the coordination to grab them, yet struggled with fatigue as she tried to open the loose knot. When Elly knelt down to assist her, Zo looked to her gratefully. The switch between dream and reality in this location had always been instant, she only hoped she was right about this.

"I'm thinking, if Daniel can't take this..." She decided to forgo finishing her sentence in favour of swallowing the berry. She held both the potion and

Daniel's hand tightly. Her friends faded from sight, as they did so she felt a gentle hand on her shoulder, guiding her. She recognised the sensation of the touch. Other than the disappearance of her friends, all remained the same, it was similar to falling prey to the spell of the forest.

"My gift to you, Thea." Seiken never actually appeared, yet he spoke to her directly. It seemed that, although she had been right about there being no time delay in crossing over, her assumption that Daniel would follow, simply because they were in contact, had been wrong. It was fortunate Seiken had been there to help. She placed her trembling hand on Daniel's neck to check his pulse.

Taking a deep breath, she fought back the fatigue and focused on her magic. Silent words filled the air around her, she moved her hand over his clammy forehead as her other gripped her shoulder tightly. The sting of thorns and the numbness of sensation indicated her healing artes had responded as expected. Poison was one thing, even in her own world, that could not be healed with magic. Cuts and scrapes, minor ailments, and even wounds of severity could be addressed, but afflictions such as these needed remedies not magic. As the pain from Daniel subsided, she knew the poison now displayed its final symptom. Removing her hand from her shoulder she drank the potion, the container falling from her hand as she reached out to support her weight before continuing once more. It took her every effort to force back the fatigue and pain which threatened to prevent her from completing her intended actions, but the strength of her will alone was enough to keep her going.

* * *

They had been absent for almost fifteen minutes. Their friends were worried for so many reasons, and with just cause. They had already been warned about the dangers of Darrienia once night had fallen there. Elly had prepared the berries and stood rolling them across her hand. She had just been about to suggest they follow them when, to their relief, they returned. Zo sat breathlessly, supporting her weight on her arms before collapsing. Eiji and Acha rushed to Daniel. Elly, however, watched Zo carefully, she was deathly pale, small traces of blood lined the edge of her mouth as she lay trembling unable to move her body further.

"His temperature's droppin'," Eiji stated removing his hand from Daniel's forehead. "Pulse strengthenin', breathin' is less shallow," he continued, relief filled his every word. Daniel seemed to swallow, taking the remaining antidote, which still remained within his mouth. It was almost as if the poison itself had been somehow removed, surely it was impossible for a remedy to work this quickly.

"What did you do?" Acha whispered, looking to Zo as she lay gasping desperately for breath. No matter how hard she tried, she couldn't seem to take in enough air, her chest was so tight she felt as if she was barely breathing at all. Even had her life depended on it, she would not have been able to move. She felt as if her entire body was drained beyond the point of exhaustion.

"My rune... is sacrifice," she gasped unable to force any more words into an audible volume. Her stomach burned as she fought the urge to vomit.

"What she means is, poison is an ailment magic cannot resolve, so had she tried to do so here, even with her rune, nothing would have occurred. If, however, she even attempted to heal him in Darrienia, his wounds and conditions would transfer to her. Effectively, she just poisoned herself, with a herbal poison, taken from Daniel, just moments before it would have killed him. It was a stupid and foolish thing to do, but..." Elly paused as she looked to Zo gently and smiled, she stroked her hair affectionately as it clung to her clammy face. Zo closed her eyes, unable to keep them open any longer, despite making the effort. She could feel Elly's tender, soothing touch through the darkness.

"But," Eiji continued, "It's that foolish act that saved his life." He moved around Daniel checking his life signs once more. "In another few minutes, his heart would'a stopped."

"How are you feeling?" Elly continued to stroke her hair, beads of sweat still ran down her pale skin as she lay shaking. "You overexerted yourself, you should have caught your breath after waking from the tree's slumber." That had been an understatement, more than that had been needed before anything else should have happened.

There was no doubt that what Zo had just done had drastically shortened her lifespan. Elly could feel the years which had been lost as she once again managed to somehow bypass the preservation laws of magic. They would have to be careful, if possible, she needed to prevent her from using her skills further. If she continued these reckless acts there was a high chance her body would surrender before her spirit. It was almost as if the source of magic sensed that she had lost her will to live and no longer protected her from overexertion. It seemed as long as she could maintain the spell, the forces were now content to allow her to do so, but such an act was reckless. It was doubtful Marise would be able to repair the damage being done, and it was a certainty she would never retrieve the lost years.

"Then, Daniel..." she protested, but she couldn't speak any further.

"Okay, shh." Elly continued to offer her the only comfort she could. "Seriously, how are you? You took a concentration of poison that within moments would have stopped his heart." Zo gave a weak smile, touched that Elly seemed so concerned, yet she had to wonder if it was truly her she worried about, or Marise's vessel.

"Cold," she shivered, but when Elly touched her, she found her feverish, her flushed cheeks accentuating her paleness. "Daniel?" she questioned again, forcing the words. Eiji nodded at her meaningfully, seeing this, she allowed her eyes to close once more. The voices faded into the darkness. She feared resting in case she would wake in Darrienia, yet the next thing she heard was Eiji's voice.

"—normal, she seems t'be recoverin'." Zo opened her eyes, the sun had moved to the final quarter of the sky. She had seemingly slept for hours. Still tired and weak as the herbal medicine fought the remnants of the poison, she moved shakily to look beyond the figures hunched over her to Daniel, whose eyes were now open as he turned to smile weakly. As they both lay sleeping in a dreamless sleep, Eiji had run between the two of them, checking their recovery during the forced breaks in tracing the path back to Collateral. It had been too complex to do in just one stage. The energy required dictated he had no choice but to attempt it in segments.

"You did it again," he whispered, feeling his energy returning, he moved to kneel beside her. "Zo, you're bleeding." Daniel pointed to her shoulder, the wound had gone unnoticed to both Eiji and Acha. The ground beneath her was stained with blood.

"I promised you," she whispered, grabbing Elly's hand to pull herself up, Elly helped to steady her, supporting more weight than she would have hoped necessary. "We need to leave, right?" In response she simply nodded, now both of them were able to move, it was better they return to Collateral to rest a while longer before returning to Darrienia. Zo could be examined by the healer there; if nothing else, he could replace some of the lost fluid. She was sure they still had some of Marise's blood stored there.

"Y' sure..." Eiji began; his sentence cut short by her answer.

"A little tired." She moved her hand to cover her wound.

"What happened?" But he saw the answer as he looked to her, her fingers were covered in blood.

"I needed to take my mind off the poison, amongst other things, it's just a little sore." Elly smiled, she had already known her reasoning. From the moment of her return the wound had been obvious. It was a skilled level of Hectarian who knew their limits and worked to overcome them by placing a third factor into the equation, something they could focus on so the true tasks would be unhindered. This was how she had overcome the self-preservation law of magic and why she had lost so many years from her life.

"When we arrive back at Collateral, I am taking you to The Medic," Elly insisted. She knew the damage she had inflicted would have easily torn the stitches, but this was not important, it was vital, now more than ever, that she recover quickly. The healer in Collateral, specifically the one who called himself The Medic to set himself apart from the others, had everything they needed. When she and Marise planned an adventure, they would always visit him. Marise never saw the point in storing blood with him, she had never needed it. It was only now that Elly was grateful she had conformed to her wishes, it would speed Zo's recovery time greatly. Acha picked up Zo's satchel; once she and Daniel had returned safely, Acha had busied herself carefully replacing its contents.

"Zo." Aside from her satchel, Acha held something in her hand. "This was in your hand." She passed her the tattered, folded, slightly damp sketch of her mother and father. She had wondered exactly how it had come to be with her, especially since it seemed Kezia had not handed it to her until they left. Nothing about this place made sense, but she decided not to question it, nor had she decided to mention that the man on the photo was the same one whose path they had crossed in Abaddon, surely Zo knew this already. "Also..." She opened her hand, within her palm rested a delicate stone flower, upon it was carved a symbol.

"When did y'..." Eiji glanced at the rune in surprise as Daniel took the satchel from Acha.

"When I was trapped I met a young girl, she gave it to me in hope that just a fragment of her would escape." She looked sadly at the rune as she recalled the young girl. "Zo, I know I have betrayed you, hurting you and turning on you without a thought or reason. I see now how wrong I was to trust anyone's word over yours. When Sofia told me those things, I thought, because she appeared like a Moirai, that the words she spoke were true. I'm not asking for your forgiveness I don't deserve it, just for a chance to earn your trust. I will do anything, please just one more chance." Eiji slipped away to occupy himself on creating the gateway to the portal.

"You're right Acha, you've had your chance." Elly tightened her grip as Zo faltered slightly. The silence seemed to stretch on forever as Zo looked at her deep in thought, before she gave a gentle smile. "Acha, you came to get me from a place no one else could, you came with only the desire of helping those I care for. You never gave up hope, and you rose to help Daniel without a thought. I never lost my belief in you, you just lost yourself along the way. Besides, if I had been honest with you from the start..." Zo hid well the misgivings of the words she spoke, she doubted she would ever be able to trust Acha again, how could she? Regardless of this, there wasn't much time left. They had to complete their quest as soon as possible, misgivings and distrust would only hinder their pace. For now, she could at least pretend to forgive her, she could mimic the actions of trust and friendship Acha herself had previously displayed. After all, if not for her, Daniel would not have survived.

"Nothing would have changed," Acha admitted honestly. "Even if you had told me yourself, when Sofia came—"

"Who is this Sofia you keep mentioning?" Daniel moved to stand beside her. He was now able to almost comfortably hold his own weight, whereas Zo still relied heavily on Elly for support.

"She was a Moirai, or so I thought. When she betrayed me, I saw her true form, Aburamushi." Acha wondered why she had been so ready to believe a stranger over anyone else. Why had she been so foolish?

"We've seen him too," Eiji interjected once the entrance was finished. The time they had rested had allowed Elly to instruct him in reconstructing the route Aburamushi had sealed. It had been a lengthy process, but completed quicker than Elly had expected. "He posed as Acha t'lure us here, and as Seiken before in Darrienia." Eiji groaned and looked to Zo. "I was meant t'tell y', Night has taken Seiken."

"I know," she replied, as Elly helped her through the portal.

Chapter 25

The Cave of Mysteries

The small figure was almost lost amongst the books she had summoned. None had dared to return to their shelving until they were certain she had finished with them. She had been asking her questions for some time, summoning endless stacks of literature, and scanning their pages for anything that could be of assistance.

"I'm so sorry Miss Lain, I can't find any records of the forest other than those I've already provided." Elisha finally began to dismiss the texts. There were no more questions she could ask, no more wisdom to be gained on this subject.

This had been the first time that Lain had ever truly needed her assistance and she had been completely useless. She had questioned and searched repeatedly, since they had first retrieved the young lady from the tree, for something that would aid with their current dilemma. But there was nothing, no information on how to remove the vines which prevented her from breathing, nor on how to break the forest's hold over her.

Elisha had put all her efforts into finding something, anything, which could be of use to them, but with every book she tried things had become more hopeless. The only remotely feasible option she had found had involved a very delicate and complex surgery, but it was doubtful even that would work given the alien entities introduced into her body. She stared into the mirror, like her, the library was exhausted, unable to offer her further assistance. She could only pray that by some miracle Zoella survived.

Since she had arrived there, she had become quite fond of the people whose lives she watched on the silver surface of the surrounding mirrors. She hated the thought that anything ill would befall them if she failed to complete her role. When she first accepted this position, she had never imagined it would be so involved, so exciting. She felt as if she had been watching a play being performed before her. She not only enjoyed following their lives, but as an added incentive she had a vast library at her call, allowing her to use both its and her knowledge to aid the travellers on their way, as if she were influencing the course of events with her intervention.

Elisha stood slowly, as she dusted herself down the last of the books filed themselves away, back to their familiar resting places.

"I have found out so much about you Miss Lain." She approached the capsule in which Lain slept, unsure if she would hear the words. "I never would have thought you had accomplished so much. Night's calling on me soon, perhaps he can offer an answer." She glanced up to a nearby timepiece on the wall as a knock echoed, she hadn't realised it had already grown so late.

She removed the wired helmet which linked her to the sleeping Lain. The helmet itself was no longer necessary to communicate with her. The bonds they shared had grown quickly, however, in times of intense concentration, it helped her to focus. Lain still begged her to find something, but it was hopeless, there was not another book, but now Night was here, perhaps he could help.

There was a slight pause before the door opened, Elisha had known her master would call at this hour, but she was unsure about the company he would bring, would he be trusted with Lain's secret, or should she work to conceal her? Without answers, she knew she would have to read her master's cues. He and his guest now approached, yet she was still unsure what action she should take.

She glanced to the capsule desperately, doing so saw her vision quickly drawn to the surface of a mirror as a wave of relief flooded through Lain. It was such a powerful emotion that Elisha, unlike Elly, could not hold back the tears as the tension drained and the person, who had seemed fated to die, moved before her gaze.

"Elisha." Night smiled. "This is—"

"Seiken," she exclaimed, wiping her tears with the back of her hand. She saw Night smile softly at her. "I know you from here." She pointed towards the mirrors, which Seiken took the time to study in detail. The same relief, which had filled her just moments ago, now flooded through him as his vision rested on the image of Zo. The extent of his relief made his heart ache, not only because she was alive, but because the reason he now stood within this room was because he had agreed to betray her.

He watched her closely, his throat swelling with pain. This very second she was attending to Daniel before starting to concoct a strange potion, despite the obvious fatigue her asphyxiation caused. It was an action that was against his better judgement, by pushing herself so hard in her current condition, she was asking for death to find her, then again, if she were to die now, perhaps that would be better. He scolded himself for thinking such things, how could death be better for anyone? As he continued to watch, he saw Acha take up the mixing bowl to help, it seemed Zo either had no choice, or no objections.

"Very good. I see you have been making full use of the facilities." Night's voice answered, as Seiken focused his attention on the mirrors. "Seiken has agreed to help us, but this is not knowledge to be revealed to our travellers."

"Then, my lord, why do you present it to me?" she questioned, rather formally.

"You are now part of Lain's knowledge, should Seiken suggest anything that you know not to be entirely correct..." When the realisation flickered in her eyes, he found no need to continue.

"I understand," she bowed, "Lain will not know any falsities that come from his words, but what should happen, should she discover this deception on her own merit?" she questioned. Lain was intelligent, after all, she still held within her conscious much of the knowledge she had taken from the Gods. The last thing she would want is for Night to think she had betrayed him, should something go wrong.

"Try to dissuade her, failing that tell her of this arrangement. However, given the current situation, the instability of emotions and thoughts a new watcher can temporarily create, I would prefer it if she did not have to know."

"Very good, my lord."

"I knew you were a fine choice. Seiken and I have some papers to sign, would you care to bear witness?" Night motioned her towards the nearby table followed closely behind by Seiken.

"Papers?" she questioned uncertainly.

"Yes, for our peace of mind, whereas Seiken does not trust my words, I do not trust his heart." He looked to Seiken meaningfully. "By signing our promise to Grimitical papers, our word is bound until the completion of our contract." This was the only way to ensure the cooperation of both parties. Once these papers were signed their agreement would be ironclad.

"Grimitical papers?" Elisha's eyes grew wide. "I thought they were merely legend. Signing one, binds both parties to the vows written upon its surface, if they should betray it—"

"They pay the price, I see you are familiar with its workings. I took the liberty of drafting the agreement, if you would do the honours." She took the paper from him before handing it to Seiken, who sat on the opposite side of the table. He read it to himself before nodding. His vision strayed back towards the mirrors as Elisha read their contract aloud. Night watched carefully, as the forest was his brother's domain, he could not intervene in anything occurring there, so perhaps he could allow this Oneiroi one final expression of his love.

"By the law and judgement of this sacred parchment, so is it written, that in exchange for release of his world, the returning of his people along with their freedom, Seiken, son of Crystenia, is bound to Night by this life-force contract, to aid him where asked in the task of leading The Chosen, as needed, in order to achieve the desired goal, leading ultimately to the retrieval of the final Grimoire.

"In exchange, Seiken, son of Crystenia, must unquestioningly assist Night in the fulfilment of the tasks required of him. Night must remain true to his word and not devise any technicality, which would result in the contract being void. Just as Seiken, son of Crystenia, must offer his complete service without betrayal to Night.

"Full cooperation of each party is expected in each instant. The signing of this sacred parchment is an acknowledgement of their agreement to the conditions and the binding of themselves by blood and life-force until the contract's completion. Should betrayal occur, the life-force of the one dishonouring their agreement will be forfeited.

"Upon completion of the tasks above, the contract will release those bound to it." Elisha took a breath as she placed the parchment upon the table. "All that remains is for you both to sign." She disappeared for but a moment, returning with a small knife which she placed upon the table.

"I trust this is to your liking?" Night was the first to sign, he drew the knife across his palm and rubbed his hands together before placing both upon the contract. The signature used for this type of agreement was not one made by a pen, or by the swearing of an oath by the water of Styx, it was an imprint of the hand where a person's future and life expectancy could be predicted. Should either of them betray the arrangement, the parchment would change these subtle lines of fate, ending their life in an instant.

Night looked at him expectantly. He knew exactly what this boy wanted to do, he had seen it in his eyes and had already resigned himself to allowing this one final act of compassion.

"Do what you must before you sign, after you have left your mark you cannot act outside of my wishes." Seiken nodded in surprise, he needed just a moment to concentrate on helping Thea one last time. He knew all too well this would be his last chance, only he could offer her something that she needed so desperately. At this moment she nursed Daniel as she attempted to cross into Darrienia's version of this forest. He had to admire her ingenuity, but things would not work as she intended, not without some intervention. He looked to Night gratefully and nodded in appreciation for not only this gesture, but the trust that it implied.

The workings of what he had to do were complicated, he took a moment in silence, he paced back and forth as he tried to accomplish that which she needed. He only stopped as his eyes fell upon a strange capsule. Although part of him was now somewhere else aiding Zo, like a sleeping animal there was still part of him that remained awake and alert, watching for any danger. It was then he saw her, a young lady suspended in sleep. She wore a black skin tight suit which concealed all skin from her neck to her feet. Her long blue hair was about waist length much longer than the version of her he had seen walking with The Chosen.

"That's..." he gasped in surprise as he approached for a closer look. Elisha grabbed the parchment from the table and ran over to prevent any further advancement, positioning herself between them.

"Elaineor? Yes." Night answered, still standing at the table in the centre of the room. He had to admit he was impressed, it was a special gift to be able to send just part of your consciousness away to complete a task. This small demonstration had explained exactly how he had been able to assist them despite his capture, but having witnessed this act himself, he knew how to monitor for this activity. Other than being considerably weaker, it was not too different to the omnipresence used by the Gods.

"But how?" He paced around the capsule curiously, never in his years had he beheld something of this nature.

"All will become clear," Night answered as Elisha passed Seiken the parchment, encouraging him to once more approach the table. Night knew he had now finished his business and was simply stalling before he became a traitor to his heart. He couldn't blame him, it was a difficult decision to make. Choosing between your heart and loyalties was never easy, but with so much at stake he also knew there was really no other decision. "But first, business." Night pulled the chair out for Seiken. As he sat, Night stood over him whilst he read the contract once more. Seiken took the knife and once more looked at the image of his Thea.

"I'm sorry," he whispered.

* * *

After seeing The Medic, by Elly's command, and taking the rest of the daylight hours to recuperate a little, they had crossed once more into Darrienia. All were still weary from their eventful day, a tiredness that, even in the land of dreams, slowed their pace as they walked through the plains in the direction of what seemed to be a range of mountains. It reminded them a little of Phoenix Landing, in the sense that they could see the slow curve of the seemingly impassable barricade before them.

It had been an uneventful journey, one that would have taken far longer had it not been for Elly's suggestion of seeking passage from the castle's wizard. In the light of a new night, it seemed all their previous misadventures had been forgotten. Castle Iris bustled with life as they readied themselves for the coming festivities. The castle's wizard had been using his talents to entertain a small group of children. It was during this act that Elly had approached him, asking if by chance, he would consider performing a vanishing act of epic proportions. They spoke in hushed tones as she gave the details of what would be his most spectacular performance. It was a request he could not refuse. The crowd grew silent as he enticed them all by his words. The children leaned forwards in eager anticipation to see if this wizard, could indeed, make five people vanish into thin air.

They had appeared almost exactly where Elly had requested. She missed the days when a ruler would possess such a fine calibre of man in their employ. With magic all but extinguished, wizards had become almost as rare as Hectarians. They now masked their talents from the world, as if to imply their skills had also vanished with the loss of the Hectarian artes. The only place these feats even took place anymore were in the dreams of those who had once held the potential to be great. There was no denying that the sealing of Hectarian artes had made an impact on the power available to the wizards, but still, it was not as if they relied on the source of this magic to fuel their own.

"So where now?" Daniel directed his question to Elly, the person who had led them since their arrival. She had been guiding their movements for some time now without a hint as to their target. All they knew for certain was that they were getting closer to the distant mountains. Elly did not answer their queries. She remained oddly silent, almost lost in thought as she either failed to realise she was being addressed, or deliberately ignored them, that was until they reached the foot of the first mountain, where they stopped to rest outside the entrance to a cave.

"From here, you must venture through the Cave of Mysteries." Elly smiled at Daniel, a slight flicker of amusement crossed her eyes as she spoke the next words. "I shall wait at the exit." She raised her eyebrows waiting for the questions that were sure to follow. She had waited a very long time to speak these words. It was a feat of her past that, although tedious at the time, she was very proud of.

"Can't we just cut through like you?" Daniel questioned, almost as quickly as she had anticipated. He wasn't exactly sure the nature of this cave, but if there was a way for Elly to pass through, then surely they could do the same.

"You misunderstand." She grinned, taking such pleasure in the words that followed. "I have already defeated this cave. Every riddle, every question and I, like any who can stake such a claim, step through straight to the exit. Even in Darrienia, these rules apply," she explained. She found herself wondering if they would make it through without assistance, she hoped so. If they ever thought to seek it out in their world it would lead them to a place beyond all imaginings. Here, however, it simply took them through to the other side of the mountain, at least for now anyway; places like these in the land of dreamers always had changing purposes and destinations. Daniel shifted uncomfortably, beginning to feel the pressure building as Elly explained what was expected of him. "Do not worry, it will be an experience." She patted him almost mockingly on the shoulder.

"Fine, what is this place exactly?" he questioned, taking in the appearance of the strange cave which stood before them. It seemed to be made from an unfamiliar rock that seemed alien to its surroundings, and shared no similar composition to the mountain or area around them.

"This place was constructed by the Gods. In this world it gives passage to those deemed worthy to pass through to the Mountain of the Spirits. Should you choose not to journey this way, you are looking at a three-day hike, one you may not survive. Attempting the cave should prove less fatal." She moved as if to enter, this warning was only true of this world, in their world the Gods had constructed it for an entirely different purpose.

"How does it work?" Again, Daniel was filled with questions, but this time they seemed to be nothing more than an exercise in stalling.

"When you enter, you will find yourself in a large area, with a number of possible exits. Each tunnel represents an answer, whether you are correct or not, the path you choose will open. The only difference being, the more mistakes you make, the further from the exit you become, until time runs out and you remain trapped within." Elly stepped into the cave to vanish before their sight. It had been almost as if the darkness within had simply swallowed her whole.

Daniel hesitated for a moment longer as he thought over what had been said. He only hoped that, as the one she had deemed most suitable to lead them through, he would not disappoint them. He took a determined breath before stepping inside, followed closely by his friends.

The cave's mouth sealed to leave them imprisoned within a circular room. It took a moment for their eyes to adjust to the darkness. Around them, wooden torches burnt within iron sconces to fill the air with the sweet smell of rich wood. The area, although stone in appearance, had a strange polished texture to it, more like a marble than the granite it appeared to be. In the centre of the room stood a small altar, resting upon it, to bring the stone tablet to a comfortable reading height, was a white marble lectern. This central feature overlooked three sealed doors, above each door something was written.

"Speak," commanded a mighty voice as Daniel slowly approached the stone tablet. There was a pause whilst the one who addressed them awaited their response. Daniel thought back to Elly's words as she had briefed him on his task.

"I, Daniel Eliot accompanied by my fellow travellers, Zoella Althea, Acha Night, and Eiji um..." Daniel looked to Eiji, it was only then he realised that he had never had a formal introduction, before Eiji could answer the voice had continued.

"For what purpose do you venture into our world?"

"We seek passage to the Mountain of the Spirits." Short and simple just as Elaineor had instructed. He would not speak the reason behind their wanting to visit there, in this world that alone could see their request rejected.

"I trust you accept the rules of this passage?" the voice questioned.

"Yes sir," he answered, hoping he had understood all that Elaineor had told him of this challenge. He now would be the only one who could trigger the opening of a door. He would be responsible for guiding them safely through to the other side, this thought alone made his heart pound and his mind empty.

"Begin." In the room a large hourglass mounted in one of the stone walls rotated, the sand slowly filtering through as words appeared on the stone tablet before them. Daniel read the text aloud.

"Bird women, swine, ogre, I have faced many a beast, Scylla and Charybdis to name a few. I have sailed the kingdom of Hades. Most in my time knew me, yet to some I was nobody." Above each of the three sealed exits a name was written, to the far left, Odysseus, to the centre Sisyphus, to the right, Ulysses.

"I guess we hafta choose one, but how do they open?" Eiji paced between them as he looked at the solid wall which blocked each path, not daring to touch one in case it was accepted to be their answer.

"Speak your answer Daniel Eliot, the door shall open before you." The voice resonated through the silence until it once more faded into nothing. Looking at the doors he spoke his thoughts to his friends.

"My initial thought was Ulysses, he did all of those, but Odysseus and Ulysses are the same. Before he left on his travels he was known as Odysseus, but as he travelled for ten years against the Gods who forced him from his way, they began then to call him Ulysses."

"You can only choose one," Zo whispered, looking at the draining hourglass.

"Odysseus," he stated firmly beginning his approach to the relevant door. He knew that technically both answers were correct, yet one of them would not be the required response. It concerned him the type of question they had been given. If they all followed this suit there was a chance that a technicality could see them sealed within these walls forever. He had finally decided on Odysseus reasoning that Ulysses was nothing more than an alias. Even he was unsure why this one man possessed two names during his life, perhaps the key to the answer of that would have revealed the solution expected, unfortunately, it was not a fact he had ever encountered.

As they approached the wall that sealed their path, the brickwork faded as if it had been nothing more than an illusion. Like the entrance to the cave, nothing but darkness stood before them as one by one they stepped through into the dark void. Entering the next room, they felt the strangest feeling of déjà vu. The room was identical in every feature to the one they had just left moments ago. This place was clearly designed to disorientate the traveller. It was easy to lose track of both time and distance in a place where each room was identical to the last. For some reason, knowing each room moved them either towards or away from their target, none of them had considered that it was in fact, simply the same room they had entered and any movement made was simply perceived.

Another pedestal stood before them, Daniel approached the centre to read the question aloud.

"By three golden apples I was forced to wed, but shifted to lions as we hurried to bed." It seemed this question was a little more vague than the last. Daniel was glad he was so well versed in this world's history, as he studied the names above the door, he reminded himself of the tale.

Melanion had fallen in love. The hand of his desired was not without its challenges. She had stated she would only marry a person who could defeat her in a race. Many had tried, staking their lives for the hand of the fair maiden, for this was the only wager they were allowed to make. Melanion had beseeched Aphrodite for her aid. To ensure his victory, she presented him with three golden apples, knowing the one he desired would be unable to resist them. Each time she began to catch up he threw an apple to the side, seeing the delicious fruit she altered her path slightly to collect it, confident she could regain any advantage lost. Each time he threw it further afield. It was by these delays he won the race and was granted her hand in marriage. In his haste to bed his wife, he forgot to honour his sacrifice to the goddess and so, as punishment, Aphrodite turned them to lions. He looked to the doors, the name on the tip of his tongue as he studied the names carefully, Athena, Atalanta or Minthe, he knew the answer.

"Atalanta." He pointed the others towards the central door, and they moved on into the next chamber.

On and on the questions went as time slipped through the hourglass. They could only tell the sands were running low, unsure how long the trickling sand allowed them. The questions merged into one another in a seemingly never-ending barrage.

"I have but a brief mention in old history, I was the first born of the elemental gods. Day and light, dreams and destruction, friendship and love, are but a few of my children."

"That's easy," Daniel stated, he, without a doubt, knew the answer to this one, although had it not been for all he had learnt from Elly, he may have answered incorrectly.

Night was the answer he would have given, that was if he had been unaware of the unusual history of this god. The god known as Night had once been an aspect of a far greater goddess, one Zeus had attempted to force into mortality for her refusal to participate in the Titanomachy. Night had been the result of this action and was created a mortal man who had, by some unknown deed, managed to obtain the immortality that had been stripped from him. The answer this tablet sought was the name of the goddess who had set into motion the very creation of the universe, and had given birth to such beings as dark spirits, sleep, death, pain, strife, as well as the other entities listed in the question, and no doubt many more.

Nyx was like Gaea in the sense that even if their names were forgotten, their presence alone would reaffirm their existence. By trying to force her to the mortal realm, Zeus had severed only the part of her that could not exist without faith, a part of her which took on a male guise and on its separation became a being, then by his own actions a god, in his own right. It could, in fact, be said that Night was a child born of Nyx and Zeus.

The old world, the one said to come before theirs, a time referred to as O.G.E, or Old Gods Era, may have possessed the same cycles as the current one, it was even hypothesised that another world existed before that one. His teacher had taken a keen interest in Nyx, seeing but a brief passage of reference to her throughout the texts. He had always been intrigued as to how one of the great goddesses could have been almost erased from history. It was rare for any to know her name, and most now thought her to be the god Night due to his own activity and stories within their history. Maybe in time, they would forget and erase him from their minds, but before they could do that, they first had to face him.

"Nyx," he stated the name almost viciously, seeing the sand trickling away he pushed them through the opening door. As they stepped through, they found not another identical room with another puzzle awaiting them, but a passageway leading towards the light. They had reached the exit. They had barely passed through when the door closed heavily behind them sealing the cave, awaiting the time the next challengers would enter.

"What took you so long?" Elly stood leaning against the side of the cave as they emerged. It was clear from the sun's rays that they had not been as long as they had anticipated. The sun was still low in the sky, perhaps two hours had passed since entering Darrienia. A good hour of that had been during their trial through the cave. "Personally, I chose Ulysses, it was, after all, how he was referred to in the stories of the listed trials, and a name is an identity in itself." She cast a meaningful glance to Zo. "You made a few mistakes, but you did far better than I anticipated. Come on." She smiled warmly at Daniel, passing him a small gold coin, he looked at her curiously. "That is your return passage," she stated. She knew he would find a use for it at some point, even if it was just as a memento which served to remind him of happier days. That was, if any of them survived.

"So how many times did you go through that to earn your free passage?" Daniel quickened his pace to walk beside her, curiosity gripped him as he awaited her answer.

"Until there were no more questions." She disclosed with a wink. He opened his mouth as if to reply but failed to find the words. Elly could scarcely believe she had shocked him into silence, then again, she had been granted the gift of time. She distinctly remembered spending almost a quarter of a century simply passing back and forth through the caves. She could have taken them through with her, had she desired, but she was more interested in seeing how they would fare. Their fate was already in safe hands, the cave had understood all too well they travelled with her. This test had been nothing more than a game, that and a distraction whilst she had taken care of some pressing matters.

"So the place we're heading, what do we expect to find there?" Acha questioned. The area, on which they had emerged, was filled with trees and grassland as far as the eye could see. The Mountain of the Spirits stood proudly on the far side of the peninsular.

The nearby mountains paled in comparison in both height and majesty, and seemed to bow before its presence as it towered above them to reach beyond the clouds. The area, like the one in their own world, was found on a small peninsula. The access by land obstructed by the towering giants.

Unlike Phoenix Landing, it was not a complete circle of these deadly peaks, there was a small access point by sea, but the jagged rocks which lined the elevated cliff face meant none would attempt to reach it by such means. It was not as isolated as an onlooker would first think. The journey here was, in fact, an easy one, for those who took the time to look.

If any of them had visited its counterpart in their world they may have noticed the small imperfections this facsimile possessed. It lacked Poseidon's temple, a number of the majestic waterfalls and crystal clear lakes near its base, and various other features, which would have provided nothing more than a simple convenience to their journey, such as the cave entrance found at its very base. Lacking such things meant that, when they reached their destination, there would be no choice but to brave its jagged rock face in an attempt to access its inner depths from the opening they would find near its peak.

"The final rune," she answered simply once everyone had taken in their new surroundings. She had thought this much would have been obvious. There had been five runes, and this was the only location they had not visited which still bore a riddle, surely they realised their journey was nearly at an end.

The grassy plain and trees soon gave way to the rocky shale of the mountain terrain. They had walked in silence across the quiet sanctuary until they had reached the very start of the upwards climb. As they looked up each one of them felt tiny in comparison to the mighty giant that towered above them. Its immeasurable heights disappeared through the clouds, perhaps even so high as to intrude on Olympus itself.

"The Mountain of the Spirits!" Eiji exclaimed, he had been hiding his excitement about visiting this great landmark since they had first seen it on the horizon, after passing through the cave. Even he was filled with awe by standing in such close proximity and failed to hide the nervous anticipation which consumed him. His master had told him many tales of this place. It was one of the areas his journey to learn from the elements would have taken him, a place his master had so often visited. He could barely believe he now stood before it, he felt humbled in its presence as he imagined the greatness that lay within. "It's a place of legend, the very home of the elemental spirits, deep within its core, gnomes forge armour and weapons, in its clear streams and lakes the nymphs are said t'play—" Eiji went to continue, but his excited manner was abruptly tamed by Elly's interruption.

"You think only of the benevolent things. This place has many a tale. It was the holding place of the Star of Arshad at one time, and that is just the tip of its lore. Such powerful places attract many creatures both good," she looked to him then back towards the mountain, "and evil. There are creatures sleeping in its depths that would freeze your blood if you so much as caught sight of them, creatures more terrifying than your worst nightmares could even begin to comprehend. Despite the dangers, somewhere within, the final rune awaits our arrival. After this, we head home before setting out on the final journey." Zo knew instantly whose home she referred to.

"Home?" Zo questioned, a joyous lift to her voice. At the journey's start she had been so sure she would never step foot in Crowley again, Elly had been certain her presence would only endanger those residing there. The thought of returning filled her heart with a strange peace. It seemed she would be given the chance to gaze upon the quiet life she once had one final time before leaving it behind forever.

"Yes," Elly answered bluntly; she moved closer to Zo, dropping her tone as she did so. "Given the choice you do want to say goodbye, correct?" Zo felt her stomach sink at her words. It seemed Elly too knew the outcome of this journey after all, or perhaps there was more to it than that, perhaps she too saw the power of her inner darkness and knew that now, even without drawing the sword, little by little she was losing parts of herself to the blackened void. Daniel stared at her in alarm. He had felt all too clearly the sadness and inevitability of her emotions. It made him wonder what Elly could have said in hushed tones to prompt such an instant response, one so unexpected she had failed to shield it from him in time. "Also, there is something we need to collect before our journey is truly over."

"I would like that, thank you." Zo smiled sadly. In her mind a single line reminded her of the truth, something she had heard such a long time ago, before any of this even had come to pass. The prophecy clearly stated to win, she had to lose everything. They were so close to the end of their journey now she could almost feel the hand of death upon the fragments of herself she fought so hard to retain. She looked at her friends as they walked around the mountain's base. Elly was busying herself scanning the slopes of the mountain in search for the most efficient way to reach its peak. Eiji walked absent-mindedly, his head craned back as he attempted to take in each part of the mountain, so was surprised when his foot caught a small protruding rock. Acha reached out, grabbing him before he could tumble to the ground. She smiled to herself as she thought back over their time together, then back further to before all this began, to the late evenings with Daniel and thoughts of her home.

"I was beginning to wonder." Daniel slowed his pace, placing his arm around her shoulder carefully. He felt her flinch slightly at his touch, but despite the pain, she continued to smile. The happiness reflected within her eyes making the gesture contagious.

"What?" she questioned as she stopped, her vision focusing upon him intently, taking in his every detail, his dark eyes, his brown hair, and his kind smile. The rest of them continued at their normal pace allowing them a moment of privacy.

"If you had a genuine smile left," he admitted quietly. He thought back over the entirety of this journey. She had smiled so much over its course, a smile she used as nothing more than a shield for her true feelings, a smile to cover her fears, worries, and pains. But this time was different, this time it reached her eyes, making them shine brightly. He never realised how much he had missed it, until it was no longer there. He was glad to see she had not completely lost it. "What were you thinking?" He had failed to capture the thought that had brought such joy to her eyes.

"Just how lucky I am to have such great friends." She smiled her true smile again, not letting it fade as the thoughts of her friends gave her a warm, rich feeling. For just a moment, she found herself thinking, *'If I should die now, I would die truly happy,'* she buried it quickly, her innocent thought had been a little too close to the truth, but even if she knew her time was running out, for some reason the smile just would not fade, not this time. They continued on towards the looming mountain.

"I never imagined it'd be so..." Eiji paused as he approached the rising cliff face. Elly had directed them expertly to this place. It was clear to see why, the mountain slopes seemed far less dangerous. From this point onward it would be a steep and difficult climb. "High," he finished, his vision straining upwards. There was no way to estimate exactly how far above the clouds it rose, but one thing was certain, it would prove to be a challenge.

"This is no time for procrastination. We can rest at the first overhang," Elly stated approaching the mountain's base. She began climbing, guiding their path as she did so. She had the strangest feeling that if she hadn't taken such a definitive measure they would have stopped, stalling over conversation. It was something they did not have time for, not if they wanted to reach the summit well before nightfall. This mountain would not be a good place to spend the night. They had to attend to things here quickly.

Elly was more skilled at climbing than any of them first expected. It seemed her feet effortlessly found the most secure footing as she skilfully led them. It was a sheer climb, as such they had secured the rope between themselves to ensure safety should anyone miss a step. The pace was steady, with no pause for breath as they pushed upwards. They seemed to be progressing at a good speed. The ledge was almost within reach as the more serious signs of fatigue started to set in from the constant progression.

Acha saw Zo's hand reach down for her as she started to navigate around to climb the ledge. Acha had brought up the rear in this instance, the pace had been hard. She took the hand, grateful for any assistance she could get. It was a small ledge, smaller than it had first appeared from their lower vantage point, but still, it was large enough for them to all sit with their back against the mountain, allowing them to avoid the strong winds that whipped down its sides.

Zo took advantage of this momentary reprieve to find a root from her satchel. She broke it into small sections placing one within her mouth to allow her to chew it throughout their next climb. She had correctly assumed this would not be a lengthy pause. It was clear to Acha, who had watched her struggle with the climb, that her shoulder was causing her tremendous difficulties. She could see the slight hesitation, and the shifting of extra weight to her legs, each time she had needed to take any weight on her injured side. She had been surprised to see the offer of assistance. Despite the immense pain the climb had caused her, Zo had once more extended her hand, an action which assisted Acha's climb to the overhang.

Scolding herself again, Acha wondered how she could have been so blind as to not see her gentle heart. Guilt filled her thoughts as she recalled the numerous times she had betrayed her. Zo had done nothing more than try to help those around her, regardless of the personal cost. Since the forest, things had become so much clearer. There was no way Marise was just a front, an alias, they really were two completely different people. This filled Acha with a new fear, ultimately there would only be room for one of them, it was impossible not to see the damage her actions had caused. Little by little, each of her betrayals had eaten away at her friend's resolve, her determination. Now she could see things clearly, she could only hope her actions would not be the cause of a greater tragedy. Her actions had given Marise power, she could only pray that Zo still had enough of her own to resist and suppress the inner darkness. Acha glanced down over the area they had just climbed, unable to bring herself to look at Zo any longer. She was so ashamed of her actions, so fearful of the events she had set into motion. Looking down, she saw they had covered at least twice the distance she had expected.

"It is a long climb to the opening at the summit," Elly advised sternly. She was surprised at least one of them, for instance Daniel who was always so full of questions, hadn't thought to query how she knew there was an opening. It seemed the group had simply become accustomed to her being correct, this made things far easier. "We cannot afford to rest any longer, spending a night on this mountain would *not* be a wise decision." Elly looked to Zo sympathetically, the root she was chewing would be slow in taking effect, but they both knew they could not wait for its reprieve. Even before Elly had spoken, Zo, as if knowing her thoughts, had risen to her feet ready to continue.

"Well actually." Seiken appeared before them, he glanced between them briefly, before moving slightly to ensure his presence was not taking up too much space on the already crowded area. "You only need to climb to the next ledge." He pointed to a small overhang to the far right of them; one even Elly had failed to notice until he had pointed it out. "There's an entrance there, from that point it's pretty easy travelling." His gaze fixed on Zo, a strange sadness reflected in his eyes. She looked at him questioningly, asking for the answers behind the weighted expression. There was something final, mournful, in his gaze.

"I thought you were trapped," she questioned lightly. It wasn't a challenge to his presence here. She simply wanted to prove to the rest of them she had no doubts about who it was that stood before them. It also gave him an opportunity to explain his presence, one they were all anxious to hear. His expression alone implied the severity of something that had recently occurred.

"I was. It's a long story. To summarise, however, Night attempted to convince me to betray you in exchange for his withdrawal from my home and the freedom of my people. I was so close, Thea, so close to signing the contract. In fact, he was so certain I would agree that he overlooked the opportunity he had presented for me to escape. I think I have made a terrible mistake. What if he now harms them because of my actions?" His conflicting emotions reflected clearly in his worried brown eyes. He looked so tired, it was clear how much he questioned his actions.

"He won't, he needs them alive," she answered, her voice held a conviction her mind did not share. She had become quite skilled in deception now, she could say anything if it would offer a little comfort. Even if she knew it wasn't true. "You said he wanted you to help him, how?" She glanced at her companions, perhaps if they were to understand more about what had been requested of Seiken, they could protect themselves from any trickery that may await.

"He didn't say exactly, although it involved betraying you. All the time he was explaining what he would offer me for my cooperation I thought about the implications. I was so close, Thea, so close," he admitted shamefully as he looked down towards his feet, "I had drawn the blood ready to sign the agreement, but then I realised, although it's true I want to save my people, how could I claim to be worthy of their respect knowing how I had achieved it? I have such faith in you, Thea. I know you won't let us down." As he smiled, he took her hand in his and the sadness almost completely vanished from his eyes. "It won't be long until he finds me, I must keep moving. I will help all I can, but you *must* hurry! I fear for the lives of my people now more than ever." His voice seemed to grow more desperate as he glanced around. "If you don't, I fear not one of us will remain for you to save. I shall find a safer place and return. Be careful, this mountain is treacherous." With those words he vanished, leaving them to begin their climb to their new destination.

The ledge was not as far away as they had anticipated, in fact it seemed they had barely climbed at all when they set foot upon its stable surface. True to Seiken's words, the ledge concealed an entrance into the mountain, an entrance which, like most places within this world, seemed to absorb all light.

"Okay, so we just go through and our target's at the end?" Eiji glanced into the pitch-black entrance trying to see what lay just inside its walls. "But let's say we do get this other rune, what then, what we meant t'do with them?" He looked to Elly for the answer. Until now they had been blindly following the map, passing through the fixed locations and retrieving the runes without a thought to what lay ahead. There were two places they had left to visit that were fixed locations, here and Crowley. It had been Elly who had decided here was their destination, it had been the only place left unvisited with a riddle. But as the journey's end drew closer, he had started to focus on the unknown. Once they had this rune, this final key, what happened then? Would a door magically appear before them leading them to Night's tower, a place of no world, yet of them all, and if so, what did they do once they reached this place?

"Aren't they supposed to be some sort of key to releasing Seiken's people?" Acha looked at the small pouch Zo now held in her possession. She was examining the runes carefully. A concerned look crossed her features as she searched in vain for any indication of what they were required to do with them once they had been recovered.

"Well, if that's the case, where's the door? I mean, we've been told they're bein' held in Night's tower. If these were keys t'get in how could anyone else enter without them? And if they all had their own keys, wouldn't it have been simpler just t'ambush them and take theirs? I think the whole thing is crazy!" Eiji ranted; he glanced at Elly again, she seemed to be listening in silent amusement as they debated the issue. He began to feel that she was withholding some very valuable information; but if nothing else, at least it seemed she knew what to expect. Perhaps when the tension caused by their anticipation died, she would share it with them.

"True but what else have we got?" Acha questioned as she looked to Elly sharing the same feeling as Eiji regarding the retention of crucial knowledge.

"We were told to find them, we found them. We must believe that everything will fall into place," she answered in reply to their looks.

"Well, I know, but considerin' the 'eyes' were meant t'be pursuin' us, and Gods forgive me for sayin' this, the only things we've really had t'contend with are the troubles brought about by this world. It's almost as if they want us to succeed, if that's the case, then why?" Eiji wasn't sure if it was the cave itself, or the dark foreboding feeling he had about what lay ahead, but he knew one thing for certain, the longer he could stall, the longer he had to try and pinpoint the morbid feeling which radiated from the depths of the gaping mouth that stood before them.

"That's not strictly speaking true." Daniel looked between them, there was a general air of discomfort that seemed to envelop everyone except Elly. "They captured you, also I'm convinced that, behind everything that has happened, they will have been manipulating events to suit their needs, manipulating this world to make it seem that way, to trick us into lowering our defences."

"We have no other information, and the runes being removed would not necessarily be a bad thing for them." Elly restarted the conversation. As she spoke, she made the first definite move towards the cave, leaving the others unable to hesitate, knowing they had no choice but to follow her into its unmapped depths. "I am sure we will know more once the last rune is in our possession. Perhaps this ends with a trade."

Zo briefly hesitated outside the entrance, a small thought rested on the horizon of her mind. A thought she couldn't quite hear, yet it seemed to call to her with such power, such warning, it seemed impossible that she couldn't interpret it.

"Wait," she called entering the cave as she realised her friends had already proceeded inside. She ran, quickly following the figures just in front of her who were already submerged in darkness. "What do you mean?" she asked as she caught up with Elly. The lingering thought now forgotten in the moment of panic as she realised she was being left behind.

"Each time a rune has been located it has been within a place of magical power, a significant place in both our worlds. This power forces certain areas of this ever-changing world to remain the same and stay bound to our own. With each rune taken, or fixed location breached, we have released the magics sealed within. The power accumulated in their vicinity must somehow be absorbed, it is not beyond belief to assume that they may be the ones receiving it. We have now passed through every place since our journey's start—" Elly was aware she hadn't answered anything, and she would attempt to keep it that way. She could not reveal that she knew the progression of their quest, and since no one else knew what to expect, she had to appear to be guessing.

"Except Crowley," Eiji interrupted. "It's nowhere near here. It's the one place we've yet t'visit," Eiji added; a slight smile crossed Elly's lips shadowed by the darkness of the cave. Before them there seemed to be lights of some kind which provided a slight relief from the all-encompassing darkness.

"So what you're saying is, that is where the door must be!" Acha exclaimed in excitement. Elly turned her gaze skyward before turning back to face them with a smile.

"Must be." She shook her head, if they weren't going to listen to what she had subtly tried to tell them, she was not going to help them any further. It was lucky that Eiji had interrupted her when he had, she was unsure why she had felt inclined to prepare them anyway. It seemed the attachment her watcher had developed for these people had exposed her slightly. It was clear how much Elisha enjoyed following their little adventure. She would have to be more restrained in the future.

They finally approached the lighter area they had seen before them. The light itself seemed to be generated from strange rocks embedded within the cave wall and floor. They emitted a slight luminescent glow. The light was a gentle yet bright green, enough to clearly allow them to see what lay before them. As they passed the first one, Daniel stopped briefly to examine it. He couldn't help it, the rock was fascinating, he had never seen anything quite like it.

The gentle trickle of water and the echoing of footsteps were the only sounds to be heard through the silence. Occasionally they would pass a small water source which bubbled through the ground, creating small pools of spring water. These tiny pockets of water would fight their way through the mountain to create some of the majestic water features, such as the streams and waterfalls, hidden lakes and pools, that lay enshrined within. Elly stopped as they passed a rather large expanse of water, and carefully sampled it. The climb, although shorter than expected, had been exhausting for those she travelled with, as such they had seriously depleted their water supplies. Confirming it was safe, she filled her leather skin, suggesting that they did the same.

"How much further is this tunnel?" Acha asked, as Zo and Eiji began to fill their own leather skins. She found herself surprised when Elly gave an answer.

"About another half a mile," she stated, once Acha had replenished her own supply, she stepped aside to allow Daniel's approach.

"Wait, where's Daniel?" she questioned suddenly, as she realised he was no longer amongst them. She was not the only one who had noticed him missing in this instant, until recently he had been walking beside Acha. Zo clearly remembered seeing him. She had felt a silence through their bond, so had been relieved when she had glanced back to see him walking beside her. It had seemed he was experimenting with their connection and had found a way to isolate himself from her.

They began to cast their vision around the darkness of the caves for his silhouette. Zo, unknown to the rest of them had another method she would use to locate him. She probed for his mind, his thoughts, but nothing returned.

"When did you last see him?" Zo looked to Acha. She knew she would receive the same answer, he had been with them just before they had stopped for water. Surely, he knew better than to wander off or stop without saying something. But that thought alone concerned her. The fact was he did know better, yet at the same time he had done it several times since this adventure began. But this time things were different, surely, he wouldn't dream of doing something so foolish here. She felt a sick panic began to rise within her, as she wondered how could he have disappeared so completely when the path they walked was a straight passage. Zo squinted down the darkened tunnel in the hope to catch a glimpse of him, but there was nothing. It was almost as if he had vanished into thin air.

* * *

Daniel stopped briefly as they entered the area possessing the strange glowing rocks. He glanced to his friends, they hadn't noticed he had stopped but he was only a few steps behind. He wouldn't stay too long, but he couldn't pass up this opportunity. They were incredible, the gentle green light seemed to have no explanation. There was no light entering the cave so it wasn't a reflective property, and since they were virtually transparent, he could clearly see they didn't pass through to the outside surface of the mountain.

He touched the cool surface, there was no heat, so a thermal reaction was unlikely.

It was true, his friends were only a matter of feet away, but this hadn't made the slightest bit of difference.

It was almost as if the darkness itself had reached from the wall to encase him. Silencing him in its unyielding shadow as it dragged him backwards into the void. He could clearly see his friends, but he had lost his connection with Zo in the instant the unknown presence had touched him. He cried out as a small wisp of blue cloud shifted to take his form, it moved quickly to catch up with Acha. Through the grip of the darkness, he could just see himself being scolded for falling behind. The darkness trickled over him, pulling him deeper into it. He screamed their names, but no sound left him, his voice absorbed by the shadow.

He felt as if he had been swallowed by the darkness. Turning slowly from the place he now stood, he could see nothing but blackness. If not for feeling the solid pressure of the ground beneath his feet he would have lost all orientation. He stood paralysed.

'*I wouldn't move too much if I were you.*' A voice whispered; he strained his vision expecting to find a pair of eyes watching him mockingly through the otherwise silent prison. He wondered if there was a possibility that he could navigate his way through the unyielding darkness and find a path to freedom. He raised his right foot to carefully probe the area before him, yet found no further ground in any direction. All the time the creatures laughed. '*It's a long way down.*' Daniel cursed to himself, it was clear they could see him even if he could not see them. He had hoped given time his eyes would have adjusted. If he could see a little of the place he was standing, he was certain he could find an escape route, but it seemed there was not even a single source of light anywhere in the area.

From his assessment, the area he stood on was no larger than a small stool. He cursed his foolishness. Only moments before his abduction he had warned his friends about letting their defences down, but that was exactly what he had done when he stopped to examine the unusual rocks. He hadn't, for a second, considered there would be any danger. He had ventured off alone so often without incident he was sure he would be safe, especially since they had only been a few feet away from him. Again, he cursed his foolishness.

'*You're hoping they'll come back?*' one of the voices whispered. '*They won't come back for you, they can't.*' Daniel wondered if this statement meant he was still trapped within the mountain. If that was the case there may still be a chance to escape. It was doubtful that this single area was the only place in a huge area of nothingness. If he could somehow work out how far it was to the next ledge, how far he would have to jump before reaching something else, he may be able to find a way out. Then again, with the trickery of these creatures, he could just as easily find himself in mid-jump, only to have the area he was about to land on vanish to send him plummeting to his death. Without being able to see, he couldn't know for sure what lay ahead. His balance faltered, everything grew silent. He cried out to Zo with his mind, hoping he could somehow bridge the distance, but as hard as he tried, he couldn't reach her. He swayed, still weary from their previous adventure, the fatigue once more catching up to him.

Although Zo had succeeded in healing him yet again, the sheer amount of times this had occurred and the severity of the injuries had begun to take their toll. He hadn't wanted to worry anyone, but since the last battle with Marise he felt so fatigued. He had simply dismissed it as exhaustion, brought about by the continuous battles he had fought for his life.

He hadn't wanted to burden anyone by letting them know how he felt, after all, Zo was in a far worse condition and she said nothing, she just continued in silence. They both suffered more than they revealed, especially since the incident with the poison. Despite the healing and the remedies, they had both been severely damaged by it.

Her presence brought him comfort, at least with someone else to worry about he found the pain he felt subsided. He clutched her satchel tightly, his hand rummaging through it slightly as he wondered if she had thought to pack anything he could use as a source of light. His hand found nothing but a collection of herbs. When Zo needed light, she could simply conjure it. He could only hope any relief she would feel from the root would last until they found him. He knew without a doubt she would be looking. Zo would not rest until he was safe, regardless of what dangers she would have to face. A long time ago she had made him a promise, a promise to protect him, but vow or not, she would come. He wobbled slightly again, through the darkness, despite his situation he just hoped that she would be safe.

※ ※ ※

"Daniel!" Zo shouted, her panicked voice joined with the chorus of her friends as their voices echoed through the cave. Nothing but their own voices answered them back, or at least they hoped they were their own, but after the incident in the minefields they weren't so sure.

"Maybe he wandered off?" Eiji's cautious tone failed to convince anyone, he had been there when Acha had scolded him for falling behind. This had been just a few minutes before they had stopped to refill their water and noticed he was missing. Eiji raised his arm to silence their shouts. "Somethin's wrong," he whispered, feeling the disturbance through the earth. Within seconds of his observation they felt the ground begin to tremble. It shook with such force it knocked them from their feet. The mountain quaked and groaned, shaking free a huge cascade of rocks and soil to rain down mercilessly from above.

Eiji had barely managed to get to his feet when he leapt upon Acha, forcing her from the falling debris. He protected her until the last of the bouncing rocks had settled and he felt the danger subside. He blushed, suddenly, remembering himself as he lay on her protecting her from the rock fall. He moved quickly. "Sorry," he whispered seeing her surprise. But Acha's surprise stemmed from elsewhere. She had always felt the raw aura of power that surrounded him. It was a power so immense that, as their skin had briefly touched, to her amazement, nothing had happened. He had been unharmed, unaffected by her curse.

When the dust cleared, they looked around in dismay. The path they had walked had been completely sealed. It hadn't seemed as if enough rocks had fallen to create such a blockage, yet it now stood sealed before them. With the entrance unreachable, they could only hope what lay before them was not only their success, but an exit, or they too may be lost to the treacherous mountain.

The fallen rocks seemed strangely organised. Instead of the appearance expected, it looked more like a perfectly constructed wall, a barricade without the slightest gap or area for light to filter through. It was almost as if the mountain itself pushed them onward.

Zo knelt at the edge of the rubble. She ignored the intense pain in her shoulder as she frantically dug into the rocks, throwing them aside in the hope to create a passage through. She had to find Daniel. He had to be back there somewhere. She knew he was very fatigued, after all, her healing wasn't perfect. He had been suffering from all his injuries. She began to panic, wondering if she had cast her gaze towards the floor. Her mind telling her he was lying unconscious just through there, waiting to be found. Despite this pretence she knew that if, by some miracle, they broke through to the other side, he would not be anywhere to be found, but the path being closed behind them just seemed so permanent.

Her fingers clawed through the obstruction, yet despite her efforts, there were no visible indications of her efforts. It seemed almost as if each time she removed a rock, another took its place in the endless barricade.

From time to time she paused to clutch her shoulder in an attempt to relieve some pain before she dug again. Her friends just watched her, unsure exactly what more to say, it seemed their voices remained unheard through her frantic attempts to clear the path. She clearly blamed herself for not watching him closer. She held herself responsible for his safety, but worst of all she, like them, knew that *they* had him, but still she dug.

It was Elly who finally approached, her hand extended out to Zo's injured shoulder and squeezed it hard enough to stop her actions, hard enough to paralyse her for a moment as the pain exploded. Zo, as she cowered away from the pressure, wondered what she had been doing, what she had hoped to achieve by delaying. Elly released her, satisfied she had gained her attention.

"It is no use," she whispered softly. "We cannot get through. Even if we did, you know as well as I that we would not find him." Zo gave a defeated sigh hearing Elly's words, her hand once more gripping her shoulder where Elly had triggered another painful spasm. "His best chance is if we succeed. They will not kill him, yet." As she spoke, she helped Zo to her feet, turning her gently away from the rubble as she encouraged her to walk the only path left open to them. Zo glanced back once more before she finally accepted that Elly was correct, they had to continue.

'*Daniel, I'll find you, whatever it takes,*' she thought. A thought she put such power behind, she hoped, wherever he was, he would hear it.

* * *

The heptagonal room Seiken had been guided to was magnificent. It was constructed from a delicate combination of glass and stone, permitting those within to gaze upon the ever-shifting realms of the outside world. It was clear this place stood at the very peak of Night's home. The intricate glass work spiralled upwards, gaining dominance over the stonework until the almost pure glass ceiling arched above them.

The carefully orchestrated angles of ascent meant that the roof itself became a heptagram. Its shape enforced by the delicate stone threads which traced its every pane. It was a symbol Seiken knew well. The heptagram depicted universal balance and represented a very old force which called upon the seven grand powers of planetary magic. Given Night's origin and power, it was unsurprising his home utilised such ancient forces, after all, being of Nyx granted him unique insight relating to the very power of creation.

Seiken closed his eyes. He could hear the music of the universe resonating from the tower. Each of the razor-sharp points of the seven-sided star playing its own note of the musical scale as it passed from realm to realm. The music of the heavens was not for all to hear, few did, and even fewer knew how to utilise the chords. Dragon charmers were the last who had done so, and there had been none discovered for a very long time.

"Magnificent isn't it?" Night took pause to enjoy the harmony. This was his favoured place, however, he did not frequent it often, lest he grew accustomed to the power and magic within. It was an area he reserved only for special occasions, a place which seemed fitting for the events that would soon transpire.

He motioned Seiken towards the only piece of furniture within the otherwise empty room, a small chair. It looked out of place within this grandeur, it was a place so full of primal forces and energy that there was no room for anything else. It was no doubt a gesture to ensure his comfort. When there was nothing for him to attend to, he had been requested to remain here.

Almost in the same instance as he sat, the stonework on the wall nearest to him distorted. A large black hole grew as if some strange force had drained away the wall, deforming and warping the area until a new feature appeared. Its heavy, timeworn bars gave the impression this prison had always been there. The cell itself was shrouded in darkness, a darkness so all-consuming that it blocked any light which attempted to penetrate it.

"That was easier than I anticipated." He smiled.

"What are you going to do with them?" He couldn't help but wonder who the first to fall prey to his deception had been. The darkness acted as a double-edged knife, its captive could not see out but nor could they see in. Perhaps, he reasoned, it was better this way. If they were able to see him, they would know the truth of his actions, and that despite what he had said, despite his words of trust to Zo, he had, in fact, betrayed them after all.

"That is not your concern, but I suppose it can do no harm. I plan to use them as a bargaining tool. You see my daughter would never aid me of her own free will. That is something I have learnt just by watching her these past weeks. She is so much like her mother, although with her mother, I never felt the need to pursue what seemed like childish dreams. She was everything I needed, nothing else mattered as long as she was safe." Night stopped as he realised he had drifted far from topic. "So I needed something in the way of persuasion. It's simple really, the Grimoire in exchange for the lives of her friends." He finished the sentence as if he had never sidetracked.

"But why go to all this trouble, why set up the fake runes, the quest, for something you could ultimately do yourself?" This had bothered Seiken for some time. He had wondered why a god would resort to such petty measures to obtain something, why one with such great power would have to rely on the actions of mortals to achieve his goal. He wondered if Night would answer. Since they had signed the contract, all his questions had been met with satisfactory responses. He wondered if this would still hold true, if the god would tell of his weakness, of why these mortals were essential to his success. To Seiken's surprise, he answered.

"On both counts there you are wrong. The runes are not fake, but true enough are useless now. They were key magical seals that reinforced the fields restraining the Severaine. Once removed, the energy used to create the seal vanished and weakened the restraints. I needed their cooperation to remove the seals, things created by mortal hands can only be removed by them. On the second account, the Grimoire cannot be taken by my hands. The Hoi Hepta Sophoi ensured this was so by protecting all from my touch. On the last tome they placed a further restriction, only one of my flesh who is pure of heart can take it from its final resting place. They thought with this protection I would fail to regain all my powers. They did not realise I had a child of my own already. Their oversight is why I can continue my quest today, why I am confident I shall achieve my ambitions."

Whilst Night spoke, Seiken thought back to the moment Acha had told them the truth, she had been outside Zo's door when she admitted she was the daughter of Night. Although he was a captive, he had seen every part of their adventure. At the time it had seemed like Night was mocking him, the only things he had not known about were the times when Aburamushi had taken his form to mislead them, but through this agreement with Night, there was no need to have anyone else beguile them. He would be the one who was responsible for whatever happened from this point forwards.

"There is one thing I don't understand, why put her through all this, don't you have any consideration for her feelings at all? For the hardship you have forced upon her, for the dangers you have put her in?" This entire situation was strange. Seiken couldn't even begin to understand why Night would willingly force his daughter into such dangerous situations. Surely there must have been an easier way.

"I have observed every step of the way, ensuring she was not in danger, but what you must understand, what I am doing is more monumental than all of this, you, me, everything. I love my daughter more than you could know, her mother too. She was a remarkable woman, she alone could justify the salvation of human life. She was the one exception to that pitiful race, the one redeeming feature that made me forget my ambitions. If it meant I could be with her, I would gladly have stayed powerless, but that time, that peace, was buried with her. My daughter is very much like the woman I loved so dearly, but I have done what is required, all things considered..." Night paused again. It was in this moment that Seiken saw it, the shadow of regret in Night's eyes. Although he had hidden his feelings well, Seiken had seen the desperation. He was not happy with what he was doing, but there was something far greater than himself, a desire so immense that it was a cause worthy of such a sacrifice.

Night looked to him and knew he had dropped his guard a little too far. He had revealed more than he'd ever planned to. He cursed his mistake, why was it, that despite their situations, he found this boy so affable? Maybe it was because they were of similar mind, despite how it may appear, they were not dissimilar, both would do what was needed in order to obtain something they desired. They had both followed their paths. The wisdom and knowledge exchanged in conversations with this boy was unfailingly like those he had shared with the great gods of times past. This Oneiroi seemed old and wise beyond his years.

"Enough of this. They are awaiting your guidance." Night broke the silence once more as he ordered Seiken to the business at hand. Seiken nodded already understanding what was required as he vanished before Night's eyes.

Night watched through the gossip crystal as Seiken appeared before them, he gave a sigh. "All things considered, even now, I wish there was another way," he continued quietly, but he knew all too well there was no alternative. If things didn't progress as required, everything would be for naught, and all would be lost.

* * *

Led by Elly they continued to walk down the dimly lit passage, following its every bend, in silence. Within half a mile—the distance Elly had so accurately stated—the tunnel ended abruptly as it opened out into a massive cavern. The height of the room was so great they couldn't even perceive its dimensions through the darkness. They stood on a wide ledge overlooking an enormous chasm that, by their calculations, was nearly as long as the room was wide. A cloud of darkness formed a single straight passage across, it seemed to be suspended in mid-air, as if a dark thundercloud had become trapped.

Eiji walked warily to the edge to peer down. He was convinced the rift would reach as far as the very centre of the earth, and the heat which rose from below it did little to disprove this theory.

"So what now?" He wondered if perhaps they were meant to somehow walk over the cloud, although looking at it he saw it towered higher above them than he first expected. With his first line of reason impossible, he wondered if perhaps it was nothing more than a trick to send them plummeting to their deaths.

"Once across the bridge, there is very little distance left to your final rune." Seiken took Zo's hand in his, for a split second he hesitated before they touched. As she looked to him, she found herself staring deep into his eyes, an action he too returned. This time, there was something different in the weight of his stare, now more than ever, she felt a sense of longing.

"There's a solid bridge under all this?" Eiji questioned, it made sense now, although there was still in doubt that played in his mind as to whether or not it truly existed. As he looked again, he saw the surrounding clouds did seem to curve around as if to shield something from view, but his instincts warned him something about the bridge felt unnatural.

"Another thing," he continued as he reluctantly released Zo's hand. "Once upon the bridge, you must not stop. Do not hesitate, that is, if you want to live." Seiken walked to the edge to look down into the vast empty space. He closed his eyes for a moment, feeling the heat from below as it warmed his face. "Once you reach the other side, do not attempt to cross back using this route."

"Why?" Acha pulled Eiji further from the edge of the chasm. Over the last few minutes he seemed to be getting closer and closer as he tried to catch sight of the bottom. She had images of him plummeting to his death before they had even set foot on the bridge.

"Its sole purpose is to be an entrance, do you understand?" But before they could even answer he had disappeared, Zo cursed silently. She had wanted to ask if he knew anything of Daniel.

"There's somethin' very strange about that guy. It's still him isn't it?" Eiji questioned, approaching Zo. He knew if anyone would be able to tell, it would be her. The way they spoke, the way they were together, seemed almost as if they had known each other a very long time.

"Yes, he seems distracted, maybe it's because…" she paused for a second as she remembered the other part of the prophecy that she had heard long ago. She pushed it from her mind, she could not afford to doubt him. "He has a lot of burdens to carry now. The future of his people rests on our success." She thought back once more to the prophecy that she had fought so hard to ignore. Now she remembered it fully, she knew the dangers that lay in their future.

"Still, I do not recall anything like this at the top if we had entered there." Elly paused, as if waiting for some sort of confirmation. They exchanged glances, none of them had been here before, how could they answer such a statement? There was a passing moment of silence as they realised that Elly must have been here at some point. When she finally spoke again, she didn't answer any of their unasked questions, she simply said. "I must admit it does seem to have been a shortcut."

Elly had been so accustomed to Zo carrying her satchel that she was surprised to find it not within her possession when she had moved to take it from her. It had completely slipped her mind that recently it seemed Daniel had taken to keeping possession of it. This action served only as a reminder of the deep bond of friendship they had formed, but since he was no longer amongst them, neither was it. Elly gave an annoyed sigh. It had seemed like such a good idea at the time to place the rope in there, it was far easier to access than the backpack.

Elly made some silent calculations, in the absence of a rope, this would have to be adequate. Elly unravelled the thin thread slowly, before moving to attach the first end around Acha's waist. Once she was happy it was secure, she moved on to Eiji, then Zo and finally herself, ensuring she had left enough slack between them. She hadn't explained her reasoning, she felt the action itself was more than explanatory.

"It is not rope, but it will have to suffice," she stated knowing full well that this tiny thread would do little to hold the weight of someone if they fell. "Come on, let us make haste." With that Elly began to lead the way towards the bridge, and since she guided their path she allowed no pause for arguments or delay.

As they drew near to the ominous cloud, welcoming them through the darkness, there stood large, brilliant white columns. The distance separating them was such that one could only hope to pass through in single file. As the darkness began to shroud their vision, it was by these pillars their path was guided.

Elly set a slow pace as they began to walk across the pitch-black bridge. Zo, unaware her friends were doing the same, held the string both in front and behind her, monitoring it for any change in the slack which would indicate any of them had encountered danger. Of course, she wasn't sure exactly what she could do, should there be an abnormality in the tension, but the act of being able to monitor them gave her a small amount of comfort.

On entering the bridge, Acha repeated to herself Seiken's warning to keep walking. Since entering, she had felt a strange sinking feeling in the pit of her stomach. She had barely entered the darkness when she heard hurried footsteps behind her.

"Acha?" the voice questioned; it was one she knew at once, one that filled her with such relief.

"Daniel, you made it." Her smile was evident through the tones of her voice. She could hear his laboured breathing behind her as his pace slowed to match hers. "What happened?"

"Thank goodness you passed through here. I was trapped within this darkness, abandoned on a ledge." He still seemed to be quite breathless as he spoke.

"If not for hearing your footsteps I never would have known where to jump." The relief in his voice was clear.

"Daniel, this bridge is dangerous. You must not stop," she repeated the warning he would have missed. She couldn't wait to see Zo's face when they stepped through the other side.

"Thanks, I thought I was finished." His voice returned to normal, the fatigue previously heard had all but vanished. She felt his hand fall gently on her shoulder as they continued to walk through the silence of the bridge. "It's okay, we're out. Zo!" he called. Acha wasn't sure how he had known she walked with her eyes closed. She heard Zo call his name, relief filling her voice. "We made it, I'm safe" Acha smiled, feeling the change of texture beneath her feet as it mirrored that of the cavern's floor. She stopped, placing her hand on his to give it a gentle squeeze as she turned to face him.

Her heart leapt and her stomach dropped as she realised what she had done. The cloud was still so thick she could see nothing. If she had only opened her eyes, it would have been fine, wise to the deception, but she had stopped. The hand upon her shoulder began to change. She felt the bones crack and alter, the skin stretching to become something unfamiliar, unnatural. She felt the slackness in the lifeline before her as it severed. Fading into the distance, she heard their footsteps, the pretence of her company kept alive. Imprisoned within the stifling grasp she felt herself growing weak. When the creature's claw pierced her flesh, for reasons she could not explain, it was unaffected by her nature.

They had been on the bridge walking at the same steady pace for perhaps ten minutes when Zo heard Daniel call her name. She fought the urge to stop and continued to put one foot before the other, despite the fact it had become more difficult, now his voice seemed to come from right behind her. She had taken to heart Seiken's warning, but her fears of him being trapped within this mountain played on her mind. What if he could only reach her through this dark place, what if he was trapped here? She swore she could hear his footsteps, to her it sounded almost as if he was walking behind her. She tried to block out his conversation, his requests for her to wait just a second so that he could catch up. It was a difficult thing to do, ignoring the pleas of her friend, but she focused on the darkness before her and kept moving. If he were trapped here, she would have to find a safer way to return for him.

Elly had been enjoying the silence brought by the stifling darkness as they walked the bridge. She already knew its nature, so she cherished the moment while it lasted. She hadn't needed Elisha to warn her of the dangers, but she had done so all the same. Elly had no guilt for her past actions, she had no reason why she should need to hesitate or reach for anything this bridge may try to tempt her with. She had just started to think that the bridge, knowing she would not falter, had decided to bypass her to focus its efforts elsewhere, when a voice spoke to her.

"I told you to go the other way but no, you were so fixated on your treasure that your actions sacrificed each of us." A young anger filled the voice as it challenged her from the shadows, it was one she knew from so many centuries ago.

"It was necessary," she stated coldly. "Besides, you would be dead now anyway." Although she found herself surprised at the accuracy of the voices from the past, her pace never slowed. She wondered, for that split second, if they truly shared this dark walk with her. Elly gasped as a hand firmly gripped her shoulder, she hadn't considered this place would use physical persuasion, despite the grip, she continued.

"But you killed us." A slightly older voice spoke now. Elly smiled as she remembered its owner. He had been wise for his age, at thirty-two he had already found various lost treasures and solved some of the most tedious clues and riddles. He was a man gifted with great intellect, it was just a shame he hadn't applied it on their final journey. Alien to her nature, she began to explain, to speak to them as if they were truly present.

"No, I saved you. Because of me, you lived that extra time until your death. You never would have lived to share my journeys if our paths had not crossed and do not forget that, all of you. I took you all from certain death. Think of all the adventures and the life you would have missed if I had not. I hold no remorse for what happened, I warned you of the danger, but your eyes were too filled with the gold to listen. You lost your own lives with your greed.

"We went to collect only one item, one item that, when I left, I passed to the nymphs, an item which saved the life of one of the heroes of this world. It was your own greed, when you lined your pockets, that signed your death. I did warn you." Elly realised she had stepped from the bridge and the voices had long fallen silent, they had possibly even been oblivious to her scolding.

She walked at the same steady pace as Zo followed behind, Eiji was next to emerge from the shadows, the rope still taut behind him.

Elly began to unfasten the lifeline from herself, seeing that Zo had already done the same, just then, as they were about to celebrate their safe crossing, the tension from the rope still attached to Eiji fell slack. Its jagged edge informed them all it had needed to. Turning towards the bridge, he was about to take his first step back into the shadows when he remembered Seiken's warning. He stopped, just as Zo had reached out to restrain him. Seeing his intention change, she released him. He reached forwards to place his hand into the darkness, knowing it was a foolish thing to do even as he did so, but the rope had only just fallen, that meant she had been mere seconds from emerging. Surely, he would be able to find her. He was convinced that, if he acted quickly enough, he would be able to reach her before it was too late. His hand fumbled through the darkness meeting only emptiness.

The cloud shifted and swelled as he felt himself propelled backwards through the air, the force of Elly's reaction almost choking him as she wrenched him from danger's path. The darkness twisted and stretched before their eyes, as if an unseen presence was trying to force its way through. Eiji felt the cold fear wash over him as he watched his would-be attacker fight for freedom.

Elly shook her head, placing the thread into her pocket, in less than an hour they had lost two members of their group. It seemed things had become far more serious.

* * *

Daniel was unsure how much time had passed since he had been abandoned by his captors, and now, he had even lost the rope. He had thought it a fantastic idea to throw the rope out in hope that it would reach something solid, that way, he could at least make a mental map of his surroundings. On his first attempt, as if mocking his efforts, it was snatched from his grasp, nearly pulling him from his feet. After this they had left him, almost as if they had been waiting to see what aid he would have in his possession to ensure he would not be given the chance to escape. He had tried to lower himself to his knees in the hope he could bring himself down to sit on the platform, but each time he crouched, his exhaustion nearly toppled him, and he did not trust his skill to land on the tiny area.

He had known for some time he was about to reach his limit. His muscles burned, and his body trembled under the force of trying to remain so perfectly still. He could only hope that somehow, when he fell, he would manage to land on this small ledge. Then it happened. He had prepared himself for this moment, and yet, as his balance failed, he screamed all the same. He reached out, hoping his hands would find something to grab onto. He let out a terrified cry as he began to fall. Hundreds of thoughts rushed through his mind in just the few seconds it took before he made contact with the ground.

All around him, the mocking laughter echoed as Daniel lay sprawled out across the floor. Little by little, light began to filter into the room. The darkness had been simply part of their game, a source of amusement for his captors. He groaned, although he had fallen only just a short way, the impact had sent splinters of pain through his already aching body. He looked around to find himself imprisoned within a small cell. He looked with disdain at the place from where he had fallen, annoyed to discover his first assessment of the place he stood to be accurate. It wasn't that the ledge he had found himself on had been the size of a stool, it was a stool, well a stone raised in the cell designed to be sat on. There were three in total which he could now distinguish through the fading darkness.

He felt a draught as something fell before him, shrouded in what appeared to be a blackened cloud. The dark blanket faded to reveal the unconscious figure of Acha. He moved slowly to pull himself beside her, his body rigid and aching from the immeasurable time he had been standing.

"Acha?" He shook her gently as he tried to rouse her. "Acha?" She lay motionless, her breathing shallow as he assessed her injuries. Moving her carefully, he saw a small streak of blood on the back of her neck. It wasn't common knowledge, but the place where the tiny drop smeared was a place used by Bengaulds to induce sleep into their victims, so that they could silently carry them away.

The Bengauld was a legendary beast which could project images or sounds into its victim's mind, whatever was needed to steal a look from them. But once seen, regardless of the guise they played in, their image would shift to their natural one, that of a mighty beast. Their index claw extended naturally to create not only a sharp weapon, but the spike they used to pierce the victim's flesh and render them unconscious. Many people mistook these creatures for the ones from ancient mythology, beings who would follow travellers after nightfall, to look back while being followed by such a thing would mean their death. The mythology was similar so he could understand the confusion, but the nameless beings that hid in the shadows never abducted their prey, they simply devoured their life-force. Of course, these creatures weren't always nameless, fear had erased their name from existence, but as the lurking fear of the dark always remained, they became immortal; for as long as there is darkness, there will always be the fear of that which resides within.

Other than the one small injury, Acha seemed unharmed, the only thing he could do for now was leave her to sleep until the effects from the Bengauld had subsided. With nothing to lose, he stood slowly to approach the bars of the prison in hope to gain some insight into where they were, or even how to escape.

Looking through the cast iron bars, he could not believe what he saw. As he looked upon the shifting landscapes through the magnificent glass, he could only stare, paralysed as his mind tried to understand what it was he beheld. It was impossible for him to know how long he had been sitting, mesmerised, before he finally managed to pry his eyes away. It had been the familiar image of the moon that had finally broken the trance to allow him to study the room. With the exception of a small single chair before the bars of the prison, it was empty.

A new light filled the surroundings. It was not a reflection of the passing worlds, but from an opening. To the right, a door closed, the sound of footsteps echoed coldly through the air as they approached the small prison. Before their owner had reached his line of vision, Daniel heard a familiar voice greet him, although he couldn't quite place its owner, he knew he had heard it somewhere before. It was a voice he knew he should have remembered.

"Welcome home," it stated in salutation; these two words somehow reinforced what Daniel had noticed without really taking note of. They were no longer in Darrienia. "Don't worry, the others will be joining you shortly." As the figure moved into sight, Daniel felt his jaw drop.

"You, but why?" He gazed upon the figure, his raven black hair tied neatly back. Although he no longer wore the clothes of a traveller, Daniel recognised him instantly, but perhaps not for the reasons he should have. The figure who stood before him, wearing a mighty shroud of darkness, was the same person who had come to Zo's aid. This however, was not how most would recognise him. Had Daniel's mind solved the equation quicker he would have known the name of the person who stood before him, without the need to await the introduction.

"It is good to see you again Daniel Eliot, allow me to introduce myself, I am Night." He gave a small bow. A long drawn out silence seemed to pass as Daniel stared at him in disbelief, unable to answer his statement. In that moment he cursed his stupidity. His mind had drawn its own perceived image of Night, and thus, since the figure before him bore no resemblance to the one he had imagined, the possibility had never occurred to him. The consideration that the person who had helped them when things were at their bleakest was, in fact, their enemy, had not crossed his mind. The more he considered events, the more he reprimanded himself. It had been so obvious, who else would know about the danger and problems they faced, who else would help them? Daniel cursed under his breath. This whole time, everything they had been doing was all part of his design. He had manipulated them well, but his plan still remained unclear.

Acha had listened silently to the exchange between them, as all fell silent she found the strength to pull herself to sit. Her voice uncertain as she beheld the figure who addressed them.

"You're my father?" The man who stood before her now bore no physical resemblance at all to her father of eras past, yet just as it had been when she had observed him through the gossip crystal, her instincts knew he had spoken the truth. "You look so different now." Her observation was more to reinforce to Daniel that she had not known who this person was previously. Like Daniel, she recognised him as the one who had aided them, but she also recognised him for another reason as well.

The father she had known had brown hair, and had appeared commonplace, exactly the opposite in regards to what could have been said about the magnificent figure who now stood before them. He possessed an unearthly beauty, a radiance and power. She had expected him to feel evil, the air around him to be tainted by his deeds. She had thought even had his appearance changed over the years that she would have known him, she had been wrong.

"Acha, immortality does wonders, this is one of my preferred forms. The one both you and your mother beheld was but a guise I took as I was forced to mortal flesh. I am sorry, but I must keep this brief, I have so much to do. After all, I am expecting visitors, although what kind of host would I be to leave you without some company?"

"More creatures I suppose?" Daniel spat as he moved reluctantly to sit on the stone stool. He wondered what possible company Night could leave them in. He had visions of horrors coming to plague them while they awaited rescue, but his next words seemed to dismiss his imaginings.

"No, not at all. I need you unharmed." Night turned his head to the side. "Seiken, I trust you shall take care of our visitors."

"As you wish," he answered shamefully, as he stepped into sight. Until now he had been too distressed by his actions to reveal himself. When the darkness first began to dissipate from within the bars, he had intended to speak with them. Instead he found himself retreating from view, too ashamed to face what he had done. He had some difficulty returning the injured, confused looks from both Daniel and Acha as they glared at him. "I thought you wanted your daughter to find you?" He looked to Acha as Night's footsteps continued towards the exit.

"That is not *my* daughter," he stated coldly, before exiting the room. Seiken stared after the figure wearing his confusion clearly.

"Traitor!" Daniel screamed, lunging himself towards the bars as if hoping they would somehow give under his weight. He thrust his arm through in an attempt to seize the one responsible. "We trusted you!" Seiken could not meet his gaze. He pulled the chair closer to the cage, remaining just outside their reach. He was aware of his actions, he would face their accusations. Nothing they could say would make him feel any worse than he already did.

"I did what I had to," he apologised, still unable to answer either of their betrayed stares, instead he occupied himself by looking at the large grey stone bricks which created the floor. The shadows from the chair twisted as light changed with the movement of the realms they entered.

As Daniel looked upon the one who had betrayed them, he suddenly realised the boy who sat before him must have been no older than himself. Seiken had always carried himself so well that he never noticed the almost insignificant difference in age their appearance held. At this moment, Seiken looked ashamed and troubled, whilst doing all he could to avoid their challenging stares. He seemed so young, for some reason noticing this cushioned his anger. Daniel too had made his share of mistakes, and it was only now that he realised the weight of the burden Seiken was forced to carry. The fate of his entire world lay on his shoulders. He was responsible for the lives of the Oneirois, they all depended on him. He had done the only thing he thought he could in order to meet their expectations.

"I don't understand, why?" He approached the bars calmer now, questioning if the situations were reversed—and he had been responsible for the lives of so many—if he too would have taken the safer route, the one that guaranteed the safety of his world and race.

"When I found out the runes were meaningless, I knew that even with your help there was no way to free my people. They're dying, Daniel. They've been away from our world's energy for too long. Even should you have succeeded, it would do no good. Night is the only person who can release them, don't you see, can't you understand? The lives of my people rested on me, I had to accept his proposal. The needs of the many must *always* outweigh those of the few." Seiken's voice, although soft, was filled with a desperate plea for them to understand his reasoning. He truly hadn't wanted to betray them.

"The runes are meaningless?" Acha raised her hand to silence Daniel before he had a chance to speak again.

"Yes, but I too was fooled by this pretence until the truth was revealed. The runes were simply physical manifestations of the seals to a great power. Seals created by people as a protectional barrier. Each one you have removed has weakened this restraining force in your world, and destroyed the anchor that bound its seal to ours," he explained desperately.

"Great power?" Daniel questioned. His stomach churned at the implications of what Seiken had just said. If Night's goal was to unleash something more powerful than the chaos that would ensue by the dissipation of the barriers separating dream from reality, then everything they had done, everything they thought they had accomplished, had been exactly what Night had needed them to do.

"I don't know the details." Seiken mumbled, it wasn't a lie as such. Seiken had come to the conclusion by himself some time ago, to state this now would only raise further questions about the extent that he had betrayed them, and from the look on Daniel's face he could see he had already realised what this great power could be. "He just said a great power was hidden somewhere in your world that he wanted. As I said on the mountain, he offered me a trade, my world, my people, our freedom, if I aided him. All I needed to do was lead you astray in the Mountain of Spirits. Although what I told them was true. They will soon reach the holding of the final rune, but there was a much safer way to travel, one which meant his minions would not have been presented the opportunity to take hostages. I had no choice, my people are dying," he stressed. "As their heir, I am responsible for them. I did what I needed to for their sake."

"Seiken, you should have had more faith in us, in Zo. She made a promise to free your people, somehow, no matter what, she has always been true to her word, regardless of the cost." He looked to Acha who nodded in agreement. This was something she too had learnt throughout their travels. Daniel continued the conversation, asking the question he had wanted to before Acha had interjected. "What was it you were saying about his daughter?"

"He told me the entire purpose of your quest was to guide the actions of his daughter, or that was my understanding. Only I don't think it was as straightforward as that, or why bring her here and not even attempt to acknowledge her?"

"I'm not his only daughter," Acha answered, recalling the picture they had retrieved in the Perpetual Forest. Daniel did not seem as shocked as Seiken regarding this statement. Just moments before Acha had spoken, he had realised the truth. He had found himself thinking back to the times he had previously met Night. Both times he'd only had one interest, one *real* interest that was. Daniel once more cursed his stupidity. He should have realised when they had met in the arena. Night had given Marise a very specific warning.

"What has Night told you of this game?" Daniel questioned sharply, as he suddenly realised the true horror this spelt. If their assumptions were correct, Night already had the means to obtain everything he desired. He already had one of his blood, who is pure of heart, and now he had the means for a trade. It was just as Elly had implied.

"Nothing really, only to live she must win, to win she must lose everything." Seiken glanced up to Daniel, this time he held his gaze in shared alarm.

"Even herself?" As he thought back to something Zo had once said. "All along," he whispered. "All along she knew, to win *she* had to lose."

Chapter 26

The Final Key

There was a heavy silence as they slowly made their way through the small passage which led from the bridge. They knew better than to look back in hope to see Acha emerge, but still both Zo and Eiji had cast backwards glances a number of times, until the path they walked obscured their view.

The remainder of their journey was very short in comparison to the tunnel they had previously navigated. The same soft green light radiated from the stones embedded within the timeworn passage, but the air was now dry, almost stifling. Another large opening spanned before them, a place where natural light seemed to filter through, from this alone they knew they were nearing the end of this path. As they reached the entrance Zo, found herself relieved they had not lost yet another person. She had walked slightly behind, allowing her to keep a cautious vigil on both of her remaining friends.

The pathway guided them towards a large dome-shaped room, its surfaces were completely smooth as if by some strange design. Surrounding the room, like a moat, was a gap at least a foot in width, it seemed there was not a single place the central floor met with the outer walls. Peering down into the small rift it was easy to see the bubbling lava just thirty feet below which filled the air with a sticky haze and nauseating heat. Zo hesitated. Her subtle movements, whilst Elly and Eiji examined the area before them, now meant that she took the lead, no one was going to risk stepping on this seemingly hovering platform, not until she had confirmed it was safe. She was not going to lose anyone else. The area before her did little to calm her nerves as it seemed to rise and drop slightly as if the heat from the lava was all that kept this large stone afloat.

A pale sand blew in the breeze from the opening clearly visible on the adjacent wall. It seemed the floor of this rock had been coated in this fine substance. In the very centre of the room, bathed in a column of silver light, hovered the final rune. The light seemed to fall from the peak of the mountain itself to encapsulate it. Zo, her heart pounding, made the jump across the small rift, the hot pockets of air almost unbearable as they rose from below. The platform, to her relief, remained solid, unaltered by the additional pressure of her weight. Satisfied the ground was secure, she looked up to beckon her allies across, but to her horror, her vision fell upon the empty walkway. It seemed they had disregarded the need for caution and had not only already followed her across, but now stood examining the suspended rune as they tried to unlock its secrets.

Eiji hesitantly extended his hand towards the suspended object. He knew, by instinct alone, this rune was meant for him. Doubt gripped him as he delayed its capture to pace before the column of light, recalling the dangers faced when retrieving the other keys.

"Is this it?" he asked cautiously. He continued to pace, stopping briefly at every turn to once more look at the strange light. The rune itself hovered at the perfect height, it was almost as if it welcomed them. He raised his hand again, this time getting a little closer to the light before he pulled back. "No corpses, no monsters, can it be this easy?" He began to pace again. "It's hoverin', like the area we stand on, what if when I take it this area collapses? Then again, that already happened at the court and has little t'do with spirit. Unless that is, it refers t'what we become when we die tryin' t'retrieve it." Elly and Zo continued to watch him cautiously as indecision gripped him. For the first time he stopped talking to himself and looked to them for answers.

"It is, as you say, the rune of spirit," Elly confirmed as she glanced over its carved surface, it was unmistakable, it looked like a diamond resting upon an upside-down V. Her comment, as intended, offered no real assistance.

"All the other runes we have retrieved had challenges based on their purpose. Sacrifice had the corpses of those sacrificed to Aburamushi, balance, the falling building, power, the heir and the demon, and innocence was manipulation based on exploiting that trait. Maybe its trap is linked to its purpose," Zo continued, realising that Elly's comment had been more helpful than she had first thought. From those few words she had understood completely what Elly had meant, almost as if words were not necessary between them, this unnerved her a little. This understanding, this closeness, meant Marise grew stronger still.

Eiji began to examine the light again, as if hoping that by looking upon it once more it would somehow provide him with all the answers he desired.

"True, but what can be related t'spirit? Do we summon the ghosts of a million dead to feed off our life-force?"

"There is only one way to find out," Elly prompted. Eiji nodded, raising his hand with a firm look of determination. This time he would seize it. He thought of Daniel, Acha, and Zo, all of whom had obtained the runes meant for their touch. He could not let them down. "But," Eiji let out a sigh of relief as he heard this word. His hand once more dropped. "I am not too convinced about the nature of the light used to suspend it." Elly was not concerned over who would be the first to handle it, it was meaningless as Marise had proven when she had obtained the rune of power in her stead.

Remembering this, she reached within her pocket to retrieve a handful of leftover narca berries. Casually, she flicked one towards the field. No sooner had it touched the shimmering light it seemed to shrivel, passing through the phases of ageing until it became nothing more than dust. A look of horror reflected on their faces as they noticed exactly how much of this substance surrounded them, a dust they had previously mistaken for sand. Eiji snapped his hand back quickly to hold it protectively as he took three large paces backwards.

"I nearly touched that!" he exclaimed, taking another step away for good measure. "So we just need t'dislodge it somehow. Without actually touchin' it." He glanced towards Zo who, following his lead, invoked the element of fire. The reaction occurring above her skin as the flame's spark grew and twisted, expanding in size and power until it filled her palm. Directing it towards the field, she watched in anticipation, hoping that Eiji would be both quick and coordinated enough to catch the rune. As the flame passed into the light, the fire died, evaporating into ashes. There was just one other option, it would have to be jolted loose by something with enough length that it would be dislodged before the field's magic travelled to the person controlling the object. Zo glanced to her sword and then to Elly. Not a word had passed between them yet Elly still answered.

"There is no guarantee," she answered cautiously. "Perhaps if Eiji and I were to take some of the force, then the light you would make contact with would not be as potent, then maybe, but—"

"Do we have any other option?" Zo had already snapped free the fasten releasing the weapon from her belt. "We need all the keys to open our path, and I just know Daniel and Acha are waiting somewhere on the other side." She readied her sword before there was a chance for protests. She had to do this quickly, while she was still confident she could. She moved, slightly adjusting her grip on the hilt.

"But if you misjudged even a millisecond..." Elly began, but the look of determination on Zo's face told her this was not a subject open for debate.

"I am ready." Zo nodded to Eiji. Elly gave a slight sigh as she passed him a handful of berries. It was clear she had already committed herself, besides it was not the worst decision she could have made. "I will create a life field around the blade using magic, hopefully, that will leave me with time to dislodge the rune as it feeds on that."

"We will have to make sure the berries make contact at exactly the same time in order to draw enough energy. Are you ready?" Elly looked to Zo doubtfully, she gave a firm nod adjusting her stance as the first berries were released. Their timing, as anticipated, had been terrible.

She whispered softly, a life field, similar to those utilised in healing to push life from the elements to the recipient, appeared around the sheathed weapon. The spell formed a pale blue light encompassing the sword, again the berries hit the field, by now their timing was perfect, but their supply of berries rapidly dwindled. She took a breath, shifting position slightly as she watched the berries leave their hands. This was it, their timing was perfect. She felt herself tense as she swung her sword. She felt the solid resistance of the light as it began to feed upon the life field. In that moment she cursed her stupidity.

Elly and Eiji could only stare in horror as time itself seemed to slow. As her sword struck the barrier, her hair began to fade losing its vibrant shades until no colour remained at all except an aged silver. The pale blue aura, which surrounded her, turned as black as night. The berries evaporated to dust as the sword grew closer and closer to the rune. It made a slight cracking noise as the sword struck it, dislodging it from the barrier. Her scabbard followed in the same slow motion until it broke through the barrier's side, and time suddenly returned with great vengeance, rushing forward at an accelerated pace to correct the distortion.

Eiji moved quickly, his hands fumbling as he failed to catch the rune. The force of her strike had propelled it faster than he had anticipated. He felt its rough texture across his fingers, his desperate attempt forcing him off balance. He stumbled, his footing lost sending him tumbling to the floor. The rune struck the ground before him as it began to roll towards the edge. His feet tried to gain traction against the dust, his balance still faltering as he pursued. He wasn't going to make it in time, he could already feel the lava's heat as they neared the edge. He thrust himself forwards in one desperate, final attempt to seize it. His arms trying to halt his acceleration as Elly's foot appeared before him to step calmly upon the rolling object. She moved her leg quickly to avoid the coasting figure which threatened to knock her over. She looked at him, shaking her head as she bent to collect the rune.

They approached Zo cautiously as she clipped her weapon back onto her belt, unsure exactly what to expect, unsure what damage the life draining field would have caused. Her hair was the colour of age, they both hesitated for a moment, not knowing what to say to get her attention so they could assess the damage. She turned to look at them, nothing about her had altered except for her hair, which shone a ghastly white. She gave a slight shrug, shaking her head gently, as she did so it returned back to its original rich copper brown. The colour trickled down from the roots almost like running water to restore it back to its same vibrant shades, although perhaps a little redder than before.

"I am an idiot," she announced, her voice still held a tremor of shock. She couldn't believe she had done something so foolish. "I did not take into account that my rune was sacrifice, fortunately I altered my attunement in time."

"Darkness?" Elly questioned in surprise, surely she didn't mean dark magic. She didn't possess that skill, she would have known.

"Yes, although I chose to follow the path of nature, I am not as pure as you may think." Zo paused as she suddenly realised that no one in this room would consider her pure, especially since they knew her past. Despite this, she continued anyway. "I studied the darker artes for a long time as a child, before finally choosing my path. Before I could truly embrace my powers, there was much I had to learn. To heal effectively, you must also know and understand the fundamental aspects of death." She couldn't explain what she had done or how it worked, she understood it well in terms of the magic and how it felt, but, no matter how hard she tried, whenever she attempted to describe her actions, even to her mentor, the result was nothing more than a confusion of instinct and energies. She could not find the words to portray how she had altered her spell and magical affinity, so that she could use the rune of sacrifice to gain the advantage.

The darker artes were not only the summoning of dark masses and powers, but the ability to utilise large amounts of life energy; but she would never dream of using those powers to call forth a being reflective of the magic itself. The power needed for such a thing may see her lose herself, not to the darkness, but to the power or even the being that she called. It was this fine line between control and destruction that, before the removal of this magic, had seen the Hectarian branch known as summoners, become virtually if not completely extinct. That type of power was too dangerous, too wild to control. The style of magic she used was far gentler, far safer.

"I don't understand," Eiji interrupted. "Y' created a life field by magic, t'counter the effects of the light right? Takin' life from around y' t'give t'the field." Zo nodded. "As the rune of sacrifice is in y' possession it took it from y' life instead, so what y' sayin' is, if y' cast a spell of death t'take the life-force from y'self or somethin' around it, and transfer it t'somethin' else, then under the rune's powers y' actually take its life-force?" Eiji frowned, as he confused himself more as he tried to make sense of what had just occurred. But he wasn't the only one, Elly too seemed to wish to question this further. Marise had never managed to grasp any aspect of this magic, or charms for that matter. The skills Marise used came naturally, she had an instinct for the forces she could manipulate, but Zo, Zo seemed to have no boundaries, it seemed she could manipulate forces beyond comprehension.

"Close enough," she smiled; she didn't want to confuse things more by trying to explain the basic concepts behind it. It had taken her months of study before she herself finally had grasped the intricacies safely.

"I never knew you could use these artes." Elly stated. In all the time she had known Zo, until this very moment, she had believed that Marise's magic was, on the most primitive level, the same as that used by her. Zo was far more proficient in healing, but the quality in the offensive power between them balanced any real power differences. This one demonstration left her filled with questions. It appeared there were a few more differences between them than she had initially thought. It seemed just as Zo could not use the sword to Marise's full potential, Marise could not utilise magic to hers. After all, she had just switched between them instantly without hesitation. Even those proficient in neutral artes needed the binding time to expire before recasting to call on the opposing forces, yet she had overlapped the expiry of one with the creation of another. It was unheard of, impossible, or so she had believed until she had just witnessed it.

"Well," Elly spoke after a few moments of silent contemplation, "there is just one place we must journey now," she stated, leading the way from the cave. They followed her quickly, still feeling uneasy about the giant floating platform. Once on the solid ground which led to the exit, Eiji stopped and—for possibly only the second time since their journey began—he opened the map Seiken had presented to Zo. She had already seen the result of their actions upon it, he had not. So when he opened it to discover the only thing upon its surface was the island of Crowley he had been surprised.

"It seems the other places on this map have vanished?" He turned the map over repeatedly in his hands in concern. He wasn't sure when this specific map had appeared in his possession, the two had been taken, passed, and shuffled around so often that if it wasn't for the symbol on the one he had found, he wouldn't have known which was which.

"That is because the magic which made them fixed points was dispelled when we passed through or took the runes from them." As Elly spoke, Zo felt a sharp tingling as Seiken placed his hand upon her back. For a second it seemed the air around them changed, growing briefly dark as the scent around them altered. As quickly as he had appeared, he vanished, without so much as a word. Unaware of his fleeting presence or the change around them, Elly and Eiji continued to study the map.

Once they had finished their examination of the single island on the paper before them, they took their first definitive steps out into the sunlight. Zo heard herself gasp, she glanced over the incredible view. Somehow, they were no longer on the Northern providence of Albeth, which was home to the Mountain of the Spirits. They had, against all reason and probability, emerged on the island of Crowley. They stepped out from what now seemed to be a solid wall of stone on the small mountain they had climbed to reach the very first entrance they had used to Collateral. From where she stood now, she could almost see her home.

"How'd we get here?" Eiji questioned, looking at Zo, as if he knew she possessed the answer.

"I think it was Seiken. He was here just a moment ago," she answered, still unsure of exactly what had happened.

"I didn't see him." He glanced around expectantly. He couldn't believe they had covered so much ground in just a single step without the use of a portal. Seiken seemed to have somehow manipulated the area to ensure they were exactly where they had needed to be, part of this unnerved him a little. He traced his hand across the solid wall they had just emerged from, confirming there were no illusions, or portals hidden deep within its core. There was nothing, no indication of anything that would offer answers as to how the feat had been accomplished.

"You were busy studying the map. I think he is concerned about the time it is taking us, so where possible, he is assisting us," she explained. She was painfully aware how long this quest was taking. She knew how much his people must be suffering, after all, their world sustained their life-force. Being away for extended periods would be like one of them being without food and water, eventually it would kill them. She could only estimate how long the Oneirois had been kept from their homeland. Seiken had mentioned that there had been other pilgrimages before theirs, and from what she understood, the abduction of his people had been a gradual process, who knew what they suffered even now.

"There are a few hours until sunset, shall we survey the area so we know where to begin tomorrow?" Elly turned to look at Zo, only to discover that she had already begun her descent of the mountain side. Hearing Elly's words, she turned back to face her in alarm.

"Tomorrow?" she exclaimed, now waiting for them to catch up. "But—"

"We do not know what dangers are ahead. We cannot risk getting caught in the dark. I know you are worried about your friends, but there is no benefit to rushing. If something were to happen because we acted in haste, there is *no one* to come for us. Let us just be grateful for this advantage. If not for your friend Seiken, it would have taken us longer to get here. As yet, I have not located this world's version of Collateral, meaning we would have been walking from the Mountain of the Spirits. These amulets work two ways, they both help and hinder." Elly smiled to herself, she knew neither of them would have considered that they could reach Crowley in their world and then remove the charm. It had been something she was planning to suggest, but doing so was pointless now.

"I guess," she muttered quietly, as some of her enthusiasm died. They continued down the mountain at a slower pace.

* * *

As they entered the town, the thing which surprised Zo most was that Darrienia's Crowley, was not too dissimilar to the one she knew. It wasn't that she had expected anything less, after all, the fixed points of this world were almost identical to their counterparts, but she had no real recollection of seeing the other places. She was surprised at the intensity of her feelings towards something she knew to be nothing more than a facsimile.

As she looked over the townsfolk, she realised that not a single one was actually a resident of the town she knew as home. Despite this, the image before her forced her to recall many memories. She thought back to how Daniel's father had tried so desperately to find someone who knew her, during his excursions. All things considered, she was now grateful he hadn't been able to discover the truth behind her past and disappearance. She smiled to herself, knowing that when they awoke, they would return to the place she loved so much, the real location of this facsimile. Her return to Crowley would almost mark the end of her adventure, but when she did return, there would be little choice but to seek the aid of Daniel's parents. His family knew this town better than anyone, and so, she needed to carefully consider exactly what she was going to tell them.

"So how will we know this door?" Eiji's voice was enough to pull Zo from her daydream, she turned to join the conversation. In Daniel's absence, she knew this town better than any of her two remaining friends, as such, it was her they called upon for an answer. "I guess it'll be the one legend says no one can pass through, with a similar place in our reality." Eiji responded to his own question, still looking to Zo for a response. She shook her head. In all her time on Crowley, not once had she heard such a legend, and considering her frequent visits to Elder Robert, she had heard some pretty outrageous ones.

"I cannot say I have heard of a place like that. There are a few underground ruins, maybe we could enquire?" she suggested. It was only a small island, hearsay and legend were easily evident. She was certain that if such a place had existed she and Daniel would have visited the location at least once, yet she had heard not so much as a whisper about anything which seemed to fit the description of what they now sought.

"Ask around, for what?" Zo turned to see a young boy on their heels. He had been following them at a distance since they had first entered the town, but it seemed he had finally built up the courage to approach them. He stood nearly three foot tall, topped with a messy head of dirty blond hair. He rocked back and forth on his heels as he waited enthusiastically for their answer.

"We're lookin' for a door," Eiji began, but before he could continue the young boy interrupted, his tone filled with excitement.

"Well, there's plenty here, my pop Tony, maybe you've heard of him?" The boy rolled his eyes as they shook their heads. "My pop can make anything." He stood proudly with his chest pushed out as he glanced between them excitedly.

"Not that kind of door, we're not lookin' t'buy one. The one we seek has been around for years, it doesn't open," Eiji finished what he was going to say before he was interrupted. The young boy laughed at them before he ran away.

"What good is a door that don't open?" he called back mockingly as he disappeared into a nearby house. Eiji gave a frustrated sigh.

"Maybe I can be of service?" Zo glanced towards the familiar voice, there before them stood the old man from the mining village, although he now wore different attire and was no longer covered with soot, there was no doubt that it was him.

"Isn't that the guy from the minin' village?" Eiji questioned, almost as if he had read her thoughts.

"Mining village? Can't say I know of such a place." He smiled gently as he looked at the travellers, he wasn't sure exactly why, but he felt indebted to these strangers, for whatever reason, he felt compelled to assist them.

"Do you think you can help us?" Zo couldn't help but recall the previous aid he had offered, help that had resulted in them being trapped in the mines, and ultimately the kidnap of Eiji. Judging by the expression on his face, it seemed Eiji too had the same unpleasant taste that this particular recollection brought.

"Well, I overheard yer dilemma. I was a renowned treasure hunter in my day. It just so happens there's quite a few ruins around here, one of which has never been excavated, yer see it's sealed, but not by a door." He paused as he rubbed his clean-shaven chin for a moment before he continued. "Maybe the door yer seek is metaphorical?" Zo and Eiji exchanged glances and smiled. Elly, on the other hand, did not seem too impressed by the interference of this man.

"What exactly do you mean?" Zo pressed, in hope to grasp a clearer meaning of how this place was sealed. If she could gain an understanding of it, perhaps she could determine if there was a way to break the enchantment, or at least give her time to think it over as they sought it.

"I mean no one can enter, it's sealed by magic I suppose," he shrugged. In truth he was uncertain if this was truly the restraining force, after all, such things had been dormant for as long as he cared to remember, and he had long forgotten both its power and appearance.

* * *

"He said we'd find it somewhere in this area," Eiji reflected. Their walk here had been precisely as the elderly man had described, and now, they found themselves on an open plain, littered with the occasional tree. It was a place Zo, who knew the island well, did not recognise.

Elly's pace had slowed considerably since their arrival here, almost as if something weighed heavily on her mind. Her vision was focused on the ground as they walked, with each step she observed the subtle change in colour and texture of the grass they walked upon as it grew darker.

"Do y' think he was lyin'?" Eiji questioned, breaking the heavy silence. He cast his vision quickly over their surroundings unable to find an indication of anything that would be of assistance to them.

Elly, instead of responding to his posed question, gave a slight sigh leaving them to investigate further. She decided to rest beside one of the nearby trees, an act allowing her a moment of peace as she sat in silent contemplation.

"I didn't sense any—" Zo's defence of the elderly man's intentions was interrupted by his appearance.

"Young 'uns these days." His voice had startled them, his approach was hurried as he moved to join them. He looked to Elly and winked before turning his focus back to them. "Yer can't see it, can yer?" His foot struck the ground beneath him, the impact causing a metallic sound to resonate through the air. "I was thinking, if yer gonna try and break the seal, I wanna at least watch. All my life I've tried to gain access to its mysteries." Eiji approached, noticing the change in the texture of the greenery as he assisted in removing the mossy grass from the metallic surface below. Grabbing the indention, the elderly man began pulling forcefully. The metal seal opened with a hiss, exhaling the warm stale air from within. Once open, he hurried inside, not waiting for them as he made his way into the darkness.

He waited for them to catch up, for some reason they seemed a little hesitant in following his enthusiastic steps as he raced inside. It was almost as if they questioned his motives. When they were barely a few paces behind him, he once more bounded forwards in youthful steps, although he had scarcely enough time to gain his full momentum before he once more was brought to a halt. Elly and Eiji stepped aside allowing Zo, who had walked at a slightly slower pace, to approach what was clearly the end of their journey. A large opaque barrier stretched floor to ceiling, blocking the path before them, its surface shimmering with the multitude of the elemental colours.

"Well my dear, how do yer propose on breaking the seal of the ancients?" he challenged. He narrowed his eyes, slightly trying to peer through the field as he had done many times before, but the shifting barrier concealed all that lay beyond. He stepped aside as she approached. Her hands traced its surface carefully, her eyes closed as her magic told her all she needed to know. Moving slightly, she found the very centre of the barrier, her palm resting firmly on its surface. It was a different kind of magic to that which she was accustomed, she simply needed to name and command it.

"Earth." As she whispered its name, the field seemed to shimmer a rich bronze as it responded. A shade which vanished to conceal itself beneath her hand before spreading outward to contain itself within one section of the field. Its finest point touching her hand as it extended out to reach the cave's wall. "Air." A pale green shade whipped quickly across to greet her touch, separating itself from the remaining colours that shimmered across the undivided surface. "Fire." A vivid red-orange met her call. "Water." A rich blue wave swept quickly past their vision. "Spirit." A brilliant white swirled around the colours. "Darkness." The foreboding black took its place, its colour so dark it seemed almost as if a hole had absorbed part of the barrier. "Light." A clear area appeared over the coloured field.

As she called each of them, they had separated themselves to claim their own domain. The colours now spanned from her hand, extending from the centre to the outer edge of the barrier, each element pure in its own colour and equal in size to those around it.

"I release you." Her voice was filled with silent power. A quiet buzzing, almost like the sound of a hummingbird's wings, echoed through the cave as the field vibrated shattering into tiny fragments. The multitude of pigments swooped and buzzed around them, filling the cave with a sea of tiny colours, darting back and forth, before finally fading into the walls surrounding them.

"Well I'll be. That's quite a trick young lady," he grinned. "All those before yer failed time and time again, but I said to myself, there's something special about these ones. Come, come, uncharted territory awaits!" Without waiting for them to move, he rushed ahead, but it soon became apparent there was very little left to this so-called ruin. The small passage had opened into a single room, and it was empty. There was no treasure and very few carvings could be seen on the walls. But there was one in particular that attracted their attention.

"The door?" Eiji approached the intricate six-foot carving, looking over its surface where delicate twists and designs showed the skilled craftsmanship.

"Perhaps." Zo approached, she studied it intently as she ran her hands across its surface. "Only, there don't seem to be any indents for the keys to fit." She looked to Elly for answers but instead noticed something else. "Where's he gone?" she questioned as she realised the old man no longer stood amongst them.

"It seems he awoke," Elly suggested, finally breaking her silence. Hearing her explanation, Zo turned her attention back towards the carving to study it further, her lips pursed in annoyance. "We can explore further tomorrow," Elly advised, turning to lead them back down the short route they had walked. She knew the end was drawing near, the atmosphere surrounding them had altered in ways she could not begin to explain. There was a part of her that had wanted this escapade to last. It had reminded her so much of the old days. When they finally stood before their target, nothing would ever be quite the same again. As much as she had awaited this, now that the time drew near, she was filled with a strange emptiness.

"Unless the locks appear by magic, I don't see how much further we can go. There was nothing behind that door but solid rock," Zo revealed, her mind clearly preoccupied by other thoughts. As she had traced the door with her hands, she had sent small waves of pressure through the surface, but there was no gap behind it. There was nothing there but solid rock, and no aura of magic.

"Funny isn't it?" Eiji mused as they exited. "We travel all this way only t'end up right back where we started. In fact, that first fairy ring we slept in is here somewhere." Eiji pointed into the distance. Many things had changed since they last found themselves on this continent, and not just the scenery. The entire journey had changed each of them in ways they had never expected.

A deeper understanding of this world had tempered them through their journey. Although Darrienia once had several fixed locations, it also possessed fixed passages, places such as fairy rings which would connect the world to its counterpart, areas that imposed upon the boundaries of their worlds. A tether that it seemed would never alter even if the area surrounding it did. The first time they had arrived here, they never would have considered they walked the island of Crowley, although it was a fixed location, there was in fact only a small fragment of this area which remained unaltered, the rest remained open to interpretation.

"It will be the safest place to rest tonight," Elly stated. "If we return now, perhaps we can discover if this door exists in both worlds. But I am certain you both observed that it was nothing more than a carving." There seemed something almost distracted about the manner in which she spoke. For the first time, in her own way, it seemed as if she was not encouraging them to move forwards.

"Don't worry." Eiji put his hand on her shoulder comfortingly mistaking her distraction for concern about their mission. "We'll still find a way, after all, that's what we're meant t'do"

"And besides," Zo continued. "Maybe the key is back home." Elly heard the doubt in her words. Since she had examined the etching of the door, it seemed as if her very demeanour had altered.

Zo was unaware if anyone had spoken during their brisk-paced walk. She only knew that, on raising her gaze from the ground, she found herself amazed that they had already reached the fairy ring. Stepping over the mushrooms carefully, she looked out across the landscape.

"It's hard to believe this is the first place we slept." Zo couldn't help but wonder what would have happened, how their journey would have differed if, on their arrival, they had taken an alternative path.

* * *

"How are they?" Acha questioned, her back now resting against the bars so she would not have to look upon the face of betrayal. She could tell that Seiken knew exactly what they faced without the need to keep vigil, that was how he had known when they had needed his aid the most, and how he had been able to so smoothly mislead them. The only real danger on the bridge they had crossed would have come from the creatures, the one thing he didn't warn them about, and the reason she sat here now.

"It's hard to say. They have discovered there is no further path for them in Darrienia." A deep-rooted sadness filled his voice, if only there had been another way. If the circumstances had been different, maybe she would have been able to save them, but sadly, he would never know. "They are about to make the final journey to Crowley. It won't be long now." He felt detestable for having betrayed them like this, but ultimately no one would really get hurt. Night would receive the Grimoire, Gaea's star would be revitalised, and they could all part ways and life would move on. Even this line of reason brought him little comfort. Something Rowmeow had said, years ago, kept repeating in his mind. For some, life would not continue. There would be casualties. He had forgotten all about this prophecy and wondered if she had too, then again it was doubtful she had even heard it.

"I don't believe this!" Daniel's voice was filled with silent rage as he continued to pace back and forth within the constraints of the small prison, as he had done for hours. "We went through all that and for what? Nothing!" His voice rose as his anger boiled. "What was the point, were we just some kind of entertainment, does he enjoy sending people on unavailing quests just to watch them fail? Because, let's be honest, there was *never* any chance we would win. Is this the nature of his game?" The level of frustration he felt rang clearly through his enraged tones. There was never any possibility his game could be won. They had been destined to fail from the onset. He continued his tirade until the sound of Night's voice startled him.

"Now, now, Mr Eliot." Night moved into view, he wasn't sure exactly when he had entered the room, but Seiken's expression implied it had not been long ago. "I'm surprised one of your intellect hasn't realised yet." He looked to Seiken. "Don't you have business in need of attending elsewhere?" At his words, Seiken vanished from sight, leaving them to wonder what fresh betrayal their friends were about to face. "All this was merely a test. I had to ensure she was ready. After all, she is the very image of her mother, her courage, her spirit, and her heart." Night smiled with hidden meaning.

"Ready?" Daniel questioned abruptly. "Ready for what?" His voice filled with demand, desperation to understand his intentions, and what this was really about. If he could learn this, maybe he could warn Zo if a chance was presented to do so. He had already ascertained their position in the prison was, for the moment at least, permanent, but perhaps he could find another way to warn her, perhaps he could force his thoughts through to her.

"To seize the final Grimoire of course. That's what this entire endeavour has been for. Each time you retrieved a rune you not only destroyed the enchantment which hides the Grimoire, but released the Severaine's protectional barriers too. This whole distraction was an ingenious scheme to lead you here to the very moment which will be upon us shortly. I simply needed to know that she would make the right choice."

"Choice?" Daniel grabbed the cold iron bars, his knuckles turning white as he glared angrily towards Night.

"In situations like these, one always likes to believe the choice to be made is straightforward. The needs of many must always outweigh the needs of the few, the fate of the world versus those you care deeply for. It's a decision people so often cast judgement on, after all what choice is there really? To save everything at the expense of one, or risk destroying it all to ensure its safety. I had to know what her choice would be when the time came, would she think the same as myself and Seiken?" Night smiled meaningfully. "She is so much like her mother."

"And her choice?" Acha questioned, but the only answer she received was a smile.

* * *

Zo didn't wait for Elly and Eiji to appear in the small busy inn within Collateral. When she awoke, their beds were empty, but she knew as yet they had not crossed over. They would soon appear, and it was her intention to be gone. It had been a wise decision to acquire a room and not to stay within the shared sleeping quarters. It would have been quite distressing for both parties should someone have taken an apparently empty bed, only to have someone appear within as they completed their journey back from Darrienia. As the first rays of dawn flickered on the horizon, she had already procured a horse from the stable hand, and had fled through the street she knew, without a doubt, led back to Crowley. But it was not the entrance they had previously used to arrive here, instead, it was another, located upon the small island, the gateway which Elly had used when first bringing her to the continent. There were things she wished to attend to away from the eyes of her friends, things which needed addressing before the final darkness descended upon her.

The sun had barely flickered past the mountains on the horizon when Zo had ridden into Crowley. She dismounted quickly outside Daniel's home, slapping the horse on the rear to send it back to its master. The horses in Collateral were well trained, and could always find their way home, no matter where their rider took them. Forgetting all the courtesy she would normally show, she rushed into the house.

"Angela, Jack?" she cried, desperately hurrying from one room to the next. As she entered the consultation area, she saw Angela already standing to greet her, concern reflected in her eyes that came with hearing the desperation in Zo's voice. She quickly excused herself to escort Zo into the sitting room. No sooner were they free from the prying ears of the patient when Zo flung her arms around her, clinging to her desperately as she sought but a moment of comfort from a person who had been like a mother to her.

She winced against the pain as Angela wrapped her arms protectively around her trembling figure. Feeling her distress, she pulled away, forgetting all the questions as her personality shifted into the role of her profession. It was a remarkable change to witness, from her reaction alone Angela had known exactly where to focus her attention. Before Zo had even realised what was happening, it was too late, Angela had skilfully slackened her top and seen the ghastly wound.

"By the Gods, Zo," she whispered seeing the horrific—expertly treated—injury that pierced her shoulder. She turned her around confirming that it had, as she suspected, pierced straight through. Before Zo could speak, she felt the sting of antiseptic as Angela rubbed it against her wound. "What happened?" Zo couldn't find the words to answer. In that instant, it was all she could do to hold back the tears.

"I'm fine," she lied, stepping back to quickly replace the loosened clothing and cover the wound. She had never seen such a serious look in Angela's eyes before, she steadied her breath. "Something horrible has happened, they took Daniel!" Angela placed a hand on Zo's uninjured shoulder, she had wondered why Daniel had not accompanied her. It was clear in her mind now what had happened. During their travels, they had clearly been ambushed, during which Zo had been wounded and left for dead. Whoever attacked them then must have taken hostages, but why? It was true that her family was well known because of her reputation as a physician, but surely any doing their research would know they had little to offer as a ransom, and no demands had been received. Despite being one of the most respected and sought-after physicians in the Plexus, her fee normally resulted in an exchange of services or commodities, as she believed it should. It had been a long time since she had taken paid work from the Plexus. These days, they simply sent clients to her when they deemed it necessary. She just couldn't understand why someone would take him.

"Who, who's taken him?" Angela questioned, as she tried to remain calm. Panic filled her stomach despite her knowing the most sensible thing she could do was to obtain as much information as possible. Considering the wound, it was a miracle that Zo had made it back at all. A fraction in either direction would have been fatal, and that was no doubt why their attackers had not ensured her fate. They had assumed she was already dead, the fact she lived was a testament to the skills of whoever found her.

"There's no time to explain, but you have to believe me, I'll get him back. There are some sealed ruins just outside town somewhere, I just need to know where they are," she pleaded desperately.

"The only ruins around the town, are just north of your home Zoella," Jack advised, hurrying through the door in alarm at having found it wide open. She looked at him, nodding in acknowledgement. She knew exactly where he meant. The light from the window faded slightly as something passed by.

"Don't worry, they won't hurt him. Not if I get there in time, but I have to find that door." She looked back to Daniel's mother. "I promise, I won't let anything happen to him." Angela nodded, the words bringing her a small amount of comfort. Whatever the situation was, at least it seemed there was a chance for it to be resolved, but by what means she couldn't imagine.

"You sound as if you know these people," she remarked, wondering if perhaps, on their travels, Zo had finally found someone she knew, a place to call home. If that was the case, what trouble must she have become involved with for this to be the result of those actions?

"She does." Elly appeared at the door; as she spoke, she knocked quietly before stepping into the lounge. "It is her father." They all looked to Elly in surprise as Zo's stomach sank to the floor.

"My father?" she echoed uncertainly, thinking back to the times she had encountered him. If not for the picture discovered in the Perpetual Forest, she would never have realised who that stranger was. "No, my father's the one who's been helping me all this time. He would never..." She looked deeply into Elly's eyes, searching for any indication her words were false, but as always, they remained unyielding to such emotion. She looked to Angela, apologetically as she realised the truth. Daniel and Acha had been taken hostage in order to manipulate her actions, to ensure she did whatever was needed. Without the need for further words or explanations, Elly turned towards the door.

"Do you have the location?" she questioned; Eiji hovered outside, not wishing to intrude on this already delicate situation.

"Yes." Zo closed her eyes for a second, trying to make sense of this new information, how could it be true, how could the one behind this be her father? If this was really the case, then the responsibility for this whole situation lay with her. At least the anger and confusion this brought would prove a useful spur to guide her forward. She had to correct the situation while there was still time.

"Good, we cannot afford to waste any more time," Elly remarked, escorting Zo through the door.

"This is all my fault. I'll send him back to you. I promise," she vowed, glancing back towards Jack and Angela as Elly led her forcefully away.

"What was that all about, who were those people with Zoella, is everything okay?" Jack asked, taking his wife in his arms, he held her close as she trembled. He had known, from the moment he saw her, something had been terribly wrong.

"I'm sure it will be." She began to cry, finally allowing herself to feel that which she had held back in Zo's presence. Jack placed his hand softly on the back of her head, stroking her hair as she wept gently against his shoulder. "Someone has Daniel. It seems they want to trade him for something in the ruins," Angela explained, having pieced together the information as best she could. Jack pulled back to look at his wife.

"The ruins? But they were excavated a long time ago. I should know, I led the team. We took everything, it's all now in Albeth museum," he stated, as he took his wife by the hand. "He will be safe, I'm sure of it, but I think it's time we talk with Elder Robert."

Chapter 27

The Echo of the Ancients

"It's not quite what I was expecting," Eiji mused, looking at the clearly marked mining tunnel leading into the underground ruin. The entrance, unlike its counterpart in Darrienia, was neither concealed, nor barricaded. Zo and Daniel had not explored this ruin, simply because there was nothing really to visit. They had walked past it on occasion, but there really was nothing spectacular about it, no force driving them to investigate it further. She had just been ready to lead them inside when she caught sight of a figure hurrying towards them.

"Jack!" she exclaimed, there was an obvious tone of apprehension lining her voice. Jack had never warmed to her, and now she was responsible for the danger his son faced, she almost feared this confrontation. They waited just outside the descent as the tall man with pepper coloured hair rushed towards them with purpose. "What are you—"

"No one knows these underground ruins like me. I led the first expedition down here you know." He smiled; his voice was filled with pride as he moved beside them, taking a few moments to catch his breath. "I'll take you, although I'm not sure what good it will be."

"You mean..." Zo's voice was filled with disillusion as her stomach sank, fearing the words that would follow.

"Yes, everything in here was excavated to the museum in Albeth," he confirmed. Excavation crews could be brutal. If there were any carvings of interest it was not unheard of for them to chisel them out of the surrounding area, then ship them to the museum. After all, people preferred to see the genuine artefact instead of a charcoal stone rubbing.

"I think we shall take a look around, just in case, Mr Eliot," Elly insisted calmly, in response to the panicked looks from both Zo and Eiji.

"Very well Elaineor. Now do you mind telling me exactly what kind of trouble you and my son have found yourselves in?" He ruffled his hand through his hair, looking between them questioningly.

"Talk and walk. You can guide us." Elly glanced back to him for but a second, before she continued securing her string to a nearby tree. "And you can explain," she glanced to Zo.

When Elly had finished securing the twine, she removed two small lanterns from her bag, passing one to Eiji they started their journey into the mine.

The ruin was no larger than that they had found in Darrienia, it was, all in all, rather unspectacular. The walls now possessed empty nooks and shelves where all its contents had once been displayed.

"And this is it," Jack announced as they entered the large square room the single corridor had guided them to. Despite his familiarity with this ruin, he seemed eager to read the tales written within. Elly raised her lantern, casting shadows on the delicately carved walls. "This area housed very little, a few scraps of ancient technology and some crystals, but as I said, they are all now in Albeth."

Elly seemed to be paying his words little attention, although to say she was ignoring him would be inaccurate. She watched him very closely as she studied the walls, the carvings, and as expected of any well-versed adventurer, she examined the secrets hidden within. The stories, which were written in ancient symbols, told a selection of tales regarding the current gods, which seemed strange given that Jack had advised ancient technology had been found here, a technology which pre-dated the gods, whose tales were inscribed here. If this had truly been the case, it begged the question of who had displayed it here and why.

"Here," Elly whispered, grabbing Zo gently to pull her before the same carving of the door that she had studied within Darrienia. As she stood before it, Elly checked the walls for traps and openings. Despite this, she never lost her vigil on Jack, who seemed strangely fixated on the historic tales. Even now, as she addressed Zo, she watched him through the corner of her eye, wondering if anyone else had noticed.

Examining the door once again, Zo could clearly see there were no indentations where the runes could fit, but she already knew what she had to do. In old shrines and passages, the constructors often carved such a thing on the wall to hide the location of a real door or passage, a passage which would lead to the tomb's greatest artefacts. Even now she could feel the emptiness behind what should have been a solid wall. She knew there was only one thing to do, but that didn't make the situation feel any less uncomfortable. Jack would finally be given a reason to confirm his misgivings about her. After this there was no return, but with time as short as it was now, it didn't really matter anymore. She could already feel the final thread, the last remnants of her control, begin to fray. It wouldn't be long now. It was only by her sheer will and determination to be true to her word, and protect those she loved, that she managed to stand before them now, but she was getting so very tired.

Jack had never known her secret. Her Hectarian abilities had been something shared just between herself and Daniel, although on occasions it had seemed that Elder Robert had his suspicions, given some of the comments he made in her presence. His conjecture was justified, given the situation surrounding their first encounter, but she couldn't be sure. She had tried so hard to keep her skills a secret from all she encountered. She didn't want people to be afraid of her or treat her like an outcast. Jack, without reason, already avoided her as much as possible, how could she ever hope to gain his trust to keep her word if all he saw in her were lies and the reckless endangerment of his son's life? After what she was about to reveal, she was certain that he would see her how the people of her own town of Drevera had, and label her a monster.

She took a breath as she focused her mind, reading the forces which surrounded her as she called upon them for their power. A gentle wind began to rise around her. Feeling the energy race through her body she reached forwards to place her hand firmly on the wall's surface. Releasing the energy she had received into the wall she braced herself for what would follow.

It was an enchantment she knew and used, even without incantations, her understanding now reminding her such words were meaningless. She needed only the desire and will to summon forth her powers. Having realised this, she understood Elly's expression when she had previously called forth her power through rhyme. It was something she appreciated the need for as a child, it helped to focus the young energy and clearly state the desire, but it was something only a child did. Something that was best left in the past as maturation saw the realisation and manipulation of the elements to meet her desire by intention alone. This particular spell gathered a large amount of energy from the forces around her. On entering her body, they concentrated into a condensed force so that, as she willed it from her hand, it created a pulse of pressure strong enough to repel an object. It was something she had practised a great deal as a child.

The last time she remembered using it, it had been on a far larger scale than this one, but the details even now continued to elude her. From the small flash of insight she had gained, she could only decipher that she had been defending someone, someone very important. It was a memory she had fought to remember for so long, but something seemed to keep it from her, almost as if her will to forget was stronger than her will to remember.

She released the energy, her hand moved quickly as she waited for the wall to crumble beneath the force, yet instead, it swung open as if she had merely pushed it. She looked sheepishly to Jack as she awaited his reaction. Even someone not versed in magic would recognise the gathering and expelling of energy in this manner, but as he returned her look, he didn't even seem surprised. Elly raised her hand to the door her hand stopping just a few inches in as if blocked by an invisible force.

"Eiji, could you escort Mr Eliot home?" She gave him a meaningful look, unseen by Zo; Eiji nodded approaching Jack.

"Okay, y' go on without me," he stated softly as he tried, without luck, to escort the protesting figure away. Jack refused to be led, he insisted on following them until the end, demanding that they allow him to do all he could to aid in the retrieval of his son.

"Do not worry, we will find you when we are finished. There is a barrier system in place here, one only maidens may pass through from this point onward. Neither of you meet the requirement I am afraid. It is an old, now redundant, rule for temples and shrines, maidens were less likely to pilfer their offerings. We will come for you once we have what we came for." With no other option, Jack finally surrendered to the enforcing hand of Eiji as he led him away. There was a long drawn out silence as they waited by the door until they had left.

"Elly, will Eiji be all right?" She already knew what would happen when they left. It had been painfully obvious since the moment the door had opened.

"Your father knows he is under my protection," she replied simply.

* * *

Eiji led Jack through the passage, making idle, yet strained, conversation as they walked.

"It's a shame about the barrier, but it's a well-known protection as Elly said. I would'a loved t'have seen what was behind that door. So, Mr Eliot, how long has Zo been staying with y'?" He followed Elly's string through the tunnel, rolling it back onto its twine ball as he did so. He knew they wouldn't need it to navigate back. He was unsure why she had even used it, after all it was an easy walk, with one or two turns along the way.

"I don't remember now. It seems like she's always been here," he answered simply, he really wasn't one for conversation it seemed.

As they stepped outside, they both squinted against the brightness of the midday sun. Eiji knew he had very little time left in which to act. With a quick glance around, he located what he needed and, without hesitation, erected an impenetrable water barrier across the ruin's entrance. At least this way he knew no one else would be able to enter. Zo and Elly could finish what they had started. If he was wrong about the situation then, on their return, Zo would simply be able to dispel it, otherwise it would vanish anyway when he left the area. With his presence no longer there to control it, the manipulated element would simply revert back to its original state. Hopefully, seeing its obstruction there now would be enough of a deterrent. He saw Jack's posture alter slightly as if the action had surprised him, yet he continued walking at his steady pace.

"So how'd y' know we were comin' here. What's it y' really want?" Jack stopped walking, when he turned to face Eiji there was surprise in his features, despite there being no further need to continue with the pretence.

"What do you mean? My wife told me you were after something in the ruins, I wanted to help," he answered. His performance was admirable. Jack seemed genuinely outraged that his intentions were being questioned. Although Eiji had seen his reaction when he had quickly summoned the barrier, he hadn't thought to question it, almost as if he had understood his actions. He was certain he was right about this.

"Look, quite simply I don't believe y'. Mr Eliot has never met Elly, yet back there y' called her Elaineor, nor can he read the writin' of the ancients. Daniel told me he was an explorer, but as it stands not one person has worked out a translation for them. The only ones who knew it were Hectarians, and the language was forgotten when their powers were removed. Their magic of old allowed them t'read it with ease, once it had been extinguished, not one of them could break the complex codes, and finally," Eiji stated taking a quick breath. "Mr Eliot, nor anyone for that matter, knows Zo can use magic, yet y' weren't even a little surprised. Y' assumed since she used it freely before us it was common knowledge, y' made only one mistake, Aburamushi, y' assumed." Despite the confidence held in his tone, he wasn't really sure about anything he had just argued. He felt the all too familiar warmth of embarrassment beginning to swell within him as he realised it was possible he had, in fact, just challenged Daniel's father.

There was a long silence during which Eiji had plenty of time to build his doubts further. He started to question what his instincts had told him, after all, he had arrived shortly after Elly, maybe she had introduced herself then. There was a small possibility Zo could have taught him to read the ancient scripts, and there was no reason why Daniel's father wouldn't know Zo was Hectarian, but when she had used her abilities, it seemed as if she had been waiting for some reaction from him. He was right, he had to be, otherwise he could never look this man in the eyes again, wasn't that why Elly had sent him out? She had made the most logical decision, to sacrifice him so they could complete the mission at hand. There was no such thing as a maiden barrier, the Gods did not fear men looting their shrines. Any foolish enough to do so would be punished, they would rain down judgement. Thieves, were not something a god feared.

"Well, I guess my plan did have a few oversights. I never did find my answer. But you see, whereas there may have been a minor flaw in my plan, in the fact that you saw through my disguise, there was a fatal one in yours. You're mine," he growled coldly as he changed back to the appearance they had first set eyes upon in Darrienia. Aburamushi knew his time had almost expired, he felt the pressure of the faltering life-force through the trace which bound him to her. When Zo vanished, so too would the magics which linked them.

He would now have to rely on Night to keep his side of the bargain, or his time would also soon expire.

"True as that is, I am also under Elly's protection." Eiji had felt for a long time that Elly had more to do with Night than she had implied. She had known of his involvement in seeking Zo, which came to reason she knew something of his motives. Over the last hour things had become very clear to him, and it was only now he realised the extent of the truth. The one person who possessed knowledge of events beyond what was possible, the person who had been guiding them, had been Elly. He realised now she had been misleading them all along. Elly did not work for Blackwood, which was why she could state so honestly that she had no intention of returning Zo to him. She had other plans, she answered to Night. He felt his stomach sink as he realised Zo was now alone with the worst possible person. He had willingly allowed himself to be sacrificed so they could continue to achieve their goal, however, he now questioned the true motives behind their presence there, he only wished he had realised it before.

"Under Elaineor's protection?" He glanced around mockingly. "Funny I don't see her anywhere. Besides, alive does not mean unharmed," he threatened, his answer serving as confirmation of Eiji's fear.

"Lead the way." Eiji smiled to himself, he had initially only joined this adventure in the interest of self-preservation, but now he would gladly risk his life to protect those he had walked beside. The outcome of this confrontation was inevitable. He could only hope that if he cooperated he could somehow leave a trail to aid Zo in the finding of Night's tower, although given his recent realisation, he doubted she would need it.

* * *

"Are you sure he will be all right?" Zo questioned again, looking into the darkness that lay behind them. Her father now had all of her friends, she never would have thought that the person who had been helping her all along was one of Night's spies. It made sense now, how else could he have known when he was needed the most? She had to wonder if Night had deliberately fashioned this course of events, if he had sought her father in order to facilitate the situation. It was strange, she had felt so safe within his embrace. She would never have considered he had been the enemy all along.

"I should think so," Elly answered honestly; she knew that no harm would come to them as long as Zo continued to cooperate.

"Another thing, it has been bothering me for some time," Zo started, she was stalling. She did not wish to take the first step through the door which now lay open before her, she did not want to walk this path until she was certain where it would lead. "How did Aburamushi get to be here anyway?"

"Since Acha gave him the mark of boundaries, he too can cross over between here and Darrienia," she answered simply.

"Elly." Zo paused as she took a deep breath, fearing the words she was about to speak. "There is no door is there?" It was something that she had wondered since their arrival in Darrienia's Crowley. It was a question she had feared to ask, a question she already knew the answer to. She had felt it when they had first entered the ruins, but she still didn't understand, why bring her here? There was nothing she could do, nothing she could offer in return for her friends. She had been wondering what could possibly wait within which would give her access to Night's tower and how the runes were connected to the equation, but she just couldn't see the destination that lay before her.

"I never said there was. If you recall I believe it was Acha who made that assumption. I simply advised that there was only one place we needed to go, and the door *I* was referring to, you have just opened. Besides it is not a door you are here for, although in some ways I must admit, it is a key."

"Another one?" Zo looked to the small pouch of runes, as she did so she realised the truth that had been alluding her. She had known something was wrong when she studied them outside the Mountain of the Spirits. The runes she held were not keys at all. Since they had been removed from Darrienia they had become nothing more than useless rocks, with symbols carved upon their surface. Their energy had been slowly fading since they first obtained them, but she had thought that as they met with the door their power would somehow rekindle to reveal the path. The runes were useless, the keys were non-existent, so what was their purpose? Suddenly she had the answer, but surely she was wrong, what was being expected of her was impossible.

"The only one, that is if you *want* to save your friends. There is only one thing you can use to bargain with, and you are the only person with the talent to retrieve it."

"The Grimoire," she sighed with a sickening realisation as everything fell into place. It had been she herself who had obtained the other six under the name of Marise Shi, and now she was required to complete the task, after all she was the only person who still contained Hectarian powers, the only person who could have opened the way to its location. But what about Acha, wasn't she needed to obtain it? "This whole thing, it was never about Seiken or his people."

"Not as such, no. We needed to get your attention and break through the boundaries in order to release the seals so this resting place could be discovered." It had been very difficult to get everything to take shape. Years ago, Seiken had shown just how much he was willing to give for her. Their history meant that, even without her memories, a part of her would always remember him. She would feel the desire and obligation to protect him. The difficult part had come just before his capture, they had needed to ensure he discovered the importance of the one selected to free his people, to ensure that he would visit her.

Despite her initial agreement to their game, there was no commitment until she first arrived in Darrienia. Until that point, she had been free to change her mind. They had to ensure she wouldn't, without either of the two parties becoming suspicious. It had been difficult, but they had accomplished it.

"Now, step through the door, finish what you started all those years ago. It is the only way to save the lives of those you care for." Elly motioned for her to enter. With no other choice, she did as instructed. Elly smiled to herself, it seemed so long ago when she first approached Marise with this quest, and now it was finally coming to an end.

As Zo walked the corridor, she knew all too well what lay ahead, everything suddenly seemed to make so much sense. Elly had been far too knowledgeable. She had answers to any questions they might ask, both genuine and fictitious, dependent on what she wanted to reveal. It was confusing, there had been times throughout their journey when Elly had truly seemed regretful of the situation. She seemed to sympathise with her, even desire to protect her from harm. Had everything been nothing more than a pretence all along, could it be all this time she had been just a guide to ensure they did not stray from the pre-planned path?

Zo followed the short walkway, amazed at how much insight she had gained in just a few short steps. Her mind was filled with questions and doubts. At some point along the journey, she had begun to trust Elly, actually trust her, not just the feelings she initially had towards her. She had considered her a friend, a comrade, but it seemed these attachments were one sided. She had been fooled all along, she should have known better. Elly clearly only had loyalty to Marise, why had she expected things to be different? Approaching the entrance to the shrine, she hesitated in the shadows. These would be the final steps of her journey. She could only hope she had the choice to walk the right path.

"Stand before me." A voice from within the shrine beckoned as if it sensed her apprehension to approach. Zo could barely force one foot before the other. The room was filled with all manner of treasures as far as the eyes could see, it was a sight to behold, gold, jewels, weaponry, armour, knowledge, everything an adventurer might seek, could be found within these walls. On the wall opposite to where she emerged stood a wooden door, it looked strangely out of place in the marble construct in which she had arrived. She felt herself drawn towards a magnificent statue, its grey marble surface untouched by time. It stood proudly beneath a large arch at the far end of the room, surveying all that was stored within. The finely carved male figure seemed to look directly towards her, its arms stretched out as if to welcome her into its domain. "Zoella Althea, you have entered the chamber of the ancients, a library of hidden knowledge from times past, present, and future. It has long been told of your coming, tell me, what is it you seek? Tell me, and I will grant it to you, if it is within my power." The deep voice echoed throughout the chamber, glancing around for the first time she noticed that Elly was not standing beside her. For some reason she hung back in the shadows.

"Sir." Her voice trembled as she spoke. She tried her best to steady it as she continued. "If you can give me anything I desire then..." She glanced towards the area where Elly lurked. Even now she could feel the predatory gaze as it encouraged her to complete the task before her. Taking a breath, Zo made her request. "I wish my friends, Daniel, Acha, and Eiji to be free and appear in Albeth castle alive and well, and for the race known as the Oneirois to be returned safely to their home world free of Night's control." Zo let out a sigh of relief seeing that Elly had not intervened. If this being could grant her anything, this was her request. She knew Elly was skilled in battle and therefore could not risk them appearing before her, or even in the area. Albeth castle was the most secure place she knew. It was protected by an enormous moat and, as a relic from times past, it possessed incredible defensive capabilities. The knights of Albeth trained and lived there, it was possibly the safest place in the world.

Elly smiled in the darkness, impressed by her choice of words. She had expected her to attempt something like this. The level of thought she had given this quick decision had surprised her, after all it would have been of little benefit if her friends were freed but remained within Night's tower. She had thought this through very well, to the extent she would place them at Albeth castle. If the being could fulfil her request, they would lose the advantage, even so, Elly did not seem in the slightest bit distressed. In fact, she seemed almost amused.

Even now, Zo refused to surrender. She refused to give them what they wanted, however, there was but one thing she could leave with. Elly knew this girl better than even she could believe. It had been an essential part of her duties to learn about her, her thoughts and feelings. She had to understand her completely in order to predict her movements and choices. The intelligence she gathered had been carefully reported to Night, ensuring everything they planned would push her towards the crucial point. Through the entire journey, most of this game's players had been his pawns, pawns carefully played to lead the king into mate, to ensure that, when the final move came, she would take the only path she could, right into their trap.

Night had planned infinite moves ahead. It had already been confirmed that, if such a request were to be made, there was no way the tired echo of the ancient watcher could possess the ability to fulfil it. He had been leading them all this time and now she had fallen right into his trap. This request of hers was simply a futile attempt to delay the inevitable.

"I am sorry." The voice answered regrettably. "That request is not something within my power, Night is a god, even I cannot penetrate the seals into his domain. The home of a god is outside my reach." Zo gave a sigh, she understood now why her request had not met with alarm and was once more forced to consider exactly how well everything had been planned to leave her with but one choice. There was only one other thing she could ask, but surely it was impossible for this being to grant, after all, she did not meet the criteria.

"Then," she paused, trying not to choke on the bile brought about by the words she would speak. "I seek the Grimoire that resides within your care." She closed her eyes, forcing free a tear. There was something strangely empty in knowing that, once she had this tome, she could free her friends and at the same time liberate Seiken and his people by proposing a trade. Its release for their freedom. A trade with a cost more astronomically high than any of them would at first realise, a trade it seemed to be her destiny to make.

She had known all along there was but one conclusion. She knew and feared the darkness which even now attempted to steal her last moments. She knew the cost, the price that would be paid to keep her promises, and with no other option she had to continue without hesitation. There seemed to be a long silence before the voice spoke once more.

"Impossible." Although Zo had known Acha was the only one who could remove it, the answer still came as a surprise, so much so that even Elly shifted in the shadows.

"But sir, you said anything, you don't understand, if I can't have it he will kill my friends, and the Oneirois will die which will ultimately bring about the destruction of our own world. Please," she begged falling to her knees before the statue. If she couldn't retrieve the Grimoire everything would be lost. If it had been Acha who had stood here in her stead then there would have been no cause for concern, but in her absence, Zo had no idea what she could do next. Without the tome, everything they had endured would become meaningless.

"If it were still within my possession, I would not hesitate in granting your request." It was at this point, Elly stepped through the door. She looked surprised, this game had been planned to the very last detail. This was the final move, she had to obtain the book. There was no room for mistakes.

"What do you mean not in your possession?" Elly questioned sternly, moving to the centre of the chamber, her shadow covered the area in which Zo knelt as she stood behind her. "How can that be? Only one with the blood of Night himself may remove the tome, you look upon his daughter." Zo heard herself gasp as she felt herself begin to tremble. Were these words really the truth, she was Night's child? Her breath became laboured as her throat closed, waves of panic swelled within her. She had known her father had her friends but she had thought him to be of Night's employ, she had not considered the two had been the same. Nausea washed over her as she felt herself growing increasingly weak, the shock of the truth challenging her control over her weakened body. In that moment it was as if all energy had left her.

"Lain, have you learnt nothing, what is a book to distinguish blood line? Although the Hoi Hepta Sophoi used their life-force to seal them, such a condition is impossible but for the Gods. Do you really think mankind would be granted such power? Although you were correct, the book *should* have resided here, but it has never been within these walls," the voice admitted.

"But sir, how is that possible, what about the magic barrier which surrounds it?" She seemed more desperate than Zo. The thought that the Grimoire would fail to reach its destined location had not even been a consideration.

Zo shifted position as she tried to force herself to stand, but in her weakened state of shock she had no choice but to remain kneeling before the statue. She could only question her next move, there was only one benefit to the Grimoire not being where it was destined, Elly did not know where it was either. This, however, did not change the fact she needed it in order to fulfil her promises, finding it was the only chance she had to secure her friends' safety. Once Night discovered the truth, there was no telling the repercussions, especially if he thought his hostages now possessed no value.

"The details are unimportant. Did your hunting days teach you nothing, or in your slumber, have you forgotten? Lain, return to your master, tell him what he seeks is not here." Elly turned on her heel before walking towards the wooden door, she was leaving. She knew the echo could not have refused to present the tome when it was requested, or lie about its location. Zo was no longer a concern to her, not now. Her remaining time was limited, her presence unwarranted. There was no harm in leaving her to live out her final moments while she presented these unforeseen circumstances to Night. All had been for nothing, Zo hadn't even needed to be preserved, she had been useless. As the door opened the image of the outside world changed. The exit here could act like a portal to any known location. Zo had not recognised the glimpse of the land Elly had departed into.

"Sir," she asked finally after a long stretch of silence had allowed her to gather her thoughts, "what became of the book, who has it now?" She still knelt before the statue.

"Even I cannot answer that. It is beyond my field of vision, but I can tell you many years ago, before you were born, an adventurer came to my assistance. With no other way to repay him I presented to him the only thing within my possession. I felt I could trust him to guard it. As he pulled me from the brink, he told me of his many adventures. I knew then that even should he say where the book originated, no one would believe him, thus we knew it would be safer in his possession than sealed within this shrine."

"Yet, you still stand vigil here?" The shock had slowly begun to recede now, although she still trembled uncontrollably the feeling to parts of her body slowly began to return as the numbness began to pass. She found her mind wandered now, if the book was never here then why did he still remain bound within these walls?

"Not only must I reside here for when you came, I must also remain for those who shall walk this path after you. We are always provided with the beginnings and ends of our time. It was written that you would arrive, just as it is written that Night will regain his power." Zo smiled at his answer, his words rekindling her hope to drive the remaining numbness from her body.

"Then I find the Grimoire?" Optimism filled her voice as she gained the strength to once again stand before the statue. If Night's rise to power had been foretold, he had to have received the power from all the Grimoires.

"Find? You cannot find that which isn't lost, but I can tell you that you will stand before your father shortly. Take care of what you must, and then, when you are ready, open this." A small box appeared before her on the floor, it was of simple design, no bigger than her palm. "Since I cannot give you what you seek, I can at least do this for you. It contains just enough power to take you to his domain. This is the limit of my magic." The voice answered the unasked question. "I am sorry there is nothing more I can do to aid you."

"Not at all." She smiled walking towards the door, by giving the tome away, this being had given her one gift she was extremely short on, time.

* * *

"Night." The summons of a familiar voice saw the prisoners moving themselves to the cage bars, allowing them a clear view of the unfolding events as Elaineor finally arrived. Once Seiken had departed, the chair had vanished, it seemed they were not expecting any further company. Night had remained with them from then, his steady gaze staring out at the ever-changing scenery. When they heard only one set of footsteps, they were more than a little relieved to realise that Zo had not accompanied her. Night turned to greet her from where he had stood, silently observing the movement of the universe. He had been waiting patiently for some time. His movements remained calm despite the expected excitement, given what her return should mean.

"Ah Lain, you have returned," he glanced around. "Alone I see."

"Night," she began again. "It appears that the Grimoire never reached the shrine." She stopped to bow slightly as she stood before him, not even acknowledging the place her former comrades were held.

"So you have returned with neither the Grimoire nor my daughter. Tell me, when can I expect her?" Something about his tone made Daniel shudder.

"She will be arriving shortly, she is just attending to some personal matters I believe. She will come even without the—" Elly was cut off by Acha's forceful cry.

"Elaineor!" The power behind her voice commanded complete attention. "You betrayed us! All this time you were working for him!" Elly slowly approached the bars, remaining just out of their reach.

"With him," she corrected. "And who are you to talk about betrayal?" She moved to once more address Night. "It seems the rumours of the blood seal were nothing more than that, yet still, somewhere out there, unknown to the one who should have been guarding it, the final Grimoire awaits us. I think now would be the opportune time to return Marise. She could locate it easily, I do not see why we should delay any longer." She smiled, soon it would all be over. With Marise returned they could complete the task asked of them and then they could watch the birth of the new world.

Soon Zoella would be permanently removed from Marise. Soon they would be together again, hunting treasure and killing all who opposed them in their quest for victory. At the same time, she could not deny her feelings towards Zo. At first, she had just been an obstruction, but she had grown quite fond of the girl. Through their travels, she had shown a strength that Elly hadn't realised she possessed, regardless of this Marise was her only concern, her best friend. She could not let fleeting moments of guilt, or feelings towards the girl, destroy what she and Marise had, or the adventures which awaited them.

"A reaction I anticipated from you. Let us allow her these final moments, who knows, she might just surprise you." Night smiled.

"It will not take her long to realise she cannot find the Grimoire, then she will no doubt come in hope to retrieve her friends." Elly, for the first time, did not seem too convinced with her response. She could not estimate how long she would spend looking. It may be necessary to enforce a time limit on her. Surely, she would quickly realise how hopeless the situation was, how impossible it would be for her to locate a single book in a world filled with them. It would be a difficult task for her and Marise, but together, if they combined their resources and abilities, they would no doubt be able to find it, after all, they had located the other six. Once she realised the futility of her mission, she would come here to try and bargain for her friends' lives. She would certainly come to them, but there was no way of knowing exactly how long they would be made to wait.

Chapter 28

Darkness Falls

Zo sat alone in her cabin. It seemed that Elly had stopped here briefly before meeting her at Daniel's house. To her surprise, when she had walked through the door, she had found a fresh set of clothes awaiting her, placed where she could not fail to see them. Almost as if acknowledging her fate, once having seen to all she had needed to, she had autonomously changed into them. Sitting there now, she realised the place had never seemed so cold and empty. Even before she had met Acha, and Daniel was at college, it had never seemed so desolate. Her home had always been a place that welcomed her. Even on her first night here, it was warm and comforting, but now it almost seemed to mourn her, like it knew what would come to pass.

She scolded herself for the feelings of self-pity which spread through her. Despite her best efforts she couldn't dispel the despair. It had been much worse since returning from seeing Daniel's mother. Angela had such faith in her that there had been no question she would soon be reunited with her child. It had been difficult to maintain the enthusiastic front. She had not explained much of the situation, just that Daniel and Acha would be returning home soon. Angela had tried to make her promise that she would return to them, if only to say goodbye, but no such promise had been made. It had been difficult for Zo to reveal only as much truth as was needed, and explain how, once they were safe, she could never return in fear of the danger it would bring. Angela hadn't understood. Leaving there that final time only proved to darken her already blackened mood. She loved the people here so much, leaving the first time had been difficult enough. Her desire was to spare them any pain, but when Daniel returned with his tale, that was exactly what it would bring. It would have been better if no one had known what had happened to her, if she had simply left and never returned. At least then they all could have kept the pretence that she was alive and well. But soon things would end and the darkness it would bring was unstoppable.

There were just a few more things which needed to be taken care of, things that needed attending to while she still could, things that would, hopefully, relieve some of the burden her actions would cause. Removing the small musical ball from her cloak's pocket, she listened to its slow sombre melody, glad that Daniel had returned it to her. If he hadn't, it would have made things more difficult. Turning it over in her hands a few times, her fingers traced the intricate carvings until the music stopped. When all was silent, she spoke to herself, holding the small sphere tightly. She knew she should be preparing herself for what lay ahead, but instead continued to sit, staring into the musical ball, talking to it gently as if to offer it comfort.

"Thea." Seiken spoke softly as he gazed upon her. He was here now to present the time limit, he was to inform her that she had two hours, two tiny hours in which to find that which would free her friends. Seeing his figure appear in her doorway, she feared that sleep had taken her. It took a moment, as she unconsciously checked the surrounding energy, to realise that he had once again crossed over into their world.

"Seiken," she whispered, her voice lost for a moment in the sadness. "Seiken, am I glad to see you. It is terrible. Night has everyone, the only chance I had was lost. I did as you told me, I gathered the runes, the keys, but there is no door," Zo despaired, forcing back the tears. She knew the truth, even why he was here, but that did not make her wish to confide her feelings to him any less. Despite what he may have done, it seemed nothing could dissolve their unique bond.

"Oh, Thea," he sighed, pulling a chair across the floor to sit beside her. "I feel responsible. I brought you into all this." He couldn't help but wonder, if he had stayed away from the very beginning, things would have turned out differently. As soon as their paths crossed in Darrienia, her fate had been sealed. If only he had listened to their warnings, if only he had stayed away from her. He touched her gently, sending tingles through her hand where their skin met. It was a familiar touch, one which offered them both comfort.

"No. My father did. This whole thing was a ruse from the start." She clenched her fists beneath his touch. It seemed Seiken blamed himself, but if not for her then none of this would now be happening. It would have been better for everyone if she had never existed.

"At first," Seiken began, he knew he owed her an explanation, despite the fact she had not asked. It seemed she already knew of his deception, he could feel it. His contract with Night had reached completion, he had done everything he could to assist him in the collection of the Grimoire and manipulating the events to meet his needs. The fact that the tome had not resided in its destined place had no effect on their agreement. He was now free to speak as he saw fit, nothing he could say would change anything. He had volunteered to present the time limit in Elly's stead. It was his only chance to see her one last time. He understood that the final part of their agreement, the release of his people, would not occur until she stood before Night. At that point they would be free and both sides of the contract would have been fulfilled. But how could he tell her that he had come to ask her to walk into her own death for the sake of the Oneirois, for him? After so long of fighting to keep her alive, he would now ask for her to die. "I knew something was wrong, one by one my people seemed to disappear. Mortals, with the same marks as yourself, passed through to quest for something. I heard rumours of a game, it seemed people were wagering their life for something they desired, but with my people being free, before death could take them, they would find themselves awake and the mark would vanish."

"There have been people before? Tell me what you know of these games." She wondered if perhaps there was something that had been overlooked. She couldn't bring herself to look at him, not because of his actions, or due to what she knew he came to ask of her, it was simply an attempt to make things easier. Avoiding his gaze, her vision focused unseeingly through the window, she couldn't blame him, but wished he could have trusted her to keep her word. There was no resentment, no bitterness, with so little time left why waste it by focusing on the negative things? She was just happy to see him one more time.

"I know you can't win," he stated earnestly. He gripped her hand to offer what little comfort he could. He wanted to tell her to remain here, hide herself away and live her remaining days in peace. Who knows, maybe over time she would find the strength to reclaim that which had been taken by the darkness. He wanted to ask this of her, but he could not. Even if he did, she would refuse. She had sworn to protect her friends and Zoella Althea kept her promises, no matter the cost.

"I must, I have to find a way." Her voice filled with quiet determination as she stared at his hand upon hers.

"He has given you two hours, but even if you win, you'll still lose." Seiken felt his heart swell as the pain of his words took his voice.

"I know that!" she snapped, blushing on hearing her own harsh tones. She pulled her hand free from his touch, her voice once more softening. "I knew that when I first agreed to play." He looked at her in stunned silence. She had changed so much since they had first met. Despite being on the verge of losing herself, her inner beauty, her confidence, shone through, regardless of all she faced. He pushed the thought from his mind as quickly as it had entered. Now was not the time to contemplate his feelings for this mortal. The damage had been done and it was more than he could bear. It was too late to question his decision. He had chosen to betray the one he loved for the good of his people, and knew for their safety he would do it again.

"I'm not talking about your friends," he stated softly.

"I know." Her answer shocked him more than she had expected. "I know what I must lose, but I made a promise to save your people. I made a promise to Daniel to protect him, and to his mother that I would see that he returned safely. I will do everything within my power to make sure I adhere to those vows." It was then Seiken noticed her clothes and realised the truth. The act of changing into them had been symbolic of her acceptance of what was to come.

"How could you know?" Somehow, he had failed to notice before, but she truly knew the price. It begged the question of how she came to know the cost of that never spoken to her. The prophecy was sealed within his own world, none but his people knew of it.

"I knew from the moment I saw you that it could only end one way. It started a long time ago, it seems like forever as I sit here now. I was about seven, the other children hated me because they knew I was different. They would tease and bully me, mostly because I spent so much time with Amelia.

"She had been the village witch before Hectarian powers vanished. Although she could no longer perform Hectarian magic, she taught me how to use mine. Step by step she guided me through incantations, potions, charms, everything. I was different, and that was why they hated me.

"I remember one day she had been teaching me the theory behind herbal lore. I was so excited at the thought of trying it that as soon as the lesson was over, I rushed straight to the forest. But the other children were already there waiting for me. That was the first time I saw you. I ran to the lake, it is only a small island, like here in so many ways. I sat washing myself. I was only young and already I saw how upset it made my mother when she saw how the other children treated me, so I had quickly become skilled at hiding it.

"I sat crying quietly into the lake as I washed my muddy clothes. It was then I heard the gentlest voice, a voice so soft and pure it seemed to be that of the lake itself. It whispered words of comfort, but as I looked to thank it for its words, there was a clear circle upon its wind rippled surface. Within it, I saw your face, exactly as you are now, you haven't aged a day." She paused; it seemed Elly was not the only one who never aged, the Oneiroi before her also shared that trait. She smiled as she fondly remembered. "I saw a beautiful land behind you, filled with bird song and trees, it seemed so peaceful."

"You could see me?" Seiken interrupted, he felt himself blush. His magic was meant to be one way, a means to look out, but somehow it seemed that all this time she had seen him.

"That wasn't the only time. I have vague recollections of fading dreams, and whenever I was sad or lonely, I would see your face." She paused thinking back, she remembered but snippets, but felt through them the importance of these stolen moments and the bond that grew through them. "The last time I remember, before we met in person, was just after I had been taken to Blackwood," she stated. She knew this would not have been the last time their paths had crossed, it had become apparent that it was his magic which had combined with her own to seal Aburamushi. Even if she couldn't recall these events, it seemed he had been protecting her through the darkness. "I was so homesick. I hated it there so much. I was alone, studying all the time and, despite my hopes of meeting others like myself, I was the only person studying, with the exception of trainee guards. I sat in my room that evening brushing my hair over and over in the mirror trying to capture the scents of home, the next thing I knew, I saw you.

"This time it seemed you were sitting in a large room, although I couldn't see much as the mirror seemed to face the door. I watched you watching me, just behind you someone entered, along with what I thought at the time to be his pet cat. I tried to warn you, but it was too late, before I could speak the hand had gripped your shoulder." Zo paused thinking back, from Seiken's expression she knew he too remembered this night well...

..."You spend too much time watching this mortal. Your obsession has become unhealthy." The man whose hand rested on Seiken's shoulder seemed angry. This man was Seiken's father, the ruler of Crystenia. "If ever your two paths cross here outside a dream, she will lose everything. I forbid you from using this kind of magic. For both your sakes, leave her be." The figure was every inch the image expected of a king who was fit to defend their homeland in battle. He was built as a warrior in both size and physique, his rich brown hair fell just below his shoulders, it shook side to side with the disappointed motion of his head as he addressed his son.

The small black and white cat, which had accompanied him, jumped upon the table to sit before the mirror. Although it spoke only in its native tongue, all, including Zo, had understood the words he spoke.

"You must be aware of the prophecy, the prophets told of the meeting of two, a mortal from Gaea's star and a prince from ours. The Chosen will be unable to escape their fate. A challenge will occur where to live is to win, but to win is to lose all."...

...Zo looked to Seiken meaningfully as she finished her tale of what she had witnessed. She knew from his expression that he too clearly remembered that moment. Knowing this, she spoke the remaining words of the prophecy aloud for the first time.

"To live is to win, but to win is to lose all. One shall be lost to Night," she paused.

"The other will lose everything and be lost to the darkness." Seiken finished, at the time he hadn't realised the 'Night' Rowmeow had referred to was a being. As he was reminded of these words, they scared him. He had spoken a similar prediction himself to Daniel, not recalling the words had been from a prophecy. His throat swelled as he fought to retain his composure. She had known this, she knew and still pushed on, knowing she would lose from the start. Seiken wondered: If he had been in her position; if he had known that to accept their challenge was to accept his death, whether he could have still agreed.

He looked at her searchingly, they both knew what lay ahead. She had known all along it would end this way, so, why, why had she agreed, knowing what the cost would be?

"Why did you watch me when I was upset?" she questioned gently. He seemed to have grown deathly pale as he realised the extent of his betrayal. He had not just misled her, he had guided her into the prophecy, and his betrayal meant she would sacrifice everything.

"I watched you always, Thea. I found you intriguing." Smiling at his words, she passed him a small pouch containing the runes that they had worked so hard to retrieve. "How could you agree to play their game if you knew, why would you make that promise, knowing the cost?"

"I don't remember much, but I know I owe you this much, if not more. The door these will now open is not one I can reach. It is a door which leads from Night's world to yours." She sealed his fingers around the bag holding his hand for a moment longer than was necessary.

"Thea, there is no door." Zo simply smiled, taking a mirror from the table. She waved her hand over it to reveal the place Seiken's people were being held.

"You realise, I learnt this from you." She had seen him do it so many times, she wondered if she could use the same magic he did. She tried and studied until finally, one day, she too could see to another place, as long as a surface could hold a reflection. "Seiken, magic is a wondrous thing, you have it yourself, yet for some reason you have always used mine." It wasn't a question, but Seiken answered anyway. He was surprised she had realised, every time he had helped them it had been by tapping into her own powers to use them as if they were his own.

"After my father caught me once more ignoring his wishes, he banned me from using magic. He took it from me and passed it to Rowmeow, who has guarded it since. He always told me, he would know when the time came to return it," he sighed. "I can only utilise other people's now, that's how I could help you all those..." He paused as he decided not to continue, she already knew he used her powers, if he left the sentence there, she would just think he meant during this journey. He had doubts even now that the divide between Zo and Marise had degraded enough to allow her to recall the era of darkness, a time when their paths had once more been intertwined.

"I see, well take these runes and place them in these five points," she pointed to a wall. "I have empowered them so that they will link together to create a door for you, but they must be placed in the exact order, ask Rowmeow to restore your powers, if he will not, simply speak these words." She handed him a small piece of paper, on it was a small diagram and the incantation he would need. "This will invoke the pentagram to summon a door which will lead to your world."

"But how is that possible?" He had been certain there had been no way to leave their captivity. The enchantment she spoke of was a knowledge possessed only by immortal beings. It was something that, within the confines of the prison, none of their race had been able to successfully create. The magic needed to conjure the doorway's foundation had been repressed within their holding cell, if these runes truly possessed the magic to create it, he could take his people home. It was far better they believed her to have rescued them, than realise the truth of his actions.

"Night's tower does not exist in this world, or any. It is beyond reach, existing in no one world, just like Olympus. By using this you're simply activating a passage to the dormant world by awakening the part of Night's tower which exists within Darrienia." She watched as Seiken's eyes grew wide in surprise. It was impossible that she could know how to do this. He had only seen it described in one place before, in an ancient diagram found within Crystenia.

"How do you know this?" He rose to his feet, as much as he wanted to stay and remain in her presence longer it was time for him to leave. He could not be selfish, he could not let her waste her final hours with him when she should be searching for the means to free her friends. On his return he could liberate his people, even should his actions be discovered, he knew that Night would allow this, there was nothing left to lose.

"I read it once, any five objects could be used, but since we went to all the trouble of getting these..." she didn't continue, she didn't feel the need to. "Seiken, please tell my friends I will be there shortly." She spoke the words so he would not have to.

"I..." he lowered his gaze to the floor. He felt ashamed at having let her down after she had tried so hard. If he had just waited, had more faith, then she would have fulfilled her promise after all, but it didn't matter now, it was too late. His actions, his impatience, had firmly sealed her fate. She was the one he had wanted to protect more than anything, yet by his own actions he sealed her fate.

"Seiken, it's okay, you did what you had to, what was expected, as did I. Now once more I must do the same." She smiled, gently turning her gaze back to the parchment on the table. With his business concluded she expected him to have vanished. She tapped the pen on it before signing her name, she would need to use one last bit of magic to ensure it didn't arrive until this was over.

"My people." His voice startled her as the letter dispersed into the air, she had been so convinced he had left she hadn't felt the need to confirm it. "They thrive in your world's darkness, perhaps I could visit you." Seiken spoke softly, his voice barely above a whisper.

"That—" she began, her words silenced as his cold hands touched her face. He lifted her chin gently as he leaned towards her. She felt his lips on hers with gentle pressure. He pulled away, tears hanging in his eyes as, before her gaze, he vanished.

She thought about what Seiken had said, wondering if he knew that once Marise appeared this time, the person he knew would no longer exist. She would simply cease to be. The darkness she would be forced into would not be the same as her former prison, it would be the dark void of nothingness, of non-existence. She touched her lips still blushing. She had done everything she needed to, she reached inside her discarded trousers to remove the small box the echo of the ancient had presented her with. As she opened it, it seemed almost as if it held the sky itself, the white clouds spilling out to surround her. As the white blanket embraced her, she heard the ancient's voice.

"Did you find your answer?"

"Yes, everything you said was correct. I never did believe his stories." She smiled, as a feeling of weightlessness drifted over her. The echo of the ancient had given her the answer quite plainly. He couldn't return her friends because the home of a god was outside his reach and the location of the Grimoire was beyond his field of vision.

* * *

Anticipation seemed to fill the air with tiny sparks of electricity, sending tingles across the flesh of all within the room. The stage had changed, the almost casual atmosphere filled with tension.

"Zoella Althea." As Night spoke her name, Daniel rose to see her approach. Even from this distance, through the bars of the prison, it was difficult not to notice the change. Her hair seemed almost red now, a shade which had been gradually becoming more apparent as they travelled. The once subtle copper lowlights seem to have overpowered her own tones, as if displaying a physical manifestation of her inner struggle. The fact that she now wore the clothes of that murderer only emphasised these changes. He gave a heavy sigh, Night had been right after all, she *had* come, and she had done so empty-handed. He shuddered to think of what she had decided to offer him in exchange for their safety.

On entering, her gaze only briefly scanned the magnificent room. She did not pay attention to her surroundings, or to Night and Elly who stood in the centremost position. Her vision's sole focus was upon her friends trapped within the small prison. It seemed alien in the now otherwise empty room. She paid Night no heed as she rushed towards them to place her hand over Daniel's as he stood gripping the bars, so tightly his knuckles had turned white. She cared little that both Night and Elly awaited her attention. She would get to them in time. First, she had to ensure her friends were safe, that no harm had come to them.

"Zo, you came," he whispered sadly. He had known she would, yet this did not stop him from hoping otherwise. He had hoped that, regardless of what it meant for them, she would, for once, be selfish and act in her own best interests. It had been the best opportunity she would be given, she was free from Elly, and there was no one to force her hand into submission.

"Of course I did." He cringed to see her smile. It was *that* smile, the one she had used so often to cover her pain. The once powerful barricades which sealed him from her inner thoughts had grown fragile. He was certain that, should he try, he could easily penetrate them, but he would respect her wishes, her privacy. He could already feel her fear as her cold hand on his trembled slightly. Seeing her now reminded him of something his father had said a long time ago. Something he had never really observed until now, *'Being brave and having courage is doing something despite being afraid,'* and that was exactly what she was doing. He couldn't help but notice there seemed to be something more to her fear than just facing Night. When the time came, he was sure she would tell him, perhaps it was the fear of losing the battle to Marise. It was difficult not to see the changes she had suffered since he had last seen her. Now more than ever, although it was his friend who stood before them, she looked almost like Marise.

Night stood waiting patiently until she turned to address him. He had waited this long, a few more minutes were of no consequence, especially when everything he sought would soon be within his grasp. Looking upon him, she tried to extinguish the fear she now felt towards the stranger who had helped them through their journey. Someone she had once felt so safe and secure with, now brought out the most deep rooted fear she had ever experienced.

"I knew that I recognised you," she said coldly, finally turning her attention to him. She wondered just how much her companions knew. It didn't matter now anyway, it would all be over soon. Her friends surely realised this even if they hadn't admitted it to themselves yet, just by looking at her it was apparent how short her remaining time was. "As a child I was always told such great stories about you. Mum told me my father was a great practitioner of the artes, that he left in order to protect us. I had never seen your face then, in the Perpetual Forest I saw a sketch from my childhood." She pulled the tattered drawing from the waistline of her tasset, the same sketch which Acha had handed her outside the forest.

In the drawing, Night was smiling as he stood behind her mother, one arm wrapped around her, the other placed tenderly on his unborn child.

"There you were, the stranger who, over the last few weeks, always seemed to save me. I was told my father was filled with wonderful ideas, how wonderful do you think she'd find them now? Maybe I should have told her, but I was scared, scared if you realised I was there you would hurt her too." She screwed the paper up, throwing it aggressively towards him, but being so light it failed to even reach him.

Night picked it up from the floor, carefully unfolding it to admire the drawing upon its surface, as he looked at it, he smiled. There was something sad, almost lonely, in the expression. It was there but for a moment then, just like the picture, it vanished.

"Now there would be a trick worthy of Hades himself," Night goaded, his expression was as cold as his tone as all signs of weakness had vanished.

"What?" Zo challenged.

"Well, if you can bring her back from the grave then I will gladly listen to anything you have to say."

"The... grave?" Zo questioned, as she fought to regain her breath, she couldn't be dead, could she? No, it was a trick, it had to be. If something like that had happened, surely she would remember. The impact of his words had struck so hard that she didn't hear Daniel call her name as she sunk to her knees before the god.

"Oh, what's the matter, don't you remember?" he stated bitterly. "I remember it perfectly. You failed to protect her, just like you failed to protect your friends."

"Protect her? I don't understand," she whispered.

"Don't listen, Zo, he's lying. Mr Venrent would have told you. He's just toying with you." The words barely registered as Daniel called out to her.

"Mr Venrent?" Night questioned. "Eryx would no more tell you than he would help you."

"You're wrong," Zo cried. She couldn't believe how pathetic she felt. How his mere words had reduced her to her knees. It was ridiculous, just like when she knelt before the statue in Crowley, her trembling legs disobeyed her command to stand. It was like a physical reminder of how weak she had become. It was all she could do to retain control, all she could do to hang on to existence a moment longer, she had to. "Mr Venrent loved my mother, he'd do anything to help me."

"You're right, he did love your mother. So much so that he crossed from Darrienia to be with her. He threatened to reveal my identity and endanger your lives further. I did what was needed to ensure that never happened. I arranged for him to give you the potion, he didn't do it to help you, quite the contrary. In return he got both his sight and youth restored." Night smiled. "You failed to save your mother. You failed to protect her, do you intend to repeat the same mistake here?" Zo opened her mouth as if to speak, there was a brief pause as she changed her mind about what she would say.

"If you loved my mother so much, why didn't *you* save her?" But before he could answer, Elly interrupted, this conversation was getting serious. If they went into the details, only the Gods knew what could happen. Losing Kezia had wounded Night more than anything she had seen, and she had seen a great deal, after all, she had served him since he had shed his forced mortality. She had never seen a god in such turmoil, her death had devastated him. Simply abandoning their life together had driven him to face those he knew would seal his powers, and this had been far worse.

"I see you came empty-handed," Elly interrupted approaching cautiously as Zo knelt on the floor before her father. Just by looking at her, Elly could already see she had surrendered. Even if she hadn't, there was so little left that she didn't have the strength to resist anymore. Her very existence held on by an already fraying thread. Night's tale had weakened her resistance, he had bluntly stated something she had repressed for so long. She would gladly do as they wished to ensure her friends' safety, especially now. Elly smiled triumphantly, she may not possess the Grimoire, but there was another task this faltering life-force could accomplish.

"No," Zo stated soberly. "I had what *he* wanted all along. I just never re-alised it. I was given it years ago by an amazing person, he was filled with such wondrous stories about everything. Even his firewood was enchanted." She looked at Daniel meaningfully, in response he clutched her satchel pro-tectively. He understood completely, she was buying them time. She would bargain for their freedom, and in order to retrieve the book in their pos-session, Night would have to release them. It was then, on discovering this deception, they would make their final stand against him.

"Impossible, we would have known if it was in your possession," she snapped stepping forwards as if to challenge her. Her advance was blocked as Night stepped between them.

"Lain, leave us," he commanded. She opened her mouth as if to object, but instead simply turned sharply and left the room. What did it matter whether she was buying time or truly did have what they sought? It would all finish the same way, even now Marise tore her way to the surface extinguishing all remaining light. Soon there would be nothing left. "The Grimoire?" he prompted.

There had been a strange commotion from the prison where the Oneirois had been restrained. Night knew, although his daughter now appeared to stare through the window into the vast landscape of Tartarus, that it was not the nightmarish image her vision found. She was ensuring they had the chance to utilise the escape she had prepared. The scenery through Night's windows constantly shifted as parts of the tower phased through all realities and all dimensions. It seemed fitting that this was the landscape witnessing these final moments.

"It appears you could have helped them after all." Night had known she would, given time, devise the means to assist them; but in order to ensure the prophecy was realised, he had to ensure events were guided before the chance of another option could even have been considered. As soon as Seiken had agreed to Night's trade, all was predetermined. "It was pointless really, they would have been free in just a moment, after all, he did fulfil *his* side of the bargain. Still it was an ingenious plan, I expected nothing less from my own flesh and blood. Now about the Grimoire," he pressed, wondering if it could truly be within her possession. He could not feel its presence but her eyes held no sign of deception.

"There's one slight problem." She pulled herself to her feet slowly. Her body tried to object but this time she refused to give in. She pushed it harder, glancing towards the cage. "It is in there." She pointed much to the surprise of both Acha and Eiji. "Although I could ask for it to be handed to me, if I were to do so there is no guarantee you would release them, so here are my conditions.

"A fair trade. My friends go free and you are *not* to harm them, the same applies to Seiken and his people. In exchange, I will not only give you the tome I have, I will release it for you. That is what you want is it not?" She knew he wanted it to be her that released the book. He could threaten her friends, but she was confident he would agree to her demands. He wouldn't lose anything, he would just gain her cooperation.

"Zo what are you doing?" Daniel interjected, as Acha and Eiji exchanged puzzled glances. It was just as he expected, this ruse would give them the chance they needed. It was essential that he assisted her by any means possible.

"That seems fair, and you will release the Grimoire, you understand what that means?" he questioned, despite knowing that she did, he was unsure why he even asked.

"I know." The prison swelled and deformed, the bars vanishing as the gaping hole distorted from behind, forcing her friends from it as it vanished to leave only the solid wall in its stead. They rushed to her at great speed as they tried to place themselves between her and Night, fearing that it would do little good. Daniel looked for the opening they needed to make their retreat, it was preferential to facing a god.

"You really are your mother's child," Night smiled; he would allow them these few moments. Daniel embraced her tightly with little concern regarding the spasms of pain he caused through her shoulder. He held her so tightly, she thought he would never let go.

"Why did you have to come?" he whispered sadly as he held her. At least now they were free, they could protect her. Surely united together they could escape the clutches of this god. It would be their most difficult challenge yet, but he was certain they could do it. There was nothing they couldn't overcome together.

Zo knew none of them had fully grasped the situation. They still anticipated a final battle, a last chance to foil the plan of this being. They didn't realise it was a strength she no longer possessed, even now the final pieces of the fraying thread which allowed her to continue her existence had begun to break. If nothing else, at least she could take Marise with her in this final act. She just needed to hold on until the rite's words were completed, then she could release her fragile grasp on the world, leaving Marise to pay the price of her actions. Their misinterpretation of the situation was a small comfort to her at this moment. Daniel was so relieved to see her safe, he didn't understand what she had agreed to; nor had he noticed the subtle movements she made to remove him from between her and Night as they had embraced.

"I have every faith in you Daniel Eliot." She smiled pulling away, her fingers skilfully sliding her satchel from his grip. It was then he caught a glimpse of a thought she had tried to keep sheltered, but as the hold on herself faded so did her ability to shield the truth. She saw the fear and questions which clearly lined his pale features as he stared at her in horror.

"What have you done?" he questioned in a stunned whisper, her hand squeezed his shoulder gently, sliding down to his chest. By the time he realised what was about to happen it was once more too late. The force of the blow propelled him backwards in an all too familiar fashion, his body colliding with his friends. Their eyes filled with questions as they struggled to their feet. They were meant to face this threat together, to overcome his evil. That was what heroes did, against the odds they would win. What was she thinking? Zo looked to them apologetically as the air between them shimmered, her action leaving them with only one route accessible, their escape.

Daniel tried to catch his breath as his world spun slightly, winded by her sudden attack. He approached the field in disbelief, trying desperately to push against it, to pass through it like Elly had previously, but it firmly blocked his way, it blocked the path between them. Both Zo and Night were out of their reach. He thought this had been nothing more than a ruse. He had been wrong.

Kneeling on the floor, Zo glanced towards her friends as she began to empty the contents of her satchel, wondering why she was being so careful, after this, she would have no use for them, like her, they would be forgotten. Night placed his hand on her shoulder encouragingly as he felt her hesitation, but Daniel saw the hidden meaning behind the gesture, he was showing them his claim on her. He looked to Daniel and began to explain.

"Every time a Grimoire is located, it must first be released before its power returns to me. In the past, I have just had messengers bring it to me and read the incantations written upon its surface. Although their pronunciation lacked finesse, the desired effects were brought to fruition. The tomes were sealed with a life, as such the cost to reverse it is the same. This is the only way to release a spell formed by the sacrifice of another." Daniel banged against the barrier trying desperately to break its seals as Zo shifted her position to turn her back to him. Fresh tears filled her eyes as she felt the rawness of his pain through their bond. In order to do what she needed to, she had to look away.

'*Is that what you've agreed to?*' his voice screamed to her mind, fear and anger mingled through the challenge of his thoughts. '*Is it?*' he demanded.

'*To win, I have to lose,*' she replied simply; there was a sound of tearing as she split the lining of the bag. This was another line she had heard before, the prophecy in its entirety was built on small fragments, those within Seiken's world and those within their own.

"What's she doing? I emptied it back at the Perpetual Forest, there's nothing in there," Eiji stressed, but seeing her actions made him recall the weight of the empty satchel. All too soon he realised what it meant. He looked to Daniel in horror, surely there was some mistake.

"Daniel, you always said I would lose something in there." She pulled a small rectangular object from the bag, covered in a finely embroidered white cloth. This cloth had probably been the reason it had been concealed all this time. It had been on this fabric that she had spent hours recalling the various shielding and protection charms. She had valued this gift so much that it seemed only fitting to use this to keep it safe during her travels. If not for this, she was certain they would have realised it was in their possession sooner. She turned her head slightly to look at him, it was a gesture she could not maintain for long. "I left it there for safe keeping, and well, I guess I forgot about it." She had made a deliberate choice to bring it with her, securing it, as always, inside the lining of her satchel for safekeeping. That way no matter where she went, it would be close to her, a keepsake to remind her of home, but never had she thought that this battered faded notebook could be of any real importance.

"That's—" Daniel gasped, unable to believe that she had within her possession the desperately sought Grimoire. He couldn't believe she had spoken the truth, he was certain she had simply been stalling. It wasn't possible, it seemed to defy all logic that something of such power had been in their possession all along. Even if his life depended on it, he would not allow her to do this, not if it meant losing her, that was after all the intended outcome, to win she had to lose everything. He thrust himself against the barrier with such force the impact knocked him from his feet. If she gave him the final Grimoire then she was doing exactly what Night had expected of her, choosing those she cared for most over the needs of the many. That wasn't the way it was meant to be, they were meant to face this threat together.

"The book that Elder Robert gave me for saving his life? Yes." She smiled, softly looking towards them once more. As long as they were safe, she could do this. Turning to face Night she rose to her feet, the Grimoire now clasped in her trembling hands.

"Damn it, Zoella!" Daniel snapped striking the barrier with his weapon. He couldn't understand why Eiji and Acha weren't helping him. If they could shatter this protection, they could still save her. "I made a promise, don't you make me out to be a liar," he warned. She did not turn back to look at him.

"Daniel, you kept your word, I never lost myself." Eiji grabbed him before he struck out again.

"Damn it Zo, that's not—" He stopped; his words froze in his throat as she slowly opened the book. The air seemed to grow heavy.

"Daniel, don't," Eiji whispered. "Don't make this any harder on her." It was only then he realised why they had not intervened. Nothing they could do would change things, not in the way they wanted. He hadn't wanted to accept what his eyes had been telling him. His best friend had been dying for a long time as Marise extinguished her light with the darkness. He had forced himself to believe that, no matter what, Zo would have somehow been able to repel the stifling darkness that consumed her. But she had known the truth, known that there was no glorious victory awaiting her and now, her final act was to sacrifice what little fragment of herself remained to save them.

In the presence of her father, the once faded writing on the book's yellowed pages began to grow darker as blood red ink bled onto the page to reveal the words in the ancient text. Taking a deep breath, she once more comforted herself with the thoughts of the happiness she had known. Happiness she would never have experienced if not for all the darkness. Without Marise she would never have found herself on Crowley, she would have stayed in Drevera, never knowing friendship. She would never have picnicked or shared stories with friends, she would never have lived, and although the darkness is what brought her to this moment, she was truly glad that she could die having lived, rather than lived as if she were dead. Her mind now calm, she began to read.

There was only one spell within this book, the one to release the powers sealed within it. A bright light encompassed her as she recited the ancient text. The foreign words sounded like poetry to those who listened. She paused briefly, turning back to take one last look at her friends, she gave them a warm smile closing her eyes before saying the only remaining words, then finally, she allowed herself to let go.

"Díno ti zoí mou." Which, in the ancient language, translated to mean, for this I pledge my life. Although there were many different interpretations it always resulted in a sacrifice of some kind for the one who had spoken them. It was a vow repeated by those pledging their service to another. Daniel had never realised until now they had been words spoken from a Hectarian spell, a spell to trade a life for a cause.

Throughout the room the sound of whispers seemed to fill the air. As the final words were spoken, all of them heard a gleeful sound, although but a whisper it called to their hearts.

'*And that makes three.*' Somewhere in the distance, the shrine of Geburah crumbled.

The light, which surrounded Zo faded, transferring through the air into Night. As his powers returned, the words of the ancients whispered on an imaginary breeze that swept over all present.

A strange smoke filled the air, in that split second Daniel swore he saw another figure join her, its hand plunging into her chest. She faltered, jolting back under the force of the pressure, as the hand pulled back, her body followed its movement until another figure shared the smoke. It collapsed forwards towards the one who had removed it, before both vanished.

The air around them cleared, as the smoke faded, so too did the field erected by Zo. The two remaining figures turned to look upon them, but the one who stood with Night, was no longer their friend. Even with Zo's sacrifice, Marise had remained.

"Oh, I guess I should have mentioned," Night said in an artificial tone of forgetfulness. "It's just a small thing really." He smiled placing his arm around Marise, "I promised *I* wouldn't hurt you," Daniel felt himself gasp as Marise turned to look at them. Unlike before, not a trace of Zo remained. As she stood there now, she looked like an angel of death. "But I never did mention anything about anyone else." He looked from Marise to them meaningfully. "Are you still here?" he questioned, watching in amusement as the three of them found the strength to run. He would let them leave, he owed them that much at least. He would even let them return to their own world when they left his tower.

"I have just confirmed all seven of the barriers in Darrienia were completely destroyed in both worlds." Elly re-entered the room in time to see Zo's friends leave with haste. "Mari!" she exclaimed joyfully.

"Lee." Marise acknowledged her presence as she watched the space where Daniel had stood only moments ago, she was going to enjoy this.

"Does this mean?" Elly embraced her gently for a brief moment. She looked different. Now there was no trace of Zo she seemed more powerful, more complete.

"She is gone for good." Marise smiled pulling the leather tie from her hair and running her fingers through its fiery red shades. "Zoella Althea is gone for good. Hades himself collected her," she stated, raising her hand to touch where his hand had penetrated to tear the life-force from her. She was glad he had taken her. For a moment she feared the hand was reaching for her instead, which had no doubt been her plan. Despite Zo's attempt to let go and fade from existence before the reaper came, something had kept her here, almost as if she had still been connected with something of this world; something which had acted as a tether refusing to release her, and so, there had been just enough of her left to satisfy the cost. Had there been a fraction less, it would have taken her as Zoella faded into non-existence. Marise doubted that her survival had been part of her plan. Zoella had been certain that she would fade, leaving Marise to pay the dues.

"For a moment, I must admit I had my doubts," Elly admitted adjusting Marise's hair slightly.

Night retrieved the open Grimoire from the floor, it had fallen where Zo had last stood, just to the side of Marise, who looked to him with excitement as she eagerly awaited her instructions. Night was, after all, so much more imaginative than Blackwood.

A look of concern crossed her eyes. Her thoughts of Zoella had made her question something, she drew her weapon. The sword was magical in nature, thus it was possible that her favoured blade—forged by the combination of their magic and essences—had ceased to be, now that one of the life-forces had been extinguished. She breathed a sigh of relief as the blade appeared after only a short delay. Even if her disappearance had not affected the blade, she had her concerns that Zoella would have found a way to destroy it, had the thought crossed her mind, she would have.

"Well," she stated, her sword still drawn, "I think they have had a large enough head start."

"Before that." Night raised his hand, a single motion which prevented her from taking another step. "There is something else you need to attend to." Elly nodded; this wasn't concluded until one final task had been completed. Elly linked Marise, escorting her from the room. She glanced back at Night before she left, she couldn't help thinking, that for someone who had just achieved everything he desired, he didn't seem content.

*   *   *

Night stood at the window, watching his daughter's friends as they fled across the open plains towards the entrance of Collateral. Their adventure had been the most exciting yet, ending with his victory. The previous people he had sent to Darrienia were merely pawns, sacrificial pieces used to test the effectiveness of his musings, their tasks paling in comparison to the true objective of his game. But now there were more pressing matters to attend to, he had to pay a visit to an old friend. Despite what Elly and Marise thought, things were far from over.

Chapter 29

Repercussions

They had scarcely reached Zo's cabin from the entrance of Collateral when the tremors began. The ground shook with such unexpected force, such power, that it knocked them from their feet. The ground beneath them split and rose as if some mighty beast tried to force its way free from the depths of the underworld.

"What was that?" Acha gasped, struggling to her feet to follow Daniel into what had been Zo's home. He hesitated at the door. Even now he could see her rushing around, bottling herbs, and preparing food for their picnics. The image distorted as another tremor shook him back to reality, forcing him to lose the fantasy he had so desperately fought to retain. "Eiji, what's happening?" Acha cried. She hoped Eiji would possess some insight into the situation, he was more in tune with nature, with the environment, than any of them. The furniture vibrated as the impact of another shockwave forced it across the wooden floor. They knew they had to take shelter, the worst was yet to come.

"I think..." he paused; it was better to explain the entire story. "A long time ago, my master told me a story, I thought it nothin' but fiction t'explain why the magic between us and Hectarians was different. Before the world we know, the races before us sealed away a magical power, I guess it was the Severaine. It was a raw magic that ran riot. Durin' that time, it was we who served the land and lived at the mercy of its every whim.

"One day the Gods, swayed by the words of Gaea and Hecate, allowed man t'seal it. They created nine seals across the world. Seven were said t'be

715

so strong that they crossed over t'another world, the world of dreams. It was said this occurred because everyone dreamt of this peaceful world, and these barriers were said t'be the strongest of all." Eiji realised, as he said this, that there had only been seven fixed points in Darrienia and two of these did not possess runes. Seiken had mentioned that there had been others who had journeyed there before them, perhaps this had been their doing. Whatever the reason, when they passed through these areas, the remaining energy had dissipated, destroying what remained of the seal's delicate threads. He knew they had been destroyed, after all, the map of Darrienia they had received from Seiken was now completely blank. "The strongest barriers were held not only by magic, but the will of the people who believed in the world they were tryin' t'create, each seal was home t'a key aspect of the world itself, an aspect of the nature contained within the Severaine.

"Before they managed t'seal it completely, it sent forth a huge power which changed the shape of the planet. Lands sunk and continents rose, the earth spat fire and almost all life was purged. The survivors were said t'be people who, despite the age of technology, still knew how t'live with the land, they devised their own means of livin' with the world, and thus the force passed them over.

"When the Severaine was sealed, the power between the Elementalists and Hectarians began t'alter. It became apparent this energy had been the source of the Elementalists abilities, and since Elementalists are only able t'learn from another, when the world was destroyed a large portion of the magic they used was destroyed with it. This meant they could only utilise powers of the basic elements around them, earth, air, fire, and water."

Eiji knew the story had been altered through the course of history, but for so long he had thought it nothing more than a fairytale. The story he recited was a combination of the various events throughout the history of the planet from its creation. Few were aware of the numerous cycles which stretched behind them, the numerous times the Severaine had devastated the lands before being restrained, after all, its release signified the end of an era. Its purpose was to purge and heal the poison, and shape the face of the new world as a new ruler found themselves upon the Throne of Eternity.

Old scriptures, such as the tales of Kronos overthrowing his own father Uranus, were no longer told, nor were the tales that came before those. The Severaine was the great destroyer of history. Since its initial imprisonment, the Severaine had bound itself to the Throne of Eternity. Each time a new god seized control, its seal would shatter and its powers would be unleashed. It did not matter if it had been sealed by god or man, the only difference being, anything created by the hands of man could also be destroyed by it, which was why they now faced the issue of its release without Zeus having lost his position.

"What's this got to do with the tremors?" Acha braced herself as the earth rumbled and trembled beneath their feet.

"Well, Seiken told us we had destroyed the barriers. I'm willing t'bet the reason Marise didn't follow us was so she could finish what we started by collapsin' the final seals. The problem bein'," Eiji found himself having to raise his voice over the volume of the earthquake. "If the stories are true, the Severaine has been sealed for aeons, I bet the runes we collected also acted as a cushion t'prevent these powers bein' absorbed.

"But, since we destroyed them, the power will be returnin' t'the Severaine and I think that's what's causin' this shift in the elements." Eiji released the wall as the tremor subsided. "But if that is the case, it could mean the very end of existence." He looked to Daniel desperately, if his theories were correct, the release of the Severaine meant the beginning of the end, for everything. At the best they could hope for years, at the worst, weeks maybe months. It all depended on the power this force currently held. "Daniel were there any other theories? Please tell me I'm wrong, Daniel!" Eiji shouted, he shouted not to be heard over the noise of the pounding barrage of rain, but to encourage his friend to listen. His words seemed to fall on deaf ears as Daniel focused his attention on a small sphere that had found his hand as he sat against the wall. Finally he shook his head. As the next tremor struck, a tiny sound could be heard, hearing its music Daniel finally found the strength to talk. The swelling in his throat making the words difficult to force.

"Eiji, is there anything we can do to stop this?" Daniel's voice seemed hoarse and alien to their ears.

"Unless we knew." The tremors stopped, Eiji lowered his voice. "Unless we knew where t'find the final two seals and face Marise, we've no chance, but—" Before he could continue, Daniel had risen to his feet, his angry stride filled with determination as he left the safety of the shelter.

"Maybe we can find the answer in Darrienia?" Acha pulled her sleeve up sharply, as if to demonstrate the point, but only rain streaked skin met her gaze where the branded flesh had once borne the mark. Daniel wasn't listening anyway, he had already left. This was not how it was going to end. He would not accept it. Even if it cost him his life, he would change it, somehow.

"Brace y'self," Eiji called, feeling another tremor stir deep within the land. The rain, as quickly as it had started, stopped. The sky was once more blue, the sodden ground the only visible evidence the rain had even fallen.

"Daniel, you can't go out there. You don't even know where to look." Acha called after him. Eiji wrestled with the door against the strength of the wind, its power so great that its attempt to rip it from the frame had started to warp and buckle the wood under the sheer force. He could see Daniel being battered by the violent gale as he walked away, his arms crossed and his head down as his cloak whipped around him so fiercely it threatened to choke him.

"Daniel," he called, but with the sheer force of the howling winds he wondered if the cries had even reached his ears. "Daniel," he yelled again, quickening his pace as he pursued. The sky grew dark so quickly it was almost as if all light had been extinguished. The blue sky turned black within a matter of seconds, and another torrential downpour began. "Daniel," he said again, his hand grabbing his shoulder. As soon as the first drop of rain fell they were soaked to the bone by the wall of water which hit them, each drop falling with so much force it felt like hail. "I was wrong, it's t'late. The final seals have already been broken. That's why this is happening. Can't y' feel it? It's already t'late," Eiji stated; he felt a great energy gathering around a force which seemed to continually grow in strength as it prepared to step into their world once more.

"I, I can't just do nothing." His whisper was almost lost in the violent winds and drumming rain. The sky above them was now completely black, lit only by the frequent flashes of lightning, the thunder roared with such force the ground trembled.

"Y' right," Eiji shouted over the wind. "Y' need t'help the people down there, help them secure against the storm, help the men build guards against the raging tides of the rivers and seas. Daniel, y' need t'help y' family."

"But—" His protest was cut short by Eiji's angry interruption.

"But nothin'! Zo promised y' mother y' would return, do y' wanna make her a liar? Do y' think she did everythin' she did just so y' could throw y' life away? No, she did everythin' she could t'keep her promises, but the last one she made, it is up t'y' t'fulfil. She couldn't take y' back herself," he screamed. Daniel looked at him as he truly understood his words.

"Let's go," he said slowly. He wanted to hunt down the people responsible for this and make them suffer like he did now, but Eiji was correct, there was nothing he could do. He had faced Marise before, it would be suicide, but there were people here right now who could use his help. He could always leave later. Eiji was right, he had to show his mother that Zo had been true to her word, and he had to help save those who this whole journey started out to protect, the people of his home. If not for her love for them she would never have left with Elly, none of this would have happened. For him to selfishly stand by and watch that which she had cherished so much be reduced to nothing, so that he could throw his own life away for a chance of revenge, would make her very angry.

He could not lose sight of the things that were important, and for now, it was to safeguard his home and to protect those whom Zo had wished to. He would protect them with the same effort and determination she had placed into their journey.

* * *

"Daniel." His mother met him at the door, she threw her arms around him to embrace him tightly as she kissed him on the forehead. He tried to pull away which only succeeded in making her grip him even tighter. She looked behind him to see who had followed him home. "Where's Zo?" she asked softly. The last time she had seen her, she had seemed to carry the weight of the world on her shoulders. She had spoken of not returning in fear of putting people in further danger, saying she would continue to travel, maybe even go home, but something about the way she had spoken had sounded so final. Worry traced her gentle features as she embraced her son. There was something strange about the last time they met, something that made her fear for the situation they had found themselves in. The smile Zo gave before she left was filled with such sadness, her expression revealing the truth, she would not return. As she left, her vision had traced every part of the village as if she was committing to memory something she knew she would never see again.

"She chose t'stay with her father Mrs Eliot." Eiji answered for him, unaware of the wet trail they left as she motioned them into her home. Discussing what had happened was not appropriate, that much was clear from the obvious stiffening of Daniel's posture as she had asked the question. They would not speak of the events to his mother, at least not until Daniel was ready. For now, perhaps it was better if she didn't know the price paid for their return.

"Her father?" Angela questioned without even trying to hide the surprise in her voice. "You mean the man who took Daniel. Why, why would she do that?" she demanded.

"Ah, she explained." Eiji felt himself blush at being caught lying, he scolded himself silently as he realised how Angela knew. It had been in this very room Elly had told Zo that her father was the one who had her friends, so of course she knew that it was he who had endangered them, but she did not understand the situation surrounding the events. Eiji decided it was better to keep it this way. "There's no time t'explain, we must secure the village, barricade the river." He diverted the topic to matters of a more pressing, immediate importance. He was thankful when she accepted the turn of conversation.

"You're right, we need all the help we can get," Angela replied. "Jack is already down there, but last I heard it was a losing battle, the currents are just too strong. I'm sure they could use some more manpower." She pulled away from Daniel, who looked at her sadly and nodded. "I'm sure an Elementalist would prove useful as well," she added, smiling softly at Eiji.

"Acha, you help Mum gather supplies and evacuate to higher ground. Leave a signal, so we know which way you're heading." He looked back to Acha from the door, he was trusting her with the most important task, to protect his mother. She nodded in understanding before he closed the door behind them as he and Eiji once more rushed out into the rain.

* * *

Finally, the men returned, praising each other for the hard work as they walked into the town, their excited chatters filled the air.

"Couldn't have done it without you kid." Jack smiled as he heartily slapped Eiji on his back. It was a friendly slap but held enough force to knock the wind from him. Eiji took a few staggered steps to regain his balance. "How you held back the water while we laid the first bunker, genius." Eiji felt himself blush with all the unwanted attention. Stopping suddenly, Jack gave a deep laugh, it seemed his strong willed wife had disobeyed Daniel's plan. They had hoped to return to a village that looked almost ransacked, but this was not the scene they gazed upon. Everything was undisturbed, and if that wasn't a clear enough sign, Angela opened the door and waved to them. Although she was barely visible through the sheet of rain, he could imagine her defiant smile. She certainly was the woman he married, stubborn to the very end.

"Mum, Acha, I thought you were evacuating!" Daniel scolded; he had known Acha would have met with some resistance, his mother was very wilful. If she didn't want to do something, they could very rarely force her hand. This was something the Physicians' Plexus had soon discovered when trying to force her to conform. Her steadfast beliefs were but one of the reasons she was held in such high esteem as a physician.

"Daniel," his mother stated in a firm voice. "This is our home, there's not a person here who doesn't feel the same way. If we stay here we have more chance of surviving. The mountain cliffs are treacherous and unstable at best, and although the rivers are rising, there is a long way for them to come before the waters reach us. With all the tremors, the old and the young of the village don't stand much chance, so we decided to remain here. Where would we go anyway?" Daniel looked to Acha, she did the only thing she could and shrugged. She had tried so hard to change their minds, she had even attempted to show Daniel's mother the entrance to Collateral, but she refused to even leave. Elder Robert knew of these portals if things became really desperate, and if the time came when there was no other choice but to evacuate, they would do so with his guidance. Despite her best efforts to convince Angela otherwise, neither her, nor the inhabitants of the town wanted to be relocated.

"We managed to barricade the river, erect a number of additional ones too for when it passes the first." As Jack entered from the rain, he ran his hand through his wet hair, sending sprays of water in all directions. He wasn't really surprised to find the town had not been abandoned, quite the contrary, he would have been surprised if they *had* been convinced to leave. No one wanted to leave their homes, even if it meant they were in danger.

Before Jack had returned, he had seen everyone to their homes. The last to leave him was Elder Robert, who seemed exhausted from the whole event, exhausted, yet filled with excitement. Jack could have sworn he had heard him let out a squeal of delight as Eiji had stepped forwards to control the water's flow. It was a sight to behold, the waters stilled, allowing clarity of vision into that which otherwise escaped their view. Even the river fish were visible through whatever force he had used to restrain the turbulent currents.

Before returning to his wife, Jack had thanked them all for their hard work. Hopefully, with these measures in place, it would be some time before the barriers were breached. If this rain continued there was no telling how long their countermeasures would last, but at least there was time to make other preparations and plans.

"How long do you think this will keep up for? Like it or not, we may have to consider relocating to Albeth." Jack looked to his wife, she had a determined look which warned him they would be doing no such thing. He chuckled to himself, that very look was one of the reasons he had fallen in love with her.

"Well," Eiji began, embarrassed to find himself once more the centre of attention, it seemed they turned to him for answers. He wasn't sure if this was because he was the stranger, or an Elementalist and thus believed he may hold secret knowledge of these things, perhaps they were right to a certain extent, he could feel things they couldn't. "This'll calm eventually when the stored energy is exhausted, and the Severaine manifests in our world." Eiji thought about how lucky they were that it was released so soon after they had destroyed the seals this alone would have prevented it from storing energy. If this much damage was being caused by the power it had built up over such a short time, he feared to imagine what it would have been like if the seals hadn't absorbed the energy in its stead. Eiji realised they all waited for him to continue, he quickly obliged. "The rivers will calm, the tremors will stop, but that's when the real danger will begin. Mankind, if they survive this burst of energy, will fall once more t'its power like it did before. The elemental creatures, creatures y' believe only t'be myth, will awaken once more from their slumber.

"Y' see, without the Severaine, there wasn't enough magic t'maintain their life-force and so they were forced t'hibernation leavin' no trace of their existence, even for those who looked, but with its release they will wake once more t'walk the world." Eiji paused to wonder, if perhaps, these creatures had resided in Darrienia. He shuddered as he thought back to the dragon they encountered. If beings such as those were to be unleashed here, they would have an even smaller chance of survival.

"Why now?" Jack questioned, drying himself on one of the towels Angela had handed them. "Why after all this time?" He wasn't unfamiliar with the legends of the Severaine, after all, his son studied it and took great pleasure in telling them of his discoveries. It was not an easy topic to find information on, so Daniel had revelled in every line of discovery, but the thought of such an immeasurable power existing sealed within the world, even now seemed so far-fetched.

"It was written on the tablets of the Gods that this would happen and also that Night would rise again," Daniel answered simply. He answered before he had realised they did not know about Night. They did not know what they had lost for this prophecy to be fulfilled. The world did not share his grief, they would never understand the cost.

"Daniel what are you talking about? Twenty-three years ago, Night was sealed away. I don't know much, but I do know that. The Hoi Hepta Sophoi saw to it that he could never return." Jack thought back, Daniel hadn't quite been born then, it was just himself, Angela, and Adam. He forced his mind from the dark place of his memories and tried to remember more about the time Hectarian magic vanished, yet although he had lived through it, he could barely recall anything. It was almost as if it had never happened.

"Twenty-four." Daniel corrected, "Twenty-four years." He knew how long it was, almost to the day, and not because he had read it, but because it occurred just four months before Zo's birth. A few more months and they would have been celebrating her birthday, but she had only been twenty-three, what kind of a life span was that? He blinked back a few tears quickly before anyone could notice. "You don't have to believe me. If I were you, I wouldn't believe me either, but I saw him, I saw him with my own eyes. We were there when he obtained the final Grimoire, a book that all the time had been kept in this village." Daniel's mother, seeing him tremble, sat him gently before the fire wrapping him in a blanket. She watched in concern as he fought back waves of powerful emotions.

"Daniel, what exactly happened while you were away, and where's Zo?" As she asked, Daniel rose to his feet and left silently up the stairs.

"Mrs Eliot," Eiji addressed her quietly, as Daniel left.

"Angela," she corrected, as her concerned features followed her son's trip to his room. It hurt to see him like this, was all this caused just because Zo had decided to leave him behind, because she didn't return with them? Surely, he knew she'd come back to visit him some day. There was no way she could stay away, no matter how far the distance between them.

"Angela then," he conceded, "it's a long and complicated story, one I don't think y' son is ready t'tell yet. Give him time, when he's ready I'm sure he'll tell y' everythin', perhaps when he makes better sense of it himself." He phrased it carefully, aware that while he held her attention, Daniel glared down the stairs at him, warning him not to speak of the events that had occurred.

Another tremor shook the house as Daniel made his way to his room. The houses here had been designed in such a manner that movements of the earth were of little consequence. Elder Robert had once bragged that the gnomes had assisted the designing architect to ensure nothing could destabilise these buildings. Closing the door behind him, Daniel thought about the last time he had seen her here, how she had rushed through the house straight into the guest room where Acha had lain. That was when all this had begun. It wasn't long after, that Elaineor had come for her. He collapsed on his bed for what he knew had to be the last time, he already knew he could not stay and it wasn't solely because he could see her ghost everywhere he looked.

Marise had made it clear she had a score to settle. If she did come in search of him, he would hate to endanger the lives of those around him. To stay would mean condemning all those he loved. It was silly, but he now understood the choice Zo had made when she had decided to leave with Elly and Eiji. He had been angry at her for sneaking away with the stranger from her past. But now he faced a similar problem he saw clearly that, no matter who faced this decision, there was really but one choice, to protect those you cared for, to sacrifice your own happiness and comfort to keep them safe.

He turned the musical ball over, his fingers absentmindedly tracing the patterns, in some instances finding pieces that would turn and alter. As he watched the movement of his hands, it seemed almost as if they moved with intention, as if he somehow understood on some level what was required of him. As the designs realigned, he could hear the changing in the tones. He had imagined its inner workings at great length. Reactive to both touch and moods, he was certain that emotions somehow engraved themselves within its delicate design. Suddenly, the tones began to change, distorting slightly. The music became a voice, a voice he knew instantly as Zo's. The symbols, as if celebrating his success, shone a vibrant yellow, and the words became clear.

"Daniel." He heard her voice so clearly that, for a brief moment, he had looked for her, but he soon realised it came from the sphere. "I hope you enjoy this gift, it is part of the ancient technology of those who came before us. Those who were ultimately destroyed by the Severaine's power. If you're hearing this, we both know what this means, either I am an idiot and left it out where you could play with it." Daniel smiled sadly at her comment. "Or you found it, but I guess we both know why really.

"Every millennia or so, the world turns a complete cycle, at the end of this phase, as the world is purged, most of this technology is buried and long forgotten. You know the story about the Hectarians and Elementalists who survived, but what you may not know is it was said that, near the beginning of this cycle, some of the Hectarians altered themselves to become part animal, meaning their instincts would be heightened, so they could have more warning if ever this catastrophe was to happen again. This is the theory behind why we have two different types of Méros-Génos, just something I thought you may enjoy, but that itself is not common knowledge compared to the other theories. Sorry, I am getting sidetracked, and I have very little time and so much clarity. Anyway, it seems Night has found a way to bypass the cycle by sending us to Darrienia. He had us destroy the barriers which restrain the Severaine in that world, I am still unclear on his motives.

"You probably know this already, and I am not sure how long this will last, so I'll get to the point. The people who came before us developed many things, somewhere out there is the knowledge you need. The Severaine was contained once by these people, and it can be done again, after all, if the technology they used had been destroyed the seals would have been broken simultaneously. Since we had to remove a physical manifestation of them in order to collapse them, it stands to reason that the device is still out there, and in working order. If you can reactivate it at the source then the barriers would reappear, and the seal would be restored.

"Daniel, somewhere forgotten by us, lies a vast library of information. If you can find it, you can find the answer. I know you can undo what I have done. There is so much I still have to tell you..." her voice wavered, almost as if something had caused her to break focus.

"Thea." Seiken's voice intruded as the sounds began to fade.

"I believe in you and, forgive me, I am sorry," she whispered before all fell silent.

Daniel lay on his bed, unable to stop the flow of tears, how cruel could she be? It was bad enough to lose her, but just as he was trying to come to terms with knowing he would never see her again, never hear her voice, she found a way to contact him, leaving him a message from beyond the grave. As he sobbed into his bed, the sphere seemed to rotate backwards, as if resetting to its starting point. He distracted himself from the grief, if he were to surrender to it now, he may never be able to do what she asked. He forced back his raw emotions, focusing on the small sphere, trying to discover how to reactivate it. He was glad it was something he could hear again, especially since he had taken in so little of what she had attempted to tell him. He had been so focused on the sound of her voice, of being able to hear his dearest friend one more time, most of what she said had been lost on him.

* * *

"Eiji, Acha!" Daniel galloped down the stairs, he had listened to Zo's message many times before his eyes finally dried. Now he understood and he was filled with a new energy, an energy clearly reflected in his voice. He would do it, he would do this one last thing for her. How else could he face her in the underworld? "There's a way to stop it, there's a way to stop the Severaine! I have to find it." Eiji looked up from his steaming cup of hot chocolate, surprised to hear the determination and anticipation that filled his friend's voice. Until now he had been unsure what to say or do that would help Daniel through his grief, but it seemed he had found a way to weather his despair.

"Daniel, what makes y' so sure?" As comforting as it was to see his friend's enthusiastic mood, there was part of him that believed this may just be his way of coping, finding something else to occupy his attention. It was a common reaction to avoid facing grief.

"I have to pack, there's so much to do, I just want you to look after my mum okay." He smiled at them, he knew, or at least believed, that neither of them had homes to go to, he had never really given it much thought.

"You're leaving again?" his mother sighed softly as she moved to embrace him tightly. A gesture he skilfully dodged as he hurried towards the kitchen.

"Mum, somewhere out there is the knowledge the ancients used to seal the Severaine in the first place. I have to find it." As he spoke, his hands enthusiastically thrust a collection of provisions into his backpack. Suddenly the only thing he could think about was leaving. He glanced quickly around the warmly lit room, confident he had all he required. He moved with renewed energy towards the door but was pulled back by his mother, who once again embraced him.

"Okay." She smiled softly, disguising her concern and worry the best she could. He was no longer her little boy, when had he grown into the young man who stood before her now? Despite, for the first time, truly seeing him as the man he was, a part of her still saw the image of the child she needed to nurture and protect. He had inherited too many of her traits, like her stubbornness and determination, for her to even entertain the idea that words could change his mind. "You do what you have to, and when you are ready come home." She brushed her hand affectionately through his hair, her voice soft, understanding that this was something he needed to do. Despite every instinct, every intuition, telling her otherwise, she knew there was little purpose in warning him of the dangers. There were no words she could use to sway his actions, and even if there were, she knew better than to use them.

"Y' really believe there's a way?" Eiji questioned as Daniel's enthusiasm became contagious. The change in his posture, everything about him seemed so certain, so filled with hope that he was starting to wonder if this really was more than just a way to hold on to her memory, and even if it was just that, what harm could it possibly do to embrace it?

"Yes, but the journey won't be an easy one. That's why all I ask of you is you remain here, stay safe, and watch over my family." He glanced between his friends, if they were to agree there would be no reason to look back. Eiji could keep the raging waters at bay, and Acha could keep his mother company in Zo's stead. He swallowed the lump in his throat as he considered his last thought. No one could fill the place of his best friend, she had been such a big part of this village, of their lives. In honour of her memory he would succeed, and do that which she had asked of him.

"We stand a better chance together." Acha added, removing her gloves from their place before the fire, all too aware that once Daniel had gathered all he needed, there would be no time for delay.

"It'd be a shame t'part ways now." Eiji agreed. He glanced around at their water-ridden belongings which still lined the floor. None of them had very much, and what they did own certainly didn't seem like the equipment expected to be carried by adventurers determined to preserve their world. With very much the same feeling as Acha about the importance of time, he started to gather their belongings. "Why don't y' explain the details as we pack." He was eager to know what great new idea was responsible for the sudden and complete change in Daniel's mood.

"Better yet," he stated, the excitement radiating from him filled the room, transferring his feelings of optimism to everything it touched. "I'll let her tell you." His fingers traced the markings on the sphere expertly as they realigned at his touch. He placed it on the table before them, taking a moment to hear her voice once more, before using the moment of distraction to sneak past his mother. Her distraction was only momentary, her son's attempted disappearance had not been unnoticed and although she had questions about the situation they found themselves in, her need to understand the events better was overpowered by her need to be with her son.

"Daniel." His mother's voice stilled his hand as it reached for the shelves containing her extensive collection of medicinal compounds. He turned slowly, looking to her. In her hand she held a satchel. His stomach sank. For a second he had thought it was hers, but it couldn't have been, it had been torn apart and discarded, forever forgotten on the floor of Night's tower. "Zo left this for you." She continued quickly, as she saw the questions line his eyes as a small part of his enthusiasm died. "She came to visit me before she left to get you. What happened? Why did she feel she couldn't return?" As Daniel's mood grew sombre, she instantly regretted her questions. The excitement drained from the air so rapidly, his mother could find no more words. He approached her, his hand lifting the satchel from her.

"Thanks," he whispered; she brushed her arm comfortingly down his, before leaving him alone to examine the gift. He sat on the floor, his hands tracing the embroidery on the corner of the right flap where she had sewn his name. His hands had started to tremble as his grief threatened to once more consume him. He attempted to restrain it, knowing if he were to embrace these feelings now, he could not do that which was required of him.

Opening the satchel, he forced a smile, a smile that grew more sincere as he examined the contents. She had filled it with herbs, each stored in the most ideal way to preserve them, clearly labelled detailing the contents, properties, and what aliments they could be used to treat. Folded to one side was a small leather belt possessing small loops as if to hold something. It was then he found the glass phials, as his fingers traced over their labels, he saw only a third were of any benefit to the health. His spirits started to lift once more as he read them. The ideas, the brilliance of what she had done, once more rekindling the flame of excitement within him.

When they first met, and her childhood memories began to return, she had told him how she had explored the darker aspects of nature. Seeing this, he had no doubt she had spoken the truth. Within the clearly label phials were poisons and compounds most, were in fact, for his protection. She had done things with herbs and chemicals that he had never dreamed possible.

He replaced his belt before finally closing the satchel after he had safely tucked away the small notebook containing a list of herbs and their uses. He had much knowledge in the field of medicine, but this notebook would have been a scripture for even the most skilled physician. It seemed she had been preparing it for a long time, no doubt, like the staff, intended to be a gift for a happier occasion.

* * *

The world as they knew it was changing. Sodden earth met their feet with every step they took. The world was eerily silent as if even the animals waited with baited breath to see what would occur. Penetrating the boiling clouds of the darkened sky, small strands of light fought their way through to dapple the land. The forests seemed different now, the air heavier as they searched for the portal to Collateral. The unearthed roots of ancient trees made the uneven ground unfamiliar. There was a foreboding presence, something immense, something powerful, a pressure which bore down upon them, making breathing a laboured task. It was a sensation that only Eiji recognised. It was magic, heavy stifling magic as the air once more became saturated with that which gave the ancient creatures life, that which would once again call them into being. The world was changing and to survive they too would need to adapt.

Daniel stopped just before the portal, turning back to take a final look. The forest, which had once been so familiar to navigate, had become alien, not unlike the lands they had travelled through to arrive here. Mountains had cracked and split, yet the town itself was, for some unknown reason, still untouched by its new master's hand.

He wasn't sure exactly what they quested for, or how they would know when they found it. For now, they had taken the very first step, a step which would hopefully guide them to the ancient knowledge they sought, and that was all that was important.

* * *

Darkness encompassed the caves. Upon the endless walls, stone carvings were carefully displayed, their content, symbols, and languages long forgotten. Their depths stretching on further than any one mind could even begin to fathom. Darkness was their friend, it preserved the precious tales, the precious stories of those who had walked the path before.

Three figures, perhaps once humanoid in appearance, stood huddled against the darkness. Their ancient predatory eyes unhindered by the lack of light as they gathered in the central chamber. They had been the keepers of these stories, the watchers of these lives, since the beginning of time itself. The most recent adventure had been secured in its new position, the latest in a long line of tales which told the history of this world's heroes, or those who should have walked that path.

A new tablet stood before them now, the atmosphere growing tense as they eagerly awaited the next names to be dealt by the hands of fate. As they watched, waited, they were unaware the old story still had chapters left to be inscribed, unaware that those who remained had now embarked on a journey to do something none before them had done, to oppose destiny itself.

The figures grew impatient, normally the next Chosen were named as the story of the former ones drew to a close, each story was marked with a beginning and an ending.

"Impossible!" the almost human voice screeched, the keening echoing through the countless millenniums which surrounded them as the tablet before them cracked. Nothing such as this had occurred before, it was unprecedented. A new story had indeed begun, but it was not a new tale. It seemed that events were no longer as predetermined as they had believed. Could it be this continuous cycle would finally be brought to an end? Something in the fates had shifted, something was different now, but what?

Dear reader,

We hope you enjoyed reading *Darrienia*. Please take a moment to leave a review in Amazon, even if it's a short one. Your opinion is important to us. The story continues in *Severaine*.

To read the first chapter for free, head to
https://www.nextchapter.pub/books/the-severaine

Discover more books by K.J. Simmill at
https://www.nextchapter.pub/authors/kj-simmill

Want to know when one of our books is free or discounted for Kindle? Join the newsletter at http://eepurl.com/bqqB3H

Best regards,
K.J. Simmill and the Next Chapter Team

About the Author

K.J. Simmill is an award-winning British author with books released in both the fantasy and non-fiction genres.

She is a qualified Project Manager, Herbal Practitioner, and Usui Reiki master, with certifications in various fields of holistic therapy. More recently she has completed training and qualifications in Special Education Needs and Disabilities (SEND).

In her free time, she is an avid reader and a passionate gamer.

Printed in Great Britain
by Amazon

85720000R00420